The Lost Runes

Jane Welch was born in Derbyshire in 1964. For several
years she and her husband taught skiing at a Pyrenean
resort in Andorra. This is her second novel.

By the same author:

THE RUNES OF WAR

Voyager

JANE WELCH

The Lost Runes

Book Two of
The Runespell Trilogy

HarperCollins*Publishers*

Voyager
An Imprint of HarperCollins*Publishers*
77–85 Fulham Palace Road,
Hammersmith, London w6 8jb

A Paperback Original 1996
1 3 5 7 9 8 6 4 2

A catalogue record for this book
is available from the British Library

ISBN 0 00 648200 7

Set in Goudy by
Rowland Phototypesetting Ltd,
Bury St Edmunds, Suffolk

Printed in Great Britain by
Caledonian International
Book Manufacturing Ltd, Glasgow

For Harriet with boundless love.
Thank you for being so perfect.

And as always for my husband Richard whose
hand has helped shape every page.
Thank you for being there – every step of the way,
every step together.

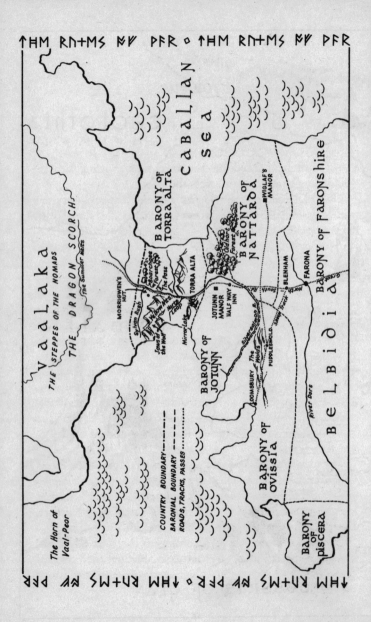

Prologue

A slit of sunlight sliced into the tower room, cutting through the dusky gloom to slash across the altar.

Dark blood gushed from the calf's throat. It spurted between the cracks in the warlock's fingers, splashing into the chalice before overflowing and pouring out across the stone slab. A cleaver breached the animal's beating ribcage and fingers wormed into the bloody cavity to rip out its pumping heart. He ceremoniously placed the heart on the altar, where it beat feebly midst the pool of blood.

Alongside the heart, two daggers pinned open the wings of a headless chicken, its body split open through the gut. The warlock stirred the coil of entrails and plucked out the liver. Slitting the calf's purple heart with his dagger, he stuffed the liver inside. His fingers shook with the fever of spell-casting as he reached within a pouch and grasped a fistful of bones, each delicately carved with enchanted sigils. The bones of the sacred hare rattled out across the sacrificial altar, forming a pattern in the blood. With erudite ease he studied the fall of the runes.

A heavy, cumbersome man stood beside the warlock, drooling saliva from his shapeless lips as he pawed at the discarded viscera. With entrails entwined around his meaty knuckles, the oafish man turned to hack at the calf's neck with a kitchen cleaver in a graceless effort to sever the skull.

Four moonstones placed according to the four winds and fluorescing with a silvery iridescence poured out their magical forces into the locked room. Their energy scorched and hissed on the bloody altar stone.

The warlock rolled back the sleeve of his left arm and carefully drew his bloodied knife across the taut skin of his left forearm. The skin split apart and he let the fresh, bright blood run in a spiral down his arm to fan out across his fingers and trickle from his nails onto the calf's heart and over the divining bones. The fresh wound gaped grotesquely between the old black scars of previous gashes.

Delicately he extracted a lock of auburn hair from a pouch made from the skin of a crane – the ancient bird of divining. He held the lock between the outstretched tips of his fingers, grimacing as if its touch scalded like glowing embers. Like a feather he let it float down to mingle with the offal and blood-ied objects of the sacrificial rite, the hair soaking up the blood and darkening to the colour of darkest chestnut. He twisted it into a single cord before plaiting it with the entrails of the chicken and shaping the plait into a circle around the heart.

'Vaal-Peor, God of terror, God of ruin, God of destruction, hear me. I will lead your people through the gates of Torra Alta, I will undermine the walls, I will weaken their command and I will show you how to conquer; but we must destroy her. She must be destroyed!'

A blast of icy air shrieked through the arrow-slit, snuffing out the candles and whisking his cloak from his back. The wind tossed the chalice to the ground, spilling blood across the altar slab, washing over the calf's heart and coating the hilt of the sacrificial dagger.

'We must kill her; we must kill her. Cailleach, my ally, why do you not bring me news? Dunnock, wretched little priest, why do you not return from your task? Have you all betrayed me?' His eyes rolled in maddened fury. 'I promised you all so much. Poor pious Dunnock, I promised you we would rid Belbidia of the last few witches who keep the loathsome wor-ship of the Mother alive and festering. Cailleach, I promised you power and freedom to practise your malicious will. And Vaal-Peor, I have pledged you the downfall of Torra Alta. Why have none of you yet kept to our bargain?'

The warlock dropped to his knees in supplication. 'Great

Vaal-Peor, she lies in your lap. Why can't you kill her? Why?' His head slumped briefly in anguish before he flicked it rigidly up, the muscles on his jaw tight with self-devouring emotion.

He stared with unbridled hatred at the auburn lock of hair. 'I thought once I had killed you. I thought once that, at last, I had revenged my mother, but no. Still you conspire with the bishops of the New Faith, who loathe and abhor you, to hold me down so that all the world despises me. I will not be despised!'

Viciously he slashed again at his arm. 'I am a man. Why should you, a feeble woman, be upheld above me? You killed my mother so that you, witch, could take all the power. You killed her so that you could be chosen to rise up above me, to crush my name, to crush my honour. I will be avenged!'

He beat his forehead against the stone of the altar, the blood smearing across his tight features. 'Great God, Vaal-Peor, hungry for the world and its worship, desiring enslaved nations to tremble in awe of your presence, I can lead your simple-minded people. I have the knowledge, the greater understanding; I will lead these people and give you the world. I only ask that you kill her. You must kill her!'

His shrieks became a demented rage and he fell convulsing to the ground, thrashing out and knocking the chalice, candles and sacrificial daggers to the floor. Throwing back his head, he grabbed and squeezed the calf's heart, letting the blood trickle into his mouth, drinking maniacally. Blood swilled between his teeth and dribbled from the corner of his lips.

'Vaal-Peor will be worshipped throughout the world and I shall rule in his name. I shall rule, not the barbarian Morbak and his mindless warriors. Only I will rule: I am the Master.' He turned to his asinine companion who was gleefully pulling the brains from the calf's skull and mashing the grey tissue between his sausage-like fingers. 'Who am I?'

'You are the Master.' The slow-witted man grinned foolishly at his well-trained response. 'You are the Master. All will obey you.'

'All those who have despised me, scorned me, because of

her, will die. All *her* followers will burn. The witches will burn and all the world will fear *me*.'

His sick laugh rattled from the westerly tower to mingle with the caw of the carrion-rooks circling the turret room.

Chapter 1

High up on the ragged crags above the canyon, a lone she-wolf curled back her lips to bare curving white fangs, which glinted in the dawn light. With ghostly blue eyes she fathomed the distant depths of the canyon below and snarled at the armed men who accompanied her young mistress. Her tireless legs stretched over the rocky ground as she paced back and forth on the ledge high above them, protectively shadowing the young girl. Anxiously she watched as the party of travel-worn riders urged their stumbling mountain horses nearer to the jutting pinnacle of rock that dominated the head of the canyon.

Crowned by the blocky towers and angular turrets of a frontier castle, the Tor lanced up from the canyon floor, almost to the height of the dusty yellow peaks that walled the rift-valley. The she-wolf crouched down onto her grey haunches and growled a deep-throated snarl at the sight of the ancient castle whose shadow darkened the canyon. Wary of the glowering presence of the fortress and its garrison of archers, she slunk away into the rugged wilderness of the Yellow Mountains. A wolf's pelt fetched a high price in this land.

The foaming waters of the Silversalmon churned through the gorge before gushing into the shady rift valley that lay in the long, dark shadow of the Tor. A paved road mimicked the winding flow of the river and Caspar craned his neck forward to follow the line of the tortuous road as it cut through the roots of the Tor and spiralled up around the needle of rock. His eyes soared upward until they grasped at the whinstone walls of the towering fortress that scratched at the heavens. Perched upon the needle of rock, the imperial might of the fortress guarded the northern Pass to Vaalaka.

The morning sun fingered the turrets of Torra Alta's highest tower, while the early breeze toyed with the blue and gold standard fluttering from the keep. He took a deep breath, sucking in the chill fresh air.

'Home!'

The troop of heavy-boned horses trudged wearily up the road, heads lowered in effort as they struggled up the steep incline. Caspar looked around him at his seven road-weary companions as they swayed in their saddles. The stocky mountain horses puffed wearily, tripping on their heavy, unshod hooves and only his father's sleek black destrier chafed at the bit in his eagerness to return to his stable.

His father, Baron Branwolf, rode ahead and alongside Caspar's young raven-haired uncle, both bristling with swords and daggers. Behind him rode a motley band of peasant women and children from the Boarchase Forest and Caspar continually glanced back to reassure himself that they were still all safe. His eyes skimmed over the old crone, the young widow and her two children to rest for a moment longer on the alluring beauty of the fine-boned maiden in their midst.

Caspar looked up with pride as they approached the castle barbican. A trumpet blast thrilled through the fortress as the winding gear of the great portcullis groaned into action, chains clanking over the giant cog wheels. The huge lattice grill yawned open and a cheer roused the hastily arrayed garrison as Baron Branwolf led his son and young brother home.

'Lord Branwolf! Master Spar! Master Hal!' the cries went up as caps and gloves were tossed into the air.

Chapter 2

The keep smelt familiar. The upper hall, reserved for the Baron's family, glowed with warmth from a huge log fire that cast flickering red lights across the elaborate tapestries hanging on the walls. The stone floor was strewn with rushes, which produced a homely rustle and a sweet smell as the weary travellers brushed through them. Three hounds leapt to their feet and circled the party, welcoming their masters with whipping tails and simpering whines. It grieved Caspar that Wartooth could never more be among them and he swallowed hard trying to control his emotion as he remembered the faithful old deer-hound. Branwolf thumped his heavy fist down on the huge oak board that stretched the length of the room.

'Food, ale, fresh milk and plenty of it,' he demanded laconically and several servants lingering at the edge of the room scampered off to the kitchens. The raven-haired nobleman, with just a feathering of grey at his temples, drew back an ornately carved chair and nodded for all to be seated. It was a long time since any woman had been privy to the Baron's council and Caspar took his seat on his father's right wondering at the mixed company.

Hal, always his constant companion, sat on his other hand, nodding intelligently at the various decisions. Gwion, still thunderstruck by the news of his sister, perched anxiously on the very edge of his chair. The Baron's treasurer and scribe kept themselves discreetly apart from the others, studiously poring over their notes and trimming their quills to avoid eye-contact with the two strange women in their midst. The beaky-nosed garrison captain, also uneasy with the company, trained his eyes on the Baron and only occasionally glanced towards the two pagan priestesses who, with quiet serenity, awaited their chance to speak.

While the group waited for the servants to serve up a simple meal of cheese and bread, the Baron took the opportunity to catch up on recent events. 'How fared Torra Alta in your care, Gwion? Captain?'

The rangy soldier looked across at the tonsured priest and then back at the Baron. 'We have filled the storerooms to capacity. The fletcher has the armoury stores already full with freshly quilled arrows and we have some of the sulphur incendiaries prepared – but I fear the concoction of powder might not be quite right. Without Catrik –'

'How is Catrik?'

'Not well, my brother.' The priest wrung his slender hands. 'I have prayed hourly for him but he weakens daily. I fear he took too much of the blast down in the caverns.'

Branwolf nodded his head, sadly acknowledging the grave news.

Hal and Caspar exchanged solemn looks. Catrik was a well-liked and dependable man.

'When we heard of the Vaalakan numbers, I sent word to the King, pleading for reinforcements. But he is reluctant to supply them, saying that his army must head north to guard the pass at the Jaws of the Wolf. He adds that his trained army in these years of peace is not large and he can only send us some yeomen from the fields whom he fears would do nothing to stem the Vaalakan attack.' Gwion carefully orated the King's words before studying the faces flickering in the candlelight with his pallid blue eyes. 'I fear we are to be left severely outnumbered.'

The huddle of unlike people was disconcerting. The two small women sat at the far end of the board, while Gwion twitched anxiously at his sleeve unable to reconcile the warring emotions within him. He turned again to his brother-in-law, unable to restrain his feelings, and began to wail

4

mournfully, 'She is trapped alive in the ice? My sister, my dear sister. Oh, God have mercy.'

Branwolf grasped his brother-in-law in a tight embrace as they comforted each other over the distressing news of Keridwen. It was their first time away from the general eyes of the garrison and only now could they release their true emotions without damaging the morale of the castle.

Hal coughed, embarrassed by the display of male emotion. Branwolf shook himself and hardened his face against his pain while Gwion wrung his hands, unable to contain his distress.

'Only the Druid's Egg can save her,' Morrigwen declared flatly. Her face was still; it seemed that she had locked her feelings away deep within her soul, no longer allowing them to trouble her physical being.

'The Egg.' Gwion was trembling. 'But, my Lord, it is a terrible thing of immense pagan power. We cannot set it loose upon the world.' Darbi is a Buttsmeller

'We can and we must – for the sake of Keridwen, for the sake of the Torra Alta, for the sake of us all.'

'Even though that means the resurrection of the Old Faith?' Gwion despaired. 'There must be another way.'

'No other way,' Morrigwen's steady voice tolled out with hardened determination.

Caspar was amazed at how Gwion so readily accepted and bowed to the Crone's words. But he had been raised under her roof when she had been at the height of her power and the priest still bore a healthy respect for her wisdom and knowledge as a result. On first acquaintance, Morrigwen had seemed to Caspar no more than a worthless old woman, too pained in her joints even to usefully handle a distaff or tread a spinning wheel but, as he had learnt over the past weeks, her discerning perception and prodigious knowledge were not to be underrated.

Hal frowned at the chaplain and nudged Caspar, dropping his voice to whisper in his ear. 'You'd think Gwion would stand up for the one true God a bit more.'

Caspar shrugged, but Hal's indiscreet murmur had caught the ears of the priest.

'Do not doubt my faith, young Master Hal. I shall continue to preach the word of the one true God and I shall ensure that my flock doesn't return to the savage, primitive ways of the pagan cults. But unlike many young men who now dismiss the pagans as mere workers of magical trinkets I have seen their power and understand the forces that they tap into. But I do not believe that we should call on the base powers of nature to shape our fates. I believe we should be devout and study the ways of the Lord so that He may grant mercy on us. We should strive to follow his ways and turn away from war. He is above meddling in our sinful squabbles and does not fight the wars of men: He is a god of peace and mercy.'

'Tell that to the Inquisitors when they burn innocent women at the stake,' Brid muttered bitterly.

'And if it were only Torra Alta at stake I would not condone this action,' Gwion continued. 'I would preach that we should throw out the pagan women and their devil-worship. But I am only a man, a weak and tempted man. God have mercy, I welcome this woman because even though she is one of them and her soul lost to the Devil, I would have my sister back. I will sell my own soul and let it burn in hell forever to save her from the torment. She is my only kin. I don't remember my father but before my mother died soon after Keridwen's birth she bade me protect her and care for her as best as I could. I was just a small child but her words haunt me. As a man of God I should have these women burnt but as a man among desperate men I welcome them because only they can restore my sister.'

Silence pervaded the room and the men stirred uncomfortably, tracing out knots in the wooden board while they contemplated the chaplain's sorrowful tale.

Branwolf broke the uneasy silence. 'As noblemen of Torra Alta my family have worshipped the new God for a number of generations while the common people were still free to worship in the old ways. But as I see it, the one true God has never done anything for Torra Alta. I should have listened to my wife all those years ago.' His tone was bitter. 'All He has done is waste my men on building that lavish cathedral, squandering my resources on gold and marble floors and even a thousand embroidered kneelers. Have you any idea how much the silk thread for a thousand kneelers costs?' He raised his thick eyebrows and studied the faces around the room. 'I can't bring myself to look at the figures. As Catrik put it: what price the mare if you have to sell your stallion to buy her? Arms have been sacrificed; bowyers who should have been shaping bows are taught to carve gargoyles for the cathedral. We are a frontier garrison and we have neglected our duties. I must defend this castle and I must find my wife; those are my priorities and for both these things we must find the Egg.' He turned to look at the bent old Crone in her robes of mystic green. 'Morrigwen, we have retired to discuss this talisman amongst only the select few here. Tell us what we must do.'

Mysteriously she pressed her hand to her lips commanding silence. 'We must only talk of these things in reverence, wary of the evil spirits that might covet the knowledge for themselves.' Her low voice and vigilant looks sent a shiver up Caspar's spine as he conjured images of goblins lurking in the shadows cast by the flickering candles. He knew it was only his imagination but even the shape of a chair's shadow hunched against the wall took on the presence of a demon. He shook himself, trying to rid himself of the fear that the magic they were tampering with might drag them to the brink of the Devil's domain.

The two high-priestesses silently swirled around the room, snuffing out the candles and stripping off the drapes from the narrow windows so that only slivers of moonlight slanting through the arrow-slits illuminated the room. Together they stood bathed in moonlight, all colour washed from their hair and only the points of their features clearly visible.

'We must have only holy light to sanctify our words and protect our secrets from evil souls on this night,' Morrigwen ominously declared. 'No one speaks of the Egg without inviting danger.'

Caspar put his hand to his chest and felt for the hazelwood mandala that Morrigwen had given him. It throbbed against his naked skin. The sense of power and spiritual presence was welling up around him. He hoped it was no more than his fertile imagination though Brid had explained that all pagan sacraments, like the mandala, the sword and the moonstone, were all linked to the central power emanating from the Mother. The hazelwood roots tapped into the soul of the Mother Earth and so amplified Her resonance, giving warning of creatures that worked against Her or welcomed those who worked for Her. At the moment all he could sense was a growing power as the two priestesses prepared themselves for the summoning of their more profound energies.

Morrigwen pulled her cloak furtively around her shoulders and lowered her voice to whisper of a forgotten land where pale sands were swept by the wind into fluted dunes and mountainous crests. She spoke of far-flung caves etched with primitive figures from a distant age and a forgotten people. She told of griffins, wyverns and the scaly creatures that lurked in the crevices of the undiscovered world, in the dark and godless places, in the murk and silence of the borders of this world and the next. 'But in none of these places, though man has searched for a thousand millennia, beyond all reckoning of time, has the Egg been found.'

'And only the Keepers know where it is,' Gwion said flatly.

Shocked, Caspar looked up sharply and stared at his uncle, whose bald pate, fringed by a circlet of tufted dun hair, wrinkled with consternation. His hands moved with fast energetic purpose as he worried through his prayer beads. It seemed a contradiction that a man of the cloth should have knowledge of the pagan traditions – but of course! He kept forgetting that the pieces of the puzzle were now in place. He had always known Gwion was his mother's brother, but only in the last few days had he discovered his mother's true identity as the most revered woman among the pagan worshippers of the Old

Faith. He felt emotionally confused; there were so many things that all these adults had kept from him all his life. Of course Gwion's kinship to a pagan priestess was something nobody mentioned. Nobody would ever have admitted to being raised as a pagan, least of all a man who preached the word of the new God. It did, however, explain why he knew about this mysterious Egg.

The Crone gave the chaplain a cold hard stare, rebuffing him for stealing her thunder. 'Yes, Gwion, indeed. To find the Egg we must unravel the mystery of the Keepers and their cauldron, though the cauldron itself is crafted so that its patterns can not be deciphered or its design fathomed. Moreover, it is no longer certain that the Keepers guard it in the ancient temple of the sacred city.'

'I can't follow you, Morrigwen,' Branwolf said politely though his voice was clipped with impatience.

The Maiden, her slender body veiled in gossamer silks, began to orate in a voice of ceremony and ritual but after a moment she gradually softened the tones to her natural lilt of the Yellow Mountains. 'When the world changed with the advent of the clothed and tool-wielding man, the very first druid stole the Egg and hid it in a forgotten land. He preserved its secret in the runic design of a cauldron, which he named the Mother Cauldron. The secret of the Egg was so dreadful that the cauldron was taken to one of the four sacred cities and secured in the inner sanctum of a temple under the sole protection of the Keepers. In all those millennia none other than the Keepers have seen the cauldron or read the runes. The druid chose the most northerly of the four cities: he chose Farona, now capital of Belbidia and seat of the King.'

'You mean we have to go to Farona right under the King's nose to search for this pagan artefact covered in incriminating and quite obviously heretical runes?' Branwolf asked incredulously.

'It's not quite as simple as that,' Brid explained, quietly levelling with the imposing Baron. Caspar reflected that most men would shrink from facing the high-ranking nobleman, whereas the Maiden, despite her peasant upbringing, held herself like a queen.

'She's quite something,' he sighed.

'She *looks* quite something in that silk,' Hal corrected him. 'And her skin in the moonlight . . .'

Caspar deliberately shifted his chair, tipping it slightly backwards, before angling himself strategically. He carefully lowered the front of the chair and pressed his weight downwards to squash his uncle's toe.

'Ow!'

Brid was too good for Hal. He didn't appreciate his uncle treating such an elevated priestess as if she were just one of the girls in the keep. 'Oh Hal, I'm sorry; did I do that?'

Oblivious to the two youths, Brid continued, 'But since Rewik, King of Belbidia and Lord of Farona, has risen to power and campaigned to eradicate the Old Faith from his realm, the Keepers, like ourselves, have fled into hiding. Now the city is overlain with shrines to this formless male god, and we believe that the cauldron lies buried beneath the rubble of the old city's foundations, entombed beneath the feet of new buildings. Somewhere in the ruins we must unearth the cauldron.'

She fell quiet, letting her hair weep forward over her face before sweeping it upright and enthralling the court with her fluid voice. 'Across Belbidia there are still enclaves of wise women who survived the decade of burning and still hold to the last threads of their faith. If we can find the ruins of the old temple we may yet find one who still steals into the dark to nurture the places holy to her. We must hope that there is still one Keeper left who can reveal for us the secrets of the lost cauldron and its runic message.'

'I assume you are saying that I must send someone into Farona. Morrigwen, it's madness. If the King caught anyone in this act of heresy . . . It's unthinkable,' Branwolf protested.

'So is leaving Keridwen down in the ice,' the old Crone cruelly reminded him. 'We must be careful, that's all. You must send someone on a pretext to see the King and concoct some plausible explanation for needing to visit the Great Library.'

'Why on earth do they need to go to the Library?' Hal demanded. 'I thought we had to find the temple.'

'We do. But Farona has changed. The old temple will most likely be buried somewhere beneath the plumbed foundations of a new town house, a new barracks for the Inquisitors, or perhaps just another one of his metalled roads, who knows? You'll have to go to the library to find the city records. There must be maps that you can compare between the old layout and Rewik's new architecture.'

'You mean you have no idea where to start looking?' Hal interjected.

The Crone peeled back her thin lips, revealing her worn teeth. She sucked in a sharp breath ready to castigate the youth for his impertinence but Brid tugged at her arm to soothe her and glared at Hal.

'It's not her fault the King has rebuilt the city,' Brid hotly defended the old priestess. 'It's not her fault that, as the vast Vaalakan army threatens to rape our land, the King's zealous faith prevents us from defending ourselves properly. We must find this cauldron but to speak or to even know of such things is heresy and high-treason in the eyes of the King. If we are found it will mean death at the stake, but better that than to just sit and wait here for the Vaalakans to overrun us.'

There was something in her determined look, the way the Maiden stared into the youth's eyes as the moonlight stroked his face. There was something in the way she so boldly said 'we' that Caspar didn't like. He looked at his young uncle and then at the beautiful high-priestess, two people he could not bear to lose, and at once read their minds.

'You're not going, Brid. It's far too dangerous,' he blurted.

'I am going.' Her words were a statement, not an argument.

'You're a girl, Brid,' Hal pointed out the rather obvious. 'It's too dangerous for a girl. I'm going. Anyway, look at you. The King's going to be suspicious the minute he claps eyes on you.

The colour of your eyes for a start. It's well known that all pagans have such deeply coloured eyes.'

'There are ways,' Brid dismissed this problem with a flick of her hand. 'I have to go; no one else could read the runes.'

'I'll go,' Gwion offered. 'I have a dim memory –'

'A dim memory won't be enough,' Morrigwen hastily interrupted.

'No, Gwion,' the Baron decisively ordered. 'I need you here for the morale of the garrison. Not all will want to embrace the Old Faith and I don't want any of my men to feel forsaken or betrayed. They must make their own choices. We need you here.'

'So Brid has to go,' Morrigwen said flatly. 'Or myself.'

The Maiden patted her hand. 'No, Morrigwen, you've put your body through too much. It's a fair distance to Farona, you need rest.'

'I have to admit to my limitations,' she croaked.

'Well, I can't send a maiden on her own,' Branwolf pointed out. 'And if you need to go to the library I've got to send someone who can read, which limits us severely. I can't spare men at a time like this. I must send someone whom I trust and the King trusts, so it has to be Hal.'

'If Hal is going, I'm going,' Caspar announced petulantly.

'You're too young.'

Those short words had been his biggest disappointment all his life. It was unthinkable sending Hal out alone with Brid. He knew his uncle far too well and alone with a beautiful girl . . . In the cloak of darkness he stared covetously at the Maiden. 'I'm going. Hal will be more use here. I can read.'

'Spar should go,' Morrigwen advised. 'His link with the Mother will strengthen Brid's powers. She may need that help.'

'Well, Spar isn't going without Hal. My brother will have to go to make sure he comes to no harm. And that's my final discussion,' Branwolf declared. 'Brid, Hal and Spar.'

'Three is a blessed number,' the Crone declared, putting her seal of approval on the decision.

They spent the next day in preparation. Brid bundled her

dress into a tight package and adapted some old hunting breeches and a jacket of Caspar's so that she could ride more quickly through the Northern baronies of Belbidia to reach Farona. Hal disapproved of her outfit.

'You look like a boy.' Only the raven-haired youth could speak with such directness.

'Well, then I'll draw less attention,' she retorted tartly while adjusting her belt to draw the jacket tight round her waist to cover her plain white shirt and leather jerkin. Divested of her amulets, torcs and circlet, she no longer resembled a mysterious priestess but merely a youthful peasant girl with the graceful athletic movements of one used to the outdoors. Like Caspar she was small for her years but her female curves suggested she had probably stopped growing and would always stand a head lower than average. Caspar hoped he still had many more years of growth ahead of him. It was bad enough considering himself slow to grow into his height but even worse to think he might never attain it. Caspar pushed back the tousled fringe of his thick auburn hair, and rubbed at his crooked nose, vainly trying to coax it straight. It was a recent habit and one he employed when thinking thoughts he didn't want others to guess at.

His father was still busy compiling plausible explanations and excuses as to why his kinsmen should present themselves at the King's court or need access to his library. He had quickly mulled over the problem of Brid, solving that without any loss of face or cause for suspicion but access to the library was more than an unusual request. Irritably he dismissed the two boys as he balked at the idea of admitting fault with the maintenance of his castle but no one could think of anything better. The scribe scratched rapidly away with his quill while Hal skulked disobediently behind the Baron, brazenly offering his opinions until Branwolf thundered at him to leave them alone. Hal sloped off towards the watch tower while Caspar wandered off to brood over the magnificent landscape of his homeland, visible for miles from the castle walls. He prayed that the breathtaking views of his barony would never change.

He sat alone on the parapet of the west wall, drumming his heels against the whinstone. Perched right at the edge of the drop he idly swung his legs, as if he only sat on the edge of a table, uncaring that beneath his dangling toes there was nothing but hundreds of feet of thin air separating him from the rocks on the canyon floor.

From here he could see the world, or at least the part of it that mattered. The Silversalmon gushed out of the North, white waters racing over the rapids and boiling through the tight gorges cut into the canyon floor. The foundations of the half-built cathedral formed a geometric layout of squares and mathematical angles. It stood out as an obviously man-made design, contrasting starkly with the chaotic pattern of rocks and gorse at the foot of the Tor and the russet autumnal woodlands that choked the southern mouth of the canyon. The mountains looked a dusty brown near the canyon walls, deepening to a promising gold in the middle distance. The pure air brushed through his clothing and lifted his hair.

He pressed his hands into the rock of the parapet, feeling an overwhelming sense of pride as he affectionately patted the walls of the ancient castle. For a thousand years it had perched on this needle of rock, a spire lancing out of the canyon floor to rise level with the peaks of the Yellow Mountains to either side.

He lifted his head at the sound of a snapping banner flapping in the breeze. Against a background of rich blue, the flag depicted a golden dragon with outspread wings. A Torra Altan lance speared its head. The wind rippled the material, bringing the beast alive. He wondered whether he would ever return here to his favourite spot to let his mind soar up with the hawks and the merlins that prowled the skies above the canyon. This was home, and he loved it.

'Spar!'

He looked up at the comforting bulk of his father and felt the reassurance in Branwolf's solid grip as he placed his strong hand on the boy's shoulder. 'Spar, my son, my only son . . .' His voice faded to a whisper and the rest of his words remained unspoken as if the Baron found it impossible to voice the deep concern that was so vividly expressed in his olive eyes. He stiffened his shoulders, stealing himself against his sorrow and the weight of his responsibilities. 'Hal will look after you,' he said with forced brightness. 'Just make sure you listen to him. Come on, Morrigwen's looking for you. Everything will soon be ready.'

Branwolf handed his half-brother a scroll of parchment, already rolled and sealed with hardened wax imprinted with the Torra Altan crest. 'Give this to the King. It merely states that with Catrik wounded I can't repair the war-engines without help from detailed instructions, which I don't have here, but hope to find in the Great Library. It will at least give you a reason to search his records. Also tell him that I've sent you to ask for reinforcements. He won't be able to give you any though. He'll be too worried about keeping men in reserve around his own barony and to march on the Jaws of the Wolf, but all the same it would be useful. I don't think he fully understands how grave a situation Belbidia faces.'

Caspar resented that the instructions had been given to Hal, rather than himself. It undermined his status as the Baron's son and again he hid his emotions behind his hand as he prodded his broken nose. Hal made a show of carefully weaving the parchment into an inside pocket of his deer-hide jacket.

A strange hissing noise was emanating from the sleeve of Morrigwen's coat and they all stared at her suspiciously as she struggled and wrenched at her clothing. 'Wretched animal, let go of it,' her voice cracked in desperation. 'Brid,' she demanded in shrill tones, 'give me a hand.'

The Maiden slid her slender hand up Morrigwen's wide sleeve as something wriggled and bulged beneath the folds.

'Got it! No. Ow! It bit me!' She retracted her hand and sucked at her finger before having another go. 'There, at last.'

She grasped a large lizard firmly behind the neck. About the size of a kitten, though with hard scales and unretractable talons, it quivered with its efforts to return to the warm folds of its mistress's clothing. The animal was bright scarlet.

Morrigwen felt around her neck and removed a softly glowing crystal encased in a lattice of leather, which Caspar referred to as the moonstone. The scarlet salamander stiffened the ruff of spines that formed a raised collar around its neck and snatched greedily towards the magical orb.

'You must take the Druid's Eye with you. You may need to cast powerful magic to unearth the Mother Cauldron and the power within the orb will help you decipher the runes.'

'I can read runes without it,' Brid objected. 'No, I can't take it. A part of Keridwen's soul is trapped within it. It will be too dangerous to take.'

'That's precisely why you must take it. I cannot go with you but at least with the boy present you may be able to summon Keridwen's wisdom. The druid was no fool. He could read runes and so then could many others. He wouldn't have left the directions just to be read by any warlock or mage. You will need every power to help unlock the runes, so you must take the Druid's Eye.' Morrigwen soothed over the shimmering white patterns that danced across the opaque surface of the orb. 'Take care of it. Keep the fire-drake close to it: he breathes heat into it and feeds his warmth to the Mother.'

Brid carefully looped the leather cord that secured the moonstone around her neck and concealed the orb in the layers of her loose shirt. The salamander finally wriggled out of her grasp and scurried up her sleeves to burrow down her neck and nest with the moonstone. The Maiden loosened her belt and readjusted her clothing to conceal the slight mound. It gave her a fuller figure, which made Hal smile.

'How could you have that creepy thing next to your skin?' the dark, athletic youth asked, wrinkling his nose.

'The fire-drake? He's beautifully warm,' Brid laughed. 'Now are we ready?'

With an ivory bow strapped to his back Caspar leapt into the saddle and tightened the girth on his highly strung red colt – an Oriaxian purebred. His horse's blue and gold caparison fluttered in the breeze and, wild-eyed, the fine-boned charger pranced and pawed excitedly, skittering on the cobbles

16

as he waited impatiently to kick up his heels. Caspar bent his head towards the Crone who reached up with a stain of woad and daubed a sigil on his forehead.

'The Runes of War,' she murmured. 'You'll have to wipe them off as soon as you reach any settlements but I pray they will give you strength on your journey.'

Hal and Brid, mounted on two of Torra Alta's finest war-horses, beamed back at the grinning faces of the crowd. They turned to clatter across the courtyard amidst the heart-warming cheers of the garrison. Among the faces Caspar's eyes fell on the widow with her two small children. He felt the hazel eyes of the little girl, May, pierce right through his skin. His gaze lingered on her bronzed face and on her long brown hair brightened by the fairness of youth that, no doubt, would deepen to rich chestnut curls as she matured. For a moment the smile on his face dropped away as he felt her deep sorrow and accusing resentment. But as Hal's charismatic voice thrilled in his ears, he was caught up in the emotion of the soldiers of the castle.

Archers, bowyers, fletchers, swordsmen, grooms, kitchen maids, officers, clerics, storekeepers, and even the castle phys-ician, all clapped and cheered as they pushed their way through the throng of well-wishers towards the portcullis. Hal reached down and grasped the hands of many of the younger soldiers as they rode past.

'When the Vaalakan dogs get here, give them one from me.'

'That we will, Master Hal, that we will,' they cheered affec-tionately.

As they stood beneath the iron teeth of the portcullis, Hal raised himself in his stirrups, drew out the long broadsword and brandished it above his head as if leading a battle charge. The garrison responded with a thundering roar of approval. Caspar squeezed his heels into his colt's flank and, in truly heroic style, they galloped down the road and out towards the canyon, fleeing south away from the encroaching Vaalakan armies and towards the belly of Belbidia.

Chapter 3

As dusk sucked the warmth from the air, Caspar pulled his cloak closely around him and waited. The light was failing but there was still no sign of Hal or Brid.

His eyes searched back along the line of the road. The dusty track melted into the shadows of twilight and he could make out nothing but the black jagged peaks of the horizon against the violet of a starless sky. Beneath him, his colt was still blowing hard from their furious gallop along the Great South Road and a white foam of sweat soaked the arch of the red roan's neck. Caspar slapped the matted hide affectionately.

'They will have made it, Cracker. They'll be here any minute,' he muttered with a slight crack in his voice as he tried to reassure himself as much as the agitated beast beneath him. Despite the arduous pace the animal had endured in their flight, the colt still champed at the bit and raked the ground with his hoof, unable to stand calmly. 'Hal said make for the plains, and we're here. There's nothing more we can do.' Startling the silence of the chill night, his voice rang out unexpectedly shrill; he coughed to steady himself. 'Nothing to do except wait and watch.'

No more than a league beyond Torra Alta, the enemy was mustering at the northern mouth of the Pass. Even from here he could see as, one by one, the orange dots of the distant Vaalakan camp-fires flickered into life, blurring into a hazy glow that snaked back into the canyon. The Belbidian youth involuntarily curled his lip in disgust and wiped his mouth with the back of his hand as if ridding himself of a foul taste.

Torra Alta was braced for the most barbaric attack in its thousand-year history.

A throbbing pain at the top of his calf nagged him to attend to his wounded leg. Satisfied that it was only a tear in the surface flesh, he bound it tightly with a strip of cloth and stoically ignored the pain, refusing to allow himself self-pity. If he was to ride out into the world as a warrior he would behave as one.

His gaze turned upwards. High above the canyon floor, the distant turrets of Torra Alta scratched at the sky. Every now and then a sizzling flare from one of Catrik's sulphur bombs made its arching trajectory off the heights of the fortress before spraying out in a flash of bright sparks. A flash of violent colour lit the Tor, the dull clap of the explosion reaching Caspar's ears a moment later. The sight of the flaring incendiaries instantly reminded him of the man who had devised these deadly mixtures of brimstone and saltpetre.

Catrik was gravely ill from his injuries, suffered down in the well, and hadn't uttered a word since their return. Grey and ashen he lay on his pallet, breathing fitfully, the flesh wasted so that his eyes bulged out of his shrunken skull. Though Catrik was officially the Wellmaster, he served the high stronghold of Torra Alta more as its chief engineer. Without his advice, the soldiers had needed to experiment with the kegs of sulphur, carbon, and saltpetre to estimate the ratio of quantities needed to create the desired range and spread of devastation. But Catrik was sorely missed for more than just his knowledge of alchemy.

Like the serrated ridges and sharpened points of the Yellow Mountains, the lone Tor was a black silhouette against the northern twilight sky. It lanced upwards out of the valley floor: a pinnacle of rock stretching up above the surrounding canyon walls. It stood alone, guardian of the northern Pass between Belbidia and the wild, ice-bound territories of the North.

Fancifully, the youth reflected on the history of the frontier castle, built and governed by his forefathers to command and protect the northernmost Barony of Belbidia. The Barons of

Torra Alta had presided over their domain for a thousand years, and in the last four hundred years they had known only peace that had stretched from the Ceolothian Wars to the present day. Now the glorious tranquillity was shattered by the encroaching Vaalakans, led by the barbarian Morbak the Butcher, as their savage hordes poured out of the North to assail the frontier. Only Torra Alta stood between Morbak and the luxuriant plains of Belbidia's ripe and abundant heartland.

'We will not fail,' Caspar murmured towards the castle as if his father could hear him. 'We cannot fail. This land, our land . . .' It was impossible to express how he felt about his homeland. The stray thoughts rolled over in his mind; he couldn't bear to think of how, in a few days, the canyon would be choked with the marauding hordes. 'The Runes of War will protect you until we return.' He spoke out loud, firmly reassuring himself. 'The runes will protect them, Cracker.'

The colt whickered as if disturbed by something lurking in the undergrowth and Caspar snapped back to the present with a jolt. 'Hal! Is that you? Hal!' he shouted out despairingly into the dark. 'I'm here. Over here.'

An owl screeched then cold silence filled the boy's ears. He sank back into his disappointed vigil. They should have been here by now, he thought restlessly and his anxious thoughts were evidently read by his horse. Firecracker was becoming more restless beneath the folds of the blue and gold caparison, tossing his head and jittering at the bit, so working the boy's hands back and forth at the end of the reins. The youth didn't notice. He merely stared back towards his home, searching the black shadows in the darkening plain.

'If they made it through, they should have been here by now, Cracker. Something's happened. Something's wrong.' At least talking to the dumb animal made him feel less alone in the eerie twilight.

'Hal said to ride for the plains, to the three beeches, by the ox-bow. Those were his words. He said the beeches. If I keep going back to look for him we'll probably miss each other,' Caspar murmured to the colt as he battled with his conscience over the best thing to do. He ran over and over in his mind the nightmare of events before he had been separated from the others.

They had galloped out under the teeth of Torra Alta's portcullis and plunged at treacherous speed down the tortuous ledge that spiralled the Tor. The rocky track dropped them at the foot of the northern scarp, spitting them into the canyon. Spurred on by the cheering garrison, they were eager to strike out with haste for Farona and galloped due South towards where the canyon widened out to sprawl into the lowland plains of Belbidia. Here in the northern barony, the Great South Road was more of a small winding track that followed the roaring course of the Silversalmon beneath the dappled shade of weeping willows. Choked with red and silver birches that battled for territory, the canyon floor swept towards the escarpments whose pale buff rocks soared vertically upwards to form the walls of the rift valley. The track was deeply rutted by oxen carts and the three of them had galloped in single file along the central grass ridge between the wheel-ruts.

Not more than a mile from the Tor, they were faced with a rushing spate of river. The Silversalmon pounded against a spit of solid granite that had fallen from the canyon walls to dam the river and water gushed across the plain, drowning the track. With the way ahead blocked, they turned west, twisting through the slender boughs of the silver birch to beat their way through the woods and back onto the track.

Hal naturally took the lead, still muttering that it was crazy to take Brid into Belbidia. 'You'll only slow us up on the journey and attract attention in Farona. Look at you, Brid. You look like a boy with your hair so tightly knotted. No Belbidian lady would sit astride a horse and they definitely wouldn't wear breeches. You look terrible.'

'Such gallant words,' she smiled sardonically.

Caspar had reflected that Brid looked exquisite whatever she wore. Her small elven features and startling green eyes held a mysterious magic and her smooth feminine lines certainly aroused *his* desires. She was physically beautiful but, more than that, her calm presence and her deep understanding made her soul beautiful too.

The Maiden had looked down at the old buckskin breeches worn through on the thighs. 'I'm wearing decent riding clothes precisely so that I don't hold you up,' she retorted stiffly. 'Besides I'm not riding to Farona just to please you with my looks. I'm going to seek out the lost runes of the cauldron and you wouldn't know what they were if a druid painted them on your face.'

'I still think it's too dangerous for you. You're a girl; women are just not tough enough to ride out unaccompanied at times like this.'

'I managed in the Dragon Scorch. That's a good deal more treacherous than the civilized plains of Belbidia.'

'But that's the point: you didn't manage. I had to rescue you.'

Brid tilted her neat nose skywards and then turned to smile at Caspar. The youth's heart always missed a beat when the young Maiden looked into his eyes. 'Is he always so infuriating?'

Caspar had laughed but the sound had stuck in his throat like an ear of barley. He didn't even have time to raise his bow. As they pushed through a blackthorn thicket, the dancing tune of a blackbird thrilled the air. It wasn't until a split second later that he realized the notes were a little flat and slightly breathy. A dozen men fell from the branches above, thumping down on the ground, all their hands grappling for Brid.

Wrapped in reindeer hide and with only black bear skins covering their naked chests, Caspar recognized them immediately as Vaalakans. His fiery colt reared and lashed out with pale hooves at the shrieking warriors brandishing their double-bladed war-cleavers. He had an arrow slotted to his bow but he couldn't get a clean shot without risking Brid. As the warriors snatched at her, she twisted her bay mare round, kicking and lashing out with her small booted feet. Finally Caspar managed to loose two arrows into the blur of flailing Vaalakan arms as the flash of Hal's sword beat through the ranks. At last the raven-haired youth cut a path to the Maiden's side, his horse thumping against the flank of the bay.

'Cut hard back towards the Silversalmon,' Caspar shrieked, suddenly seeing a way clear for his uncle to get the girl away from the enemy's reach and onto the road where they could gallop to safety. The Vaalakans clawed at her throat, fighting to strip the moonstone from her neck. He loosed a flurry of arrows, some spitting the Vaalakan warriors, the bloody ruin to their torsos more gruesomely obvious without any shirt to hide the wounds. If he could just cover Hal's back, the dark-haired youth could get Brid away. His aim was hindered by his colt rearing and bucking beneath him but at least Firecracker's lethal hooves kept the Vaalakans at a healthy distance from him.

'Cut towards the river,' he yelled as he wrenched the cat-gut taut, drawing it back towards his chin. A Vaalakan raised his arm to sweep his great battle axe at Hal's thigh. Just as the muscle of the Northman's upper arm contracted into one thick wedge of tissue, Caspar's arrow-shaft pierced the bulge of his biceps. With Hal protectively covering her back, Brid thumped her heels into the bay and disappeared into the trees. Caspar loosed another arrow at the back of a Vaalakan warrior who lunged after them in pursuit. He fell in his tracks as the quarrel lodged between two vertebrae. Brid and Hal would make it now; he was certain.

'Gallop for the plains. Meet ... beech copse ... ox- ... Silversalmon. Ride for –' Hal's words filtered through the trees, half lost in the guttural shrieks of the Vaalakans closing in on him. Caspar wheeled his colt in a tight circle and looked back towards the chaos of berserk Vaalakans. He pulled Firecracker onto his haunches, halting the roan in his tracks, so that he half-reared before twisting round into the frenzied mall of the ambush.

An arm clawed out of the forest of axes. Caspar could hear the snarling, bestial growls of the Vaalakan tongue as something grabbed his boot. He jabbed back frantically with his heel but the coarse hand tightened its grip and the biceps on the Vaalakan's bare arms contracted into a solid slab of muscle.

The horns of the warrior's helmet stabbed up at him above the grimace of a hideous blood-thirsty face.

'Get away. Get off me!' It was a futile desperate cry. The boy lashed out with his heel while Firecracker reared and thrashed the air with his forelegs, shrieking like a demon. The Vaalakan's grip lessened fractionally and the boy was able to muster his panicked senses enough to get a clear aim with his bow. The enemy hand raked at Caspar's thigh, half-dragging him from the saddle. Struggling to notch the crook of the arrow onto the bow-string, the Belbidian youth kicked madly whilst fighting to stay seated on the rearing horse. One of Firecracker's raking hooves sliced his attacker. His expression-less face stared blankly at the boy. Watery blue eyes, set wide in pallid cheeks struck out from beneath the insipid white hair. The clouded pupils hazed in the mêlée of thrashing arms and whistling axes cleared and focused on the face of the young Belbidian, the expression changing to cold-hearted determination.

Caught in the horror of the stare, Caspar fumbled frantically with the bow but at last he managed to slot the arrow home onto the string. He wrenched back the cat-gut and held the string level with his chin for a split second before letting the arrow fly.

The Vaalakan's jaw dropped open into the beginnings of a horrified scream but stuck fast as the arrow split his cheek and lodged into his palate. The warrior's brawny hands sprang instantly to his speared face as he clutched at the arrow shaft and fell to the ground, kicking in agony.

Without waiting to see more, Caspar snatched up the reins and jerked Firecracker's head round to face South, seeking any avenue of escape through the tightening circle of men. Axes surrounded him on all sides, steadily drawing in like a garrotte tightening on the neck of a sacrificial animal. He wheeled his horse around, searching for an escape route. The knot of Vaalakans tightened.

'Ready Cracker?' he hissed to his mount.

The cincture of ruddy faces and long blond hair wavered

in and out of the close packed trees, but continued to close on him. The mantrap's jaw was set to spring. Caspar spurred his heels into the red colt's sides and, giving the animal his head, he charged at the southern rank of Vaalakans. He selected a single warrior, the shortest in front of him, checking that the Vaalakan brandished an axe rather than the longer reach of a pikestaff.

Caspar counted the strides: five, four, three. The Vaalakan stood his ground, drawing back the axe ready to take a cleaving swing at the war-horse's chest. The boy touched his hand to his forehead where the old Crone had daubed the Runes of War. 'Come on, Spar, confidence,' he told himself, fixing the Vaalakan in the eye.

'We can make it, Cracker,' he yelled out loud to give himself courage whilst jabbing his heels into the animal's sides, encouraging the horse to make the leap.

The Vaalakan had braced himself ready to confront a direct charge and seemed unprepared for the Belbidian to attempt to leap clear over him. He ducked down covering his head with his arms to protect himself from the scything hooves that skimmed his horned helmet.

Caspar was too intent on the man beneath him to notice the pikestaff that lanced out from the left. Its point scraped upwards along the leather of his boot and punctured the fleshy muscle of his calf. He instinctively clutched at the wound, roaring out in anger rather than pain, and pressing his horse on towards the plains.

'Go on, Cracker,' he urged through clenched teeth, guiding the agile colt to curve through the close packed trees. The fiery Oriaxian stallion flattened his ears in a determined effort to flee the ambush. Storming through the gaps in the trees, Caspar hunched low over the horse's surging shoulders to avoid the whipping branches that skimmed over his head. As they struck the open road he pushed his hand up the red roan's neck, allowing the animal to stretch out into a flat gallop. 'Faster, Cracker, faster than the wind.' The youth had no time to look behind him. Hal, he thought, said make for the plains, for the three beeches by the ox-bow in the Silversalmon. Brid and his uncle must be working through the trees ahead of him; he could hear the snapping branches and the thud of horses' hooves. There was nothing else to do but ride on.

A cross-bow bolt skimmed past his ear. One tore a strip clean out of the horse's war-cloth but they were moving too fast, dodging too quickly through the trees, for the enemy to get a clear shot. At a whistling gallop they had sped to the safety of the plains where he had waited impatiently by the beech trees. After the first long hour of fearful waiting, he had raced back several times to search the edge of the woods for his two companions. When he didn't find them he dutifully returned to his allotted rendezvous.

But he had been waiting for several hours and now the canyon floor had succumbed to the darkness of night. Should he go back and search the woods just one more time? He had already ridden back and forth over the two miles that separated the ox-bow from the head of the canyon four, maybe five times. Each time he went back he had sensed the Vaalakan spies still lurking in the trees but he had been unable to find any sign of his companions.

Under the canopy of leaves it was already dark and from the edge of the woods he could hear uncanny noises; grunts and snuffles disturbing the undergrowth. The low breathy caw of a jay chilled his flesh; he instinctively knew its note was unnatural. Surely if the enemy spies were still prowling in the trees, they couldn't have found Brid or Hal. He was certain that his companions had ridden out ahead of him, but why weren't they waiting by the beeches? Perhaps they are wounded, lying face down in the mud, unable to move, slowly painfully dying, while I'm sitting here doing nothing, he despaired. But if I keep going back to look for them they might never find me. If Hal said to wait here, that's what I must do.

He filled his lungs and cupped his hands to his mouth, mimicking the cry of a nightjar in the hope that Hal would recognize it as their private signal since childhood.

He let the cry wail out. The colt laid back his ears and tossed his head nervously.

'Steady, Cracker.' Caspar laid a hand on the animal's neck, teasing out the sweat-tangled mat of hairs. The long wait had cooled the sweat to a crisp frost that knitted the stallion's smooth hide into stiff spikes. Caspar tuned his ears for a reply but could hear little bar the rumble of the river rushing by; the whisper of the wind rustling through the last remaining leaves, which clung crisply to the tall majestic beeches; and a soaring sparrow-hawk pealing out its cry. Gradually night crept in and the birdsong ceased. The sound from the river seemed to swell, making the surrounding silence even more oppressive.

I can't just stay here, he thought fretfully; but Hal said to wait. If I don't, he'll turn back into the trees to look for me and get ambushed again. Hal will come. I must wait till he comes.

He couldn't even get back to the castle for help. He would have to return through the thick of the trees, forced off the road by the diverted Silversalmon, and in the dark alone he would have little chance of getting past the Vaalakans.

A screech from an owl split the night, making the fine hairs on the back of the boy's neck prickle. The moon slid out from behind the silhouetted crags of the Yellow Mountains and battled through dark ribbons of cloud to shine wanly from behind the pinnacle of the Tor. The pale globe crowned the towers of Torra Alta, washing them in gossamer threads of silky white light. Caspar clearly understood why his ancient ancestors had dedicated their fortress to the Goddess and her Hand-Maiden, the Moon. Mesmerized by the vision of the Moon embracing Torra Alta, Caspar conjured a picture of the lone Tor as a giant, an enormous cloaked warrior, keeping constant vigil over the gateway to the North.

Firecracker snorted and backed up nervously, warning his master of a threatening presence nearby. The slight youth unhooked the ivory-inlaid bow from his back and slotted an arrow to the string, straining to listen for danger. The colt whickered, blowing a ghostly mist of warm breath into the night.

Two red eyes glinted in the dark. Both eyes glared directly forward but unlike the harmless eyes of a deer or ibex, these were the seeking eyes of a predator. Caspar stretched back the bow-string. The eyes stalked closer, betraying the stealthy approach of the nocturnal hunter. A mountain lion, Caspar thought. He steadied his breathing, preparing to take the shot, but just at that second, the eyes vanished into the black of the undergrowth. The boy felt cold sweat prickling along his spine as his self-control began to give way to an unnerved panic: he no longer knew where the animal might spring from.

He waited. The night was still again, all life swallowed into the emptiness except for the steady murmuring of the Silversalmon. Gradually his short anxious breaths relaxed, soothed by the heavy sighs from the colt who now dozed beneath him.

Then suddenly, tearing through the chilled silence, the mournful howl of a wolf panicked the horse into a fit of thrashing hooves. Firecracker reared, lashing at the blackness with his forelegs. Wheeling and bucking, he plunged against the restraining bit as Caspar fought to gain control. Any bolting horse could run in blind panic to smash its skull against trees or boulders and in the pitch of night it would certainly be lethal. He pulled the charger's head round, trying to control the animal's frenzied impulse to flee from its natural enemy. Soon the conditioned training of a war-horse conquered over natural instinct and the wild thrashing conformed to trained manoeuvres.

A wolf. The howl of a wolf. He was no longer afraid. If there had been more than one wolf there would have been an answering cry and no lone wolf would attack so large a prey without the support of its pack. He had Firecracker in hand now, keeping the animal firmly under control and concentrating its mind on his commands rather than the threats from outside. He drilled the horse through a series of manoeuvres: reining back, wheeling on the spot and the more

28

exacting falcades where he encouraged Firecracker to throw himself onto his haunches. It was an ostentatious manoeuvre he had been practising of late. The rhythm of the movements helped to focus his mind away from the unknown terrors of the night. A lone wolf was strange so far from the security of the mountains and so close to the Great South Road and the pulse of human activities. It could only be there because of Brid. Only the priestess could draw these creatures out of their natural habitat: she must be close. Caspar's spirits rose as hope grew within him. The eerie howl filled the night air again, but this time the battle-horse stood squarely on all fours though trembling slightly beneath his coloured war-cloth.

Rider and horse remained on watchful guard, waiting with anticipation through the long hours of endless darkness, but there was nothing more to disturb the slumber of the valley. His anticipation soured to fretful disappointment.

The very thought of going on alone without Hal was simply unthinkable. They'd grown up together as constant companions and Caspar had always considered Hal more an elder brother than an uncle. Brid was different of course. He hardly knew her but was drawn by her raw beauty and the enchantment of her mysterious words. What he did know was that alone, without Brid, they would be unable to uncover the cauldron in Farona or understand its runes.

Caspar recalled Morrigwen's last instructions. *Find the cauldron and they had the Egg.* As he understood it, those of the Old Faith considered Farona to be one of the four sacred cities. In olden days the cauldron had been guarded in the inner sanctum of a temple to the Mother. Morrigwen had known the place and as the Maiden had even walked up to the altar – though she had never actually seen the cauldron: that was only for the eyes of the Keepers.

Morrigwen was unsure that the cauldron or even the temple would still be there because of their close proximity to the King's palace. But if they could find the temple's razed foundations, she had been sure in her brittle bones, that somewhere the guardians would have left some sign as to where the cauldron was hidden. She had described Farona as it once had been: the wide airy streets avenued with trees, the squat wooden huts, the stock pens and the open markets. In the past, even though the New Faith had already stolen most Belbidian hearts, the old King Sithric, Rewik's father, had not enforced the southern religion on his people.

He tried to picture the capital as Morrigwen had described it, bustling with markets and huge arenas. The temple, she explained, was east of the river Dors between the barley-corn exchange and the foreign herb and spice auction, a place of great pilgrimage in those days. When King Rewik succeeded, he destroyed much of the old city, relocating the markets to the east quarter, to make way for his regimented streets, ostentatious town houses and the vast stone halls and spires of his new cathedral. This Farona of sombre stone dwellings beneath tall roofs was the city Caspar knew.

King Rewik the Converter was not, of course, going to welcome them into his city as disciples of the Old Faith. Branwolf had rasped at the coarse black stubble on his chin, considering the problem. The rotted workings of the old ballistas of course provided Hal and Caspar with an excuse for a visit to the Great Library and Hal's mother, Elizabetta, provided an explanation for Brid's presence.

Elizabetta had moved south the previous summer and her presence in Farona provided an excuse for a young maiden of Torra Alta to visit the dowager during the troubles along the northern border. Elizabetta was Hal's mother as well as Branwolf's step-mother. With the first rumour of a Vaalakan threat, she had immediately removed herself and all her paraphernalia to a manor just south of Farona. The Vaalakans had presented the young dowager with her first good reason for fleeing her step-son's castle. Elizabetta had not fled through fear but simply because she found little joy in her redundant position in the northern wilds of the Barony now that her son, Hal, was nearly of age.

When Branwolf's mother died the widower, old Baron Brungard, had plucked Elizabetta from the King's court and promptly married the young maiden. She had relished the prestige of being the Baron's Lady, but now as step-mother to Branwolf, she resented her demotion. For three short years her son had been second only to Branwolf as heir to the Barony of Torra Alta but when Keridwen gave birth to Caspar, it was certain that Elizabetta would never again hold any position of authority in Torra Alta. Having lost her rank as Lady of Torra Alta she no longer enjoyed the wild and barren lands, preferring to return South to where Brungard had first found her.

Yes, Branwolf had decided, it would seem quiet plausible that a young maid would be sent to the sanctity of Elizabetta's home at such a time. He had explained further that if Hal announced Brid as a kinswoman, Rewik would believe her to be the fruit of some indiscretion and this would easily explain his protectiveness over her in these troubled times.

Caspar smiled wryly to himself as he remembered Hal's proud chin when he took the parchment and stuffed it inside his shirt. Anything that pronounced Hal senior to his nephew gave the raven-haired youth a satisfied set to his jaw. Never a smile – that would be too obvious and rankle his pride – merely an arrogant stiffness to momentarily replace the mercurial humour that animated the older boy's face. Perhaps it was Elizabetta's jealousy that had rubbed off on her son, making Hal snatch at anything that elevated him above his younger companion, as if making recompense for that inevitable moment when Branwolf died.

An owl hooting in the beeches above, jolted Caspar from his ambling thoughts. Hal, he prayed, please Hal, don't be lost to the Vaalakans.

A grey light seeped out of the East and was reflected by the western peaks whose tips caught the first rays of dawn, swathing the distant snow-caps in hues of lilac and mauve. As the sun warmed the air above the peaks without yet delving down into the hollows of the valley, the promise of day coaxed a slumbering mist from the cradle of the river-bed. The mist spilt out over the banks and smothered the valley floor. Dawn touched a slab of basalt. During the night it had been as black as jasper touchstone. Now the wan morning sun probed the crevices and highlighted the brush vegetation, breathing grey colouring back into the rock and glimmering over green veins of olivinite. Caspar tensed as his eyes discerned the shaggy form of the wolf, which unbeknown to him had also kept an anxious vigil through the night.

The wolf drew up from its hunched squat and stretched out its maned neck, baying out a blood-chilling howl that stopped the boy's heart for a beat. The animal cried as if berating the morning for the loss of the comfort of night, before leaping from the rock and plunging into the sea of mist lapping at the fringes of the rocky outcrop.

'Brid's wolf, it has to be,' Caspar murmured, praying he was right and that his imagination wasn't drawing him into disappointment. He traced the shadowy form as it loomed in and out of the mist. The occasional sigh of the breeze stripped drifts of shrouding cloud from the wolf as it loped on stretched and tireless legs, before finally submerging totally into the whiteness. Caspar felt terribly alone as if his last hope had slunk away with the vanishing wolf. He strained his eyes, still trying to penetrate the morning mist long after the beast had gone. The haze stirred and curled in eddies where he imagined the wolf to be lolloping under the veil of cloud and he followed the ghostly ripples. Finally his eyes fell upon a dark shadow in the foamy sea of cloud.

Gradually the shadow condensed into a solid definition that swayed in and out of the mist. Like a dream on the edge of waking, Caspar wasn't sure if it was real or imaginary. The shape appeared tall and thin as it clumsily staggered closer. He rubbed his eyes to clear the dregs of denied sleep that dragged at his lids. Firecracker snorted, sensing his master's alertness as the dark figure stumbled towards them, labouring under the burden of a small body, slumped lifelessly with one arm lolling downwards, the fingers dipping into the mist.

Nervously Caspar drew his bow, uncertain of the approaching apparition. The red colt snorted, adding his vortex of white breath to the mist. The boy levelled the bow and focused it onto the advancing silhouette.

The form swept eerily forward, gliding like a ghost, its legs shrouded in mist.

Chapter 4

That night May slept badly, haunted by the chilling howl of a lone wolf that echoed between the canyon walls. She was restless, letting her mind roll over and over the events of the last few days.

Pa was dead. Killed at the claws of some monster. Her mind choked on the thought, unable to grasp it.

She reflected on the last few days since the Baron had brought them here to the cool heights of Torra Alta. She remembered reaching back to clutch hold of her mother's skirts as they rode up the breathlessly steep road to the castle and looked anxiously towards her younger brother. Pip hadn't spoken since the Baron had returned to their humble shelter in the forest. He blamed himself for his father's death; she knew that. When Ma had healed the Baron from his troll wounds, Pip had secretly run after him in search of adventure. Pa had followed to retrieve his son, sending Pip home, while he had accompanied his noble overlord to rescue Lord Caspar.

'Take heart, children,' Ma had told them. 'Take heart; he died a hero and we must be proud of him. He died to save our future baron.' She had nodded towards Caspar who rode ahead next to the broad, cloaked shape of the Baron. Lord Caspar: she hated him. It was his fault. So proud and arrogant.

When they first approached the castle, it was terrifying. Vast ramparts of solid rock formed the outer defences and, built at an impossible height, the buttressed whinstone towers soared into the heavens. Narrow vertical slits formed the only windows, allowing arrows to be fired at any enemy on the canyon floor far below. She had clung to the shaggy draught-horse, winding her hands through the thick mane as they swayed up the road. In places the track took them right to the edge of the Tor whose sides sheered away into cliffs and scree slopes. She had been certain she was going to be sick. Her head had swum as she peered over the edge and she could imagine herself falling forever downwards. Falling, falling, falling . . .

'You'll be all right. Just keep looking upwards,' a bright voice had reassured her. She had looked into the deep blue eyes of the auburn-haired youth who sat comfortably relaxed with the steady swaying strides of his horse. He had smiled kindly. 'It happens to nearly everyone the first time they come to Torra Alta.'

He didn't speak the way she imagined. He didn't sneer at her or disregard her as merely a peasant girl but looked straight into her eyes. She thought that the son of a nobleman would be too proud to notice her but he talked comfortably, retelling, with animated thrusts of an imaginary sword, how Hal had met and slaughtered the son of Morbak in the wasteland of Vaalaka. She had been frightened by Hal.

As they were jostled through the courtyard, she had clung close to her mother and tried to understand what was happening. The Baron's young brother had stood high in his stirrups, whooping wildly and her ears had reeled from the thunder of cheers from the soldiers applauding the safe return of their overlord.

Master Hal they called him. Only that tall dark Baron on his black war-horse was called Lord by the men of the garrison. When he raised his hand he commanded instant silence and a thousand eyes watched and waited while they listened for his every word. She could see the admiration and loyalty in all their faces and knew that, like her father Wystan, every one of these men would have laid down their lives for the Lords of the Barony.

She had watched from behind her mother as the crowd

35

drew round the Baron. There was talk of witchcraft and devilry and talk of the one true God. The curate who had visited them four times a year in the Chase had once said they would burn in hell if they worshipped the Goddess. But someone had told her that Curate Dunnock was dead and now this great Lord seemed to be saying that they should embrace the Mother. Even the short little priest dressed in sombre black had said blasphemous things. She didn't understand.

'Isn't it wonderful, May?' Ma's eyes had sparkled with joy. 'We can hearken to the old woman again, like we did in my youth.' It was the first smile to brighten her mother's face since they had heard about Pa.

The Baron didn't order them to worship the Great Mother. He told them he was no man's conscience – which Pip pretended to understand but she knew it meant no more to her brother than it did to her. Lord Branwolf said they were free to worship as they wished but that he himself would follow the ways of his wife and strive to restore the Trinity of the three priestesses. The crowd was confused. Some whispered of heresy, some prayed for the Baron's soul, but many cheered, many including her mother, Elaine.

'But, Ma,' she had gasped in shock, 'your soul will burn forever in hell.'

'Oh my child, but of course, you do not know the joy and peace of the Great Mother. To worship her is to understand life, to know one's purpose, to live at ease and in harmony with the world. To follow her is to restore the balance.'

The Baron's speech had stunned the crowd. But as the implications began to stir through the minds of the people present, a murmur had risen like a swelling storm. Only the educated clerks, the higher-born officers and a few of the younger soldiers grunted in disapproval.

The Baron had instantly recognized the seeds of discordance and urged reassurance on the younger men. 'I am lord of Torra Alta and you, my people, are free in mind and thought; no slave to the doctrines while I still hold this castle. Stand with me, stand boldly, stand to the last, so that we can turn away the Vaalakans and their terrible God of ice who threatens to crush us all. With the help of the Great Mother we will be forever free!'

Drowning out the anxious mutterings of the younger archers, who looked to the chaplain for guidance, the cheer from the older soldiers and women had been deafening. 'The Great Mother! Mother, protect us and preserve the precious balance of life.' Many of those who muttered anxiously about witchcraft cheered too. 'Praise, praise the Almighty; thank God for this freedom. We will follow, you Lord Branwolf; we will worship side by side though to different gods.'

May remembered being led away to one of the soaring towers. She had followed her mother's swishing skirts, listening to her breathing heavily as they circled round and round, scaling the spiral stone stairs that twisted upwards into the unknown. The serving woman who led them eventually presented them to a circular chamber made comfortable with soft furnishings of luxurious quality. May had fingered the embroidered cushions while Pip dived onto the soft couch and smothered his face in the silk drapes. This must be a lady's chamber, the girl had thought in amazement, but there was a certain mustiness to the room as if no one had lived there for a long time.

'These rooms were used by Lady Keridwen's ladies in waiting. They say she favoured this high turret room.' The young serving woman had shrugged her shoulders as she looked round the chamber. 'Dare say it needs a bit of a dusting but the Baron said you were to make yourselves comfy here.' She had left, closing the heavy oak door behind her.

Once alone Ma had exclaimed over the Baron's words. 'May, May, my little Merrymoon, Wystan has not died in vain. His death is helping even now to restore the Old Faith. Once Lady Keridwen, the Mother, is found the order will return. The world will be at peace again.'

'It's the Vaalakans, Ma, who are disrupting everything,' Pip had argued. 'Not the one true God.'

'No, Pip, no. Maybe Belbidia is a wealthy country now but

this new God has greedy followers. Everything is politics and ceremony. But the Goddess loves us just as we are and doesn't demand buildings and treasures costing the land a sorry fortune. Even I, a simple woodcutter's wife, can see how the tithe taxes have hit us all – even the wealthy like the Baron, himself. We'll soon be a hungry nation even if we do fight off these Vaalakans.

'This new way can't understand the delicate balance of nature; the cycle of birth, death, and rebirth. They fell the trees, they kill the boar, they overgraze and over-till the soil and it all produces more and more, until one year – nothing. The land is sucked dry with no more left to give.'

'But Ma, Curate Dunnock said that God created animals and plants to be put to the service of man.'

May had watched as her mother took in a deep sad breath. 'Oh Pip, it's so hard to explain when you haven't been brought up with the true understanding. I know the preacher said that this new God places man above the animals and that it's vile to think you're a part of nature. But, Pip, we are just one more of the creatures of the earth, part of the order. The stag has his antlers, the wolf has his fangs, the fish has his fins, all of us have a gift to let us adapt to our special place in the order of things. And we have the gift of rational thought. We must not use it to destroy the balance. Every year we cut the trees without allowing time for new saplings to grow. Soon there will be only death.'

'Is that what the Baron is thinking about?' Pip had asked still confused.

Elaine shook her head. 'No, he doesn't truly understand these things. The Old Faith had been fading for a number of years before it was actually outlawed. He only wants the Great Mother to restore his wife Keridwen and to save his castle. No, he doesn't understand. It comes from something that cannot be taught but is already within your soul – like in Keridwen's son.'

'The Lord Caspar – Master Spar?'

She had nodded and turned to the window, leaning forward

into the recess so that she could peer through the narrow slit. 'You can see for miles, right up the canyon.'

For two days May and her family had barely left the circular turret-room except to join the mustered garrison when Master Spar, Master Hal and the high priestess had departed on their quest.

May had glared resentfully at the auburn-haired youth on his high-stepping charger, which scattered archers from beneath its prancing hooves and jittered restlessly at the bit. She had remembered the embracing, protective love of her father and resentment bored out of her eyes. For a second he seemed confused, almost hurt by her gaze and she had hurriedly bowed her head and stepped into her mother's shadow. As the three riders galloped down the road, the crowd had surged forward, hanging over the parapets to cheer until they were no more than dots streaming out across the valley floor.

At last dawn squeezed through the arrow-slit and slanted across the chamber floor. May slid from her bed.

The castle seemed quieter now that the two noble youths and the Maiden had gone. Already the men drilled in the courtyard below and a watchman marched along the crenellations, signalling with sharp blasts on his horn. They moved with alert watchfulness, wary of the massing threat in the canyon below. Above them all fluttered the standard of Torra Alta, the gold dragon embossed on a brilliant blue background.

As she watched from the tower May thought that the garrison seemed subdued. The men bowed their heads, heaving huge engines across the cobbles to their new strategic positions. The thought of the impending attack muffled their voices in solemn anticipation. Bursting into the heavy silence came one explosive crash after another. She hated the yellow flashes from the incendiaries that they hurled over the battlement to test for range. All that day she jumped every time the bangs split the quiet to echo back off the canyon walls. But she had been told their purpose and understood its importance.

On the third day there was quiet.

The Baron strode through the courtyards and marched along the crenellations, muttering a word here and a word there, encouraging his men. They were ready now; there was nothing left to do but wait. The tension grew with the expectant silence. The castle walls and tower crenellations were lined with idle archers who checked and rechecked their bow-strings and nervously twitched at the quills on their arrows. The castle air was turgid with expectant silence.

May crawled into the narrow window recess and stared northwards along the line of the Silversalmon. Something glinted at the edge of the water. A grey shadow lay across the land. Her heart thumped. Pip squeezed in beside her and stared, slowly moistening his dry lips with his tongue.

The alarm horn blasted three short sharp notes from the watch tower, repeated every minute. Elaine snatched both her children to her bosom and clung tightly. There was no need to say anything; they all knew the Vaalakan force pressed against the Torra Altan threshold.

A sharp knock on the door broke up the huddle. Elaine swept to the door and pulled on the great iron ring. Standing on the threshold was the stooped form of the Crone.

'Come, Elaine.' Morrigwen said no more as they followed her down the spiralling stairwell, along the dark corridors, and through the courtyard until they reached the central keep. None of the servants or soldiers spoke as they scurried to their posts. The only sound was of leather-shod feet slapping on the stone cobbles and the persistent warning blasts of the horn.

'You must stay here now,' Morrigwen said softly as she stroked May's head. 'And you, little one, can keep everyone's spirits up with a cheerful smile. We'll all need it.'

May stared warily into the dark stone hall. The floor was cold and bare, the rushes swept clear as a precaution against fire. The hollow chamber echoed with the clatter of looms and the constant rhythmical, hissing tread of a spinning wheel:

the anxious faces of women and children raised to stare at the newcomers. May frowned resentfully and stepped closer to her mother. After several polite introductions, Elaine gave her children some carved wooden toys to play with and ushered them into a quiet corner.

Pip was disgusted. 'Can't I have a sword, Ma, or a bow? I want to do my bit too.'

'Don't worry, young lad,' one of the serving women said helpfully. 'No doubt there'll be too much work for us all to do soon. And then they'll want you down in the wellroom, I shouldn't doubt, and then you'll be sorry you ever had hands to work with.'

'Elaine,' Morrigwen appeared from behind a heavy velvet drape, which sealed off a stairway leading upwards out of the lower hall. 'I need your help. Bring your daughter too.'

The red-haired widow fixed her eye on her son. 'Now, my little imp, don't go pestering any of the soldiers. I don't want to hear you've been causing trouble.' May followed after her mother, keeping her expression sombre to mimic the adults. The old priestess looked terribly tired, and frail. She had seemed so strong when she rode along with the men but over the last few days she seemed to have aged.

The old woman smiled at her mother. 'I've missed my Keridwen for so long – such years of sorrow; and now Brid has gone into Farona. It's so good to have you two here with me, two others from the forest. It fills some of the emptiness.' She smiled at May. 'You're quite like my beloved Brid in many ways, little one – but blessedly not as headstrong, I dare say. Now, Elaine, do you know anything about herbs?'

'A little.'

'Good, but you don't need to know too much so long as you do as I say. Now keep quiet; we don't want to disturb him.'

They had climbed up two flights of stairs from the upper hall into the smaller chambers above. The old Crone climbed stiffly and stopped frequently for breath. She pushed open a heavy door and led them into a solar near the top of the

41

tower. A man, breathing heavily in short rasps, lay on a couch and moaned as they crept into the room. 'I need someone to sit by him; the castle physician can do no more for him and he seems to have taken a dislike to me. I guess he is one of the men that will cling to the New Faith. Gwion certainly did a good job,' she muttered bitterly. 'The garrison needs him and Branwolf is anxious that he survives. You'll have to sit by him.'

'I'm only glad to be of help.' Elaine spoke softly. She had said very little since she had heard the tragic news of her husband's death and, except on the occasions that she spoke of the Great Mother, she had withdrawn into herself. She sat quietly by the man's pallet.

'If he stirs, call me immediately. That's all you need do for now.'

'What's his name?' Elaine asked.

'Catrik. He was injured down in the well and has been like this for weeks apparently. Try not to let him talk in his sleep or move too much.'

May sat with her mother. It was long, tedious work watching over the old man. He stirred only occasionally and once or twice blinked his eyes open to stare dreamily at Elaine's face.

'Keridwen,' he groaned and then drifted off to sleep.

'You must look very like her. It's just what the Baron said when he was delirious,' May whispered.

'Hush, child. Don't wake him.'

Morrigwen returned later in the day with a pestle and mortar and some herbs.

'Here, this will give you something to do. Can you grind them up? We may need them in the next few days.'

The Crone swept soundlessly from the room and when she had only been gone a few minutes the slap of heavy boots echoed up the stairwell. May leapt to her feet and edged closer to her mother as Branwolf marched into the room. He tried to step lightly as he approached the sick man but the floorboards still creaked beneath his weight. He nodded in greeting and Elaine curtsied, keeping her head politely bowed.

May watched her mother and then mimicked her movements.

'Has he stirred?' Branwolf's voice rumbled in his throat.

Elaine shook her head. 'Hardly at all.'

Branwolf's shoulders visibly sagged as he sadly crouched next to the man's head and felt for his damp hand.

'Hello, old friend,' he whispered warmly. 'You've been asleep on us for a long time but the old woman will heal you now. I'm sure you'll be better soon.' He sighed and was silent for a moment. 'They're here. They appeared at the head of the valley this morning. We've got the soldiers making your spicy little explosives, but we need you to wake up, Catrik. Come on, old man, you can pull through. You can't let us young ones take all the credit for your good work. You're a tough old boar; you can make it.'

Catrik moaned. His eyes briefly blinked open. 'That you, my lord?' The words were barely audible between the rasping breaths. 'Spar, Master Spar . . . ?'

'He's safe. We got him back. You don't need to worry. He's gone with Hal to get help from Farona.'

Catrik shook his head. 'The moonstones . . . expl . . . explosion . . .' He slumped back in utter exhaustion, wheezing. His lips were trembling and his skin no more than a pale ash, deepening to blue around his mouth and eyes.

'Just rest now, Catrik. It's all right. Spar is safe. And you don't need to worry about the moonstones causing havoc in your wellroom. They must've all been destroyed or lost in the explosion. The Captain searched everywhere for them and he says they've gone.'

Branwolf rose to leave and nodded a farewell to Elaine. May felt uncomfortable. She didn't like the way the Baron's eyes lingered for just a moment too long on her mother.

'Watch over Catrik, May.' Elaine rose and walked morosely towards the arrow-slit, straining onto her toes to get a glimpse of the canyon, but from here she could only see the peaks of the Yellow Mountains.

May took her responsibility seriously, even watching the pulse in a vein on the man's wrinkled temple. He was muttering incoherently in his sleep. Nervously she soothed his brow and whispered like her mother had done.

'Hush, Catrik, sleep. All will be well.'

'No!' He turned his head from side to side. 'It's the Devil's stone. He tried to kill Spar with it. I know he did.'

'Master Spar's safe. Lord Branwolf says Spar's safe. The Devil won't touch him.'

'Spar's safe,' the old man relaxed, muttering her words over to himself.

'Yes, Master Spar's safe.' She felt embarrassed referring to the Baron's son in such a familiar way but realized that everyone in the castle called him Spar. Still she shuddered at the thought of him aloof and superior on his dashing charger.

Catrik had been sleeping peacefully for over an hour when the chaplain glided silently into the room. Smaller than most men in the garrison, with neat hands and a quick eye he had crept stealthily into the solar.

He looked at May, not seeing her mother, but when Elaine stirred he gave her a quick sharp look almost of shock. It was rapidly veiled. May felt that he must have realized she was hankering after the old ways and disapproved. The chaplain smoothed his hands over the long black sleeves that covered his arms and tightened his thin lips into a smile. 'Ah, yes, it's Elaine isn't it. Yes, well, I'll sit with Catrik now. You can take a rest and go back to the others.'

Father Gwion knelt by the man's bedside. They heard him chanting a psalm as they crept out of the doorway and coiled down the stairwell back to the tense atmosphere of the lower level of the Keep. A few women still worked anxiously at their looms while others had climbed to the windows and reported back on the inactivity from the outside world.

'Nothing, nothing at all. They're just sitting there at the head of the Pass.'

'I wish it would just hurry up and start. I can't bear this waiting any longer,' one of the younger women wailed.

A fat old woman, with ruddy cheeks and red hands from honest hard work, sighed calmly, replaced her bobbin and looked slowly up from her work. 'Don't say that, Rosalind; just be thankful for every last healthy breath you can draw. The only thing you can be sure of is that when it does start it'll be far worse than you can possibly imagine.'

'Cheer us all up, won't you, Maud?' a sharp voice rang out from behind a half-worked tapestry.

May studied the gathered serving women and decided that the suspense of waiting for the Vaalakan attack was fraying their nerves. All the preparations for war had been completed and they had returned to their needlework to distract their fraught minds.

Pip was wide-eyed with excitement.

Elaine gave him a sharp look. 'What have you been up to?' she scolded him.

'Nothing, nothing at all,' he said casually and gave May a quick surreptitious look, throwing his eyes towards a quiet corner of the room. Obligingly she glided casually through the groups of muttering women to the secluded corner that Pip had indicated as their secret meeting-point.

'I've been all over the castle,' he hissed with wide-eyed excitement. 'I've explored everywhere – the armoury, the stores, the well, the stables – everywhere.'

'Pip, you were told –'

'I know, but there's a locked room.'

'So?'

His eyes shone with wonder. 'I looked through the keyhole.'

Chapter 5

The dawn light caught the man's face, filling in the contours and defining the features. With heartfelt relief Caspar lowered his weapon and sagged into his saddle. He let out an exhausted sigh as the tension sank out of his body but rapidly stiffened again as a youth's angry voice rang out across the mist.

'For love of horse and hunting, Spar, give me a hand!'

Finally stung into action, Caspar leapt from the saddle, yelling with delight and relief. 'Hal! Hal! I'm coming. What's happened?' He sprinted through the mist towards his uncle. 'Brid!' he cried helplessly as he took in the image of the inert Maiden sagging in Hal's arms. 'Brid; what's happened to her?' In despair he looked on the girl's blanched face and the stains of blood that seeped through her jacket. Her head bobbed up and down senselessly to the rhythm of Hal's strides. The older youth took a few more valiant but exhausted steps until he reached the mossy bank sloping up above the moving mist that hugged the river.

Almost callously, Hal let his burden slump from his arms so that she crumpled into a heap on the ground with a painful thud. He then dropped to his knees and sank down beside her.

Caspar couldn't quite take it all in. Finally he steeled himself to ask, 'Is she dead?'

Hal avoided answering his nephew's question, but turned angrily on him instead. 'I've carried her all night. Right from the edge of the woods. Where the hell were you?'

Caspar was too intent on Brid to follow his uncle's train of thought. He crouched over the girl's prone body and eased his cloak under her, carefully enveloping her in the protective folds. He gently laid his head onto her breast and listened intently for the rhythmical pump of her heart. He jumped then steadied himself as he realized that the croak escaping from the layers of her clothing came from the salamander. He prodded it aside, carefully avoiding touching the moonstone and listened again for the Maiden's heartbeat. His own pulse and short, hard breaths were roaring in his ears, but he could hear no sign of life from the girl. 'Is she dead?' he demanded again.

Hal sighed. 'She'd better not be. I've carried her miles looking for you; if I thought she were dead I'd have left her with the Vaalakans –'

'Hal! How could you?!'

'If she'd been dead, it would hardly have made any difference to her now, would it? I knew she'd be hopeless. A mere scrap of a girl. It was bound to happen. So much for the magic runes, eh Spar?'

'So much for the runes,' the nephew agreed as he stooped over Brid's body, searching tentatively for injuries. His overlong fringe flopped over his eyes and he wiped the strands back with his fingers, smearing the woad stains that the old Crone had daubed on his forehead. A crust of black blood matted the girl's coppery brown hair at the nape of her neck and Caspar teased the dried blood away to reveal a purplish bruise and grazed skin. 'Get some water, Hal; we need to wash this. What happened?'

'Everything,' the dark youth replied dismissively. His usual bronzed skin was drained and sallow with fatigue. With a weary sigh he pushed himself up from the ground to unhook the canister of fresh water from Firecracker's saddle pack. He handed it to Caspar and slumped down again, massaging his thighs.

For a moment Caspar let his attention focus on the exhausted face of his uncle, taking in the sullen olive eyes sunk beneath dark brows and crowned with thick black hair. He had never seen Hal look so worn. He turned his attention back to the girl, wondering what they should do to help her, and at the same time pressed Hal for more information. 'You've got to tell me what happened. Where are the horses?'

Hal groaned and lay back on the moss, throwing his arm across his face to bury his eyes in the crook of his elbow. 'I thought we were clear so I yelled at you to fight your way free. But she blundered straight into a Vaalakan, a great brute of a warrior. He took a swipe at her, which she at least had the sense to dodge, but then he struck again and her horse took it full in the chest, just beneath the breast plate.'

'Oh,' Caspar commented inadequately.

'I got alongside just in time to run the butcher through, but not in time to help Brid,' he sighed remorsefully. 'The horse fell, trapping her beneath him. Fell hard too. I reckon she hit her head.'

'Mm . . . there's another mark colouring up by her temple,' Caspar drenched a torn-off strip of his shirt in water and draped it across the girl's brow. Perhaps the touch of the Silversalmon would bring her new life. He didn't know if it would help but he was eager to do something. She had saved his life twice with her powers and knowledge of the physics: he couldn't fail her now when she needed him. Hal had fallen silent so Caspar pressed his uncle for more information. 'Then what happened?'

'I put the poor beast out of its misery. It was thrashing and I couldn't get the girl clear. Anyway I eventually managed to drag her out and sling her over my saddle. We were very close to the track but in the fray my horse had taken a glancing blow to his hock. I didn't notice at first but as soon as we were in the clear I realized he was limping. Then of course, I couldn't get up a decent pace to get clear of the woods. I was hoping you'd had the sense to keep running for the open plains and weren't felled by the Vaalakans and lying half-dead at that thicket.'

Caspar nodded, acknowledging the concern for his safety.

'You know, those spies must have already been waiting for us.' Hal suddenly broke off from the thread of his story. 'How the hell did they know we'd be setting out for Farona? I'm sure it wasn't just chance: they were deliberately going for Brid and the moonstone. How the hell did they know?'

'Quite!' Caspar agreed. He remembered the traitor Dunnock lying dead near the cairn at the edge of the Vaalakan tundra. 'How on earth *did* they know?'

'Well, just when I thought we were completely in the clear, one of the Vaalakans got a lucky shot at us. My horse staggered beneath me with a crossbow bolt through his flank. I had to cut its throat too. Messy business.'

The younger boy shuddered at the mention of the crossbow, remembering the agony when he had been pierced through the ankle by an enemy bolt.

'Then I saw *him* in the midst of the ambush.' Hal's voice lowered to a chill whisper. 'I'm certain it was him again.'

Caspar raised a questioning eyebrow.

'*Him*, Scragg: huge Vaalakan brute with half an ear missing. Why didn't I kill him in that arena when I had the chance? I should have killed him with his own axe,' he added with bitter feeling.

'That Scragg won't forget that you humiliated him in front of his own men.' Caspar shuddered at the thought and tried to shrug away the uncomfortable memories of their captivity in the clutches of Morbak's cruel-hearted warriors. He nodded back towards the canyon. 'The Vaalakans will feast well on horse flesh tonight.'

'Mm, but they'll feast well on us too, if we don't get a move on.'

'They can't follow us into the plains.' Caspar sounded convinced but then his tone altered. 'Could they?'

'No army of course can get through the Pass as long as Torra Alta holds fast; but one or two spies . . . ? They couldn't last long in Belbidia but all the same I've had this pricking sensation between my shoulder blades ever since I got out of range from the woods.'

'Maybe that was the wolf.'

'What wolf?'

'Brid's wolf. It's been around all night.'

'Oh. Well, it's a shame you weren't as smart as the wolf at finding people. Anyway what were you doing here? I told you to wait by the birch trees beside the ox ford where the Silversalmon enters the plains,' Hal said accusingly.

'You did not!'

'I did! I wasted hours looking for you. I thought you were dead or stupid enough to go back looking for me in the woods where those spies were lurking.'

'Don't flatter yourself, I wouldn't go back to look for you. Brid maybe, but not you. Anyway you said the beech trees after the ox-bow,' Caspar protested.

'You heard wrong –'

A moan from Brid instantly stopped their bickering.

'We've got to find help for her as quickly as possible.' Hal suddenly became decisive. 'The nearest village, Willowbourne-by-Forge, won't be any use; there's only a smithy and an inn there if I remember rightly. We need to get to Baron Bullback. He's got a big court; he must have some sort of physician.'

'Will it be all right to move Brid though?' Caspar's voice was full of concern. 'I could go back for help. Morrigwen –'

'And how long will that take? The Vaalakan army was nearly at the foot of the Tor when we left. The canyon will be crawling with them and we might not make it back let alone succeed in getting that old woman out here. We've got to take her south.' Hal's fierce eyes glared at the doubtful face of his younger kinsman. 'Well, do you think we've got much choice?' his uncle demanded, irritation fringing his words.

'No. No, I guess not.'

'We can't just sling the girl over the saddle. I'm sure that wouldn't help her injuries so one of us will have to ride and support her.' Hal continued without pausing for breath. The need for decisions and action had renewed his vigour. 'I've walked all night, so I'm going to ride.'

Caspar resented his companion's arrogant tone and the way he automatically placed himself in charge, but he knew that Hal was right so he didn't argue. He didn't have the energy to argue; he was too preoccupied with worry over the slender girl. *If she dies we'll never find the runes and then we'll never find the Egg and then Torra Alta will fall. And we'll never free my mother.*

He looked at the darkening bruises that swelled the skin around her eyes and found himself praying that the Mother Goddess in all her love for her high priestess would open those beautiful vibrant green eyes again. 'Don't leave us, Brid,' he begged. 'We need you.'

Firecracker stepped out, tossing his mane and shying at every twisted twig or broken branch that lurked suspiciously on the verge of the Great South Road. The curb chains, which seemed to have very little restraining effect on the horse, jangled every time the red colt snatched at his bit. Hal's body lurched uncomfortably forward, his arms almost dragged from their sockets by the tireless animal at the end of the reins. The darkening colour of his face showed that he was obviously becoming frustrated and irritated by the horse's unquiet gait.

'What on earth possessed you to choose this brute? He's useless as a war-horse. No obedience at all. I'm telling him to walk and he just dances along like some silly spring lamb.'

'He's the fastest. No horse could outrun Cracker.' Caspar eagerly jumped at any conversation that distracted him from the ailing Maiden.

'I suppose that's great if you're retreating but he won't make much of a charger. If you ever get big enough to carry armour, this horse would crumple under you.'

Caspar sniffed, ignoring the insult. It was no good rising to Hal's goads because he always won the argument in the end. 'If you relaxed a little and didn't stiffen your back as much he'd be a more comfortable ride.'

'Don't try and teach me horsemanship. This animal needs a firm hand and telling what to do. I just want him to walk,' Hal declared in frustration as the animal stole three jittery sideways paces to avoid a curved stick that twitched in the morning breeze.

'Telling Cracker to walk, is like commanding you to sprout

wings and fly. Anyway you've got it all wrong; you don't tell a stallion anything. You can order a gelding, you can tell a mare but you can only ask a stallion, as they say. And this one, well . . .' Caspar reached up and pulled affectionately at one of Firecracker's smooth pricked ears, 'you have to suggest.'

'Don't be ridiculous; he's just a dumb horse.'

'Well, if that's the case, don't grumble when you can't manage him.'

'Huh!' Hal fell into a sulky silence, grunting as he eased Brid's limp body to rest against his other shoulder and swung his cramped arm to restore the blood flow. They paced on in silence, Caspar occasionally breaking into a jog to keep level, sometimes catching hold of the rippling caparison to steal a tow.

Where it had been nearing winter in the harsh mountains, it was still mid-autumn as they entered the temperate climate of the lowlands. They were still too far north for the production of the Belbidian grain, but already the soil smelt different: a rich loam that oozed fecundity and sprouted the dense lush grasses which fed the Jotunn Ox.

As the sun climbed towards noon, they reached Willowbourne-by-Forge and were greeted by a young boy in a grubby smock. He stopped dead in his bare feet and gawped at them, the stick he had been carrying slipping from his hand as he bolted back towards the circle of huts that crouched sleepily around the smithy. The rhythmical chime of hammer on anvil pealed out across the fields where a dozen of the high-crested, black-faced oxen grazed contentedly. The peasant-boy's flight through the village sent chickens squawking to either side and a squeal of piglets skittering to the safety of their mother.

The furious alarm of honking geese, brought nervous eyes to the cracks in the doors. A few braver herdsmen stood with pitchforks at the ready whilst they anxiously decided on the nature of the advancing nobility. None of the villagers spoke though one backed in towards the cave of the smithy and enticed the owner out to take stock of the Torra Altans.

What the blacksmith lacked in height he made up for in the breadth of his shoulders. The sleeves of his smut-stained shirt were pushed up over his elbows and his muscular arms looked as if they would burst through the seams. A well-worn leather apron protected him from the sparks off his anvil. He took his time looking the youths up and down before a broad smile filled his flushed face.

'It's nought to fret over, Bill, me lad,' he spoke to the anxious youth whose grip was white around the shaft of a pitch fork. 'That there crest on the 'orse's clothes-like is certainly of Belbidia and, if I ain't mistook, it's of the northern Barony. That be the dragon of Torra Alta. Aye, villagers, these ain't the wicked Northmen. Be that not right, young master?' He finally looked up and addressed Hal. 'You, Sir, and your squire are of Torra Alta.' He tugged at his thinning fringe in deference to their rank.

Typical, thought Caspar. Everyone automatically assumes that I'm Hal's subordinate. Then he supposed that since he was walking and Hal was astride the magnificent charger, it was a natural mistake.

'Good-day to you, Blacksmith, we certainly are. I am brother to Baron Branwolf of Torra Alta,' Hal replied courteously. His announcement was met with an awed gasp from many of the younger cowmen who had evidently had little contact with the outside world. 'But we need help.' He curled back the fringe of the cloak, which swaddled Brid protectively. The Maiden stirred and moaned but still didn't open her eyes. 'The maid here is injured; we need help urgently. Is there anyone here with herblore or physics?'

'No, Sir, the nearest physic be the priest at the Manor – that be the Baron's manor – another three leagues yonder,' the smith informed them, waving one of his blackened arms southwards.

Another three leagues, Caspar thought in dismay, glancing anxiously at the limp body of the Maiden.

'Thank you, and good-day,' Hal replied in what Caspar thought was a slightly too arrogant manner. The raven-haired noble snatched up Firecracker's reins a little too positively, causing the colt to prance sideways nearly trampling on an inquisitive young urchin who had stepped too close.

'Damn horse,' Hal muttered under his breath.

'Wait, please wait, me Lord,' a nervous voice broke out from behind the protective back of the smith. A large round woman, with full skirts and a huge bosom which sagged heavily on her belly, waddled forward. 'I've borne several childer into this world and treated 'em all, bless 'em, for their cuts and grazes. Let me look at the wee lass and see if there ain't nought I can do for her.' The peasant-woman smiled warmly, pushing up her ruddy cheeks so they looked like two round apples.

'Well, . . .' Hal began, obviously uncertain of the woman's capabilities and then continued more decisively. 'Here, Spar, give me a hand.' Caspar stretched up to reach for Brid's thankfully light body, as his uncle lowered her down.

With motherly care the woman folded back the hem of the cloak to examine the Maiden and the smile on her face froze. She stepped back in fright, busily wiping her hands on her apron as if ridding herself of some contaminant.

'What is it, Edith?' the smith grasped at the woman as she turned her horror-struck face towards him. 'Make some sense woman. It ain't the Plague, is it Edith, not the Plague?'

'Oh! Oh! No! Worse. It's . . . oh! . . . Come away don't touch it. Stay back,' she shrieked at her husband as he turned to look at Brid.

'Stop gibbering woman, just tell me –' His voice fell flat as his eyes fell on the injured girl's face and he too stepped decisively back. He swung round on Hal and Caspar. 'Wherever it be that you found her, take her straight back. And leave now. We don't want no trouble here.'

'Don't be ridiculous, man.' Hal snorted patronizingly. 'The girl's injured, not infectious.'

'That ain't a girl; that's a changeling. I don't know where it were you found it but you be taking it back, ere its people come looking for it and steal your souls away.'

'Come on, Hal, let's get out of here; these people are mad,' the younger boy said contemptuously as he eased Brid's limp form into Hal's arms.

'Don't you be taking that thing towards our Baron's Manor,' the woman shrieked. 'Take it back now or it'll be the perish of all of us.'

'It's only the bruising that makes her look strange,' Hal insisted, struggling to balance Brid in a comfortable position.

'It ain't, Sir. You've been led away from the right if you thinks so,' the smith answered curtly. 'It's got the features of a near full-grown lass but it's no more the size of a childer. The skin is unnatural bronzed-like and it's elf-shot – got the elf-look – like the fairies of Oldhart Forest.' The smith stepped out into the road. Hammer in one hand, he picked up a length of chain that swung from the door of the smithy. 'I'm a feudal bondsman to my Lord Bullback, and a faithful retainer. Walter! Bill!' he called for support from the villagers. 'We cannot be letting you past to threaten his household.'

'Stand aside, churl!' Hal roared.

'I will not be standing aside for the works of the Devil, be you the brother of a baron or the brother of a king.' The smith was bravely defiant though he cast anxious glances toward the hilt of the great runesword. 'Walter, bring your fork and shoulder me.'

'I'm not too sure, Jack.' The yeoman looked hesitant and shifted his weight between his feet. 'The way I be seeing it, our Lord Bullback has enough proper armed retainers of his own, who will protect his household a merry sight better than the likes of us. I ain't one to be interfering in the ways and business of nobility an' the like.'

'Nor I,' the other yeoman ventured.

'Just stand aside, man,' Hal ordered. 'I'm not about to run one of my own countrymen through, but the welfare of Belbidia is at stake.' He put his hand threateningly on the carved dragons whose interlocked claws formed the hilt of his sword.

'Oh Jack, do as he says,' shrieked the woman. 'Let them away from here. Come away, Jack; come away.'

'I stand firm! I'm no coward.' The smith's obstinate jaw was set tight.

'Oh, this is so frustrating,' Hal grumbled under his breath and then bent forward towards his nephew. 'Get yourself ready, Spar.'

Twisting his wrist through the stirrup leather and securing a firm grip on the pommel of the saddle, Caspar gritted his teeth.

'Ready!'

Firecracker exploded forward and Caspar pulled his feet up underneath him, bouncing against the horse's flanks for the few strides it took to draw level with the blacksmith. Hal roared out. His foot, on the opposite side to Caspar, kicked forward with the heel aimed at the stocky man's chin. The blacksmith, despite his brave words dodged sideways and made no attempt to pursue them as they galloped a hundred paces beyond the village boundary and drew to a halt. Caspar uncurled his legs and stretched his toes down to find firm ground before untangling himself from his handhold on the saddle. The horse was excitedly pawing the ground, lathered up after the brief exertion and eager to continue the gallop.

Caspar turned to take stock of the villagers. Evidently there wasn't one amongst them foolhardy enough to give chase. The youth instantly dismissed the threat of the smith and turned his attentions to Brid, whom Hal clasped tightly under the crook of his arm, trying to shield her from the buffeting ride.

'Is she all right? Is she any worse? Check on her, Hal; check on her.'

'Oh stop nagging, nephew. I can't do anything on this mad boxing hare of a horse. Here, we'll swap. We'll just get out of sight of those village oafs and get reorganized.' He looked back in disgust at the frightened villagers and regretfully sighed. 'Branwolf said that since the coming of the New Faith the country-folk had become more superstitious than ever.'

They paced on for several furlongs with Caspar firmly gripping Firecracker's bit, endeavouring to restrain the beast. The road twisted on, following the banks of the Silversalmon, which was lined with tall grasses, crisp and full-eared after the long dry summer that had swelled into the ripeness of autumn. Now in the month of Hunting the rich sward had tarnished to bronze. A sanctuary of weeping willows gracefully dipped their branches to taste the fresh waters of the Silversalmon and the two youths decided that they provided suitable cover from the blacksmith's superstitious eyes. They drew to a halt and exchanged places, carefully supporting the injured Maiden.

Caspar knotted the reins and hooked them to the raised pommel to allow him the freedom of both his hands. He positioned Brid so that she sat sideways across the colt's withers, putting one arm around her back and letting her head flop against his shoulder. With his other hand he twitched the fur-lined cloak aside and anxiously examined her face. Her eyes were shut and a dark, yellowing bruise spread from one temple towards her left eye, which was now puffed and swollen. Her breathing was shallow but slow and rhythmical. He heaved a sigh of relief; at least she didn't seem any worse.

'Why hasn't she come round yet? Shouldn't she have woken up by now?' he asked Hal, feathering his calves against the colt's sides, trying to suggest a calm forward gait. The movement reminded him of his own injury to his leg but he determinedly dismissed it.

'I haven't the faintest,' replied Hal dismissively as if he, too, refused to dwell on such sullen thoughts. He stepped out to keep level with Firecracker's high-stepping walk. 'How do you stop that animal from prancing?'

'Oh Hal, will she be all right? She's been in this half-dead state for a whole day. Are we ever going to get to Bullback's Manor? She needs care.'

'She should never have come with us. What good is a girl on a quest? We could find this cauldron without her. It's only a matter of searching Farona's ruins and she's just going to make life difficult. She's already had an entire village in hysterics because of her looks. She's a heretic, a pagan and I'm not happy that we're taking her to a cathedral city. No doubt our

57

souls are already in peril from what we're doing to save Torra Alta and the witch, Keridwen.'

'Don't you dare speak about my mother like that!' Caspar was livid with rage, suddenly fearful that Hal was right. Would all the people of Belbidia fear him and hate him when they realized that he was the son of a witch? They could all understand why his father had fallen in love with such a beautiful woman but that didn't make Branwolf a warlock. No, but being the flesh and blood of a witch? Pagan blood ran fresh and hot through his veins: would he burn in hell for it? Father Gwion would tell him; he would understand better than anyone else.

Carefully he drew his hand across the Maiden's brow, teasing away a strand of her soft brown hair that had escaped the matted braid. Brid was normally so defiantly capable, always in control, always driven by a purpose that demanded no compromise. Now she lay helpless, relying solely on their care for her survival, her diminutive form enclosed in his guarding arms.

She was quite the most beautiful creature he'd ever seen. Despite the gruesome swellings and the unhealthy colour of the bruise that marred the right side of her face, the fine features and full bowing lips pulled at his heart-strings. He gently squeezed her closer, hoping that Hal wouldn't notice the subtle change in his pose. He felt the thrill of her proximity pulse through his youthful veins. 'Oh Brid,' he murmured and then flushed, embarrassed by his own emotions, and decided it would be more honourable for him to focus on the road ahead.

He had been so absorbed in sighing over the fair creature in his arms, that he had taken in little of the surrounding view. The snaking road had slipped from the vast plains of grass to coil through the secluded umbra of a drooping willow glade. As they turned the last bend and rounded a languishing willow bough that rested on the riverbank, the road brought them out into the open. Suddenly they came face to face with the long horns of a Jotunn bull.

The sight of the massive white bull with its black head made Caspar jerk his colt to a halt. The impenetrable black of the creature's satanic face made it almost impossible to discern its eyes. Warily he sized up the great beast. The fatty hump at the base of its neck was as high as a plough-horse's withers but its back was flatter, twice as broad and covered with deep muscles that rose and fell like the swell of the sea. Its face was flat and broad across the cheeks and distinctively heavy-boned between the eyes compared to the female ox. What struck Caspar most was the arc of the horns, like the tusks of some legendary beast, curving upwards into two sharp points.

The tips of the horns deliberately lowered to challenge the travellers.

'Hal,' the boy whispered, not wanting to attract any more attention from the great bull. 'What do we do now?'

'Well, I'm not getting off the road for a cow.' A defiant stubbornness girded the young man's voice. 'We'll just shoo it out of the way and –'

'Don't be stupid, Hal. That creature's massively powerful; look how it's broken through the fencing. You've got to think of Brid. Jousting with a bull isn't going to help her injuries.'

To their left a field of heifers lazed in the mid-afternoon sun, mulling over the grass and ignoring the escape of the animal. The bull, whose powerful shoulders were hunched into heaps of muscle, took a threatening pace forward and scraped at the ground with a cloven hoof.

'We've got to do something,' said Caspar.

'Well, you run and hide in the field and I'll get this animal out of the way,' Hal boasted refusing to allow himself to be intimidated by a domesticated beast of burden. He stretched up a hand for the runesword and drew it from its scabbard.

'Don't be daft, Hal; that beast won't be stopped by you. Look at it.'

'If you're going to be a coward, you can hide behind me, nephew.' Hal's bravado had got the better of him and he stood with sword before him, preparing to take the bull's charge.

'For the love of honour, Hal, I'm thinking of Brid. We'll go back and find a way round.'

A plume of dust swirled up in front of the bull where its snorting breath stirred the ground. Caspar wisely urged Fire-cracker to step lightly backwards, though the stallion, like the older Belbidian youth, showed no signs of fear in the face of the horned brute. Hal still stood his ground, waving the sword about like a herdsman's stick to try and drive the over-sized beast back to its pen. Caspar fell into a dilemma: it would be far more prudent to search out a safer path, through the fields and away from the bull, but he knew his uncle was too stubborn to make a timely retreat and they had to stay together.

'Out of my way, you ugly cow!' The raven-haired youth twisted the blade in the air, swinging it over his head, the repeated slashes whistling through the air like the beat of an eagle's wings.

He's been practising, Caspar thought, deciding it would be wise to unhitch his bow from his back but, with Brid in his arms, he found it impossible to notch an arrow to the cat-gut.

Rather than enticing the bull to move aside, the sword appeared to agitate the beast further. The great ox now swayed from one foot to the other and started to pace steadily back-wards with horns lowered, preparing to make his charge.

'You reckless half-wit, Hal!' yelled the younger boy in despair. It was now too late to make a retreat.

A bellow from the Jotunn Ox roared towards them and dust spat out from behind its cloven hooves as it plunged forwards. Hal stiffened and took a step back, shocked by the speed of the bull's charge, before gathering his composure and leaning into the sword again. The bull skidded to a halt, bracing against its comparatively short front legs that sank low to the ground as they absorbed the pressure from the massive weight of its chest and shoulders. The bull backed up again, ready to make its next charge, leaving the boys to guess whether this would be a full assault or another feint to scare them off. Hal returned the bull's roar with his own thin shriek and lashed forward with the sword but the animal didn't waver. Instead it threatened with snorting nostrils and raking hooves that tore at the dirt. Caspar was mesmerized by the points of the great horns, which spread to a full arm's length. They had few cattle at Torra Alta and he didn't know much about them except that they gouged people with their horns.

The next charge was ferocious and direct. It was ten strides from the foolhardy Hal, when a grey flash leapt out from the ditch at the verge of the road and wrapped itself around the oxen's neck. Confused by the ambush, the bull swerved to the right, tossing its elephantine head and twisting back and forth to free itself from the snarl of gnashing teeth that ripped at its throat. For a split second Caspar thought it was a mountain cat – the attack had been so rapid and agile – but then he realized it was a wolf.

The bull wrenched his head upwards, finally freeing himself from the canines latched to his throat, and the wolf cartwheeled into the air with her long legs splaying outwards. The ox lowered his head and, as the flailing wolf spun in the air, he ripped his horns upwards, tossing the wolf clear over his broad back. The wolf yowled in pain and fell in a sprawling heap on the road, scrabbling to her feet, with a red slash across her flank. She slunk forward on her belly, snarling with lips peeled back to show a row of dagger-like teeth. A trickle of blood flowed freely from the torn flesh around the bull's neck. The two beasts stared at each other. Creeping up onto her haunches, the wolf prepared to pounce.

Quite suddenly the great ox wheeled round and cantered clumsily towards his pen. Apparently the over-sized beast had decided that these intruders weren't worth the effort and stood four square in his pen, looking startled and confused by his injuries. The wolf silently vanished.

'You're an idiot!' Caspar declared as the breath soughed out of his taut body and he pressed Firecracker forward. The colt danced and jittered as he swept past the broken fencing, his hocks springing beneath his hindquarters. 'Where did the wolf go? It'll probably die of its wounds.'

'So!' Hal replied churlishly, obviously brooding over his poor judgement at taking on the ox.

'That's Brid's wolf.'

The taller youth strode silently ahead, brandishing his sword, practising his battle skills to fill the awkward silence, but after a mile or so he turned with a solemn face towards his nephew.

'The ox looked so slow and cumbersome. They're always so docile under yoke. I didn't realize . . .'

The Baron's son knew these words were meant as an apology and that Hal was furious with himself. Caspar, too, was still so angry that he could only bring himself to grunt by way of an acknowledgement. 'Brid won't be pleased about the wolf.'

'If she ever wakes up to find out,' Hal muttered somewhat callously.

'She'll be fine, just as soon as we can get help for her. She has to be,' Caspar replied, drawing the Maiden anxiously closer. 'Look!'

They had reached the Manor's lodge gates and Caspar paused for a moment considering their plan. 'The blacksmith said that Bullback's physic is a man of the cloth, remember? We'd better make sure she hasn't got any pagan objects on her just in case the priest wants to examine her.'

'She always has that leather pouch full of herbs. You'd better take it and put it in your shirt,' Hal agreed. 'And the moonstone of course.'

Caspar untied the tresses of the leather pouch nestling against Brid's bosom and wove them around his own neck. The leather was still warm from rubbing against her skin. He eased out the smooth glow of the moonstone protected by its latticed pouch, extracting with it the red salamander that clung tightly to the orb.

'How could she go round with a lizard crawling over her breast?' Hal complained.

'We have to have the salamander. Its heat keeps Keridwen – keeps my mother – alive.' Caspar looked at the scarlet scales and wondered if the fire-drake wasn't paling a little, as if some

62

of its fiery nature was being sucked from it. He carefully avoided touching the actual crystal, fearful of arousing any prophetic power or distant images that the orb could force into his mind. He knew if he touched it, he would again feel the horrible suffering of his mother as she lay trapped in the claws of the glacier. He slid the moonstone into his saddle bag and the fire-drake scrabbled after it to curl possessively around the mystical glow.

A sweep of elegant beech trees crowded round a pair of vast wooden gates that were studded with bullets of reinforcing metal. The open gateway drew them on to a track that twisted through the woods. Eagerly they swung off the main highway and the trees thinned to give way to fenced fields of grazing cattle. The soft leaf-mould covering the drive turned to baked-hard loam and finally smooth cobbles, which announced the approach to a grand dwelling. Caspar shuddered at the sight of the huge grazing herds, scanning the number for any more stray bulls, but the pastures seemed only to be grazed by cows with the occasional large, seasoned calf. The shadows were rapidly lengthening and, as they turned the last bend, the boy realized how exhausted he was. He hadn't slept since the night before last and his arm was numb from supporting Brid.

By the time they reached the broad moat, which lazed around the sprawling manor, it was dusk. The drawbridge was down and there were no sentries on guard, which surprised the two youths. They were born and bred in a frontier castle and it was anathema to them that any main approach should be left unguarded. Belbidia had known four hundred years of peace, but Caspar was still shocked by the complacency in Jotunn. After all they were only two days' ride from the northern border and the threat of Morbak's barbaric hordes.

Firecracker's hooves clattered over the bridge and they passed two sleepy out-cottages still without being challenged.

'Shouldn't some soldier step out and demand something like friend or foe?' Hal suggested with a raised eyebrow.

They clattered noisily into the courtyard fronting the manor. The hall itself was already in the shadow of darkness, lying in the lee of the old Jotunn Castle which Baron Bullback's ancestors had deserted in favour of the greater comfort of the manor house. The centuries of peace had eaten at the foundations of the old castle and it had mostly decayed into rubble. Each season more and more of the great stones had been carted away to build pens and shelter for the valuable oxen. A welcoming glow of firelight flickered through the arched windows and the Manor looked warm and inviting.

'Still no watch,' Hal grumbled disapprovingly. 'Haven't they heard of Vaalakans?'

'They probably have every faith in Torra Alta,' his companion suggested wearily. 'Here, give me a hand.' He eased Brid down into Hal's upstretched arms and then slithered from the saddle to approach the grand oak doors. They were black with age, filling an archway high enough to ride through. Fashioned into the shape of a bull's head, a carved knocker hung beneath a latched peephole. He raised the knocker and beat it hard against the door so that the noise boomed out through the hall within. He stepped back to study the coat of arms engraved into the masonry above the lintel. The shield bore the head of a bull with a salmon leaping between the horns. Impatiently Caspar rapped at the door again. 'Open up! We urgently need help!' Almost immediately the small plate covering the peephole was snatched open and a face with several teeth missing appeared in the gap.

'Who knocks at this hour?' the face demanded, looking the boys up and down. 'Ah, I see. Torra Altans,' he decided without hesitation, allowing Caspar no time to answer. The face vanished, followed by the scrape of metal bolts being drawn back and the great doors swung outward, letting a wash of warm light flood out into the evening shade. 'Sirs, welcome and step inside. I'll get a groom for your horse and announce you to the Baron.'

'Thank you,' Hal replied courteously and carried Brid over the threshold into the hall. 'Spar, bring my sword. I don't want it left in the stables.'

'It would please the Baron if you left your sword in the

weapon room, just to the left in the hall.' The servant looked anxiously at the mighty broadsword.

'Naturally,' the youth assured him. 'But get help quickly.' Hal nodded at the girl's body furled in his arms.

Since the taller youth was cradling the injured girl, Caspar took the sword and hooked it carefully over a bracket in the weapon room. He prayed that no curious hands would unsheath the sword to reveal the incriminating runes on its fuller, but decided they had no option but to leave the weapon here. He shuddered as a cruel energy from the cold white metal pulsed through his body. A sense of cruel blood-lust emanated from the enchanted blade, contaminating him with its gruesome desire for destruction. Hurriedly he turned to concentrate on his surroundings and tried to push away the sinister feelings. The weapon room guarded a mere half dozen bows and two long swords nailed decoratively to the wall. He was disappointed at the poor display after the vast weaponry of Torra Alta's garrison, though he was impressed with the suit of armour hanging in the corner. Armour was too heavy and impractical for the rough terrain of the mountains and the sight was rare to his young eyes.

He returned to his uncle and whispered in a low voice so as not to offend the Jotunn household, 'Bullback might have a real suit of armour, but it's all rusty.'

Hal nodded but his eyes still anxiously pierced the dimness of the weapon room. 'I hope you put it in a safe place; that sword is priceless.'

'How could I forget?' Caspar retorted.

The old retainer shuffled back into the Manor, leaving the Torra Altans to wait in the stone entrance and disappeared behind two further arched doors. An aroma of roast meat wafted temptingly through to the outer hall.

'It's a few years since we last paid a visit here,' Hal spoke quietly. 'Do you suppose he'll remember us?'

'I don't know, but I hope there's someone here who can help Brid. Why are they taking so long?'

A rich voice boomed out from the inner hall. 'From Torra

Alta you say. Well, who? Is it Branwolf?' The doors were suddenly flung wide to reveal a bulky man with full ruddy cheeks and a generous belly. Still holding a knuckle of beef in his hand, he greeted them with a warm toothy smile, and a greasy handshake.

'Well lads, what brings you to my table? Branwolf needs my help, eh?' He looked them up and down and his brows knitted quizzically as he took in the body wrapped in Caspar's cloak. 'What's this? Have you had some trouble?'

'We need your help. It's a bad head wound –'

Caspar didn't have to explain. The Baron was instantly goaded into action, yelling orders to his servants to immediately summon Father Rufus, his priest.

'He's skilled with herbs and all the humours or whatever it is these people do. Now bring the poor lad this way. There's a quiet solar through here where he can be treated.'

The Baron had made the natural mistake of assuming their injured companion was a boy but Caspar didn't feel he had time to explain. He followed Hal into the chamber where a low couch covered in ox-hide was pushed against the wall. Hal gently rolled Brid onto the couch and arranged her limbs so that she looked comfortable, whilst Bullback ordered a fire to be lit and arranged for pitchers of boiled water. After a few minutes Father Rufus appeared in the doorway.

He was a thin man in an otherwise well fed household. The sharp points of his shoulders jutted up into the coarse brown habit that loosely covered his body. Beneath his hood his hair was white and his eyes looked too big for his starved, sunken face. He carried a large leather bag in one hand and a small earthenware ewer in the other. As soon as the man stepped into the chamber Caspar felt the hairs on the back of his neck prickle and the talisman that he wore concealed around his neck now felt cold and heavy. He gawped nervously at the priest who squared up to him.

'You'll have to stand aside, young sir.' Like his body the priest's voice was thin and sharp. Reluctantly, Caspar drew aside to let the priest examine Brid. She won't like this priest, thought the boy, perplexed by his conflicting loyalties. He knew that neither he nor Hal could help her but it still felt like treachery to let the pagan priestess be tended by a priest of the New Faith. What was he thinking! Suddenly Caspar was shocked by his own thoughts. Here he was anxious to defend a pagan from the touch of a holy man. He shuddered and inwardly muttered prayers to himself, fearful that the Devil might possess his soul.

Father Rufus's thin white hands folded back the cloak and he took a long hard look at the girl's bloodless face. His brow knotted into a frown and for a second Caspar thought he was going to react like the blacksmith's wife but the priest merely tutted at the injuries.

'A girl,' Bullback exclaimed in surprise. 'Oh dear me, poor thing, a maid won't be strong enough to pull through such an injury.'

'There's been a lot of swelling at the base of the skull, but it seems to be draining downwards away from the brain. I hope you've kept her as still and quiet as possible.' The priest didn't wait for a reply but Caspar felt a guilty flush colour up his cheeks. 'Here, young lad,' again the old physic seemed to have lost any deference to rank, 'help me roll her onto her side.'

Fortunately Brid's small frame made the task easy and the priest loosened the matted braid at the back of her head and combed back the strands to examine the wound. He tutted disapprovingly again. 'This should have been treated a day ago. She's tough to have survived but if she's lasted this long, I'm sure she'll pull through. If I leech her now the sanguine pressure should be released by morning.'

He tilted the ewer and shook it vigorously until five black leeches fell out onto his palm. He put the pitcher down and pinched a leech between his thumb and forefinger, placing the slug-like parasite onto the nape of the girl's neck so that it could suck her blood. Caspar felt queasy at the sight of the amorphous squirming creatures. It seemed so unnatural to inflict the beautiful, defenceless girl with the revolting blood-suckers.

'She needs peace and quiet. I'll sit with her but the rest of you must leave. My Lord,' the priest addressed Baron Bullback with a semblance of respect, 'if the Lady Cybillia would be so kind as to sit with me for propriety's sake, I will call you if there is any change.'

Hal looked up sharply at the mention of Cybillia's name and Caspar vaguely recollected a thin gawky girl with yellow hair, surprisingly slender for any of Bullback's offspring.

'Well, I've a good side of ox roasting by the fire, Hal. Are you and your young brother ready to join me? I think you must have a tale or two to tell.' He took an uncertain look at Brid's pallid face as she groaned, mumbling in her sleep and calling out for Morrigwen. She raised her hand to try and wipe away the leeches on her neck but it slumped feebly back onto the couch as if she didn't have the strength. 'A girl! You must be fleeing from the Vaalakans already.'

Reluctantly Caspar left the room and followed after his uncle and neighbour. He was so concerned about Brid that the normally galling remark, about being Hal's younger brother, washed clear over his head.

Chapter 6

Small puffs of smoke rose lazily from the old-fashioned central fire on the floor, filling the inner hall with a blue tinged fog. The heat warmed the room and a large spitted ox was laboriously turned over the sizzling flames. The black metal of the spit was turned by a small tread-wheel worked by a hound who paced tirelessly for the promise of a portion of the roast. A sweating, red-faced kitchen boy basted the dripping carcass with a carved ladle. His sleeves were pushed up and he nudged his brow against his shoulder to wipe the trickling sweat. The rafters of the hall rose to a conical peak where a hole served as a chimney to draw away the smoke. The walls were draped with colourful tapestries depicting hunting scenes, some with views of the babbling Silversalmon with spring salmon leaping up river, but most were of Jotunn Oxen grazing or under yoke. The far wall, however, was of naked stone except for a single-edged sword, supported on brackets and draped with a simple white sash.

The weapon instantly drew Caspar's eye and, without being aware of his actions, he protectively rubbed at his neck. It was an unadorned sword that flared out from the protective quillon of the hilt to form a gruesome cleaver-shaped blade. He remembered the crusader's sword from previous visits; it had induced many a gory tale of blood-shed in distant lands, which the Baron of Jotunn had revelled in relating. Under the sword a black oak table stretched the lordly width of the hall, basking in the heat from the fire.

'First, I must know whether you are here because Torra Alta has fallen,' the Baron declared, drawing a carved-back chair from the centre of the refectory table, 'otherwise I won't be able to eat.'

'No, no, when we left the Vaalakans were not yet at the foot of Torra Alta, but –'

'Enough!' Bullback raised his hand to cut Hal short. 'That's all I need to know. You've obviously been on the road a long time and now I know that Torra Alta's steadfast, we've got time to eat before you tell me what's happening. Without good hospitality you'll rush the details.' The Baron indicated two chairs facing him and waved the youths to sit.

Food, thought Caspar gratefully, reaching straight for a knuckle of beef from a jointed roast, and tearing out a ravenous hunk with his teeth. There were several other places laid at the table but the dirty plates strewn with half chewed bones and crusts of bread showed that several people had already eaten and left. The servants rushed round, hurriedly clearing away the remains and scattering the bones to three happy dogs who lazed by the fire. Bullback explained that he'd sent his family away so that they could discuss the welfare of Torra Alta and the reason for their sudden arrival in private. 'My boys are out of course, still organizing the drovers. It's a hectic time of year for us ox breeders. But we don't want the women folk disturbing us with their prattle, do we now?'

Caspar was glad that Brid wasn't able to hear such a remark.

'You'll need some wine to wash that down, Hal and young – ? '

'Spar – Caspar, that is.' He rubbed at his crooked nose to disguise his irritation at being forgotten when Hal was so clearly remembered.

'Hm, yes, wine for you both?' Bullback suggested, snapping his fingers at one of the servants who waited patiently behind him. 'The food is good and plenty and the Caldean wine is strong and mature,' the full-bellied lord boasted. 'It will loose your tongues and I cannot listen well on an empty stomach.' The Baron raised his horn goblet to receive the Caldean red that his servant poured from a leather bladder. He took a long breathless draught before allowing his arm to drop heavily back onto the board, letting the blood-red wine spill out over the rim. His hospitable grin reappeared, framing his strong white teeth.

The irrelevant thought that you'd need teeth like that to eat such a feast slipped into Caspar's head as he surveyed the fare before him. Crowded onto the table a selection of roast meats, some hot and some cold, rested on square wooden boards. The spaces in between were filled by chopped vine fruits, some that Caspar didn't recognize and he imagined were imported from southern climes. There were no vegetables of any sort but plaited breads and bowls of nuts added to the variety. The two youths tucked in greedily.

'You both look as if you haven't eaten for a week. I see I've finally got some healthy competition at my table,' the Baron laughed, leaning back from the oak board to make room for his stretched belly.

Hal raised his goblet to the Baron by way of reply since his mouth was too full to speak clearly.

'If you tire of beef and venison, there's always boar. I've already eaten myself,' Bullback announced between long draughts at his horned goblet, 'but I can always manage some more boar.'

Caspar followed the nobleman's gaze down the length of the table to the wild hog's head set on a pewter platter with an apple caught between its tusks. He shuddered inwardly, remembering the fate of the Belbidian piglets that they had driven through the Boarchase Forest in front of the Vaalakan spies to create a distraction.

'My word, you've stopped eating lad,' the Baron teased. 'You youngsters need all the meat you can get. You want to get as big as your brother here now, don't you?'

'He's my uncle,' Caspar formally replied, hoping that his irritation didn't show. And Hal continued the oft-worn explanation that the two kinsmen had repeated at every new occasion they could remember.

'Ah yes, yes indeed. Old Brungard remarried, I vaguely remember.' The news didn't seem to alter the Lord of Jotunn's view of his visitors, but he used the new knowledge as an occasion to make another toast. 'Your good health, young knights.' He raised his goblet and Caspar politely did the same. He took an enthusiastic gulp but then had to struggle to disguise the spluttering cough induced by the wine's rugged flavour.

'Steady lad. Not used to the stuff, eh? Better have some bread with it. I think it's pretty good stuff myself – a special import from Caldea.' The Baron's cheeks were becoming slowly redder and his friendly grin broadened at a similar rate.

'Yes, Sir,' Caspar choked, lowering his head to conceal his embarrassment. To Caspar's amazement Hal had emptied half of his goblet already. He wondered how he had managed it until he discovered that if he drank and ate so that the liquid mixed directly with the meat and bread, it slipped more gently down his throat.

The heat from the fire and the warmth of the wine ruddied his cheeks. He felt guilty eating such a robust meal when Brid was lying so ill but, as Hal had pointed out to him before they sat down, starving themselves would do nothing to help her.

'Serve up a pitcher of wine,' the Baron ordered one of his servants. 'Better still set it by the fire to warm and then you can all leave us. We need to talk.' The servants swung the roasting ox aside from the fire and released the dog from the tread-wheel.

'Yes,' Hal agreed gravely with a tone that his nephew thought was a little thicker and deeper than usual. He couldn't decide whether it was the effect of the wine or whether Hal was trying to sound more adult. 'We need to talk: there is much to discuss.'

The Baron pushed his hands forward, sweeping the wooden board and tossing a knuckle joint to the dogs. 'So,' the Baron looked back and forth between the two youths and satisfied himself that their bellies were full. 'What brings two young noblemen and a maiden away from Torra Alta in such times as these? The primitive barbarians can't have chased you from the mighty stronghold already.' He laughed at his joke but it fell flat on the two Torra Altans.

'The Vaalakans are not to be scoffed at, Sir,' Hal corrected him. 'We are indeed under a grave threat and the murderous hordes will soon be leaning heavily on the battlements of our home. The fortress will stand fast but there are too many Northmen to repel and how long the garrison can survive on their siege rations is difficult to say. We ride to Farona to seek help.'

The Baron's jaw dropped in stunned amazement and some of the colour drained from his glowing cheeks. 'By the Saints, by the Sword, Torra Alta, it's the country's shield, it's . . . it's unassailable. No ropy band of Northmen can destroy her, by God, Torra Alta's . . . well, Torra Alta's Torra Alta!'

'Their numbers are vast.' Caspar's words were slightly slurred but the talk of the threat to his homeland cleared his head as if he'd been doused in a pitcher of iced water. He picked up the empty horn in front of him, gazing into its depths and rolling it back and forth between his palms as he solemnly recounted their tale. He explained about the wells beneath Torra Alta and the caverns. He thought about adding colour to the story by describing the dragon, but when he reached that part of the tale, Hal with pursed lips and a disapproving frown surreptitiously shook his head at him. Glancing anxiously at the crusader's sword, he related only the suitably relevant parts of the tale, such as being captured by the Vaalakans and their journey by troll to the camp. He improvised about their escape, making no mention of Brid, feeling that any mention of witchcraft and sorcery would not be well received by his host. 'We were tied in a stockade but there was a sharp stone, which we used to fray at our bonds. I pretended to be taken ill and moaned like a peasant dying of plague.' Caspar had no idea what that would sound like but it suited his purpose and the Baron seemed impressed. 'When the guard came and bent over me, Hal smashed the stone onto the back of his skull, seized the man's dagger from his belt and sliced his throat from ear to ear.' Hal grinned approvingly at this unexpected part he had played in the escape. 'Then we ran.'

'Here we are gorging on meats fit to feed a king and yet within months Torra Alta's food supply will be gone and they'll be staring starvation in the face,' Hal expanded, thrusting his knife into the saddle of venison as if to drive home his point.

Three seasons from the time we left the glacier, thought Caspar; that's all we've got. He shuddered and looked up at the crusader's sword hanging on the wall. They had to save his mother; they had to get her out of the ice; they had to save Torra Alta.

'Good Lord, Good Lord!' the Baron stammered, too shocked to string a sensible sentence together. 'I had no idea. The oxen – you know, I've been so absorbed. Have to select the future stud bull from the pick of the calves and weed out those for cutting. Always relied on Torra Alta for protection . . . never thought. Come to think it, I thought it was strange when the messengers stopped riding by – but the oxen, you know – didn't give it a second thought.'

'We were ambushed by enemy spies in the canyon. We cut loose but the girl's horse fell and she was injured. My horse took a fatal crossbow bolt just as we were nearly out of range,' Hal continued, his voice racing as he remembered the speed of the action.

'But the girl? What was Branwolf thinking of sending a girl out without a sizeable escort at a time like this? A sister?'

'Well, um, sort of I guess,' Caspar replied vaguely, as Branwolf had instructed.

'Ah, I see.' The jowly cheeks of the Baron nodded up and down and he gave a knowing wink. 'One of Branwolf's dallyings bore fruit, eh?'

Feigning embarrassment, Caspar avoided the man's grin.

'So Branwolf's sending all his young ones to safety,' the large man voiced his personal deduction.

'No,' Hal was politely indignant. 'Only the young lady. We are delivering her into the safety of my mother, Lady

74

Elizabetta, south of Farona. But we ourselves are riding south to take council with the King and to get help for Torra Alta.' The simple half-truth seemed to be the most prudent disguise for their covert activities.

'Mm, I see,' said the Baron, not sounding the least bit convinced and obviously preferring his original conclusion. 'At the moment, the two of you appear to be walking to Farona. But I'll see to that; as soon as the girl is well, I'll see you all mounted and then you can continue your journey to the safety of Elizabetta's home. Now I need more wine.' Bullback rose from the table, pushing his chair backwards and toppling it against the wall. 'I need to think this all through. Torra Alta ... It doesn't seem possible, by God.' He tipped a half full pitcher of wine, slopping a generous helping of the Caldean brew into his horn goblet and sat by the fire, staring into the embers. 'Here, help yourself, lads.' The Baron carelessly waved his hand towards the pitcher and the two youths rose to join him.

The younger boy found that he was now beginning to enjoy the choking flavour after several goblets had mellowed his palate. He lowered himself onto the bench, which squatted by the hearth-side, and had the uncanny sensation that the seat was rolling underneath him. He gripped the seat to steady himself.

As the Baron brooded silently over the news of the Vaalakans, which had obviously come as a shock to him, Caspar guiltily remembered that the heady wine had eased his worries over Brid. Suddenly he decided to go and check on her. He half rose and Hal caught his arm. 'She'll be all right,' he hissed. 'Sit down and stop making a fool of yourself.'

After several minutes of brooding silence the Baron abruptly stood up. 'You'll take Cybillia with you of course. I need my boys here – we'll have to protect the oxen – but I want my daughter as far from the northern frontier as possible. If Branwolf is sending his young girl to Farona so will I. You'll have to take her.'

'No!' Hal stood up to meet the Baron full in the face. 'We

can't. Send her with servants if you must, but we can't take her. Brid's injuries have delayed us too long.'

'Nonsense,' the Baron of Jotunn was obviously quite used to having his own way. 'I can't spare any men at a time like this; I need them all to protect the oxen. But I want Cybillia taken as quickly as possible to safety. After all we're only two day's ride from Torra Alta. If you were ambushed this side of the fortress I can't take any risks. You have to take her. I will, of course, provide the horses and supplies you appear to be sorely lacking. You cannot refuse your neighbour this courtesy.'

Caspar saw that indeed this was true and reluctantly nodded.

'And I suppose Helena had better go too, by God.' He mentioned his wife only as an afterthought.

Hal sat down on the bench and slumped forward, holding his head in his hands and groaning as if he were in pain. The Baron ignored him. 'Yes, there will be a lot of arrangements to be made in the morning. I hope the young lass is fit because we don't want any delays. The servants will show you to a chamber. I'm going to bed.' He was about to stride out of the room but turned on his heels and climbed onto a chair to reach up for the cleaver-bladed sword. 'Northmen, thousands and thousands of them! And then an ambush!' He stroked the flat of the sword and tested the edge as if to reassure himself and then marched off, taking the sword with him.

'I now know why Branwolf always calls him the Ox,' Hal moaned. 'It's not because of his name, or his size, or because he is Lord of the Jotunn Barony where the great Ox is bred. It's because he's as stubborn and as bull-headed as that black-faced beast we met on the road. Come on.' He pulled his young kinsman to his feet and took him by the arm, since Caspar seemed to be swaying precariously, grunting as he took the strain of his nephew's intoxicated body onto his shoulder. 'You're too young for this, aren't you? Come on; let's go. One foot then the other.' Caspar merely groaned in protest. 'We've not slept for two days. Let's find this chamber, nephew.'

The young boy slept fitfully, falling in and out of dreams where white-haired men with bludgeons and axes leapt out from behind black-faced bulls. The bull kept changing shape, until finally its thick hide fell away to leave a screaming skeleton. The scream went on and on and then with a start Caspar shook himself awake to find it was morning and that the scream was real. Hal was already awake and struggling with his breeches. Caspar followed suit and together they rushed out into the main hall and followed the agonizing shrieks to their source. They found themselves at the door of the chamber where they had left Brid in the care of Father Rufus.

The room was bustling with people. For a heart-stopping moment Caspar thought that Brid had died during the night and someone had screamed on discovering her body. But as the shrieks started again Caspar recognized Brid's voice, shrill and defiant.

'Get that beast away from me.' She was standing on the bed with her back to the wall, her gown torn and falling indecently away from the smooth lines of her body. She didn't seem to care about her half-naked state but howled abuse at the priest as she clawed at her neck to remove the last leech and flung it right in the priest's face.

The man was praying, seemingly for the salvation of her soul. The riotous screams of several other women added to the confusion. A coarse-featured serving woman stood amidst the pieces of a shattered pottery pitcher, which she had obviously dropped in horror. Another middle-aged woman, grandly dressed in scarlet robes, her ample girth partially disguised by the tight lacing of her bodice, lashed the air with a shrieking tongue. The serving woman was senselessly screaming and pointing at Brid.

'Sorcery! Witchcraft and sorcery! She's like the fairy people from the forest. A changeling.'

The noblewoman, whom Caspar decided must be the Lady Helena, was shouting with more purpose for her husband. 'Bullback, bring the sword, the sword, Bullback. Cybillia, get out of here before you are bewitched.'

The fair-skinned maiden rushed from the room, sobbing, before Caspar had even realized she was there.

'Shut up!' the Baron's voice roared. 'Shut up, shut up!' The crack of a bull whip split through the high-pitched screams and finally Bullback's deep throaty voice quelled the riot. He looked around for an explanation. 'Helena?'

'Where's your sword? That whip's no use. Where's the sword for using on heathens?' The noblewoman was obviously a match for her husband and was unperturbed by his anger.

'What are you talking about, wife?' the man demanded looking down on her as if she were mad.

Lady Helena pointed coldly at Brid. 'My maid recognized it at once. It's a changeling and look how it defies the good Father Rufus here.'

The Baron frowned, obviously thrown off his stride by the unexpected revelation. He thunderously examined the people in the room. 'Rufus? Have you an explanation?'

The priest was carefully extracting the leech that was entangled in his wispy hair and Caspar secretly admired the man's composure whilst praying he would say nothing to condemn Brid.

'I am a man of the cloth,' Father Rufus declared pompously, 'and as such, if the work of the Devil were in this poor child, the good Lord would have shown me first.' He paused to slide the leech back into the flask and then continued. 'Certainly I would know before this serving woman.' For once in his life Caspar was relieved that the priests of the New Faith were all so stubbornly arrogant. 'It is my opinion that the girl's blood is poisoned by the wound from the pagan Northmen. And certainly she will need purgatives to cure her.'

'There! You see, Helena?' The Baron seemed totally satisfied by the priest's explanation. 'Your serving woman has heard too many folk-tales. Her family live too near the Oldhart Forest where their heads are stuffed with superstitious nonsense. Of course there's nothing wrong with the girl; she's one of Branwolf's brood from Torra Alta and he's a good pious man.'

'And the chaplain there has worked tirelessly to see to the construction of the new cathedral,' Father Rufus added earnestly. 'He would never let a nest of heathens fester in the heart of Torra Alta. Now, I know they have trouble in the very far north in the Boarchase but that's virtually in Vaalaka and a long way from the castle and its chaplain. Any man of the cloth would smell sorcery a mile off and call in the Inquisitors,' the priest reassured the Lady of the Manor. 'Since the beginning of this last decade it's no longer been possible for a creature from the dark worlds to lurk in the castle at Torra Alta.'

It struck Caspar that if Father Rufus had really known what had recently happened at Torra Alta he would be reaching for the verses from the exorcism.

'We must be ever vigilant against the work of the Devil,' Lady Helena sniffed by way of apology for her outburst and swept from the room.

'Now child, . . .' Rufus turned towards Brid who trembled with rage, still ready to howl abuse at him.

Caspar anxiously pushed himself forward and snatched up the cloak lying on the floor to wrap it around Brid. 'Look, she's just frightened and confused after her injuries. You're a stranger to her. Leave her with me and Hal and perhaps we'll be able to calm her.'

Father Rufus nodded in agreement and stood aside to let the Lord of the Manor pass through the door in front of him.

'How dare you!' Brid snarled at the two youths when the door closed. 'How dare you let that man touch me! I am defiled.'

'What did he do?' Caspar was shocked. 'Has he hurt you? I'll run him through!'

'Hurt me! Hurt me! He's a priest of the faith that burnt my mother; and you let him tend me! My soul is damaged beyond repair.' She angrily rejected the cloak that the embarrassed youth was trying to put round her shoulders. 'My soul is so injured that it will never crawl to Annwyn and my ghost will limp through the shadows forever.'

'Oh Brid, stop it, please,' Caspar begged, trying not to look at the cup of her breast and the pink nipple that jutted through her torn bodice as she tore at her hair in anguish.

Hal was showing no such decorum. He blatantly studied her with an amused look on his face and shook his head at his nephew's hopeless attempts to quiet the Maiden. 'Here, let me sort her out.' He shouldered Caspar out of the way, grasped Brid by the remains of her clothing and wrenched her towards him and off the couch.

He stared her straight in the eyes and then slapped her hard across the face just as she opened her mouth to scream again. Her jaw dropped open in surprise and then her face blackened in anger. She lashed out with a return slap. Taken aback for a split second, Hal turned his cheek and blinked before smiling back at the defiant priestess. He smacked her again; this time leaving red finger marks on the side of her face.

'Hal!' the younger boy objected. 'She's been injured.'

'Well, if she's able to make that fiendish noise, she's obviously feeling better. Aren't you, Brid?'

To Caspar's half relief and half disappointment, Brid began to rearrange the calf-skin jerkin to hide her nakedness and slumped back onto the couch. A pouting sulk shaped her lips. 'I feel awful. I've got a sick headache and my temples are pounding.'

'I'm not really surprised after all that shrieking.' Hal was unsympathetic. 'Are you going to be fit to travel? We can't keep you here very long after that outburst.'

'No, I'm not! Where's my pouch of herbs, that . . . that priest creature was going to poison me. Why did you bring me here? I would have healed quicker on my own.' She fumbled through the layers of the cloak, frowning stiffly.

'I've got it,' Caspar explained, scrabbling at his neck for the strings of her pouch.

Brid's possessive fingers clutched at the tools of her trade and sifted through the crisp leaves of dried herbs and the tubular shapes of roots and other diverse specimens that she used in her herblore. She selected a strip of wrinkled, greyish-brown willow bark and Caspar recognized it as the medicine she had administered to relieve his pain after he had been shot with the Vaalakan crossbow bolt. She chewed on the bark, wincing as the movement of her jaw pressed on her temples, and gradually began to relax as she sagged back against the wall with a sigh.

'I suppose you've got the Druid's Eye as well,' she assumed, gathering her usual composure.

Caspar nodded and the diminutive Maiden relaxed a little, drawing her arms protectively across her body and looked suspiciously round the room. 'You left me alone with that priest!' She lifted a pitcher, from the floor near the bed and swilled its contents. 'He's bathed my head in water, hasn't he? You left me alone and you let a priest of the New Faith bathe my head in water,' she accused.

'You were covered in blood.'

'Yes, but it might have been holy water; he might have baptised me.' Her face lengthened with the dismaying thought. 'My mother died to save her soul from baptism. I watched her burn.'

Hal remained calm. 'Brid, he's convinced you're not a pagan so I know he won't have tried to anoint you with holy water.'

'I'm sorry, Brid,' Caspar started to apologize, feeling very guilty about inflicting the priest on her. 'I knew you'd be upset, but you hadn't woken up in over a day and we thought you might die.'

She shrugged. 'I'm sure, as Hal says, there is no harm done but wasn't there anywhere else you could have taken me?' Brid pulled the cloak up round her shoulders, shivering. She looked awful. All the usual bright colour had evaporated from her face. She looked wan and tired and the ugly stain of the bruise round her right eye disfigured her fine features. Though the priest had cleaned away the crusted blood from her skin, her hair was still matted and clogged with earth and stale blood. Caspar reflected that she looked much as when they first met her, disguised as a hideously deformed creature.

'We tried at the village.' Drawing up a stool, the boy squatted down and spoke softly to try and win back the Maiden's trust. 'But you produced the same outburst from a woman there. She said you were a changeling, just like Lady Helena's maid was shouting. They think you're an elf-child.'

'It's perverse, isn't it?' Like pearls of dew, tears were forming at the corners of the girl's forest-green eyes. 'Once the most truly devoted followers of the Great Mother, it's the women who are the most afraid now. Once the new religion has poisoned their hearts they follow it like an ugly old maid who's found a lover for the first time. But they still have the intuition; they still have the stronger sight and they see the things that men don't see, especially the ones closer to the land, closer to nature. They have a pricking feeling in their blood but their New Faith twists and deforms their thoughts and they're eaten up by superstition. It's so sad, so very sad. How shall I ever bring the love of the Mother back into their damaged hearts?'

Hal interrupted impatiently, 'This isn't the right place for one of your sermons, Brid.'

'And you hit me!' The girl flushed red again.

'You were shouting and I'll hit you again if you restart that caterwauling and what's more, I'll hit you harder,' Hal threatened behind the shield of his brash smile. 'I'm a lot bigger than you and it'll hurt.'

Caspar couldn't decide if his uncle was joking or not but he was amazed at the way Brid, normally so defiant and independent, was quelled by Hal's words. There was a different look creeping across her face almost of admiration, he thought jealously. He'd been kind to her whereas Hal had hit her; and now there she was looking with big, wide astonished eyes at the dark youth.

'For the love of life, Brid, you look awful. You look like a relic,' Hal exclaimed callously. The poor girl ran her fingers through her hair and looked at the sorry mess in dismay. 'Now listen, you've got to bite your tongue and behave with as much grace and decorum as your wild temper can manage. We need Bullback's help with horses to get us safely to Farona and we don't want his suspicions aroused any more than they are already.'

'He's too absorbed with his precious oxen to notice much,' Caspar interjected.

'No, Hal's right,' Brid admitted. 'I didn't handle it well. I came round all confused, seeing that priest with his leeches and that harridan screaming "changeling" at me; I thought I'd been taken prisoner or something. The last thing I remember was charging through the canyon, and then suddenly being surrounded by shrieks and screams. What was I meant to think?' She took a long deep breath to steady herself. 'I was caught off guard. Morrigwen told me to be careful, but I wasn't prepared for this.'

'I'm sorry Brid,' Caspar apologized again.

'So you should be; you shouldn't have left me,' she flared up again, obviously prepared to listen to Hal but still furious with Caspar. 'You at least should have known better.'

'Father Rufus wants to give you some purgative herbs to cleanse the poison from your blood,' Hal explained. 'Unless you at least appear better we'll have to let him in.'

'No! You will not let him near me.' Brid quieted her voice. 'I will be contrite and demure and as soft-headed as a Belbidian maid is meant to be; but his leechlore will do more harm than good and will only slow our progress. I'll use my own herbs, thank you.'

'Well, get yourself together, wash up and pretend you are well enough to take breakfast with us. Can you manage that?' Hal asked, assuming a role of command.

'I can manage anything,' she retorted defiantly. She rummaged through the leather scrip that contained her precious herbs. 'Since the bleeding has stopped I need some Ovissian ribbed melilot to open up the veins and help clear away any stale, clotted blood.' She extracted a herb, which to Caspar looked like long-stemmed clover. 'It'll make me sleep too, so give me a few hours and I'll be a lot better.' She raised the herb as if in a toast. 'Let me rest and keep that priest out. Say I want that girl, whoever she was, to help me with my dress or something. That should keep that leecher away from me.'

'She's coming to Farona with us.' Caspar felt it was as good a time as any to break the news to the pagan priestess. 'Cybillia and the Lady Helena.'

'Well, as long as they don't slow us down.' She tentatively pressed at her temples and winced at the pain. 'I still can't think straight.' After a moment's reflection she murmured, 'Cybillia,' and then repeated the word as if she'd been mulling over the name in her mind. 'It's a good omen and the Mother always smiles kindly on three women together.'

'And perhaps we'll have fewer outbursts from the peasants along the way if you can hide between them.' Hal raised his eyebrows a little disapprovingly at the young priestess. 'Come on, Spar, we'll leave her to her potions and give her time to make herself look . . . well, look more normal. But,' his voice lightened and he produced one of his charming smiles, 'I'm glad you're well again, I guess.'

'Huh!' Brid sounded scornful as they pulled shut the old arched door on her. Hal and Caspar turned to walk down the corridor back towards the main hall only to be confronted by Father Rufus and the Baron.

'How is my patient?' the priest demanded.

'You just frightened her that's all. She simply requests the help of the gracious Lady Cybillia,' Hal continued in his most courtly of voices. 'She says she feels thankfully better and won't be needing any more medicines. She said specifically to apologize humbly to you, kind Father, for her tantrum,' the noble youth improvised and Caspar hoped that Brid couldn't hear his uncle through the door.

'Well now, that's good,' Father Rufus flustered, 'but I should check on her to be sure.'

'No, no. No need,' Hal said hurriedly. 'She begged me to send for female company only. She's a little shaken and a woman's comfort –'

'The Church is all the comfort she should need,' Father Rufus announced indignantly. 'She should look on me as the voice of God and not as a man.'

The arrogance of this self-righteous man was painful to Caspar's ears and he was very relieved when Baron Bullback, an essentially practical man, pulled the priest away. 'No good arguing with womenfolk, Father, no good at all. You've done an excellent night's work and we're all very grateful. I'll fetch Cybillia. Isn't there prime or matins to attend,' he suggested which brought a sense of urgency to the man's gaunt face and he scurried off without further argument. 'He's sometimes a little over-zealous,' Bullback explained under his breath. 'Come on, it's a whole eight hours since I've eaten. I can never think on an empty stomach.'

The hall was bustling with life. Four young men with the same burly, thick-set looks as the Baron, but without his heavy bulk around the midriff, were listening with angry faces to a herdsman at the door.

'Yes, sir. A wolf. The prize bull beyond Seven Beeches. The pen was ripped apart. Couldn't say if it were rustlers or the bull itself, sir, but the stud bull is distressed. He has fang wounds all round his neck. He'll patch up but . . . a wolf, my Lords, a wolf.'

Caspar felt his neck flush and he nervously pressed at his nose to disguise his expression.

Hearing the news, Bullback strode purposefully over to his four sons and the herdsman. 'Get a huntin' party together, lads, right away. Scour the pastures; comb the woods: I'll have this wolf.'

We'd better not tell Brid, Caspar decided and then thought sarcastically that if ever the Vaalakans did break out into Belbidia they'd never get through the Jotunn Barony. Bullback alone would hold them off in fervent defence of his oxen.

The Baron's sons urgently strode out of the hall, leaving the Torra Altans alone with Bullback and his wife, Lady Helena, who was already tucking into salmon and sweetmeats.

The lady of the house welcomed the boys to her table. 'My dears, Baron Branwolf's offspring, Hal and . . . and . . . ?'

Caspar bowed politely to the Lady of the Manor. 'Caspar, Madam. I'm Baron Branwolf's son and this is Hal, my uncle.' He stressed the word uncle.

'Yes, dear yes, I remember you. I'm not an old dowager yet.

Now my husband says there is danger from the Northmen and you have agreed to escort myself and Cybillia to the safety of the King's court. It's very kind of you to offer, but tell me, is the situation really so very grave?'

Whilst eagerly helping himself to poached salmon Caspar explained the story again. Lady Helena was persistent in insisting that the two youths filled her in on the details that her husband had neglected to tell her.

'I'm afraid my protective husband didn't make it quite clear. He feels that women are too sensitive to be made fully aware of state affairs.' She smiled coldly at the Baron who didn't look up from his plate. 'Cybillia must leave at once, but of course I cannot leave my sons.'

'What?' The Baron was obviously not quite as deaf to his wife's words as he liked to pretend. 'What! My Cybillia travel alone with these young lads! Noble or not they are still boys.'

'No dear, of course not,' Helena replied patiently. 'But her maid can go with them. That will be quite proper enough for me.'

'No! Helena, no!'

'Oh yes! Yes, of course, I know Cybillia is so very precious, but so our my sons and I'm not going.'

'You will obey me, Wife,' the Baron roared, trying to reassert his authority. A few months ago Caspar would have been very shocked to hear this display of domestic discord. A lady defying her lord seemed unthinkable, but after meeting the two pagan priestesses he now believed women were capable of almost anything.

'I am staying,' Lady Helena replied simply and without temper. 'And that's that. The serving woman, Hetta, can go.'

'Infuriating woman,' Bullback muttered and thumped his empty tankard on the table. The young kitchen boy, who last night had been basting the spitted roast, scurried forward and tilted a pitcher of ale so that the golden liquid sloshed into the cup. The Baron grunted a word of gratitude and turned to his visitors. 'Well, Hal, Spar, tell me what you need and we'll get organized. When do you think your sister will be able to travel?'

It was a while before they returned from selecting horses for Hal and Brid, and inspecting Cybillia's palfrey. Caspar had been very dissatisfied with Cybillia's cream gelding. He complained that the animal's chest was shallow and the pasterns too upright and so the horse would have difficulty keeping up and would go lame easily on the hard dry roads. Bullback was not to be persuaded, saying that the horse was safe and without vices and that he wouldn't have his daughter on any animal that might frighten her. Caspar had a natural horse sense and he selected, by way of compromise, a heavy-boned pack-pony for the luggage, reasoning that if the girl's palfrey went lame, she could at least manage the plodding nature of the sturdy mountain breed. They chose a chestnut mare for Brid with strong clean legs bred for hunting stag, and without any hesitation Hal selected a piebald mare of over seventeen hands for himself. He looked at his nephew for approval, who obliged by nodding reassuringly. 'A bit slow for my liking but the conformation's good.'

'She'd carry a knight in full armour as easily as carry a child, wouldn't you old girl?' Bullback reached up to slap the mare's black and white neck. 'Her real name's Warrior Queen but we call her Magpie. Used to ride her m'self for preference but she's a long climb up for my old bones.' He laughed, rubbing his stomach, suggesting it was his excessive weight rather than his age that made the tall horse difficult for him. 'She's very quiet around the oxen. Steady and bold in all other ways of course but she's particularly good round the oxen. Valuable animal but, if she helps you to protect my precious Cybillia, I'm happy for you to borrow her.'

They were still discussing the horses when they returned to the Manor. Caspar persisted with his loud protestations over the choice of the cream palfrey despite the withering looks from Hal, which warned that he was verging on rudeness. Only the sight of Brid and Cybillia waiting for them in the great hall silenced his complaints.

'Brid! How do you feel?' Caspar asked anxiously, forgetting his manners as Hal shouldered past him to make an elaborate and gallant bow, sweeping his fingers to touch the ground before the Lady Cybillia.

'It is a great honour, fair maiden, to have the privilege of addressing you.' That special tone had crept into Hal's voice. Mellow and rounded, it was a tone that the dark youth only ever used when talking to girls.

Caspar cringed as Hal's inflated words offended his ears. He also noted with a stab of anguish that Brid wasn't paying his concerned question the slightest heed but was pouting suspiciously at Hal's advances towards Cybillia.

Cybillia rose elegantly to her feet, standing almost as tall as Hal. Her willowy fragile looks were accentuated by the light gown, which fell in straight lines from her shoulders and the long loose hair that swung to her waist in a sheet of strawberry blond. She modestly pulled a wrap around her shoulders and bobbed Hal a demure curtsy.

'Your hair is like sunlight,' Hal began.

'Spare me,' Caspar muttered under his breath and the Baron gave Hal a withering look of disapproval.

'Don't forget yourself, young man. Cybillia is a lady.'

The girl's porcelain white cheeks flushed a feminine pink and she tittered nervously. She sat back down next to Brid: the pair contrasted like day and night. Cybillia was softly feminine with delicate movements and demure composure. Seeping with a deliberate air of helpless vulnerability, she was the epitome of courtly charm. Caspar wondered how two such ox-like people as Bullback and his wife had managed to raise so delicate a lamb.

Brid, on the other hand, was roughly dressed in calf-skin breeches. Her hair, now washed, was a mere bronze compared to the golden brilliance of Cybillia's locks and her tanned skin and hardened hands betrayed her peasant upbringing. However, to Caspar she had fire and zest, the love of life and the joy of nature, all of which the other girl lacked. Despite the disfiguring bruising, the boyish clothes and the fact that she'd kicked off one of her boots and was sitting cross-legged on the bench, she was nonetheless decidedly appealing to Caspar's young heart.

His thoughts were broken by a disturbance in the outer hall. Bullback's four sons burst into the room, letting their boar-lances and hunting bows clatter to the ground. The eldest rushed forward and with the flat of his hand slammed an object down onto the table. 'There Father, what do you make of that?'

Chapter 7

'We shouldn't be doing this,' May protested, slinking behind the heavy velvet drape that hid the stairwell.

'No one will miss us, so we can't get into trouble,' Pip reasoned, as they crept up the back stairs from the lower hall. 'Ma's much too busy.'

He led her through gloomy passageways until he stumbled on a low arch in the wall of the corridor. It led to a flight of damp cold steps that crept down into the dark.

'I'm not going down there,' May protested, wrinkling her nose at the dank air and shuddering at the thought of the dark.

'You've got to. It's the only way we can get to the west tower without being spotted crossing the central courtyard. It's only dark for a short way,' he reassured her. 'There's a whole network of cellars and tunnels down there. I haven't explored half of them but I've found passages that lead to the north tower as well as the mews by the west courtyard. If we take that one we can slip through the west courtyard without anyone seeing us and then I can show you the tower. Come on.' Pip turned and skipped down the steps before May could argue. She took one look at the cold blank walls around her and plunged after her irrepressible brother. She didn't want to be left alone in this deserted underworld.

She could hear the light slap of his bare feet as she felt her way along the cool walls but for a moment she could see nothing. She tried to ignore her racing pulse, telling herself it was childish to be afraid of the dark. Nevertheless she edged her hands forward tentatively, wary of plunging into a spider's web. At last a shaft of grey light fell from a grill in the ceiling and she could see the shadowy outlines of her surroundings. She bit her lip as she heard a rat scratching somewhere to her right and covered her face as she pushed through a curtain of cobwebs. Strangely she was no longer afraid of confronting a spider now that she could see. She was only afraid of them when they surprised her in the dark.

Pip was waving her on with excited impishness. She sighed in resignation. The tense inactivity over the last few days had aroused her younger brother's roguish desires for exploration. He would be quite incorrigible now, seeking adventures to make up for the tedious hours imprisoned in the lower keep, forced to watch the women rattling away at their looms.

For the last couple of days the Vaalakans had remained inactive, like some brooding monster. They camped just beyond the range of the castle ballistas, mustering their numbers and regaining strength after their long march. By day their numbers stretched to the northern horizon, lying like a smouldering fog over the canyon floor. By night their blazing campfires lit the black sky with an unnatural red glow, as if the earth's crust had cracked open and the flames of hell leapt up from the Devil's pit. The hungry mass of barbarians seemed to suck at their very air. The castle population grew fractious with weary anticipation, half-dreading the moment of full attack and half-praying that it would come quickly, so that at least the waiting would at last be over.

Ahead of them the tunnels split and Pip stopped and muttered to himself uncertainly for a moment or two, searching the bare walls with the palm of his hand.

'Are we lost?' May asked irritably. 'I knew we'd get lost.'

Pip merely grinned at her, his teeth flashing a bright white in the half-light. 'Now would I get us lost, May?'

'Huh!'

'Well, not this time anyway. Look, the passage is marked. There's a strange sort of sign carved in the wall.'

Despite her worries, May couldn't help her own curiosity as she fingered the score marks. She was only worried that they were disobeying the Baron's strict orders and so would disgrace themselves in their new home if they were caught and she didn't want to do that. Though she missed the Chase, she had almost become used to the giddy heights of Torra Alta and was pleasantly surprised by the friendliness of the castle inhabitants. Whenever they had met a fletcher or even the roughest looking soldier they would generally have had time to ruffle Pip's shaggy hair and give her a cheerful wink. The castle women, though generally more reserved than their menfolk, always had a smile and a nod for their mother.

She had expected the people of this austere fortress to hold themselves above the common folk, imagining that even the servants and retainers of the Baron would assume an aloof air of superiority above the woodsfolk, shepherds, trappers and boar hunters. But they were no different. Even the Baron acknowledged them. Though his face was tight with worry as he paced purposefully through the courtyards or marched the parapets, he always had a cheerful word for every one of them when he visited the keep – especially her mother.

The tunnel led purposefully upwards to a flight of steps where fresh air and bright sunlight flooded down to light the way. May could smell the wholesome aroma of horses stabled on fresh straw. Pip went first, looking furtively around him as they emerged in the west courtyard. They hunched low, creeping secretively through the shadows at the back of the stables and falconry mews until they reached the sheer upright masonry of the curtain wall on the west fringe of the fortress. They slunk beneath the battlements until they arrived at a stone archway recessed into the cloistered wing adjoining the deserted west tower.

The corridor was dark, lined with small oak doors blackened by linseed oil. Set between the grimy black of the walls, an occasional patch of brighter stone marked where presumably a large tapestry had hung for a great many years but had now been removed. The west wing was utterly deserted. Each door was no more than five feet high as if this part of the castle had been built by a smaller race of men. Several passageways led off the main corridor and by the time they were half way along its length Pip was looking left and right uncertainly.

'I think it's this way,' he decided. 'Yes, definitely. Here it is.' He hurried towards the foot of a circular stairwell that emerged from the base of a huge curved wall. 'This has to be the foot of the tower. You know, May, this castle's *enormous*.' He dragged out the word to give an impression of vast scale and spread his arms wide. '*Eeenormous!*'

'There's as much built down into the rock of the Tor as towers above it,' May commented. 'We could get lost here for ever.'

'No, look. I told you they were here,' he said, indicating the narrow opening of a stairwell. 'These go up forever. I reckon they lead right to the top of the tower and it's the highest in all the castle.'

Pip was certainly right about that, May reflected as she stopped for a moment's breath. Her legs ached and she was beginning to feel giddy as they twisted round and round, following the spiral staircase ever upward. Pip was even beginning to slow now and she leant against the outside wall of the stairwell to draw breath, rubbing her thighs to ease the ache. The stones were dipped in the centre, worn through by the endless passage of feet. A dark line ran level with her hand where countless other hands before hers had rubbed against the stone, but now the tower seemed deserted.

Pip skipped ahead of her and, determined to stay with her mischievous brother, she again heaved herself up the endless ascent. The spiralling steps became steeper and narrower so that she wearily stumbled and clutched to the sides of the wall as a giddy sickness swirled in her mind. She wondered how far she would tumble if she slipped. Even the arrow-slits, which lit the way with thin chinks of light, were becoming more intermittent and the air more close.

'We're nearly there,' Pip panted excitedly. 'Only a few more flights.'

Only a few more, May groaned inwardly, willing her legs to haul her up the endless steps. The stairs finally led them to another low-ceilinged corridor and May stumbled wearily forward. Pip walked quietly to the end of the passageway and stopped at the seventh door along. Capped by a pointed arch, it was smaller than all the others, being no more than May's own height. Instinctively the girl recoiled from it.

Pip rattled the handle. 'It's locked.' Disappointment clouded his face.

'Well, perhaps they're all locked,' May pointed out breathlessly. 'Perhaps it's to tell us we shouldn't be here.'

'Well, it was open before. They all were.' He tried another door and it swung open to reveal a plain chamber, which housed nothing but dust and cobwebs. 'They're all empty like this one. Apparently far more people used to live in the castle and all those with families had a room to themselves.'

'Oh yes? And how do you know that?' May asked incredulously. She decided that her brother was making it all up.

'I asked one of the guards. Anyway you can try another yourself. Any one of them; they're all empty in this tower.' He looked quizzically at the small locked door. 'But that one was open last time and it led to a corridor and more steps and another door – and that door *was* locked – and I saw something: a magical *glow* through the keyhole.'

She dragged at her brother's arm. 'What glow? Come on, I don't like it here. Just leave it. We should be getting back before we're missed.' The soft-hearted girl plucked impatiently at her brother's small hand. 'Pip, leave it. We'll go back to Ma. It's probably where they store explosives or vats of oil or whatever it is that they use for defending the castle.'

Pip shook his head. 'What right up here out of reach? Don't be daft. Girls! No, the storerooms are right by the central courtyard. The man there showed me the mountain of arrowheads. He said everything had to be in easy reach of the keep.' He nodded knowledgeably at his sister as he relayed the information. 'We've twisted through miles of corridors to get here. Look at the dust everywhere except on this door. It must be in use and up here alone it must be for something special.'

Pip was right, she conceded, but if it was something special they definitely shouldn't be here. He rattled the latch and May looked nervously back down the corridor.

'What if we get caught?'

'We'll say we got lost.' Suddenly he froze. 'Listen!' he demanded, putting his ear to the door.

Pressing her head against the dark panels of the wood, May struggled to calm her breathing. She was certain she could hear a scratching, snuffling noise, though muffled and distant.

'I know there's something alive in there.' The small tousled-haired boy felt through his pockets for a knife and began picking at the lock, twisting the blade back and forth.

'Don't,' May begged, hardly able to breathe. He merely turned and grinned at her as a satisfying click came from the lock. The door slid noiselessly open. It didn't lead into a chamber but into another corridor, whose roof pressed over their heads so any full grown man would need to hunch double to move through the passage. At the end of the corridor another set of steps spiralled up into darkness. Muffled noises drifted down the stairwell.

Pip went first, his bare feet noiselessly padding on the worn stone. As they crept up the steps, the shuffling and grunting became louder. They climbed on as the walls closed in tighter around them and the worn steps became narrow, treacherous ledges. At the top they came to another half-sized door.

May felt the blood drain from her face and fingertips as a stifled scream escaped through the keyhole. She pressed herself back against the wall but Pip, curious as ever, slunk forward and peered into the narrow crack. He looked steadily for at least a minute and then urgently gesticulated for his sister to look too.

She shook her head at him, but he whisked the air with an impatient hand and glared at her insistently. Reluctantly pressing her eye to the keyhole, she could see no more than a black cloak swaying just beyond the door.

She couldn't see the man but the voice, thin and angry, was cold with hatred and laced with bitterness. 'They must be stopped. How could that fool Northman let them slip through like that? But a letter to the King will still stop them. We must expose the girl for what she truly is. A brief, anonymous note will raise his suspicions.'

'Yes, Master, yes.' This second voice was eager but indistinct, the words slobbering as he drooled over his S's.

'But we can't be too direct. We can't have it traced back to me. *You* will have to go now that fool Dunnock has failed us. Just when I needed a man who cares more for the New Faith than his own country, the half-wit went and got himself killed.'

'Half-wit,' laughed the second deeper voice. His chortling abruptly stopped with the sound of a sharp slap.

Although May instinctively sensed an intense evil in the words, she could make no sense of their meaning. She swallowed hard, watching in transfixed horror as the black cloak stirred aside from the keyhole, revealing the mysterious glow that Pip had described. She could only stare agog at the shimmering white light that came from what appeared to be four glass spheres placed on a stone table. At first she imagined they were candles encased in globes of glass but she was puzzled by the light. Not only were there no flickering flames but the spheres emitted a ghostly white glow, rather than the warm yellow flame of a candle. A sleeved arm reached out to stroke one of the orbs.

'Ahh, I can see them,' he sighed with triumph but his thin voice quickly deepened into raw frustration. 'But those idiot Northmen have let them escape again. They are in some hall, some large manor with many servants. How is that fool shaman going to get at them now he's let them slip so deep into Belbidia? They must be stopped. I'll have it whispered that the girl is a witch and then Rewik will do our work for us. The Inquisitors in Farona will soon unearth her. The Vaalakan fools may have let them slip through their fingers, but the Inquisitors never fail.'

'Yes, Master. So clever, so very clever.' The voice was deep but flat as if not truly understanding what was happening around him.

'You will have your reward, Ulf. You will share my power, if we succeed.'

'Yes, Master, yes.' The voice gurgled with saliva.

'Now we must seek further guidance.' There was a squawking and flapping noise that came unmistakably from a chicken. May swallowed hard as she sensed a rush of evil emanate from the room. She couldn't see the man's face. Only his long-fingered hands and a portion of his back were visible, the outline indistinct because of his black cloak. With horror-struck eyes she watched him pin the shrieking bird down onto the table. With frantic movements the fowl flapped its wings in a futile bid for freedom. May cringed at the sound of one last terrified squawk before a cold silence slunk into the room, broken only by the satisfied breathing of the two men.

'Are the signs favourable, Master?' the dull voice asked greedily.

'There are many forces working against us, Ulf. Look at the twisted innards and the swollen liver. I must finally attend to the other one: her presence is now strong in this castle. I have already tried to dull her powers but I must do more. She must be removed from the field of play.'

The cloaked man moved slightly to the right and May's stomach churned as she watched him sifting through the entrails of the slaughtered fowl. Pip nudged her, as he tried to peep through the keyhole again.

'What was that?' the voice growled from inside the tower room.

They shrank back from the door, pressing themselves against the cold stone wall. Trapped in the claws of silence, they stood trembling, unable to breathe or move. The door creaked open. May bit her tongue, praying that her pounding heart wouldn't betray them. The door swung wider so that a stud on the panel pressed against her cheek as she turned her head sideways and silently drew in a breath, trying to make herself as thin as possible. She could smell the man's meaty breath as it rushed in and out of his lungs. She closed her eyes, held her breath and prayed.

'Nothing Master. Must've been a rat.' The door swung to with a heavy thud.

They didn't wait to see more. Stealthily they retreated, fearfully creeping inch by inch back down the stairwell. It seemed an eternity before they reached the low passageway and the endless spiral of the main stairwell. They raced down the steps and, too frightened to worry about slinking through the cloistered west wing and round the back of the mews, they burst straight out into the open of the west courtyard.

'Hey! What are you doing here?' The air was thick with the smell of sweet straw and the sound of contented munching from the horses in the stables. 'You can't come thundering into the stables like that, you know. You'll start a stampede. Now clear out of here.'

With their hearts still pounding in their mouths, they fled straight through the inner courtyard as startled soldiers looked at them in disbelief. May was too frightened to brave the dark of the tunnels that wormed beneath the castle courtyards, preferring to face the wrath of the adults if they were caught outside the keep without permission. Breathlessly they charged into the lower keep and May flung herself into her mother's arms, sobbing.

'Ma, ma!' Pip wailed, clinging tightly to Elaine's skirts.

'Hush, children. Whatever is it?' she soothed their heads.

'Ma, we saw a man murder a chicken and pull out its innards.'

Elaine looked at them aghast and then relaxed. 'No, you didn't. You two are always seeing strange things. Snakes turn out to be twigs and monsters turn out to be boulders in the dark. I know it's terrible that your father has gone but you mustn't let your mind play tricks on you. You've spooked yourself down in the cellars. Maud guessed that's where you'd gone. She saw you creep out behind the curtain. I've been worried sick for you. Now don't you go doing that again. '

'But, Ma . . . ,' Pip objected.

'Don't you "but Ma" me. Now, I've been waiting hours for you, worried sick. And the Captain was looking for you earlier,

Pip. He says that they could do with your help in the wellroom.'

'Wow!' His eyes blazed with excitement, his fears instantly banished. 'They want me to help?'

'I'll show you the way.'

'You don't need to,' Pip called over his shoulder as he charged off through the room, upending a spinning wheel and dragging a trail of yarn ten paces across the floor.

The flame-headed widow turned to her daughter. 'How could you have run off like that? These are serious times; you can't behave like a child, May.'

May cursed her brother for tempting her into behaving so irresponsibly. She was beginning to feel that she must have imagined it all and it was only her fear of the spiders in the dark that had conjured the strange images. Her mother's smooth practical tones made her feel certain that there must be a plausible explanation for what she'd seen. Typical though: Pip had already raced off. He always escaped any punishment, leaving her to bear the frosty looks of the adults. She missed her father; he never used to scold her.

She was saved from further reprimand by the arrival of the old Crone hobbling into the hall. Her blue eyes sparkling with those mysterious flecks of white, quickly scanned the women in the lower keep before resting on the red-haired widow. Impatiently the old woman beckoned them to her. 'So at last, you've found her.'

Elaine glared at her daughter. 'Yes, at last.'

'Good, come on; I need you to sit with the old Wellmaster again. He's too ill to be left on his own. You only need to sit with him to see if there's any change, so I can get back to my work. We will need a lot of herbs and potions as the weeks wear on.'

May wondered what sort of work the priestess meant and imagined cauldrons full of newts and sheep's eyes.

The old man was no better and if anything a little worse.

Morrigwen frowned over him and muttered to herself, 'I don't understand it. He should be better.' She stood up wearily.

99

'It's almost as if his spirit's broken. He just doesn't seem to have the will to get better.' Abruptly she fell silent and stood up, shakily putting a hand to her forehead. She began to sway precariously on her feet.

Elaine ran forward to support the old woman as she suddenly doubled up, coughing fitfully. 'May, get some water. Here, sit down,' the red-haired widow scolded, 'you've been driving yourself too hard.'

The Crone shook her head. 'I'm just too old, far, far too old; but I can't die. I cannot die until the worship of the Mother is restored and Brid is old enough to choose a new Maiden to take her place. I must not die yet, though my bones yearn to return to the cradle of the Mother. If I die now the Trinity is lost for ever.'

She took the cup from May but clutched her tightly for support as harrowing coughs shook her bony shoulders. Her clothes hung on her as if she were no more than a bundle of twigs knotted together with yarn.

She sucked at the water and took steady deep breaths. 'That's better, that's better.'

'You were all right when we rode back from the Boarchase,' May whispered, 'so I'm sure you'll be right again soon. Perhaps it's living in this draughty old castle.'

'No, I'm just another day older,' Morrigwen sighed.

Chapter 8

Lines of trepidation contoured Bullback's face. He took the measure of the metal shaft with his hand and flicked his perturbed eyes towards his four sons who anxiously crowded in on him.

'Where did you find this?' he demanded.

'By Flat Meadow Hidage off the road from Seven Beeches. We've got a dozen more.' The son thrust a fistful of bolts under the Baron's nose. 'The ground was strewn with them. We found some wolf tracks: they lead off towards the forest. By the look of the prints it was dragging one leg but we lost track of it in the forest.'

Caspar glanced anxiously towards the young priestess. Her eyes were wide, her pupils momentarily dilated to black pools at the mention of the wolf, but she rapidly calmed herself and set an expression of disinterest on her deep red mouth. Only her eyes betrayed her thoughts.

Bullback's son continued, 'The footprints vanished and then we found this.' He presented his father with a shaped wooden shaft about two feet long. 'Where can this have come from, Father? We've got an odd sort of rustler out there.'

'That's a handle from a war-axe, boys. We've got trouble in our Barony. Summon the yeomen, call up the tithemen.' He turned one of the bolts, inspecting it more closely before continuing, 'And those – those are crossbow bolts, an uncommon weapon in Belbidia anyway, but these ones – they're certainly not of our fashioning. Here, Hal, take a look. What do you make of them?'

The two Torra Altans were already squeezing their way

between the large jostling shoulders of Bullback's tribe. Caspar took one look at the broken axe and the crossbow bolts and his heart pounded in his throat. Despite his determination to show no sign of cowardice in front of his neighbours he felt his skin turn a clammy white. 'Vaalakans.'

'Vaalakan spies,' Hal corrected him. 'The crossbow is carried by their scouts and spies rather than regular troops. They're on our trail. Brid, are you ready to travel? We'll have to leave right now. Bullback you must set your men to finding these barbarians and I'm sorry we can't possibly escort your daughter now: the road will be too dangerous.'

'If any Vaalakans have reached this far south I want Cybillia removed immediately. I'll provide you with a full escort of men to the borders of my land and then you'll be safely into the heartland. Cybillia, my sweet, get yourself ready. You're leaving right now.' The Baron glared defiantly at Hal and the youth shrugged, realizing it was pointless to argue against such determination.

Brid was on her feet, still looking frail and ashen but she set her teeth hard and nodded. 'I'm ready! Cybillia?' She looked questioningly at the flaxen-haired girl.

'Oh dear no! Oh heavens, so soon; I've so much to pack.'

'No, you haven't,' Brid replied simply, returning to her normal, commanding self. 'Put some warm clothes on and some sensible boots. You don't need anything else.'

'But I can't cope without my wardrobe,' she whined. 'Especially not if I'm going to the capital. Father, please, I don't want to leave.'

'It's for your own safety, my child. I don't want the heathens to get any where near the fairest maid in all Belbidia. Now hurry along, my sweetest.' The Baron's voice was indulgent, a tone he appeared to reserve solely for his only daughter.

Within the hour, the three Torra Altans, Lady Cybillia and her maid, Hetta, were assembled outside in the courtyard that fronted the Manor. A stable lad was being spun round in circles, trying to restrain Firecracker and calling for help, but even with the assistance of two grooms, they were unable to steady the beast. Caspar strolled over and relieved them of the stallion's reins.

'Rather you than me, Sir.' The groom was rubbing his hands where the leather had bitten into his skin. 'That's some animal,'

Effortlessly Caspar swung up into the saddle. Religiously he checked on the girth as well as the leashes that strapped his quiver and other baggage to the back of the saddle. The caparison was folded into a neat roll and strapped to the rear of the cantle since Firecracker was generally more biddable without the war-cloth flapping around his legs to excite him. When he was satisfied that everything was in place, he looked round to see if his companions were ready.

Already mounted on her chestnut hunter, Brid drew the cowl of her cloak up about her ears and clutched onto the high pommel of the saddle for support. She did not look at all well.

'Will you manage, Brid?' the young boy asked with concern.

'Of course I'll manage,' she retorted. 'It's those two you'll have to worry about.' Brid's friendly disposition towards Cybillia seemed to have changed since she'd witnessed Hal's enthusiastic greeting of the noble maiden. 'We need to move fast but with those two . . .' She waved a dismissive hand towards the serving woman and the Lady Cybillia, not needing to say more.

'Keep him still, boy, keep him still,' Bullback's daughter berated the stable lad. 'Father, make this boy keep Diamond still. I can't get up if he's making him play up and dance about.'

Caspar's face dropped in dismay as he took in the picture of the placid cream gelding with its head hanging calmly level and despaired at the side-saddle.

'Hal,' he whispered, 'how on earth is she going to manage on a saddle like that?'

'Don't be ridiculous,' Hal looked snootily down from the back of Magpie's lofty back. 'She's a lady; all ladies ride side-saddle.'

'It's like tying your feet together and trying to run,' Caspar retorted.

Cybillia, dressed in a vivid scarlet habit with gold trimmings, lace collar and ruff, was still wailing at the palfrey for its disobedience. Caspar noted with irritation that the docile mount only moved at all when the girl wrenched hard on the reins merely to steady herself.

'He moves every time I get close to him. Father, do something.'

Poor brute, the youth thought to himself, it's got a mouth as hard as granite. Two grooms were now steadying the cream gelding whilst Bullback himself lifted the maid into the saddle. 'There, there, rose-petal, it's for the best.' The Baron made soothing noises to his precious daughter. Lady Helena hung back, keeping her distance from the farewells. Nobody paid much attention to poor Hetta who had been dumped into the saddle and was gripping tight with both hands, looking very bewildered and nervous.

The Baron stroked his daughter's hair and pinched her cream cheeks. 'There, my sweet child, your fair hair is worth more than all the golden wheat in Belbidia and your beautiful face will win you a lifetime of smiles. You'll outshine all the beauties at the King's court.' He kissed her tenderly on the forehead, before finally adding with a catch in his voice, 'Now look after yourself.' He slapped the palfrey's rump, so that it slowly paced forward with the others, and dabbed hurriedly at his eye.

Five armed retainers escorted the young nobles as they set off along the road taking them south towards Farona. It's over a week's hard ride to the capital even on the smooth, firm Great South Road, Caspar thought in dismay. It'll take more than a fortnight with those two women. Why can't all women be more like Brid? At least she knows what she's doing.

Brid, however, looked very much the worse for her injuries and nudged her chestnut mare forward, quietly joining the centre of the group. Hal was far too busy sidling up alongside

Cybillia to worry about details like the pack-pony. Caspar resentfully took the lead-rein, hoping that Firecracker wouldn't kick out at a strange pony so close on his heels. The two saddle-bags on either flank of the pony were dwarfed by several bundles all piled one on top of each other and stuffed with Cybillia's courtly gowns, hoops, head-dresses and veils. The whole pack shifted from side to side as the pony ambled forward. Despite Brid's protestations, the young mistress had insisted that she must have all her best gowns and head-dresses. They were piled in neatly wrapped bundles one on top of the other. Caspar couldn't understand why noblewomen needed so many different things to wear. Brid after all had only packed one dress. They turned south out of the avenue of beech trees and wheeled onto the road, the sharp clip of the hooves dulling to a more peaceful thud on the earthy surface.

They rode on in silence, with Bullback's retainers covering the rear now that Hal had pushed his piebald mare forward to take the lead. The dashing youth drew his magnificent sword, practising his battle-thrusts with artful grace. At least he had the sense to move away from the Jotunn retainers so that they would be unable to see the runes on the unsheathed blade. Hal had persisted in trying to break into a conversation with Cybillia but, while she was fretting over the fresh state of her palfrey, such a task had proved impossible. And now, Caspar cynically presumed, the battle drill was laid on solely to impress the willowy maiden. Brid looked up from beneath the fringe of her cloak and studied Hal's body as it flowed from one thrust to the next well-balanced sweep. He might not be impressing Cybillia but he was certainly impressing Brid, he thought sulkily. Not wanting to be excluded from the company of the priestess, he eased Firecracker forward only to find his arm being wrenched back as the pack pony dragged reluctantly on the end of its lead-rein.

By the time he drew level with Brid she had already trotted forward to ride alongside Hal and he had to fall in beside both of them, having missed his opportunity to talk to her alone. The girl was complaining about the Jotunn maidens. 'Our quest is vital to Torra Alta; you should have refused to let them come.'

'You were quite happy about them earlier. Something about the Goddess blessing three women together,' Hal reminded her, not in the least worried by her scorn.

'That was before I realized that they were total imbeciles on horseback and no more than a burden,' the girl continued, tilting her nose stubbornly into the air.

'Seems to me, Brid, that you were quite a dead weight when I carried you right from the edge of Torra Alta to the plains. You were a burden all night, and it's only because of you that we had to stop here in the first place.'

'You won't manage any of this without me,' she retorted. 'You wouldn't know a rune if the ancient Druid himself etched it on your nose, so you can't even begin to call me a burden.'

Hal glanced anxiously over his shoulder at their Jotunn companions. 'Sh! Don't talk of runes so loudly in their presence,' he warned.

The girl tossed her head arrogantly and looked back at the other females with disgust. 'Look what following a male God has done to them. It's made them less than half women and I doubt if they'd understand anything we were talking about anyway.'

Hal laughed. 'Cybillia looks all woman to me!'

'Well then, she's too much for you.' Brid's quick remark merely brought a disgusted grunt from the youth who turned to examine his sword of white metal. He tested the sharpness of the blade by scraping the back of his fingernail across the cutting edge: it was too sharp to test on flesh.

As the miles wore on Caspar had an uncomfortable feeling of being watched. A buzzard circled overhead and he hoped it was just its penetrating eyes that he felt burrowing into his backbone. He worried over the enemy crossbow bolts. How could any Vaalakan track them into Belbidia itself? They'd have to be in heavy disguise: northern Belbidians were always wary of strangers, having much wealth, property and stock to guard against rustlers.

'Would we be safer off the road?' Caspar suggested. 'The enemy wouldn't be able to track us as easily.'

'I'd thought of that,' Hal was immediately tuned to his nephew's train of thought, 'but we'll be more vulnerable away from the busy traffic on the road. And even if Bullback hasn't already got them, there can't be many of them otherwise they would have tried to jump us already. And we don't really know for sure that they're following us, do we?'

Brid shook her head. 'It's too much of a coincidence.' She dropped her voice so that the others couldn't hear. 'They were after the Druid's Eye, I'm certain of it. They weren't trying to just kill us; they wanted us alive so that we could reveal its secrets. They went straight for me as if they knew I was carrying it. They want her dead; they want Keridwen dead so that we can never rescue her. But to do that they have to free her from the glacier. So they need the Egg as much as we do.'

'But how do they know about the Egg?'

'How did they know that we were leaving Torra Alta and heading South?' Hal said by way of reply. 'Anyone could have overheard us, but why would any Torra Altan want to help the Vaalakans? It's terrible.'

'Why is she still alive?' Caspar asked, clenching his mouth to stop his lip from trembling. 'If the Vaalakans want Keridwen dead, surely Vaal-Peor would have crushed her in his blocks of ice?'

'That's one thing I do have the answer to,' Brid replied softly. 'Whoever put her in the ice chose badly for them and well for us. The Great Mother must have been working hard to protect her high-priestess. When they threw her into the freezing water, they couldn't have realized that they were at a significant point of power on the mantle of the Great Mother Earth.'

'The cairn?'

She nodded, casting furtive glances at the retainers behind them. 'It marks a point where lines of energy running through the bones of the Mother converge and concentrate. That's why Vaal-Peor has been unable to completely destroy her.'

'So they still need us and the moonstone,' Caspar concluded, anxiously looking behind him into the shadows. 'That's why Kullak and Scragg set the ambush.'

'Bullback will get them,' Hal said in firm, reassuring tones. 'And a huge Vaalakan warrior, with blond hair and a lack of decent clothes won't get far into Belbidia in one piece.'

It was already their fifth day of travel by the time they made the busy courtyard of the Halfway Inn and the soft hues of twilight bathed the sky. The Inn marked the southern borders of the Jotunn Barony, half way between Torra Alta and the capital itself and was welcomed by all. There had been no sign of any suspicious movements along the road and the thought of a Vaalakan ambush became more and more ridiculous as they pressed deeper into the populated plain of central Belbidia. For the retainers, however, the threat of the Vaalakans to their now distant families was spreading through their nervous hearts like cold creeping through an unlatched window in the midst of winter. They fretted to return North. Now that they had fulfilled their duty in delivering the Baron's daughter to the safety of the heartland, they were eager to return to their home village, anxious to protect their own families. The party of five retainers decided to start their homeward journey that night rather than wait until morning.

'We won't be spending the night, Sir,' the oldest retainer explained. 'Without the young ladies we'll get three leagues towards home before the night really takes hold and they'll be safe enough here with you. It's a large inn and the Baron did say this was where we were to take you.'

Carters and mule-drivers stowed their wares in the Inn's stalls before eagerly heading for the merry chatter of the tavern, where they were beckoned by a warming fire and the wholesome smell of roast ox. The Inn was bustling with life. A few itinerant tradesmen and merchants were gathered at one end of the room, separated from the locals by an open fire that dominated the centre of the hall. On the other side, shielded by the wafting fumes from the fire, a huddle of herdsmen and drovers happily exchanged stories over the frothy tops of their ale tankards. A general buzz of life and merriment filled the atmosphere. The sight of the armed young nobles with their impressive weapons and the cloaked women brought an instant silence to the room. A serving wench with a buxom bosom, gawped vacantly over a tray of hot soups and ale that she was carrying to the table nearest the door. The innkeeper elbowed her aside and stepped forward.

'My Lords, welcome.' He instantly recognized their noble bearing that starkly contrasted with the mannerisms of the rustics and travellers who normally patronized his public house. 'I'll find a quiet corner for yourselves and your ladies. You'll be wanting food, the best we have naturally, and wine. Would you prefer wine?' The innkeeper was obviously a little thrown out by the unexpected travellers. 'Whenever the Baron passes through he sends messengers in advance . . .'

Hal raised his hand to stem the innkeeper's constant torrent of anxious words. 'I'm from Torra Alta; we don't hold with as much ceremony as the lowlanders. Ale will be fine and something more refined for the ladies.'

'I'll choose for myself,' Brid announced stiffly, which raised a few eyebrows on the nearest table. She followed the innkeeper to a secluded table near the rear of the hall, cordoned off by a lattice of struts that formed part of the framework of the inn. Once they were alone Hetta spoke for the first time in several hours, quietly addressing Cybillia. 'My Lady, will you excuse me. I'm not hungry; I'll wait in the chamber for you but –'

'Yes, Hetta,' Cybillia waved her aside without a thought. Caspar found it strange that the girl could be so offhand with her servants and yet so demure amongst nobles. He put it down to upbringing. The four of them sat around the wooden table, Cybillia fastidiously sweeping her chair before she deigned to delicately lower herself. She sat with a stiff back and disdainfully nibbled at the slices of ham laid before her.

Brid pushed her plate away and propped her head up in her hand, resting the grubby elbows of her calf-skin jacket on the table.

'You must eat, Brid. I know you still feel bad but you must eat,' Caspar coaxed her, half-anticipating a tart remark, knowing that Brid never liked to be told what to do.

Much to his surprise she nodded at him. 'I know; you're right. I'll have something in a minute. I felt better in the fresh air outside but the heat is making my head swim again.' She pulled the scrip of herbs out from around her neck and rummaged inside for some more of the pain-killing willow bark. 'I'll be better in the morning. I just need another good night's sleep.'

Cybillia's dusty blue eyes focused on the leather pouch and her smooth brow puckered into a band of furrows. She returned to her meal without commenting and Brid glanced with resentment at the Jotunn lady. Caspar realized, of course, that Cybillia's presence greatly inhibited Brid's freedom to express herself. He was not surprised when the pagan Maiden picked up her plate and went to sit alone by the fire, pulling the cloak around her hunched shoulders. Her coppery brown hair flowed loosely over her back and in the glow of the embers it rippled with streaks of gold. The naiveté in Caspar's heart made him yearn to protect her from the pain.

'Did I say anything to offend her?' Cybillia asked meekly.

'I'll talk to her,' Caspar offered, glad to have an excuse. 'All the terrors of the Vaalakans must be catching up with her,' he apologized to Cybillia for the young girl's unsociable behaviour. 'She's not her usual self.'

The heat from the fire blasted Caspar's face and he rubbed his crooked nose, trying to push the gristle straight again. The subconscious action helped him to organize his thoughts. The heat from the fire was fierce and he wanted to nudge the bench back a pace but at the same time he did not wish to annoy the brooding priestess. He wondered how best to start a conversation but any brilliant ideas eluded him. She didn't look up as he sat down beside her but continued to study the flames.

The fire was very like the one in the central hall of the Jotunn Manor. It was placed in the middle of the room without a chimney so that the smoke slowly spiralled up into the rafters before drifting out through a vent at the apex of the beams. A circular pattern of cobbles surrounded the blackened stone of the hearth and Caspar presumed they found it a satisfactory way of heating the rooms.

'Aren't you surprised by the fire?' he asked Brid, thinking it was an innocuous question that might draw her out of herself.

'I thought fires were fairly standard at this time of year,' she retorted sarcastically.

'You know exactly what I mean: the central circular fireplace. I've only seen them in peasant's shacks and the like,' Caspar explained himself.

The girl finally turned and gave him a half-hearted smile. 'Yes, I knew what you meant. I'm sorry, Spar, I know you mean well but having to conceal my faith – it just hurts so much. I've fought all my life to uphold what my mother died for and it feels like a betrayal.'

'But we've all got to go through this for the sake of Torra Alta and to find my mother so that you can invoke the power of the Great Goddess. We need Her protection and She'll understand a few white lies if your motives are right.'

'Not that you'd know anything about it but I hope you are right,' she sighed, finally tearing off a strip of ham from the joint on her plate and eating it absent-mindedly. 'You're right about the fires though. It shows how old traditions still linger in the most surprising of places.'

'What do you mean?'

'Oh, you wouldn't know, would you?' she laughed teasingly and for the first time in days Caspar felt his heart lift as the sound of her musical laughter filled the air. Several heads were drawn by the enchanting sound. 'All these pious followers of the New Faith, they don't know either.'

'Don't know what?'

'About the fireplace,' she giggled as if laughing at a private joke. 'And to think of that fat Lord of Jotunn with his great crusader's sword and that self-righteous skeleton of a priest all sitting cheerfully round it every day. You know it's strange:

Torra Alta succumbed to the New Faith many generations after the insipid contamination by the southern He-God had crept up through the rest of Belbidia and yet these ancient rites are still here at the heart of their lives. The Goddess is still with them though they don't even know it.' She smiled with renewed vigour at her companion. 'It gives you hope, doesn't it? It gives you hope.'

'You still haven't explained about the fire,' Caspar coaxed her.

'Oh yes, the fire. If you clear away the hot ash from the ancient hearth you will find inscriptions laid there by the founders of the house. Only they're laid in a stone that's dull and the same colour as the rest of the hearth's fabric. When it's hot, however, the inlaid stones glow to reveal the inscription. At night their prayer to the Goddess is carried up in the smoke to touch the moon.'

'Then you can never read them because the fire covers them up. How do you know they are there?' the boy objected. His eyes were smarting from staring with unblinking lids into the fire.

'You can just see them in the embers but to someone who doesn't know runes, they look like scratches or accidental scars in the stone work. They are tree runes though, which look less like writing than the spell runes so unless you know what you're looking for it would be hard to see them in the fire. There; see?' She used the end of a charred branch to scrape away the fire from a patch of stone near the centre, revealing a pattern of glowing scars on the black stone. 'They could just be glowing bits of twig. They're hard to read in the fire so fools like the Baron of Jotunn don't even know they're there.'

'What do they say? All I can make out are lines with different numbers of bars crossing them.' Caspar was fascinated by the idea of secret writing.

'I can't read them without seeing all of them and I think we'd attract too much attention if I swept the whole fire aside. Those marks though are two tree runes representing phagos, the beech, for ancient knowledge, and uilleand, the honeysuckle, for hidden secrets. Maybe the people who built this fire knew that the New Faith was coming and hid all their knowledge and prayers in the tree runes, here in the fire to preserve them.'

'What are tree runes exactly?' Enthralled by the talk of the magic, Caspar felt lost in the enchantment of Brid's talk and the lulling sweet smell of hazelwood.

'Every tree has a property, a characteristic of its own, and each of the trees of power are given a sigil bearing the symbolic meaning of that power. For instance do you know what wood is burning here?'

'Yes, of course; it's hazel.'

'Mm, mainly hazel, but there's rowan in there too. I can't see it but I can smell its presence in the smoke. I can feel its power.'

'Well, what do they mean?' Caspar asked with avid curiosity.

'Coll, the hazel heightens powers of intuition, helping to bring inspiration, and luis, the rowan brings protection against evil enchantment. They are both female trees but what we should be burning tonight is tinne and duir, holly and oak.'

'Why?'

'Oak is for solid protection like a great door locking out the enemy from our home and holly is for strength in fight. There are enemies about. Can't you feel them?'

Caspar glanced anxiously round the room, taking in first the glowing faces of the local herdsmen and ox drivers who were happily engrossed in tales or idle board-games. Beyond them sat merchants and tradesmen who travelled north to barter for the prized Jotunn cattle. The travellers were sitting apart from one another, silently brooding over their meals without making much conversation. A few were studying Hal and Cybillia, now deep in their own conversation, but Caspar sensed no malice, only lonely interest from the strangers.

'They all seem innocent to me,' he replied, feeling inside his shirt for the carved talisman given to him by the old Crone. It felt warm and comforting which he had learnt to interpret as a sign that there was no danger.

'I can feel something,' Brid replied. 'There's an evil, malicious soul wishing us harm.'

She followed Caspar's searching gaze around the room until it stopped at Hal and Cybillia who were leaning towards each other. Hal was offering the young lady a sliver of venison that he held provocatively in his fingers. He edged the morsel towards her mouth, but she coquettishly turned aside and blushed to match her scarlet gown.

'So demure, so sweet,' Brid spat the words scathingly. 'She's such a perfect lady, all grace and charm. Ribbons and bows for muscle and bone, giggles and shrieks for brains. How could he?'

The younger boy was secretly pleased that Hal was concentrating his affections on Cybillia. It meant that his uncle no longer monopolized Brid's company and that at least left him with a fighting chance for her favours. He doubted, however, that Hal's latest infatuation would last: they never did. 'Are you sure your sense of evil isn't just . . . well, you know because of Lady Cybillia and Hal?' He nodded towards the couple wallowing in each other's gaze. He tried to put his meaning across as delicately as he could, suspecting that Brid's judgement was being clouded by a certain envy, but he obviously hadn't been as tactful as he thought. Instantly he regretted his words.

'Jealous?' She spoke the word softly with no hint of defiant outrage or denial and her composure almost concealed her true feelings. 'There is no time for jealousy in my life. I have far more important things to worry about other than Hal and that stick-like girl.'

The boy was still berating himself for his insensitivity and made a mental note to keep any hint of such tactless thoughts to himself in future. Such remarks wouldn't help his standing with Brid at all. They sat side by side in silence, the inexperienced boy racking his brains to think of a starting point for a conversation while the Maiden receded back into her brooding shell.

'I – Do? . . .' No, it was no good. Everything he said seemed so contrived that in the end he gave up and had to be content with just being near her.

It was Brid who broke the silence with words of such unexpected candour that they shocked the boy. 'I know he never liked me, but at least he used to view me with interest, you know, with that look.'

Lust; that was Hal's one and only look for women. He didn't see girls with any other form of interest and thought that in all other ways they were a nuisance, getting in the way of good hunting and fishing. Caspar didn't think that such a comment would be polite or constructive and was lost for words. 'You can't take Hal seriously,' he said blandly as he stumbled for something innocuous to say.

Brid frowned at him as if she was trying to fathom some meaning but couldn't. 'I know I shouldn't be thinking of anything else but the Mother and the fate of Torra Alta, and I really didn't give Hal a second thought until that girl turned up; but now . . .'

She left all her words unsaid. Caspar studied the furtive look she stabbed at the couple in the corner and thought, but now she feels ill every time my dear uncle drools over Cybillia. 'But you're a high-priestess,' he blurted, though at least in a low whisper so that no one could hear. He couldn't believe that someone dedicated to their religion could succumb to such human feelings. 'You shouldn't think –' He swallowed his words as the Maiden glared at him haughtily.

'You mean that because I'm a priestess I can't think or behave like a girl.' The stiff effrontery relaxed suddenly and she waved her hand as if dismissing her umbrage. 'I suppose it's not your fault you were brought up with the New Faith and so can't understand. They believe that celibacy is holy: we believe that the love between man and woman is the celebration of nature and there is much power, much magic woven at the time of joining. After all, think of Keridwen and her devotion to your father, Branwolf.' She smiled teasingly at Caspar's wide-eyed look of embarrassment but then the corners of her mouth flattened and she sighed, 'But it wouldn't be so bad if Hal didn't look at me with such disgust.'

'It's probably just the bruising on your face.' It was the only sympathetic comment Caspar could think to say. He felt at a loss to understand why Brid could feel anything for his uncle who was always so callous towards her. 'Hal's very affected by that sort of thing.'

Brid tenderly pressed the swellings under her eyes and grimaced. 'I haven't got any hyssop to quickly cleanse away the bruising.' She cast a furtive look regretfully towards Hal. 'He risked his life saving me and carried me all that way. I must have meant something to him.'

'Hal is very noble and brave,' Caspar spoke confidently but inside he was praying that Brid would stop hankering after his uncle and notice him instead.

'Yes, he is noble and brave – and fickle. The moment he laid eyes on that creature he forgot all about me. And don't you dare say it. Don't you dare say he's the brother of a baron and she's a noble lady of high birth and I'm not.'

The younger boy didn't think that Cybillia's birthright made much difference to Hal's desires. Hal, like his step-brother Branwolf, was motivated more by female curves than titles and Caspar secretly felt that the barmaid, with her low cut dress and flirtatious manner, as she swayed her hips around the room, held as much of Hal's attention as Cybillia.

'It's late,' Hal called over to the pair by the fire. 'We'd best get some rest.'

The landlord led them to their rooms, apologizing for the lack of space and the meagre nature of the furnishings but Caspar reassured him that it was quite satisfactory. Hetta appeared nervously at the door, having prepared a room for her mistress. Hal made a lavish bow, tenderly kissing the noble-woman's hand before retreating into the room that the land-lord's wife had prepared for himself and Caspar. They were about to get into their beds when there was a wail outside the door and sobbing noises.

'Not again. These damn, silly females will be the downfall

of all Belbidia, I swear,' Hal angrily declared. They opened the door to discover Hetta cowering behind her mistress, sobbing fitfully that she wouldn't sleep in the same room as Brid.

'Why ever not, Hetta? Brid's a gentle lady of high birth. You can't expect her to sleep in the same room as the gentlemen, now can you? You get back in here right now.'

'I can't, I can't Mistress Cybillia, I can't. Whatever Brother Rufus says she's got the look in her eyes. My soul don't feel safe near her.'

Caspar realized where Brid's sense of distrust had come from. The Baron's desire for his daughter to have female escort for propriety's sake was becoming a problem.

'Father Rufus is never wrong, Hetta. Now pull yourself together.'

'I'm not being disrespectful, Mistress, but she's been touched by elves; there's no mistake.'

At this point, Caspar sensed that Brid's patience was about to give way as he watched her eyes narrowing into a vicious squint. Hal gently took her hand and pulled her towards him. 'I think it will be all right if our little kinswoman sleeps in our room. Since your maid is so obsessed with witches and devilry I think I'd prefer it if my innocent niece was not left to sleep in her presence. What do you think, Spar?'

Caspar readily agreed that they would all pass a more peaceful night if Brid was in their protective care. The priestess tilted her neat little nose into the air, pouting arrogantly at both the maid and her mistress as she calmly marched into the chamber across the corridor.

Caspar felt that the air was rigid with the intensity of Brid's concentration as she fought to control her temper. He was worried that she would burst with rage if she had to continue this pretence much longer. Please Brid, for all our sakes you must keep your head, he prayed silently to himself.

Furiously stripping the bedclothes off Hal's couch she hurriedly prepared a soft pile of blankets for herself so that she could sleep discreetly in the corner. She kept her head down so that her hair fell like a curtain over her face, hiding her emotions. 'You'll have to share Spar's bed,' was all she said.

It was hard to sleep. The inn was full of strange noises and Hal's elbows kept digging into his shoulder. The blankets weren't quite big enough and every time Hal moved, he pulled half of them with him. Caspar wrenched them back.

'Stop that!' Hal complained.

'I thought you were asleep.'

'Well, I'm not.'

'What are you thinking about?' Caspar whispered after a prolonged hush.

'Torra Alta, the Vaalakans, Branwolf,' he sighed painfully. 'Even if the castle walls do stand for three seasons, the food supplies will have long since been depleted by then. It's going to be tough. We need to find this cauldron fast so that we can get back to them.' He fell silent for a moment and then added more cheerfully, 'And Cybillia – don't you think she's exquisite?'

'No. She's spoilt.'

'You're still hung up on the witch-girl, that's all,' Hal retorted, protecting his latest infatuation. 'She's a sight dressed like a boy. And all those bruises!'

'I don't suppose the precious Cybillia would look quite so refined if she'd bravely fought off a Vaalakan ambush.'

'It's a shame your little witch isn't quite so hung up on you, isn't it?' Hal's words cut deep into his soul and the sensitive youth rolled away, snatching more than his fair share of the bedding.

'We need to get her to behave like a civilized, god-fearing, Belbidian lady. Rewik will smell her out and have her burnt, if she keeps inducing hysterics in the servants. He's not called the Converter for nothing, Spar. I'm sure she should put her dress on; it would make all the difference.'

'You can't ride properly in a dress, with all those bows and frills snagging on the horse's legs,' Caspar objected, defensively repeating Brid's words.

'Cybillia can.'

It was no use arguing with Hal. He would always win the

last word. Caspar lay silently staring into the empty blackness of the room, listening to the sounds that filled the pub. A group of late revellers could be heard singing merrily below them. Floorboards creaked as people made their way up to bed at last. An owl hooted, but gradually the noises lessened and he was only aware of Hal's regular deep breathing.

The youth didn't remember falling asleep but suddenly he was being roughly shaken by the shoulders and someone was calling his name.

'Go away!' he grumbled in his half-sleep, imagining that it was his old nurse waking him for chapel, but with a rush he realized where he was and sat bolt upright, blinking in the half-light of dawn. Brid was fully dressed and desperation sang out of her eyes.

'Spar, wake up. I heard the wolf bay out a warning. There's something wrong.'

Still uncertain about what was happening, Caspar tried to take in his surroundings. He could hear nothing until a shiver ran the length of his spine and the haunting howl of a wolf broke the tranquillity of dawn.

'That's your wolf. She's alive.'

'I know she's alive, Spar. She's warning us, that there's something wrong.' There was a hint of frustration in the girl's voice.

'What's happening?' Hal was finally awake and without pausing to consider Brid's sensibilities threw the bedclothes off and reached for his breeches. 'Who's out there, Brid?'

'I don't know.' She was standing at the window, peering out into the dull grey mists of early dawn.

'Vaalakans?' Caspar felt for his hazel talisman. It ached with cold and he shuddered at the thought of the cold-hearted God of Vaal-Peor. 'It can't be though; they couldn't have got through Jotunn. They couldn't have got past Bullback and his men.'

Brid was busily twisting her hair up into a braid. 'I don't know. All I know is the wolf is crying out to warn me to move on fast. Perhaps the Druid's Eye will tell us more.' She reached inside her jerkin and beneath the folds of her homespun shirt to withdraw the moonstone. The fire-drake clawed at the tresses but she unhooked the talons and rapped the lizard on its nose. The spiny ruff raised threateningly but eventually the salamander gave up the struggle and retreated to the folds round her collar, spitting at Hal in disgust.

'God, Brid, did you have to bring that creature. It only attracts more attention.'

'Yes, I did,' she hissed. 'It feeds its warmth to Keridwen. Now shut up. The stone might show me something. Don't you touch it, Spar, though. You will only reveal your mother, because of the strength of the link between you. Let me concentrate.'

As her slender fingers caressed the smooth glowing surface of the orb, shimmering lines of energy rippled away from her touch as if she had tossed a pebble into a pool. Dark clouds scudded across the surface before swirling into an inward spiral that drew their gaze down into the dark centre. Caspar felt his mind being sucked into the whirlpool, dragging his thoughts down into the depths of the crystal.

'Torra Alta,' Hal murmured as in the far distance they glimpsed the buttressed towers perched on top of the pinnacle of rock. A rain of arrows fell from the arrow-slits into a carrion pit of Vaalakans swarming vulture-eyed around the foot of the Tor. The canyon was choked with the berserk tribes of Morbak's massed armies.

'Father,' Caspar muttered nervously. 'Father.'

The vision swooped towards the back of a silver-haired woman who stooped low, staring out over the battlements. Suddenly she turned on her heel and looked upwards, her flecked blue eyes staring straight out of the heart of the moonstone. Her lips moved as she spoke Brid's name but the image was soundless. The eye of the moonstone soared upwards away from the castle, sweeping across Jotunn and the dark green meadows with their grazing herds. Gradually the image dulled over.

'You're losing it, Brid,' Hal snapped irritably. 'It's not showing us anything.'

Her fingers hooked into claws as she tensed her hands, gritting her teeth with concentration. The image went angrily black as if it were struggling against her will. Her eyes blazed with a fury as they bored deep into the crystal's heart and then dimly four points of light appeared. They didn't flicker like a candle but produced a steady soft glow. A calf's head with blood oozing from its nostrils turned to stare directly at them. A hand reached out and they all involuntarily flinched back. The arm was striated with black scars where a sacrificial knife had repeatedly drawn blood. A Vaalakan axe handle lay between the points of light and around the man's neck hung a chain of ibex skulls. The eyes of the calf's head had been dug out and from the bloody sockets a pair of pallid blue eyes stared out at them.

Brid wrenched her hand off the moonstone. She was quivering slightly. 'I shouldn't have done that,' she mumbled regretfully. 'Whoever it was saw us.'

'Who saw us?' Caspar demanded.

'I don't know,' she replied in tones of exasperation, 'but they did, and they've got four stones with powers of sight. He's using them to trace the great Druid's Eye.'

'So they know where we are?' Hal was incredulous. 'How did any Vaalakan get hold of the moonstones?'

'Dunnock?' Caspar suggested. 'The Captain said they couldn't find the moonstones down the well. Perhaps he took them when he took Sandstorm.'

'I hadn't thought, maybe you're right. Anyway that's obviously how they know where we're going. That's how they set the ambush.'

'We've got to conceal ourselves from the Sight,' Brid said urgently. 'Wherever we run, they'll find us unless we first conceal ourselves.'

The wolf howled again.

'Well, and just how do you propose to do that?' said Hal sceptically as he sat down on the corner of the bed to pull his boots on.

'We need to perform a rite. If we're going on with Cybillia

and that dumb maid of hers we'll have to include them as well. We need to hide ourselves as well as the Eye,' Brid said simply, as if it were one of those things that you do every day.

'Can't you say your chant without them knowing and then we can get moving.' Hal was anxiously examining his sword and feeling the edge of the blade for any burrs that might need honing.

'You really don't understand, do you?' The Maiden had changed from the subdued girl of the night before into a priestess, clear in her mind of her mission and purpose. 'If we are to ask for the protection of the Goddess it is not a simple and obvious thing like saddling up a horse. It's a skilled rite and Cybillia will know. I think we should leave her behind.'

'No,' both boys replied in unison.

Hal's motives were obvious but Caspar explained further: 'We can't. Firstly, if they've tracked us here, as Brid says, they'll know about Cybillia and Hetta being with us. As soon as she steps out of the Inn they'll probably try and take her to get more information about us. She'll only have to step out onto the road, wondering where we have gone, and that'll be it. She's a lady of Belbidia, my neighbour's daughter; I will not abandon anyone of Belbidia to such a fate.'

'I still say we leave Cybillia and Hetta,' Brid decided coldly. 'We stand a much better chance of sneaking out without them and our mission is more important than they are.'

'No.' Hal was firm.

'Why not? It's the only chance we've got.'

'We're still in Jotunn. If we abandon Cybillia, Bullback will have our blood. He knows we're going to Farona and he'll drop everything to get there and he'll see us all hung – or more probably burnt. We can't leave them behind: it makes us look guilty in the eyes of every noble in Belbidia.'

'You're right,' Brid conceded, 'but they still have to be with us when I perform the ritual.'

'What – here – now? They'll be terrified. Witchcraft is their biggest nightmare,' Hal protested.

'Well, you'll have to persuade her. I'm sure you have some

influence over the gracious Lady Cybillia, don't you?' Brid's words were sharply pointed. 'Oh, don't look at me like that: I wasn't being serious. We'll have to give them a draught to make them sleep soundly. They only have to be present at the rite. They don't have to be awake.' Brid dipped into her scrip and curled her fist around a sprig of herbs, whose hairy leaves and creamy yellow flowers were veined with purplish lines. 'Faronan henbane,' she winked at them, 'and the tiniest fraction of wolfsbane just to speed it up.'

Lady Cybillia's room was dark. The shutters struggled to hold back the fingers of light that dawn pushed out as feelers into the land of night. Brid tiptoed over to the noblewoman's bed while the two youths crept close behind, trying not to wake the young mistress and her serving woman. A floorboard creaked and the sleeping maiden stirred.

'I told you not to waken them,' Brid whispered in frustration. 'This is going to be much more difficult now.'

'Who's there?' Cybillia's thin voice whispered anxiously through the dim light. 'Who's there?'

Brid pounced forward and clamped her hand over the girl's mouth. Cybillia kicked and struggled as the priestess smothered her breathing and forced the potent herbs between her clenched teeth. Caspar was frightened that all the commotion would bring another fit of screams from the serving woman. He stumbled in the dark but as his hands broke his fall on the small bed in the corner of the room they fell on empty sheets.

Just before the Faronan henbane took hold of Cybillia's mind the girl was able to lash out and caught the priestess across the cheek with her nails. She convulsed and retched at first but eventually lay peacefully drawing deep even breaths. Caspar studied her anxiously. Her heart seemed to be barely beating: he prayed Brid knew what she was doing.

'The maid's gone,' Caspar anxiously informed the others. He moved over to the window and eased open the shutters. A grey light fell across the beds. Lady Cybillia lay with her mouth open and a thin trickle of purple juice bubbled at the corner of her lips. Hetta had indeed gone. All her clothes and belongings had vanished.

Brid sighed, 'Well that's one less to worry about.'

'We'll have to find her.' Hal's face set in concern. 'They'll get her, won't they?'

'We can't,' Brid was adamant. 'We're too late. I only hope she's too stupid to give them any helpful details. Or more likely they'll realize she's of little consequence and won't risk drawing attention to themselves in the middle of enemy territory when there's bigger prey to go after.'

It seemed so brutally cold-hearted but, staring out onto the cool light of dawn and seeing the sparkling dew that brought a magical beauty to his beloved country, Caspar agreed. Of course he hoped Hetta had caught up with the Baron's retainers but if she hadn't, this was war and they had to think of the greater good. They had to succeed and find the cauldron with its tale of the Druid's Egg, otherwise all this beautiful land was lost.

'Look, can one of you help me?' Brid implored, trying to stuff Cybillia's arm into a ruffled sleeve. 'What does she have all these ridiculous frills for? If you bundle up her clothes, I'll get her dressed. We can't leave any of her stuff behind; it'll only start a search party and that'll probably lead the Vaalakans to us.' Brid flung various frilly garments and lace articles disgustedly aside and forced Cybillia's lolling head through the scarlet material of her riding habit. Caspar ravelled the various garments and several layers of petticoats and hoops into a tight ball and drew the bundle together with one of the ribbons.

'I hope that Salisian wolfsbane won't do any harm.' Hal looked uncertainly at the lack of composure in Cybillia's unconscious face.

'She'll just be a little groggy that's all,' Brid reassured him, but without raising her face to meet the youth's accusing eyes. 'You'd better carry her down to the fire quickly, before the landlord rises.'

They sneaked down the stairs, Hal struggling a little more

with the dead weight of Cybillia than he had with the petite frame of the young priestess. The floorboards creaked and groaned pitifully but none of the late revellers stirred to challenge them and the Inn was otherwise silent. Lowlanders were not renowned for being early risers. To Caspar's relief there was still no sign of early morning activity in the scullery as they crept past on their way to the tavern. The central fire had burnt low so that only a few curls of charred wood glowed a deep red in the very depths of the hearth.

'Rowan,' Brid sighed with satisfaction as she drew in a deep breath through her nostrils. 'I was wrong last night: we do need rowan.' She hurried to the wood pile stacked up neatly by the archway that led through to the kitchens. 'But this is all hazel,' she said in disgust. 'No, wait, here at the back.' She wrenched out several chopped logs from the rear of the pile and laid them onto the fire. Then taking her knife she sliced a tendril of hair from her head and then took a lock from Caspar and one from Hal. 'Fan the fire,' she demanded. 'Get some smoke going quickly. We want to get this done and be out of here before anyone hears us. Now let's see, a lock of fair golden hair from the lady.' Her voice was like warmed, sugared milk as she hacked off a fistful of hair right from the front of Cybillia's golden tresses where it would certainly show. 'It's better to have too much than too little.' The fire was beginning to catch and she looked on approvingly. 'Good, now we're ready.'

After Hal had laid Cybillia tenderly onto the bench, which Brid had turned to face due East, the priestess instructed the two youths to stand one North and one South of the fire whilst she took up her position to the West.

She plaited each lock of hair into a braid and tossed them one by one into the fire. Caspar's heart caught in his mouth as he suddenly realized that she had entwined Hal's hair with her own, braiding it into a twist of black and bright brown. The red and golden locks of his and Cybillia's hair were scattered separately. The hair caught, flashing into life, and instantly shrivelled as it singed into vapours, flicking out bright white sparks into the red flames and filling the hall with a pungent smell.

'Hurry up, won't you,' Hal worried. 'The whole inn will be awake soon.'

Brid ignored the agitated youth and drew a deep breath, inhaling the smoke. It whispered out through her mouth like the breath of a dragon as she began to chant: 'Protect us Mother, hide us in the rowan smoke and close the eyes of the Druid's stone. Protect us from the sight of Vaal-Peor's cold heart. Mother, protect us from the Vaalakans.'

The smoke seemed to hover over the fire, no longer spiralling upwards, growing thicker and more oppressive about them. Brid held her arms out with the palms lowered as if she were pressing the smoke downwards. Slowly she began to circle her hands and the smoke began to stir, gradually swirling withershins, like a whirlpool spinning round them. Caspar felt the particles of charred smuts fill his lungs as the dense, brown fog enveloped him inside and out. He could see nothing but the swirling clouds of mist and his three companions no longer appeared as people but as points of light.

The priestess used simple plain words without the intricacies of rhyme and Caspar instinctively felt that their sincerity and lack of rhetoric added to their power. As Brid lifted her arms the heavy pall that shrouded the fire billowed upwards, eagerly seeking the hole in the roof before dispersing into the atmosphere. Caspar suddenly realized he felt drained of energy as if a great force had sucked the power out of him. Brid too looked frail, but she offered him a satisfied smile.

'There. It's done. Just be careful not to touch the Eye. As long as we don't try and reach into its heart it will only reveal the hazy view of the rowan smoke to the other lesser stones. The concealing spell will last for as long as we don't delve for its images.'

The moonstone still shone with a pale silvery incandescence, though Caspar noticed subtle differences in the patterns where thin traces of grey wisps marbled the pure white surface.

'We'd better go before the house stirs and we start a witch-

hunt,' Hal reminded them. 'It's bad enough having Vaalaka
after us, but the whole of the Jotunn Barony . . .' He reached
inside his shirt for a small pouch that chinked as he drew it
out and generously left four silver coins for the landlord. Brid
and Caspar between them, picked up all the baggage whilst
Hal wrapped his arms around Cybillia. For two paces he carried
her before him in his arms so that she looked serene and
comfortable but then he grunted. 'This is too difficult.' He
bounced her up so that she folded over his shoulder and her
arms lolled down.

'Quick,' Caspar whispered, 'someone's coming.' They crept
out to the stables to find one of the grooms already up. He
seemed surprised to see them and stared at the dead weight
of Cybillia thrown inelegantly over Hal's shoulder. He seemed
to bite his tongue as if holding something back before decisively saying, 'Morning, m'lords, m'lady,' as if he had decided
it would be too improper to interrogate nobility about their
own business, however strange. He gave a curt bow but quickly
hid his expression by busying himself with the horses. 'I saw
the smoke and thought it were a little early for folk to be
rising in these parts hereabouts. Mainly draught oxen and beef
here, you see. Don't rear them for milk here. The grass ain't
quite right so they tell me. 'Orses seem happy enough so I
don't see why meself. Now I'm forgetting me business. You
want your 'orses now I'm sure.' He dropped the curry comb
into a wooden bucket of tools and then looked at them. He
couldn't contain himself any longer. 'The young lady all right?
Not me place to ask, but –'

'Mmm she's fine. Still sleeping. Not used to the landlord's
good ale,' Brid improvised. Cybillia was slowly coming round
and her pitiful groans fitted well with the lie.

The groom gave her a sideways look.

'Well, as I says, not me place, you know.' He turned away
from Brid and grinned at Caspar. The man's garrulous nature
was obviously distracting him from his suspicions. 'I've 'ad the
Devil's game with that Oriaxian youngster of yours, Sir. 'E's
kicked a panel out of his stall and all. Now I've been dealing

with 'orses all me life, that's three score years I don't mind telling you, and I've never seen the like yet. How the good Lord thought fit to create such a spirit in an 'orse, I couldn't tell. He's more of a cat, a mountain cat, than an 'orse. Tried to eat me cold beef pasty last night too, you wouldn't believe it.'

Caspar could believe it all too well.

Cybillia was in no fit state to ride so Hal cradled her in his arms as he rode high above the others on his piebald mare. They abandoned Hetta's horse and hitched the pack pony and the cream palfrey to Brid's saddle, since Firecracker was not being very accommodating that morning. Hal gave the grateful groom a fistful of copper coins and they turned south onto the road. They kept their eyes open for signs of the Vaalakans and for a trail that would lead them off the main highway.

Chapter 9

The storm broke, thunder heralding the release of the first slashes of stinging rain from a bloated sky. It eased the still, sultry thick of the air.

For the last few days May had felt unable to breathe for the pressure of turgid anticipation hanging in the air. Their preparations complete, the men stood at their posts, endlessly waiting and watching as Morbak's army swelled beneath them. Like the thunderheads brewing on the horizon, the Vaalakans held all at bay. But now the suspense was over.

Predictably they attacked at dawn.

As rain lashed the fortress walls the first savage assault beat against the outer ramparts at the base of the Tor. With barbaric frenzy the warriors hurled themselves at the lower defensive earthworks and the abatis of sharpened staves that cinctured the foot of the towering rock. The Belbidian counter-attack of sizzling flares arced from the towers of the fortress far above to shower down on the exposed heads of the enemy. Pungent sulphur smoke and raucous angry flashes from the explosives filled the canyon and stopped the Northmen in their tracks.

A huge roar of victory bellowed out from the men of Torra Alta's garrison. Branwolf stalked the crenellations, the Torra Altan standard in one hand and his sword in the other, rousing the men's spirits as they hurled their missiles at the enemy far below.

May didn't dare look out through the arrow-slit, though her brother angled his face to peer intently through the narrow crack. He described the roaring Silversalmon boiling around the eastern foot of the Tor, protecting them from any attack against that quarter. In more horrifying detail he reported on the scene to the north and west, where the road snaked up around the pinnacle of the rock. Here the Vaalakans raged like a thrashing tempest.

When the savage noise first started May had wrapped a pillow around her ears and buried her head under the blankets. But even though she could no longer hear the yowling screams of attack she could still feel the very stones of the mighty castle vibrate under the shock of the enemy forays as they hammered against the roots of the Tor.

'Got him! Got him!' Pip drew back an imaginary bow and whooped with delight as a bare-breasted Northman clutched at his chest and fell to the floor, a quarrel splitting his ribs. The Torra Altan archers steadily spat arrows into the throng, and though uncountable numbers pressed at the foot of the Tor, not one Vaalakan made it beyond the first earthworks that bristled with staves at the foot of the scree slopes.

May didn't exactly hear Morrigwen's voice above the frenzied screams of blood-lust welling up from the canyon floor but somehow she knew the Crone wanted her. The feeling of certainty unnerved her and she wanted to be wrong as she ran up the stairs to Catrik's sick-room where she was sure she would find the high-priestess. With foreboding she realized she wasn't wrong. Morrigwen leant against a window, looking more frail than ever as a racking cough shuddered her spent frame.

'Fetch your mother,' she gasped. 'Fetch Elaine.'

Instantly sensing the urgency in the old woman's voice, May scampered down the dark stairwell to summon her mother. The second the red-haired widow heard Morrigwen's wheezing breath and took one look at her ashen face she immediately sent her daughter to tell the Baron of Morrigwen's deteriorating condition.

'But Ma! I can't. The Baron won't want to be troubled at a time like this.'

'That's for him to decide,' Elaine told her firmly. 'It's our duty to tell him. Now go.'

The rain stung her eyes as she stood in the courtyard, scanning the parapets for the bold figure of the Baron.

'Get out of here, child,' a soldier ordered angrily and with outstretched arms sought to usher her back inside the keep.

'But, sir, it's urgent. I must see the Baron.' She ducked under his arms and raced into the open courtyard. She clutched her hands to her ears and cowered to the ground as a blinding yellow flash, followed by the crack of an explosion, shuddered through the castle. When she lifted her eyes again, she saw the bedraggled blue and gold of the Dragon Standard drenched in the rain. Side-stepping the men, she scurried between their feet and looked up into Branwolf's disbelieving eyes.

'It's Morrigwen,' she cried before the Baron could angrily dismiss her. 'She's very ill. And I'm sorry, I shouldn't be here, but . . .'

'You did well to come.' The Baron's rain-streaked face hardened into lines of concern. He thrust the standard into a soldier's hand as he leapt off the parapet, swept May up into his storm-drenched arms and raced through the courtyard towards the keep.

Elaine was easing the frail old woman onto the couch in the corner of the tower room, as he flung open the door and charged in. May wriggled from his arms and clung to her mother's skirts. He scooped up Morrigwen's hand and felt the bony wrist for a pulse. May looked out from behind her mother and anxiously stared at the Crone's ashen face. She looked at those dark sunken eyes and despaired at how the crepey skin, discoloured like ancient parchment, draped from protruding cheek bones.

'Morrigwen,' the Baron whispered urgently almost as if in pleading.

'I know, my boy, I cannot die. If I die, the Trinity dies and Keridwen with it. Believe me, the thought never leaves my mind. I am weak. Brid no longer reaches out to me as if she fears to use the Eye because of some malevolence in the channels of magic. I am weak without my Brid.'

'Hush, don't talk. You must have food. Elaine will stay with you.' He looked towards the little girl still drenched from the rain. 'May, go to the kitchens and fetch a jug of broth and soaked bread. Keep feeding her.' He gently squeezed Morrigwen's hand. 'I must leave you. There's the small matter of a few thousand Vaalakans still to attend to.' It was lightly said but didn't quite disguise the heavy responsibility in his voice.

May fled out across the courtyard, splashing through the puddles and slipping on the worn cobbles as she ran towards the castle kitchens. They were housed just across the central courtyard in a low stone building that backed onto the east tower. The old kitchens had originally been housed in the keep but years of peace had allowed them to be relocated to a more practically designed building.

She cringed from the twang of bow-strings and the steady whistle of arrows flying through the air, but her fears for Morrigwen's welfare overcame her terror of the horrifying noises storming the canyon. Avoiding the recoil from a catapult engine that suddenly lurched backwards against its restraining ropes, she caught her toe against the edge of the great rune-etched heartstone. Recovering her balance, she was bewildered by the urgent shouts and yells that blended to a meaningless barrage of noise. Suddenly so close to the men, she could discern an individual cry above the general chaos.

'Steady it down, men.' The Captain strode through the ranked archers, repeating the Baron's commands. 'We need to keep them off; we need to hold them back; but we don't want to waste arrows. Mark your man before you loose your arrow. The fletchers will have no peace till this is over.'

May was glad that she couldn't see over the walls. She could only hear the determined shrieks and cries of the besiegers and didn't have to look into the wild savagery of their eyes. Every now and then a determined enemy surge brought a warning blast from the castle bugler and, with frenzied activity, a flurry of arrows spat out from the archers. Each burst of rapid fire was followed by heavy silence. The Torra Altans, she noticed, no longer wasted their energies on cheers each time they quelled an approach but merely stared down expectantly, waiting for the next move. Nerves were fraught.

She cringed as the ropes and pulleys groaned and creaked under the strain as the great ballistas were wound back into their firing positions and loaded with shot. She ducked as the huge wooden levers smacked into the crossbeams, catapulting their lethal rocks out across the canyon floor. The shrieks from below were terrible. Still, as they all knew, each ton of shot felled only a handful of men and many thousand Northmen pressed forward to take their place.

With great relief she turned through the arch that led to the kitchens and heaved the heavy door to behind her. She found herself inside a vaulted hall filled with delicious, steaming aromas and the bustling activity of the kitchen servants. Long trestle-tables were neatly pressed against the outside walls, sagging beneath the weight of pots, vegetables and joints of salted beef wrapped in muslin. To her left she could see into a dark, cool store-room, its shelves stacked with honey, dried herbs and precious kegs of salt. Another side-chamber contained rows of dripping tallow ready for shaping into candles and a cauldron of lard that was being boiled up with soda to make blocks of soap. The room emitted a peculiar, rancid smell like over-ripe meat compared to the fresher pungent aromas of the herbs. Servants scrubbed at pots and pans, dipping them into vats of water. Their skin was red-raw from the work, though they chattered amiably. In fact there was so much noise from clattering pans, bubbling cauldrons, simmering broth and raised voices that the violence of the furore outside was banished from within the kitchen walls.

Across the room, two young boys were struggling to carry the stiff carcass of a hind towards the cook's chopping table and it was only at the fourth attempt that they managed to heave it up onto the scrubbed surface. A broad-beamed woman pounced on it with a heavy cleaver as she began to quarter the animal ready for a big game stew.

'Where is that lad?' The cleaver split through the bone with effortless ease as the cook took out her anger on the meat.

She spoke directly to a lithe, young woman who was shaping balls of suet pudding to float on the stew. 'I've got an army to feed as well as I can on as little as possible. The good Baron wants miracles from me. "Got to eke out the supplies," he tells me. All of this I have to cope with, which I do mighty well, now don't I, Rosalind?'

The younger woman nodded quickly without looking up from her work. 'Oh yes, Cook, mighty well.'

'Mmm.' The cook brushed aside a stray grey wisp of hair from her face before tearing apart the knuckle joint of mutton, seemingly satisfied by the woman's placatory response. 'Now look at the state of my kitchen. What good Master Catrik would have to say about it all if he were well, I don't know. We're behind with the cleaning and we'll be up half the night setting things straight. It's heavy work. Them big pans and the cauldrons take some moving and when one of them pans is half-full of stock now, I don't mind you saying, I can't lift on my own now, can I?'

'Oh no, Cook, 'twould take a full grown man to lift that.'

'My point entirely. That's it entirely.'

May kept shyly hidden by the door, not daring to interrupt the woman while she seemed so dangerously angry. She eyed the butcher's cleaver warily.

'Now we normally has young Ulf, but where's that great lad now? He weren't useful for nothing in this world apart from doing the heavy work in my kitchens. Now all I've got is these two little mites and, bless their hearts they struggle away with the heavy loads, but it's hard for them.'

'That it is, Cook.' Rosalind looked sympathetically towards the two young lads now grunting under the heavy sacks of flour.

'So, where is he? That's what I want to know. The Captain's never gone and posted *him* on the garrison wall, has he?'

'No, he couldn't have done.' The younger woman sounded dismayed at the thought. 'It's not his fault but he's apt to them fits and he's not really quite all with us, is he Cook? Though we shouldn't speak harshly of the afflicted. Talks to himself and looks at you funny like.'

The cook nodded. 'He knows his work here in the kitchens but he'd cause chaos out there with the archers. He'd unsettle the men. Might start pointing a bow in the wrong direction.'

Rosalind laughed at the thought.

Cook frowned reproachfully. 'Well, I don't think it's funny. It's a bit much him not being here when there's so much work.'

The lithe kitchen helper smartly rearranged the expression on her face to one of more sombre disapproval. 'Like as not he's mooning out one of the top windows at the enemy. Morbid man he is. I caught him trying to eat a lamb's heart the other day. That was bad enough, what with there being little food to go round now we're on siege rations, but it was raw and dripping with blood, I'm telling you. That Ulf, he's not right at all.'

'Right or not I need him here.' Cook tossed her head towards the two young boys as they dragged a sack between them across the flagstone floor, grunting in their efforts. 'Ulf could carry that in one hand. When I get my hands on him he'll know about it.' She struck the cleaver into the wooden board before scooping up sections of chopped meat and piling them onto a platter ready for the stew. 'Nobody's seen Ulf since last night, so where he's hiding I can't think.'

May felt her face go clammy at the mention of that name. Since her mother had accused them of making up tales, she hadn't dared speak of the sickening sights she and Pip had seen through the keyhole of the turret room. Besides she was almost certain herself now that her imagination had deceived her. Perhaps they'd only witnessed the gruesome sight of Ulf having a fit. She instantly dismissed any thought of the man as the cook suddenly turned and glared at her hovering by the door.

May squirmed as the woman's brow wrinkled into a frown. 'Who are you, child? Oh yes, the widow's daughter. Now, have you come here to help? Bless me, you look like a drowned rat.'

May looked down apologetically at the puddle around her feet where the rain had dripped from the hem of her dress and off the tangles of her hair. Nervously she shook her head. 'No, Cook, the Baron sent me for –'

'The Baron now?' The cook raised her eyebrows. 'She's been here all of a week and not one word to me nor the kitchen-maids, but she's already privy to the Baron.'

'But, but –' May stammered.

'Oh don't tease her, Cook. Can't you see she's frightened of you?' Rosalind laughed. 'Now don't take no notice of Cook; she only pretends to be a great grumpy bear 'cos she thinks that's the only way to get work done hereabouts. Now, what did you want, dear?'

'The priestess, Morrigwen, is very ill and the Baron sent me to fetch her some of your broth and some bread to soak in it.'

'The old woman's ill!' The cook's expression switched entirely to one of grave concern. 'I hope there's someone what can look after her right. Oh blessed Mother, preserve her. We depend on her now.'

Rosalind gave her superior an anxious sidelong look.

The cook glared fiercely back. 'I think you're too young to remember the happiness we all shared when we worshipped the Great Mother. It gave us purpose and a sense of place in this world. Now Morrigwen has returned to us. We cannot lose her now. Here, child, take this.' She dipped a pint jug into a boiling cauldron of broth. She wiped it over with a cloth and covered it with an upturned bowl before slicing several thin slices from a freshly baked loaf. 'Tell her we all pray for her.'

Taking a deep breath, May braced herself, ready to dash across the courtyard again. The rain and storm clouds turned the world to a threatening grey, brightened only briefly by the hellish flashes of brimstone fire as the ear-splitting explosions devastated the silence. She was glad to return to her mother. Elaine sat by Morrigwen's bedside, patting her hand. She had already tucked her in with thick blankets and stoked up the fire to stave off the clammy chill that possessed the priestess's frail body.

'Now you must eat!' Elaine ordered in a voice she normally reserved for chastising her children.

'Yes, you must,' May tried to be encouraging. 'Cook wished you well. She said we all depend on you.'

Morrigwen feebly smiled. 'She did, did she?' Painfully she sat up to take a sip of the cooling broth but she choked, spluttering and coughing over her bowl. 'I'm so old and weak,' she moaned. 'I've felt old for a long time but never this weak.'

'You'll feel better after some broth. Now try again.' Elaine raised the old woman's head while May anxiously ladled small spoonfuls of soup into the woman's trembling mouth. Finally the old Crone slumped back painfully against the soft pillows and closed her eyes in exhaustion. 'Tell me,' she croaked, 'tell me what you can see from the window.'

May took a stool and climbed into the narrow recess. From here she could stare out over the battlements and down into the valley. She swallowed at the sight.

'Well, our men are on the walls,' she explained quietly, trying to banish all sense of alarm from her voice. 'They're firing arrows and working those big engines, but the Vaalakans, most of them anyway, don't seem to be moving much. Some of them look like they're building something, but it's hard to say. They look like ants from here. And it's raining hard.' She didn't add that the entire northern gorge of the canyon was choked with the enemy. They lay so thick on the ground that their tents and white blond heads looked like a field of tired snow. The giant geometric pattern of the cathedral foundations lay completely submerged beneath the huge number of Vaalakan warriors. There wasn't an inch of bare ground to be seen. 'Are they making some kind of war-tower?' she asked fearfully.

Morrigwen sniffed derisively. 'You don't need to worry, May, not for a long time yet. Spar will be home soon and then we will drive them back. The Runes of War will protect us for many months yet.'

May continued to stare out through the window, studying the movements of the Torra Altan men. They were tired. She could see it in the way they leaned on the parapets and raised their bows; but she could not yet see it in their brave faces. She didn't quite share Morrigwen's blind faith in the Mother. And what if the old woman died? She looked anxiously back at her hollow cheeks. She didn't fully understand the high talk of magic and trinities but she knew it was vital that the woman lived. That much she had learnt today simply from the care-worn expression on the Baron's face.

As the long hours of the first day of siege wore on, the frequency of assaults lessened and the dreadful screaming shouts that announced another frenzied foray from the enemy became more intermittent. Long hours of silence stretched out their nerves. While her mother still sat by the sleeping priestess, May stared fixedly out of the window, mesmerized by the shape of the heartstone washed in the slanting rain. Faced with the countless enemy numbers gathered at the foot of the Tor, she could begin to see that the garrison's morale was flagging.

It was the tall garrison Captain who started to sing first. He had a tuneless voice but the rhythm was solid and firm and it lifted their spirits. She smiled as she felt their nerves steel within them as if all the castle folk were linked by one single thread of emotion. One by one the men around him caught up the refrain, drowning out his voice in a deep melody that soared up to the window of the tower room.

The rousing voices stirred the sleeping priestess from her sleep and she groaned, blinking in the soft light of the fire. Elaine carefully drew a shawl around her angular shoulders, while Morrigwen stared dreamily into thin air. May looked sorrowfully at her glazed eyes, which were now dull and lifeless. Sadly she remembered their once extraordinary colour, the vivid blue flecked with white, as if fragments of the moon had shone out from her soul.

'They are singing, Merrymoon,' she croaked in her dry old throat. 'Listen to them sing.' May could see the pain in the old woman's eyes. 'Sit with me, Merrymoon, and sing too.'

'I don't know the words,' she whispered studying the old woman's face. Her colour seemed a little healthier after her sleep. 'But how do you know my real name?' she asked curiously. No one had called her by her real name in years, not since Curate Dunnock had expressed his disapproval and insisted that her family called her by the new shortened name of May.

'I know everything about you, child. You must learn the songs of Torra Alta. This is your home now. Torra Alta is your destiny.'

Morrigwen's movements were slow and awkward as she brought a shaking hand up to grip the girl's arm. May could feel the obvious pain as the woman flexed her swollen knuckle joints. The old woman's glazed eyes suddenly focused and with the lucidity of fierce determination she felt them pierce through to her soul.

'Promise me this, Merrymoon, you will not let me die. You must sleep by me and see that I do not die in the night.'

Outside the relentless driving rain thickened into streaks of sleet.

Chapter 10

They rode in silence, hearing only the constant clip of the horses' hooves on the paved road. The early morning hush was broken by a startled partridge flying out from the long grass at the verge of the road. Dawn warmed the air and a mist rose out of the river, smothering the water meadows and shrouding the grazing oxen, so that their disembodied grunts appeared to come from rumbling ghosts. At last the first shrill notes of a blackbird ushered in the dawn chorus and the air was suddenly alive with song.

'I think we ought to cross the river,' Brid mused. 'I want to get off the road and into Oldhart Forest: they'll find us on the road.'

The Silversalmon swirled around the horses' flanks and the cream palfrey stumbled on the rocks that rolled beneath the currents. They had found a ford easily enough by following the oxen tracks in the churned mud to where they converged on the river crossing. The oxen's cloven hooves had cut deep shafts where they had sunk up to their hocks in the squelching mire. Away from the muddy banks, the water was high with a fast running current that dragged round the horses' fetlocks.

'It must be raining in the mountains,' Caspar muttered, looking at the swollen waters. Firecracker pranced, all four of his hooves breaking clear of the rushing current, spraying water high into the air and showering the others.

The noise and the touch of the fresh droplets on her face must have roused Cybillia from her drugged sleep because suddenly she was awake and whimpering.

'What's happening? Oh, I can't swim. The water! Hetta,

help!' She was silent for a moment and then howled, 'Where's Hetta?' She clung tightly to Hal, and wrapped her arms around his neck, making it difficult for him to see where he was going or to accurately guide his mount. But Magpie stoically waded on through the water, following Firecracker's lead until they reached the far bank.

'Hetta left with the other retainers,' Brid coolly replied, as the horses scrambled up the far bank. They churned their way through the mire towards a strip of water meadows that separated the river from the golden bank of oak forest beyond. 'Don't you remember?'

'I don't remember a thing beyond yesterday afternoon.' The girl looked a little green.

'It must have been all that wine and ale.' There was a hint of pleasure in Brid's voice as she wove her tale. 'That's presumably why your head hurts so much.'

'But Father doesn't allow me to drink!'

Hal flashed the priestess's marred and bruised face a look of displeasure before turning to the perplexed damsel enfolded in his arms. 'Now you've got to be brave, Cybillia. We've crossed the river because we think there might be Vaalakan spies trailing us and we want to throw them off. They won't expect us to leave the Great South Road.'

'But isn't that dangerous, leaving the road?'

'Now look, I know what I'm doing, and you'll just have to trust my judgement,' Hal replied authoritatively. Caspar felt it was a good thing that the young girl hadn't inherited her mother's more independent spirit.

The flaxen-haired maiden seemed to accept Hal's words with meek compliance and no longer pressed him with difficult questions. Her face had turned from green to white and she clung ever more tightly to the young warrior. 'Oh Hal, will I be safe with you?'

'Don't worry, sweet lady, I shall protect you from every foe,' he assured her grandly.

'I'm going to be sick,' Brid muttered, tugging irritably at the rope that tethered the two riderless horses to her saddle. 'Here,' the small girl with the coppery brown hair focused on Cybillia and demanded, 'now that you're awake, you can take this mule of yours off me.'

'But, I've got to stay with Hal.'

Hal beamed from ear to ear and looked with devotion into the maiden's dusty blue eyes. 'Much as I would like to hold you in my arms, it's not practical, Cybillia. We'll make better time if you ride your own horse,' he explained, transferring the girl to her cream palfrey.

They squelched through the mud and brushed through the tall meadow grasses swaying in the meadows that skirted the oak forest. The grazing cattle stirred and ambled away from the horses as they approached. Each of the black-faced beasts was branded with a symbol burnt onto its flank and Caspar puzzled over the markings for a moment until he recognized the outline of two buckets beneath a strange squiggle. He remembered the symbol from his lessons on Belbidia's political divisions: it was supposed to represent a milk yoke. They had just entered Jotunn's neighbouring and rival Barony of Nattarda.

'Rustlers,' Cybillia announced, displaying unexpected signs of mettle in her voice. 'They're Jotunn oxen and the Nattardans have stolen them!'

'How can you tell? They all look exactly the same; they all have the same markings – white bodies and black faces – and that's definitely the Nattarda brand.'

'He steals all his cattle from us. Look at them: they've got good bones and heavy muscling round their quarters, which means they've been bred for draught work not beef. Everyone knows that the best draught oxen are bred in Jotunn. These have to be stolen. I know my oxen and those are Jotunn – my oxen.' The girl was rigid with indignation and obviously felt that Hal should reclaim the rustled cattle immediately. The dark youth, however, was not as endeared to the horned beasts as she was.

'Well, maybe your father's sold them to him. He sells oxen all across the kingdom and beyond, after all,' Hal suggested.

'Not to Wiglaf! Never!'

'We can't do anything about it, Cybillia.' The youth puffed out his chest and continued in his most reasonable and commanding voice. 'We've got to lose ourselves in that oak forest until we're certain that the Vaalakans aren't able to follow us.'

'I don't believe there are any Vaalakans. No one would ever try and invade Belbidia: we're too rich and too powerful.'

'All ripe and ready for the picking, you mean. Listen, Cybillia,' Brid warned, 'you're not in your father's house now, and a few oxen are of no importance whatsoever compared to the safety of the realm. Just concentrate on keeping your horse going. That's all you need worry about.'

'Hal, you can't let her speak to me like that,' Cybillia pouted.

The youth looked apologetically at the damsel's distressed face. 'I'm sorry Cybillia, but Brid's right. I'll get you safely to Farona and it'll be easier on you if you don't trouble yourself with any more worries.'

The baron's daughter fell into a quiet sulk and lagged behind on her palfrey, muttering about her oxen, her mud-splattered skirts and her sick headache as they slipped into the semi-umbra beneath the crisp autumnal leaves of the oaks.

As they followed the trail deep into Oldhart Forest, the canopy of golden leaves rustled over their heads as if the trees were whispering to each other. Squirrels skittered back and forth, scavenging for acorns and Firecracker shied at their jerky movements. The oak branches gradually closed in tighter around their heads, sometimes catching on the rider in front and whiplashing back into the one following.

'Can't you steady that beast down, Spar? He'll set the others off,' Hal complained.

The path twisted and turned, taking them deeper and deeper into the forest, where it branched and forked. At every junction they halted to discuss which way to go.

'That'll take us west again. We turned west last time: we need to go south again,' Caspar protested.

'If anything that's north, not west; but it's definitely the right way,' Hal argued.

'We're lost. I knew it; we're lost,' Cybillia wailed, gripping tightly to the pommel of her saddle. 'I want to go home. I want my father.'

The closely interwoven branches scattered the sunlight, making it hard to decide which way the shadows were falling. Even Brid was confused, turning her mare round and round, trying to look for a landmark. 'We've been past this tree before. It's got a badger set in the roots. I knew I shouldn't have let either of you two lead. We'll turn right. And Hal, that's west, like Spar said. You should listen to him sometimes, you know.'

'Huh! If we waited for Spar to make all the decisions we'd still be deciding whether or not to cross the ford.' The insult was accompanied by one of Hal's most charming smiles, which made it impossible for Caspar to take the remark seriously. But to add to the injury, Brid laughed delightedly at Hal's humour, filling the forest with her gay laughter. Brid's laughter echoed back at them, tossed from one tree to the next; they instantly ceased their bickering and fell silent.

'The trees are laughing back at us,' Caspar whispered, twisting his head from side to side, worried that the trees would close in on him.

'Shut up, Spar, you're frightening Cybillia,' Hal warned, but he looked none too comfortable himself and placed his hand on the hilt of his sword for reassurance.

'Let me past. Spar,' Brid demanded, 'if you take the pack-pony, I'll lead the way and then we'll get away from the heart of the forest quicker. It's not well travelled here and the place is undoubtedly full of dryads. I have a feeling that we may be intruding.' She unhitched the pony from her saddle and handed the lead-rein to Caspar. 'Look, we went left last time; I remember the bole of that tree, so we'll go right.'

Firecracker insisted on crabbing sideways along the narrow trail and Caspar's arm soon ached from being stretched by the lead-rein. The pack-pony was being stubbornly slow, resisting all the boy's attempts to encourage it forwards. As the branches continued to cramp closer together, compressing the stifling space between the forest floor and the tree canopy, Hal had to flatten himself forward onto Magpie's back. Her height made it difficult for him to pass easily beneath the overhanging boughs. Brid squeezed her horse past a bramble and the thorny whips of the stems lashed back at Firecracker who squealed in excitement and bucked, throwing out his heels to kick the pony behind him. Caspar fought to keep a firm grip on the lead-rein as the pony wrenched its head from side to side, trying to escape the stallion's heels. The more Caspar struggled, the more the pack-animal fought back. The horse's natural instinct to bolt from any threat swamped all its schooling. Again Firecracker plunged forwards and angrily flicked back his heels.

'Easy. Steady now!' Caspar urged but to no avail.

'Can't you do anything? Oh please, Diamond's all jumpy; he feels like he's going to run,' Cybillia's plaintive voice added to the confusion.

'No, I can't,' Caspar angrily shouted back, gritting his teeth with the physical effort of controlling the wayward horses. 'Hal, get hold of her horse before we have some real trouble on our hands.'

Magpie remained reliably quiet, totally ignoring all the fuss that Firecracker had instigated, and ambled over to Cybillia's palfrey without showing any signs of excitement. 'Now this, Spar, is what you call a real war-horse, not that fickle wild beast of yours,' Hal pointed out as he reached down to take Diamond's reins firmly in his hand. 'I've got him now, Cybillia, don't worry. Spar, do something with that wild animal before you get pulled in two. You look quite ridiculous.'

It was too late: Firecracker's sharp hoof connected full in the chest of the small mealy brown pony and the beast finally succeeded in wrenching its tether out of Caspar's grasp. The squealing pony smashed through the brittle, lower branches of a tired elder, before tearing through the brambles between the mighty oak trunks. Within a moment the animal was gone.

Despite the excitement Diamond still showed no signs of bolting, standing quite still with only his startled eyes expressing his fright.

'Oh Mother!' Brid swore, which produced a confused frown on the other girl's alarmed face. 'You'd think it would be a simple matter to ride through a forest. I thought you could handle horses.' She glared at Caspar who was busily turning his stallion round in a tight circle in a vain attempt to quiet the beast.

'Well, I did say that Cracker didn't like the strange pony.'

'You didn't, actually. Come on,' the girl sighed, kicking her horse round in irritation. 'You and I had better get him. Hal can stay with the girl.'

Once moving forward purposefully, Firecracker's stride smoothed to a flowing trot as they followed the trail of broken branches and flattened undergrowth into the forest. It was impossible to ride any faster because of the dense thatch of trees and Caspar dipped and weaved to avoid the snatching branches. Without having to think, he guided Firecracker with gentle calf nudges to ease the horse around the boughs of the great oaks.

'He won't go far,' Caspar said optimistically, but after several minutes of difficult work, forcing themselves through the brambles, he was beginning to grow doubtful. Brid's chestnut hunter had a tear in its flank, which was beaded with tiny droplets of blood, where the talon-like spikes of a blackthorn had scratched at her as they squeezed past.

'He'd better not go far. It's going to be hard to find our way back.' Brid looked round her in concentrated concern, mentally noting each tree as they passed.

'Don't worry, Brid; we've left an unmistakable enough trail.'

'Hm,' she sounded unsure. 'It's not that I'm worried about. It's just that there's something odd about this forest. It's so old.'

Caspar shuddered, again feeling as if the trees were watching him with warty eyes.

They pushed on. As the forest thickened, Caspar had the

distinct feeling that the ground was gradually sloping down towards a hollow. The air had become heavy and cloying as if it hadn't been disturbed for a thousand years. An uneasy feeling was creeping through the boy's bones as he remembered Cailleach's forest and the snake-like hands that had dragged him to her lair. A shiver ran up his spine and he rubbed the back of his neck. Dead twigs appeared to wriggle and uncurl on the forest floor, feeding his over-active imagination. Ugh, snakes. He shuddered and then wondered why he was thinking of snakes. It's just a forest, he told himself and I'm only looking for the pony. But he still had the unshakeable feeling that he was intruding.

'This is irksome,' he whispered.

Brid turned her bruised face towards him. Despite the ugly markings, she shone with radiance as if a core of happiness had been lit within her soul. 'This is wonderful, you mean.'

Caspar wondered if some tree-magic hadn't infected her brain. 'There's no birdsong; it's all gone quiet. I don't think we should go any further. We can manage without the pony. Come on, Brid, let's go back.'

'What are you afraid of?' she sighed in a dreamy voice. 'It's beautiful. The forest's so old. The trees are ancient. Here, time seems to have stood still beneath their boughs, capturing the essence of life from the age before man fought against the Mother. There's nothing to be frightened of, look at the trees. They are all the old trees, the ancient trees of knowledge and enchantment. Their roots reach far down into the earth towards the heart of the Mother and bring her love and her bounty up to her children. This is an ancient place of love. Your fear clouds your instincts, Spar. Stop being afraid.'

'I'm not afraid!' he manfully stiffened his shoulders. 'I'm not afraid. But why isn't there any birdsong? Tell me that. It's not natural. It's like that place where that green demon lived.'

'There's no birdsong because they are listening to us. There hasn't been anyone here in thousands of years. This is an undisturbed place, a quiet place, uncontaminated by the meddling ways of man.'

As they rode deeper into the forest, Brid became radiant with a deep fulfilling joy. Tenderly she stroked the deeply creased bark of a chestnut, then the smooth greenish moss that clung in a thin veneer to the pale bark of a beech. 'Phagos, tree of knowledge, I have never met one as old and wise as you,' she murmured reverently. 'It's a long time since the dryads have met people,' she sighed.

'You're wrong!' Caspar said, briskly coming to a halt. 'Listen!'

'What? That's only your fearful imagination again.'

'No, listen: it's laughter.'

'Probably only a stream,' she suggested, fondling the weeping tendrils of a silver birch. The perimeter of the forest had mainly been oak but now there was an increasing number of different species that scraped their lower branches over the backs of the two riders as they pressed deeper into the depths of the wood.

'Brid, listen,' he whispered harshly and grabbed her by the arm, pinching her slender limb tightly in his grasp. 'Stop talking to the trees and listen.'

Haughtily she brushed his hand away and sternly frowned at him, but then her eyes flicked away towards the faint sound that came in brief snatches through the trees. It was like a murmur borne on a gusting wind, only the air was still. Brid raised herself in her stirrups, straining forward, trying hard to catch the tatters of noise. Caspar opened his mouth to speak but she signalled to him for silence.

There! There it was again, rippling and merry, the sound of carefree laughter. But nobody could live here, Caspar thought to himself. Then the blood chilled in his veins as he imagined the elves, pixies and hobgoblins that the folk from Willowbourne-by-Forge rumoured of with such fear. Perhaps these were people from the fairy world. Brid urged her chestnut mare forward but Caspar was gripped by superstitious fear.

'Brid no, they might be elves, or something.'

'You're quite simple sometimes, Spar,' she chided him.

'Elves! Where do you get such ideas from? There's no such thing.'

'You sound like Hal,' the boy complained. 'If there are dragons and trolls and green monsters with six arms, and all those things that the lowlanders say can't exist just because they haven't seen them, why can't there be elves?'

'Elves,' she laughed throwing back the heavy braid of her coppery brown hair that had wound itself snugly round the front of her neck like a scarf. 'Elves! There's no such thing because they are not in the *Book of Names*.'

'No smoke without fire,' the boy retorted.

'Huh! Elves; that's just the talk of superstitious fools. You know what elves really are, don't you?'

Caspar shook his head.

'They're the old people. You know the old tribes of Belbidia, the people I'm descended from – and you too in part. That's why we're smaller than the others. When the trade routes first opened up, long before the Dragon Wars, a taller race came from the East and gradually outnumbered the old people. But there was little strife between them, because the old tribes retreated to the wilder more desolate or hidden places, though they were often despised because their ways were different. Ever since man first raked at the Earth's fair mantle with his churning plough, he's been wary of the old people who farm nothing but only gather the natural fruits of the Earth and cull the excess of the deer and boar. But since the New Faith has soiled our land the old people have become the targets of fear and hatred.' Her voice swelled with passion. 'The villagers think we worship devils, and what's so strange is that we don't even believe in the Devil. Such a monstrous idea could only be an invention of this new male-led faith.'

Her eyes were alight with wonder and she abruptly covered her lips with a finger as the sound of laughter undulated through the still air. 'I didn't think there could be any left, not in the heart of Belbidia, but the forest is large ... The old tribes,' she whispered reverently, 'their blood runs pure in my veins and in the veins of your mother, Spar.'

'We shouldn't disturb them,' Caspar warned, still uncertain of Brid's explanation. He wasn't at all sure that the laughter wasn't some trick of an evil tree-spirit. He still couldn't understand how the pagan priestess could believe in spirits and yet still not believe in elves. Even his old nurse had warned him about elves. Brid, however, was riding on regardless of his protestations and he couldn't possibly let a young girl ride alone and unprotected into danger. He looped Firecracker's reins over his pommel and reached back for his quiver of arrows and the ivory-inlaid bow.

The laughter grew louder and Caspar slotted one of the arrows to the bow-string. They were still gently moving downhill but the trees were thinning out and, between the interwoven twigs of an ancient leafless beech, Caspar could see a glade. He nudged Firecracker a pace forward and froze as one hoof snapped a dry twig. In the still of the forest the noise was as loud and abrupt as one of Catrik's sulphur bombs and the merry laughter instantly stopped.

There was a deathly silence.

'We'd better show ourselves,' Brid decided. 'Don't frighten them and, for the love of the Mother, put that bow away.'

Caspar, however, still felt it was prudent to remain armed. He dipped his shoulder to avoid the overhanging branches and followed Brid into the clearing. As the horses stepped out onto the grass, there was a squeal from a small naked child, black from head to toe with mud. The child ran to hide behind a phalanx of six men, all armed with bows that were aimed nervously at the intruders. Caspar jerked his ivory hunting bow from side to side, fixing at each in turn, trying to decide which one to shoot first if they attacked. The defending woodsfolk yelled over their shoulders for help. Brid held her palm high and forwards in a universal gesture of peace and welcome. The small dark people looked uncertain and continued to shout for help.

'Put your bow down, Spar,' she hissed. 'You don't need it and besides if there were only one of them you wouldn't stand a chance.'

Caspar's masculine pride was wounded. He was considered very handy with a bow in Torra Alta, and the castle garrison was reputed to have the finest archers in all Belbidia. What did these half-naked little men know about weaponry? Nevertheless, he lowered the bow and glared back at the woodsfolk. They were dressed in deer-skin but were mainly bare above the waist. All were small and slight of frame, but this did nothing to dull the ferocity with which they guarded their cluster of wattle and daub huts. The archers continually glanced anxiously towards the central hut and even Caspar felt relieved when finally the figure of an old grey-haired woman appeared in the entrance and hobbled into the glade.

She too was small, but her appearance was made considerably more striking by her headgear. Crowning her silvery hair were the head, antlers, and complete hide of a white stag. The animal's cloven forefeet dangled from her shoulders, half-covering the nakedness of her wrinkled, sagging breasts. Around her waist she wore a belt hung with hares' feet and eagle talons and, beneath the sinister adornments, a tattered buck-hide formed a simple skirt that reached to her calves. Her feet were bare.

The woodsfolk seemed to defer to her for guidance, immediately obeying her as she waved them aside and instructed them to lower their weapons. Her eyes were full of wonder as she stared up at Brid on her horse and, without a word, the ancient woman fell to the ground in awed veneration.

Brid slid from her saddle and ran to the tribal shamaness, taking her hands and drawing her up. The old woman's eyes were full of tears and her mouth was moving as if she wanted to speak but the words wouldn't come. Instead she raised her hand to touch her breast just above her heart, then raised her arms above her head, touching her fingers together to form a circle with her thumbs and fingers. Brid returned the sign.

'It is I who am honoured,' the Maiden's voice was soft and gracious. 'I did not know that there were any of the old tribes left; I did not dream there were any left who still lived in the sacred groves in the old way.' Tears, half of joy and half of sadness, rolled silently down the girl's bruised cheeks. 'I didn't know there were any complete tribes of the old ones left.'

The ancient shamaness opened her mouth and moistened her lips. 'So long I have lived midst the trees,' her voice cracked. 'It is many generations beyond the reckoning since last we stepped openly over the green plains. Their bones are no longer white and dry but merely dust, who last could walk freely in the dales and valleys of the land. We hide from the big people. We stay in the forest. But now you have come to us. The Maiden. The Maiden has come to bless the soil and the fruits and bring new fertility to our home. Now may I die happy. We will light the fires and celebrate.'

'Come,' Brid said simply, taking the hand of the shamaness. 'We must talk.' She led the woman away to the far side of a carefully constructed pile of dry branches and twigs that had been laid out ready for a bonfire. With great ceremony the ancient woman took a smouldering ember from an ever-burning fire, which was guarded in a pot that swung from the lintel of her door. She drove the ember deep into the heart of the crisp bundles of kindling. As the dry twigs caught and crackled into life, the two women crouched on the ground, huddled together in deep conversation. The old woman raised her withered hand to tenderly touch the bruising on the priestess's face.

Despite the gulf between the potency of Brid's youth and the shrivelled years of the crone, there was a clear resemblance between them. Brid had the same large eyes, small neat nose and mouth, and the same distinctive, heart-shaped face. It was the eyes that Caspar found particularly striking as he looked about him at the several pairs of eyes that were studying him with fascination. They were all brilliant and shining, and either green or blue. There were no hazels or browns or greys. Brid had those green eyes and he knew that he had the same vivid blue eyes just like his mother and it was quite plain that they shared common ancestry. From his father's side he had inherited a little more height but he'd always feared that he was never going to be as tall as Hal. Brid, however, was purely one of them. If she changed her clothes, or removed half of them – a thought that Caspar shamefully dwelled on – she could stand amongst these people and be sister to half of them.

Brid had been so enraptured with the wonder of finding the lost tribe that she had abandoned Caspar, who still sat dumbly on his horse being gawped at by the six bowmen. He grinned sheepishly at them, but they continued to study him icily. Firecracker sensed that the tension had evaporated from the air and snorted, tossing his head so that his curb-chains jangled and he began to stamp, anxious for some movement.

Eventually one of them spoke. 'Did you send the horse?'

Caspar was so taken aback by the abruptness of the question that he couldn't think what they were talking about.

'The horse,' another one added emphatically and pointed to the heavily laden pack-pony happily grazing in the shadows at the edge of the glade. Meeting these strange primitive people had made the young nobleman completely forget why he and Brid were here in this forgotten part of the kingdom.

'Oh, the pony,' he said stupidly.

'Yes, the pony. Did you send it?' the archer persisted.

Caspar still wasn't quite sure what they meant by 'send', but he presumed the men were wondering where the animal had come from so he nodded in agreement, trying to help the conversation along.

The bowmen all grinned and, lowering their bows, gleefully invited Caspar to ride forward into their glade and join their festivities by the fire. He kicked both his heels up over the back of the saddle, dismounting in one neat athletic movement, and tethered Firecracker to the branch of an oak. Caspar lowered himself onto an upturned log and looked around him, taking in the lie of the hidden forest village. One by one, the children and the womenfolk ventured out of their huts to inspect the strangers and gather round the fire. He wondered how long Brid was going to be absorbed in conversation with the shamaness. He felt sure that, by now, Hal would be fretting over their long absence.

The children were fascinated by him, climbing onto his lap,

pulling at his auburn hair and inspecting his woven wool shirt. The homespun fabric was in itself uninteresting but the children were intrigued by the gold and blue designs that adorned the yoke and collar. The stitched boars, stags, hunting bows and most importantly the heraldic dragon made the boy instantly recognizable as a member of a powerful and wealthy family.

No matter how many times he pulled them off and placed them to sit away from him, they instantly returned to cling like fleas. As his frustration grew, the menfolk fell about with laughter. Little by little the boy's shyness faded and he laughed merrily along with them.

At last Brid looked up from her conversation with the old woman and opened her arms to the children who still swarmed over Caspar. They fled to her, chirruping in excitement, pulling at her thick braid and untwisting the strands so that they could wrap themselves in her hair. Brid's carefree laughter mingled freely with the children's.

'Brid, we must take the pony and get back to the others. They'll be worried,' Caspar tried to interrupt.

'Oh no, they can wait; I must give these people my blessing.' One by one, the people of the village came up to speak to her and receive the blessing from the Maiden, the youngest part of the Trinity of high-priestesses. When the six bowmen who had originally confronted them came shyly to speak to her, she giggled and turned to Caspar. 'They're thanking me for the pack-pony. Apparently you've made a present of it.'

'I didn't!' But he instantly realized that he must have misunderstood the woodsfolk and his heart sank in mortification.

'They want to say thank you. I think you've been most generous.' She grinned at his helpless expression.

'Oh Brid, can't you explain that I made a mistake?' The bowmen's faces dropped in disappointment and Caspar knew at once that he didn't have the heart to retract the gift.

Brid smiled wickedly. 'And of course the packs. We can replace everything necessary in Farona: Cybillia's clothes will be a very suitable offering for the women. They can cut them up and make all sorts of shawls, bedding and bags with them.'

'Brid, you can't!'

'I can. Cybillia doesn't need them.'

Caspar felt that the gesture was made more out of spite against Cybillia than generosity towards the old tribe but he didn't like arguing with the Maiden.

'The men have a gift for you in return,' she informed him and Caspar rose politely to receive the offering. They held out a plain bow. It looked very simple and unworthy in comparison to his own richly carved and ivory-inlaid weapon. Nevertheless, he took it graciously and thanked them politely, feeling that the swap for the sturdy pack-pony was not quite a fair one. However, as his hand closed about the shaft of the bow, he was struck by how comfortably and naturally it fitted his grasp. He examined it more closely. What at first appeared to be a single solid arc of wood was on closer inspection a laminate of many different materials glued and tightly bound together.

'The core is of many thin strips of holly bound in sinew.' The oldest bowyer spoke proudly of his handiwork. 'Then we wrap the wood with bone from the stag; bind it with gut and finally take the glue from the hooves of the stag to seal it. We first form the bow in a crescent like the waning moon but, when we string it, we bend the bow against its natural curve to form the waxing moon. You'll find it strong, strong like the holly, but still light and fast, like the stag that leads the running deer through the forest.'

Caspar was impressed. He stroked the curve of the bow and twanged the tautness of the string. He thanked them again, this time with heartfelt sincerity.

Brid nodded in satisfaction as she admired the weapon. 'The holly has the blessing of strength in fight. It needs no runes to enhance its power, all the magic is intrinsic in the materials.'

An old man, who had been guarding Firecracker from the curious meddlings of the younger members of the tribe, ambled over and lowered himself stiffly onto the log next to Brid and the shamaness. He smiled at her without speaking and bent to pick up a twig that he snapped in half before idly tossing one half into the fire and thoughtfully watching it burn. Once it had crumbled into curls of glowing embers, he turned to the other half still in his hand and used it to scratch marks in the soil at his feet. His actions appeared almost absent-minded until he nudged the old shamaness and pointed to the patterns in the ground. She looked at him quizzically but when he pointed to Firecracker, she rose and hobbled over with him towards the red roan.

Caspar jumped to his feet and rushed to hold the horse's head to make sure his temperamental charger didn't cause any trouble.

The old woman was examining the breast plate that wrapped around Firecracker's chest. Caspar couldn't understand what was so interesting about the horse's harness. The breast plate was merely a beaten plate of metal with the crest of Torra Alta emblazoned on it. The emblem showed a rearing dragon with a lance piercing its skull, but the smith had not been painstaking when forging the metal and the pattern was indistinct and scratchy.

'He is a Seeker,' the old man declared. 'Look, it says so here on the horse. I can read the runes,' he said proudly, obviously wanting to exhibit his knowledge. 'He is a Seeker.'

'There have been no Seekers for as long as the common reckoning, since before the big people came,' the old woman said, contradicting the man.

His puffed chest deflated. 'But I can read the runes,' he insisted. 'Look.' He traced his finger over the crest, drawing out lines. 'It is the sign of the Seeker.'

Brid's face was tense with concentration and disbelief but then her eyes widened with amazement. 'Mother! I never noticed. Spar, look at the pattern.' She traced out the rune with her finger: R. 'The rune "Rad", meaning a long journey by horseback; it is the rune adopted by the Seekers. The old man's right. I don't believe it.'

'What's a Seeker?' Caspar asked, not understanding what all the fuss was about.

'Before the Dragon Wars, when the old tribes lived freely throughout the land, there were in their number many Druids. From these learned men a select few were chosen to form a sect known as the Seekers. They dedicated their lives to the scholarship of the runes and quested across the known world and beyond to bring us enlightenment. You are a rune Seeker.'

The boy examined the coat of arms and agreed that the more distinct lines formed a pattern, but the runes still meant nothing to him.

'What runes are you seeking, my child?' the shamaness asked.

'The runes that will lead us to the Egg, the Druid's Egg.'

'Don't speak so boldly of such a thing.' The crone clutched at his hand and her eyes filled with tears. 'Who knows what powers are listening, what spirits are lurking in the trees? Only a Seeker can find the Egg of Power but many covet it and if they know you are a Seeker they will hunt you till you lead them to it.'

'But there isn't anyone near to hear me,' Caspar protested.

'I didn't say any*one*; it could be any*thing* – so hush! If you find the Egg, the tides of the world will change. We will be free, the old ways will return and the lands will be ours again. But,' her head drooped and she looked sadly at the ground, 'it is a thing long since lost. Out there in the open world there is a new God and he has hidden the runes that tell of the Egg. The runes are lost.'

'We will find them. We have to find them. The Goddess herself has sent us on this quest. There is a worse evil coming, far worse than the big people or even their new god. There is a cruel cold God, Vaal-Peor, who is driving his people out of the Northlands and they come in their thousands, hundreds of thousands and they know only cruel death. We have to stop them lest they bring the snows with them. We will find the Egg,' Brid added emphatically. 'We have to.'

'You are going to look in the big settlement? I have heard of the big settlement. Some of the youngsters sneak out to explore the outside, creeping through the dark so as not to get caught by the big people. Some of them return to tell their tales: some we never see again,' said the old woman with heavy sadness. 'Of what I hear, the big settlement is an evil place,' she warned. 'Where once were dales and tall noble trees, now the broken bones of the Mother jut high into the air, unable to heal.'

Caspar listened politely but couldn't understand what the shamaness was talking about.

'I should have known that you were looking for the runes. There have been omens; harbingers of change. The wren was not caught on the eve of the winter solstice; the hawthorn didn't blossom; the beast is abroad and there have been wild men hiding in the shadows. At the signs of such evil you have risen up again to protect us all, the old tribes as well as the big people. We must all rise up and be counted.' She thrust her arms dramatically outwards. 'You must take care and hurry.'

Brid agreed: they had delayed too long in the depths of the forest. She kissed the old woman on her forehead and hugged many of the children tightly to her before finally mounting her horse and slipping back into the gold and coppers of the autumn forest.

'What was she talking about, what beasts and men?' Caspar asked feeling uncomfortable at the pagan rituals. He shuddered as he realized that his mother must believe in the same things.

'She must have meant be careful of Vaal-Peor and the Vaalakans,' Brid said distractedly. 'We've been too long. Come on, hurry.'

It wasn't my doing that we were so long, Caspar thought disgruntledly but hurried on all the same. He ducked and winced as a holly branch scratched across his face. 'And what did she mean about the Mother's broken bones,' he asked still puzzling over the last words of the shamaness.

'What?' Brid was obviously still lost in thought, brooding over the miracle of finding an entire tribe of the old people. 'Oh, the broken bones of the Mother. The stone buildings of course. The materials are dug up out of the earth and piled high on top of each other. When the old people build houses they only use materials that grow on top of the earth that will one day rot and return to dust. They don't disturb the ground or do any damage or harm that would forever change the surface of the Earth. The stones are the bones of Mother Earth. The old tribes will not harm her, do not change her; they simply love her.'

Birdsong returned to the forest and Caspar felt that the world beneath the trees was indeed a calm and carefree place. He felt warmed by the tranquillity. But then the sudden cackle of a magpie's warning cry rattled through the trees. He had the eerie sensation that something strange was following him; that something insubstantial crept along in their footsteps, keeping to the shadows and hiding behind the thick boughs of the oaks. For a moment even Brid was startled but then she smoothed her furrowed brow.

'Probably only a dryad,' she said reassuringly.

Caspar still tried to shake the creepy feeling but then his concern for Hal pushed the superstitious fears from his mind. He was concerned that his uncle would be beside himself with worry. He didn't know precisely how long they had been in the depths of the forest because the sun had not been clearly visible through the interwoven fingers of the branches overhead, but he guessed it had to be at least an hour. He wondered whether it was mere coincidence that the pony had bolted into the sacred grove or whether the Mother had deliberately guided the animal there. He fingered the string of his new weapon that was slung over his shoulder alongside his elaborate hunting bow. It was a rare gift and he yearned to try it out and show it off to Hal.

'I can see the trail,' Brid shouted gleefully, as she pushed her horse past an elder, letting the pliable branches whip back into Caspar's face. Firecracker snorted and twisted round the bough of the tree, brushing past the scratchy twigs until the youth too could make out the rough clearing and the leafy path that formed the trail.

'Hal!' he shouted eagerly to warn his uncle of their approach. 'We're back, we're here. Hal!'

There was no reply.

'Hal! Hal!'

The red-haired youth shielded his face in the crook of his arm as Firecracker forced his way through the branches of a holly bush and at last they were into the clear of the forest track. Caspar anxiously looked left and right, up and down the trail for any sign of their companions, but they were not to be seen. Perhaps they had misread the tracks of the bolting pony and mistakenly followed another route to a different path altogether. Perhaps they were lost. Perhaps Hal had got tired of waiting and gone off, or perhaps . . .

His train of thought was broken by Brid suddenly spurring her horse and breaking into a canter, careering wildly up the track. Firecracker spurted after her, never to be outdone in a race. They went a hundred paces before Brid yanked her horse to a skidded halt directly in front of the stallion and Firecracker nearly collided into the back of her. Brid was already on the ground, leaving the chestnut mare to stray free.

Caspar finally realized what Brid had seen, as she extracted a shred of bright cloth from a forked branch. The cloth was a deep red, fringed with a scalloped decoration of gold thread. There was no mistaking that the scrap of cloth had been torn from Cybillia's dress. Caspar's heart sank with a cold sense of foreboding.

Brid held the cloth up to him. Her face paled. 'They've gone. They've been taken . . .'

Chapter 11

The marks of a struggle scarred the earth. The crescent-shaped clods, clipped out of the hard-packed soil of the track, showed where churning hooves had circled rapidly in their dance of combat.

Caspar dismounted, dragging Firecracker behind him by the reins as he stooped to read the spoors. He traced the hoof prints further along the trail only to find more shreds of clothing and broken branches where the trees on either side had been crushed by the battling horses. Splashes of bright blood speckled the pale bark of a silver birch and its roots sucked at a pool of dark liquid that stained the forest soil. Caspar prayed it wasn't Hal's blood and the same thought was obviously uppermost in Brid's mind.

'Hal,' she murmured, clutching at her breast. 'Hal . . .' Her words were lost as the first rain for weeks splattered down through the dry branches onto the dusty hard track.

'Vaalakans.' Caspar spoke the name of their enemy as if it were a profanity.

'But they couldn't have traced us here, so deep into the forest. They couldn't, not after we used the rowan smoke to hide our images in the Eye,' Brid objected.

Caspar raised his eyebrows, thinking that perhaps she hadn't been concentrating quite hard enough when she cast the spell. Perhaps she had been too busy thinking about Hal. He didn't however dare make such a remark to Brid's face. 'It has to be Vaalakans; no one else would attack us in our own country. Perhaps they're not using magic to track us; maybe they just used their eyes and ears.' His voice became shrill and panicky as he thought about the enemy so close at hand. 'We've got to find them.'

He vaulted onto Firecracker's back and trotted off at an urgent pace, hanging low over the horse's shoulder to search the ground for spoors. He hadn't gone more than fifty paces when something caught the corner of his eye and he ground Firecracker to a halt. He leapt to the ground to investigate the shape, wrapped in bright emerald cloth, lying just out of arm's reach beneath the fronds of a bramble. He found a branch and began digging in the bush with it, scraping the thing towards him over the ground.

'What is it?' Brid asked kneeling beside him.

'Don't know,' the boy grunted as he managed to hook the object and drag it out. He stepped back in revulsion and dropped the branch, but Brid went forward and picked it up without any squeamish inhibitions. 'Don't touch it!' he warned her.

'Well, it can't hurt me now, Spar: it's dead.'

'But it's a hand! A severed hand.'

She gave him a cold look, making him feel as if his reaction to the repulsive limb had been both childish and weak. He shook himself and edged forward to take a closer look. The hand was large and rough with dark coarse skin and short stubby nails that had scratched a hard living. Well, at least it wasn't Hal's . . . or Cybillia's for that matter.

Brid tossed the limb back into the brambles. They mounted in silence and pressed their horses into a controlled canter, which was the fastest pace they could safely manage through the woods.

How long had they gone? Had Hal been taken dead or alive? Where were they being taken to? Caspar's anxious thoughts stormed in his mind. The more he fretted, the faster he kicked Firecracker on and the eager beast stretched out into a fool-hardy gallop. The red mane sprayed up into Caspar's face as he crouched low over the colt's neck to avoid cracking his unprotected skull on the rapidly passing branches. Once or twice the bough of a tree smashed against his thigh, tearing rents in the buckskin, but he didn't notice: adrenaline roared through his blood, cutting out all pain. He concentrated on one thought. Rescuing Hal.

The track seemed to go on for miles but Firecracker never tired as Caspar urged him to maintain the reckless pace, while his mind spun through the various calamities that might have befallen his kinsman. Even if we'd been gone several hours, the attackers may have only just ambushed Hal and they might not be that far ahead. Caspar reminded himself to be cautious of recklessly charging into their midst and being captured as well. He hoped Brid was far enough behind to stay well out of danger.

Daylight ahead warned him that he was approaching a clearing. He reined in, halting Firecracker, who was now steaming and streaked with foaming sweat.

'Steady, Cracker,' he murmured. 'Easy now.' He tried to edge the stallion forward but Firecracker was too steamed up after the gallop to walk calmly and crabbed sideways in jittering steps. The boy halted and tethered the animal to a tree, so that he could creep forward, unnoticed, to inspect the clearing ahead and avoid blundering out into the open.

The high pitched screams of a girl made it quite plain that at last he'd caught up with Cybillia and his uncle. As he crept forward the shrieks became louder and more fearful. 'Get your filthy hands off me, you . . . you beast! Get your hands off me or my father will hunt every one of you down and have you hanged, drawn and quartered.'

The shrill feminine cries induced only a peal of ugly, deep laughter.

'The Baron, you know, 'e'll 'ave us. The great and mighty Baron. I'm that scared,' a squeaky voice taunted her.

Caspar's only relief was that the sneering jeers were spoken in a foreign accent that he didn't recognize, but which was definitely not Vaalakan.

'She'd fetch a pretty price in ransom then,' another voice spoke more calmly. It was a rough hard voice grinding in the throat like someone who had drunk too much ale all his life.

'Mmm, a pretty price. So lay your dirty little hands off her, Squit; she'll be worth more if you haven't pawed her.'

Caspar listened to their voices and decided that though they were all using Belbidian as a common language between them, they were of several different nationalities. It was customary practice throughout the countries of the Caballan Sea to converse in Belbidian since the country traded more widely than any other and the practical language was well understood.

A pitiful wail for mercy whimpered from the Jotunn damsel, followed by a male howl of snarling anguish that was silenced by a heavy thwack. There was a second of silence before Hal's bitter tones sliced through the air. 'I'll kill you. I swear I'll kill you if you touch her again.'

Hal, you're alive, thought Caspar gratefully, as he racked his brains for a plan.

'You look so dangerous all trussed up like a jack-rabbit for the spit,' Squit's voice sneered again. 'You're in no position to threaten me; you ain't *my* lord.'

'I said I'll kill you.' Hal's voice was no more than a hiss. 'And I will.'

'Squit! Get over here. Bolga, keep that pip-squeak under control.'

Caspar crept round through the dense undergrowth and sneaked towards the edge of the glade to get a better look. He wriggled forward under the low branches and peered through the camouflaging sprigs of withered bracken.

A large scruffy ruffian, with slate-black skin, had his fist closed roughly about the neck of a small soldier and was cuffing him hard across the ear. There was a stifled cry of pain. 'If the boss tells you not to touch the merchandise, Squit, you don't touch. See?'

Caspar judged there was at least a dozen men circled around Hal and Cybillia. Most of the mercenaries were clearly foreigners but, judging by the varying accents, differing skin tones and the variety of their dress, they were from far-ranging lands. Some were almost sleek black, others bronze, but a few had the reddish-brown tones of fair skins burnt under the southern sun. The Jotunn maiden was bound with her hands behind her back. Hal was tightly wrapped from head to toe in several twists of rope and was kicking and struggling to free himself. You must have given them a hard time, Hal. Caspar grinned to himself. A small number of men were moaning softly at the edge of the glade and two others were digging a large rectangular pit. 'How big do I have to make this hole for Ostro and Troas?'

'Better make it big enough for three; Xavios don't look too healthy without his arm,' another remarked callously. 'Who'd 'ave thought that one man, not even full-grown and all, could get all three of 'em. Experienced men at that.'

Swinging Hal's mighty runesword, a middle-aged soldier strode back and forth. He had a bald pate and an old scar across his face that lifted his mouth into a permanent and ugly snarl. 'The Baron of Jotunn, eh? Well, the barbarians didn't tell me about *that* now, did they? Makes it different, see, don't it? Makes it very different.'

'Just let them go, Gatto.' A young self-assured man stood up. He had a distinct Belbidian accent though his skin was almost as dark as the foreigners'. 'Your decisions haven't been so perfect lately. We were meant to be going to the northern frontier to offer our services to Belbidia like you promised and instead this. Let these kids go and let us at least try to make an honest living, warring.'

'We can still do that. Doesn't stop us just because we're making some good money on the way. I can take the Northmen's money and then kill them.'

'But these are Belbidians and Belbidian nobles at that. You told us that the Vaalakans were after travellers dealing in magic. I'm not harming any Belbidian.'

'Getting a bit above yourself, ain't you?' The old leader strode over to his challenger and stared the young man down. 'You'd be nowhere without me and just you remember that. Once a mercenary, always a mercenary. You lost your rights as a Belbidian the moment you joined me.' He shoved the tall, mutinous man away. 'Listen men, the Baron of Jotunn is a wealthy man. The Northmen offered us five hundred gold crowns – a lot of loot – but that was for all of them, all five of them. We've only got two.'

Hetta got away then, Caspar thought with relief.

'Well, that's got to be two hundred crowns,' one of the grave diggers calculated.

'Yeah or nothing at all with our 'eads crushed by their axes, more like,' the small waspish mercenary added pithily.

'Listen to our little Squit here,' Gatto continued. 'We don't know much about these big men with their axes, do we? Don't even know that they've got the money. But I know the Old Bull of Jotunn's loaded. He'd give us ten times as much just for his daughter alone.'

A feathery touch on the back of Caspar's neck made the youth start and he swung round, ready to lash out.

'Oh, Brid,' he breathed, 'it's you. What are we going to do?'

'What's happening?' She wriggled down next to him and twitched a spray of bracken aside to clear her view of the glade.

'Mercenaries,' Caspar whispered. 'There's a Belbidian amongst them. The Vaalakans have paid them to capture us. Shh! Listen.'

The defiant mercenary rose to his full six foot height and spoke out again. 'I'm not happy about any of this. We've come north because we heard there was a war brewing and that Belbidia would pay for our services. But I did not bargain on fighting against my countrymen.'

'Does it matter, s'long as they pay us?' Gatto growled in his deep rasping voice. 'You can clear out if you're not happy.'

'We're free-lances not bandits. We're paid to fight not steal helpless damsels.' The Belbidian-born mercenary had dark brown hair with streaks of blond falling from his crown where it had been bleached by the sun. Close-set brown eyes beneath straight brows glared defiantly at his leader.

'My! We have got moral now, haven't we?' Gatto mocked him.

Caspar stretched sideways to reach Brid's ear. 'We need a

plan, Brid. How are we going to get them out of there?'

'I don't know.' There was a touch of alarm in her normally calm voice. 'I'm thinking. There's a lot of them.'

The unmistakable shriek of Firecracker's raucous whinny abruptly shredded the atmosphere.

'They've got Cracker. I'll kill them! If they harm my horse, I'll kill them.'

There was a growing commotion in the glade as one of the men on the trail shouted for help. 'There's more of them out here. Look what I've found? Two more horses.'

'Get out there and find them; they're only kids. Get out there and bring them to me. I want my five hundred crowns,' roared the bald leader, his scarred face blackening.

'That kid there got three of us even when we surprised them,' one of the soldiers remarked as he started to look anxiously round the perimeter of the glade. 'If there's any more with swords like that we'll have a few more limbs missing.'

Brid was tugging Caspar by his collar. 'Come on, follow me.' They snaked backwards through the bracken until they came level with a holly tree. 'Give me a leg up.'

Caspar cupped his hands to form a stirrup so that Brid could step into his palms and he hoisted her high enough to reach the lower branches. From there, she swung her legs up to hook them over a bough and then disappeared into the thicket of the spiky leaves. Her arm dropped down to give Caspar a hand up in turn. Ever since the youth had seen her effortlessly scale the lofty branches of the silver-fir in the Boarchase Forest, he could never again be surprised at how swiftly the girl climbed trees; but the strength in her small hands still took him aback.

'They won't find us up here,' she reassured him.

The spikes on the holly leaves pierced Caspar's skin and scratched his face but the tree gave far better protection, with its thick dense evergreen foliage, than any of the graceful beeches or oaks. He brought his feet up close so they didn't hang down beneath the concealing protection of the boughs and twisted round to get a better view, trying to breathe as quietly as possible. He needn't have worried about being heard since Firecracker's squeals drowned out all other noise in the forest.

'I need some 'elp with this 'orse. 'Ere someone give me an 'and. I bet this animal's worth more than all the pearls in Belbidia. For God's sake someone! I can't 'old him.' Firecracker backed into the glade, dragging a square-shouldered, solidly built man with him. The mercenary tried desperately to grip onto the reins and control the wild-eyed beast but Firecracker was too strong, pulling him over and dragging him through the mud.

The old leader with the balding head strode forward. 'Call yourself a soldier, when you can't even manage a dumb horse?' He strode purposefully forward, raising the sword as if to take a swipe at the horse with the flat of the blade.

'Oh no,' Brid murmured.

'Don't worry.' Caspar was surprisingly calm. 'Firecracker's a war-horse: he knows about fights.'

The sword whistled through the air towards the roan's muscle-contoured rump but, Firecracker, with ears laid flat, threw his heels high in the air and lashed out viciously. The metal of his shoes tore into the man's forearms, throwing him backwards. The sword arced out of the mercenary's grasp and spun through the air, falling at Hal's feet. Gatto squealed with pain, clutching at his wrist.

'Get them, Cracker,' Caspar urged. The hot-blooded colt was spinning nervously round, kicking out at anyone who came within reach. 'Now's our chance,' he whispered to Brid. 'With all that commotion I can get them.' Raising his bow, Caspar aimed directly at the leader's face. He narrowed his vision until he focused only on the ugly scar puckering the man's cheek and the deep lines gouged around the eyes from squinting against a blistering sun. The youth's vision suddenly lurched to the right as Brid jabbed him hard in the shoulder.

'Don't be an ass, Spar; you'll get us all killed. You can't get the full score of them with one shot and they'll have us before you can loose a second arrow.'

'I want that horse.' The leader was red with anger. 'I'll get a great price for a horse like that. Get a rope round its neck. And get a hold of the other one too.'

Brid's chestnut mare, though more docile than Firecracker, bucked and struggled against the restraining reins while a smaller mercenary hung onto her bridle. In the commotion the bundle containing Brid's dress worked free from the straps securing it to the saddle. It flapped against the horse's belly before being trampled into the mud by the stamping hooves.

Firecracker was now loose and surrounded by a ring of men who were closing in on him. Their chainmail glinted beneath the loose fabrics of black surcoats, which declared their free-lance status, unaffiliated to any overlord. A heavy, slow-moving man approached fearlessly from the front, advancing determinedly to take the horse by the bit. Just as his hand touched the bridle, the red colt reared and raked the air with his flailing forelegs. The hooves smashed down on to the man's skull and he collapsed to the ground without even a cry. The other mercenaries fell silent and gradually started to back off. One of them reached for his bow.

'I'll slow that animal up,' he snarled slotting an arrow to the string.

Caspar moved fast. No one was going to injure his horse. He swung his new bow forward and aimed straight at the man's head and without pausing for thought let the arrow fly. It hit the man through the eye socket and pierced clean through his skull so that the quarrel spat out at the back of his head. His mouth fell open as if to scream but he merely fell silently backwards. For a brief second the group of mercenaries stared in disbelief at the blood oozing from the mutilated eye. But then, with the rapid response of trained men of action, they were speedily reaching for their weapons

'The tree! Up there in the tree!' One of them pointed very much in Caspar's direction. Brid was already swinging down.

'Quick, Spar, before they spot us.'

The men were slashing through the undergrowth and Caspar released another arrow at the large ogreish man making the fastest approach. The boy was stunned at the power of the small light bow. The arrow struck the man's chest, effortlessly piercing the tanned leather of his protective coat and bore through the soft tissue of his belly. The mercenary fell forwards, clutching the arrow's shaft, watching with horror as the thick bright blood squeezed through the cracks in his fingers and soaked into his gambeson.

There was no time left to fire another shot. Caspar leapt down from the tree and turned to look for Brid. Like a wood sprite, she had vanished silently and without trace into the forest. Panic gripped him. He could feel the mercenaries closing in and he couldn't decide which way to run. Hal! He had to rescue Hal. He fought his way fiercely back into the deeper thickets and skirted round the perimeter of the glade, trying to make his way around to the far side to throw the mercenaries off his track.

Apart from Hal, Cybillia and the dead and wounded men, the glade was empty, though he could hear the bandits thrashing through the undergrowth in their attempts to reach him. A bramble twisted round his leg and anchored its thorns into his clothing. He slashed the leggy branches with his knife and pushed himself backwards through the rest of the bush. At last he was at the edge of the glade nearest Hal. Firecracker was grazing on the short grass with his ears pinned back, listening for more trouble. Brid was already there.

The priestess had retrieved the great runesword and was struggling to slit the rope that tethered Hal. The moment the raven-haired youth was free, he grabbed the hilt of the sword from the Maiden's hand and sprinted over to release Cybillia. For once the girl wasn't shrieking. It took Caspar just an instant to take in the scene before he ran to where the horses were ranked. He untethered Magpie, as well as Brid's mare and took a fast looking bay, rather than Cybillia's steady palfrey. He reasoned that if the mercenaries gave chase the lithe bay was going to be a safer bet than the slothful palfrey. Brid was by his side and she hauled Magpie and her mare out into the glade whilst Caspar held the bay and collected Firecracker.

Hal threw the delicate girl unceremoniously into the saddle

and within seconds they were all mounted. With white frightened hands Cybillia snatched up the reins and twisted her wrist through the long dark hairs of the horse's mane to give herself more to clutch onto. Caspar took hold of the bay's bit, uncertain that the girl would manage the animal, while Hal lashed through the tethers of the mercenaries' horses. With heavy slaps from the flat of his blade, he sent the animals bolting ahead down the forest track.

It had taken only a minute of frenzied panic to free Hal and the girl and to retrieve the horses, but it was a minute too long. The squealing animals and the cries from one of the wounded men, alerted the mercenaries and now the men were crashing back through the undergrowth.

'Let's go!'

Hal led the charge out of the glade only to be met by the large Bolga and the rat-like Squit. They barred the trail ahead with swords at the ready. It took a second for Caspar to reach for his new bow which snagged on the intricate detail of his old hunting bow. He struggled frantically to separate them whilst staring helplessly at the ogreish man advancing on Hal.

His uncle had the advantage of being mounted but Magpie responded slowly to his commands. He was having difficulty positioning her and couldn't get his right arm clear to cut and thrust at the moon-faced oaf. At last Caspar had the bow free and snatched an arrow from his quiver, a movement so natural and so well trained that within a split second he was ready to shoot. But Hal now blocked his line of sight.

There was a resounding clash of metal as the swords connected, the great runesword peeling out its toll of warning, singing its song of death to the world. The mercenary backed off in astonishment as the hard-edged, tempered steel that cased his sword shattered into a dozen jagged fragments, leaving only the pliable iron rod at the blade's core protruding uselessly from the hilt in his hand. Stunned, he stood defenceless against the mounted warrior and his mighty sword.

Hal skilfully wielded the sword and Caspar remembered his uncle's constant sparring with imaginary partners as they rode down the peaceful paths of Belbidia. All that time he'd thought Hal was showing off but it was now proving to be invaluable practice.

Six other mercenaries were now closing in on them and one of them pressed the hilt of a sword into the big man's back. The ogreish Bolga was stretching his hand backwards to take the sword from his comrade and Hal turned Magpie to make a fresh attack. Caspar's line of fire was suddenly clear. The power of his new bow was staggering, spearing clean through the neck of the man so that blood spurted from the wound. But it didn't kill the blundering mercenary instantly; he fell to the ground, making throttled noises, his eyes bulging in pain.

Now a dozen armed men were all about them. Caspar let three more arrows fly and Hal had dispatched two of the braver mercenaries before there was an agonized squeal from Cybillia. Squit had dragged her from the saddle and now had her pinned in his throttling grip with a dagger to her throat. Even though the two Torra Altans had slashed the mercenary numbers, Hal instantly lowered his sword in defeat, not prepared to risk the life of the damsel.

'Hal, save me, help me,' the girl's shrill voice wailed. 'Hal!'

He looked at her in despair as the men closed in on him. No one approached Caspar, still too wary of the red roan's heels and the accurate power of the bow, but like his uncle, the small youth fell into submission. Only Brid fought on. She kicked and lashed with her heels but the reach of her knife was too short to cause any real damage.

'Now we've got four of them – and fewer men to share the loot with,' Gatto roared with hard-hearted callousness. 'Get the ropes.'

'No!'

The tall Belbidian mercenary stepped boldly forward. 'I won't let you. They're Belbidians and the children of noblemen. I'm paid to fight foreigners and defend any country from invasion, not to sneak like a thief to steal the fledgling heirs of my own country.'

'We 'ave got 'igh and mighty all of a sudden, Ceowulf, for a man always prepared to kill for the 'ighest price,' sneered Squit.

'Not my own countrymen,' he hissed, 'and certainly not defenceless girls.'

All eyes were focused on the defecting soldier as he approached Squit with menacing purpose.

'Stay back, or I'll kill her,' Squit fretted. A thin trickle of blood ran from the point of his blade as he pressed a little too fiercely against Cybillia's white neck. She was rigid with terror.

Caspar twisted slowly and imperceptibly round, raising the bow inch by inch, hoping that all the attention would remain focused on Squit and the defector, whose sword was now raised for attack. Cybillia screamed hysterically as the blade gouged a little deeper into her flesh, slitting the superficial layers of her skin.

Now's my chance, thought Caspar. He had to be accurate. Squit's head only reached a hand's breadth higher than Cybillia's and if they suddenly moved . . . But he had to take the chance. He snatched the bow up and in one fluid action the string was taut and the feathers drawn level with his chin. Squit's head filled his focus and he honed his gaze in on the spot between the man's slanting eyes. There was an unforgettable crunch as the arrow pierced Squit's skull and a perfect circle of blood haloed the shaft where it bored into his forehead. Cybillia swooned in a dead faint, collapsing over the body of her captor.

'I was going to kill him!' Hal cried, lashing out with his sword the moment another soldier came forward to attack.

It was the tall mercenary who picked up Cybillia, whilst Caspar covered him with his bow. The dark, sunburnt soldier flung Cybillia's body over the front of the bay and leapt up behind, wielding his own sword menacingly at his former confederates. Two more slashing blows from Hal's runesword opened a gap in the mercenary line and the new fellowship of Belbidians spurred their horses towards the clear track ahead.

They galloped hard for nearly a league, Caspar well to the lead, but still restraining Firecracker so that the others were out of clear sight. Hal remained to protect the rear, glancing regularly over his shoulder for any sign of pursuit.

Cybillia's limbs flailed against the flanks of the bay, and the tanned warrior had a fierce grip of her dress to stop her sliding. He battled to keep the billowing skirts from floating up into his face. Brid was high in her stirrups, her cloak flying out behind her like a banner as she whipped her horse on. Caspar looked round repeatedly to make sure she was still there and, it was only when he judged that the other horses were tiring, that he eased the pace and waited for them to draw level.

'Are they following?'

'No sign. It should take them a while to catch their horses,' Hal replied breathlessly. Caspar noticed a streak of blood from a gash on his temple. His uncle must have been wounded in the fight.

Cybillia was coming round and howling pitifully. 'Help, help! Put me down.' Panicking, she kicked frantically with her legs and the bay bucked fractiously.

'We can't slow up yet,' the stranger warned, gripping Cybillia more tightly. 'We've got to make the safety of the road. Here, young lady, keep still,' he snapped irritably. 'We've got to keep moving.' They pressed on at a steady canter. Cybillia moaned, her fists white with anxious tension where she clung to the saddle-flaps to steady herself.

At last the forest began to thin out and the path widened to a track that led into fields and pastures. A line of willow trees to the right marked the course of the Silversalmon and they blinked in the full sunlight after the subdued umbra of the forest.

Caspar halted to take his bearings. The riders relaxed for the moment, taking in the lay of the land and wondering where they could ford the river.

'Please,' Cybillia murmured pitifully. 'Please, put me down.'

Hal kicked his heels over the back of his saddle, landing

quite heavily from the long drop off Magpie's back, and put his hand to his temple for a moment. He studied his palm as he felt the warm blood.

'Are you all right?' Brid asked anxiously.

He dismissed her fears, 'Mm, just a graze,' and hurried over to help Cybillia down from the bay. The tall stranger gripped her under the armpits while Hal reached up to take her by the waist, lowering her gently to the ground. She was sobbing. Mud and sweat from the horse were smeared across her delicate face, which was now streaked with tears.

'Why didn't you stop? You didn't stop. I could have been hurt.'

Hal put his arms round the girl and she clung on tightly even though she scolded him endlessly.

'It's all right now, Cybillia, they've gone. You're safe.' Hal tried to reassure her as she buried her soiled face in his shoulder, shaking with sobs. He tenderly stroked the back of her honey-blond hair. 'There, you're safe. Come on, ride behind me; we'll get moving towards the road.'

'He was going to cut my throat; he was going to kill me,' she started up again.

'Poor thing,' Brid sighed.

Caspar studied the beautiful face of the priestess, which showed a paradox of emotions. Her jaw tightened and her cheek muscles twitched at the sight of Hal embracing the frightened girl, but there was also a glint of deep concern in her eyes. Her sympathetic nature and concern for the injured finally won.

'You're all right now, aren't you? Let me look at your neck.' Brid jumped lightly from her horse to examine the cut. Cybillia's trembling body quieted under her soothing touch and Caspar was struck by the power of Brid's comfort when she wished to offer it. 'There, it's not deep. It won't leave a mark. Now, you get up on Magpie and then we'll get quickly across the river.'

Hal smiled thankfully at the girl in her breeches and leather hunting jacket, though he couldn't quite disguise the grimace he cast at the deep stains of yellow bruising that gave her a jaundiced look. 'So you hadn't forgotten that not every maiden in Belbidia is as tough and as hard as you are?' He turned to look gently at the fair girl who clung tightly to him. 'Now come on, let's get you up on Magpie.'

She looked doubtfully up at the big piebald horse. 'I don't think I can.'

'Of course you can,' Brid interrupted as if she were a mother encouraging a small child. 'If Hal gets up first, I'll give you a leg up.'

The blond young noblewoman watched Hal climb onto Magpie's back and shook her head uncertainly.

Brid turned away to look at Caspar and threw her eyes skyward in a gesture of frustration and silently mouthed, 'For the love of the Mother!' before continuing to coax Cybillia. 'Now look, Magpie's very safe and gentle. Here we go: one, two, three.' She knelt down and cupped her hands to make a stirrup for the girl's foot and lifted her up towards Hal. Cybillia looked down, still with the imprint of fear on her face.

Without bothering with the stirrups, Brid vaulted cleanly onto the back of her mare almost as if to prove her superior abilities.

The stranger was anxious. 'Come on. They want you alive for the ransom, but if they catch me, I'm dead. Another mile and there's a bridge back onto the main road.'

The bridge was a solid construction of stone arching over the quiet waters of the Silversalmon. Here the river was untroubled by rapids and waterfalls but ran smoothly through the plains of the Belbidian heartland. The still, smooth surface of the dark water belied the undercurrents and the speed of the flow. They reached the bridge at a pace. As they struck the flagstones, the thud of the horses' hooves turned to a clatter as they thundered across. The stranger kept looking anxiously over his shoulder, but once they reached the broad sweep of the Great South Road he relaxed and reined in to let his horse draw breath. Just ahead, a herd of oxen was being driven at a leisurely pace by several honest looking herdsmen. 'No one will attack in full view on the road,' he sighed with relief. 'There'd be too many witnesses.'

Caspar looked at him suspiciously. They hadn't had time to question the stranger and he had a natural distrust of anyone that could be hired to fight. It seemed to him that there was a basic lack of honour in anyone who fought for a price. The art of battle was a craft, an ultimate test of skill or prowess. To be a warrior was a glorious honour – or so he had always thought when his imagination had been lost in the old legends and the tales of the Dragon Wars. But now he had tasted the bitter cruel cut of war in the soft comfortable flesh of Belbidian life and his delusions and fantasies were changing. To fight for your country, to defend your lands, to protect your women – he gave Brid a look of yearning – was the highest honour; but to steal a slice of someone else's war was a different matter altogether.

From the back of the tall piebald mare, Hal was able to look down on the well-built stranger and Caspar instantly recognized the look of disgust on his uncle's face. The mercenary was dark and swarthy as if he'd spent many years in the heat of distant lands. His skin was thick and leathery and his hair, though a dark brown, had streaks of gold where it had been bleached by a scorching sun. Beneath his surcoat he wore a hauberk that chinked as the heavy charger jogged with prancing steps, the feathers around its fetlocks floating on each high-stepping stride. The bay had an arching crest to its neck and bore its noble head neatly beneath its pricked ears, displaying the breeding and the highly schooled nature of a true war-horse. Caspar wondered if they hadn't inadvertently stolen the chief mercenary's mount. A silk surcoat covered the man's mail, a cloth of black that rippled with each stride, but he bore no badge or emblem, just the black unassigned colour of a mercenary. The lone knight didn't bother to talk to them and evaded Hal's glowering looks by fixing his cold eyes firmly ahead.

'I don't know who you are,' Hal declared abruptly, 'but we

don't want your help and we don't need it. I think after you have explained why you and the other bandits attacked us, you should leave.'

The warrior did not reply at first but merely turned to examine Hal, letting his self-assured eyes run up and down the youth's body as if slowly and carefully assessing him. The sun-scorched free-lance studied the blood-stained breeches, the clogged, oozing wound beneath the dark hair and the arrogant jut to the youth's chin. He saw fierce determination in Hal's olive eyes and glanced over the youth's tight wiry muscles, the clean look of young fresh skin, and the lack of armour. As the mercenary's eyes fell on the sheathed rune-sword, his eyebrows lifted slightly giving away the very first hint of emotion.

'Quite a sword for a young boy,' he laughed.

'How dare you! If you do not explain yourself and your reprehensible actions I shall be forced to draw it against you, stranger.' Hal was bristling with indignation.

Caspar felt that his uncle needed some support and drew his bow. 'You're at very close range and I never miss. Now answer our questions, traitor.'

The soldier spoke quietly but forcefully. 'I am no traitor.'

'You're a Belbidian, aren't you? A Belbidian prepared to take money from the Vaalakans. That makes you a traitor in anyone's book.'

The mercenary sighed, seemingly unshaken by the accusations. 'Now, listen, young knights; Gatto made the deal alone. I didn't question the Vaalakans; I didn't even meet them. Gatto led us to believe you were gypsy travellers dealing in magic, so naturally I thought you couldn't possibly be Belbidian. Witchery and Belbidian are contradictory. No doubt there's fewer Belbidian pagans than cripples cured at the shrine of St Anne in Ildros.' He glanced almost imperceptibly at Brid as if a thought had flickered through his mind and then returned his attention to Hal. 'The moment I realized who you were, it changed everything.'

Hal grunted as if not yet satisfied. 'What were you doing

with them anyway? None of the others were Belbidian. Why were you with them?' he demanded.

'It's a long story,' the soldier began. 'A long story.' As Caspar listened to the warrior's tale he relaxed and his faith in the man grew. He began to feel relieved by the comfort of having an older, more experienced man in their number. He was amazed by the man's tales from far southern lands still plagued by dragons and other beasts. But at last the warrior fell to explaining about himself. 'I'm from Caldea; at least I was from Caldea. I am the youngest son of Baron Cadros.'

Caspar had only been as far south as Farona, and then only once on a state visit to the King, but of course he knew much about Caldea. It was the southernmost Barony of Belbidia, cut off from the rest of the country by the bay of Caldea to the east and Dorsmouth estuary to the west. Linked to the mainland by only a narrow isthmus, Caldea had once been a country in its own right before some ancient King of Belbidia had conquered it. Caspar couldn't remember the exact date, but the King was called Peppin, which he had thought a most ignoble name for a monarch.

The stranger continued, 'He made me join the monastery of St Wulfstan's at Tartra to learn the scriptures. You see there was no place for me in the castle. My brother would, in his turn, become Baron, but I was one son too many and there were no lands for me. My father wanted me to renounce all worldly goods and take up the cloth. I wanted to go out into the world and be a man. I wasn't much older than you, I suppose, when I finally had the courage to leave, lured by tales of knights on golden plains of sand. Rumour had it that they wanted men to fight off a plague of lizards, which were creeping out of the desert. I had to go; I had to escape from the cold stone walls and the enclosing cells of the cloisters. I know all of them, all the words of the one true God, but I have seen too much of men to turn to God now; I am not a man of worship.'

Brid's blazing green eyes and hard cold stare became liquid like dew drops on the green buds of spring and she smiled approvingly at the stranger. 'Your name, son of Cadros? What should we call you?' Her voice had the soft lilt of the mountain folk unlike the smooth, clear-cut pronunciation of the high born nobility, which made any baron or his offspring impossible to place geographically by voice alone.

The stranger frowned at her again with that same look of curiosity on his face.

Caspar supposed Brid was someone who did look a little incongruous in their company. Her face was severely bruised but thankfully the staining was at last beginning to fade. She handled her horse like a boy with neat precision and sure confidence. She was tiny, with neat small features and at first glance she could be mistaken for a young child, but her cool self-assured manner coupled with the taut roundness of her budding figure and the pouting allure of her lips revealed her true age as that of a maiden on the verge of blooming into womanhood. Caspar, in his most whimsical of moods, compared her to ripening fruit just as it matured to its full, honey-sweet opulence, reaching that single day when the harvest is perfect to pick.

'I am no one. A youngest son has no right to a name,' he said in a way that portrayed every ounce of his bitterness, 'but I'm known as Ceowulf.' Then he added with a self-derisive laugh: 'Ceowulf, Wyvern-Bane, by my more recent acquaintances but I find that a touch extravagant. And you, young lady?' He bowed with courtly manners. 'May I have the honour of knowing your name?'

Brid tilted up her proud chin and filled her lungs to declare her sacred ancestry. 'I am Brid one of –'

'Us. One of the household of Branwolf, Baron of Torra Alta,' Hal cut in rapidly to prevent Brid announcing her pagan fealties.

'I was going to say that,' Brid uttered under her breath to Caspar, in tones too low for Ceowulf to hear. 'I'm not a complete fool, you know.'

'He's just worried after the way you reacted in Jotunn,' Caspar apologized for his uncle. He'd also been afraid that the

Maiden would proudly declare herself. She had a long title, Brid the Maiden, Daughter of the Moon and One of the Three, but the heartland of Belbidia was not a place to declare such a position. He knew that Brid had fought all her life for her faith and considered it a sin to deny the Mother so he knew the pretence weighed heavily on her soul. Her mother had burnt at the stake for refusing to be baptized into the New Faith and Brid must feel she was betraying, not just the Goddess, but her own mother as well.

'Anyway,' Hal was saying, 'tell me more about the wars and the foreign weapons and the armies.' The youth had obviously dismissed all his suspicions of Ceowulf's motives and was openly admiring the man. Caspar reflected that his uncle and the Caldean mercenary had much in common: Hal too had no land to inherit and there seemed to be a natural empathy between the pair.

The sun-washed stranger told them of the deserts and sand-storms that swallowed entire villages, and of the nomads in tents of camel-hide, and of the violent skirmishes and border raids. He told of the kingdoms of the deep south where the wyverns swarmed and devoured entire herds of goats and had a particularly sweet tooth for young girls. Cybillia gasped in horror at this part and clung more closely to Hal. Caspar felt his eyes widen and gape with wonder at the fantastical details of worlds beyond his imagination. Ceowulf was a true adventurer.

'It was there that I met Gatto. He's from Camaalia. It's said that he used to be the Captain of the King's guard and highly acclaimed at that. He personally trained the King's knights with lance and sword until he fell in love with Princess Delfina and so fell out of favour with the King. Camaalia is said to have the finest knights of all the countries of the Caballan Sea but, even so, he admired my skill with a lance. He trained me further and then took me south to the jungles of Lonis to fight the Cagog Nomads who were slaughtering the tribes-men of Tantony. Over many years and mainly due to Gatto's unparalleled bargaining skills, we made a large fortune – a fortune that we lost in the storms off the cape coming here. And when we washed up in Ceolothia across the sea from Belbidia, we heard tales of a war brewing to the north. I had planned to return home when I had amassed enough wealth to buy my own lands, but I had too much pride to be thrown back into dependence on my family. There is always money to be made in wars and it was an ideal opportunity. We were on our way north to offer our services at Torra Alta when Gatto cut a bargain with the Northmen.'

Caspar felt his eyes widen with amazement over the daring tales from far-flung shores and Ceowulf smiled at his youthful innocence.

'I'm sure I was once as raw and impressionable as you are now,' the solid man laughed. 'Stories always sound so thrilling and heroic but when you are actually there in the bloodied mud and heaving slaughter of battle . . .'

'Tell us,' Brid clutched at his arm. 'Tell us about the Vaalakans.'

'I didn't see them. It was Gatto who spoke with them: he always made the deals alone, probably to get a better cut for himself, I guess. Anyway, he said there were three of them, cloaked and travelling secretly. He described them as big men, broad-chested with thick forearms like woodcutters or loggers. He said they were travelling on the Great South Road in a wagon, taking ox horn south to the market and they easily passed for cowmen grown big and burly from their work. Gatto said he hadn't recognized them as Northmen because their hair was a flat dark brown so I presume they dyed it with root or something.'

'Black root,' Brid suggested.

'Anyway, Gatto finally smelt out that they were not what they seemed when they approached him with an offer. He noticed their eyes were grey-blue, pale and lifeless like a wolf's, and it didn't match their hair. As mercenaries you learn to look out for things like that – anything out of place. There are always sinister people scavenging for pickings at the edge of a war; you have to be wary of them. Anyway, they offered him money and once Gatto has a smell for money he doesn't ask too many questions; he says it lowers the price.'

'How did you track us?' Caspar asked, suddenly realizing that the Vaalakans as well as Gatto were still looking for them.

'Well, Gatto said the Northmen had lost track of you after the Halfway Inn when you left the road. They've been searching along the west side of the Silversalmon and the road, and the Vaalakans wanted us to search the wooded areas because, as people delving into magic, you'd be drawn to such places. Seems he was right. Gatto arranged to meet the Vaalakans back at the cross-roads north of the Inn in two days' time if we were successful in capturing you. They even gave him a handsome amount of money up front to ensure that we showed up.'

'That at least gives us a good head start on the Vaalakans,' Hal deduced with relief. 'I'm sorry, Cybillia, that you've been caught up in this.'

'Why do they want us so much?' Cybillia asked, with innocent fear blanching her face. She pressed the thin cut at the base of her neck gingerly.

Hal shrugged. 'Ransom, or maybe because Spar and I know details of Torra Alta that could be vital to a Vaalakan attack, I don't know? They might think we know Torra Alta's weaknesses.'

'Torra Alta doesn't have any weaknesses,' Ceowulf laughed.

'Only one,' Hal replied seriously. 'We can't keep the supplies coming in. They will starve if we can't drive back the Vaalakans.'

'We can probably hold them off but there are too many to drive back,' Caspar added.

'So,' concluded Ceowulf. 'You're either running away from the threat of siege and starvation or you're riding south to get help from the King. Judging by your fierce bravery in combat I think I can safely plump for the latter.'

Hal nodded. Caspar was glad that Ceowulf didn't ask too many questions.

'Well then, I'd better see you safely to the nearest town and alert the reeve so that he can give you an escort. Your back needs covering. Gatto will still want his money.'

'No.' Hal lowered his voice.

'Why not?' Cybillia demanded.

Ceowulf studied them all curiously.

'Now this is not something a young lady should be troubling herself with,' Hal soothed her, while nodding to Caspar and Ceowulf to draw away from him and the young lady of Jotunn.

Caspar trotted on ahead and waited for the tall dark man to draw up alongside.

'I perceive a tale of cloak and daggers,' Ceowulf curled up his lip as if he found it amusing to see how these young noblemen took themselves so seriously.

'We take secret documents for the King and they are for the King alone,' Caspar improvised. The last thing they wanted to do was to alert any local reeve to their plight. Authorities asked questions, which they might not be able to answer. Vaalakans wouldn't risk following them into Belbidia without a very good reason and he certainly didn't want to draw attention to Brid. Even this mercenary obviously suspected something. 'We don't want any local interference.'

Ceowulf nodded and looked at him sideways. 'Can't say I'm all that keen on explaining myself to the local townsmen either. No doubt you have good reason and I'm not really in a position to judge; but you're not safe out here alone. The Vaalakans knew you were heading for Farona and Gatto won't take all that long to muster the horses and lick his wounds. He'll find you easy enough to track if you continue straight along the Great South Road. They'll find an opportunity sooner or later when there are no herdsmen around. We need to move out west and approach Farona from a more unexpected angle. That way we'll throw him off our trail.'

'*Our* trail?'

There was a long silence while the self-assured free-lance contemplated the thick mane on his horse's withers, then he lifted his head and nodded. 'I have no home and no purpose: you need help and protection against Gatto. The least I owe you is to ride with you to Farona. Then maybe I can ask the King for a position in his army. But for now, at least, I can do something for Belbidia by offering you my help.'

Caspar nodded gratefully and offered his hand in friendship.

Chapter 12

The water smelt familiar. Cool, fresh: the sound was comforting. But the heat was in the air again. Must wait. It burns ... burns ...

Where are the thieves? They've stolen the glow. I remember the glow, but it's gone. I can feel the heat – nasty, scorching heat. He missed the cool, wet rocks of his home.

The mountains would be safe. The air was fresh and sharp, and the eagles shrieked somewhere in the emptiness high above him. There would be a cave in the mountains, somewhere to hide from the burning in the sky. He hated the smell and the noise, the constant shrills and twitterings of the birds. Too much noise all around him.

He gnawed at his claw. His tail limply dragged behind him and the pain in his head ... He coiled up his long neck and tucked his snout under a foreleg. The pain ... But that was nothing compared with losing the glow. There was nothing else like it. He had loved the taste of the bright metal objects that had lined his nest in the cool caverns. They had always been there. His old mother, she had described them as bright and glittering. He couldn't imagine what bright and glittering was; he no longer cared for them: but the glow ...

He could *see* the glow.

The stumps on his back ached. They nagged at the back of his mind and he fluttered them feebly. At night he dreamt he could spread them into vast wings and glide through the emptiness above his head. He moved on, sniffing out a place to hole up.

The mouth of the cave was tight. He squeezed his snout

into the entrance. It smelt dank and wet and cool. He sighed. He needed the rest. His tongue caught the heady scent of bear. Cubs squeaked and squealed. His jaws snapped as his great snout darted forward.

The meat was good. He curled up contentedly, coughing on a fur ball that stuck in his craw. He tried to coil his tail around him but it was too limp. These bears were different to the hairless bears, he thought. The hairless bears have sharp, sharp claws. They scream and squeal; they smell like little, weak creatures; they move with feeble sickly movements; but they have sharp claws.

He knew it was his eye. The pain was like the burning that fell out of the sky but more intense and deep. It hurt round the rim, where he had first seen the glow. He felt nothing, he sensed nothing at all from the centre, but he knew his eye was still bleeding. He could taste the acid of his own blood dripping down his snout.

They have powerful claws. One or two on their own seemed unthreatening, like the bear cubs. He smacked his jaws together contentedly. But they flock. They pack together like the howling wolves only into vast numbers – numbers that shake the earth. Then they are deadly.

He feared them. He feared nothing that crawled on the surface of the earth except for the naked bears. His mother had feared them and his grandfather had feared them. His grandfather spoke of a time when he could roam free on the surface. Both his mother and grandfather could see. His own world had been darkness. A world of rich sounds, of touch, of smell – until he had found the glow.

She had dropped it. She was in the caverns, running. He had heard the light patter of those little feet. She was running; she was frightened. Frightened creatures make easy supper. I didn't have to crawl up onto the surface for supper; it was running towards me. Pitter patter, pitter patter: little soft feet running through the long twisting tunnels.

Then I saw the glow; pure light, a circle of wonder. I saw the glow. I forgot her and saw only the glow. There were more feet running. They slapped the ground more heavily. I concentrated only on the glow. The glow had life and fire and energy. The glow had power.

She screamed. I remember the scream. So much pain. Like the scream of a wildcat when you crush it in your jaws. I forgot to kill her. Only the glow mattered. She dropped it and for the first time I put my claw on the glow.

I felt the thrill of ancient power. She was still there though, in the glow. It was confusing. I knew she had gone. I heard the other one drag her away out of the tunnels, but I could still feel her presence in the glow. At first I felt her terror and the heat of the power, but then I felt a terrible pain of cold at the heart of the stone, an aching cold loneliness.

He understood loneliness. His grandfather had died and then his mother – he understood the emptiness of being alone. He remembered her chewy scales and brittle bones, of course, but after she had gone there was only terrible loneliness, which only the glow could fill.

He could see the glow.

Now it was gone. The naked bears had taken it. The creatures with the sharp claws had taken it. He must have the glow.

He could smell its trail. He could sense the shimmering power of the glow imprinted on the bones of the earth. He was blind and so he lived and breathed and moved by vibrations. He tracked his prey and sensed their movements, knowing when to strike because of the vibrations. But more than that he was the last of an ancient breed and he knew the power of the earth. He knew he was born from the earth and he understood Her sensations and tremors. The naked bears were taking his glow south.

It was quiet now. The birdsong had ceased and the burning pain that fell from the emptiness above had gone. Cool moist air bathed his parched scales.

His dragging tail slowed him up. His claw was regrowing now where the sharp-toothed naked bears had stabbed between his talons. It was sore but it didn't slow him up. Only his dragging tail made progress difficult. He heaved his belly over the jagged rocks and slithered along the valley floor, coiling southwards following the trail of the glow.

They had taken it towards the great rift in the mountains and into the Old Nest. He said they had piled stones over the entrance and from there they could spit claws and fangs that would pierce even the armour-plating of a Fire Being's scales if struck with an unlucky blow. His grandfather told him never to go near the Old Nest but if he had to, he must keep his snout low to protect his maw and keep the fire in his belly burning. He must always keep the fires ready.

But he had no fire. What should have been a vicious heat within his belly was an aching cavern of loneliness. He had no fire. But the glow had made him feel like he had fire. He needed fire; he needed the glow.

But the glow had moved on again.

He slithered down out of the mountains towards the southern plains, where the grass was wet, lush and soothing on his underbelly, but he knew there was danger. Few men lived in the mountains. The mountains had caverns, grottoes and caves but out here, beyond the mountains, it was flat. He could smell them everywhere. They would spit their claws at him.

The glow was moving away, along a smooth hard surface. He licked the worn rock and felt the tremor of feet scurrying along it. He turned away into the empty places. He couldn't follow on their beaten course. He would move away where he could find hills and cover. He would track them from a distance. He would wait. He smelt horse and remembered his stomach. Horse was good. A quick and easy kill, plenty of meat; horse was good.

They had moved towards the plains where the naked bears flocked together in vast numbers to nest. He would bide his time and wait for them to come out. They would move to an empty place soon. He would wait for the glow.

He sucked in cavernous lungfuls of air, filling the great bladder beneath his throat. He threw back his neck and was about to roar out his furious pain but instead let the air waffle out, fluttering through his stretched nostrils. He had to be careful. The naked bears had sharp claws.

Horse was good but he could only find it where he also smelt large numbers of naked bears. He soon discovered that sheep were just as easy to kill, came in large numbers but lived further from the nests of naked bears. They were found in hollows in the rolling hills. Here the air was damp and it stroked his scales with a constant drizzle that was cool and refreshing. He enjoyed killing sheep. They huddled together. One swipe of his claw killed three or four at a time. He ate several of them but soon he had gorged himself on so many that he didn't bother to eat them anymore and just enjoyed the killing for its own sake. It made him forget his solitude and filled his time as he waited for the moment when the glow moved out into the open.

He knew the glow had gone into a wood but he didn't like trees. He couldn't squeeze between the branches and if he had to fight his way through them he knew he would draw too much attention. Then flocks of naked bears would hunt him down. They hunted in large numbers. Grandfather had said that thousands of the Fire Beings had been killed by the little creatures. They hunted in packs like wolves, only they could throw their claws.

He wanted the glow.

He could hear the sheep bleating and the noise angered him. He killed a few more so that he could sleep peacefully.

He woke with a start. His tail hurt less and he could move more freely now. He stretched out his long neck to ease the stiffness of sleep and lumbered up onto his squat legs, wondering what had disturbed him.

He stood still, letting the vibrations shimmer through the earth to feed his senses. He quivered as the throbbing energy pulsated across the land. The glow was moving towards him.

Chapter 13

The jostling flanks of oxen barred the road ahead as the cumbersome beasts ambled along. Their udders were a bloated, stretched pink and they lowed in deep groans, yearning for the relief of milking time. The oxen were white with black faces, still the Jotunn breed, but they had softer contours and less bulk of muscle around their necks and quarters. The Nattarda brand was scorched into each and every rump. Perhaps Cybillia had been right about the other cattle; maybe they had been stolen, Caspar mused.

The herd was three score in number and blocked the road entirely. The herdsmen made no effort to clear a path, as if they presumed that milking was the most important event in life, taking precedence over all. They milked through storms and drought, on every feast day and even on funerals and deaths: nothing else took precedence, so why should a company of nobles push the cattle aside?

A constant rattle rose from the clash of horns as the interlocking points knocked against each other. At least the presence of the oxen and the general activity on the road protected the travellers from any attack. This road didn't have the same ring as the metalled Great South Road. They had crossed the river and taken a beaten-earth track that slunk beneath the tall hedges and steep banks dividing Nattarda's meadows. The road linked Wiglaf's capital with the town of Loomsbury in the heart of the Barony of Ovissia. Ceowulf suggested that if they headed west into Ovissia they could then take the road from Puddlewold back into Farona. None of them were keen on the idea. It always rained in Ovissia and it was a long way off their route, but at least heading west would throw Gatto off their scent.

'Ovissia of all the places,' Caspar groaned.

'What's wrong with it?' Cybillia asked innocently. 'Surely it's better than Nattarda?'

'Nobody likes Ovissia,' Hal proclaimed with emphasis. 'I mean, all those sheep. Sheep are so . . .' He looked at his kinsman, raising his eyebrows for any suggestions.

'So ignoble.'

'I hope they treat their flocks better than the Nattardans treat their oxen. Look at them: it's unnatural,' Brid suddenly burst out passionately, raising her voice above the noise of the cattle. 'How could they leave the poor creatures until their udders are fit to burst?'

'They're only oxen, Brid, not women.' Hal sounded irritated by Brid's thoughts – thoughts that seemed so far removed from the pressing dangers. He looked anxiously over his shoulder for any signs of pursuit. 'We need to get further away from the Great South Road and these beasts are blocking the way.'

'I still think we should have made straight for the nearest town and its reeve,' Cybillia continued her over-worn statement.

'What here in Nattarda? Beg help from Wiglaf's men?' Caspar asked, trying to divert the girl's attention.

'Oh no! He's a dirty rotten thief. No, Father wouldn't like me to go to him for help. It's bad enough just being in his barony.'

'Prejudice is a marvellous thing sometimes, don't you think?' Brid suggested with a mocking glint in her eye. Ceowulf hid a smile behind his gauntlet.

'There's enough milk and beef in front of us to feed an army for a year,' Caspar remarked, thinking fearfully that within a few months the eked out, salted rations at Torra Alta would be meagre and rancid.

'Oh no,' Cybillia objected. 'You can't eat Nattardan beef; it's tasteless.'

Hal patted her on the shoulder as if to tell her not to worry herself about these things, but Brid had less tolerance where Cybillia was concerned. 'You must go around with your ears stuffed with ribbons and your eyes full of dusting powder. There's a siege at Torra Alta; the castle is cut off from supplies and there's a thousand fine warriors in the garrison. Come spring they'll be eating their own horses and if they last to see the summer they'll be boiling their boots for stock.'

'It'll be summer before we get through this lot,' Hal cried in desperation. 'Hey, you man, clear the way there. Let us through!'

The drover turned his head and tugged at his fringe, politely acknowledging the presence of nobility, but moved on with the same unhurried laziness as the oxen.

Ahead, the farmstead, with its wide courtyard dominated by open stalls, was like a pot of sweet nectar to the many milkmaids swarming towards it. They came from all about, skipping through the meadows and clambering over stiles, one here one there, running to join a friend. Quickly they gathered, ten, a dozen then maybe a score in all, happily making their familiar way to the dairy. The rumbling drone from the oxen drowned out the gay chatter from the dairymaids as more herds converged on the creamery.

'It's getting late and it'll take forever to fight our way through all those oxen. We could see if we can find hospitality here at the farm, rather than waiting till the next inn,' Hal suggested.

'We could, indeed,' Caspar agreed, considering his empty stomach. The day had been so hectic that there had been no time to eat and now he realized just how hungry he was. 'Besides it's a dairy; they should have loads to eat.'

Born and bred on the beef ranges of Jotunn, Cybillia had an entrenched prejudice against the produce of the neighbouring barony. Her face was like sour cream. 'A dairy! You expect me to stay in a dairy. Me, the daughter of Bullback, Baron of Jotunn, stay in a Nattardan dairy? I'd rather sleep on the roadside.'

'Well, do that then,' Brid said with exasperation rather than malice. She looked tired and irritable. Caspar worried that the combined stress of permanently concealing her faith, along with worrying over Morrigwen and Keridwen, would be taking a heavy toll on the young Maiden. 'If you won't come with us, no doubt the Vaalakans will find you a sweet and tender morsel, easily stolen like ripe windfalls. They'd probably let you entertain all ten of them.'

'Brid! Control yourself!' Hal flared up in anger. 'Your ugliness from the bruises has made you mean, mean and small minded. Cybillia is a fine and delicate gentlewoman; your common vulgar –'

A sharp cuff to the side of his head silenced Hal instantly. Caspar, whose face was red and bloated with rage, had come hot-blooded to the defence of the young Maiden. He had wanted to leap at Hal and drag him from the horse, but Cybillia sat coyly before him. However angry the boy became, he was fully aware that Belbidian noblewomen were too delicate to be brought that close to a scuffle. Hal turned his head slowly and his eyes formed into slits like the narrow, sinister slits in a vizor.

'Excuse me,' he said to Cybillia with controlled politeness in his voice, 'I have some business to attend to.' He slowly dismounted and stood beside his horse, glaring up at his nephew to meet the challenge. They didn't need to bandy words, tempers coming flushed and ready to their unrestrained natures. Caspar launched himself at Hal, sending Firecracker, suddenly riderless, into a wild-eyed dance, and they rolled around in the dust, frantically burying clenched fists into each other.

Cybillia's startled face was covered by anxious tight fists as she looked down in shock. Brid was smiling calmly; some of her own pent-up feelings being released in Caspar's temper. Ceowulf laughed.

'Well, I'm glad some things haven't changed in Belbidia. I was beginning to think the whole of Belbidian youth had turned to softened butter.' He jumped down from his horse and pulled the freckled boy off his uncle. Ceowulf was a strong man, probably in his early thirties though the leathering effect of the southern sun made him look older than he was. His greater size and weight made it an easy task for him to separate the youngsters. 'You'll stampede the oxen and no self-respecting farmstead is going to open the doors to you if you behave like this. What was your father thinking of when he sent two kids like you as an escort for young ladies? Haven't you had enough of fighting?'

Caspar was not pleased with Ceowulf's patronizing tone. He dusted himself down, shaking the grit out of his jacket and stomped off to retrieve Firecracker.

Hal and Caspar led their horses forward in silence with their heads proudly tilted skywards, pretending that nothing had happened. Ceowulf didn't seem that concerned by their behaviour, finding it more amusing than childish. Cybillia was looking prim and superior, while Brid for the first time was smiling at Caspar in welcome comradeship. His step lightened and he returned to his thoughts of supper. Nattarda, after all, was famous for its cheeses.

Brid reached back behind the saddle and rested her hand on the mare's swaying quarters, stroking the chestnut hide where her pack should have been. She looked down at her grubby leather breeches and sighed. 'I should really have a dress to put on. It would look more seemly now that we're in the heartland.'

A dairymaid with a mop of steely hair came nervously forward as the gentlefolk approached. The younger ones hung back, preferring to stay in the safety of the gaggle, tittering gleefully at the sight of the fine and handsome warriors. Only the older, more matronly woman came forward and bobbed a curtsey at them. 'Would you be wantin' me to fetch the master for you, fine Sir?' she said, directing her questions at Ceowulf as the most senior member of the party. The soldier nodded and she hurried off at quite a pace for someone of her girth.

The farmer soon appeared at the entrance to the stalls, brushing wisps of straw from his clothing. His sleeves were rolled up and he wore no jacket despite the coolness of the early evening. He was flushed from hard work.

'My Lords, I would have greeted you earlier, but it's milking time, you know.'

Inside the farmhouse everything was clean and white; the stone floors were washed and bare, the walls were unadorned and the furniture was functional. The home wasn't poor or sparse through a lack of means but more out of a desire for functional cleanliness. The farmer's wife, a well rounded woman, brought two heavy pitchers of frothy milk and placed them on the table, beaming broadly.

Large windows let the evening sun pour through into the airy refectory. The broad table was freshly scrubbed and the walls were lined with shelves covered in row upon row of round cheeses. The strong, sweaty smell of ripe cheese was everywhere but, after a while, Caspar got used to it and was no longer aware of the odours. The farmer's wife was a busy efficient woman who enjoyed working, and seemed very ready to welcome them with the offer of food.

'At any other time,' she said, 'the maids would be waiting on us, but it's milking time. The herds are big. We've just bought up the neighbouring farm and their creamery isn't up to my Perry's standards so we've been bringing them here. There's too many of them at the moment: we'll be culling off the poor milkers, but Perry will still have to build another milking hall.'

'Are you going south to avoid the troubles?' the farmer asked, finally returning from his duties. 'We hear there are bands of wild men raiding the northern frontier.'

'There's an army,' Hal explained. 'A massive army, organized and intent on invasion.'

'But Torra Alta,' he objected. 'An army is nothing to Torra Alta. We've all heard about Torra Alta. I even send cheeses there. They like the hard-rind cheeses if I recall rightly. No one can get past Torra Alta: it's an historical fact.'

'No one can get in either,' Hal retorted with just a hint of exasperation in his voice at the farmer's innocent complacency. 'The Vaalakans are encamped on the north side and it's the only way up. You can only approach Torra Alta by the road which by now will be within enemy range. A goods wagon wouldn't stand a chance of getting through, so the garrison will eventually starve if we can't get help.'

'I just can't believe it; no one can starve in Belbidia. Even the peasants are fat.' He looked incredulously at the youngsters. 'Mind you, you're all a little bit spare. This young lady has touched nothing.' He nodded at Brid. 'And for two growing lads you should eat more and worry less.'

Caspar suddenly didn't feel hungry anymore. He thought of his father facing the barbaric hordes and then of his mother. He tried to blank out the image of her frozen scream venting her perpetual torture as she lay entombed within the Vaalakan glacier. Twelve years entombed in the pain of near-death: the thought was unbearable. He stabbed at the cheese, imagining it was the belly of a Vaalakan. Suddenly he was desperate to race on to the capital. He couldn't stop, couldn't wait for rest or food; he had to find the whereabouts of the Egg so that he could free his mother.

Farmer Perry and his wife were chatting politely with Ceowulf while still plying more food onto their plates. Smelling the fare, Caspar forgot that he didn't want to eat and eagerly took another mouthful. Rich broth thickened with cream, fresh crusty bread and slices of more varieties of cheese than the boy had ever seen, was a welcome and filling meal even if simple and plain. Cybillia was displeased at the lack of meat and pushed away the cheese platter ungraciously.

The dairyman explained that meat was an unnecessary item when they had all the healthy wholesome food straight from the dairy. Cybillia didn't seem convinced but Brid concurred with the farmer. 'Too much meat,' she said, 'slows the brain.' It was a little dig at Cybillia but the Lady of Jotunn didn't pay her any heed.

The maids were returning from the milking-parlour ready to help in the kitchens and clear the farmer's table. Their ruddy cheeks, washed and scrubbed, shone like polished apples and the smell of soap clung to their skin.

'Can never be too careful when it comes to dairy cows. Any

tiny thing can mar the flavour and quality of the milk,' the dairy farmer explained.

The cook, who had also been busy with the milking, arrived with a steaming bowl of bread pudding laced with stewed autumn fruits, again simple but wholesome. She beamed proudly at the guests, who seemed to greatly approve of her culinary skills, judging by their empty bowls. Her eyes slowly skirted the room, studying each face and nodding a polite greeting to the nobility gracing her master's kitchen. Then her eyes fell on Brid. She stood stock still, her mouth gaping open, and dropped the dish with a crash onto the flagstone floor. Warm milky liquid splattered across the room.

Farmer Perry rushed to her side. 'What is it, Meg? What's the matter?' She was unable to speak and for several seconds she stood horror-struck, then she pointed straight at Brid and began screaming hysterically. Perry dragged her from the room, deeply disturbed by his cook's emotional behaviour, and a huddle of anxious and confused maids scurried in to mop up the mess. From the distant kitchen, muffled cries of, 'Elf! Sorcery! Changeling!' came ringing through the pristine corridors of the echoing farmhouse. Everyone stared at Brid.

'We'll pay you for your hospitality,' Ceowulf rose diplomatically from the table, 'but our errand is pressing and we must get a few more miles under our belts. There's still some hours of daylight left and we should be moving on.'

'Yes, yes, I'm sure you should,' Farmer Perry replied distractedly, edging nervously away from Brid. 'There's a priory not one league from here, right on the border before Ovissia. You'll make that sure enough by sundown.'

The cook's cries came back down the corridor. 'She'll put a spell on the cows. The milk'll turn sour in the udders. She'll turn the milk.'

Brid kept a low profile, pulling her cloak around her and as Caspar touched her arm to offer his comfort, he could feel her trembling. Her eyes were moist and she didn't speak.

A mile down the road, Ceowulf broke the contemplative silence of the five companions. 'I don't know what's going on here, but I'm not so dumb as to think you're just travelling south to get to Farona; you're far too secretive. And as for you, Brid, you can't afford outcries like that. That scene back there will attract attention for miles. All the villagers in Nattarda will know you've been here; and if they know, the Vaalakans will know. So, are you going to tell me what this is all about?' He looked expectantly between their young faces.

Brid wouldn't meet his gaze and Hal and Caspar stared back with their jaws clamped. Cybillia just looked bewildered as she bumped along in the saddle, clinging fearfully to Hal's back.

Eventually Hal replied coolly, 'We didn't ask you to come with us, and if you're not happy you can leave. The three of us have to see King Rewik, and Cybillia is under our protection through the journey. You are just a mercenary.'

'Protection, from a couple of kids!' Ceowulf scoffed. 'And if I told Rewik about what I'd seen and heard today, he'd consider your requests for just as long as it took to arrange your trial. He's not called Rewik the Converter for nothing. I've read the scriptures and I've studied theology for more years than I care to remember.' He paused to draw breath and then continued in solemn monotones: '". . . And fear the small people with the bright eyes. Fear the women who walk in the tree groves for they walk not with the one true God but with the gods of the dark world, the gods of lust and base natures. Beware their smiles lest they beguile you."

'I also know that Torra Alta is a wild and remote territory where Belbidia's dark and ancient secrets could hide without disclosure. I know Rewik won't receive this girl favourably, even if you're too young to know it.'

Cybillia clutched her cloak tight to her neck as if trying to protect herself from any evil spirits. Prayers formed on her lips as, with wide eyes, she observed Brid warily from beneath her hood.

'As I said,' Hal continued sternly, 'we didn't ask for your escort and we'd probably be happier without it.'

Ceowulf shook his head. 'You don't have to be so guarded,

you know. You misunderstand me. I have seen too much death, too much slaughter. I've been fighting wars for fifteen years, and they all die the same – heathen, pagan, the followers of the one true God – they all die painfully, slowly and alone. Side by side in the battlefields, death treats them all as one. I read the scriptures throughout my youth, and they told me that God was on the side of right and that he would defeat the heathen enemy. But I've seen the truth ... No hand of God wields a shield to protect the good or the meek. Never the meek! They are swept aside and trodden under foot, dying in the swill of blood and mire.'

'So?' Caspar remarked, suspiciously. 'So people die in battle. Why does that mean we should trust you?'

'I won't say it out loud, but I know what Brid is and I'm just saying I don't care. I no longer believe in the one true God – or any other for that matter. I have wasted my life fighting for everyone else's countries and now I'm going to do something worthwhile and fight for my own. Brid is fighting on the same side and it means nothing to me that she comes from an older world with a different set of beliefs.'

'Let him come,' Brid said quietly. 'Let him come. He needs to prove his worth, to himself and to his estranged family. You can trust him because he's not afraid of me.'

Both the boys grunted in acquiescence, realizing that Ceowulf's skill at arms was an undoubted asset while they rode under the constant threat from the Vaalakans. Cybillia was more in a state of shock, seemingly unable to comprehend the horror of what the others were talking about.

'Father Rufus said she was just injured and that made her behave badly, but my old nurse said she was a changeling and that cook screams in terror. Then Father Rufus said he would know if there was anything suspicious about her.'

'What are you talking about, fair Cybillia?' Brid jeered. 'Are you calling me a witch? Are you frightened that I'm going to cut your heart out and boil it in my cauldron?'

Cybillia's eyes widened and she buried her head in the folds of Hal's bearskin cloak, her breath coming short and sharp.

'I do believe she's going to faint,' Brid sneered.

'I'm not. I don't believe you're a witch; I think you're just nasty to me because of Hal.'

The dark-haired youth reached his arm backwards to squeeze her reassuringly. 'Don't worry about Brid; she's harmless.'

'I'm not harmless,' the young girl hissed, 'and I am a priestess. I am one of the Three and Daughter of the Moon and in my own country I will declare it loudly and proudly from the peaks of the Yellow Mountains to the southern beaches of Caldea. I worship the Goddess in all Her forms and guises and I will preach Her love and Her teaching. And particularly today of all days just before an eve of such astrological importance.'

Caspar reached over and grabbed her arm. 'Brid, shut up; that's the type of talk that got your mother burnt. You've got to keep quiet.'

Brid laughed. 'You didn't think I'd be such a fool as to let her remember all this, do you?' She kicked her horse forward to draw level with Magpie. Thrusting her hand over Cybillia's horrified mouth, she forced a spray of purple-veined Faronian henbane between her lips. 'Sweet dreams, sweet Cybillia. No one sneers at my faith.'

Hal clung onto the damsel who swooned in his arms and he looked furiously at Brid. 'You are so stubborn and arrogant. Why couldn't you just keep quiet? What if she's too frail to take these poisons?'

The priestess sighed. 'Faronian henbane alone doesn't work that quickly; she's only fainted. But when it does take effect it'll muddle her mind. I had to do it: the damage was already done. After everything Ceowulf said, we had to be sure that she wouldn't remember anything.'

The mercenary appeared totally unperturbed by the violence of the Maiden's actions and, with courtly composure, smiled at Brid. 'I'm impressed with your titles. But I must apologize; I would never have spoken so openly had I known that the young noblewoman wasn't privy to your plans.'

'Hal was right though,' Brid also apologized. 'I shouldn't

have made such an outburst. I didn't have to be secretive at home in the Boarchase Forest where we are isolated from the rest of Belbidia by the Yellow Mountains. Secrecy is not in my nature.'

'Now, look at her.' Hal was furious as he studied Cybillia's lolling expression. 'No one will take us in for the night, now. Not only will they think you are a changeling but they'll think Cybillia's carrying the plague. That was just mean spite, Brid.'

'We'll go to the priory like the farmer suggested,' Ceowulf calmly announced, pushing his horse between the dark youth and the belligerent girl.

'What? With Brid! They won't even have to look at her to know she's a witch: they'll only have to breathe in the air to smell her malice.' He wrapped his arms around Cybillia, cradling her gently. Caspar was horrified by the cruelty in his uncle's words but he didn't want to say anything in case he stirred up a bigger argument.

'I was being practical.' Brid calmed herself and dignifiedly tilted her nose. 'We can't let Cybillia jeopardize anything.'

The youth grunted his displeasure. 'Well, we can't go into the priory – not unless we leave Brid outside.'

'We can,' Ceowulf disagreed confidently. 'They would never suspect her. A witch would never march voluntarily into the house of the one true God.'

'But her eyes . . .' Hal protested. 'I mean look at her; she looks like an elf, so fine-boned.'

'Yes, but so does your younger brother here.'

'Nephew!' Hal and Caspar corrected in unison. Caspar was horrified. He had never thought of himself in those terms. He always imagined that he would be heavy-boned and muscular like his father when he grew up and this lightness of bone was merely a stage he would grow through.

'Nephew then,' the free-lance corrected himself. 'Spar might have the eyes of a heathen but nobody is accusing him – though of course his ancestry must be traceable straight back to the old people.'

Caspar felt uncomfortable. Ceowulf seemed to know too much about all these matters.

'No, you wouldn't suspect Spar because he speaks like a Baron's son, he rides a nobleman's horse and he behaves just how you would expect him to do. Brid on the other hand . . . Well, here's a girl of peasant upbringing – a soft mountain lilt if I'm not mistaken – but with an educated vocabulary and just far too capable with a horse. And she's just too quick to argue with young noblemen. No maiden I know would argue with a man, let alone a man of higher rank. Once they're married now . . . well, that's different. The best thing Brid can do is act as if she were Cybillia's maid, and try not to speak too much. Shame about the clothes though.'

'Mmm, that's more like it,' Hal smiled triumphantly. 'Brid needs to behave with a little less arrogance. We'd all like that better.'

Studiously avoiding Hal's glare, the priestess spoke with dignity as she defended herself. 'I did have a dress with me but I lost it in the struggle. I was waiting until we got a little nearer to Farona before pretending to be one of Belbidia's empty-headed noblewomen. Keeping up the pretence for so long would be too hard and we wanted to get to the capital as quickly as possible. I can certainly do it but I'm never going to act as Cybillia's maid.' She shortened her stirrups so that she perched uncomfortably on the saddle, slackened her grip on the reins, and rounded her back as if she'd never sat on a horse before in her life. 'Oh my fair neighbour, what'll ever become of her?' she wailed as she bounced awkwardly in the saddle.

The mare's chestnut ears were laid flat and its normally long fluid strides shortened to jilting steps. As they brushed past some sorrel growing at the roots of a tree, its head lunged for the tempting shoots. Brid flapped helplessly, her small feet tapping against the saddle-flaps and never reaching the horse's sides.

'Yes, but don't lay it on too thick, will you?' laughed Ceowulf.

From a distance they could see the priory set back from the road. The entrance was guarded by a high wall and a yew hedge. A tall stone building with arched windows and doors, slate roofs and tall ornate chimneys stood in the shadow of a vaulted chapel. A quadrangle fronted the cloister and two solid oak gates sealed off the religious retreat from the outside world.

Brid halted abruptly in front of them, slid off her mare and raised her hand to rap on the smaller, inset door built into the main gate. She froze abruptly, her hand poised in mid-air, and then slowly withdrew.

'What's the matter?' Hal demanded.

'I don't know,' she whispered. 'I just don't like the place. It's somehow wrong.'

'Well, of course you don't like it. The priory is built for the worship of the one true God.'

'It's not that,' she said uncertainly.

'No,' Caspar agreed. He dismounted and touched his hand to his chest where the mandala was hidden beneath his shirt. 'No. I can feel it too.'

He was suddenly gripped with panic that finally his soul had been totally possessed by the Devil. Why else would he fear a house of God? He was filled with a terrible sense of lonely desolation at losing his faith. He still believed in the one God; he didn't want to become a pagan. He feared hell and the fires of the Devil. He tried to steady his thoughts. Could he really think that a priory was an evil place?

'The saints preserve me from the whimsical fancies of my nephew.' Hal threw his eyes heavenward, spurred Magpie towards the gates and, rather than knocking with his hand, kicked the door with his boot. 'Open up in there. We've travelled long on the road and need shelter and help. Open up.'

Chapter 14

The shutter in the door snapped open and two eyes and a nose appeared in the gap. The eyes were hazel beneath tufted brows that had grown thick and long with age. Wrinkles outlined the eyes, feathering out into crows' feet, which hinted at an energetic, mobile face. The nose was long and broad across the bridge, grown a little gristly with age but there was nothing sinister in the man's expression. The voice was gentle and welcoming but Caspar still had a sense of unease. He liked it less as the hinges groaned beneath the weight of the gates and he stepped into the quadrangle. The monk kept his hands folded in front of him, using the loose sleeves of his habit as a muffler and his head was bowed beneath a brown cowl.

He spoke slowly and warmly but wasted no words. 'God bless you on this evening.'

Ceowulf nodded in reply. 'And you. We beg for shelter. I have in my charge a young lady who has taken sick – nothing serious. She had a bit of a fright on the road and fainted. Her horse shied and took off.'

'There is always a place here for the needy.' He snapped his fingers and two novices ran forward to take care of the horses. 'Your weapons,' the monk said politely. 'You can leave them in here. I assure you they'll be quite safe, but we can't allow you to bring them into the sanctuary of the priory.' He nodded towards a round gatehouse that squatted next to the heavy oak foregate. Caspar pouted at the gatehouse, reluctantly placing his two bows inside. He was only satisfied when he saw that the monk had securely padlocked the strongroom.

They were led across the quadrangle to a low building set

apart from the stone cloisters. A hideous gargoyle leered at them from the lintel above the door. Set aside for laymen, the hostel was served by two novice monks whose feet shuffled soundlessly beneath their robes. They showed them to two cells with pallets and blankets where they could put their belongings and then led them back to a large table in the middle of the hostel.

'Welcome, travellers, to this place of solace.' The younger of the two monks smiled thinly at them offering a wooden bowl of plain stock thickened with barley. 'When you have eaten, you may join us at evensong. You will hear the chimes.'

'We will gladly join you,' Ceowulf said calmly, 'except the ladies of course. One is unwell and naturally the other must stay with her.'

'Of course,' the monk agreed and left them to themselves.

Caspar was thankful that at least Brid didn't have to suffer through a ceremony in praise of the one true God. He looked at her thoughtfully. 'Will you be all right if we leave you here?'

She looked uncomfortable, hooking her thumb into her sleeve and fraying the material but she raised her head and smiled. 'Yes, I'll be fine. I think you should go; it looks better.'

The vaulted chapel was dark and smelt of spice. Caspar pressed himself close to a thick circular pillar and tried to pray, but his thoughts simply wouldn't reach out towards any god: he had too many prickling sensations trembling through his veins. All around him the monks chanted in an unmelodious drone. There was a lack of joy in their voices though he didn't find that strange at all. Their cowls were reverently swept back so that their tonsured heads reflected the flickering candle-light. They looked eastwards at the large altar spread with a lavish gold and purple cloth, bearing golden candlesticks and finely detailed offertory plates. The flames from the candles leapt up towards the wheel of a stained-glass window depicting saints with their hands clasped together in prayer. Everything was how it should have been except . . . He wasn't sure. Something didn't seem right.

Of course he'd never been in a priory before and no doubt the congregation of a garrison chapel would behave differently but there was a lack of emotion on their faces. There was certainly no sense of rejoicing, but then he had never felt that at Torra Alta either – except, of course, on feast days when everyone sang out from the depths of their lungs. But neither was there that look of reverence or pious self-righteousness, nor even of boredom, which was quite usual at the chapel of Torra Alta. There everyone fidgeted from time to time, shuffled their feet or coughed or at least showed some sort of emotion. The monks here seemed simply too restrained.

Beside him, Hal was singing tunelessly while Ceowulf was looking furtively around. The free-lance's dark eyes caught the expression on his anxious face and the big man stooped down to his level. 'I'm not happy about this, Spar,' he whispered.

'Nor I. We should return to the girls right now.'

Ceowulf pursed his lips and shook his head. 'The service will be over in a moment. We'd attract suspicion walking out now.'

Caspar waited fractiously and at the first opportunity sped back to the hostel.

Brid and Cybillia were gone.

The novice looked at them with steady emotionless eyes. 'Oh no, they both left with our brother from the herbarium to find some medicines for the lady.'

Brid would never do that, Caspar was certain. She carried enough herbs with her and would never have asked for help from a monk, especially not on Cybillia's account. 'Hal,' he whispered into the back of his uncle's black hair. 'This isn't right. He's lying.'

Hal's eyes narrowed. 'What type of monks are you? What have you done with them? We are powerful men in Belbidia: you cannot hope to get away with this.'

With clenched fists, Ceowulf advanced on the monk. His large frame enveloped in the sinister black surcoat looked fiercely intimidating, but to Caspar's amazement the monk showed no signs of alarm. The door burst open behind him and a score of robed men pushed forward, standing shoulder to shoulder.

In the centre of the group was the abbot who they had last seen leading the evening prayers. 'You see,' the abbot proclaimed, throwing off his brown robes to reveal a short white tunic, 'you have come to us on an auspicious day. You are here on the feast of Lokki at a time of a grand alignment in the heavens. Lokki has brought you to us.'

The robed men advanced.

How could we have been so stupid to leave the weapons at the gate, Caspar thought in despair as he punched out indiscriminately. Ceowulf flattened several of the men with his fists while at first Caspar lashed and struggled, but eventually resorted to scratching and biting as his arms were pinned to his sides. He was plunged into darkness as a musty sack was tied over his head.

'Praise Lokki, the feared one of darkness,' the manic chants rang out.

They were dragged along smooth stone floors and then thumped down a flight of steps. Caspar was disoriented but he judged they were spiralling downwards.

'We will deal with these troublemakers tomorrow, since they cannot leave this place alive. But their blood must not contaminate that of the virgins on this sacred day that comes but once a century.'

Was this pagan enclave some cult of the Mother? After all, Brid too had said she recognized this night as having special significance. Could this be one of the Mother's sects that had remained hidden in Belbidia through the decades of burning? Is this part of the religion that we are turning to for help against the Vaalakans? He was sure that all paganism was supposed to be linked. Is this my mother's religion? Is this devil-worship my ancestry? Caspar despaired. Brid talked of sacrifices: was this just another guise of her earth magic? He felt sick to the core.

A wailing filled his ears. Cords of rope tightened around his body and he felt himself being lashed to a post. The sack was ripped from his head. He tried to scream but an excited man in a white tunic stuffed a rag into his mouth and bound it viciously.

Struggling at his bonds, Caspar wrenched himself from side to side but the friction of the cord only burnt into his skin. He could take very little in at first; everything was happening so quickly. Ceowulf and Hal were there beside him. Ceowulf had a split cheek where he had been punched with a hard object. His head was slumped forward and his body hung limply against his rope bonds. Hal was fighting furiously but he was also tightly bound, his screams of outrage muffled by the rag in his mouth. The blood of anger pounding through his head flushed his cheeks to a furious red. They seemed to be in a closed space, the rough walls reminding Caspar of the caverns beneath Torra Alta. It was dark and the only light came from seven giant candles the height and width of a man.

The monks, all now divested of their disguise, were alive with zealous energy. Their eyes flickered with arousal and the muscles on their faces worked into tight knots with the thrill of anticipation. The chamber buzzed with chanting: 'Lokki, Lokki, Lokki.'

The abbot, robed in a white tunic that went only to his knees, held the severed head of an animal in one outstretched hand and a sickle dripping with blood in the other. It was probably a goat but Caspar couldn't tell for certain; there was too much blood. No, it wasn't a goat. It was a rare breed of sheep with straight horns over a foot long that stuck up like spears from its disembodied head.

He dragged his eyes away from the satanic sight of the ram's head to scan the chamber for any means of escape. But where was Brid? He could see Cybillia slumped on the ground before a cold stone altar. Was she already dead? Then he remembered the herbs that Brid had thrust into her mouth and prayed that she was still only drugged and unaware of the terrors around her. Another girl, probably a peasant too terrified to scream, was already bound with her arms outspread over the slab of the altar stone. But where was Brid?

'God of darkness, ruler of death, deity of doom, we are your servants. We give you the blood of this maiden.' The abbot raised the head of the ram above the peasant girl's chest, aiming to gouge the two points into her breasts and thrust the horns deep into her body.

Oh dear God, great mighty Father, defend us from these pagans, Caspar prayed. Where was Brid? Had she betrayed Cybillia? Was she really no more than one of these barbaric demons who thirsted after human blood? He looked in horrified disbelief at the priest in his white tunic. The points of the horns would be blunt compared to the raw edge of a knife. The death would be slow.

Fear stormed in his mind. But he was sure Brid was not evil. She had feared this place just as he had done; but why hadn't they brought her forward to be sacrificed? Was she to be spared because she was one of them – a pagan? Brid believed in many gods, a whole pantheon of gods, not just the Great Mother. She might be dedicated to the worship of the Goddess but was this Lokki one of her Gods too?

At last the priestess was dragged into the chamber. Caspar was almost relieved to see how she frantically resisted them with flailing limbs and sharp nails.

'Women of the new God, tonight your blood will flow in praise of Lokki. Fear him,' shrieked the abbot. 'Fear him! Dread him!'

Brid stared him straight in the eye. She didn't cringe or scream or tremble, but stared at him steadily, her fierce green eyes stabbing into his soul.

She threw back her head and laughed. 'You expect *me* to fear Lokki. You little men with your half forgotten rites, hiding miserably behind the guise of the new God; you, who fear the outside world so much, do you expect me to fear your God?'

The abbot looked up in shock. His trembling hand raised his sickle and raked it through the air as if clawing her towards him. 'You! You will die first.'

'Die!' she laughed. 'Die? I am One of the Three. The Goddess speaks through me. I cannot die.'

The chanting in the chamber suddenly collapsed into a stunned silence before a general murmur of unease threaded through the congregation.

'See! My soul burns with fire. The life-force of the Goddess channels through me. You cannot kill me: I have the immortality of the Primal Gods.' The men around her recoiled away, releasing her arms. She ripped open her jerkin and woollen shift. In the dim light of the chamber the moonstone round her neck glowed brightly, the silver white light shining through her spun silk shirt just above her heart. 'The light of the moon shines from my soul. I conjure demons from my heart.' She thumped her chest and a thin shriek squealed out. Coiling up around her neck and weaving through her hair, the salamander clawed over her face and perched on the top of her head with its spiney ruff fanning out. It spat viciously at the strangers. Then its snout stuck open to reveal its forked tongue while it shrieked painfully.

'Fear me! I am the living Goddess before you,' Brid blazoned. 'You, who have never seen your God, fear the one that stands before you now.'

Quaking at the sight of Brid's blazing soul, the abbot fell to his knees. He turned the ram's head so the horns thrust upwards, laid the skull on the ground and hurled himself onto the lance-like horns. Jets of blood pumped from his chest and soaked into his white robes. 'Lokki, take me,' he gurgled.

The monks threw themselves to the ground, babbling in fear.

Brid tossed her head back to let her voice ring out demonically. Despite himself, Caspar was afraid of her. She no longer seemed like the small peasant girl with playful eyes and the simple love of life and he really could believe that she was a terrible creature with a demon burning within her soul. He knew it was only the moonstone but in the dimly lit chamber it shone brightly. The scarlet salamander shrieking on her head was only the pet fire-drake, but in this evil underworld it looked like a devil. No one in lowland Belbidia would have ever seen a fire-drake before.

Brid wasted no time. She ripped the sickle from the abbot's hand and trampled over the supplicating priests to release first Hal and then the others.

'We'd better get out of here fast,' she hissed. 'I haven't got any more tricks up my sleeve.'

Ceowulf slung Cybillia over his shoulder while Hal and Caspar dragged at the petrified peasant girl. Brid skipped over the bodies and fled towards the spiralling stairs that led up into the chapel above. Although the monks had fallen into panic, perplexed by the abbot's slow and agonized death, they would see that Brid wasn't truly a goddess the moment she started to run up the stone steps. A goddess simply wouldn't run away. The chapel was still heady with the smell of burning incense, juniper and cloves to hide the smell of blood.

Outside it was dusk. The watchroom and the stables were unguarded. They only had to get to their weapons. Thirty monks represented no threat to Caspar once he had a bow in his hand.

The strongroom door was of course padlocked. Ceowulf frantically searched the half-shadows of twilight for a suitable rock to hammer against the metal lock.

Caspar wasted no time. He ran to the stables and flung a bridle over Firecracker's ears. Shrieks and angry yells echoed through the cold stone halls of the priory. They didn't have much time.

'Sorry about this, Cracker, but we need a door kicking down.' He leapt onto his horse and clattered through the quadrangle to the door of the strongroom where he turned Firecracker so that his lethal heels faced the padlocked door. He backed the horse up, holding him tightly against the curb chains, while spurring him forward at the same time. The colt didn't like it. He threw up his forelegs and lashed angrily with his hooves. Finally Caspar gave him a sharp yank in the mouth and the horse bucked, flinging back his hind hooves. There was a satisfying splinter of wood. Where the wood had split, Ceowulf pounded it until the screws holding the padlock tore away from the broken panelling. The door swung open and they fell over each other in their desperation to reach their weapons.

'Spar, Brid, get the rest of the horses,' Hal ordered. 'Ceowulf and I will hold them off.' The dark youth already had an arrow slotted to Caspar's ivory bow. As the string twanged, the arrow whistled through the twilight air in a high arc to strike the ground right at the feet of the first devil-worshipper who came bursting out of the priory. He froze in his tracks, daunted by the accuracy of Hal's aim.

Breathlessly Caspar leapt to obey his uncle's orders. He heaved the saddle up onto Magpie's back and left Brid to buckle up the girth. Within minutes they had the horses ready and led them out into the quadrangle. Hal threw Cybillia across the front of his saddle; Caspar hauled the young peasant girl up behind him and they fled through the gates back onto the beaten track. Ceowulf took the rear with his sword flashing in the starlight.

They galloped for several miles – not because there was any threat of the devil-worshippers' following them out into the open countryside, but because they ran from fear.

'Where's the nearest town?' Caspar yelled over the sound of the hooves to the girl clinging to his back. She was too frightened to speak. She bumped and bounced precariously behind him and, fearing that she was about to slide off, he reined in to a walk. As he slowed the others drew up beside him.

The girl's petrified hands hooked into his cloak. She was breathing in fast shallow breaths and her eyes were black with fear.

'There's a barn ahead.' Ceowulf pointed to the outline of a black roof against the midnight sky. 'We'll shelter there and see what we can do for her.'

The barn housed an ox and her small long-legged calf who slept curled up in the straw beside her. Above their heads, the rafters supported several roosters who strutted up and down their perches at the sudden disturbance. Brid drew out the moonstone from beneath her layers of clothing and held it aloft so that they could see.

'Now that's what I call baring your soul,' Ceowulf laughed. 'So that's how you did it.'

The peasant girl shrieked at the sight of the glowing orb. 'Demons!'

'It would be kinder if you could help her to an oblivious sleep, like Cybillia here,' the knight suggested. 'Let her forget the whole thing or at least only remember it as a nightmare.'

The priestess nodded, scrabbling through her herb-scrip for a scrap of Faronian henbane. The girl backed away as Brid approached but Ceowulf caught her and held her firmly while the Maiden pressed the herb onto her tongue.

'Ow!' Brid yelped and jumped backwards. 'She bit me.'

Terrified the girl shrieked and struggled in Ceowulf's arms. He gripped her firmly, refusing to let her escape until the drug took effect. For several minutes she moaned and shuddered before finally her eyes began to dull and she swooned in the knight's powerful arms.

'Leave her to sleep in the straw. If we leave before dawn the farmer will discover her in due course. She must live locally and they'll take her home. She won't have any tangible memories of us,' Brid assured them, squeezing her fingers.

Hal carefully wrapped Cybillia in a shawl and laid her on the straw. He smoothed her golden hair from her cheeks. She was breathing deeply and steadily with a calm resigned look on her fair face. 'Well, thank God she didn't have to witness any of that. She would probably have died of shock.'

'Thank me, you mean,' Brid corrected him. 'I was the one that got all of us out of there.'

Hal gave her a sidelong look, his dark eyes almost invisible in the dim light. 'And are these devil-worshippers like the hidden enclaves of Goddess-worshippers we are looking for? Is this Lokki one of your gods?'

She held up her hands in a defensive gesture and slumped wearily into the deep straw that rustled around her body.

'What you witnessed was corruption and imbalance,' she despaired. 'No, they are nothing to do with me. The true worship of the Mother has virtually been driven from this land. Only tiny glimpses of the Old Faith have persisted but, unguided, they seem to have become distorted and sour. I'm sure it was originally built as a priory but just imagine the unnatural imbalance of such an isolated community – a group of secluded and fanatical men closed off from the outside world. They read of demons in their scriptures and they come to fear the merciless Devil more than their all-forgiving God. Petrified by threats of hell and purgatory, they turn to the Devil, worshipping him with the deeds of evil they believe he thirsts for.'

She fell silent for a moment, staring into the heart of the moonstone while Caspar struggled to understand her theological argument. 'But I do not worship evil gods. I believe in the balance of life's cycles which of course includes death and so perhaps that is what the priests of the new God confuse with devil-worship. Death in itself is not evil: without death we cannot be reborn. It is a sadness, but if the plants do not die they would not nourish the soil. If the grass wasn't killed by the cow there would be no milk, no cheese, no beef and we would not be able to eat. And if we did not die we could not return to the earth to nurture the soil so that the cycle of life can continue.'

She sighed profoundly and Caspar was about to speak, thinking that the Maiden had finished her sermon, when she snapped up her head again and, with campaigning energy, continued her soliloquy. 'But these men, too civilized, too distant from nature, hunger for ceremony. In that way they are like the followers of the New Faith. They feel closer to their gods if they can perform intricate, mysterious and lavish rites but all the time they get further from the truth. Worship need only be in your heart. If you rejoice in the beauty of nature around you and trust in the love of the Mother, you need nothing more.'

'Wise words for a young girl,' Hal said half mocking, though

Caspar detected that his uncle was really impressed with Brid's clarity of vision.

The priestess laughed lightly, shaking off the fears of the sacrificial chamber beneath the priory. 'They are old words passed down through the generations. The wisdom is old even if it is proclaimed by a young voice and I can't take any credit for it.'

Brid was awake even before the roosters. She nudged them all gently, though Cybillia needed quite some shaking before she woke up. The baron's daughter groaned heavily as Hal pulled her to her feet. She frowned at her surroundings but said little as they led the horses out of the barn and left the poor peasant girl to sleep safely in the straw.

'We'll ride on to Puddlewold,' Ceowulf decided, 'and I'll search out the reeve.'

Brid agreed. 'Someone needs to do something about those men, but now that we've slipped through their fingers, I doubt they'll hang around to get caught.'

'No, you're probably right,' the knight agreed, 'but all the same we've got to do something.'

'What men?' Cybillia finally asked. 'And my head hurts again and I feel horribly sick. And I look such a mess! My dress is torn, and my hair!' Her voice was rising into a shrill wail. 'Hal, look at me: my dress!'

'I'll buy you a new one,' the youth offered, which seemed to distract her.

'Oh you will? Oh, Hal! Satin . . . If I'm going to Farona it must be satin.'

Hal raised his eyebrows and chinked the purse that hung from his belt. 'We'll get some fine wool here in Ovissia, when we reach Puddlewold.'

'Wool!' The noble maiden was disgusted. 'Wool is for peasants. I want satin.' There was no defiance or anger in her voice. It was mere matter-of-fact statement and she looked offended when Brid laughed.

'We'd better get something for you too, Brid,' Ceowulf

said thoughtfully. 'You can't go into Farona like that.'

Hal looked at the two girls and compared them in his mind. Though Cybillia, with her long golden hair and thin willowy figure was blessed with traditionally good looks, he still appreciated Brid's healthy femininity. But after this last affair with those pagans he felt distinctly uneasy around her. A pagan was a heathen was a barbarian; Vaalakan, devil-worshipper or witch. There was something sinister about all of them. True he'd never seen Brid tear up an animal or drink its blood, but she was a pagan, so who was to say that she wouldn't? He wondered at Branwolf and how easily he had turned to the Old Faith. Hal decided that this change in heart probably wouldn't last indefinitely – just long enough to drive back the Vaalakans and fetch home his wife.

It had started to rain. The only comfort was that it made Cybillia cling more closely to him with her head resting on his back, but everything else was miserable. Ovissia had a heavy soil, and the rain soon turned the unmetalled road to mud. At first they crossed through lush pasture, but the countryside gradually became more hilly and wooded and the road dipped in and out of dales. Wan sunlight dappled the ground where it sifted through the overhead branches. A wood-pigeon, with its feathers ruffled up, shook off some of the water as it sat pathetically in the bare branches. They climbed up to where the ground had been tilled on the far side of the wood.

'Too wet out here for crops,' Brid muttered.

The deep furrow lines came right up to the edge of the track and the rain drove the loamy soil onto the road. The horses were tiring as they staggered through the mud. Clouds of steam rose up from Magpie's back, filling Hal's nostrils with the pungent heady odour of horse.

Ovissia, he thought in disgust. Every wool merchant who came from the area to sell his wares to Torra Alta's garrison complained about the dank weather and the perpetual grey skies. To think, if it hadn't have been for Brid they could have continued on the Great South Road and sought help in

Nattarda to combat the mercenaries. Instead they had to pro-
long their journey by moving unexpectedly west to throw
the Vaalakans off their trail. All of this because of Brid's
pagan faith. No self-respecting lowlander would have anything to do with paganism, and nor should a Torra Altan.
Branwolf was obviously unhinged by his wife's plight
otherwise he would never have turned to the Old Faith for
help.

He looked at Brid. She was quite beautiful in her own way,
though it was a shame about her arrogant self-will and lack
of decorum. Perhaps Keridwen had been more gentle and
rather more feminine in her ways otherwise how could Branwolf have been so smitten – unless, of course he'd simply been
bewitched by her beauty?

Imagine though, Spar the son of a witch. I always knew
there was something sinister about him. It was one thing Brid
being a pagan and Branwolf marrying a pagan but Spar . . .
Spar would be a baron one day. Women were apt to be a little
light-headed so if Keridwen and Brid were pagans, did it really
make any difference? But Spar . . . It was all a little too close
to home.

He didn't like being involved in all this paganism but he
had no choice: only the Mother could save Torra Alta. Torra
Alta was home even though it would never be truly his. It
was where he belonged and the place he loved more than
anywhere in the world.

Sheltering from the rain, a flock of sheep had gathered
beneath the widespread boughs of a sycamore. Hal decided
the wool merchants had not exaggerated: Ovissia really was
wet. The rains from the western oceans wept persistently onto
the wolds, drenching the rolling limestone hills and drizzling
over the small hamlets nestled in the soggy valley bottoms.
The barony of Ovissia was large but sparsely populated, the
principal livelihood being sheep farming – an extensive farming activity requiring few crofters to tend the animals. There
were a few towns based on weaving and spinning, from where
Torra Alta bought its thick woollen shirts; Loomsbury and

Puddlewold being the largest. Puddlewold not only had a cathedral but a nunnery as well.

He groaned inwardly. Brid was still moaning about the Ovissian farmers ploughing up the better drained slopes. He couldn't understand why she took exception to the deeply tilled earth. Surely it was a good thing that these people were trying to better themselves? I mean, who would want to do nothing but rear sheep? They must be infested with ticks the whole time.

'Yes, but,' Brid argued, 'tearing up the sodden earth like this, it's futile. The crops will only rot in the ground. Surely they don't need to. Wouldn't it be better to leave the place undisturbed? There's nowhere for the hedgerow creatures to shelter and breed. They'll be no foxes, no hares, no stoats, nothing, if they continue like this.'

'They've only ploughed up small areas, Brid. Look at the rest of the wolds; they're all green.'

'I know, but where will it stop? When they've destroyed the last otter, the last kingfisher, the last deer and the last badger?'

'Badgers!' Cybillia exclaimed. It was the first time she had spoken for some while. 'We don't want badgers: they're a terrible vermin, carrying all sorts of disease and transmitting them straight to the oxen.'

He smiled inwardly. Cybillia wasn't as empty-headed as that pagan priestess always made out. When it came to oxen she always had something to say.

'Old wives' tales,' Brid pronounced with a patronizing air.

The going was heavy away from the tilled fields where rotting piles of turnip tops stank worse than wet dog – or horse for that matter – he thought to himself. The edges of the road were deeply rutted where carts hauling bundles of wool had sloshed through the mud and cut deeply scored marks into the clay beneath. They rode in single file down the raised centre of the road and were all cheered when Ceowulf's deep voice began thumping out a marching song. It lifted all their spirits and when they rose to the top of the next rise and saw Puddlewold nestled in the valley bottom with a rainbow arching above the cathedral spire, Hal was considerably heartened. Perhaps, at least, they'd get a good meal here.

Puddlewold consisted mainly of a haphazard collection of thatched cottages, all brightly painted almost in defiance of the weather. The horses' hooves turned to a rattle as they clipped onto the first cobbles of the town. The doors of many of the townhouses were swinging open, which surprised him since the first thing he'd do if he lived in Ovissia would be to barricade himself against the weather. A few dogs skulked through the streets but otherwise the place was empty. Hal and Caspar exchanged puzzled looks, but as they trotted through the market town it soon became clear where all the townsfolk had gone.

Cobbled and overlooked by taller buildings, the town square was thronging with people. An angry mob gathered around a circular tower with a huge clock face. Shepherds shook their crooks and stamped their clogged feet. The clogs looked uncomfortable but perhaps they were more waterproof than leather boots. Farmers shouted angrily and the women gossiped in anxious huddled knots at the edge of the crowd as a man climbed the steps in front of the clock tower, thrashing a hand bell.

'Hear ye. Hear ye. Sheep murderers abroad. Gather your hounds; gather your staves and bows. Sheep killed in Three Mile Bottom. Wolves, wolves here in Ovissia.'

An astonished gasp escaped from the shocked faces in the crowd. A few isolated cries wailed out as several of the women fainted, but most of the crowd stood in stunned silence until one red-faced farmer took up the angry cry. 'Muster the hounds. Muster the hounds.'

A roar swelled to fill the town square and the crowd surged behind the farmer.

Ceowulf halted. 'Somehow, I don't think now is such a good time to visit the reeve. To the men of Ovissia, a few sheep will be hugely more important than a few mad monks in their shire. I'll tell the King when we get to Farona instead.'

'Wolves!' An agitated woman wrung her apron and trotted

home, her clogs rapping on the cobbles. 'Wolves! Hundreds of dead sheep!'

Hal looked suspiciously at Brid. 'Where's that creature of yours?'

She shrugged and blinked in consternation. 'One sheep maybe but she wouldn't kill hundreds; that's just ridiculous. Anyway wolves aren't like foxes; they don't kill just for the fun of it.'

'We'll ride on,' Ceowulf said decisively. 'We can take the road to Farona from here. There's bound to be an inn soon and then we can rest. We don't want to get involved in any more troubles.'

Caspar was becoming entirely exhausted by Cybillia's constant wailing. She was beside herself about her appearance; drenched like a water-rat with her bright scarlet skirts smeared and splattered with mud off the road and her once fabulous hair in tangles. She had declared in frail sobs that she would die if she didn't have a bath within the next hour and the youth's impatient eyes scanned the landscape ahead for any sign of a likely inn. The wolds, however, rolled on from one green dale to the next without any hint of a smoking chimney or welcoming light from a window. Dusk was rapidly approaching and Ceowulf became uneasy.

'We must find an inn and get off the road out of the dark. We need a nice noisy inn, somewhere we can blend in with the crowd. The more merchants and travellers the less out of place we'll look. And Brid, lovely though you are, you'll have to keep your head down and your hood up. We don't want to arouse any more suspicion. We'll have to do something about the way you look tomorrow.'

Caspar spirits soared as he glimpsed the first sight of a twinkling lantern ahead and he was very relieved when the sound of a creaking inn sign welcomed them to a tavern. At last Cybillia could have her bath and they could have some peace.

The Ram's Head Inn looked inviting though they were all displeased by the name after their experiences in the priory.

It had a small arched door that creaked open to reveal a low beamed ceiling dancing with the shimmering shadows cast by the firelight. There were no travellers, only local small-holders and shepherds who chatted idly after their hard day's work. Ceowulf strode straight towards the innkeeper, pressing a gold coin into his palm.

'Find us some privacy – a table at the back and see we're not disturbed. Also a chamber right now for the young lady here.' He indicated Cybillia standing morosely next to Hal. 'If you could have a maid draw a hot tub for her we'd be most grateful.' He produced another gold coin and the innkeeper beamed gratefully.

Without a word to her companions Cybillia swept after the maid so that she could wash and repair the damages of the journey. The others all sighed with relief. Not even Hal, it appeared, could stand any more of her wailing laments.

As the maid escorted the Jotunn noblewoman to her chamber, the innkeeper led the Torra Altans and Ceowulf between the closely packed tables to a room at the rear. The mercenary continued to take charge of the group, which Caspar found reassuring. 'We'll have some of that good food I can smell. Mutton pie is it? And a jug of dark ale. And sweet milk for the lady.'

Brid made a face but tactfully didn't complain. She managed to keep her head bowed submissively and followed meekly after the men so as not to draw attention to herself.

The room was small and had possibly been a stable at one time but it was now swept out and fitted with plain wooden tables and benches. It was warmly lit and a fire crackled and spat in a converted metal manger. The ale loosened their tongues and Caspar could feel a growing warmth towards this strange free-lance. Hal liked him, that much was evident, admiring his skill with a sword, and was engrossed in the tales of distant battles and far-flung lands. The younger boy could see that his uncle had a special bond with Ceowulf since both were not only of noble birth but also younger sons without lands or a birthright to inherit. Despite the difference in age, there was a natural understanding between them that eventually enticed Hal away from caution to pour forth their tale.

'The Druid's Egg,' Ceowulf sighed with a lowered voice. 'It's mentioned in the Scriptures. An ancient power. Locked in its shell.'

'How do you know about the Egg?' Brid sounded horrified. 'You're a mercenary . . . You're from a barony that was one of the first in Belbidia to succumb to the word of the new male God; you shouldn't know about such ancient things.'

'I didn't just read about the word of the one God. We were taught many strange and mysterious things about the Old Faith and its abstruse powers. We were taught that the one true God fights continually against the darkness that is manifest in the old beliefs. In the teachings of the New Faith you, Brid, represent those powers of evil. The learned men of the cloth know much of the things that you hold sacred. I was also taught that the Egg is in some way lost. The priests found this idea easy to believe since the secret of the Egg was only guarded by a priesthood of women.' He grinned apologetically at the New Faith's attitude towards women. 'I myself have always found that women can always put their hands on a lost item when their husbands have been searching for it for days.'

'Quite right,' Brid agreed. 'But the Egg isn't exactly lost. There are runes that will lead us to it.'

'Why runes though?' Caspar queried. 'I never understood what power runes have over normal writing. Does it matter what characters form the spell?'

Brid looked at him as if he had asked why is the sky blue or why does night follow day. She spread her palms across the table and looked across the room into the fire. 'Runes,' she whispered. 'They are the writing of the Gods. They are older even than man. Legend has it that when the first druid discovered their existence he had no conception of their meaning and dedicated his life to understanding their occult powers. He sought long and hard to discover their secret, scouring the world, but for many long years he could find nothing. He studied the oceans, the patterns in the stars, the formations of the migrating birds and the flow of the currents in the rivers but none gave him any clues to the meaning of the runes. After many years he had gained untold knowledge but he was still no nearer to ending his quest. Then he found a dragon. This was many millennia before Torra Alta was built, in the time when beasts could speak. He promised the dragon a share in the knowledge of the runes if he helped him in his search for their meaning.

'So they took to the air and flew across all the world, faster and faster, until they passed through the sky to the world beyond. Through mists and ice-clouds they flew on and on into the world of fire beyond. Faster and faster they went until they burst through the ring of fire that surrounds the world and passed into Annwyn. Here in the firmament, the gods were so impressed by his bravery that they bestowed on him the understanding of the runes. He and the dragon flew back, bringing the runes through the ring of fire and the land of mist and ice, then through the clouds and back to earth. But the runes held so much secret power that the druid feared to share them with the dragon and withheld his new-found knowledge. Thenceforward all dragons have hated man and would never more speak in his tongue and vowed to destroy him.'

'You mean he broke his promise to the beast?' Hal was disgusted.

'I'm afraid so. But if the dragons had the knowledge of the runes, the tools of the Gods, think of the terrible might they could have wielded. But the druid, though a learned man, was not a Belbidian. If he had been a Belbidian he would have lived up to his promise.'

Caspar wondered at this extraordinary tale and how the warring between man and the great beasts had started. He shuddered as he remembered the monstrously deformed dragon that had crawled out of the depths of the earth to seek the moonstone and to destroy them. He vividly remembered Wystan's savage death at the dragon's jaws and recoiled from the thought. Hastily he diverted the subject.

'What I don't understand,' he sighed, trying to sound pensive as if he had been thinking about more important things, 'is why the women of Nattarda and Jotunn were so afraid of Brid. The Torra Altan women weren't afraid of her.'

'Now that question is sadly very easy to answer,' the young girl said, the weight of sad times hanging heavily on her heart. 'It's because of the forest, the people in the Oldhart Forest. It's less than a day's ride from the dairy and rumours grow faster than brambles.'

The priory had put all thoughts of the Oldhart Forest from their minds and Caspar had not yet thought to tell Hal about their experience there. As the priestess explained about the ancient tribe, he realized how the lowlander's folklore about changelings and elves had come into being. Brid looked so like them that the old women, who were more sensitive to the hidden natures in people, believed her to be one of the changelings from their tales that had grown up around the ancient oak forest. The Old Faith had been rooted out from the plains of Belbidia many generations before, leaving the lowlanders with very little memory or understanding of the old ways. They therefore feared the pagans far more than did the peasants of Torra Alta, who still remembered them for who they truly were. The fleeting glimpses of small, secretive, half-dressed folk from the Oldhart Forest had only added to the lowlanders' fears. The older women, like the blacksmith's wife and the cook from the dairy, had recognized Brid as one of them.

They rested well that night and in the morning they struck out along the heavily rutted highway that linked Ovissia to the capital. Officially it was known as the Wool Trade Route but it was more commonly derided as the Sheep Track. As they marched out of the wolds Caspar sensed a surge in his friends' spirits. At least the dreary clouds had lifted and they could see the clear Belbidian skies again. Cybillia was refreshed from her sleep and her hair, like golden threads of silk, was tied in a bow to disguise where her locks had been raggedly cut. Hal smiled at her appreciatively. Cybillia smiled back but her eyes seemed bewildered and she complained that she remembered very little of the last few days except something vague about bandits in a forest.

'Oh, I *know*,' Brid exclaimed with wide shocked eyes. 'They were big men and they shouted a lot. Dreadful, sinful revellers. I was so frightened but this kind knight came to our rescue and chased them off. We told the local reeve, though, so you don't need to worry,' she lied.

'But I don't remember.'

'How awful for you, dear.' Brid looked sympathetically at her. 'It must have been the shock when the ruffians stole Diamond. Shock does such strange things to the mind.'

At least thought Caspar, Cybillia appeared to remember nothing about Brid's true identity, though he worried that the priestess was laying her act on a bit thick.

Brid brushed out her hair so that it drifted in a silken sheet down her back, letting the curling tendrils soften the contours of her sharp-featured face and sweep across her forehead to veil her eyes. Again she shortened her stirrups and slouched in the saddle, turning out her elbows and holding her hands high so she worried at the horse's bit and looked utterly help-less. She seemed to be ignoring Hal who chatted constantly to the Jotunn noblewoman. Much to Caspar's delight she smiled warmly at him – almost with encouragement, he felt fancifully – though he was disconcerted by her apparent change in character. The only thing that she didn't manage to conceal was her insatiable interest in their surroundings. Brid had so much enthusiasm for life.

'You're doing well, Brid,' Ceowulf muttered encouragingly. 'Nothing that a good dress wouldn't hide now.'

'Satin!' she said emphatically. 'I *must* have satin!'

Caspar reflected that it was fortunate that they had Cybillia with them. Brid had undoubtedly never met a Belbidian noble-woman before so at least she could study Cybillia and so learn how to behave like one. Even the lilt was beginning to fade and she drew out her vowels quite convincingly. Those green eyes though ... He wondered if his own eyes were as distinctive.

The Ovissian wolds with their green fields and dry stone walls slowly gave way to the arable lands of the central shires of Belbidia. Now in autumn the fields were hog-haired with stubble and teams of oxen laboriously ploughed the golden remains of the crop back into the black-peat soil. Paradoxically, the sheets of dark denuded humus gave the landscape a barren, infertile appearance with its lack of vegetation. The further south they journeyed the more the landscape changed. The fields were vast. Caspar felt small and insignificant, lost in the featureless acres of unfenced fields where the wind swept over the plain, tugging wisps of drying soil into the air and whisking them over the bare plains. The fine earthy dust was swept in drifts over the road and Caspar turned his face to protect his eyes from the grit.

After riding for some time through the starkness of the harrowed peat fields they came to the first harvests of winter wheat and late turnip fields. The tubers were grown as fodder for the oxen but also regenerated the soil, putting back some of the nutrients that the wheat sucked out. Dotted through the landscape, windmills groaned in the breeze and endless teams of smock-clad peasants led donkey-carts from the towering grain stores to the cranking mill wheels. The plains looked very different from the last time Caspar had ridden south towards the capital. Then, the landscape had been a rippling, yellow-gold sea of corn, the vast fields of barley and wheat producing the real wealth of Belbidia.

They travelled on for several days through the uninterrupted plains of northern Faronshire before joining the leveed banks of the River Dors that cut through the heartland of Belbidia. The river with its high banks, reinforced to protect the flat land from flood, at least provided a welcome break in the monotonous landscape. Caspar was pleased to see the roofs of a town ahead, hoping that they might stop for a refreshing drink at one of the local inns. Faronshire was renowned for a wheaty brew of ale, but his father had forbidden him to try any the last time they had travelled to the capital.

As they neared the cross-roads at Bleham, where the main Wool Trade Route from Puddlewold crossed a lesser road the travellers encountered an increasing number of gentry and finely dressed merchants. Cybillia politely nodded her head at every richly dressed passer-by and Caspar noted how she fluffed out the curls and waves of her flaxen hair before each new stranger drew level. Brid studiously did the same. Bleham itself was a small market town and the moment Cybillia's eyes touched on the sign over a dressmaker's she squealed with delight.

'I have to. I must,' she insisted, flinging herself from the saddle and moving as fast as her dignity would allow towards the shop. 'I can't see the King like this.'

'Help me down,' Brid unexpectedly demanded.

'What?' Caspar asked taken aback. Brid had certainly never needed help dismounting before. 'Oh yes, of course, I forgot.'

'Satin,' she said sensuously and gave him a wicked grin.

The older youth didn't reply but looked at Brid with a critical eye. 'Just choose something like Cybillia's. At least then you won't stick out like a speckled hen amongst peacocks.'

Ceowulf touched her arm. 'But don't get anything green; it'll only accentuate your eyes.'

'Can't you disguise them?' Hal suggested, 'like you did when you helped us escape from the Vaalakans.'

'I can try.' The Maiden looked doubtful. 'Well?' she added more stiffly in her normal soft accent. 'Aren't you coming in with us, Hal?'

The dark youth merely looked at her blankly.

'Money?' she prompted him. 'We weren't all born with silver-spoons in our mouths, you know. I thought you were going to pay for all this.'

Hal reluctantly disappeared into the dressmaker's leaving Caspar and Ceowulf to guard the horses.

'Come on then, young knight,' Ceowulf said. 'There's an inn along the road. They'll be ages.'

He was right. It was some time before they re-emerged and both girls seemed peeved with their experiences.

'Dreadful,' Cybillia exclaimed. 'The stitching is all coarse with loops in it.' Her purchase was neatly packaged and furled in plain cloth to protect it from being soiled on the last few miles of the journey.

'Nothing, but nothing, fitted.' Brid angrily strapped her new bundle to the back of her saddle, appearing not to care whether the dress would be crumpled or not. 'It's about six inches too long and I had to pull the silly hoops off the inside before I could walk properly.' She cast Hal a black look as if to say that the dress was entirely his fault.

'And what is that?' Caspar exclaimed almost unable to speak for laughing. Hal sported a felt cap with ornate pheasant tails sprouting from the brim.

'They say it's quite the thing here in Faronshire,' he replied haughtily.

'And, I chose it,' Cybillia proclaimed, as if that left no doubt that the article in question was beyond criticism.

The heartland of Belbidia was vast, covering as great an area as Torra Alta, Jotunn and Nattarda in one. The empty, relentless miles of flat, ploughed land sapped at their stamina. With many leagues still to cross before they sighted Farona, the travellers were dusty and weary from the long road. Cybillia, despite her new dress, had begun to mope again, whining on and on about the loss of her fine clothes, and what a dreadful sight she would be before the King, wearing a dress with such dreadful stitch-work.

'And my hair!' she wailed. 'What happened to my hair?' For the hundredth time on the journey she examined the jagged cut at the front and looked suspiciously at Brid. Even Hal, who until now had basked in the courtly and restrained nature of the maid's infatuation, was beginning to tire of her complaints, preferring to listen to Ceowulf's tales. But Caspar felt sorry for her. None of this was her fault. She wasn't brought up to cope with physical hardship and he was thankful that at least Brid's drugs had relieved the girl from suffering the memory of the mercenaries and the horrific rites of the devil-worshippers. She was far too sensitive and delicate to bear the stress of such atrocities.

It was late in the morning when Farona finally appeared on the horizon. As they approached the capital, the road became increasingly busy with mule trains and merchants, but these never outnumbered the grain wagons delivering wheat to the windmills or taking flour into Farona. Countless granaries lined the road, raised off the ground on stone, mushroom-shaped pillars to keep the rats and mice out of the grain. Caspar was surprised to see a smoky heap of barley ears burning alongside one of these elevated buildings. Brid slipped from her horse and scooped up a fistful of ears, still unburnt at the edge of the smouldering heap and stuffed them into her leather herb-pouch.

Hal raised his eyebrows at her.

'Ergot. It helps in childbirth,' she explained.

'Well, I sincerely hope we're not going to need it,' the raven-haired youth laughed.

'You never know what you're going to need. It also causes hallucinations and rots living flesh if used in large quantities. That's why they're burning it.'

At last the spires of Farona glinted before them in the full noonday sun, standing like the points of a crown around the central cathedral that dominated the landscape for miles around. Even from this distance the cathedral spire seemed to frown down on them. 'It must be as high as Torra Alta,' Caspar observed.

Brid shook her head. 'No it's not. It only looks so tall because everything else around here is so flat. Torra Alta has to compete with mountains and still stands out like a lanced knight in a field of foot soldiers.'

Caspar nodded though he was still impressed by the magnificent arches of the transept and the ornate turrets and domes above the nave. The soaring spire swept his eyes heavenwards, as it stretched up to grasp the home of the deity.

'It's obscene,' Brid sneered, her lips curling with disgust. 'It's like –'

Hal cut her short. 'Just remember that we're approaching Rewik and you've got to behave.'

'I'm hungry,' Caspar complained. 'Can't we stop, for something to eat before we enter Farona.'

They dismounted, stretched their legs and unpacked the last of the supplies from Jotunn. Strangely, now that the great city was so close, Caspar was in less of a hurry to get there. Somewhere within Farona's walls he knew they should find clues to the whereabouts of the cauldron, but the threat from Rewik loomed large. Caspar imagined the King's eyes glowering down at them from the upper turrets of the cathedral. He imagined them searching his soul for the worship and dignified praise of the one true God but instead unearthing the heresy of the pagan faith that was growing within his soul. He fought against the deeper instincts within him, which every day seemed to draw him closer and closer to the Old Faith. He could only imagine that these instincts were inherited directly from his mother, but still he feared them, dreading that it meant his eternal damnation. Determinedly he clung to the philosophies of the civilized world and the reassurances of the one true God. But the love of the Mother Goddess was simple and unadorned, without ceremony or pretence, developed through instinct rather than indoctrination. Its simplicity made him feel naked and vulnerable beneath the piercing threat of the cathedral.

'What about Branwolf's scroll?' Hal suggested, spluttering through an over-large mouthful of salt-beef. The food was tough and he gripped it fiercely with his teeth to wrench away shards of the meat. 'He might have written something unexpected about Brid or Torra Alta's defences. We ought to find out; he wouldn't let me read it.' Hal and his nephew had edged away from the others to talk privately between themselves so as not to arouse any suspicions in the Jotunn maiden.

'We can't look at the scroll; it's sealed,' Caspar objected when they were beyond earshot.

Hal reached inside his hide jacket and pulled out the roll of parchment, teasing away the ribbon that was wrapped around the waist of the document like the laces on a bodice.

'Hal, you can't,' the younger boy insisted, as Hal slid the tip of his dagger underneath the Baron's wax seal.

'I can,' Hal grinned. 'Watch.'

'Don't. The King will know if the seal's been tampered with. He'll kill us.'

The raven-haired youth was still grinning with the dagger poised to slice the seal open as if he were teasing his nephew. 'You're not frightened of the King, are you?'

'No, but –'

'Oh, Spar! We'll be able to reseal it.' Brid had crept over to join them and her green eyes shone with excitement. She nodded at Hal in encouragement. 'Go on. We can't take the King a message without knowing precisely what it says; there might be something unexpected. Just be careful and see if you can peel the wax up without snapping it.'

The red wax was imprinted with Baron Branwolf's insignia of a dragon and Caspar looked on the broken seal in shame, praying that his father would never learn of their childish deceit. The curling characters of Torra Alta's scribe swirled across the page and the Baron's scratchy signature sprawled uncomfortably beneath.

To Great King Rewik the Converter, King of Belbidia and Lord of the Kracka Isles.

Dear Cousin,

I pray for God's divine guidance in such forsaken times as these when the accursed pagan threatens the Faith in this holy land of Belbidia. The sacred foundations of our new cathedral will, as you read this letter, be desecrated by the barbaric infidels as they swarm out of the north to attack my ramparts. Their aim is to spread the foul heresy of the pagan and to destroy the enlightenment of the New Faith that has so raised this noble country out of the ages of darkness and sin. The might of Morbak's army is so vast that he will press heavily against the great walls of Torra Alta and I fear for the safety of your Kingdom. I fear you will be unable to ease our plight here in Torra Alta with reinforcements because a sizeable proportion of this plague of barbarians, issue of Satan, are attempting to pierce the frontier at a high mountain pass known as the Jaws of the Wolf. I pray God gives you strength as you lead your army to meet the invaders.

My loyal kinsmen bring you these letters of vital news. I pray they arrive safely. I send them in person for they are learned and there are few in my garrison who have the knowledge of letters. I beg of you to allow them access to the records of the great libraries of the capital. The request is strange at such perilous times as these but I need information about the building of engines and siege contraptions to further fortify the walls of my fortress. My loyal servant who is the only master of design and engineering within my walls is gravely injured. We no longer have the knowledge to prepare these machines of war. As your loyal subject, I will stand firm and hold the Pass at Torra Alta for as long as our strength and supplies will hold. I send you my prayers in your own fight. God will preserve our souls as we remain faithful to him and drive the pagan from this land.

Your feudal subject,
Branwolf, Baron of Torra Alta

The colour from Brid's cheeks evaporated and she looked suspiciously at the scroll. 'Drive the pagan from our lands! He begs for the help of the male God of the south. Your father writes as if he would be the first one to strike up a witch hunt. He's using me and Keridwen to save his castle from the Vaalakans and then he'll turn straight back to this new God.' She looked angrily at Hal and Caspar. 'Just like you are.'

'I never said I had turned to the Mother,' Hal protested.

'Look at his words,' she insisted. 'He let the King's Inquisitors burn women in his Barony, burn even my mother. Why should I trust him now?'

Caspar put a placatory hand on her shoulder. 'He couldn't very well say anything else to Rewik now, could he? If the King even vaguely thought the Old Faith was rising again in our barony and that we were the instigators of it, he'd have us burnt for heresy as well as hung for treason.'

Brid looked anxiously towards the threatening spire that dominated the skyline.

Chapter 15

The solid gold gates of the city were wrought with the patterns of the Belbidian coat of arms. The crest of the Barony of Faronshire and the emblem of the city were woven into the tracery at the top of the gates. The intricate designs proudly declared Rewik's status not only as King of Belbidia but also as Baron of Faronshire. The sight of Torra Alta's crest, the rearing dragon with a lance struck through its head, filled Caspar with pride. The noble beast represented the power and dignity of his homeland, making the King's personal insignia of the scythe and wheatsheaf seem weak and almost undignified in comparison. The boy smiled proudly.

'At least they've had the sense to close the gates,' Hal remarked. 'The complacency of our fellow countrymen was beginning to sicken me but at least the King realizes there's a war brewing on his frontiers.'

Behind the gates and idly watching their approach stood a liveried watchman. 'Who seeks entrance to our fair city? Your names and your business?' Though his voice was dignified and solemn, the tone was dull and weary as if the watchman had unnecessarily uttered those words too many times before. 'Declare yourselves or be denied.'

Caspar wondered what authority had chosen the words of the watchman's challenge, thinking that they sounded pompous and contrived. 'He's going to ask friend or foe, in a minute.'

Hal, as always, was the first to step forward and took the responsibility of announcing himself and his companions to the watch.

The Faronan cast a cursory glance over them and frowned

at Ceowulf in his black surcoat. 'You knight, why do you not bear the colours of your barony?'

'I have been abroad in the South for many years and my colours have been shredded in battles,' Ceowulf explained patiently. 'I return now to offer my services to the King as Belbidia comes under threat from the Northmen.'

The watch acknowledged their right to enter and proceeded to slide back the three locking bars that secured the gates. The golden gates were so heavy that they could only be drawn open by two draught horses, which spent their days harnessed to the gold barriers. As the watch cracked a whip, they laboured forward, leaning their thick necks into their collars, inching open the bright metal of the glorious city gates. Fire-cracker squealed and danced, fretting at being made to stand still for so long.

Once inside the city walls, Ceowulf looked critically at his young companions. 'We'll have to stop and clean up before presenting ourselves to the King. We look like vagabond gypsies.' He pointed to a small tavern sheltering under the eaves of the tall, upright buildings to either side of it. 'That looks perfect for us; we'll stop there.'

The Barley Sheaf was a simple timber-framed inn with low overhanging eaves and a coil of woodsmoke seeping out from its chimney. It looked homely and comfortable in the sprawling city, standing between two forbidding buildings of bare stone. The Torra Altans were instinctively drawn to it.

'Baths?' Ceowulf queried the innkeeper. 'Baths for all of us.'

Caspar was taken aback. He didn't need a bath. He'd had one this year already and he didn't want another. 'Wouldn't a wet flannel do?'

'No.' The knight was emphatic. 'You need to smell right as well as look right.'

'Baths are dangerous,' he muttered. 'If you get your whole body wet you catch cold and get pneumonia.'

'Well, you might in Torra Alta but you won't here,' Ceowulf assured him.

'Water's still wet, whatever barony it's drawn from,' the freckled youth complained.

The innkeeper led the ladies to one ground floor room and the two youths and the Caldean free-lance to another further along the same corridor. Caspar eyed the cold stone floor suspiciously. He was sure it would aggravate any health problems, though a roaring fire in the hearth did at least do something to placate his dislike of this extraordinary rigmarole of washing in a bath. Before long three tubs made from half-barrels were filled with steaming water and Hal and Caspar stripped off their clothes and tentatively slid into the water.

'We had baths regularly in Caldea. And in Glain,' Ceowulf told them, plunging into his bath, his well-built bulk displacing gallons of water onto the floor, 'they have baths every single day.'

'Every single day!' Hal echoed incredulously, lathering his hair vigorously and sloshing water across the room. 'Doesn't their skin rot?'

'God, look at this,' Ceowulf complained. 'You're supposed to keep the water in the tubs not wash the floor with it.'

Hal retaliated against this remark with a sodden sponge, which missed Ceowulf's face by inches before smacking against the wall. The knight's eyes cautiously reappeared over the brim of his bath, wary of any more damp missiles.

Squeezing the soap between his palms, Caspar grinned as it shot through the air, catapulting against Hal's tub with a resounding thud. The dark youth's face, unrecognizable beneath the foaming soap with his lathered jet-black hair sculpted into two short horns, appeared triumphantly over the top of his tub. He stuck out his tongue before submerging into his bath again and another tide of water sloshed over the edge of the tub.

Caspar reflected that baths weren't quite so bad after all.

They finished long before the two young ladies emerged from their separate chamber, and contented themselves with finding a quiet corner of the tavern where Caspar practised drinking the mellow-tasting beer without spluttering. He hiccuped loudly and looked up from his tankard with a frothy moustache.

'Well, at least you're doing better with that than with the wine at Bullback's. That Caldean red just about choked you,' Hal laughed.

'God, not the export stuff!' Ceowulf chortled. 'It's wicked. Bullback can't really drink that; it tastes like the inside of a dragon's belly.'

All three of them fell instantly silent as two young noble-women swept elegantly into the room. The eyes of several strangers turned and someone in the corner, a merchant by the cut of his loose, brightly coloured gown, gave a low whistle. Hal and Caspar both instantly reached for their weapons, angrily rising to defend the two ladies in their care, but Ceowulf pulled them diplomatically down. 'Don't make a fuss. It was a harmless gesture.'

Caspar hardly noticed Cybillia, even though she looked more like a chrysanthemum than a girl. A dress of soft pink with cream sashes and bows fanned out from her hips. A tight constricted bodice squeezed her waist and her bosom was demurely veiled with lace. Her hair was quite dazzling, falling in a smooth cape to her shoulders and was alive and fluid with colours like rippling wheat in the halcyon days of harvest. Hal was making a fool of himself by bowing low and twirling his new hat with what he obviously thought was a courtly flourish. Caspar found it quite irritating. He would take the first oppor-tunity he could to see the demise of that particular item of headgear. Cybillia's misty eyes raised to meet the youth's enthusiastic gaze and her cream cheeks flushed a delicate pink to match her gown.

Caspar looked straight past Hal, who was fawning over the pink chrysanthemum, and gazed with astonishment on Brid. She'd grown, she'd definitely grown, standing at least as tall as he did now, which made him feel rather inadequate. Draped in a robe of soft blue that clung to her narrow waist and smooth hips, she tottered forward, taking short feminine steps. She looked nervous and uncertain, unlike her usual serene self, and after a couple of steps she had to hitch the skirt up above her ankles to avoid tripping on the hem. However, she let the folds of her robe swish from side to side and managed to copy much of the graceful courtliness required of a Belbidian lady. Her hair was streaked with gold, disguising the coppery tinges of her soft brown hair, and smelt of camomile. Ringlets played on her ivory white cheeks and blue ribbons swept her hair into a broad braid interlacing the locks. Her big, *dark* eyes blinked at Caspar and they sparkled with tears. She dabbed at them with a finger of her lace glove as she swayed forward, catching her hip on the back of a chair and waited politely. Caspar stared up at her, still unable to believe that this was the same girl.

Ceowulf leapt to his feet, drew a chair back from the table and dusted it with his sleeve. 'Dear lady, pray, be seated.'

Brid blushed obligingly.

'How have you done that?' the younger youth asked in disbelief.

'Done what?' Brid squinted at him as if she couldn't see too clearly.

He nodded at her, indicating her general appearance.

'Well, camomile lightens the hair so there's not a trace of red and I found these ridiculous shoes.' She looked down at her feet, revealing the raised heels on her sandals. 'They're designed specifically so that you can't walk properly but obviously that's the whole idea: the more hamstrung a girl is, the more appealing these men of the New Faith find her. Anyway, they've given me a couple of inches. Then a bit of powder on my face. That's all really. Not much to it.'

'No, but your eyes. They're virtually black. I can't see any green in them at all.'

'Good. It was the best I could do. I thought about using drops of a red or brown dye to try and conceal them, but I'd soon blink that out. I thought about wearing a veil but I've not seen anyone else wearing one so that might look suspicious. The only thing left was belladonna.'

'Belladonna?'

'It translates as beautiful lady,' she explained. 'It's usually called deadly nightshade – terrible stuff, a deadly poison, but if you take it in very small quantities it dilates the pupils and gives a flush to the cheeks. As the pupil dilates you see less of the iris until the eye is so black that you can no longer see the green. Morrigwen told me that women in some southern countries take it all the time because big wide eyes like these are meant to make you so much more beautiful. But to be honest I can't see very well and it's given me a maddening thirst. Why women have to make themselves so handicapped in order to look beautiful, I cannot imagine.' She took a deep breath. 'But needs must.'

'It's disgraceful this gown,' Cybillia declared forcibly in a voice that was vaguely reminiscent of her mother's. If she didn't get exactly what she wanted, the only daughter of the Baron of Jotunn would undoubtedly get more difficult as she grew older. 'At the first opportunity I will go out and find the best dressmaker and have a dozen made up to my own design. Look at this stitching, Hal, look at it.'

'It does nothing to mar the brilliance of your beauty,' he said fervently.

She blushed again and wafted her eyelashes appreciatively.

'Well!' Caspar declared. 'Are we ready to meet the King?'

Rather than jumping to his feet, Ceowulf sat back and spread his hands on the table. 'Oh, the impulsiveness of youth,' he despaired with a weary smile and tutted at them. 'Now look, just sit down and hold your horses.'

Hal thumped heavily down into his seat, showing his impatience at being delayed. 'Well?'

'I'll find a messenger to announce our arrival to the King's household and make an appointment. You can't just charge in unannounced, not in Farona.'

'But there's a war on. Surely these courtesies can be waived?'

'No, the King is very particular and the court would only throw scorn on anything you had to say, if you behaved in such an unseemly manner. I mean, a couple of young kids charging in all breathless!'

After a frustrating hour of waiting, in which Brid managed to drink several tall goblets of water, the messenger returned. He solemnly informed them that the sovereign would receive them just before sundown.

'Sundown! Doesn't the King realize it's important?' Hal exclaimed, kicking a stool in unsuppressed frustration, so that it skidded across the stone slabs. A few heads turned to frown at him and Cybillia and Brid simultaneously put their hands to their mouths and gasped. Caspar wondered how long Brid could keep the pretence up.

The vivid green rims of Brid's irises were starting to shine around her black pupils when an arrogant blast from a bugle announced the arrival of the King's escort. She hurriedly reached within the intricate layers of her clothing for her herb pouch. She had refused to leave it with the salamander and the moonstone, which were carefully hidden in her saddle-bag, explaining that you never know when you might need a certain herb. She took a single shiny black berry and nipped off the smallest amount with her teeth. 'At least as the light fades it won't hurt my eyes as much,' she whispered as she followed quietly behind Cybillia, tottering on her high heels. Caspar hoped it wouldn't be too long before she could return to her usual self. He missed her air of self-confidence, which had a comforting way of rubbing off on him.

An armed escort of seven guards, dressed brightly in red and yellow with their tunics fringed in black, snapped smartly to attention on the backs of their perfectly matching cream mares.

'Your escort, my lords!' A soldier bearing the Belbidian standard bowed his head.

Ceowulf nodded in acknowledgement.

At the start of every street the bugler blasted three sharp shrills on his horn and the townsfolk scurried to the pavements, clearing the streets. 'Make way!' bellowed the standard-bearer. 'Stand aside for the lords of Belbidia.' With each blast the red colt shrieked furiously and plunged into his bit as if he expected to make a battle charge.

'Steady there, boy,' said Caspar, soothing Firecracker's neck. 'Easy now. There's no battle afoot.'

They must have looked quite a spectacle: an array of brilliant colours contrasting against the dark solemn streets of Farona. Firecracker's blue and gold caparison and the purple saddle-cloths of the Jotunn horses were almost as gay as the vivid splashes of colour of the ladies' pink and blue dresses. Even Hal's new hat added to the display. And as they paraded ceremoniously through the streets of the capital the crowds cheered. 'Noblemen of Belbidia! Proud Belbidia!'

Hal took off his ostentatious hat and waved enthusiastically at the assembly, his flamboyant gesture and natural charisma rousing a delighted cheer. The standard bearer surreptitiously threw a frosty glare at him and Ceowulf calmly reached out to steady the Torra Altan's hand. 'Dignity, Hal, dignity.'

'To hell with dignity,' he snorted, rising in his stirrups and tossing the cap into the air. 'Three cheers for Belbidia!' The roar from the crowd was deafening and Caspar found tears of joy pricking at his eyes as he became swept along in the tide of patriotic fervour. Hal, like his half-brother Baron Branwolf, knew how to stir a crowd and excite their passion. Caspar had no idea how they did it.

The capital was just as Caspar remembered. Tall buildings, storey upon storey, overhung the narrow streets, trapping the constant chatter of people and the laughter of children in the echoing alleyways. At first glance the constricted alleyways appeared to be decorated with gay banners, though Caspar quickly realized the so-called banners were actually lines of washing strung between the eaves of the houses.

They were conducted along the main state road that guided them from one ornate square to another, each faced by grand townhouses with fine pillars and majestic though stern façades. Farona was a city of merchants and these were their houses.

Scampering urchins, laughing and squealing with delight at the sight of the war-horses, were shoved roughly aside by the escort of pristinely dressed soldiers as they tried to snatch at Firecracker's caparison. Caspar grinned at them. They were not much younger than himself and he understood their excitement. They grinned back and waved frantically in delight, their bare feet and obvious poverty jarring with the luxurious wealth of the grandiose houses. He knew his father would have been displeased by this sight. Baron Branwolf had taught his son not to expect their people to lay down their lives to protect Torra Alta if they didn't share in its bounty.

'What good is gold,' Brid sighed, 'what good is gold if you can't buy food with it? Are these children meant to lick the gold from the gates to stave their hunger?'

Caspar was surprised at how closely his own thoughts mirrored Brid's and he nodded at her in understanding.

'The Great Mother gives of herself to feed all her people. She blossoms with fruit and grain to feed all the children of her land not just those with gold . . .' she preached on in hushed tones.

'Brid,' Hal hissed, giving her a meaningful stare of warning to hold her tongue. The Maiden evidently resented taking orders from the dark youth and she looked straight through him before turning to smile at Caspar. The young boy felt uneasy about the Maiden's sudden change in affections, especially since she had shown a suppressed preference for Hal. Maybe his uncle had snubbed her once too often.

The palace stood alone, hemmed by a green park and encircled by beech trees. It had once been a fortress: castellation crowned the top walls and round towers braced each of its corners, but somehow despite all its grand architecture it looked wrong. The drawbridge was down with no chains or winding gear to raise it again and the mullioned windows seemed out of place. Where once arrow-slits carved narrow slots in the walls, now the stonework was knocked out to form large, square, airy windows. It gave the palace a shocked, staring expression. The moat at least remained filled and peaceable ducks up-tailed and dabbled in the roots of lilies.

The standard-bearer shepherded them forward and announced them to the palace guard. The horses' hooves boomed out as they trotted across the outer courtyard and passed under a high arch into the inner courtyard of the palace. Stable lads scurried forward out of the mews, politely taking their horses. Caspar patted Firecracker's neck and pulled his ear affectionately. 'Try and behave yourself, Cracker,' he entreated.

They were escorted in silence over the smooth tiled floors of the palace's long halls and corridors. Every wall was richly decorated with tapestries. The scenes, however, were vastly dissimilar to the tapestries in Torra Alta or Jotunn. Here they depicted grim men with sober faces in worship and vast scenes from the scriptures. One even depicted a large old man stretching down out of the sky to touch the earth. Caspar sensed Brid's trembling outrage as she glowered at the representation of the Mother Earth as a creation of this wizened old man.

She gripped Caspar's hand: her touch cold and tight. Her hand felt so small, so delicate and he felt every pulse in his body quicken. For a moment he assumed she was frightened but as he looked at her set jaw and clenched fists he realized he was wrong. She was trembling with the effort of controlling her outrage.

'Give me strength, Spar,' she murmured. 'I must deny my love for the Mother in this palace of faithless men, and it hurts. It cuts so deep. My own mother would have died rather than go through this dissemblance.'

There was nothing he could say so he simply gripped her hand more tightly, willing her courage through his touch. It seemed so strange that this girl, who was so unequalled in her strength of character, should now suddenly be shaking as they approached their king.

A court page led them further along a final corridor, which was lined with a series of vaulted arches. At the end of the corridor a pair of studded oak doors were firmly closed across the throne-room archway. The palace page raised the pommel of his ornamental staff and solemnly knocked three times in the centre of the doors.

A formal voice sang out in a chanted, ceremonial response,

muffled through the thick oak, 'Who craves audience with the King? Declare yourselves.'

'They know it's us, don't they?' Caspar remarked. 'The King sent for us at this time.'

'Of course they know it's us,' Ceowulf informed him gently, 'but Faronans love their ceremony.'

Hal was about to answer the voice on the other side of the doors but the palace servant raised his arm to silence him and continued with the formal introductions. 'Standing here in humble readiness to pay honour to Your Majesty is Lord Caspar of Torra Alta, son and heir to the King's servant Baron Branwolf. With him is Lord Hal of Torra Alta, brother of Baron Branwolf. Also begging audience is Lord Ceowulf of Caldea, youngest son of Baron Cadros; Lady Cybillia of Jotunn, only daughter of Baron Bullback; and Bridgetta of Torra Alta, kinswoman to the Lord Caspar.'

Caspar felt privately pleased that, without prompting, the palace page had announced them in order of rank according to the custom and tradition of Belbidia. It was so rare that anyone recognized him as the higher ranking of the two kinsmen. His father's suggestion for the identity of Brid was cleverly devised. To announce someone without a title but to declare them kin was a common and accepted practice for hinting at the connection without declaring the word bastard: that would have been far too coarse for the civilized courts of Belbidia.

Brid however was still not happy about it. 'I had a father once you know. He was a blacksmith,' she hissed under her breath and Caspar felt quite shocked. Brid had never mentioned her father and, since she seemed so untamed and defiant with men, it didn't seem probable that she had ever been subjected to male authority. 'The Inquisitors speared him through the heart when he tried to protect my mother.' Her hand was trembling. 'They would have killed me too if it hadn't have been for Morrigwen.'

The muffled voice on the far side of the door was a few minutes in replying, but finally the voice boomed out, 'Rewik,

King of Belbidia, Emperor of the Kracka Isles and Lord Duke of Faronshire, Defender of the Faith, bids his subjects welcome and enter.' The doors glided noiselessly open despite their great weight and the page stooped to present a practised bow, brushing the polished flagstones with his fingertips.

The throne-room was bright and airy after the gloomy corridors. Coloured light flooded in through the stained glass windows, some falling as the natural warm orange glow of sunset and some as the coloured rays of the rainbow, split into spectrums by the curves of the decorative glazing.

Rewik was beset by clerks and scribes petitioning him with rolls of paper. The courtiers scraped and bowed, smiling obsequiously in their efforts to win the favour of the thin austere man. Caspar found himself frozen to the spot: it had been one thing to accompany his father to meet the King but another to approach alone and uninvited. Ceowulf hung back and nudged Hal from behind. 'You and Spar go forward; I'll stay with the ladies. The King doesn't need to see all of us at once.'

Even Hal was reluctant to approach His Majesty, knowing him, by reputation, to be a hard and difficult man. Rewik turned his thin beak-like nose towards the party and rose from the carved throne. 'Torra Alta. You bring me news of Torra Alta. Come forward at once; I must hear how my subjects fare on the northern frontier. Messengers have been thin on the ground of late and I've had no word for weeks. I'm raising an army, but I need information. Don't just stand there. All of you now, come forward and present yourself.' His words were softly spoken in a thin reedy voice that cut through the respectful hush of the court.

All five of them shuffled forward though Caspar made a concerted effort to square his shoulders and walk proudly as befitted his status. It was Ceowulf who first bowed low and Caspar took his cue from the more experienced man.

'Oh get up!' Rewik snapped his fingers at them. 'Come right in close. I need to hear the news. I didn't expect to see you Caspar. I expected messengers but I didn't expect the old Black Wolf's son. Am I to believe that he fears for your safety?

Or do you bear a message that could only be brought in person?'

Hal rustled through his breast pocket and produced the crumpled parchment, holding it forth to the King. 'We were attacked by rustlers in the Oldhart Forest and the seal was damaged in the scuffle, Your Majesty.'

The King nodded wryly, not even bothering to challenge the truth in Hal's statement but raised an eyebrow just to let them know that he wasn't born yesterday. He took the parchment and sat back, scanning it carefully and without comment for several minutes of hushed silence. 'So, I must take the army north-west to the Jaws of the Wolf, but still Branwolf asks for reinforcements. That request is easily answered: I cannot supply them. I must keep men in reserve to defend Farona.'

So, Father was right about Rewik, Caspar thought, nervously pressing at his crooked nose.

'I've only had garbled information from half-witted messengers of late. Tell me Branwolf's mind and what he considers of the enemy's movements.'

'The full Vaalakan assault will be split, with one half attacking Torra Alta and the other the Jaws of the Wolf, though this is still supposition. When we left only the very first of Morbak's men had crossed the wastelands between Vaalaka and the northern border.' Caspar drew a breath and studied the King's face to see if he was making himself clear. Rewik glared at him intently, swallowing hard in concentration, and the boy continued. 'Morbak's army is too vast to move quickly but, from the angle of their approach, my father suspects that half of the Vaalakans will turn westwards.'

'If he goes that far west, why doesn't he assault from the sea?' Rewik sounded as if he were correcting the boy and Caspar didn't dare contradict him.

Hal coughed and cleared his throat. 'No. They can't attack from the sea. Even if they had a suitable fleet, they cannot get out of their ports because their seas are now frozen both winter and summer. They will make their second attack overland through the Jaws of the Wolf. It is the only undefended Pass in the Yellow Mountains.'

The King sat forward and looked attentively towards his subjects, snapping his fingers at the council who stood on his left hand and dismissing the rest of his court. Four men came forward, two dressed in the garb of generals with grand swords, chainmail and black silk tabards embroidered with the King's yellow and red crest. They had been listening with acute interest and stepped eagerly forward. In stark contrast, the other two men wore long white beards and shuffled forward on walking-sticks, mumbling continually to each other.

'I will hear your news of the Vaalakans before I deal with this matter of the siege-engines.' Rewik dismissed Hal's attempts to discuss access to the Great Library.

The King flicked his gaze past Caspar and Hal and focused sharply on the two girls. Caspar's breath quickened as he feared that the King might notice something untoward in Brid's appearance but he didn't seem to see beyond their colourful dresses.

'I imagine these young ladies are here to seek shelter away from the troubles on the northern border.'

Caspar was dismayed that even Rewik dismissed the Vaalakan invasion as troubles, and stumbled over his reply. Smoothly Hal interceded, 'When we are concluded here, we intend to escort Lord Caspar's kinswoman to my mother, Lady Elizabetta who now lives just south of Farona. Lord Bullback asked us to request that you give his daughter, Lady Cybillia, safe housing here in the palace.'

The King nodded, dismissing the problem of the two girls without a moment's wasted thought. He snapped his fingers at a page and muttered discreetly to his servant. The page scurried forward, bowed low before Brid and Cybillia before leading them towards a side-chamber where they could wait comfortably without worrying over the state battle plans.

They spent that whole evening in conference. Hal, with

help from Caspar, drew out plans of the enemy's movements, adding their estimation of Vaalakan numbers and the type of weaponry that they carried.

'That's impossible,' one of the wizened old men confronted the two Torra Altans. 'Impossible! Vaalaka is a poor barren country: it could not raise an army ten thousand strong let alone more than one hundred thousand.'

Caspar had felt doubtful in his own mind about the numbers until he had actually seen the column snaking through the vast wilderness of the Dragon Scorch of southern Vaalaka. He had listened to Branwolf as he spent conscientious hours correlating battle charts and recording numbers from both foreign wars and Belbidia's own distant past to estimate the numbers. Caspar did not doubt his father's judgement. The column of white-blond men with their bear-skins and make-shift weapons stretched from the starved tundra of Vaalaka to the head of the Pass.

The boys were weary and deflated when finally Rewik dismissed them from his court, refusing to be bothered with the issue of the siege-engines until the following day. Ceowulf was angry as they joined the two girls, declaring that Rewik's generals were complacent and arrogant and knew nothing about warfare. 'I've seen cities overthrown by nomads; I've seen knights cut down by foot soldiers. Without great commanders and skilled tacticians, war is just a game of numbers and Vaalaka is a vast wilderness full of wild and desperate men. These foppish fools have lived too long in the sweet sop of the heartland.'

There was a keen sharp look to Ceowulf's gaunt face. The pupils in his dark brown eyes contracted into pinpoints of anger. Caspar decided he didn't quite understand this man. There was surely an innate disloyalty in the heart of a mercenary but Ceowulf appeared to have a noble soul willing to die for the love of his country.

'My Lords, my Ladies,' a brightly dressed page, wearing ridiculous shoes that curled up at the ends, entered and bowed low before them. 'It is my honour to escort you to your chambers.' They followed the soft pad of his smooth soled shoes along the endless corridors of the palace. Both of the youths strode out, striking the floor with their heels to produce a smart, manly click as they walked. Hal had tried to deflect the King's offer of hospitality, saying they would stay with his mother, Elizabetta. The King, however, insisted that if they were there on state business it was his privilege to demand that they accepted state hospitality. It was impossible to refuse the King.

The bed was uncomfortably soft and Caspar couldn't sleep. The enveloping covers made him feel as if he were drowning in warm waters that were lapping up and stealing his breath. He woke with a start to find the bedclothes over his face and he struggled to get free. Something else had awoken him though.

The palace servants had latched the shutters closed when they retired and, without the flickering light of a candle, the boy's eyes could see nothing in the pitch of the room. He knew someone was there. He heard no step, no breathing, no creak of the door; he could just sense the living pulse of a body close by. He touched his chest, reaching for the mandala. It was warm and comfortable like a sleeping hound curled up at the foot of its master.

'Hal? Hal? Is that you?' He spoke in a half whisper, sensing it was an intrusion to speak louder in the darkness. There was no reply. Someone sat beside him and reached out to take his hand. Caspar pushed himself upright, pulling the covers up to his chin, but the light touch was still on his arm. 'Hal?' he asked uncertainly even though he knew it wasn't; Hal would have flung the door wide and prodded him hard with his boot to see if he were awake.

'It's me.' Brid's soft lilting voice sang in his ears.

Caspar's heart leapt into his throat and his pulse quickened to a dreadful pounding. He didn't dare speak because he knew his voice would catch or squeak like a little boy's. And at a moment like this, when a lady comes unbidden to the dark of a gentleman's chamber, well, that was the very last moment you wanted your voice to sound high and squeaky. The youth coughed, trying to clear his throat.

'Brid!' He coughed again; the pitch still needed lowering an octave. 'Brid what are you doing here?' He hoped that wasn't a stupid question; after all she'd been smiling favourably on him all day, squeezing his hand as they walked towards the throne-room, and given Hal only black looks. She squeezed his arm tighter.

'I couldn't sleep either,' she whispered.

'How did you know I wasn't asleep?' the boy asked, trying to keep the conversation open, trying not to say anything that might spoil the magic spell that had brought this wonderful budding woman to his bedside. He wasn't exactly experienced in talking to maidens in the middle of the night and he wasn't entirely sure of the best approach. Should he take her hand, should he stroke her hair, should he pull her towards him? He didn't know. Instead his fingers clutched tightly at the bedclothes and froze.

'Oh, I always know if you're awake or asleep: I can sense your breathing. You were bound to be uncomfortable in a place like this,' she shuddered, gripping tighter and producing a sweet pain as her nails dug into his skin, 'where the walls are so thickly spread with the worship of the new God. It makes me feel uncomfortable too, so alone – so afraid. I can hardly sense the presence of the Mother. I've never felt like this.'

Caspar didn't like the implication that he was intrinsically drawn to the Old Faith but he had a haunting feeling that the Maiden was right. His fear for his contaminated soul, however, was completely submerged in the rush of emotions that concentrated his mind on the girl's tantalizing presence. 'Oh Brid,' he tentatively put his arm across her shoulder but barely touched her skin in case the weight of his arm offended her. She inched a little closer to him. 'You never have to feel afraid when I'm near you.' It was a stupid thing to say and he knew it; but this was one of those stupid situations when almost anything he said would have sounded wrong. Hal, of course, would have said all the right things to make her feel desirable and kindle the spark of lust in her heart. Caspar sighed; it was no use trying to be his uncle – he had to be himself.

'Spar?'

'Hm?'

'Tomorrow we have to search the libraries, the almanacs, the tombs, we have to search everywhere and if they realize what we are looking for, you know what will happen? We'll die at the hand of our own king, for trying to find the only thing that can save his country. It seems so wrong, so absurd. I've never been afraid before, but here in this palace, I feel alone.'

'You're with me,' Caspar finally found the courage to pull the girl towards him, bringing her close so that he was breathing in her sweet warm breath. He knew his pulse was racing feverishly and he hoped she wouldn't realize how nervous he was. He didn't really take in what she was saying about the danger of seeking out the sacraments of the Old Faith beneath the very nose of Rewik the Converter. He didn't really care what she was saying; he was only aware of the closeness of her body, knowing that her thigh and his thigh were only separated by the thin layers of bedding. Caspar didn't share Brid's fear: he only felt the stirrings of thrilled excitement.

'It's funny, Spar, we've lived such different lives and yet I feel so in tune with you; as if in past lives our fates were entwined together. I feel as if I've known you ever since ever, since the beginning of Annwyn.'

The boy wished he could think of something equally romantic and poetic, but his brain was only fixed on what she was wearing. He wondered when it would be appropriate to slide his hand gently down her shoulder. Her night-gown, evidently provided by the palace, felt as if it were of shimmering silk, the sensation tingling on his fingertips.

'We've shared so many of the same things: the same rare ancestry for one and we were both deprived of our mothers.' She sighed pensively. 'And of course we both in our different ways care too much for Hal – though I hate to admit it.'

Caspar's heart stopped. What in one breath was sweet music now clashed with sudden discord and he realized he'd made an embarrassing mistake. Brid wasn't here for him: she was here to talk – literally talk – and what's more, about Hal, of all people. He couldn't believe it; Hal was always spoiling things for him. Sighing heavily, he thanked God, or possibly the Mother, that his actions hadn't betrayed his thoughts and that he had done nothing to embarrass himself. He felt the sweat of excitement chill on his skin and he sighed deeply, trying to expel the arousal from his body. She was still talking but the youth was concentrating on calming his own clamorous thoughts and didn't take in everything she was saying. At last he was able to focus clearly on her confession. 'You're so easy to talk to and you always seem to understand. Hal is so infatuated with that . . . that prettied-up, spoilt brat. I don't know if you're old enough to understand such things . . .'

Old enough! Old enough! Caspar's thoughts cried out in despair. *She thinks of me as a mere child. No wonder she didn't consider the impropriety of sneaking to my bed-chamber in the middle of the night. Not old enough!*

Brid was still talking as Caspar struggled to regain his dignity.

'. . . and I feel so guilty. All that should matter is the Mother and the search for the Egg but I can't stop loathing Cybillia because of Hal.'

'Cybillia?' Caspar began to relax and moved across the bed to let her sit more comfortably beside him. He no longer had to think what to say but the words came easily and naturally. 'She's not so bad. She'll improve greatly away from her father, who's obviously always doted over her.'

'She'll improve greatly away from Hal, you mean,' she snorted with a laugh that sought humour in every situation.

Caspar laughed too, releasing all his tension. The situation was so absurd. Now that he understood that Brid was here with no improper thoughts in her mind, he felt a paradoxical degree of prudish indignation. It seemed quite wrong to visit a man's room in the middle of the night though it was clearly apparent that Brid's culture and upbringing saw nothing untoward in her behaviour. Anyway, he thought with annoyance, she considers me too young.

'Since you weren't raised with the natural laws of the Mother, you may find it difficult to understand. The New Faith believes that priests should be celibate otherwise they compromise their worship of that god of theirs, but we believe the opposite. The union between man and woman has deep and potent power, bringing life and posterity to all. Anyway,' Brid dismissed her own thoughts, 'Hal intrudes on more important things. Tomorrow we must go to the library. Somewhere hidden beneath Rewik's desecrating constructions we should find the Keepers.'

Brid had been talking a long time and sleep was beginning to tug at the boy's eyelids. 'Who are the Keepers, exactly?'

'The Keepers? They are an esoteric sect of priestesses whose sole duty is to guard the cauldron and keep its runic secrets. According to legend, on their initiation into the order, their tongues are cut from their mouths to prove their dedication to keeping the secrets of the Druid's Egg,' she explained in a drowsy voice.

'How horrible! But what do you mean by legend? Don't you know?'

'No. Nobody knows,' she sighed. 'All things surrounding the cauldron are more than secret.' There was a long silence and Caspar thought she must have fallen asleep on his shoulder, but then she mumbled in a blurred, dreamy speech. 'He drives you mad doesn't he? He does exactly what he likes, doesn't care whom he offends ... But he risked his life for me, carried me all that way ...' She didn't finish her sentence but slipped into the silence of reverie. With natural ease Caspar put his arm around her shoulders and squeezed her with friendly compassion.

Yes, he thought hazily with an envy dulled by drowsiness, he can drive you mad.

Brid was silent for a while and the boy felt no need to talk either, their thoughts strolling along the same paths with the ease of understanding. Caspar felt his eyelids dragging down with sleep and he slumped deeper into the propped up pillow, feeling comfortable and secure next to Brid.

'Do you know what is really so shameful?' she asked proving that she was still awake.

'No.'

'I should only be thinking about Keridwen and Morrigwen. I should be concentrating on how we must rescue Keridwen before the Vaalakans destroy everything – the Old Faith and the New Faith. What I feel for Hal is irrelevant and shouldn't matter at all; not when there are so many things of such greater importance to worry about. I shall ignore him,' she said with a satisfied sigh. 'I have been weak and insufficiently committed to the love and service of the Great Mother. My feelings should be nothing compared to the quest we are on.'

'I'm sure you are right, Brid,' he agreed with renewed and unsuppressable hope.

'He's so handsome and brave,' she continued, immediately contradicting her last statement. 'Oh, I don't mean to say that you won't be.' Her tone was suddenly placatory as if she'd realized that she might have offended her friend. 'I'm sure you will be as equally dashing when you are a little older.'

Hal always took precedence because he was older: the old wound stabbed in his stomach but the sensation was so familiar that he ignored it. They talked in quiet whispers. Caspar's eyes grew heavier and he spoke more lazily, the words slurring one into the other. The next thing he knew a sharp beam of daylight prised open his eyelids. It was morning. His arm ached where it had lain all night underneath the weight of the girl's body as Brid had slept curled up above the covers. A palace servant was opening up the shutters and as the light fell on the bed, the serving-girl's mouth fell open.

'Oh! Oh! Excuse me, Sir, my Lady, I didn't realize.' She scrambled from the room with deep red cheeks. Caspar laughed, assuming that the woman had mistaken them for lovers. Sulkily he mulled over the irony of it all and nudged Brid awake.

'Come on! Go and get dressed.'

'I'm sorry for last night,' she sighed. Caspar was disappointed to notice that her night-gown was discreetly covered by a thick blanket, which she held tightly to her bosom. 'You'll forget it all won't you. Be quick and get Hal up; we've got lots of work to do.'

Chapter 16

'We are displeased. He should have rectified this problem many years ago.' The King stared down from his elegantly carved throne at the two young subjects presenting themselves to him. Caspar felt his collar tighten as his indignation rose. How dare the King speak of his father like this – and in front of the court too? He flexed his hands, digging his nails into his palms in an effort to restrain himself.

'But the engines must be repaired.' King Rewik flicked his hand towards a courtier wearing a ridiculous outfit of puffy crimson breeches that stopped half way down his thighs. Two spiky legs covered by tight fitting leggings stuck out beneath. Caspar thought he looked quite absurd and struggled with an irresistible urge to laugh. He avoided Hal's eyes, knowing that if they so much as glimpsed each other they would collapse into an unseemly display of giggles. Hal snorted and then coughed fiercely into his hand.

Rewik craned his neck towards the knobbly-kneed scribe. 'These young noblemen need access to the records held at the Dowager's Palace. Tell that fossil Legros that he must allow them access.'

He turned his sharp nose towards the Torra Altans. 'The Great Library is of no use to you in this matter. I keep nothing but the scriptures and scholarly works on the word of the Lord there, as I do not wish to have them contaminated by the proximity of other impure literature. You will have to go to the Dowager's Palace, where I have removed all the less worthy works to. Unfortunately you'll have to speak to our near-heretic librarian, Legros, who seems reluctant to oblige us by dying. Some charter from my father gave him life-long custody of the state library and so I can't be rid of him.'

The two youths bowed and stepped backwards away from the throne as Rewik dismissed them with a flick of a long-fingered hand.

'We'll take our young kinswoman with us,' Hal whispered loudly so that his words were audible to the King. 'She wants to see a little of Farona before we deliver her to my mother's manor.'

Under the escort of the fastidiously dressed page, the two young noblemen and the priestess strutted through the broad streets of Farona. Brid looked the very picture of a spoilt noblewoman from a rich and arrogant family. The page diligently avoided the narrow alleys that twisted secretly away like capillaries spreading out from a main artery, carrying the life blood of commerce to feed the peripheral regions of Farona. The further they went from the palace, the louder the barking of dogs, the cries of street sellers and the laughter of children became. Caspar felt enclosed by the tall buildings, seeing only a thin corridor of sky above his head that managed to squeeze between the rooftops. He was accustomed to the airiness of Torra Alta, encompassed by a panoramic sky, with the fresh air swirling freely around him. Here he felt like a hawk with clipped wings.

The streets were bustling with the flow of traffic. Wagons laden with grain and churns of milk rumbled over the cobbles on their way to the markets. Spice trains clattered on the solid pavements and the mules, led by merchants with sun-bronzed faces and loose flowing robes, laboured under their burdens. All of them, merchant, tradesmen or plain wagoner hurriedly drove their teams to the edge of the street as they noted the approach of the page, proudly displaying the King's crest on his livery.

The page never paced beyond a dignified slow march and Caspar thought they would never reach their destination. But at last they came to a broad stately avenue lined with graceful sweet chestnuts. The head of the avenue was dominated by the old stone building of the Dowager's Palace. Creepers tugged at the walls and the building's narrow, arched windows were hazed with dust. Even from the outside there was the sense that it hadn't been lived in for several years.

The page ceremoniously knocked on the dry splintered oak of the palace's front door and waited solemnly while Caspar studiously avoided looking at his ridiculous attire for fear of spluttering out his bridled mirth. Eventually, just as Caspar could feel his mouth curling upwards the unoiled door finally creaked open. An old man with a long beard plaited at the ends to form a point, glowered out at them. He wore a dark brown robe that dragged on the floor and he leant heavily on a stick.

'Hm, yes?' he demanded, the words a little indistinct due to his lack of teeth. 'Yes, yes, out with it. I'm busy, very busy.'

The page looked shocked by this reception. 'I represent the King. I have his seal here on this document. It bids you to welcome these noblemen. They want your help with some research. And mark me, Legros, the King will hear of your surly manner towards the representative of His Personage.' Having discharged his duty, the page turned on his heel and marched stiffly away.

'How does one so young get to be so arrogant?' the old librarian muttered, staring thoughtfully after the page. 'No respect for age. Now in my day . . .'

'Sir, I beg you, may we enter and begin our search?' Hal asked with the utmost courtesy whilst tapping his fingers against his thigh to relieve some of his impatient tension.

'The King never bothers with me: why should I bother with his whims? He cast me out of the Great Library, nigh on fifteen years ago now, and not once has he visited the wealth of knowledge I have guarded and preserved for the nation. When I die no one will come to replace me. What do I care for the King's wishes? These are my books. I haven't got time to help you; I have to re-catalogue. I will die before I am finished and there is no one to continue my work.'

The old man worked his chin up and down, mashing his

gums together. 'He won't send me an apprentice. All the apprentices go to copy out more of the same book for the Great Library, always just the one book of the scriptures. Here I have tens of thousands of documents and I cannot catalogue them all. My eyesight . . .'

Oh Mother, he's completely mad, Caspar sighed to himself, wondering if the old man was ever going to let them in.

'We beg of you, sir,' Hal said again, but Brid nudged him aside.

'Legros, we don't come from the King.' She reached up and took the man's hand, staring into his eyes. 'His page merely showed us the way. We come to see your books. We've come to admire your lifelong work. My name is Brid.' She spoke in the softest of voices like a mother soothing a child to sleep. 'We're from the North. There's a war, you know.'

The old man shook his head, unable to take his eyes away from the clutch of Brid's gaze. 'A war? No, I didn't know there was a war. I've ordered my subject matter alphabetically, you know, but the King doesn't appreciate it, not young Rewik. Now King Sithric was a good man; he cared about the books; but Rewik . . . your eyes are staring child. The light is too bright for you.'

'What subject are you on now, Legros?' she wooed him with soft words and bright interest in her eyes.

'Equestrian matters, but that alone will take me a month. You'd think the King would be interested in matters pertaining to the noble beast – the training of war-horses. I don't read the books; haven't got the time . . .' He followed meekly, like a pet puppy on the heel of its mistress, as Brid drew him into the panelled entrance halls. The old librarian shuffled along, nearly tripping on his robes. Caspar suspected that the garments had once fitted the man but now he was shrunk and stooped with age. His trailing gowns were probably the only things that kept the corridors swept free from dust.

The panelled walls were cracked and cobwebs as thick as birds' nests stuffed the corners and recesses of each room as the librarian shuffled his way deeper in to the Dowager's Palace.

However, as they entered the great hall, which housed the bulk of the books, all odour of mustiness and decay was banished. Every shelf and every book was dust-free and polished. In the centre of the room a low beech table supported three great tomes whose pages were covered with the inky scrawl of a plume. 'My catalogues.' The old man spread his arms widely as if to embrace a beloved child, but then he stiffened abruptly. 'Shoo!' He hurried forward with the first signs of urgency to chase away a cat that had hopped up onto the table and was advancing towards the ink pot. 'Mice, Mortica, mice. Get to work.' The cat slunk away and disappeared into the labyrinth of book shelves.

The great hall was lined to the vaulted ceiling with row upon row of boxed papers and leather bound books: gold leaf declaring their illustrious contents. Brid stroked the backs of the books with sheer wonder. 'There are so many, so many.'

'I will not live long enough,' Legros sighed, 'and Rewik denies me assistants. I shall die before the work is complete. That cat! She's put footprints on my alphabetical catalogue.' He rushed for a feather duster and delicately wafted it over the thick parchment. 'I'm very busy ... my work ... What do you children want?'

Children, thought Caspar, in disgust.

'We need to see the records of the city, the old plans and the old street layouts,' Brid said in her most innocent of voices. The old man was too absorbed in his work to be of any threat to them and Brid had evidently judged that there was no need for pretence. Moving with graceful energy, she had quickly mastered the skill of walking on her raised heels and she tilted her head upwards in her more usual composed and confident manner. She certainly no longer tarried behind the youths but eagerly took the initiative.

Legros nodded without questioning their motives. 'They're not in the hall. Come with me.' He stopped to pick up a poker and stooped towards a fire that smouldered in the centre of the grate. 'Always need a fire. It stops the mustiness and mildew and so helps to preserve the books.' He stirred up the embers until a yellow flame flickered into life, then led them to the back of the hall and through a heavy drape that sealed the entrance to a narrow stone staircase. The steps spiralled upwards. The old man laboured over the climb, stopping regularly to calm his wheezing breath. 'I shall die before my work's done,' he muttered to himself.

The staircase led them to a second floor of inter-connecting rooms where dusty piles of books lay on tables and stacked up against the walls. The windows here were so thick with cobwebs that the diffused sunlight cast no shadows in the dim chambers. Legros was muttering in despair, almost anger, railing against the dust and the dirt. 'I'll never get it done. I'll never get up here to these records before I die.'

Caspar had no fear of death, but he understood how this man had become horrified by the thought of it. He didn't fear for the fate of his soul but mourned for his work, knowing that his death would mean death of his work. The boy nodded as if suddenly recognizing the emotion. What if he died before retrieving the Egg? What would happen to his home, his Mother? If he failed, his mother would remain alive and trapped in the terrible crushing vice of the glacier forever.

The toothless man was muttering again. 'The west tower room or the east?' He drummed the floorboards with an impatient walking stick. 'The King had the books dumped here. I shall never get round to them.' The despair was terrible. Caspar wanted to say that he would give up his life in Torra Alta if there had been no danger from Vaalakans; but even then he knew it was an empty thought. He would be driven mad cooped up in these halls forever.

'We will try the west tower first. It must be the west tower.' They weaved in and out of the columns of books heaped precariously on top of one another, Brid hitching up her wide skirts to stop them from snagging on everything. Hal frowned at her with disapproval but she raised her chin and smiled with serious eyes straight back at him. Legros sighed as the door to the west tower refused to yield when he tried to push it open. Hal shouldered the low arched door until it suddenly gave way and he fell into the musty room. Legros nodded without smiling.

'They're in here . . . somewhere.' He waved his hand around the room but stopped, suddenly overwhelmed by a wheezing cough as the dust attacked his lungs. 'My work,' he spluttered. 'Equestrian matters. I must do my work.' He turned and abandoned them without further explanation, leaving the two boys and Brid to look around the circular room in dismay. There were books heaped everywhere.

'It's like the fairy tale where a girl is shut into a barn and told to spin all the straw into gold in one night,' Caspar remarked, causing Hal to shake his head in despair at him.

'Fairy tales,' he laughed. 'Even if you have to think about such things, you could try not to mention them. I mean, could you imagine the Captain at home talking about fairy tales? It's so . . . so unmanly.'

Caspar shrugged away the insult, telling himself that he really didn't care what his uncle thought. 'Well, where do we start?'

'We've got to be methodical.' Brid was pushing up her sleeves.

Hal took a deep breath, looking around him authoritatively. 'We'll work from the window back towards the door. I'll take the left hand side, Spar, take the middle and you can take the right. Ah, yes, and clear a space so that you can restack the books into it. Then you'll know where you've been.'

Twenty minutes later Caspar was still annoyed with himself for allowing Hal to come up with all the sensible ideas first because it always automatically put his uncle in charge. Brid had already sorted through half a dozen books before he got started, neatly stacking them spine out so that the titles were easily read. Most of the books were atlases of the known world, some quite modern and some hundreds of years old. To start with Caspar hurriedly piled them one on top of each other, merely wiping his hand across the dusty lettering to read it properly before rejecting it and carefully placing it on his new pile. Then an ancient atlas caught his eye. The lettering was ornate and the spelling antiquated as he thumbed through the pages. The first few leaves showed the whole of the known world. Caspar smiled at the symbols of dragons illustrated at the extremities of the map just beyond the distant lands of Waerlogis, Oria and Salise. A swirling inscription read: 'Beyond the seas that boileth with serpents is ye edge of ye worlde'. It was now widely known, of course, that there were many far reaching continents that spread beyond them. Belbidia was centrally placed whereas Caspar knew it to be a northern country and was shown larger than the tundra of Vaalaka, which on modern maps was drawn four or five times bigger.

'Spar! Get on with it will you,' Hal snapped.

With a jolt Caspar returned to his task, forcing himself to make his eyes skim only over the titles. *The Baronies of Belbidia*, *The Historical Shires of Belbidia*, *The Populations of Nattarda*, *The Principles of Seamanship*. Caspar looked at the last book and decided it was in the wrong room. The title *Belbidia and its Colonies* was upside down on the spine of the next thin book but in plain modern writing. Caspar flicked the cover open and discovered a detailed map showing all of Belbidia and the surrounding islands. It marked sites of ancient battles, old dragon haunts, rings of standing stones, ancient barrows as well as the modern towns and the roads. He was intrigued by the dragon haunts and surreptitiously slid the pamphlet into his breast-pocket, convincing himself that the maps might prove useful, though really he desired the knowledge for himself.

'Who ever had the time to write and copy all these things?' Caspar sighed. 'They must have been cooped up for years.'

'Men like Ceowulf, the youngest sons with no birthright and no lands to look after. What else have they got to do?' the elder boy replied with understanding.

Cramp was building up in the boy's calves and the floor was grinding into his knee caps. They had been sifting through the books for what felt like hours but was probably less than one. 'Maybe these books don't exist; maybe Legros has lost them; perhaps they're in the east tower room. We've not come across one book with Farona in the title.'

'We're in the right place,' Brid contradicted. 'All these books are about places. They'll be here somewhere.' She had progressed much further down the length of the room than the two boys, working rapidly with quick eyes and hands, reaching for the next tome whilst still putting down the last. For another quarter of an hour no one spoke and the room was silent but for the heavy thuds as each volume in turn was laid upon the next. Finally Brid sighed and sat back on her heels, '*Farona, the Strategic Capital.*'

The other two came over to join her. 'What exactly are we looking for?' Caspar asked as he picked up a narrow volume bound in green leather and read the spine.

'You are hopeless sometimes, Spar,' Hal complained. 'We want the layout of the old city.'

'And the new one because we need to compare the two.' Brid corrected the older youth who grunted in begrudged agreement.

'You mean one like this?' Caspar said grinning and presented them triumphantly with the book. Hal snatched it from him and opened the pages, carefully turning the crisp yellowed parchment in case it cracked or disintegrated. '*The Three Eras of Farona.* Here, look these are the chapters: the market settlement; the opening up of the trade routes; the heretical era of the last millennium; and the modern capital. Perfect. All in one volume. No charts though,' he said in disappointment. 'It's all writing about why Farona is in such a favourable position. Do people really think about these things – or even care?'

'It's here,' Brid sighed, despairing at his incompetence. 'It fell out when you snatched the book.' Hal reached for it again but she pulled it close to her chest. 'I know what I'm looking for; you can wait.' The parchment unfolded to reveal three maps, which she carefully spread out side by side. The four gates pointing towards the four winds were in identical places. The bridges spanning the River Dors and the four main streets were present on the latter two maps; whereas only a simple collection of huts and a moat were shown on the earliest chart. They ignored that one. 'The old castle, the King's Palace and the Dowager's Palace are the same on both maps, so at least that gives us clear reference points.'

'Look, turn it round so that I can see. I'll be better at this than either of you.' Hal tugged at the corner of the parchment. 'Look, I told you, it's obvious. There's the grain market on the old map that Morrigwen was talking about.' Hal bored his index finger into the parchment near the West Gate. Brid pulled the map round again so she was looking at it from the right aspect and smoothed her fingers over the sketches.

'Here,' she said reverently. 'Here it is.' The building wasn't labelled but the outline was circular with a pentagram inscribed in the centre. 'There's the temple.' She leant forward peering over the map with her wide black eyes, blinking to focus clearly.

Hal traced his finger along the main west street towards the central cross-roads and crossed over the Dors. He then followed the same route on the new map and tapped the equivalent spot.

'Oh Mother, oh no! It's the cathedral! The temple is right beneath the cathedral.' They sat in silence considering the danger of their task whilst Brid studied the map more carefully. She used her bent thumb to measure distances, lining up the transept, nave and crypt of one map with the pentagram on the other. 'The centre of the temple seems to be right beneath the most easterly part of the building, here.'

'You mean right beneath the altar. Right beneath the feet of Rewik's bishops.'

They found Legros still at his desk with the cat comfortably stretched out on the oak table, lying in a strip of sunlight that fell through a high window to warm a favourable patch. Its tail twitched as they approached but otherwise it didn't move. Legros didn't look up until he had finished the line he was writing and had carefully rested his quill across his inkwell. 'Did you find what you were looking for?' he asked. 'I shan't see you out; I've got my work to finish. You'll find the way.'

Of course they didn't need the map to find their way to the temple, but Hal kept the charts all the same. The cathedral was visible from every part of the city, and even if they weren't able to see it, they could hear it because of the bells chiming out every quarter of an hour. They made their way rapidly towards the magnificent building with its soaring spire, mullioned and traced windows and the intricate lanterns and turrets that decorated the west doors. They were firmly closed but cut in the centre of the left hand portal was a small entrance that swung open on its hinges, inviting them in. A robed priest stood in the nave and Hal asked if it was all right for them to enter.

'The house of the Lord is never closed to those who seek guidance through prayer,' he whispered, depositing two bronze platters on a casket near the entrance. He placed them down with pointed over-emphasis. Hal recognized the hint instantly and extracted a gold coin, dropping it onto the platter. The clattering noise echoed through the silent cathedral. 'The poor of the city will bless you, kind sirs.' The priest smiled and glided silently away.

Caspar expected Brid to be afraid. She had trembled in the palace and he was certain that entering the cathedral itself would be a worse ordeal but she bowed her head demurely and gathered her skirts about her to step easily through the door. She tottered forward, her movements restrained and submissive with the decorum and grace of a courtly lady but lacking her usual energy. Only when she shied away from the font, which held the sacred waters of baptism, did she give the slightest hint of being discomforted by her surroundings.

The freckled youth already felt giddy from looking upwards. He stepped backwards as the distant masonry of the ceiling above began to spin, mesmerized by the patterns of painted stars and the enormity of the huge stone pillars that arched over to touch their opposite number. Like huge giants in a marriage dance holding hands high above their heads, the columns formed an avenue drawing the worshippers forward towards the altar. Hal nudged his nephew.

'Stop gawping like that. You're staggering like a village drunkard,' he hissed under his breath. 'Try and behave with at least some semblance of propriety.'

Caspar was only able to drag his gaze away from the spectacular surroundings for a moment soon falling to gaze at the triforium. The upper windows ran at an impossible height in their arched formation, letting light shine through to the vaulted ceiling. He studied the grotesque gargoyles crouched on the capitals of the pillars, like hobgoblins ready to pounce on the sinners below.

'I've never been in a house of worship of the New God,' Brid whispered. 'I thought I'd feel some sense of evil, but, apart from the tainted water,' she smiled at him, 'I feel nothing, just a sense of – well – architecture.' She was whispering so as not to disturb the vast silence of the cathedral. 'The building is so new, the stones are so clean, the oak so pale, that none of it has a life of its own.'

The altar beckoned them forward. Brid halted at the sight of it, quite aghast.

'Mother! And they burnt us in our hundreds because they said we performed devilish sacrifices, but right here they worship before a huge sacrificial altar. Look at it. It's a stone of sacrifice. The hypocrites!'

'No,' Hal was shocked by the idea. 'No, they never make sacrifices. The altar is for the sacramental candles and chalice.'

'A chalice to catch the blood in, candles to send the fumes of the sacrifice up towards the heavens. They are all sacrificial artefacts. I should know, I am one of the three high-priestesses.'

Caspar's blood ran cold at the implications of her words. With a shudder he remembered the priory in Ovissia. 'You haven't, you couldn't have done . . .'

Hal sidled away from her, shaking his head. 'No, I don't believe it.'

Brid was so small and delicate. Her soft vulnerable form was accentuated by the silken layers of her dress and the way her long bright hair was coiled into a knot on the back of her head with curls spilling over to dangle about her face. Her big dark eyes fluttered like those of an awe-struck young lady who had never stepped beyond the threshold of her ivory tower.

The dreadful image of Brid performing such atrocious acts was impossible for Caspar to grasp. He loved Brid, knew that she was fierce and brave, knew that she was competent and hard-willed but he couldn't believe that she had the brutality to perform sacrifices, no!

The girl neither refuted nor confirmed their fears but began to study the aisle. She squinted to scan over the transept, whose wings stretched north and south from the central nave, and gradually she progressed forward to inspect the area behind the screen separating the altar from the nave. Behind the stone slab of the altar the curved recess of the apse described the easterly arc of a circle. The walls of the cathedral followed that trajectory to swell into a circular shape, embracing the chancel and its altar. Sparkles of gold glinted everywhere from the capitals of each pillar to the tassels on the kneelers. Even an enormous lectern in the form of an eagle with outspread wings appeared to be of solid gold. Caspar wondered how many boars' tusks or wolf pelts it would take to buy so much gold.

The chancel was separated from the rest of the cathedral by a stained-glass screen and formed an almost separate chamber that was clearly constructed on circular foundations. The circular walls were accentuated upwards into the supporting base of the impressive spire that stretched up into a feat of magnificent architecture. Brid glided forward to the centre and spun slowly round with an intense look of concentration on her face. Her neat brow puckered into furrows. Caspar stepped forward to join her.

'It's here,' she whispered. 'Can you feel it?' The cold, still air of the cathedral chilled the boy's skin, which was damp with the sweat of guilty fear. He dreaded what would happen if Rewik found them here or suspected their true purpose. Clutching at the mandala he felt it burn fiercely in his fist like the yearning of a hungry, adolescent love.

He nodded in agreement. 'It's definitely here. Something very powerful is here somewhere, but where exactly, I don't know.'

'It's right beneath our feet.' Brid stooped down and pressed her palm onto an eminent tombstone set amongst the flag-stones. 'I can feel the Mother's love simmering beneath these stones, incarcerated here beneath this tombstone. It's like a sarcophagus, entombing her love, sealing it away from the people.'

Right in the centre of the chamber a brass plaque inlaid into the tombstone declared that the bones of King Sithric were buried beneath. She traced the lettering. 'Look, the rune of the Mother.'

'That's an effigy. That's his head,' Hal objected

'Have you ever seen a head that round? It's a rune, the rune of the Mother. It's placed centrally and it represents Her presence. Some ancient mason has known and loved Her and set this plaque to keep the knowledge of Her presence alive even within this city that denies Her.'

'How do we get in?' Hal voiced the practical problem.

Suddenly they realized that they were not alone. Caspar straightened up, deliberately genuflecting towards the altar to disguise his actions before turning slowly and innocently towards the approaching men. He immediately recognized one of the King's generals from the day before, but not his two companions. Judging by the mitre and crook of one and the plain robes of the other they were the bishop and his dean. The bishop was in white with a purple sash and the dean wore the subdued black cassock so familiar to the two young noblemen. It reminded him instantly of Gwion. Caspar shuddered; the dean glared at them with cold hungry eyes.

'We have been sent to summon you. There have been cer-tain accusations made,' the general began in solemn tones. 'Certain grave accusations. You are to accompany me and his grace, the Lord Bishop, to the palace where the King is gather-ing court.'

Hal started to object. 'On what grounds? With what are we charged?'

The general drew his sword, the blade grating against its scabbard. The harsh sound disturbed the hush of the cathedral with jarring echoes.

'Put up your sword,' the bishop demanded in quiet tones of authority. He was in his own domain, the one place in the realm where he outranked even the King, and he had no need for angry words or a raised voice. 'I'll have no weapons drawn in the house of the Lord. These gentle folk will come peaceably to face the charges of their King as is their duty; is that not so?'

'We are here kneeling before the altar in the worship of the Lord,' Hal announced with firm conviction, his voice booming through the vaulted space.

There was a sharp intake of breath from the dean and his dark little eyes pierced them with a look of disbelief.

'You are wasting the King's time. This will be treason: today he has declared that Belbidia is at war.' The general's irritation was evident as he rattled the hilt of the sword that he had reluctantly sheathed.

And about time, thought Caspar, thinking of how many months his father had been preparing to repel the Vaalakan attack.

'They're only children. Not one of them is of age,' the bishop sighed, evidently reluctant to do his task.

'The Devil knows no barriers of age. He plants the seeds of evil within weak hearts and there, like a fungus, it grows until the Devil's canker spreads to infect every organ,' quoted the dean with solemnity.

Caspar braced his shoulders and levelled his gaze at the three men. 'We will of course accompany you to face these charges. We have nothing to hide. Our only concerns and efforts are for the safety of the realm.' He spoke quickly before Hal could mutter anything inappropriate. He sensed an intense animosity boiling inside his uncle that raged against the general and he didn't trust Hal to say anything in case he further prejudiced the Faronans against them.

Brid said nothing but stepped closer to Hal with her head demurely bowed. She brushed out her skirts just as Cybillia would have done and primly fussed at her curls, as if there was nothing of more import to concern her than her looks. They followed the bishop in solemn procession down the aisle with the general snapping at their heels. Caspar didn't have to speculate what the charges were against them; he knew. He knew they were charges of witchcraft and sorcery, charges of heresy. He reached for Brid's hand but she pushed him away.

'Stay away from me, Spar. You look too like me. If they have an Inquisitor, he will detect the similarities.'

It had never occurred to the boy that his slight frame, unusual hair and big almond eyes of dazzling bright blue made him so similar to Brid but then he did have some of the same blood in his veins – the blood of the old tribes. Brid was right; he squared his shoulders and tried to look as tall as Hal, matching him pace for pace.

Outside the cathedral a guard of ten mounted knights waited expectantly and fell into a square formation to surround the three young companions. There was no escape. They marched down the streets, gradually gathering a crowd of fascinated townsfolk. The gathering became a procession and then even the tradesmen left their stalls and shops unattended to watch the captives as they were marched under escort to the palace.

As the troop approached the permanently lowered draw-bridge, the foremost rider lifted a short brass clarion to his lips and gave three sharp blasts to announce their arrival. They marched under the portcullis and across the cobbled courtyard, the horses' hooves clattering loudly, and without further word they were escorted down the long corridors. Every door was already thrown wide so as not to delay their approach to the throne-room. There was none of the previous delays or ceremony and a deadly hush filled the lengthy room.

The King sat on his throne with a drawn face. To either

side stood twelve tall men in black robes, their heads shorn and their hands clasped in front of them. The noblemen of the city, as well as Ceowulf on the right and Cybillia on the left, were all gathered to the court and stood beneath the pillars. Huddled in a nervous group nearer to the entrance was a muttering knot of palace servants.

As they entered the room, the King's eyes pounced on Brid. They were small dark beady eyes like those of a hovering hawk, full of purpose, waiting for the precise moment to dive for the kill. His hands clutched at the arms of the throne, flexing and kneading the ornate carvings. He concentrated on the girl.

Brid have courage, Caspar willed her, have courage. They can't prove anything. Please have the courage to deny the Mother. He didn't know if she could do that, doubted that she would. As they passed the row of servants, the women backed off, clutching at their bosoms as if they thought some demon would leap from Brid's mouth and burrow through their flesh to infest their hearts. The men hissed, producing a barely perceptible sound just loud enough to make sure that Brid knew of their contempt.

When they were five paces from the throne the general raised his hand to call for a halt and the soldiers stood back, barring any escape. The bishop and the dean proceeded ceremoniously forward and took their places next to the King. The throne-room echoed with a booming thud as the studded doors were pulled to and the doorman announced: 'The room is sealed; none may enter and none may leave whilst this court is in session.'

The King rose and all those seated in the court rose with him.

'These are charges of heresy, charges of witchcraft and sorcery. In Belbidia we cleanse our lands with the purity of fire. If this court finds these charges to be true you will burn until the fire consumes the Devil in your soul.'

Chapter 17

The snow fell so thickly that it was impossible to tell the broad flakes from the grey blanket of cloud that crowded round the Tor. The air was muffled and strangely light as if the daylight had been trapped beneath the clouds. May watched it settle on the crenellations. The wind swept up from the canyon floor, whipping up the snow drifts to form white eddies that danced along the castle walls. She was fascinated by the way one flake immediately melted on the wet stone but the next stayed a little longer in its feathered crystalline form. The one after that settled even longer until the ground was quickly covered.

A raven dropped out of the grey curdled sky and left splayed, three-toed prints as it broke through the virgin snow. It shook its head to shed the hood of snow that had risen to a peak on the crown of its head.

'Come away from the window.' Ma's voice was scratchy with irritation.

'But it's snowing, Ma!' May looked round at her mother's drawn cheeks and the clothes falling loosely off the points of her hips. She had never been fat but had always possessed a certain healthy plumpness. Now she could only be described as thin. May instantly regretted the whine in her voice and jumped down from the ledge.

'It's snowing, Morrigwen.' She crawled up onto the old woman's sleeping pallet and smiled. Morrigwen was eating bread soaked in goat's milk and looked much healthier. At least she always had time for her and Pip now that she was confined to bed, while every other adult snapped and chided them.

'Well, it should snow, Merrymoon.'

'But it never snows until Snowmoon in the Boarchase.'

'Yes, but we're much higher here and it's very much colder. This snow won't melt from the Yellow Mountains until spring, probably Lenting.'

'You mean it will snow every day?'

'No,' Morrigwen laughed, which induced a raking cough from the depths of her wheezing lungs. 'No, of course it won't. It'll snow for a few days. It just won't melt because the ground is frozen.'

'But snow always melts when the sun shines.'

'It does in the forest, but here in winter there's very little heat in the sun and once the cold ground is covered it'll stay under snow.'

May looked at her doubtfully.

'Well, if you don't believe me you'll just have to wait and see.' Morrigwen gave her a self-satisfied smile.

'I'm going to help in the kitchens, May,' her mother informed her as she prodded Pip from his bed. 'And you, lad, had better get down into the wellroom. We've all got to do our bit.'

Pip groaned. 'But, Ma, you've got no idea what it's like down there.'

Her brother's enthusiasm for helping with the machinery down in the sulphurous wellroom had faded rapidly. His clothes were now finely coated with the yellow dust that he gathered off the sulphur barrels. The well water was contaminated with sulphur deposits and had to be purified before they could drink it. Once they had extracted the sulphur and mixed it with other things – though Pip hadn't been very good at explaining what precisely – they made those horrible explosives that set everyone's nerves jangling. She wished they could do a better job of freshening the water, which had an unappetizing eggy smell. The old women in the Keep sipped at the distasteful water and muttered about how they missed Catrik's skills.

Soon May was left alone with the old Crone. She seemed

considerably more lively today and her skin had a more perky blush.

'You look thin, child. Here, eat some of my bread.'

The young girl looked at the food hungrily but shook her head. 'No, you must eat it. It's very important you stay well.' She sat down at the edge of the bed. 'Tell me another story.'

'Which one?'

'The one about the wolf and the white stag.'

'I've told you that one about forty times already,' the woman groaned.

'Well then, a new one.'

Morrigwen sighed. 'Let me think. I'll tell you the story of a rich powerful man, who was tall and handsome – and very, very pleased with himself, I might add. One day as he was thundering through the wood on his big horse, frightening all the animals, he came to a little hut. He was thirsty and wanted water, so he knocked at the door of the hut and asked for some. I – The woman that lived there didn't like his tone too much and she would have turned him away except that he asked for water for his horse as well. A beautiful big black animal it was and the woman could see he treated it well, so she decided he couldn't be all that bad. Now, while he was drinking the young maiden who lived with the woman –'

'Do they have names?'

'Don't interrupt, child,' Morrigwen snapped. 'But yes they have names only you needn't know them. Well, anyway this girl was beautiful. Everything about her was beautiful, not just her face but her loving smile and brilliant blue eyes that perfectly reflected the beauty of her soul. He took one look at the lass and she one look at him and the spell was cast.'

'What spell?'

'The magic of falling in love.'

'Oh.' May felt shy.

'Well, the woman was protective towards the maiden. She wasn't convinced by the man's intentions.'

'What does that mean?'

Morrigwen looked at the young girl thoughtfully. 'Perhaps

276

you're a bit young to understand. Young lasses brought up in the New Faith don't seem to know much about life.'

'Well, I won't know anything if you don't tell me.'

'Hmm . . .' Morrigwen paused for thought and chewed at her thin lips. 'Let's see. The woman was concerned that he would court the maid without actually wanting to marry her. He was a rich and powerful man; she was just a peasant girl from the Boarchase. Men aren't always honourable in those situations.'

May thought she understood.

'The woman wouldn't let him buy the young girl beautiful dresses or present her with riches, nor would she let them walk alone in the forest. She lectured on and on at the young girl and told her it was wrong, that it wouldn't work out for her and that it would end in sadness, but the girl was very stubborn and wouldn't listen. She had already fallen helplessly in love.' Morrigwen sighed and looked clear into May's eyes. 'You know, child, the young are always like that. However wise they seem and however sensible or learned they are, they always fall in love despite themselves. You try and tell them but they always think they know best.'

'Will that happen to me?'

'You? Yes, of course you will fall in love, but you never know who or why or when.'

'I can't imagine being in love.'

'No? Well, how old are you?'

'Nearly twelve. Everyone thinks I'm younger because I'm small.'

'Another year and you'll know what I mean. Now where was I?'

'You weren't happy about them falling in love.'

'That's right – only it wasn't me,' Morrigwen said sternly. 'It was another woman from a whole life time of sorrow ago,' she added enigmatically. 'But in truth it was the old woman who was wrong. The man did love the girl and it was the old woman who was blinded by his power and wealth and not the young girl by his love. The man was honourable and they had a magnificent wedding and shortly after a son. When the sceptical woman looked into the boy's eyes her heart was filled with joy because he looked just like his mother.'

'And so they lived happily ever after,' May sang delightedly.

Morrigwen sorrowfully shook her head. 'No, life is rarely like that. Their love was so perfect that it had to be balanced by an equal amount of despair and sorrow; but that's another story, one that's yet to tell. Now you've tired me out. I'm going to sleep now. You run up to the top room and see how Catrik is getting on.'

'But I'm supposed to watch over you.'

'Yes, child, I know but you only talk and tire me out. The young always talk so much idle chitter chatter.' The Crone looked stern for a minute but then the lines round her eyes wrinkled up and she smiled. 'Go on, run along. I'm much better now.'

May moved a jug of water a little closer. 'Are you sure you'll be all right?'

'Look, I've told you. Don't argue with me. Go on and leave me alone.' Morrigwen's eyes were now tightly shut. 'I'm asleep.'

May trotted up the stairs and slid silently into the old man's chamber to check that all was well. The door was already open and Father Gwion was kneeling at the bedside, muttering prayers. As she entered he was just rising up to leave but he started as he looked down at her creeping lightly into the room.

'Morrigwen sent me to see how he is faring,' she apologized for her presence.

The priest shook his head. He moved silently except for his robes which swept across the floorboards. He kept his arms neatly folded and she felt uncomfortable as he looked sternly down at her. Apart from his tonsured head and tufts of dull brown hair, it struck her that he looked remarkably like the Baron's son and she decided they must be related. Master Spar made her feel uncomfortable too.

'I fear he's no better. Why don't you sit and talk to him a little. Perhaps that will bring his mind back to us?' Father

Gwion swept from the room and pulled the door to with a heavy thud.

May looked into Catrik's eyes and saw they were glazed and dull. His brow was clammy but cold and his face ashen. She puzzled over him, thinking he was afflicted in very much the same way as Morrigwen. He was old too and perhaps age had the same effect on them. He was not nearly as old as Morrigwen, but maybe his injuries had prematurely aged him.

She moved closer and sat by him, feeling a little embarrassed. How could she talk to someone she didn't know and who couldn't talk back? 'They told me to come and keep you company, sir, but there's not much to tell.' She paused and looked down at her knotted hands and then out of the window. 'It's snowing,' she added brightly. 'And the Vaalakans have moved very little in the last few days.'

She looked at his grey skin and the dried lips. He was spare with dark crescents underlying his drooping eyes. His breathing, snatched and shallow, came in uneven bursts and he didn't respond to her voice. She sighed, wondering if she should still try and talk to him and racked her brains for some conversation. 'Pip – my brother – has been helping in the wellroom. He's been scraping out the yellow sulphur so the men can make powder kegs with it. We haven't had to use any these last few days because the Vaalakans are just sitting down there, waiting. At least that means we haven't had to suffer those explosions.'

The man's lips moved.

May leant forward and tilted her head to listen anxiously to his mumblings.

'Explosion – The moonstone – Spar – Master Spar.' His words died away.

'Master Spar is fine. He wasn't hurt. He's gone to Farona to fetch help,' she told him simply, not knowing what else to say. She didn't understand the details herself and thought with resentment of the young red-haired youth sitting arrogantly on his elegant horse. He's only a boy; she sniffed at the thought.

'Explosion . . . del – deliber – ate. I – I saw him . . .'

Staring directly into Catrik's eyes, the girl could see he wasn't awake. There was a glazed faraway expression as if he were looking at the pictures of a nightmare storming through his head. 'Master Spar, Master Spar!' He began to thrash back and forth and raised his hands as if grappling with something. 'Master Spar, wait! Hold on, hold on; I'll get you.'

May only knew that the Baron's son had been trapped down the well by an explosion and that was how he had somehow fallen into enemy hands. Catrik had been badly injured and never fully regained consciousness. It appeared that he feared for Master Spar, believing him still trapped. She took a cloth and soaked it with some water to soothe his brow.

'Catrik, listen to me. It will all be all right. You don't need to worry. Master Spar came out of the tunnels unharmed.'

'I – I saw him . . . it was him; it was him,' Catrik continued to rave, though gradually the cooling water soothed him and he fell back into a more restful sleep.

After that, May thought it wise not to talk any more. She passed her time gazing out through the high arrow-slit at the drape of white snow that softened the angular contours of the parapets and the barbican over the main gate. She couldn't see beyond that; the rest of the world was banished by the muffling cloud of snow. It was eerie being right up in the clouds like this, she thought, and had a momentary pang of homesickness for her own small world in the forest.

She jumped as the door creaked open and snapped her head round as the chaplain slid into the room. For just a moment she realized he hadn't seen her. His face was set hard into taut lines sucked into his cheeks and his pale blue eyes focused intently forward like the piercing eyes of a wolf. His gleaming satin cowl, hooding his shoulders, looked like the folded wings of a black falcon stooping for its prey.

Nervously she jumped down from the window sill and he stopped short. For one brief moment a look of startled horror crept into his pale eyes, then he gracefully stepped forward and smiled with avuncular ease. 'Now, child, are you still here? I didn't see you. You'd better run along now and tend to your mother. I'll sit with Catrik. You must be worn out; you've been here ages. Has he stirred?'

She shook her head, preferring to lie than speak out loud to this strict-looking man. She had never been frightened by Curate Dunnock. In fact she had quite liked the funny little man and the way he fussed and chattered on; but the chaplain was a different matter. He was austere and cold despite his smooth tongue. Surely that was wrong though; surely she shouldn't be afraid of a man of the cloth. She wondered whether her time spent with Morrigwen was affecting her. Perhaps it was simply that she was gradually falling for the mystery and wonder of the old woman's tales and had been caught up in the promise and hope that the Great Mother offered. Certainly she now felt more uneasy with the New Faith and its disciples.

Thankfully she fled from the chaplain and crept out of the door. She raced down the stairwell to return to the old Crone.

The room was dark. At first she thought the woman was still asleep but as she tiptoed closer she was alarmed by the sound of her breathing. It was shallow, rasping and uneven. Morrigwen had been so much better, since they had kept a constant vigil over her, but the moment she had left the old woman alone, she had suffered a sudden turn for the worse. May crept forward guiltily.

'Morrigwen, Morrigwen, what is it?' The snow clouds outside had closed in and the fire was dwindling. She clasped the old woman's hand. 'Morrigwen.'

The Crone's eyelids flickered open. 'Brid, is that you?'

'No, it's only me; it's only May,' the young girl apologized for herself. 'Morrigwen, what's happened?'

'Vaal-Peor,' the Crone muttered. 'Brid, I can feel him in the room. He's creeping in with the snow. I can feel his cold loathing smothering me.'

May stoked up the fire, tossing on a couple of unseasoned logs that sputtered sparks and smoked profusely but at least the flames cheered the dank atmosphere. She drew the bear-skin rugs snugly around the woman's shoulders.

'I'm ill, Brid. I must not die. We must restore the Trinity. Brid! Where are you?'

May clutched at the hag's withered hands and soothed her brow. 'Brid isn't here. She's gone with Master Hal and Master Spar into Farona. It's only me here, only May.'

'I need Brid. She can cure me. But I can't reach her. She's closed the Eye from me, muffled its power. She doesn't whisper into it anymore,' Morrigwen fretted.

May looked at her in dismay. 'I'll fetch Ma.' She ran hurriedly from the room, fearing that the old woman was delirious.

The snow in the courtyard was soft and light like powdered sugar. It lifted and billowed into wisps that skimmed across the surface and collected in deep drifts against the east walls, scooping into mysterious sculptured shapes. It didn't stick to her like the wet snow of the lowland Chase but brushed off her clothing, the flakes so frozen and firm that they were completely dry. Her ears and nose stung with the bitter cold and she curled up her fingers, pulling down her sleeves to cover her fists. She left deep imprints as she laboured across the courtyard but they quickly filled as the broad flakes like downy feathers sifted out of the grim sky.

Halfway across she stumbled, plunging into a deeper drift, and stretched out her hands to break her fall. The freezing snow bit into her bare palms but she felt a strange tingling delight as she touched something hard beneath the snow. She looked down and saw the blood-red ruby glinting in the snow. For a moment she forgot the freezing chill around her as her eyes were instinctively drawn to the curious silver threads embedded in its heart. They formed a circular pattern divided into three equal sections and somehow she felt the sigil was significant. She frowned, thinking of the unaccountable sense of confidence that the ruby had given her as she rushed into the kitchens.

'Ma! Ma! Morrigwen's taken a turn for the worse.'

Elaine wasted no time and within seconds they were both racing up to the Keep. The red-haired widow urgently flung open the door of Morrigwen's solar and rushed to the Crone's bedside.

'It's me, Elaine.' Her voice was soothing and warm. 'Now, let's take a look at you.' She briefly glanced at the cold sweat that beaded the Crone's deathly white brow and reached for the pitcher next to the bed. She splashed some water into a basin so that she could mop Morrigwen's forehead.

Elaine stopped short and frowned.

'What's the matter, Ma?' May asked.

'Come here, child, and smell this.' Elaine raised the pitcher towards her daughter's nose. 'Smell it.'

'Well, it's a bit eggy, but Pip says that's the sulphur. He says the men in the wellroom complain about the water. They need Catrik to make sure the process always runs smoothly and they don't get such good results without him.'

'Yes, I know, but smell it again.'

May frowned. The water had an unpleasant odour, which she was gradually getting used to, but she couldn't smell anything else strange.

Elaine glared suspiciously at the horn cup resting beside the old woman's pallet. She sniffed at it warily. 'I haven't smelt that in years. But I'm sure it's . . .' She sniffed it again and grimaced. 'Vaalakan fang-nettle. It smells of fang-nettle. I've not come across any of that since the Dragon Scorch melt waters dried up more than a dozen years ago. A few seeds used to get blown just to the edge of the Chase but how it got here . . . ?' Tentatively she dipped her finger in and licked the end with just the very tip of her tongue. She recoiled in disgust. 'Take this to the garderobe and chuck it out.' She handed it carefully to her daughter. 'Don't spill any of it on you. It's definitely Vaalakan fang-nettle, very rare and highly poisonous.'

Chapter 18

Rewik moved in a series of jerks. He remained perfectly rigid until he snapped his head round to a new position only to return to that disquieting stillness, not a tranquil rest but a motionless tension. Caspar thought he was like some giant bird, one of those huge bald-headed vultures that he'd read about. Rewik's eyes flicked away from Brid towards an official near at hand. 'Bailiff, call the first witness.'

In broad tones the official boomed, 'The court calls the honourable Lady Cybillia of Jotunn to bear witness.'

Caspar's throat was dry. The girl had been so infatuated with Hal that they had always dismissed the possibility that she could be a threat to them. Nevertheless they had still taken careful pains to conceal Brid's identity and Cybillia had held firmly to Father Rufus's conviction that only the blow to Brid's head had made her behave so strangely. All the same the girl had travelled with them as part of the group, as their companion, and as she stepped forward into the centre of the throne room Caspar felt betrayed.

'I'll get that skinny bitch,' Brid murmured through gritted teeth. 'I shall cut out her guts while she's still alive and twist them round her neck. She won't be so pretty then, will she?'

'Speak forth child,' the King spoke in cajoling tones. 'Tell us all again what you said to my general this morning.'

Cybillia looked at the ground, swaying slightly on her feet, and mumbled something though she spoke too softly for anyone to hear.

'Speak up, child. No one will harm you.' Rewik stretched his neck forward, trying to catch her words.

'I didn't say she was a witch, I do not believe she is a witch.' Cybillia's white cheeks were flushed and she looked guiltily towards Hal, her eyes begging for his forgiveness.

'That is not for you to decide: you are too young and only a girl. The burden of such responsibility is beyond you. I just want you to repeat what you said to the general when he asked you about her.' Irritation was showing through the King's veneer of dignified patience.

She coughed politely into her hand. 'When she arrived at the Manor in Jotunn she was badly injured – a wound to her head. She had been harmed by Vaalakans and was near death. Some of the women were terrified of her because they said she looked like a changeling or a witch but Father Rufus said he would know if she were a sorceress because he had an instinct for the Devil's work. He told us firmly that it was the pressure of blood on her skull and when the wound was good again the ravings would pass.'

'Is that all you told the general?'

'Indeed Father Rufus was right. Within two days she was hale once more,' Cybillia continued in a wavering voice.

'That was not what you said.' The general stepped forward unbidden and the King jerked his thin neck round and glowered at him. 'I'm sorry, Your Majesty, but she is concealing the truth. May I have permission to relate her words?'

The King waved him on with a flick of his hand and the self-important soldier paced up and down with sweeping gestures of his hand to add emotion to his rhetoric. 'That creature,' he lanced a finger towards Brid, who stood perfectly still with a smooth and unruffled expression on her face, 'have no doubts in your mind, gentlemen of the court, that fiend is a Devil's sorceress. When the good and holy man Father Rufus administered his healing skills to save her life, she could not countenance his presence. She screamed like a banshee forbidding him – a man of the cloth – to touch her.'

'She was injured; Father Rufus said so. You are twisting my words.' Cybillia's spoilt nature no longer permitted her to keep silent.

'Silence, young Lady,' the dean interrupted. 'We are coming near the truth.'

'Such revulsion of a man of God, surely . . .' the general paused for effect, 'surely is indicative of a heathen soul.' There was a murmur of assent throughout the hall. 'But there is more. This fair lady of Jotunn has sought medicine from the King's physician because she has been plagued by nightmares and a disorientation of time. And when did these sinister happenings start?' He paused looking steadily round the packed throne room at the expectant faces hanging on his every word. 'Only since she has been in the company of this changeling. It is my belief that this elf-sprite has the power to tamper with the elements.'

There was a gasp of horror from the court and a murmuring buzz as they anxiously mumbled fears and aired their indignation to the eager ears of their neighbours.

'That's ridiculous,' Cybillia objected. She had lost the timorous waver of her voice and defiantly glared at the general, momentarily reminding Caspar of the Lady Helena. 'I will not hear such words spoken against my neighbours. I will not!' Suddenly her protests disintegrated, distraught sobs cracking her voice. 'You are twisting my words.'

'The court will have silence!' Rewik demanded in thunderous tones. 'Daughter of Bullback, restrain your outbursts, otherwise I will have you restrained.'

Cybillia clapped her hands to her mouth and began to shake with sobs.

'However the court would not have been summoned merely to hear about the ailments of a frail maiden from the north of the kingdom. There is more. Bailiff, continue.'

'Your Majesty.' The bailiff bowed towards the throne. 'A message came from Torra Alta. It is true that we are not entirely sure how it fell into my hands. I received it from a cloaked man who handed me the parchment and rode straight off with barely more than a grunt. It is an extract from the holy scriptures.' He coughed to clear his lungs and boomed out in a steady voice. 'Beware the wiles of women. Only man

286

was made in the image of the Almighty Father: woman was denied this grace. Beware those who seek with female charms and sinful seduction to lure their men away from the path of righteousness.'

A hundred eyes glared at Brid. 'It is true. Her beauty is sinful.'

Hal stepped forward. 'With your permission, Your Majesty, the message does not refer to Bridgetta. There is no reason to assume that this extract from the scriptures refers specifically to her. How do we know it came from Torra Alta? On the say-so of some nameless messenger who vanishes guiltily into the crowd?' There was an interested buzz around the court as the men of Farona pondered his words.

'I have considered that,' Rewik replied pompously, 'but I find the circumstances too strange. The scroll has no signature or seal.'

'Which means it can hardly be official or sent with honest intent,' Hal interrupted.

Rewik's eyes stabbed at his insolent cousin, demanding an apology. Hal hastily bowed and apologized for his outburst.

'But, I'm inclined to agree. I only presume it came from Torra Alta merely because the paper is headed with the crest of Branwolf's barony and, as the young lord so aptly pointed out, on the say-so of some mysterious messenger. However the question is raised: why would I receive such a warning given in connection with the Torra Altan seal? I have three visitors recently arrived from the barony. Two young noblemen and a girl, of undeniable beauty, and I receive this warning. It has to be considered.'

Caspar's mind was boiling with confusion. No one in Torra Alta would write such a thing. Surely the paper was stolen and someone meaning harm to the barony had sent it. A Vaalakan spy, someone like Kullak; would he have had the knowledge? Could Dunnock have instigated the message before he died? But he knew nothing of Brid. No, it couldn't have been Curate Dunnock. The words were well-known extracts from the Scriptures and not necessarily those of a learned man. Most men knew them since they were often quoted at wives who were becoming difficult to handle in those domestic situations where the man's authority needed a little bolstering.

Cold sweat pricked on his palms as suddenly another possibility sprang to his mind. Could his father, now content with the company of Wystan's widow, have reneged on his vow to restore the Old Faith, no longer driven by his desire to find Keridwen? Could he have regretted sending them all to Farona and was now trying to unravel his deed by exposing Brid, who would take the blame for all their actions? Surely his father would never risk implicating his son in this adventure. But perhaps he saw everything differently now that he was back in the castle walls surrounded by his men and far from the desolate wasteland of Vaalaka. It was Wystan's widow Elaine that made the boy suspicious. Branwolf had always provided himself with female company to fill the emptiness created by the loss of his wife. Elaine undoubtedly drew the Baron's attention even though he knew that Keridwen was still alive. Caspar didn't like that.

'I treat this scroll as no more than circumstantial,' the King nodded logically. 'However the evidence mounts. Bailiff, relate the details.'

'A further message, from a reeve in the far north of Faronshire, was brought to my attention for audience with the King. He told a story of a serving wench fleeing from the company of her mistress, Lady Cybillia. She refused to return to her master Baron Bullback because she feared he would punish her for abandoning his daughter. However, again she reiterates the Lady Cybillia's tale of this creature's outburst before Father Rufus. Again we have dismissed this as the ravings caused by her injuries. The maid Hetta, however, exclaimed that she saw blue, red and green smoke pulsing from the roof of the Halfway Inn where this kinswoman of Lord Caspar lingered overnight.'

'Witchery!' the court murmured in awed tones.

Hal took another step closer to the monarch. 'Sire, the

ravings of a frightened, superstitious maid. No doubt she mistook the colours of the dawn light playing in the smoke as witchcraft.'

'You have a logical and perceptive mind.' The King actually looked pleased with the dark youth's protestations. 'I like to hear justice.' He rose and stepped forward with his hands knitted in front of his chest and glided across the floor. He came to an abrupt halt in front of Brid, pushing his face close up against hers. 'However, suspicions have been raised and we must answer them. My six chief Inquisitors are away in the South in Caldea where there have been suspicious outbreaks of sorcery, particularly in the Western port of Ildros.' He drummed his fingers irritably as if contemplating the latest canker of heathen activity in his realm before snapping his head round to stare at Brid again. 'Nevertheless, I myself have some knowledge of the arts of detecting a pagan soul.' He peered at her face.

Brid blushed and lightly put her trembling hand to her powdered cheeks. She fluttered her eyelashes over big black frightened eyes.

Clenching his fists so that the nails bit into his palms, Caspar swore to himself that if Rewik raised one finger to hurt her he would tear out his throat. The treason in his thoughts jolted him into shock. I'm a loyal Belbidian; I have sworn allegiance to my king and a Torra Altan is true to his promise. How could I think such a thing?

Rewik raised his thumb and used the section from the knuckle to the tip of his nail to measure the distance between the Maiden's eyes and took her chin in his pincer-like fingers. He tugged her head to one side and pulled her hair back to look at her ears.

'Though she does not lack stature, like many of the witches we have seen burnt, there is a slightness of bone; the eyes are widely spaced; the ears are high-set. Now, my Lord Bishop, what do you infer from that?' The King turned towards the old man in the white robes but he didn't wait for a reply. 'The eyes though, they puzzle me.'

He circled the priestess like a wolf circling a lamb. Caspar's throat was dry and his tongue felt like a wad of parchment. 'Black like a cat's when stalking the shadows. Black with fear possibly. Seductive eyes, sinful eyes but they are not the colour of a heathen's. They should be a vivid green or a dazzling blue. But the accused lacks this colour. It is said that when the love of the Old Faith dwindles in a person's soul the colour of their eyes fades. Let me hear your voice, girl.'

'Your Majesty,' she spoke in rounded tones. 'What would you have me say? I pray my words do not offend you, Sire.' Brid's normally musical voice was now dull, a little shrill and without a hint of her mountain lilt. The King looked partially satisfied but tapped his toe thoughtfully. 'Not one bit of evidence would disturb me on its own, but I am still uncomfortable. There is something I cannot quite place in her looks that troubles me. If only the Inquisitors . . . Lord Bishop, what do you make of this?'

Caspar was heartily relieved that the King's Inquisitors were in Caldea and not here to examine the priestess. He rubbed his neck uncomfortably.

'Your Majesty, it is not proven that the girl is a pagan just because of her looks. It indicates her lineage but as you can see she has the same look as the younger boy, and no one is bringing charges against him.' There was a sadness in the bishop's voice, a despair at the inevitable course of the proceedings.

'Her looks declare her tribal ancestry and that is well known to play a big part in her faith,' the dean interrupted. 'No one here can deny that the small people of the old tribes, now by God's grace nearly extinct in this good land, still cling to the faith of the Earth Mother and to their naive belief that the earth, the sun and the moon are in fact deities.'

Caspar suspected the priest had been sniffing at the bishop's heels for too long and was now taking a stand against him in his eagerness for promotion. Brid was rigid, and for a moment he thought that the tumult of boiling indignation within her would erupt like a volcano.

'It is indeed well known,' the King argued.

'But yet is not proof,' the bishop insisted. 'The looks of the young boy hold up my statement. It is well known that his father is building a lavish cathedral at the foot of his castle and the boy, though of dubious origins, has been honestly brought up in the true faith. Nobody doubts his faith.'

'Ah yes, but that brings us to another point. Bailiff, bring forth the next witness.'

Caspar's tongue felt thick and dry in his mouth.

'The court summons Rebecca the weaver's daughter and under-maid in the King's service.' Again he raised his voice to a solemn chant but then spoke more softly in a normal tone. 'Step forward, Becky, and answer your King. Go on out into the centre.' Caspar at once recognized her as the maid from that morning who had opened the shutters in his chamber. Becky looked nervously around, reluctant to step forward but the bailiff encouraged her with a smile and a nod of his head.

'Now, Rebecca, my cook says you came this morning with a scandalous tale and she was so shocked that she brought it to the bailiff's attention.' The King spoke softly to the girl so as not to intimidate her but she remained flushed, twiddling her hair and unable to look up. 'Tell us again what you saw.'

The weaver's daughter looked nervously round the court and stammered incoherently.

'Speak up, Becky; no harm will come to you.' The bailiff stepped forward to stand next to her and patted her hand. 'Now look at me and tell me what you saw this morning.'

She looked into his eyes and clutched his hand for comfort. 'I saw them,' she trembled.

'Tell me from the beginning.'

There was a hushed silence in the court as all ears strained to catch her soft-spoken words. 'I was doing me duties, opening up the rooms as I does every morning and I came to the rooms, in the west wing. Well, no one had told me they was occupied so as normal I went to open the shutters and that's when I saw them.'

'And what was it that shocked you so?'

'Well, to start off with we all thought it was a bit of a lark surprising them – them being gentry and all. And truly we thought nought of it until Emmy said she'd heard them announced as kin, in fact brother and sister.'

'And why was that shocking.'

'Why?! Well sir,' she flushed a brilliant scarlet, 'they were a-sharing the one bed.'

The King flicked his gaze onto Caspar and thrust a finger at his chest, prodding his sternum. 'So, the charge against you, Caspar, son of Branwolf of Torra Alta, is the heinous crime of incest.'

All words stuck in Caspar's throat and a buzz of confusion hummed in his ears. He thought he would faint but struggled hard to find the right words to redeem himself. 'She's not my sister!' It was no good declaring that they were innocent of any lustful deeds. No court would believe that because nowhere in the civilized world would a lady enter a man's sleeping chamber without some intent of that nature. Only Brid would do that because she came from a different culture that was uninhibited by such things.

Hal's eyes were wide with amazement and when the King stepped back to take his throne again, Hal whispered at him. 'You little scoundrel, nephew!'

'She's not my sister,' Caspar declared to the court.

'In which case you lied to me,' the King roared. 'Though it is hard to believe since you both have the same distasteful looks.'

'We did not lie. We announced her as kinswoman,' Hal interceded to protect his nephew. 'She is in fact the adopted grandchild of Caspar's mother's foster-mother.' The courtiers' faces drew into perplexed confusion as they repeated the explanation to each other, even trying to work out on their fingers what sort of relationship such complexities created, but shook their heads dumfounded. 'So she is a distant kin but not by either blood nor marriage. She is not, as the court made the mistake of presuming, any bastard daughter of Branwolf.'

'You definitely led us to believe that. You announced her as kinswoman,' the King looked accusingly at the older boy.

'Your Majesty that is precisely what she is. She has no title, is not of high-birth but is still his kinswoman,' the youth continued with placatory innocence.

'Perhaps it is the rustic, uncultured manners of the North that has misled you with your choice of words.' The monarch's taut features relaxed a little and he nodded without smiling. 'The charge of incest is dropped. The Lords Hal and Caspar of Torra Alta will step to the side. The charge of witchcraft remains.'

Brid looked so small and defenceless, her big pleading eyes brimming with tears as she stood alone in the centre of the throne-room. Caspar wondered if they were real but doubted that her brave heart would betray such fear. If anyone lays a finger on her, he thought bitterly to himself, I'll kill them. Hal and Caspar pushed back against the wall, separating themselves from the blood-thirsty crowd that eagerly anticipated the drama of a witch trial.

'They can't prove anything, can they?' Caspar's voice was trembling.

Hal shrugged his shoulders. 'I don't know. I just don't know.'

Ceowulf was suddenly beside them. 'No. *They* can't prove anything. A witch can only be burnt on the testimony of her own confession. It's just that they have certain ways of encouraging a confession.'

There was a sinister undertone to Ceowulf's words and Caspar felt for his dagger, but Hal nudged him to stop.

'Her mother died at the stake,' Caspar explained, 'murdered by Rewik's Inquisitors, because she refused to deny her faith and be baptized. Brid has fought all her life to uphold her mother's beliefs and to keep her trust. It would be very hard for her to deny her love for the Great Mother. They will burn her.' Caspar put all his effort into praying for the girl, willing her to lie, pouring out his own strength through his thoughts to help her.

'This girl has done no wrong,' the bishop sighed.

Rewik slammed his fist down on the carved arm of the throne. 'Why do you defend her so? I will not tolerate heathens in my lands, be they Vaalakan or Belbidian.'

'My first sight of her was kneeling before the altar in prayer; now would any witch be doing that? Shouldn't we let this lie and get on with the far more pressing matters of the war council?'

There was a buzz of discontent spreading through the court. 'He's getting too old for his post; perhaps the dean should be given a chance.' The mutters spread round the throne-room. 'It's his duty to seek out the Devil and protect us from his black disciples.'

It was painful to hear. All these people, comfortably cosseted from the harshness of life, were unable to imagine the real threats to their civilization. They could not contemplate the horror of the barbaric Vaalakan threat because that lay beyond the all-embracing city walls; but here within the court their fear of one small girl was immense. 'Superstitious fools,' the small youth murmured.

The bishop rapped his staff on the smooth marbled floor, demanding silence. 'Let the girl prove her innocence by kneeling before the altar and having her head anointed with the holy waters; then we can have a swift and happy conclusion to this trial.'

'Let us first hear the voice of the accused once more,' the dean slyly prompted. 'Let us hear her pronounce the Creator Mundi. Speak girl, recite the Creator Mundi.'

Brid's mouth sagged helplessly open.

We are utter fools, Caspar berated himself as his heart sank. How could we have hoped to let Brid be disguised as an edified noblewoman of Belbidia. To bring her here to the palace was madness. Brid could speak and look the part but she didn't know the words of the prayer that every other living soul in the throne-room, right down to the smallest child, could recite in their sleep.

All eyes turned expectantly on Brid as she stammered hopelessly.

'The ducking stool,' the dean exclaimed triumphantly. 'First the ducking-stool and then we'll burn her. That is the correct way to prise the demon from the soul. Look at the creature. She doesn't know the words of the prayer.'

'The ducking stool! To the Old Pond and the ducking stool!' the cry was eagerly taken up. Rewik looked from one face to another, rattling his fingers on the arm of the throne, then stopped abruptly.

The elderly bishop pounded his staff on the marble floor. 'No, Sire, no! Look at her; a young girl terrorized by these accusations. No wonder her wits have left her. No!'

'That is indeed the normal way, Lord Bishop, why do you suggest otherwise?'

'These duckings have a habit of finding out the pagan but also of drowning the innocent. If there is no unnatural spirit in their body to make the pure water reject them and spit them to the surface, they simply drown. What justice is that?' argued the bishop.

He is truly a good man that bishop, Caspar thought, as he admired him for his courage in publicly standing up against King Rewik. He must have had a hard time since the old king died.

Brid was standing stock still with her eyes lowered and Caspar thought his heart would break. If he'd realized how dangerous it was going to be bringing Brid to the capital, he would have ... but no, they had to come. He thought of his mother and her twelve torturous years entombed in the Vaalakan glacier; for her sake they had to come. And for the sake of the greater good. The Northmen would bring the cruel ice of Vaal-Peor to this land and destroy them all if they did not restore the Trinity.

'My Inquisitors believe the ducking stool to be an excellent weapon in the holy fight against the Devil.' Rewik was again rattling his long manicured nails on the throne. There was a suppressed hush in the hall, a shuffle of feet, a nervous cough but otherwise silence as they waited for the King's decision. 'The innocent have nothing to fear.'

Ceowulf suddenly burst forward. 'This is preposterous, Sire. We are at war; there is a serious threat on our northern borders. At the moment the only thing that stems a flood of barbarians into this land is Branwolf. And Branwolf alone and unsupported, holds the northern passage. This girl is his charge. It would show scant gratitude to the Baron if you were to destroy one of his feudal charges.'

Rewik's face seethed up into a bloated fury at being interrupted in his own court but he restrained himself enough to listen and just as suddenly became calm and passive again. 'You are right. We will take the bishop's advice. The accused will be taken to the cathedral and we will let God's water prove her innocence or guilt.'

Brid was swaying and blanched to an off white. In that one instant, Caspar was certain she would be unable to bear the drops of sacred water. The pool would have been better; she would have died a merciful death by drowning: now she faced the horror of the stake.

Hal was rushing forward to catch her before she swooned, declaring loudly, 'My kinswoman is overcome with relief that she has this chance to prove her innocence.' But she didn't faint. She set her jaw and clasped Hal's hand for support.

Caspar thought for a second and decided against rushing to her side. Instead, as the crowd surged forward in the excitement, he pressed himself back against the cold stone walls, slipped behind a pillar and edged his way silently towards the locked doors. He wasn't going to be able to do anything to save Brid by standing by her and whimpering. Hal would give her all the support he could but no words could now reach Brid's heart. He remembered in the Dragon Scorch, how she had told the sorry tale of her mother's death. Brid would have been about four years old when she was forced to watch the very eyeballs of her mother shrivel and melt in the flames. Her mother died rather than deny the Goddess and Brid could not forget nor betray her mother by denouncing her loyalty to the Old Faith. It was one thing taking on a disguise but quite another to accept the holy waters. The touch of the sacred baptism would burn her pagan skin. She would scream with the unbearable pain. He had to rescue her.

'You can do it, Brid,' Hal whispered encouragingly. 'It's only water.' The excited crowd, thrilling with the anticipation of the witch-trial, smothered the sound of their words.

Brid's staring black eyes looked helplessly up into his. 'But it's not.'

Suddenly Hal realized that this small girl, whom he despised for her arrogance and unladylike self-confidence, was no longer acting; her trembling fear was genuine. He felt an overwhelming urge to protect her as she fiercely gripped his arm.

'You've done really well until now. This will all be dismissed as coincidence and a few silly dreams just so long as you keep it up.'

'I can't,' she gasped.

'Brid, you'll burn otherwise.'

'If you were me, wouldn't you rather burn than lose your soul, lose your chance to go to Annwyn and be one with the Goddess? If I deny Her I will forsake my chance to return to Her bosom and meet my after-life so that I might be reborn. If I publicly declare my love for Her, I might die now in suffocating flames but I will be reborn again.'

Hal wasn't sure. He'd never given anything like that any thought. 'It's only water, Brid,' he said somewhat lamely, squeezing her hand as they were led away by the King's guard. Caspar somehow seemed to have been separated from them, at any rate he could no longer see his nephew for the body of men pressing around them.

'I can't do it.' Brid gripped his hand. 'I saw my mother die to uphold her faith and I cannot betray her. How could I ever have been so arrogant as to think that I could deceive the King without risking my soul?'

Hal bit his lip. So much depended on this girl. Without her, even if they did find the runes and the mysterious Egg, they couldn't restore the Trinity of the three priestesses. Why hadn't anyone listened to him when he had said it was far too dangerous for her. Of course he wanted Keridwen free from the glacier; it was terrible to think of Spar's mother suffering in endless torture. But more than anything they must be restored so that they could drive back the Vaalakans. He believed Gwion when he said the one true God wouldn't intercede and only the powers of the Goddess would defend the castle from such numbers.

'Listen, Brid, I have had to forsake my soul and turn to what I consider heresy to save my country. You will have to do the same. I will burn in hell for my part in aiding this conspiracy to restore the Goddess. Surely for the greater good you must do the same. You have to live so that we can find the cauldron's runes. We only need the runes.'

'My powers, Hal, though. I don't know what will happen if I let the holy waters touch my skin. For the greater good, to restore the Mother I will deny my faith, and lose my right to rebirth but, Hal, will I also lose my power? Will I no longer be one of the three, with the sight and the knowledge of a high-priestess? Will I be nothing but a girl without the power to invoke the Great Mother?'

The youth didn't have any answers. All he wanted was to get out of Farona and back to Torra Alta with this precious Egg so that they could turn back the threat of the Vaalakans. He didn't understand what it meant to lose powers. Perhaps it would be like losing his sword.

'Brid, if you do this for the sake of the Mother surely she will understand your motives. She will know your heart is faithful.'

'I don't know what will happen.' Brid's words were faint but she looked at him with the firm set of resolve in her jaw. 'But you are right; we have no choice. For the greater good I must survive to restore the Old Faith and rescue Keridwen. I have to take the risk. Now tell me the words of this prayer.'

He muttered them to her once and she repeated back the foreign words with only one mistake. He corrected her and this time she was word perfect.

'I didn't know girls could learn that quickly.' He hoped she would rise to his taunt and meet him with her usual spark but she didn't even wince.

The cathedral dominated the head of the street, the long thin shadow of its spire cutting across half of the city. 'Now come on, Brid, this can't be as bad as that devil worship in the priory.'

She took deep breaths to steady herself. 'Just don't let go of me. I don't think I could walk alone. I can't see well because of the deadly nightshade. Are my eyes still black?'

He nodded comfortingly. 'You look quite beautiful, absolutely disarming in those clothes and your hair . . .'

'Couldn't I look beautiful just as my normal self?'

'Just concentrate on looking right before the bishop. Just remember the temple of your Goddess will be right beneath your feet. Good luck, Brid.'

A footman jangled a ring of keys and began the laborious process of releasing the three locks that sealed them all in the throne-room. The third one finally clicked and the doors swung inwards. Caspar's heart was pounding as he waited for the right moment to slink out of the doors. He stood in the shadow behind the oak panels, trying to make his breathing smooth and even. The King rose. Caspar snatched his chance as the court rose and bowed low before the presence of their monarch. He slipped out of the doors and walked down the corridors quickly but without running, so as not to raise any alarm. He didn't have a plan. Instinct told him to find Fire-cracker. He was strong on a horse; he could fight on a horse; but where and how and against his King . . . ? This was treason, high treason. He felt sick. But Brid! He couldn't forsake Brid.

Which way were the stables? He couldn't remember. The palace seemed deserted; they must all have been in the throne-room. He stopped to listen for any noise. There was a faint clatter of dishes, which must have come from the kitchens. He turned away down the darker, less decorated corridors, down into the narrow servant's passageways and broke into a run. A small door led to the outside world and he twisted the circular hoop that served as a handle. The latch was stiff and rusty but the door yielded and led him out into the kitchen herb gardens, which were dry and barren at this time of year. He skipped across the low hedges that separated the herb beds and scaled the wall with ease, leaping down onto the soft sloping grass that led towards the moat. From here it was easy to tell where the stables lay, not by the sweet smell of straw or the warm odours from the manure heap but because of the battering noise and the sound of splintering wood interspersed with the fiendish shrieks of a captive stallion. Only Firecracker caused so much disturbance in a stable. The horse was predictably trying to kick his way out of his prison.

Only two young stable lads had remained to tend the horses and Caspar assumed that the rest of the servants had gone to join the gawking crowds who eagerly feasted their eyes on Brid's suffering. The boys were young and a little uncertain without the grooms to direct them but they were used to taking orders and didn't question Caspar's. He scooped up Firecracker's tack in his arms, knowing that it would be far quicker if he saddled the red colt himself.

The horse was already lathered into a sweat and crushed the boy several times against the wooden slats that boarded the stable, pacing round and round in his eagerness to be free. 'Stand still, Cracker,' the anxious youth soothed as the horse tossed his head up and down, unwilling to accept the bit. In his frustration Caspar belted him with the free end of the reins, which did nothing to pacify the wayward animal, but at least relieved some of Caspar's fraught tension. It was only quick work with his hands that enabled the boy to slip the bit between the brute's teeth and within minutes he had the bridle strapped, his saddle in place and was trotting across the drawbridge. The King's procession surrounded by an excited rabble was already proceeding along the east street, taking the broad state road towards the cathedral. Caspar steered his horse into one of the narrow alleys, thinking to cut the corner and stay out of sight of the King's men.

The alleys were dark because of the overhanging eaves that

nearly touched his head. He had to duck to avoid the dripping rags and bright sheets of clothing that were strung on lines between the houses. Not all the streets were empty. A mother with a toddler nestled on her hip was hanging out her washing, able to use only her free hand and having to grip the pegs between her crooked teeth. A small barefooted boy was chasing a ginger cat and an old man shuffled along, bracing his stooped back with his hand. The man pressed himself into a door jamb, nervously muttering as Caspar passed.

He could see the cathedral spire thrusting up above the rooftops to his right but realized he needed to find another side alley that would take him that way. The beat of the horse's hooves echoed through the narrow cobbled streets and the red-haired youth became increasingly anxious that he wouldn't get to the cathedral in time. At least if he could get Brid out of there before she was threatened with the consecrated water it would rob them of the chance of proving her guilt. Oh Great Goddess, can you do nothing to protect your disciple; is there no magic that will save her; no runic spell?

He felt impotent, suddenly realizing that he was passing the cathedral and still no alley led him towards it. The fates were conspiring against him. He had passed three or four alleys that turned away to his left and he could see the corner of yet another one. He kicked his horse into a canter, though Firecracker slipped and skidded on the smooth round cobbles. A dog snarled out of the darkness of an alley, making the young stallion lurch sideways and the boy turned his head. Just for a moment he caught the image of a sinister face lurking in the shadows. The image was gone, just a fleeting picture that vanished in an instant. With relief the boy finally discovered a passageway that led straight towards the cathedral.

But the image of the man's face remained emblazoned in his mind's eye: a dark scarred face, a face that he had once fixed as he stared down the length of his poised arrow shaft. It was impossible to forget a face once held in your sight, at the mercy of your bow.

The cathedral filled the space at the exit to the alley and

Caspar looked up to take in the sheer walls and the everlasting height of the spire. It was impossible to imagine that such an immense building could have been built by man. The perspective was bewildering. The height of the walls gave the illusion that they were continually falling towards him. A crowd was gathered outside the west door, clamouring to be allowed entrance to the cathedral, but was being handed off and pushed back by guards with staves. One of the King's guards, mounted on a charger and with vizor down, stood sentry at the door. I'm too late; the burden of defeat weighed heavily on Caspar's heart. I'm too late: she's inside.

He gathered up his mount, urging the horse to pace forward at a steady controlled gait. The red roan picked his hooves up high and pranced with an energetic stride, his mane and tail floating in the air on each downbeat.

The knight lowered his lance, pointing its tip at Caspar's chest. 'The cathedral is closed. On the King's orders no more may enter.' His voice echoed inside his helm.

'I am part of this trial; the accused is my kin. I am of noble birth; you will not deny me access to her trial.' Fear for Brid reinforced the youth's courage and his voice cracked out with authority despite his lack of years.

'I have my orders.'

'Open the doors and ask one of higher authority than you, knight. I have the right, in God's name in God's house, to be at my kinswoman's trial. Let me pass.' The quiver of arrows pressed against Caspar's right knee. Both bows were hooked to the saddle and lay against the horse's right shoulder. He focused on the point of the lance in front of him, wondering whether he'd have the time to aim his bow before that lance pierced his ribcage and punctured his lungs. He doubted it.

Oh Mother, help us, he instinctively prayed, help us. He was certain that his own God would never show mercy towards the pagan priestess, and so his fear for Brid drove his soul one step closer to the Great Mother, begging for her help. But he couldn't conjure an image of the Goddess in his mind. Instead he envisaged the beautiful face of Keridwen as he had once momentarily seen her in the image of the moonstone, with the sparkling blue eyes almost of violet. He could fall into their watery depths to the infinite love, the succouring protective love of maternal devotion. Oh Mother, help me.

The crowd still clamoured to get in. ''Ere soldier, we ain't seen a witch trial in the actual city in years,' one of them cried. 'Come on, let us in. Let the squire in too. 'E's got a right, got a right as 'e says.'

'Aye!' The crowd surged forward as one entity, united by their frenzied lust for excitement. The mob now controlled each individual. The soldiers punched back with their staves but the cries of pain only brought more fuel to the mob's determination. ''Ere lads, let's shove together.'

'I've never seen a witch,' one of the younger youths cried out, managing to clamber over the shoulders of the pikemen who reluctantly beat back with their wooden staves.

The knight looked more disconcerted now as his men became preoccupied with the pressing mob. He took his sword from its scabbard and beat on the door. 'The young lord from Torra Alta demands entrance; what should I do?'

Caspar could hear the bolts of the great studded doors being drawn back. The noise instantly quelled the mob to an expectant hush and as a thin crack appeared they surged forward, forcing the doors wide open. They swarmed over the soldiers who were also drawn to ogle at the spectacle in the cathedral. The knight reined back his horse uncertainly, but short of beating back the crowd with his sword there was nothing he could do. Once they had a clear view the townsfolk instantly became calm. The smaller men at the back pressed down on the shoulders in front and rose up on their toes to get a better look at the small girl kneeling before the altar. The knight sighed and let his lance drop, realizing that the mob was not going to cause any more trouble and turned his horse to let his own eyes possess the ceremony.

Caspar hung back, taking in the view. From Firecracker's saddle he could easily see over the crowd. The cathedral was full; every seat was taken and there was a strong sense of the pressure of people. The tension of expectant thought filled the atmosphere. The energy of heightened emotion seemed to pour out of each soul to be absorbed by the surroundings, by the air and by the stones. Caspar remembered how the cathedral had had no sense of history but now, he thought, now and forever, it would radiate and pulsate with the memories of this excited throng.

'She's so small,' someone whispered.

'I saw her face. She's beautiful.'

'Aye. Bewitching!'

The irony in the statement silenced the crowd but soon the excited murmuring returned as they took the words to be some omen. 'Bewitching!'

'The women folk are saying she's a changeling, not a witch,' one of the boys announced.

'What's that?'

'It means she ain't human, not a natural being at all, but an elfin creature, something from the land of faerie.'

Brid was kneeling in the centre of the circular chancel, where they had knelt that morning and had felt the power of the Goddess welling up from the temple beneath. It was a magical scene. The light from the stained window above the altar poured down, anointing the Maiden's head, bathing her in the ethereal colours of the rainbow. She kept her head bowed and one arm stretched up to clutch Hal's protective hand. In front of her stood a semi-circle of priests: the bishop with his mitre and crook, the dean and three vergers. From this distance Caspar couldn't make out their expressions. His focus was channelled along the length of the aisle to the altar. He judged it to be about four score paces. His thoughts swam with indecision, reason drowning in his rising panic.

The bishop raised a chalice high above his head, held by just his fingertips in reverence to its sanctity. He remembered Brid telling him how it was the worst betrayal of all to allow the baptism waters to touch her. It was the ultimate denial of her Goddess and he knew she would be unable to bear one drop of the liquid. His heartbeat quickened as his thoughts touched on new terrors. The power in the holy water will burn her skin and eat through her flesh and dissolve her soul. She will scream out in pain and the King will take that as the demons within her. Then he will burn her at the stake.

He didn't know what to do. He had to stop the ceremony. Feeling for his new bow, he surreptitiously unhooked it from the saddle. He prayed that the knight wouldn't turn to look at him but, whilst the crowd remained calm and untroublesome, all eyes remained fixed on the east. He let his hand stroke the grey goose feathers of his arrows, feeling for one with short angled feathers that would give him maximum flight. He still didn't know what he was going to do. He imagined taking the shot, just as the bishop was about to let the water pour from the cup to cascade over the girl's head. He imagined the arrow flying true and straight, stopping the bishop's heart. He imagined Brid rising and turning towards him as he spurred Firecracker through the crowd, galloping the length of the cathedral, skidding on the smooth flagstones. He imagined gathering her up in his arms and charging out, but by then the doors would be closed. But then Firecracker could smash them with his hooves and . . . and . . . no, it was hopeless.

He had to do something. The arrow was slotted to the cat-gut and he raised it slowly. As he focused along the length of the shaft all he could see were the distant figures; everything else, the cathedral, the pillars, the aisle, everything blurred into the periphery of his vision. He took deep slow breaths, trying to calm his breathing and steady his heartbeat. It was a long shot; he had to be perfectly still. The back of Brid's head filled his vision. Would it be kinder? She would die instantly, innocent forever, guiltless and faithful to the last. It would be better surely than to let her burn. The death would be instant. Firecracker shifted his weight to the other foot and broke Caspar's attention. No, he couldn't do it. The Goddess must save her.

The memory of Brid's words stayed in his heart. She had preached that the Goddess would never give unconditionally.

Anyone invoking her powers would first have to do everything in their power to achieve the task. He looked again at the scene. The bishop was lowering the chalice, slowly and with the solemnity of ritual. Caspar inched his aim upwards. It had to be the bishop. It wouldn't be impossible to get to Brid. Firecracker was fast. The sprint would take only seconds. The confusion over the death of the bishop would stall any counter attack. Hal was there. The great sword was slung over his back with its pagan runes hidden from the King's eyes by the scabbard. Hal could protect Brid till he reached her. He drew back the bowstring level with his chin.

But the bishop is a good man. He means no harm and he tried to defend her. Caspar's conscience clamoured in his head. A lifetime of worshipping the God of the New Faith made him abruptly stop. *I cannot kill a man of God, not in such cold blood. There is no hatred in my heart.* Somewhere lurking in his soul the innate belief and worship of the Great Mother was rising up and stirring his heart towards Her love, but he could not deny his childhood teaching. His awe of the one God still burnt fiercely within him and to kill a man of God in front of the altar was too great a trespass. He would roast in hell for eternity. He raised his aim higher so that the focus centred only on the golden chalice that flashed out the rays of red light filtering through the stained window above. It was a very small target for such a range but he was a skilled archer; it was a possible shot. Surely the Goddess would favour him and bless him with the luck that would drive the arrow home.

He drew a deep breath, letting it sigh out evenly so that the rise and fall of his chest wouldn't deflect his aim. When he reached the bottom of his breath he would loose the arrow.

It happened all at once. Firecracker tossed his head up, champing at the bit so that the curb chains jangled. He caught the attention of a little boy at the rear of the group who squeaked in disbelief, 'He's going to shoot the witch.'

The boy's cry was drowned by the expectant gasp from the crowd as the droplets of water sprinkled from the chalice and tumbled towards Brid's head. His shot was ruined: he was too late. He let the bow drop as he watched in defeat with his mouth sagging and his heart strings tightening. He was too late; he had failed her; Brid would burn.

The moment was so filled with tension that it seemed to be suspended in time. To Caspar it seemed to take an eternity for the droplets of water to cascade from the holy chalice. He wouldn't have been able to see them except that the droplets of water were transformed into sprinkling jewels as they fell through the rays of brilliant colours falling through the stained-glass windows. The water cascaded onto Brid's head, soaking into her hair, seeping onto her skin, running over her flesh. Caspar held his breath. Every man, woman and child held their breath waiting for her to scream, waiting for the cry of anguish as the heathen heart reviled against the touch of the sanctified water, but there was only silence.

Brid rose from her kneeling position before the altar and proclaimed in loud solemn tones:

> 'O Creator mundi, te laudamus.
> Creator caelorum, te laudamus.
> O Creator omnium, te laudamus.
> Pater et Princeps, Dominus et Deus es;
> Tibi gratiam et laudem damus.'

The great cavern of the cathedral was filled with her echoing voice that trailed away into meaningful silence, a silence deeply profound and significant. The silence screamed at the impulsive youth that the pagan priestess was saved; his Brid was saved.

It was over. He felt relieved and deflated all at once.

She was now bending forward to kiss the ring on the bishop's finger. The cathedral reverberated with cheers from the congregation, though there was disappointment on some of the younger faces near Caspar, who had hoped to see the excitement of a death at the stake.

Satisfied by the conclusion of the ceremony, the King turned to leave. Brid slowly withdrew from her supplicated pose before the bishop. Hal pulled her up and held her close in his embrace before offering his arm to lead her triumphantly back down the aisle. Even here have I failed you, thought Caspar. I underestimated your courage and, like a madman, endangered us all with my vain attempts at mighty actions when all along I should have been at your side to support you. Hal is there. Hal has done everything right. I have failed. He reined Firecracker back, feeling absurd up there on his horse and rapidly dismounted, vowing never to admit to Hal or Brid what his intentions had been.

He stood aside as the crowd dispersed, bowing as the King and his bishop were escorted out by the house-guards and waited for his companions. Brid looked wan, and bedraggled by the drenching. Hal gave his nephew a suspicious look that questioned where he had been at such a time. No longer a cause for sensation, Brid was ignored by the crowd, which dispersed leaving the three Torra Altans alone. Hal lifted the exhausted girl onto the horse's back.

Amidst the tombstones they were left alone, no longer of any interest to the King and the people of the city. From beneath her dripping fringe Brid's black eyes reached out towards Caspar. 'I have lost my soul.'

Chapter 19

'Gatto's here. I saw him in a back alley,' Caspar blurted out, not knowing how to comfort the priestess.

'What!' Hal looked at him for a moment in disbelief. 'Here in Farona? We must go straight to the palace and warn Ceowulf – he can inform the King while we keep our heads low for a bit. Gatto's got some nerve coming right here to the capital.'

Brid coiled her sodden hair into a twist and wrung it out. A sheet of water fell to the ground and she dried her hands disgustedly on her dress. There was a proud tilt to her nose as she sat with dignified poise on the back of Caspar's stallion but her eyes were bathed in sorrow.

Only a short-haired hound chained to the rail in front of a stern-looking house paid them any heed as they returned to the palace. Growling, the guard-dog rushed to the end of his chain, which snapped taut on its studded collar. All the curious faces had gone: nobody cared about the lady on the high-stepping red colt; nobody cared to stare at the pain hidden behind her dewy eyes. Caspar felt her pain, but could think of no way to comfort her. He understood that she was mourning for her lost soul and inwardly cried over her scarred faith; but anything he could say would only sound hollow and inadequate.

'I still don't understand where you went or what you thought you could do,' Hal persisted in chiding his nephew.

'I just wanted to save Brid from this . . . this pain,' he tried to defend himself.

'But what on earth did you think you could do?' Hal was amazed.

'Leave him alone, Hal,' Brid cut in with unexpected sharpness. 'Just leave him alone; he was only trying to do what was right and, if it hadn't have been for our quest, he would have been right.' She softened her tone and braced her shoulders as if denying herself the privilege of wallowing in self-pity. 'Anyway we've got far too much to worry about without dragging over things past.'

'Ah yes, I forgot,' Hal sneered in his most cuttingly sarcastic of voices. 'I forgot you two have a *special* relationship.'

Caspar flushed. 'It's not like that and you know it – and you're being damned insensitive.'

Ceowulf stood sentry at the portcullis, apparently waiting for their return. He politely proffered Brid his hand to help her from the proud stallion and she slid lightly to the ground, keeping her eyes lowered, shunning the searching look in the knight's eyes. With courtly tact, the tall mercenary avoided any mention of her trial but diverted his attention to Hal, who was anxiously trying to inform him of the presence of Gatto somewhere in the city.

'I know,' the man said unexpectedly. 'I saw him in the crowd. I was waiting to warn you.'

As the mercenary and the young Torra Altans anxiously discussed Gatto's presence, Brid drifted away to stare into the dark waters of the moat. She looked too tired and spent to trouble with these new events. Her ordeal was over; nothing worse could happen to her and Caspar wanted only to comfort her. He started to move after the Maiden but Ceowulf caught his arm and shook his head at him.

'I'd leave her alone. She needs time to herself. Women pull themselves together more quickly if you leave them alone,' he advised. 'Now where did you see Gatto and who was with him?'

Caspar shook his head. 'I don't know. I just caught a glimpse of him in the shadows in the back alleys off the cathedral.'

'I saw his face in the crowd – just for a fleeting second. He'd covered himself in a peasant smock but I didn't see any of the others: they'll be keeping their heads well down in the city of course. He was talking to a stranger, certainly no one I recognized,' Ceowulf added. 'A big slow moving man draped in a brown cloak.'

'Well, that could have been virtually anyone.' Hal dismissed the information.

Ceowulf shrugged. 'Anyway, I'll alert the King immediately. But I'm warning you that whatever you've got to do here, get on with it, and get out of Farona before Gatto catches up with you – or the King gets suspicious again.' He turned as if to leave but then stopped short and stretched out his hand to Hal and then Caspar. 'Good luck; you're going to need it. Gatto is an old mercenary and no mercenary gets old without being wilier than his enemy. I'll offer my services to the King and see if I can't hunt the man down.'

Caspar nodded gratefully. Ceowulf was a welcome ally.

'Thanks,' Hal said simply but gripped the knight's hand fiercely in friendship. Then he lowered his voice to speak closely. 'And will you say farewell to Cybillia for me? In the circumstances I don't really want to return to the palace.'

Ceowulf smiled knowingly but then his brown eyes, beneath clean straight brows, drew together in a serious frown as he nodded towards the Maiden, who was staring wistfully into the waters of the moat. 'She's rare that one; look after her.' His boots clipped smartly on the cobbles as he marched across the palace courtyard, the tails of his black surcoat catching the breeze.

'I'll get Magpie and Brid's mare,' Caspar offered. 'We'll be safer from Gatto if we're mounted. We haven't got any more time to waste; we need to get back and search the cathedral – things must have quietened down there by now.' He kicked a loose stone and sent it rattling across the cobbles, letting out some of his frustration. He wanted to be on his way; he needed to find the cauldron with its runes so that they could trace the Egg and return, triumphant, to rescue his mother and repel the Vaalakans. He thought of his father desperately defending the castle. Branwolf had restricted the garrison and castle household to siege rations before they left; the first stabs of hunger would now be beginning to bite.

Brid seemed partially recovered though still a little pale and quiet. As Caspar led out her chestnut mare, she stumbled forward and clutched at the saddle-bag strapped to her horse's rump.

'The Eye,' she murmured. 'I must check on it. Spar, bring the horses round to give me some cover.'

Obediently the youth complied, wheeling Magpie so the tall piebald mare shielded Brid from general view. She peered into the saddle-bag at the scarlet salamander contentedly coiled around the moonstone. Looking over her shoulder, Caspar was immediately overwhelmed by the magnetic pull of the orb on his emotions, demanding that he reached out to delve into its mysterious heart. His hand irresistibly rose to stroke the smooth sphere of cool light.

'Don't touch it,' Brid snapped in warning. 'Look, it's clear again. The concealing rowan smoke has been washed away by the waters of baptism. The Goddess has punished me for my faithlessness and broken the spell of concealment.'

'What does that all mean?' Hal asked. 'Look, be careful.' He glanced anxiously at the palace. 'Someone might see you.'

'Someone can see us. Whoever it was with the power to reach us through the Druid's Eye can do so again.' Brid looked around her frantically and finally scooped up her skirts and ripped off a strip of petticoat. 'Here, Spar, go and soak this in the moat. The best thing we can do is keep the Eye wet and so dull its powers.' She wrapped the moonstone in the damp cloth and resignedly buckled the saddle flaps. 'We can't possibly try to conceal ourselves in smoke again, not here in Farona – even if I still have the powers to cast such a spell.' She shrugged. 'Well, let's hope no damage is done. At least we know we're not far from the cauldron. We'd better get on and find it. The sooner we get the runes, the sooner our problems will be solved.'

She mounted and led them forward, determinedly taking the initiative to lead. Caspar kept his eyes on her back, willing away some of her pain. Hal, diligently alert, snatched glances into each dark alley that ran off the main street.

They pushed themselves to the side of the street at the sound of galloping hooves. Ceowulf led a score of the household guards to scour the city and hunt down the intruders. The three companions stuck firmly to the broad busy streets to be on the safe side. DARƏi Smells big butts

The cathedral stood alone and majestic, set apart by lawns and defended from the rest of the city by an abatis of tombstones. The towering building offered no clue to its inner secrets. They tethered the horses to the trunk of a silver birch, keeping them away from the poisonous yews that were numerous around the cathedral, and decided to start their search by first surveying the exterior of the cathedral. Small arched doors led in from various angles but there was nothing secret about their positions or the well-worn paths, scuffed out of the grass, that led to each entrance.

'We're not looking closely enough,' Hal argued. 'All those doors are too obvious; there must be a tunnel or something leading in from the graveyard.'

'You mean under one of these raised tombs?' Caspar queried.

'Mmm, yes, something like that,' Hal nodded.

Brid shook her head. 'No, they wouldn't like that. They'd rather tunnel down from under the roots of the trees. People couldn't sneak in and out of the graveyard: it's too exposed. The yews would at least provide some shelter and they wouldn't have to approach too close to the cathedral.'

Her argument seemed very plausible so they returned to search beneath the drooping branches of the yew trees. Raking through the fine coating of needles and fragments of bark that had peeled from the trees, they combed the dark soil for any signs of disturbance. The ground was perfectly untouched. Hal kicked a snapped branch, venting his anger.

'We're missing something obvious. We've got to get under the cathedral.' He grabbed hold of a branch, working it back and forth till the bark began to fray.

'Leave the tree alone,' Brid snapped at him and then

pensively mused over his words. 'Under the cathedral. What is under the cathedral?'

'The ancient temple of course,' the raven-haired boy answered in exasperated tones. 'Why do you think we're here?'

'Mmm and what else? Sewers, drains, cellars?'

Caspar shook his head. 'No, churches don't have things like that. At least the chapel at home didn't, but then we didn't have a crypt either.'

Immediately he uttered the word crypt all three knew where to look. 'The library plans said the crypt is under the north transept,' Caspar said, picturing the parchment in his mind. They strolled round to the northern end of the building, looking as natural as possible.

There were three doors on the north side but only one that led into the transept. It creaked open with relative ease and they stole into the building, blinking in the dim light, trying to let their eyes adjust. For once luck was on their side: the cathedral appeared to be deserted. Caspar prayed that all the vergers, sextons and the dean had accompanied the bishop to the palace. A side altar dominated the east wall behind a vast pillar, with a girth almost as broad as the graveyard yews. The pillar supported four arches that branched from its capital. An evil-faced gargoyle grimaced down at them and Caspar recoiled from its troll-like expression before scouring the walls for an entrance leading downwards to the crypt. In both corners of the transept two small niches dipped away into shadow. On closer inspection they only led to narrow, upwardly spiralling staircases. The stone steps were built within the walls to allow people access to the corridors of the triforium where the bays of arches, grouped in families of three, ran the whole perimeter of the cathedral.

'I've found it,' Brid whispered, though the acoustics of the building caught her voice, making her words echo through the vaulted space. They all stood stock still for a moment, fearing that someone would respond to the sound of their intrusion, but silence soon reclaimed its domain. She lifted the corner of a heavy tapestry, which covered the wall behind the side-altar, and revealed a low archway. They tiptoed to the recess and followed Brid down into the dark well. The smooth regular flagstones of the cathedral gave way to rough hewn irregular limestone steps that betrayed their age. There was an instant sense of stepping back into history. Caspar could feel the presence of many other souls making that same journey down into the darkness. Even the air smelt different, too old, too stale, as if the stagnant atmosphere had been trapped down there for a hundred years.

Ahead of him, Brid in her flowing dress faded to a dim spectre as she was swallowed up by the dark. There was a whispered sigh as Hal drew his sword from its scabbard. The insidious feeling of other people all around them must have penetrated even Hal's tough hide, he thought. The sword glinted brightly as it caught the last rays of sunlight, filtering through the cathedral windows. As Hal's form darkened to match the shadows and they twisted down the spiralling steps, the light on the sword didn't fade but grew brighter and more insistent. Its silvery glow fell on Brid's face as she turned to see if the two youths were following.

'Isn't it wonderful! We're nearing a temple to the Goddess.' Her face was radiant and alive. 'The sword is singing Her praises.'

The atmosphere thickened to a cloying rancid stench and Caspar coughed to expel some of the fetid air. He held out a hand to feel for the walls in case he stumbled on the uneven steps that led them deeper into the womb of Mother Earth. At last they reached the crypt, a low-ceilinged chamber that appeared to be hollowed out of solid rock. There was no masonry work, only the worn pitted walls of limestone whose edges had become rounded with age. Hal stepped slowly about, letting the light from his sword fall into each recess in turn. Caspar shuddered with the sudden realization that they were surrounded by bodies in various degrees of decay, laid out to rest in recesses in the wall. He wondered if it was the presence of their souls that he had felt walking with them down the steps.

'I hope none of them died of disease,' Hal managed to produce a practical matter-of-fact tone to his voice. 'It's not the most wholesome way to bury the dead.'

Caspar was unnerved by the light from the runesword. Every time Hal moved, the light fingered deeper into the hollow ribcage of a skeleton or cast new shadows across a skull. When the silvery light caught the glint of an eye still undecayed in its socket, Caspar clutched at his chest, feeling certain that the dead body had winked at him. He retreated nervously only to discover that he'd backed onto a rotted and shrivelled hand that protruded from a corpse behind him.

'Stand still won't you, Spar; I'm trying to concentrate.' Brid's tone was firm as if she were scolding a child. Caspar stepped forward into the centre of the room and stood completely motionless, trying to draw comfort from the warmth of the mandala that throbbed against his chest. They were so close now to discovering the location of the Druid's Egg and finding its secret. So close.

'Is this it?' Hal asked incredulously. 'Is this the place we've been looking for?'

'Of course not,' Brid replied with indignation. 'Does it look like a temple? There's nothing here but dead bodies, but somewhere there must be a door. The temple is over there to the east.' The girl's eyes were scanning the wall in front of her, flickering up and down, trying to unearth its secret. Brid's usual command and composure had returned: she was in her element fulfilling her duties to the Goddess. Caspar presumed that in the dark her dilated pupils enabled her to see better than she had outside in the daylight. For the last two days she had moved as if permanently dazzled.

Caspar could make out nothing except the bones of skeletons nesting in their allotted shelves. At least on this side of the crypt the bones were dry and lacked the gruesome mess of congealed and rotting skin. Some still had straw-like hair, which decayed more slowly than skin, but it didn't have the same nauseating aroma of the blackened flesh clinging to the corpses on the other walls.

'There's nothing here but dead bodies,' Caspar protested.

'Ah, but we must pass through death to be born on the other side,' the priestess said enigmatically. 'These bones, you know, all these bones on this side are much older than the others, older than the cathedral. They've been brought here from somewhere else, maybe from the ancient henges.'

'What do you mean?' Hal asked, pointing the sword systematically at each skeleton, scanning for tell-tale signs of a concealed entrance.

'The ancient tribes leave their dead in stone circles out in the open and only when they have been picked clean by carrion do the relatives inhume the bones. Treated in that way the bones are still white and not old and brittle. Look; like these.' She smoothed the curve of a skull with her hand, showing not the least revulsion at touching a dead object. 'The flesh has been picked clean away, not left to rot on them like it has with the others, and the hair is much older. These bodies have come from the henges.'

The dead guarding the way to the temple of their Goddess; unremitting souls watching over the sacred shrine; Caspar could feel it now. They were there all around him watching, questioning. He pulled his cloak in around his neck, trying to protect himself from their intrusive presence.

'We must pass through death to be born again on the other side,' Brid muttered again. 'It's here somewhere. Why can't I see it?'

'It's pretty gruesome probing through the skeletons of dead men,' Hal shuddered.

'Who said they were men?' Brid contradicted him.

'Well, it's obvious, isn't it? They only bring the most eminent people to be buried in crypts: kings, bishops, knights, brave warriors.'

'And priestesses,' Brid finished for him. 'That one!' She pointed triumphantly to a small skeleton lying low down on the right of the wall. Its jaw was loose from its skull, and had dropped to rest on its neck vertebrae. 'The entrance is through that one.'

'How do you know?' Hal peered more closely at the skeleton, examining the shelf and the wall behind. 'I can't see anything.'

'It's the only woman here. Look at the hip bones.'

Caspar saw nothing different about the shape of the skeleton, but Brid was always knowledgeable about the natural anatomy of beings so he didn't doubt her words. The young girl had pushed up her sleeves and was feeling all round the dry bones, but the wall behind was completely intact and no loose stones or trap doors yielded to her touch. 'The whole thing's solid; the wall's solid; the plinth's solid.'

'Solid but separate,' Hal corrected her, running the tip of his sword along the edge of the six-foot slab.

Instantly they knew what to do. Caspar grunted as he bore the strain at one end of the plinth. The stone ground over the underlying rock as they slowly dragged the plinth away from the wall. The muscles in his back creaked as he lowered the slab and its recumbent skeleton onto the floor. He shuddered as his hand accidentally touched the bones of the feet. He retracted his hand and Brid smiled at him.

'You don't need to be afraid of her; she's probably one of your ancestors.'

Where the plinth had just been, a dark pit now sank into the earth. Hal lowered the tip of the glowing runesword into the pitch black hole but flinched backwards as something leapt out of the darkness at him and a rat ran across his hand.

'There's something in there!' he exclaimed.

'What?' Brid's voice was still calm and level. 'You two really are a couple of kids being spooked by a few bones.'

'I don't know; some thing, some demon-type thing.'

The small girl snatched the sword from the black-haired youth and strode purposefully forward. 'There's nothing evil in this place: look.' She plunged the sword into the pit. Caspar peered over her shoulder, his heart stopping as a horned face snarled out of the black. 'It's just a stone sculpture to frighten off faithless people like you. Come on.'

She crawled through the hole, grabbing onto one of the stone antlers for support and dragging the runesword with her.

It wasn't so much the need to fulfil their quest that drove Hal and Caspar rapidly after her, but a dread of being left alone in the dark with the unsleeping dead. It was a tight squeeze through the tunnel and Caspar used his elbows to drag his body through the passage. To his relief he saw light ahead, not bright open sunlight but the soft rays of light filtering down through grills in the cathedral flooring. The air smelt fresher. When he reached the exit of the tunnel Brid was already upright and standing in the centre of the chamber.

Before he could take in his surroundings Brid's voice, full of despair, whispered in the half-light. 'There's nothing here. It's all gone. They've gone.'

In the filtered light Caspar could see that the room was circular. Towards the west, two solid plain pillars blended into the wall. They marked an old entrance into the chamber but it was now bricked up with huge blocks of stone. The smooth stone floor curved upwards into cold, bare walls, and in the centre of the chamber a massive slab of square rock formed an altar. It was almost a complete replica of the one above their heads – except for the hollow on its top surface, a sort of cup-shaped dip. He wondered at its purpose for a few seconds before realizing with distaste that it must be for catching blood. There were some things about his mother's religion that he could never fully embrace.

'There's nothing here.' Hal's voice was indignant. 'Come on, let's get out of here before someone finds us.'

'Sh! Someone might hear us through the grating.' Brid's whisper cracked in her throat and for the first time he thought she was close to tears. 'The Keepers must have thought they would be discovered; they've taken everything and gone. There should be sacraments of worship, daggers, chalices, candles and it's all gone. The cauldron must have been removed before that entrance was bricked up and that must have been years ago by the look of the masonry.' She nodded towards the two pillars. 'It must have been too dangerous to keep it here beneath the cathedral.' She stepped slowly round the room, trying to unravel the riddle of past events. 'But they seem to have kept this as a place of worship until fairly recently. There's not much dust.' She retrieved the stub of a candle and fragments of a chalice that lay broken on the floor. 'My guess is that the Keepers still worshipped here although the cauldron must have been removed to a safer place elsewhere in the city years ago. But now they've gone. Simply gone!' she emphasized.

'Gone. Is that it, then?' Hal asked in scornful disappointment. 'Have we failed?'

'No, we have not!' Brid had lost none of her determination. 'They couldn't just go without leaving some kind of cryptic message for the still faithful followers of the Mother. They would have to leave some sign to tell us where they'd fled to. There has to be a message somewhere.' She clasped the altar, her fingers turning white with the pressure. 'Oh Mother, help me. Do not punish me for allowing the holy waters of that he-God to touch my skin. Do not punish me. You know my heart is true.' There was no sob in her voice but Caspar could see the tears running silently down her cheeks. She slowly raised her arms heavenward and the soft folds of her blue gown slid down to reveal her slender limbs. Incantations formed on her lips and her presence swelled, seeming to fill the room. Her will pressed against the walls. Caspar felt all the energy around him being sucked into her, focused through her body. 'Mother, accept my blood as payment.'

Before Caspar could stop her, she flashed the sword sideways and sliced a great gash into the inside of her arm. The blood was dark and thick and the skin on either side of the severed flesh parted like lips, and her blood flowed freely and unrestrained onto the cool surface of the altar. Hal rushed forward, ripping a piece of cloth from his shirt to stanch the flow but she pushed him away with amazing force for her size. Hal staggered back with dismay tightening his face.

'Brid, stop it. You've cut an artery: you'll die.'

'The Mother will take as much as she wants.' The blood was spurting out in pulses.

Caspar could bear it no longer. 'Well, the Mother is acting

through me!' He strode purposefully towards her only to feel her will reject him. He gritted his teeth and lowered his head to drive through the offence of volition that attacked him. She held him off with her free hand and Caspar thought her grip would crush his forearm, splintering his bones. The focusing of energy and gathering of her will had intensified her strength.

He didn't try to fight back. 'Brid, I'm sure the Mother wants you to stop. She must know you are faithful. You are always telling us that worship is in the heart not in the word. If not for me, for Keridwen and Morrigwen you must stop.'

Her glazed, unfocused eyes burnt through him but gradually the human look returned and she stared at him in comprehension. Suddenly Caspar felt the energy within her subside. It was as if he had been shouldering against a steel door that had suddenly given way. She collapsed in his arms and within seconds the boys had the wound tightly bound, Hal pressing the heel of his palm against the wound to allay the bleeding.

'You shouldn't have tried to stop me.' Brid's voice was faint. 'You weakened my will. The Mother wouldn't have let me die, and if I had, she would have wanted it.'

'But Brid, she allowed me to stop you,' Caspar reassured her. 'Your will is far stronger than mine and she allowed you to weaken and listen to me.'

'There isn't enough blood,' she whispered in despair.

They all looked at the pool of bright red blood that was creeping across the altar. The surface tension held it within its meniscus but it was gradually seeping towards the hollow at one side of the altar. As the excesses flowed away only a thin layer of the treacly liquid coated the table and Caspar noticed how the blood separated in places as if some force was repelling it from the rock. Gradually a pattern began to form, an interlocking pattern of lines. ᚠ ᛋᛈᚻᚦ Caspar realized at once that they were runes but he had no idea what they meant.

Brid sighed with relief. 'So simple, isn't? They've left the message in wax, which repels the blood. The runes are only apparent to anyone that would spill a coloured liquid onto the stone.'

'Which means only someone like you, because no one else would be so crazy as to pour blood all over it,' Hal remarked. There were anxious knots on his brow and he looked at Brid with concern even though he spoke callously. 'Well, what do they say? You'd better tell us quick just in case you pass out or something. Do they tell us where the Egg is?'

The girl shook her head. She was starting to look a little green and Caspar realized that she'd been through an enormous ordeal and her body had only just recovered from her last injuries. 'No, that is Lagu meaning the sacred liquid in the womb of the Mother. The cauldron represents the Mother's womb and so Lagu is the rune adopted by the Keepers. And the other runes merely say south. They've gone south.' Her voice was faltering and Caspar thought she would faint.

'Come on, let's get out of here.' Hal went first into the constricted tunnel, this time with the runesword in his own hand and muttering to himself that he'd never again let a woman touch his precious weapon. 'You never know what they'll do: women are totally unpredictable.'

Brid paused to tear off a strip of cloth from her petticoats and handed it to Caspar. 'Wipe the altar clean. We don't want anyone else following.'

He felt slightly nauseous as the warm liquid seeped through the cloth and moistened his skin. He scrubbed hard at the waxed areas until they blurred and smudged before squeezing into the tunnel after the others. Brid was struggling. Her breath was laboured as she forced her way through the tunnel on her elbows, wriggling like a worm through the ground.

It took only a moment for Hal and Caspar to slide the plinth and its guardian skeleton back into the recess to cover the tunnel, whilst Brid leant against the crypt's central pillar for support. Without pausing to ask her permission, Hal swept her up into his arms and carried her up the steps two at a time, pausing only briefly at the curtain that covered the exit to the north transept. There was still no sign of life in the cathedral. Quickly and unnoticed they slipped out the way they had come. The horses were still tethered by the naked silver birch and Firecracker welcomed them with a soft whicker that fluttered his nostrils.

'Can you ride?' the older youth asked the girl in his softest tones. 'Or am I going to have to carry you again?'

'I can ride,' she smiled back at him.

'Here,' he wiped the crypt's dust from her face and pushed back the loose tendrils of hair, 'that's better. You look like a lady again.'

Caspar brushed himself down and even though he despised himself for worrying about anything else except Brid's strength and the search for the cauldron, his anger with Hal rose foremost in his mind. How dare he play with her emotions like that? Just because he hasn't got the Lady Cybillia to fawn over he has to swoon all over Brid and confuse her again. She said she was going to ignore him and now look at her, eyes melting like butter as she stares up at his face. He forcibly pushed aside his jealous emotions, suddenly deeply concerned for Brid as her head dropped and she started to shiver with shock.

'We can't go back to the palace, not with Brid like that. We'll have to find an inn so that she can rest.'

Hal shook his head. 'Too dangerous. We can't afford to draw any more attention to Brid, not after this morning. It wouldn't take much to stir up suspicion again, and look, that herb she keeps taking is wearing off. Her eyes are dazzling green again and in the state she's in now I doubt her body could take any more poison.'

'I only need some nourishment, some warm milk and I'll be all right in an hour or so. I didn't lose that much blood.' Her teeth chattered.

'We'll go to your mother, Hal,' Caspar decided quickly.

'I don't think that's a good idea.' Hal looked mortified by the notion. 'She's not going to take too well to Brid.'

'I never thought of you as having a mother,' Brid murmured weakly.

'Everyone's got a mother,' Hal snapped as if that put an end to the conversation.

'What's she doing here?' Brid mumbled as she let herself be led by the two youths.

Caspar explained. 'When we first heard word of the Vaalakans, Branwolf sent his step-mother away to the safety of central Belbidia. Elizabetta didn't like being at Torra Alta anyway, not as a dowager. I think she felt too young to be a dowager.'

Hal threw a cloak over Brid's shoulders to conceal her wound before they moved off sedately through the streets, heading for the southern outskirts of the city. Set back off the road, a manor house with a courtyard and stabling provided a home for Lady Elizabetta. It was easily identifiable because of the Torra Altan flag and the crest over the gateway. She had taken her own servants with her and so, as they approached, the two youths were instantly recognized.

'It's Master Hal and Master Spar!' There was a great shout of delight.

'Look how that wild colt's filled out.' The stable lad proudly took Firecracker's reins. 'He's quite an animal.'

Elizabetta appeared on the doorstep with arms open wide. 'Hal, my baby, my little boy.'

Hal flushed bright red and Caspar knew why he hadn't wanted to see his mother with Brid present. She was a stately woman with big healthy bones that made her look powerful rather than cumbersome. The silken dress with bright ribbons and sashes looked totally out of place on her upright body. A wholesome covering of plumpness rounded her cheeks, not enough to make her look fat but just enough to emphasize her smooth feminine features.

'Hal!' She embraced him. 'You've grown, how you've grown. What a fine young man.' She gushed all over him despite his efforts to push her away. 'Ah and little Spar. You haven't grown quite so much I see – but you will, I'm sure,' she added dubiously.

Caspar didn't exactly dislike Elizabetta. She meant him no

personal harm but she was fully aware that he thwarted her ambitions for her only son.

'Mother, this is Brid. She's not well and needs some food and rest.' Hal brushed aside any pretence at formality.

Elizabetta looked the girl up and down suspiciously. 'Keridwen,' she said simply as if that was an explanation in itself. 'I'm not having one of Keridwen's breed in here. All those ribbons and bows and coloured hair does nothing to hide your eyes, girl. None of Keridwen's sort will ever be welcome here.'

'Mother!' Hal exploded.

'Well apart from our young Spar of course,' she added as an afterthought. 'But that girl isn't welcome.'

'Mother, you'll do this for me,' Hal demanded. 'It's terribly important. You have to help us. For me and for Torra Alta.'

'What do *you* care for Torra Alta?' she sniffed. 'It's not mine and it'll never be yours, so what do you care?'

'Mother, it's my home and if Torra Alta falls so will all Belbidia. Do this for me, just for me.'

'I don't need this woman's help.' Brid sat stiffly in her saddle though she still looked wan.

'I know what you are, girl, but don't think I'm frightened by you, anymore than I was of that peasant-girl, Keridwen. Not like all these silly superstitious people here who think you pagans have some sort of supernatural power or some pact with the Devil. You're just a small people with naive and simplistic beliefs.'

Caspar didn't bother to charge hot-headed to his mother's defence or argue with Elizabetta. She was always sharp tongued and arrogant and she had a knack of belittling him even more if he tried to stand up to her. He felt sorry for Hal though, having such a brash mother.

'Mother!' Hal was red in the face with embarrassment and anger. 'I need your help. Will you deny your only son?'

She sighed heavily. 'No, I won't deny my only son,' she agreed. 'I'll let the girl shelter in my house.'

Hal led Brid in by the hand and stood by protectively whilst

325

the servants brought warm milk and some soaked bread. Elizabetta plied her son with questions that he answered fully and truthfully, explaining about Torra Alta, Keridwen and the Vaalakans.

'Good Lord, she's alive, well I never. Well, I suppose I'm pleased for you, Spar, though I've got to say she always made me feel very uncomfortable.'

Brid squeezed Caspar's arm. 'Should Hal be telling this woman everything? She could betray us.'

Caspar shook his head. 'Whatever Elizabetta thinks or feels about us makes no difference. Her only thoughts are for Hal and she'll do nothing to endanger him.'

The middle-aged woman smiled at Caspar. 'We've understood each other well all these years, haven't we, young sir?'

The auburn-haired youth nodded at the woman. She had resented him from the moment he was born because it was he alone who superseded Hal's claim on Torra Alta. Yet she could not fully resent him because of the deep brotherly bond that he shared with her son. She was brash and stiff but she'd never do anything to harm him; Hal would never forgive her.

'Well I never, Keridwen, after all these years. That's an unexpected stitch in the tapestry.'

Colour was returning to Brid's cheeks and she was stirring a potion of ground willow bark and the oval leaves of yellow loosestrife into her milk.

'I hope you know what you're doing, young girl. Herbs can be very dangerous. I never touch them.'

Somehow Brid didn't seem to want to argue with Hal's mother. Caspar was amazed at how politely she spoke to the lady, enduring the insults however veiled or direct. Then he realized that of course, as Hal's mother, Elizabetta could do no wrong. As long as Brid was besotted with Hal, Elizabetta would be beyond reproach. His thoughts produced a sudden pang of guilt: his jealousy was getting the better of him. It was much more likely that Brid simply felt too faint to trouble herself with the dowager.

'I'm sure you're very wise and I thank you for your concern

but I have had extensive training with herbs. The willow bark numbs any pain and helps me sleep and the loosestrife should help stop any more bleeding. And if you really want to know, it's good for nosebleeds too. In a few hours I'll be fine.'

Hal went over to pick Brid up, scooping her into his arms and carried her to a solar at the rear of the manor. Elizabetta snappily sent a serving woman to accompany them. Hal was only away a short time but it was long enough for Elizabetta to interrogate Caspar. 'He's not in love with that girl, is he?'

Caspar shrugged. 'No more than he is with any other. For the moment he probably thinks he is, but she's been weakened by the traumas of the day. Tomorrow she will be strong and defiant and wilful, which he doesn't like, and then he'll wish that Cybillia was still with us. You know Lady Cybillia, Baron Bullback's daughter. We escorted her to Farona. '

Elizabetta smoothed out her skirts, shaking out the ruffles. She always sat with a perfectly straight back. Her dark hair with just a few whispers of grey about the temples was neatly and properly contained in a snood though she carefully rearranged it before reaching for her needle-point. 'Of course I know who Cybillia is but does this elf-girl really have to go with you?'

'Of course she does.'

'I won't have it. Where exactly are you going? How far are you going?' Elizabetta demanded.

'We don't know. We're going south, that's all we know. Brid will have more idea than Hal or I.'

'How could either of you let yourselves be led by a girl, and one of Keridwen's sort at that. He's as bad as Branwolf. He's got no right to be falling in love with her. It has to be stopped.'

'My Lady, I don't think that Hal's affections at the moment are really the important issue here. He's going south to who knows what dangers. Surely you should be more concerned about his safety.'

'Don't belittle me, child. Of course I'm concerned for his safety, but he's nearly a man, and men must face dangers. They must be prepared to fight – that is a glorious thing; but falling in love with a witch from the hills, that can only lead to ignominy.'

Elizabetta spoke with the standard emotions of the people from Torra Alta, voicing all the feelings and attitudes that he'd been brought up to admire and uphold. He supposed that it was wrong of him to expect her attitudes to change just because his had.

'It's Hal's position, Hal's place to fight bravely for his country and I'm very proud of him, but this, this mooning romance with that girl is intolerable. I will have to stop it.'

The younger boy sighed inwardly, torn between loyalty to his uncle and his own desires for Brid. If Elizabetta had her way, then Brid would give up her blind longing for the handsome Hal and leave the way open for him. There again, Brid had already condemned him as too young and it seemed unjust for Elizabetta to interfere with her son's emotions like that. He felt duty-bound to defend his lifelong companion.

'Isn't Hal old enough to make his own mistakes?'

'Nobody ever is,' she said flatly.

Hal returned and, with filial affection, kissed his mother on her forehead before taking a seat by the fire. He looked pleased with himself.

'Hal!'

'Hm?'

'I forbid it.' Elizabetta's voice was firm though she didn't look up from her tapestry.

The youth merely sighed, obviously quite used to disobeying Elizabetta. 'Forbid what, Mother?'

'I forbid you to have anything to do with that witch-girl.'

'You do, do you?' He seemed totally unperturbed by this outburst. 'I suppose Spar's been telling you things. You know he's jealous, don't you?' His olive-green eyes stabbed at his nephew.

Caspar was mortified. How could Hal say something so embarrassing in front of Elizabetta? He also didn't want his uncle to think that he had sided against him behind his back. There was nothing he could say, however, other than shrug away the accusation. 'Elizabetta merely asked whether you're in love with Brid.'

'Yeah, and you've been conspiring to make sure you keep me away from her.'

Elizabetta interceded. 'You should have kept Cybillia along with you. At least her father owns land. She's an only daughter – so I hear; the dowry would be huge –'

'Shut up, Mother; it's none of your business.'

'If anything was ever my business, this is it,' Elizabetta snapped, roughly pushing the needle through the material. The stitches were becoming large and uneven.

'I'm going to bed,' Hal growled at her.

'Well, just remember that I'm sleeping in the next room to Brid,' the dowager retorted.

'Do you really have so low an opinion of me that you think I'd take advantage of a stricken maiden.' Hal was furious.

'No dear, I think the world of you. I want the best for you.'

Hal stormed off and, not wanting to be left alone with Lady Elizabetta, Caspar followed after him. 'Mothers!' Hal exclaimed. 'They're impossible.'

Caspar spent the night worrying about his own mother still trapped in agonizing pain in the river of ice. Tomorrow they'd ride south. The quicker they were on their way the better.

By morning Brid seemed fully recovered. She was dressed in the old breeches and torn buck-skin jacket that she had worn when they first rode out from Torra Alta. Caspar rejoiced at the sight of her vivid green eyes as they sparkled at him. He hadn't realized how much he had missed her usual self and it lifted his spirits. She nodded a polite good morning to the lady of the house and ate ravenously at the breakfast table. It was the first time they had ever seen her eat a full-sized meal. She hardly spoke and it was Hal who first asked where they were going. The message south gave them a direction but it hardly limited their search to a manageable area.

'Haven't you worked it out yet?' Brid asked.

'Worked what out?'

'Rewik's fanaticism had obviously made Farona too dangerous for the Keepers so they've escaped and must have taken the cauldron with them.'

'Yes, and gone south as the message says. Yes, I'd got that bit.' Hal seemed particularly irritated at being put down in front of his mother.

'Farona must have been too dangerous because of the Inquisitors.'

The Inquisitors, of course, Caspar realized as everything instantly fell into place. The King had difficulty trying Brid because his Inquisitors had gone south, to the port of Ildros in Caldea.

'But, Brid, we can't follow the Inquisitors to Ildros,' he explained with horror. 'It'd be too dangerous. They'd find you out.' The younger boy pleaded, but the moment his gaze touched the determined coolness of the Maiden's dazzling green eyes, he knew his protestations were hopeless. Personal danger to Brid meant nothing. Only the quest was important.

'We'll have to be more inventive than we were in Farona, that's all,' she said calmly reaching for another helping of spiced loaf.

Chapter 20

'Do you have to wear that hat?' Caspar waved his hand at the offending article set at a jaunty angle on his uncle's head.

'I thought I looked quite dashing in it,' Hal said unabashed. 'What do you think, Brid? Do I not look quite handsome in it?'

'You look ridiculous,' Brid remarked, without casting her gaze in his direction.

'Hmm, well, since neither of you have any taste it simply proves my point.' He swept the hat off his head and examined it critically before grinning at it. 'It's fine.' He stroked the pheasant tails reverently and replaced it firmly on his head. 'We'll stop the next merchant we pass and see what he has to say. That'll put you both straight.'

A few dark, purplish leaves still clung to the copper beeches that avenued the Quertos Road leading them south-west out of Farona. Beyond the trees and to either side, the black peat soil was combed with deep furrow lines. Gulls flocked over a plough as a team of oxen tilled the ground, turning over the soil and bringing worms to the surface. The three companions were travelling fast, unencumbered by pack-ponies or Cybillia's complaints. It was at least eight days' ride to Northdown on the northern tip of Caldea and another three to Ildros, but Hal insisted they could do the whole journey in a week if they kept the pace up.

Caspar doubted it. Firecracker could make the distance in no time and led the way at a steady canter, but Magpie and Brid's mare would be unable to maintain such a taxing pace.

The landscape was a relentless sweep of arable land, punctuated only by small hamlets, stock-pens for the plough-oxen and the whirring blades of windmills. Vast grain stores, built on stone stilts to keep out the rats and mice, lined the roads and a continual stream of traffic travelled in both directions along the highway. All the heavy grain wagons were rumbling southwards while the brightly coloured spice and cloth wagons rolled northwards, bringing their exotic wares to the capital. Any of the six-wheeled wagons could conceal Gatto and his mercenaries, and the Vaalakans for that matter, but no one could keep up with the pace of the three travellers. Caspar was content to believe that they had happily outrun the enemy.

'Aha! Another merchant caravan,' Hal declared delightedly. 'I'll wager ten gold pieces that they like my hat.'

'They've all liked your hat, Hal. They look at you as if you were completely mad but they all like your hat. You've asked twenty-three merchants so far. Now is any one of them really going to say that they don't like your hat?' Brid reasoned. 'Anyway I haven't got ten gold pieces. I doubt that the entire population of the Boarchase Forest has ten gold pieces.'

'Sir,' Hal called to the approaching merchant. The youth deftly raised his green felt hat as he tossed back his black fringe. 'Sir, we have a dispute and we beg for your arbitration.' He wafted the hat in front of the merchant's astonished face. 'We need your opinion on this splendid article of attire. Is it not the very finest hat you ever saw?'

The merchant looked the youth up and down, paying particular attention to the length of the sword buckled to Hal's saddle.

'A fine specimen indeed, sir.'

'Of course he's going to say that after the way you asked,' Caspar objected. He snatched the hat from his uncle and shook it at the merchant. 'Is this not the most ridiculous hat in the world?'

The merchant studied the boy's noble war-horse and carefully noted the two bows and the quiver.

'Quite absurd.' Hurriedly he signalled for his caravan to

move forward and nodded his head in polite but hasty fare-well.

'His first answer stands,' Hal declared. 'Only his first answer can be accepted because you, nephew, intimidated him into lying. That's five hundred gold pieces you now owe me.'

Brid laughed at the absurdity of the situation. 'Five hundred gold pieces! Hal, you make the rules up as you go along. Even at ten gold pieces for each poor merchant you've victimized it doesn't add up to that and Caspar never agreed to any wager. I'm sick of the hat but if it really matters so much to you, I'll say it suits you perfectly.'

Hal flashed his white teeth at the freckled youth. 'You see, I told you it was a fine hat.'

By the morning of the fifth day the flat plains began to soften into gentle undulating downs and the first orchards of the Barony of Quertos chequered their horizon. Caspar began to get an uneasy feeling that they were being watched; but he reassured himself that nothing could have kept pace with them. The wagons still lumbered slowly along, their spoked wheels grumbling over the pot-holes, dragged by the black-faced oxen swaying to the steady inexorable rhythm of their ambling gait. Nevertheless he could not ignore the prickling sensation at the back of his neck, warning him that something was watching him. Now that Ceowulf's armoured presence was no longer there to reassure them, Caspar felt less confident and more wary of any strangers.

High in the sky, a gerfalcon hovered on the late morning thermals. Any bird could easily keep pace with them and he wondered if it was possible for such creatures to be in the service of the enemy. Several hours later the uneasiness still remained and he unconsciously pressed Firecracker for a faster gait until the others were lagging way behind. Since it was well past noon and the horses obviously needed a rest, he decided it was high time they stopped for a meal.

He dismounted beside a small irrigation pond shaded by a spinney of elms and let Firecracker suck at the still waters while Brid sorted through her saddle-bags for their provisions.

She pushed up her sleeves to cut some slivers of venison off a salted haunch, exposing the gash on her arm. It had healed to an ugly lumpy scar that had knitted unevenly on the inside of her arm. Hal curled his lip up in disgust at the sight. Brid sat between the two boys but perhaps edged fractionally closer to the taller youth. She seemed happier without Cybillia's presence and was certainly more relaxed away from the city, though she gave the occasional anxious glance west toward the apple orchards.

'We're being followed, aren't we?' Caspar asked. 'All morning something's been on our tail. It felt like the birds were watching us. Could they be working for the enemy?'

Brid burst out laughing and then gave the boy a soft despairing smile. 'Birds? They're completely dumb. They've got to be the dumbest of all animals; besides fish that is. No, it's not birds.' She seemed highly amused by the idea as she split an apple in half, examining the pattern of the pips.

'Is it him, then? The person who can see in from the other side of the Druid's Eye?' the boy fretted anxiously.

Brid looked up sharply with sudden worry creeping into her eyes. She leapt to her feet and unbuckled the saddle-bag containing the moonstone. 'No,' she breathed in relief. 'At least I don't think so. I'll dampen it again just in case. But whoever is trying to find us could do so more easily just by asking Elizabetta. You shouldn't have told her.'

'My mother won't betray us,' Hal retorted sharply. 'Besides she has a household of fifty servants; no one could get at her. I'm more worried about Cybillia.'

'We left her with the King,' Caspar reassured his uncle.

'Yes, but with Gatto still on the streets.'

'But Hal, Ceowulf is there; he'll keep an eye on her,' Brid remarked stiffly, as if annoyed by the mention of Cybillia's name. She leant forward and stole a ration of salt-beef from Hal's plate.

'You're eating a lot lately,' he observed.

She winked at him, 'This isn't for me,' and rose to walk in the direction of the orchard.

The horses were shifting uneasily. Firecracker pulled hard against his restraining bridle, making the branch he was tethered to sway viciously back and forth. Caspar worried that his colt was about to snap the wood.

Moments later Brid reappeared with her old shaggy wolf. The animal walked lovingly alongside her, pressing its lean body against her hip and pushing its toothy snout into the curve of her waist. Her hand rested on its neck, kneading the deep layers of mane. Hanging from its mouth were the floppy long legs of a dead hare, which the animal then dropped at the priestess's feet in offering.

The grey she-wolf snarled at the youths to warn them to keep a respectful distance before crouching down to lie by her mistress. There was a bald patch under its neck where the mane no longer grew and a red patch of scar tissue marred the grey skin. Brid examined it carefully.

'Poor old girl. That was the bull, wasn't it? These fools told me about it.' The wolf nuzzled the Maiden, pushing the long snout under her arm, insisting that the girl continue to stroke her head.

'I've missed you,' the priestess sighed, ruffling the mane behind the she-wolf's ears.

'I haven't,' Hal murmured too softly for Brid to hear.

The girl chatted away to the wolf as if the animal understood every word. 'You didn't like the city, did you? Nor me; I don't blame you for staying away.'

Brid tossed the hare at Hal. 'Here, skin this,' she demanded. 'We'll wrap the orb in it. The skin of the sacred hare will bring us more protection from whoever intrudes into the Eye.'

The dark youth indignantly flung the animal at his nephew. 'You do it. I'm not being ordered around by her.'

Caspar sighed and obligingly picked up the hare. It wasn't worth arguing about.

Brid's chestnut mare was decidedly unimpressed by the wolf loping alongside its flank. The horse kicked sideways, lashing out with its heels but the wolf was always too quick, jinking away just out of reach. By moonrise they had reached the isthmus that divided Caldea from the rest of Belbidia. For several miles there had been a growing sense that they were approaching the sea. The air tasted of salt as the breeze in their faces began to freshen and there was a distant roar of breakers crashing against the cliffs. As they rode down towards the narrow causeway, which bridged the lower peninsula of Quertos with the near-island Barony of Caldea, the roar of the sea was swallowed behind a headland.

Once beyond the horizon the air was thick with the heavy, stale smell of rotting seaweed and the mud-flats seeped their distinctive stagnant odour into the atmosphere to blend with the brackish smell of the ocean. There was something very dead about the area. Nothing would grow, nothing at all: the salt had sucked the fertile life from the soil.

'The tide's out,' Brid announced flatly as the first drops of rain moistened her cheeks.

'How can you tell?' the older youth asked scathingly.

'It's obvious, isn't it? The tide is pulled by the moon. I can feel her tugging on me just the same way as she holds sway on Mother Earth. Anyway the mud-flats are all exposed and everything I've ever heard about the isthmus says that at high tide the causeway is so narrow that no more than ten men can ride abreast.' She pointed towards the causeway. 'That's about a mile wide.'

Caspar had always thought that on maps this thread of land looked like an umbilical cord joining Caldea to the mother country. But what struck him now was how the sea had gnawed like some ravenous monster at the cord, as if it wished to sever the bond forever.

'If it's only that narrow how come it always looks much wider on the maps? But we'll take your word for it, Brid, and cross now whilst the tide is out,' Hal decided firmly.

'Do you know how far the causeway stretches, before you reach Caldea?' she asked haughtily, in a manner that made it quite clear that she knew herself. The rain was beginning to sting as the drops were given bite by the wind.

'Yes, it's five leagues. I remember it from the nursery rhyme,'

Caspar told them cheerfully. 'I don't remember it all but each verse ends:

'Old King Peppin led his men across the sea,

Five full leagues along the spit to Caldea.

'I always found it so annoying because Caldea doesn't rhyme with sea, it only looks like it should.'

Hal burst into a fit of laughter, clasping at his stomach and the younger boy sniffed indignantly. 'What's so damn funny?'

'You are. Only you could remember something so utterly childish.'

'Well, at least I know how far it is across; but anyway what's the problem? What does it matter how far it is to Caldea?'

'There's a spring tide. The sun and moon are pulling together. That causeway won't be so sure if the waves are breaking over it,' the girl said simply, raising her voice above the wind.

'Then we'd better go now and stop wasting our time with nursery rhymes.' Hal was becoming frustrated. 'There's no place to shelter and every time we stop it gives the enemy more time to catch up.'

'We won't make it.'

'Fifteen miles in six hours, of course we will.'

'We haven't got six hours,' the girl corrected him. 'The tide turned two hours ago. It's dark, the causeway's slippery, there's no margin for error.'

'Hal, Brid's right,' Caspar tried to argue. 'It's going to mean a full gallop and the horses are tired already.'

'We'll make it. We haven't got time to wait. How many soldiers have died in Torra Alta whilst we've been debating about the tide? We wasted too much time in Farona; it's already the month of Fogmoon. How long do you want to keep Torra Alta on siege rations?' Hal didn't wait for their reply. He turned Magpie's head toward the spit of land and kicked her hard in the belly. She grunted into a slow lumbering canter. As the great horse gathered speed, he vanished into the darkness with only the drumming of the horse's hooves still audible above the rain.

There was nothing else to do but follow. Caspar gave Brid's mare a thwack on the rump to speed her forward while holding Firecracker in check so that he didn't race past the Maiden. The wolf, almost invisible in the darkness, lolloped faithfully alongside, her footsteps silent.

The wind tore at Caspar's face. It tasted of salt, which was crusting his hair and grinding into his cheeks like an abrasive polish. The wind picked up the sand and whipped it into the air, blasting it against his face. He screwed his eyes up to protect them from the elements, cursing Hal for his bullish behaviour. But Brid wasn't always right and being a girl she would naturally be more cautious than either him or Hal. And his uncle was right: they had no time to waste. He couldn't believe there was any danger from the sea. He could only just hear it murmuring on the shore, a strange beast sleeping in the moonlight. The distant waters glistened with the silvery reflections of the slit crescent of the moon, shining through breaks in the scudding clouds. The sea beckoned like a beautiful woman calling him to explore her hidden fruits with promises of warm waters and distant shores.

Hal had slowed to let the other two catch up with him and, three abreast, they galloped across the smooth beach. A central causeway of basalt slabs ran like a spiny backbone across the mud-flats, designed to give a firm surface for wagons during flood tides, but it was easier on the horses' hooves to gallop on the sand and they made good time.

Firecracker was gradually pulling ahead, anxious to make sure he was always a length in front of the other horses. Caspar was aware that he was holding the colt back more and more as the other horses began to gradually slow. The moon was creeping higher into the sky, a thin slit of the crescent dancing on the waters. Suddenly Caspar noticed how the sea seemed much closer. Like a faint drumroll the waves were rushing over the mud-flats, galloping over the plain like a herd of cream horses stampeding towards the causeway. He looked to his right where more encroaching ripples washed in, narrowing the isthmus to half its original width. Ahead the lights of

Northdown, which huddled around Caldea's entrance to the isthmus, sparked into life and filled the freckled youth with a great sense of relief.

'Look!' Hal shouted above the wind. 'There's Caldea; I told you we'd make it.'

The second after he shouted, there was a shriek from Brid's chestnut mare. Caspar whipped his head round to see the horse floundering down on its knees, squealing in terror. Brid was thrown clear and rolled away on the ground, dragging on the reins to get the horse up again. It took a moment for Hal to turn Magpie but in seconds the two boys were rushing to the girl's side.

'Sand-serpents!' she cried. 'They've got her hindleg.'

It was difficult to see in the darkness, but wriggling shapes writhed and squirmed about the horse's hindquarters, plunging and coiling in and out of the sand, worming themselves into loops around the mare's hock. Hal charged in with his blade, chopping indiscriminately at the unnatural beasts squirming through the sand.

The horse squealed and shrieked, a terrifying noise almost like the scream of a maddened human. The other two mounts fled to a quivering distance.

'Do something, Spar, do something,' Hal yelled, furiously slashing with the sword.

Fear gripped Caspar's stomach. Snakes – he panicked – not snakes, anything but snakes. The image of the slithering arms that had silently slid out of the smoke in Cailleach's forest filled his mind. The horror of the green demon with her snake-like servile dryads had inflicted him with an obsessive fear of the creatures. The stupefied youth stared at the mare struggling for her life and at Hal grappling to save her.

'Spar, do something,' Hal pleaded.

Finally the boy seized his courage and plunged into the coiling mass of reptiles to fight alongside his kinsman.

The nose of one last snake burrowed out from the soil and whilst his uncle slashed at the neck Caspar stamped at the long scaly body. His stomach churned in revulsion as he felt the flesh give under the pressure of his boot. The unbound leg of the horse thrust wildly backwards as she kicked like a mule, hindering Hal's efforts to save her. The heel of the hoof nicked him on his shin and he swore with feeling. 'I can't get a clean cut.'

Caspar hacked relentlessly with his heel, feeling the reptilian scales break and bruise beneath the impact. Bile rose in his throat. Of all the creatures it had to be snakes, he shuddered inwardly; I can't bear snakes. The horse was beginning to weaken and, as its thrashing became quieter and more hopeless, Hal was finally able to take an unimpaired cut with the runesword and sliced cleanly through the serpent's body. Instantly the trunk of the beast fell inert and for a moment it looked like nothing more than a dead branch washed onto the beach. Then the headless coil of the serpent suddenly disappeared with a sucking, slurping noise back into the hole. The mud sealed over the top, letting out a thick bubble like simmering porridge before leaving a smooth surface as if nothing had ever been there. The horse's instinct for flight forced it to its feet and for a moment the three companions looked at her in relief.

'She's all right; look, she's putting weight on it.' Brid was gladdened; but it was immediately obvious that the mare was only gingerly touching the ground with her near hindleg.

'She's not severely injured. Nothing that cold water and a few days rest wouldn't heal,' Caspar judged, feeling the mare's leg below the hock. 'But she's not going to gallop.'

'I think the tendon's pulled.' Brid agreed with him. 'But she's going to get too much cold water any minute.'

'Well, we've got to get out of here,' Hal decided. 'Brid, get the packs off her and put them on Cracker. You can ride with me on Magpie, then maybe without a rider, the horse will make it.'

She struggled with the buckles and briskly re-strapped the packs to the back of Caspar's saddle. Hurriedly she delved into her saddle-bag to check on the moonstone and then anxiously snatched up a water canister. 'It's a bit dry,' she explained, pouring the contents of the leather flask over the faintly glowing orb to dampen its powers of sight before carefully rewrapping it in the hare-skin. She hung it around her neck, concealing the orb and the salamander in her clothing. All three of them looked towards the hungry sea whose jaws were closing towards the causeway. They set off again, pushing for a trot but the chestnut mare was stumbling and dragged heavily on the reins.

'She can't do it,' Caspar cried over the sound of the waves. 'She can't take the pace.'

'Well, we'll have to leave her then. We can't all risk being taken by the sea.' There was no indecision in the older youth's voice.

'I can't leave her to drown, Hal. Keep going. I'll catch you up.'

He pulled Firecracker to a halt and the injured mare behind him clumsily stopped short. She was shaking and held her near hindleg off the ground. Caspar looked sorrowfully into her face. 'You're a good old girl and you'd heal fine but you won't make it across the causeway and I won't leave you to drown.' He pulled his dagger out of his belt and, fondling the horse's ears, he felt for the soft point at the base of her skull where the spine joined the head. He carefully placed the point of the blade and brought his other hand up towards the hilt. 'I'm sorry old girl, but it's kinder.' He pulled hard on the dagger, gritting his teeth to make the cut as quick and as painless as he could. The thick hide resisted for a second and the horse threw its head up with her eyes rolling and wild. With a sudden spurt of blood the dagger slid in between the vertebrae and stabbed into the soft tissues of the animal's brain. She fell heavily to the ground, without a squeal or a grunt and lay totally motionless.

Caspar wiped the blade on the clean hide of her flank. 'I'm sorry,' he whispered, not knowing what else to say.

The sea was all around him now, baffling on the shallow, shelving flats, skimming over the land with the drumming noise of wing beats from a vast flock of birds. He leapt onto

Firecracker's back and with his feet not yet in the stirrups, he turned the horse southward, spurring the animal into a full gallop to beat the tide.

He'd never realized before how quickly the tide could come in. He lived in a mountainous region and, although the borders of Torra Alta touched the sea, they rarely visited the bleak, largely uninhabited cliff-lined shore. He couldn't see the others; he hoped they were far ahead and nearing safety.

Pushing his hand further up Firecracker's neck, he gave the horse its head. With the tide so close now, he could see more clearly in the moonlight reflected off the foaming waves and riding at speed became less treacherous. The red mane flew in his face, mingling with his own auburn hair and like a storm of red sand they tore across the flats.

Magpie was just ahead now. The thunder of the great charger's heavy hooves was barely audible above the sound of the waves rushing in. By the time he drew level, the lights of Northdown had become defined windows and lanterns, but the thud of hooves had turned to a splash as the waves broke around the horses' fetlocks. Caspar looked down at the water in horror. The wolf had moved to the right, up onto the higher land of the causeway and the two horses followed her example.

Two hundred yards from the safety of the beach, the waves broke across the land bridge. A ridge of white water formed a seam as the two facing tides collided. The waves crashed, locking together like the butting heads of two ibex males clashing horns in mortal combat. Water sucked and dragged at the horses' hooves and they were forced to slow to a trot, spraying water up in white droplets that caught the moonlight and drenched the riders. The breakers from the battling seas ran through each other and the ripples diverged away leaving a flat plain of water.

The horses were labouring now. Water swirled over their hocks and the wolf was swimming, her long neck straining forward and her mane fanning out as it floated in the waves. The tide was still coming in. Caspar judged that there was only fifty paces to go now, but fifty paces over dry land seemed like a mile across water.

Firecracker's feet dragged through the water and in another moment the waves lapped up under the horse's belly: his jolting movements suddenly changing to a slow floating stride. Caspar felt the stallion surge forward without any jar of hooves on rock; they were swimming. Firecracker's breathing was laboured, the nostrils snorting out brackish water. The shore that had looked so close a moment earlier now seemed to stretch away beyond reach. There were shouts from the beach.

'Hey you! You can make it. Keep coming in; you'll make it. Not far now.'

There were more shouts. A crowd was gathering. 'What are those fools doing? Don't they know it's a spring tide. Main-landers are all fools.'

'Keep coming. Not far now,' the more encouraging of the voices called across the water.

Brid's cloak floated out in a great fan over Magpie's hind-quarters that dipped under the waves. The girl was slowly floating away, slipping off the horse's back where she had been seated behind the saddle. Her body lengthened out, her feet furiously kicking to propel her along whilst her fists closed tightly onto the saddle flaps. A flash of red showed in her hair where the salamander clung to her head, keeping itself out of the water.

The beach was thronging with people now and a host of voices yelled encouragement. Caspar felt warmed by the cheers in contrast to the cold water which bit into his flesh. The leather breeches seemed to be shrinking onto his thighs and his hands were frozen, tight white balls feebly gripping the reins. He didn't know how to encourage Firecracker but believed that, unlike humans, horses instinctively knew how to swim. He had to stay still and not interfere with the roan's efforts; that was the best help he could give.

Suddenly Firecracker surged up with a great powerful kick and the boy realized they'd struck firm ground. Grunting, the stallion pulled himself forward and with great relief Caspar

343

felt the water falling away from him. The weight of his sodden cloak dragged down at his shoulders with the hem still floating in the water, but the beach was shelving rapidly upwards now and they were nearly there. The wolf reached the shore first, shaking herself vigorously, showering the onlookers in seawater, but quickly vanished into the dark of the night. The crowd was still focused on the two floundering horses and the three people struggling ashore. The moment all four of Firecracker's hooves found firm footing the horse leapt forward into a series of bucking strides, storming up the beach to be patted and thumped by the friendly gathering.

'You damn fool,' someone shouted without venom but more with anxious concern. 'You could have drowned.'

'Don't I know it,' the boy replied simply as he slid to the ground. He was drenched and shivering. Magpie heaved herself up onto the beach but Brid was still wading through the water and Caspar rushed to give her a helping hand. She pushed him away and marched straight towards Hal, who had dismounted and was coughing vigorously to clear his lungs.

Brid stopped directly in front of the bedraggled youth, whose black fringe clung to his cheeks. She raised her hand and with a resounding smack belted him viciously across his face. Hal's own gasp of surprise was drowned in the general gasp of the crowd.

He gawped at her speechlessly.

'You stupid pigheaded idiot.' She didn't shout but spat the words in quiet vehemence. 'You just blundered off. Why wouldn't you listen to me?'

The crowd was silent. All eyes focused on Hal, intrigued as they waited for his defensive reply.

'We made it, didn't we? We're here. No one said this was going to be easy, but we're here.'

'My horse isn't. Your stupid hat might have made it, but my horse didn't.'

'No,' Hal agreed, 'you don't seem to be having much luck with horses lately. Well, I suppose it's harder for a girl to keep a galloping horse on its feet.'

Brid hit him again, this time on the other cheek. She ripped his hat off his head and stamped it into the sand.

'Feisty lass,' someone murmured in the crowd.

Hal looked grievously at his mangled hat. 'You can't blame the horse on me. That was the snakes.'

'Snakes! Not again,' said one of the men. 'There seems to be a plague of them since the freak weather in the North has been washing them southwards. We've always got them of course but that and these spring tides just before a new moon make it worse. The sands are lethal now: what'll it be like when there's no moon in a couple of days' time, I dread to think.'

Caspar stood next to his uncle. 'Brid's right, you know, you should have listened to her,' he whispered, leaving the villagers to talk anxiously about the problem of the snakes.

Hal nodded at his nephew, the broad disarming grin that made him impossible to reproach, spreading across his face. His white teeth caught the light of the burning torches. 'I know. I shouldn't have done it, but I'm not going to admit that to her, am I?'

Caspar shrugged his shoulders and let himself be led by the hospitable villagers towards the warmth and welcoming comfort of the Causeway Inn.

'You lads are a couple of fools risking the life of a young girl like that. What's the tearing hurry to get across? This time of year the ferry further along the coast at Dorsmouth is much safer. I know it's off the route from Farona but at least you don't have to dice with the tide. Didn't you lads know about the tide?'

'We didn't realize how fast –' Caspar started.

'I did.' Brid cut him short.

An elderly woman was wrapping a shawl around Brid's shoulders. 'Yes dear, the women always understand the pull of the tides more. Men, despite all their fishing and love of boats, they never quite get the same feel in the blood as we women about the tides.'

'I wouldn't like to see the fishermen hear you say that.' The innkeeper then winked at the two boys. 'We have to let the women have their whims now, don't we?'

'I heard that,' retorted the bustling woman, as she ushered them towards the tavern with warm concern and a companionable hospitality that was rare on mainland Belbidia. These people lived a slower, gentler pace of life and it seemed to make them more disposed to the plight of strangers. The old man, who first spotted them on the beach, started to draw them into the inn. Caspar, however, refused to leave the horses until he had rubbed them down vigorously with handfuls of straw to bring back the circulation and make sure they didn't catch a chill through the night. They couldn't afford to lose another horse, he told himself, still feeling sickened as he remembered dispatching the chestnut mare. Poor, dumb animal. He comforted himself with the thought that it would have been a cruel end to its life to be abandoned to the waves and a slow panicky death by drowning. Caspar shuddered. It could have been all of them if something else had gone wrong. Hal was unforgivably reckless sometimes.

For the first time ever Firecracker looked tired and subdued. Caspar patted the stallion's neck whilst the roan stretched down to nuzzle at some wisps of straw. 'You'll feel better in the morning, Cracker,' he told the colt firmly. 'We all will.'

The yellow light of the inn's lanterns had revealed that the Torra Altans were no ordinary travellers and the atmosphere in the crowd had altered accordingly. There was still the warm natured hospitality but it was tinged with respectful reserve once their status was revealed by the light. The younger village boys were being collared by their mothers and pulled back from curiously examining Hal's sword but they still stared with wide eyes.

'Well, Sir, we'd best get you some dry clothes,' the old man, who appeared to be the innkeeper, announced. Someone had stoked up the fire that had dwindled down for the night and Brid was shivering in front of it, her brown bearskin cloak, typical of Torra Alta, in a sodden heap on the floor.

'Out! All of you!' The older woman took control of the

gathering crowd, opening the door to let the cold sea breeze blow through the room and pointed outside. 'Let's have you all out and give these gentlefolk some peace here. They've been through enough without being pawed to death by all of you. Now out!' The curious villagers reluctantly returned to their beds, leaving the Torra Altans alone with the innkeeper and his wife.

'I'm always last to bed,' the old man explained, talking to fill the silence. 'It comes with running the inn you know. There's always one or two that need a helping hand home.'

'Here,' the woman interrupted her husband. 'You can have these to sleep in whilst your own things dry.' The woman had already taken Brid away to wrap her in warm layers. When the boys were decently dressed, the Maiden returned to the warmth of the fire, smothered in blankets and tripping over the hem of the loaned skirt, which dragged along the ground.

'Now you sit here, dear, till all your hair is fully dried out and I'm going to look in the kitchen and see what I can find for you, poor mite. You look like you haven't eaten in days.' She pinched Brid's gaunt cheeks.

'She's always like that,' Hal said rather tartly, touching his cheek, which was still smarting from Brid's surprisingly sharp blow.

'Well, young sirs.' The innkeeper could no longer restrain his curiosity. 'By your dress you're a long way from home. There's no bearskins to be had in these parts. What on earth drove gentlefolk like yourselves across the isthmus at this time of night?'

Hal took the initiative to improvise a vague explanation. 'There's a war brewing on the northern borders, but you know that,' he said, looking at the nodding face of the innkeeper.

He pulled up a stool and sat to listen eagerly to the tale. 'We're only joined to Belbidia by the isthmus but we're not totally cut off. We get word, especially from the fishermen and the wine merchants.' He nodded at Hal, prompting him to continue.

'We're from the North where the Vaalakan army is massing.'

347

'Torra Alta,' the man said, determinedly displaying his knowledge.

'Hm, Torra Alta.' Hal looked uncertainly at his nephew, raising his eyebrows as if asking for help in their explanation, but he turned thankfully towards the door from the kitchens as it swung open to reveal the old woman carrying a tray laden with bowls of steaming broth.

'Well, here we are. Look what I've found for you.' She offered the broth first to Brid. 'Here, dear, get that inside you. I dare say that it's not such fine fare as you're used to but it's hot and wholesome and there's nothing better to chase away the cruel sea. I've even put a dram of my ginger wine in it. That'll get your blood flowing again.'

Brid thanked her with a smile but didn't get a chance to reassure the innkeeper's wife that her normal victuals were nothing special; the old lady had already turned on her husband.

'Now, Herren, what are you thinking of asking all those questions? Just leave them to rest now while I put warming-pans to their beds. Their business is nought but their own.'

'Your kindness, my lady, we'll never forget it,' Caspar said which brought a red-faced smile to the woman's face.

'He called me lady.' She blushed, showing him a gappy row of teeth framed by her smile.

Herren reluctantly rose to his feet, looking guiltily at his wife. He looked as if he was going to ask them another question but she gave him a quick sharp glance and he clamped his mouth shut. 'What about your hound?' he asked as if the thought had just come to him. 'I didn't see him again.'

'Don't worry,' Brid spoke over the top of her steaming bowl. 'She's a loner and will come back when she's ready.'

The old man moved as if to rise but, after a surreptitious look over his shoulder to check that his wife wasn't still breathing down his neck, he leant forward onto his knees and whispered, 'You folks aren't in trouble, are you?'

'No more than the rest of Belbidia,' Brid answered enigmatically before Hal could say anything of any substance.

Looking at her doubtfully the old man tugged at his beard. 'Well, I'm not one to pry,' he said in obvious untruth, 'but, though we're from Caldea, we're still faithful Belbidians and if you need help, we'll give it of course.'

'A horse?' Hal asked hopefully.

'Mm. I'm sorry about your horse, Miss. Dare say we'll find you another on the morrow. It's the high tides. It's our duty here to clear the causeway of the serpents. We have special terriers for the job but it's not safe at these spring tides. They're big worms, you know, several feet long. We lose a few dogs but we've got some new terriers now, imported all the way from Ophidia, and they'll do the job real well just so soon as the moon changes.'

He collected up the empty bowls and left them stacked precariously on top of one another for his wife to clear up later. 'I'll show you to your rooms. We get lots of travellers here, lots of merchants but it's rare that we get gentry. Would it be rude to ask your titles? But, no, it's not my business.'

'Quite right, it's none of your business, Herren.' The old woman sounded shocked.

Hal laughed, reassuring the innkeeper's wife that they would take no offence. 'I am the brother of the Baron of Torra Alta. Spar here, if he ever lives long enough, will be Baron himself one day. But we're not fond of titles in the North.'

Old Herren raised his eyebrows in fascination, obviously impressed by the rank of his visitors but his wife was less affected.

'Well, young knights of the realm, you'd better get yourselves off to bed now and get strong again after your soaking and gallivanting about in the middle of the night. If you're so important we'd best be keeping you healthy.'

Brid laid a hand on the old woman's arm and squeezed it tightly. 'Thank you,' she said simply and sincerely. 'You've got a good heart.'

Caspar had a peculiar sense that the old woman reminded him of Morrigwen though she was neither so abrupt nor arrogant. They shared the same kindly confidence that came with the selflessness of age.

Caspar didn't wake until the full light of morning had squeezed through the cracks in the shutters and fingers of light had crept across the bed and probed into his eyes. The air was filled with the constant cry of gulls squabbling over the fish offal thrown out by the trawlermen. Brid and Hal were already up though he noticed at once that the young girl still kept his uncle at a stiff distance. He smiled inwardly, hoping that Hal's thoughtless behaviour might finally sway her affections towards him.

'Won't you have some breakfast, sir?' The dumpy old woman offered him a wooden bowl full of gruel.

'Won't be a moment.' Grabbing a steaming, freshly baked roll from the table, he crammed it into his mouth. 'Got to check on my horse,' he spluttered as he dashed out of the door.

He sighed thankfully when he was greeted by Firecracker's clear dancing eyes. The young stallion threw up his head and Caspar noted that one of the stable panels already had a hoof-shaped chunk missing and was swinging loosely from a nail. Firecracker was his old self again; there was no doubt about that. More relaxed, Caspar returned to the inn to enjoy the rest of his breakfast.

'Herren's out looking for a mount for you.' The old woman was sitting on a stool, her broad hips spilling out over the seat. 'He won't be long. They've brought the first catch home so there's mackerel grilling. You'll want some of course.' The woman seemed to take great pleasure in nourishing the young-sters and Caspar imagined her in her younger days plying liberal quantities of nourishment to huge numbers of healthy offspring. He nodded gratefully, and was gratified when she delivered the largest of the fish onto his plate and gave Hal a slightly smaller one. Hal looked slighted.

'Well, he needs it more than you do.' The old woman

seemed to instinctively understand the rivalries of young males as if she'd had to arbitrate in constant family squabbles with her own growing lads. Brid refused the fish, which didn't surprise anyone.

Herren returned while they were still eating. 'It's not much,' he apologized, 'not compared to your magnificent chargers but he's got four legs I suppose.'

Brid looked the dappled cart-horse up and down and examined the rough, coarsely-spined saddle. She gave the man a smile of such feminine charm and disarming beauty that he blushed. 'He's perfect, Herren. Hal will be very comfortable on him.'

'I'm riding Magpie!' the black-haired youth replied firmly.

'It's your fault that the mare was lost, so you can take the cart-horse.'

Caspar pressed his mouth down into the collar of his cloak, which had dried out overnight, trying to hide his smile.

Hal had too much dignity to squabble publicly with a girl, especially since Brid was particularly difficult to better in an argument. He turned to their hosts instead.

'Now pray, let me settle with you. What is your charge for bed and board and what's the charge for the horse?'

'Nothing,' the innkeeper replied flatly.

'Don't be stubborn,' Hal insisted. 'We have money enough. Be a good man, Herren, and tell me how much?'

'The food and board's nothing. We'd have let anyone stay at the inn if they'd been in trouble on the causeway and the horse . . . Well, let's say that we're doing our own little bit for Belbidia – and proud to do so. Just bring him back on your way home.'

Meandering south out of the village the road was lined by flint stone walls. In its sleepy uncommitted way the road wound along the lower contours of the valleys, drawing them into the dales of Caldea. 'I feel bad not paying them,' Hal commented. 'It feels unlucky.'

'Don't say you're getting superstitious, Hal,' the younger boy laughed. 'And by the way that horse suits you. He makes a fine war-horse for you.'

The dappled cart-horse waggled its long ears to flick away an annoying fly and Hal slumped sulkily on its dippy back.

Chapter 21

May woke early. The silence disturbed her. Through the stillness she sensed the silent, hungry desire of the enemy encamped in the canyon.

'Pip,' she whispered.

He groaned and stirred.

'I can't sleep.'

'Nor I. It's nearly dawn.'

They crawled into the recessed arrow-slit and stared out into the indigo night until dawn whispered through the clear air and breathed over the tips of the jagged mountains. Slowly the sunlight slipped into the winter-cloaked valleys, the drape of white snow softening the contours of the mountains and castle walls. They hadn't seen the sun for days but now dawn broke with the vivid clarity of frost: the storm had passed.

Three short blasts on the bugle summoned the men to their posts. May was no longer startled. Every morning the ceremony was regular and undramatic as the men strung their bows, sorted their arrows and stood vigilantly at their posts. They watched and waited while the Vaalakans gathered in numbers, the smell of roasting reindeer meat wafting up to the heights of the Tor. The enemy had driven their herds with them across the barren Dragon Scorch, she had been told. The smell of the cooking meat was a regular topic of conversation in the keep now that hunger gripped their stomachs and sharpened their minds. The Vaalakans gathered their strength, biding their time and waiting for the right opportunity to attack, while the air within the castle was turgid with silent anticipation.

May and Pip slid from the recess and slouched towards their mother, who was dividing out her family's rations for the day. A few of the subdued women and children gathered to their meagre breakfast around the central table in the lower keep. 'They're just going to sit and starve us out,' Pip complained as he munched on a crust of bread and looked hungrily around for some more. Elaine pushed her plate towards the young boy and his eyes widened in delight at the prospect of an extra ration of salted beef. He ate noisily and the red-haired woman gave him a wan smile.

May's own hunger gnawed persistently at her stomach, like some rabid wolf tearing at her insides, but she refused to complain, otherwise her mother would sacrifice the very last of her own food and May couldn't have that.

Elaine pressed a hunk of loaf into her hand. 'There, my child, have that. You'll feel better.'

The girl stubbornly shook her head. 'No, you have it; it's yours.'

'Oh no, I've eaten earlier; I'm not hungry at all. You must have this.'

May knew her mother was lying. 'No, Ma, I'm not hungry either. You *must* eat it.' Her mother was small and light-boned but had never been spare. Now her face was drawn and narrow where the healthy plumpness was beginning to fade. 'Can't the rest of Belbidia send in reinforcements?' May asked.

All the other women who huddled around the table frowned at her and she felt guilty for raising the idea.

'No, my dear,' the older woman, Maud, explained without looking up from her loom. 'Not until someone designs a horse and cart that can fly. The road up is on the north face of the Tor, you take a look through one of those windows and tell me what you can see.'

May didn't need to look; she knew the enemy smothered the road and held a death-grip on the only lifeline Torra Alta had with the rest of Belbidia. Shamefully she hung her head and contemplated the meagre crust and strip of withered-looking beef before her.

Elaine looked anxiously at her children and then sternly pressed her lips together. 'This will never do. Off with you, Pip.'

'But Ma!'

'I'm tired of hearing that, young lad.'

The old woman sitting at her loom looked up and smiled at the young boy. 'Now everyone knows that all the best archers in the garrison have to serve their apprenticeship down in the well-room.'

'Really?!' Pip's eyes widened in excitement.

'Yes, really,' Maud nodded with an inscrutable smile at the young boy. He scampered from the room without another word and the woman laughed good-naturedly. 'Lads don't need food to live off; they just need dreams.'

Elaine patted her hand gratefully and then turned to her daughter. 'I'm off to help in the kitchens. You'd better get back to Morrigwen and see if you can't get her to eat today. She seems to respond better to you than anyone else and unless we get her to eat something . . .' Elaine's worry lines had deepened over the past few days. She looked sadly towards the door of the solar that led off from the lower keep and left her words hanging in the air.

Maud looked back at her loom. 'It's almost as if the Vaalakans are waiting for her to die.'

The other women all turned on her with shock startling their eyes.

May stoked up the fire in Morrigwen's solar and then peered into the Crone's glazed eyes. She was lying so still, a deathly blue-grey tinge to her skin. May's heart thumped but she nearly leapt out of her skin as the hag's skeletal hands suddenly snatched at her wrist. 'Brid, Brid, my beloved you've come back.'

May stroked her forehead. 'No, it's still only me, May.'

Morrigwen blinked and peered at the child crouched beside her. 'Merrymoon?' She sounded surprised and then snapped angrily, 'But where's Brid? I told you to fetch her. I need her herb-lore. You must fetch her, now.' The Crone's grip tightened fiercely, leaving white imprints in May's arm.

'I can't, she's gone to Farona,' May soothed. She was no longer upset by Morrigwen's outbursts but feared increasingly for her health. Her mother had ground up the last of the foxleaf yesterday and now there was nothing left to cure the old woman with from the slow, wasting poison.

'Keridwen then. I saw her yesterday; I know I saw her.'

'No, that was my mother Elaine,' the child whispered sadly. Since Morrigwen had been stricken ill, Elaine had decided it was best to keep away. She seemed to induce a near hysteria in the old woman since Morrigwen refused to believe she wasn't Keridwen.

'Don't argue with me, girl.'

May took a deep breath and stroked the Crone's furrowed brow. Fistfuls of her long silvery hair shed from her shrunken scalp and lay in a tangled web on her pillow. May dabbed at her stinging eyes and fought back her tears. Though the old woman was crotchety and sharp she had come to love her like a grandmother. She despaired at the clammy grey skin and the deeply contoured outline of her cheekbones that emphasized her sunken eyes sagging in blue hollows. She looked worse every day; her strength was failing. May cleared her throat and patted the woman's hands.

'Morrigwen, listen to me. I know everything seems confusing –'

'Don't you dare patronize me, child.'

'No, Morrigwen no. Please listen to me. You've been poisoned. It's the Vaalakan fang-nettle in your veins,' the girl tried to explain.

'Vaalakan fang-nettle! Fang-nettle! You're mad, child. No one would find fang-nettle in these parts.'

Each morning, Morrigwen raved. She was at her most confused on waking but her senses seemed to gradually return as the child explained again what was happening to her.

'Fang-nettle? I'm poisoned?' Morrigwen's hands slumped down and she stared blankly at the dark ceiling. 'I can't believe it; the weed's too rare. You'd have to know so much of herbs.'

Her breathing was fast and rapid. Slowly it steadied but she spoke in wheezy snatches. 'Bladderdock and foxleaf. I need bladderdock and foxleaf.'

May nodded. 'I know. You told me yesterday.'

'I did?'

'There's plenty of bladderdock in the broth, but we could only find a tiny sprig of foxleaf and we've given some of that to Catrik too of course. He seems to have the same symptoms as you. We searched the kitchens and asked every soul in the castle but that's all we've got and of course we can't get any more now.' She tossed her head northward, vaguely indicating the besieging Vaalakans. 'But I've kept the broth warm by the fire. You must have what we've got anyway.' May propped the woman up and patiently fed her small spoonfuls of the remedy.

Morrigwen coughed and spluttered, liquid dribbling from the edge of her mouth. She swallowed painfully, but the effort of eating quickly exhausted her before she had taken more than four or five mouthfuls. She slumped back, her eyelids sagging heavily onto the bruised skin that underlined her sunken eyes.

'You must paint the runes of healing across my chest. I'm not strong enough to eat without them.'

'Yes, Morrigwen, you've told me before, but I don't know them. You *have* to try and eat.'

'Bring me some woad and a quill. The poison is too deep in my veins for the herbs. We need a stronger magic.'

May sighed. The quill and the crushed stems of woad with their deep blue stain were already by the bed. They had tried this the previous day but Morrigwen's hands were too shaky and her eyesight too dim. The effort and frustration of trying to cast the runespells only weakened her more.

The young girl loosened the Crone's gown and winced at the sight of her hollow ribcage protruding through the gossamer layer of skin. The Crone's hand shook as she scrawled a spidery line of blue woad across her skin. Morrigwen let her hand fall away in disgust. She lay broodily silent for several minutes.

'I've tried this before, haven't I?' she sighed bitterly at last. 'Why didn't you tell me?'

'Because you never believe me,' May retorted honestly. 'You don't remember until you've been awake for a while. Now lie back and rest and we'll try some more broth in a few minutes. It's the best we can do. And you have to try, Morrigwen.'

The old Crone sagged back in resignation while May rose to tidy the bed and make her charge as comfortable as possible. 'Catrik. Why didn't I recognize it earlier?' Morrigwen wheezed. 'Not even Brid suspected; but then Vaalakan fang-nettle, it's not common.'

'Ma said nobody believed her at first as none had heard of it, but no one understands why someone would want to poison you. They think it had something to do with Curate Dunnock.'

Morrigwen's ruffled breathing rasped through the solar as May tucked the blankets round her. Suddenly she snorted and snuffled, blinking her eyes open. 'You are looking after Catrik, aren't you?'

'Father Gwion watches him hourly,' May reassured her. 'But the old man is very weak.'

'Old and weak but not so old as I,' Morrigwen muttered. 'Give me that soup, child. I must get well.' Morrigwen stoically tried to swallow the curative brew but again it made her cough violently. A trickle of blood seeped from the corner of her mouth.

'We just have to keep trying,' May encouraged her. 'Little and often.'

'You're a blessed child, Merrymoon,' the Crone muttered as she sagged into her pillow and closed her eyes against the pain of the thin light creeping through the shutters. 'But we need Brid. She must return to me. But she doesn't – she doesn't even –' Her breathing was light and quick and her words barely escaped from her dry cracked lips. 'She doesn't reach out to me anymore.' Her body went limp as sleep dragged her down into its dreamy realm.

May sat by her, clutching her hand and praying she would live. She passed the long sad hours chattering to the woman, retelling the stories that Morrigwen had told her, hoping that the sound of a soothing voice would bring a calm peace to her dreams and keep her mind closer to life. May found her own eyelids gradually dragging as the soporific heat from the room drugged her senses.

A shattering blast from a bugle horn burst the peace open and she fled from the Crone's bedside to unlatch a shutter and peer out into the courtyard. The bloated red face of the bugler in the watch tower strained as his lungs produced an urgent shriek from his horn; long haunting howls that jangled the nerves.

Slowed by the deep snow dragging round their calves, the men of the garrison scurried to the east wall where the Captain stood on a parapet. With sword drawn he slashed at a black shape that grappled for a purchase on top of the wall. May's mind swarmed with impossibilities. The wall was sheer; no one could reach its foundations because of the seething winter waters of the Silversalmon boiling around the foot of the Tor, let alone climb it. The approach was impossible. With big strides the Baron covered the courtyard, his thick cloak swept back off his shoulders. He leapt up beside his captain.

'Oil, bring the oil drums. You men,' he thrust his fingers at five men running towards him. 'Wheel that far trebuchet round and load it with slingshot. Get the oil vats. The walls are crawling with them.'

May shrank back from the whistling sound of arrows hailing down on the enemy. Fiendish inhuman shrieks pierced the chill air and she felt her heart pumping in her throat.

'Come away, child,' Morrigwen's trembling voice pleaded. 'Put the shutter back.'

May couldn't drag her eyes away from the horror below. A dark snub-nosed face growled over the parapet, its long claw-like arms slashing at the archers around it. A gurgling roar burst from its throat as it sank its claws into the neck of an archer. It finally fell with a dozen arrows sticking into its leathery hog-haired back. Five other beasts swarmed over the walls, their yellow upturned fangs drooling gluey saliva.

'Merrymoon, close the shutters,' Morrigwen ordered in sharp rasping breaths.

May slowly turned to look at the blanched face of her patient straining anxiously to raise her head.

'Trolls, Morrigwen. Trolls.'

The Crone sank back in resigned sadness. 'Aberrations. Unnatural creatures. The runespells are weak against creatures not bound by the natural laws.'

A pained human scream snapped May round and she stared out in horror at the scene below as a short-legged troll crouched over an archer, shredding his chest with its claws. Long strands of tendon and gut hung in tatters from its fangs. The Baron raised his sword and in one sweep severed the creature's head. The blood pumping out was horribly red as it seeped into the virgin snow.

As the Captain braced himself to face another troll advancing over the east wall, Lord Branwolf looked urgently around him, bellowing out clear orders. 'Get to the walls.'

The men had instinctively started to charge at the half-dozen trolls already in the courtyard but Branwolf's bellowing tones brought them to a halt. Quickly he assigned only a score of men, with swords and short bows, to round up the beasts whilst redirecting the rest of them to the walls. 'Stop any more from breaching the battlements,' he thundered. 'And get the oil over here. Why isn't it ready?'

Once the disciplined men were strategically in place, the Baron put both hands to the hilt of his sword. With the bloodlust of battle raging in his throat, he hacked at the nearest troll, which was bearing down on the Captain.

The men nobly wielding the oil vats suffered the worst losses. Though the Baron stood beside them, hacking viciously with his sword another three men were quickly felled by the heavy blow from a troll's claw slashing across their throats. May covered her eyes, but she couldn't blank out the terrible screams of pain and fear. Instantly she thought of her father and wondered whether he too had suffered such agony at his death.

The battle was bloody. Eight trolls lay heaped in the centre of the courtyard and as many men. The Baron looked sorrowfully into their faces as the last screams echoed up from below the east walls. A heat haze shimmered above the oil vats, which had disgorged their seething brew onto the fiendish animals. Archers leant out over the walls, picking off the last of the trolls as they fled with lolloping strides, swinging and leaping like great apes from one jagged rock to the other.

'Save your arrows men. Once they are out of range save your arrows,' the Captain reminded them, wiping his bloodied sword on the roach back of a dead troll. 'See to the wounded. Get them into the lower keep. Sling these trolls over the walls; their flesh is too diseased to even feed to the dogs. Let's get to work men. The day is not over yet.'

The matter-of-fact tone to his voice seemed to rally the men. Never before had they suffered losses within their own walls and the white shock showed on their faces. Branwolf sprang up onto the walls.

'This is war men. War means death and we cannot hide from it. Nor must we let it press the cold chill of fear into our hearts. These men died to save the castle and we fail them if our spirit dies with them. Now to work. Follow your Captain. Torra Alta will not fall. We have had losses but the day is ours.'

'The day is ours!' A weak cheer came from the rear of the subdued archers.

'Are we going to let these Vaalakan curs think we can be daunted by a few dumb beasts?'

'Never!' The cry was more vehement.

'Then up onto the walls, men, and show those northern dogs what we are made of.'

The soldiers lined the battlements, raised their bows into the air and filled their lungs. A thousand men hurled their voices at the sky. 'The day is ours. Torra Alta will stand. Torra Alta! Torra Alta!'

May tumbled from the window sill and found her legs buckled under her as she stumbled towards Morrigwen's bedside. Sobs shook her shoulders as she fell against the old woman. 'The day is ours,' she wept. 'The day is ours, but I saw them die.' She felt sick with fear and sorrow.

'Weep, child, weep.'

May quietly raised her head as she heard the thin cracking voice of the hag whisper out from her spluttering lungs. She dried her eyes and took deep even breaths to steady herself. 'Lord Branwolf is right. We must be strong. You must eat some soup or we will lose you too.'

Morrigwen flinched away from the spoon as the child pressed it towards her lips.

'Later, later, Merrymoon, I promise. But first go to Branwolf. Tell him he must sweep away the snow from the heartstone. The Runes of War are smothered in Vaal-Peor's snow.'

'Now?' May feared to interrupt the Baron at such a time.

Morrigwen nodded feebly. Her eyes were closed and her voice was an urgent whisper. 'Do as I say.'

As evening drew to a close, the flames of the funeral pyre leaped high towards the top turrets and Branwolf rallied the whole castle to offer their respects. May clung to her mother's skirts and felt a strange hope as the heat from the pyre drove away the chill frosts from the air. It was as if even after death the brave men of Torra Alta fought on against the evil Vaal-Peor. The circular slab of rock set at the very centre of the courtyard was now swept clear. The light from the funeral flames played over the surface of the central jewel and flickered deep in the red of its heart.

May frowned at the runes. The long evening shadows crawling over the rock defined the etched characters, throwing the angular sigils into vivid relief. She felt stronger and gladdened by their sight. Morrigwen was right. The runes must be kept clear from the snow. She could feel their throbbing energy steel the walls and gird her heart.

Baron Branwolf muttered a few words of farewell to the dead soldiers and then turned to face his men.

'War is ever a time of hardships: the pain of hunger, the pain of death, the constant threat of death gnawing at our hearts. Though the storerooms are full, you will be hungry. This you can bear because you know that it is better to be on scant rations now than to have nothing to sustain us in the months to come. Our hearts bleed for the savage loss of our comrades, who laid down their lives. But we know they died to save us all and we will gladden our hearts with ballads of their bravery and their names will live on. But today I must burden you with one more sorry hardship and I can find little solace that will soften this cruel blow.'

An expectant hush lay heavily over the crowd like a cloying fog.

'My friend, my oldest friend, has today lost his own private battle for survival. Catrik is dead.'

The bell for evensong tolled out through the canyon. A handful of younger men marched towards the chapel while the rest turned west to face the setting sun as the ancient deity slid behind the peaks of the Yellow Mountains. The sheer slopes and ragged cliffs were transformed into rivers of molten gold, cascading from the peaks to flood into the valleys as the deep scarlet of the dying sun bled out over the land.

May ran from the courtyard. Gasping back sobs, she flung open the door to Morrigwen's chamber and wrapped her arms around the hag's frail neck. Catrik had lost the battle against the poison. Catrik was a large man not nearly as old or frail as this woman. The child trembled with fear for Morrigwen's life.

'Morrigwen, wake up; you must take your medicine. If I've got to force it down your throat you must take it. Catrik is dead. The fang-nettle has eaten him up from within. Morrigwen, wake up.'

Chapter 22

Brid rode on ahead, shunning the two boys. She looked even smaller perched on the seventeen hands of the piebald war-horse, like a child, a young child. Her heels hardly reached below the saddle yet she controlled the great war-horse with as much ease as Hal, giving Magpie a long loose rein and guiding her with sensitive touches of her calves.

'Who does she think she is?' Hal muttered.

'She's a high-priestess,' Caspar replied simply. 'It means more than owning land or being a princess or a baroness. She's One of the Three and it means more than anything.'

'Humph! She's just stubborn and spoilt. She's taken my horse.'

'Well, you let her,' Caspar retorted, rather enjoying Hal's predicament.

'It would have been childish to squabble,' he shrugged. 'Oh get up, horse.' The animal had stretched its neck down again and was taking a greedy swipe at some dry, seeded grass that grew in patches along the road side. The round-bellied cart-horse ignored his protestations and ripped and munched at the shoots whilst Hal hauled at the animal's hard mouth. 'How do they ever get anything done here if they have animals like this?' Finally in desperation, he drew his sword and with the flat of the blade smacked the horse hard across the rump. Startled, its head shot up and the beast lumbered into action, trotting with heavy cumbersome strides alongside Firecracker.

When Brid reached the brow of the next gently curving hill beside a low-walled vineyard, she stood high in her saddle

364

and scanned the land around as if searching for something. She gave out a soft tuneful whistle and unexpectedly the wolf hopped over the wall, wagging her tail and tilting her head sideways in an obsequious greeting. Brid laughed and rode on with the wolf trotting alongside Magpie's hocks. The massive war-horse was totally unperturbed by the wolf as if her schooling had removed all normal sense of fear from the animal.

They climbed steadily up through chalky downs. The soil was thin and the white bones of the Mother showed starkly through the rough cladding of sparse grass. The steeper slopes were neatly laid out with row upon row of orderly vines trained onto trellises. The harvest was over and the plants were pruned back to stumpy brown stems. The valleys were clogged with brambles and the only grazing ground was given over to goats and the occasional flock of sheep on the better pastures. Caspar wondered at the striking differences between Caldea and mainland Belbidia.

The road led them due south towards Tartra, the home of Baron Cadros. The freckled youth was reminded of Ceowulf and how he had fled his father's home to wield his sword in foreign wars. On the second day after leaving Northdown they came to a fork in the road and chose the right-hand road that cut through the downs towards Ildros. At the point where the Tartra and Ildros roads met, the way was overshadowed by a ring of oak trees crowning the oval mound of a hillock.

'An ancient barrow. I would guess it holds the bones of an old king of Caldea from before Belbidia conquered the peninsula.' Brid pointed delightedly at the trees. 'And look!' She slid from the saddle, landing lightly from the long drop off Magpie's back, and brushed aside a bramble to expose the hairy heart-shaped leaves of a herb growing in the cover of the bush. 'Hedge woundwort; I've been looking for some of this for ages.' Brid nipped several sprigs off the plant and dropped them into her leather scrip.

By noon of the following day they had crossed the plateau of central Caldea and were winding down towards the sea.

There were few trees on the peninsula and the dark shades of a yew forest ahead made a welcome change from the vineyards and bramble covered downs.

'They probably planted them so they had wood for bows,' Hal suggested.

'I think they're older than that,' the Maiden contradicted. 'I think they've been there since the dragons roamed across the northern countries of the Caballan Sea.'

'You always have to try and prove that you know more about everything,' Hal complained, slouching on the cart-horse's back. Evidently, he hadn't forgiven her for the demise of his hat.

'I can't help it if your education is lacking,' she teased.

Hal laughed good-naturedly, instantly replacing his pout with a wide grin. 'Spar, what are we going to do with this shrew?'

It was not until they rode past the yew forest and over a hill laid out with withered vines, still untrimmed after the autumn harvest, that they got their first glance of the western ocean. The far horizon was crowned by the twin peaks of the Hespera Islands, rising out of a dark sea oppressed beneath a threatening mantle of grey clouds. Caspar felt the first light drops of rain touch his cheek. Brid drew the cowl of her cloak down to protect her face and the youth was aware of a sudden dampening of their spirits. To the north, the downs stretched away towards a headland and below them the port of Ildros nestled against the northern banks of an estuary.

'Remember to keep your eyes down, Brid. The Inquisitors could be all over Ildros,' Hal warned.

'I hadn't forgotten,' she replied quietly. 'We need to do a lot more than we did in Farona. Now two learned young nobleman brought up in the correct teachings of the New Faith like yourselves should be able to tell me what the saint of this place is?'

Caspar thought for a moment. 'What did Ceowulf say?'

'St Wulfstan?' Hal suggested.

The auburn-haired youth shook his head. 'No. Oh, what

was it?' He snapped his fingers irritably and finally brightened, 'St Anne, patron saint of cripples.'

'Perfect!' Brid explained. 'You can be escorting your young kinswoman to the shrine of St Anne where we'll pray for a cure.'

'A cure for what?'

'For my blindness and my deformities of course. Let's move off the road to the barrows. This will take some time.'

They let the horses graze as Brid chewed on some willow bark to deaden the pain and scrolled chips of crampbark to prevent her muscles from going into spasm. While waiting for the medicines to take effect, she sent the two youths off in search of cobwebs.

'Cobwebs seem to be everywhere until you actually look for them,' Hal muttered. 'Why couldn't she go and search for them herself.' It was not until they strayed as far as a stream, winding through the split roots of an elder, that they found any webs.

Hal offered them to the young Maiden who rested against the grassy bank of one of the barrows. 'And just when I thought you were beginning to look quite beautiful again.'

Brid threw him a brief glance – which Caspar thought veiled a degree of hurt – and said quite sharply, 'Unfortunately I need your help. I hope you are up to the task.'

The dark youth sniffed haughtily. 'We're up to anything.'

She raised an eyebrow in challenge but Hal ignored her. 'Right, that rock,' she pointed. 'I want that up against the inside of my ankle. Spar, you'd better hold it firmly in place. Don't let it move. Hal, you hold my ankle. You're going to twist it sharply downwards using the rock as a fulcrum.'

She kicked off her boot and arranged herself, gripping fiercely onto the tufts of grass that pushed up between her fingertips.

'No, stop. You can't,' Caspar protested.

Hal ignored him and grasped the slender delicate ankle in his hands, taking a deep breath. Brid screwed up her eyes in anticipation of the pain. 'I can't. I just can't do it, not to a girl.'

'You said you could do anything.'

'Yes, but, Brid . . .'

'The better the disguise the less chance I'll have of being burnt. If it's all the same to you I really don't want to get burnt and since everyone knows witches are supposed to be beautiful, we'll have to do something to make sure I'm not. Now don't go squeamish on me; you've got to do it.'

'I'm not squeamish. It's just you're a girl.'

'You're a coward!'

There was a horrible tearing noise and a pop as the ankle suddenly cracked sideways. The priestess's slender body snapped rigid with pain. The colour from her cheeks faded as if a cloud had swept across the face of the sun and she clutched her hands towards her face, her fingers in spasms of pain.

'Oh, Brid I'm sorry, I'm sorry,' Hal stepped back in horror. 'I really didn't want to hurt you.'

It was some moments before the girl could speak. She gasped in sharp breaths and reached out a trembling hand. 'You did what you had to do.' She scrabbled for her scrip and searched out more willow bark. 'Oh Mother, I'd forgotten how painful this is.'

'Will it keep on hurting?' Caspar asked anxiously. He tried to avoid looking at the twisted leg but the skin, rippled and twisted round the joint, and the nodular ends of her dislocated shin bone held all his attention. Her foot dangled at an impossible angle, pointing inwards directly towards her other leg.

She nodded between gritted teeth. 'Until we can get it straight again. Now let's have that cobweb.' She plaited the strands of gossamer together until she had finally moulded them into two flat disks about the size of a groat. She then unwrapped a knuckle of beef from its muslin covering and sliced off two very thin slivers of fat. She pressed the translucent slithers of fat into the cobweb, making each disk look white and gelatinous. Peeling back her eyelid, she patted the congealed mess in place over her pupil and iris. Tears immediately sprang up and streamed down her face; she blinked furiously. 'Now for the other one,' she muttered, bravely swallowing hard and stabbed at her other eye with the pad of cobweb. She kept her head down, rocking gently back and forth, nursing the pain for several minutes and then looked up towards the two youths. 'There,' her voice croaked slightly and she coughed to clear her throat. 'What do you think to that?'

Caspar looked into two white eyes glazed by the cobweb and fat. They were slightly raised and lumpy across the centre and looked utterly revolting. He thought he would gag. Hal flinched and looked away.

'Can you see? Does that hurt too?' Caspar's uncertain voice was thin with distress. Brid looked far too delicate to withstand such pain.

'Almost and yes, definitely,' she said a trifle acidly. 'It's like having two splinters and a bale of nettles in your eyes at the same time. I guess it keeps my mind off my ankle though,' she added sardonically. 'It's like looking through a haze. I can see light and outlines but not much detail. You'll have to take care of me. One of you get my dress for me. I'll put it on over the top of my riding gear once I remove all those silly petticoats. A dress will draw less attention. And I'll have to go barefoot. I can't wear those high heels or my riding boots now.'

'Don't be silly. You'll look a fright,' Hal argued, slicing the heels off her sandals and strapping them to her feet. He grimaced as he touched her disfigured ankle. 'And you'll have to ride the cart-horse. A respectable Belbidian lady would never be seen on a war-horse like Magpie any more than go barefoot.' He threw her firmly up onto the long-eared beast, though he apologized profusely as she caught her dislocated ankle against the stirrup irons.

There was a sweat on Brid's brow as she struggled to fight off the pain. Caspar's heart bled for her. He couldn't bear to look at her in this state, not because she appeared ugly with her grotesque eyes and deformed ankle, but because he couldn't stand to see her suffering. It seemed so unfair that she, a girl, should have to withstand these tortures while he and Hal rode around freely. Surely a man was better able to withstand such pain?

Ahead of them lay Ildros. In comparison to the dark granite of Farona's stiff stately buildings, Ildros shone with a carefree brightness. Every house was daubed in white paint, the squat dwellings umbrellaed by warm peach roofs of terracotta tiles. There seemed to be no pattern or central focus to the streets. The houses, some stepped in terraces and some huddled together around the estuary, were like a disorderly crowd gathering for a fair. They contrasted with the neat rows of Farona, which had reminded the whimsical Caspar of a ranked audience assembled for a pageant. The warm colours and carefree disorder of the town did much to raise their spirits, though they kept constantly alert for any sign of troops bearing the King's colours.

As they reached the outlying houses of the settlement, Caspar was no longer surprised by the lack of city guards to challenge them, putting it down to Belbidia's general air of complacency. With no protective wall or moat, the town boundary was merely marked by a decreasing number of chickens and small speckled-back pigs, scratching in the fenced yards of small-holdings. The animals seemed excessively alarmed by their approach. Caspar wondered at first whether they weren't scared by the hem of Firecracker's caparison fluttering in the breeze. Then he caught a fleeting glimpse of two grey ears lurking in the shadow of the deep gutter, which ran along the edge of the street. The wolf must have sensed Brid's pain and decided that her mistress needed protection.

When he looked again the wolf had gone. The pigs in their rickety sties must have caught her scent, though, because the squealing piglets continued to scamper wildly and hide behind the shelter of the troughs, as if the shadow of death were prowling amongst them. An old sow grunted to her feet and scraped the ground, threatening with her trotter.

That was the only unwelcome challenge to meet them.

Otherwise, their horses were allowed to wind through the haphazard buildings, picking their way carefully along the brick cobbled streets that fell steeply towards the centre of the drowsy town. The majority of the houses were low two-storey buildings with arched doorways and square shuttered windows designed to keep out the searing, relentless heat of Caldea's summer. Even now in Fogmoon there was a temperate warmth in the air. Brid's cart-horse slithered on the rain-wetted stones and stumbled on the terracing that cut into the cobbles, to ease the gradient of the steeper slopes. Hal grunted and flicked away his damp fringe before berating the town for its ill-disciplined design, exasperated by their search for a straight route to the town's centre. Each promising street led them into one unexpected side-cut after another but still they were unable to find a single sleepy alley that would lead onto a main arterial street.

'There's something strange happening,' Caspar said, feeling disconcerted by the echoing beat of the horses' hooves through the deserted streets. 'It's too quiet. There's just no one around.'

'They'll be sleeping off their midday meals.' Brid laughed at him as if unsurprised by his ignorance. 'The whole world doesn't have to live in the same way as Torra Alta, you know.'

Caspar was relieved to hear the uplift in her voice and hoped her pain-numbing willow bark was taking effect. The streets were becoming narrower and more confused and he pulled Firecracker to a halt as he waited for the others in case they were separated in the maze-like settlement.

'Well, we're here now, high-priestess. Right in the middle of Ildros,' Hal said mockingly but masked the insult of his sarcasm behind a broad teasing smile. 'Which way does your crystal ball say we should go now? Where are these secretive women who are meant to hold all the keys to the mystery?' Though he tried to hide his disgust in brash humour, he couldn't conceal his pained expression as he eyed her twisted ankle dangling beneath the hem of her skirt and avoided her rotted eyes.

'You're just sore because you didn't like being shown up as

squeamish,' she replied stiffly, taking him at his word rather than enjoying his sarcastic sense of humour. 'The Keepers must be here in Ildros somewhere. The Mother will give us a sign.'

A church bell tolled one solemn solitary chime, announcing the first hour of the afternoon and Hal grinned humorously at her. 'It seems the wrong God is talking to us.'

Brid stared up at him with blank deformed eyes that somehow couldn't disguise her defiant confidence. He tried to stare back with equal composure, but flinched away from the wall of white that seemed to see right through his flesh to his soul. 'Don't pretend you're being funny. You're just brooding because your so-called manly pride can't handle your sense of inadequacy at being unable to shield a maiden from pain. Just stop sulking; it only makes it worse,' she chided him in an unemotional voice. Hal's mouth dropped open in surprise at her remark.

The silent tension of the moment was pierced by the bark of a dog. But it wasn't a bark of alarm or warning nor the simple mindless bark of a dog arguing with its echo; there was pain and fear in this bark. The wolf was suddenly beside them, her hackles raised to spines on her neck.

The bark startled the lull of the streets. Abruptly it turned to a yelp and then silence, an uncomfortable silence that rested uneasily on the tranquil hush of the dozing town. Without consultation the three companions automatically moved towards the source of the noise, turning into the shadows of a stepped passageway. Hal had to crouch low over Magpie's neck as they passed under an arch spanning two buildings. He shouted angrily to Brid, ordering her to wait as she impulsively rode on ahead.

'Look, get behind me, won't you. You don't know what you're riding into. Let me go first. You can't see well enough for a start.'

'I can hear well enough. That animal's frightened and in pain.'

The rune-etched white steel of the broadsword flashed in

the sunlight as Hal drew his weapon, endowing him with all the presence of a seasoned warrior with proud carriage beneath his hide jacket and dun cloak. Jeering and urgent shouts filtered out from a back-street. They traced the sound down the narrow alleyway, which was just wide enough for the horses to walk through in single file. The backs of the houses were windowless as if they shunned this part of the city. Caspar anxiously covered the rear of the party, the palm of his hands brushing over his quiver of arrows in anxious anticipation. The vicious snarl of an animal in terror and pain led them on into a secluded courtyard. The sound of snarling animals brought deep cheers from a large gang of sinister-looking ruffians.

They weren't noticed at first. The men had their backs to them, all looking inwards into a pit, shouting, cheering and goading.

'Come on, get him, Scrapper! Get him!'

'I'll raise the wager five to one,' another shouted over the rising excitement.

'You're right. Bloody dog. This new Ophidian breed might look the bloody part but he's nothing, got none of the fighting spirit of the old Caldea Dogs. He bites every bloody man here but won't lay a tooth on the other dogs. Bloody useless.'

'He'll better two of yours,' a dark-skinned man with a breathy accent disagreed.

'Yeah and I suppose he'll cock-a-doodle-doo and all.'

'Two! He'll finish two of your Caldean dogs. If he proves himself, you'll buy him?'

'You're on, but looks like you'll need to give that yellow-livered dog a boot to gee him on.'

The furious barking abruptly stopped with a yelp. There was silence, a pregnant bloated silence. Suddenly a huge cheer erupted from the ruffians accompanied by much waving of fists and punching of the air as a horrendous snarling and snapping of jaws erupted from the pit.

Brid laid her hand on Hal's arm. 'Stop them.'

Why me? Hal asked himself, but then yielded to her pleading look and charged in with the Torra Altan battle cry ringing from his lips. The great sword whistled through a well-practised routine in a series of co-ordinated loops and arcs around his head. The men all turned at once. As one they stepped nervously back, though one or two brandished pitchforks and another swung a heavy chain. It suddenly dawned on Caspar that his foolhardy uncle was advancing on at least a dozen of the most ugly-looking men he'd clapped eyes on. He pushed Firecracker forward to stand level with his rash uncle. The clean snap of teeth, bloody snarls and pitiful yelps continued to growl up from the pit.

'Stop the fight!' Hal commanded, pointing his sword at the nearest man.

'You don't want to do a thing like that, sir.' A dark-eyed man, with his front teeth missing and his thinning hair tied into a greasy ponytail, arrogantly stepped forward. 'Why don't you kids just get your snotty noses out of our business?'

'We're not breaking any laws here,' another man snapped, the chain taut between his blackened fists. Caspar noted the scars up his forearms, old healed scars where hopefully he had been justly savaged by the dogs he so mistreated.

Caspar glared at the ring of men. He disliked them, loathed the meanness that could drive them to such mindless cruelty, but he didn't draw his bow. The men facing them were largely Belbidian and the Torra Altans couldn't afford to alert the sheriff of Ildros to their presence by maiming several of the townsfolk. The sheriff breathing down their necks would certainly draw the Inquisitors.

'We'll buy the dogs,' the younger boy shouted, trying to lower his voice to a more authoritative pitch. He pushed Firecracker forward so that the horse's presence would intimidate the men.

'Here, but what about us?' one of the men in the crowd objected, shouting above the seething dogs. 'I get nothing out of that and I've got a good wager on here.'

'And me.'

A circular pit, dug to a depth of about five feet, was writhing with a snarling mass of tooth and fur. Two large brindle-coloured dogs with docked tails and clipped ears, barely distinguishable in their entangled fury, had pinned a smaller animal to one wall of the pit.

The man with the ponytail laughed. 'I'll take your money, but you can stop the fight yourselves,' he sneered. 'We'll have a wager on that instead. He might not take to dog fights but no one can touch that white dog. He's the Devil himself.'

Caped in blood, the white dog was on his back with his fangs latched into the soft folds of flesh under the brindle bitch's neck. He wrenched his head back and forth as if trying to kill a rat until a hunk of the bitch's flesh came away in his jaws. Tearing into the bitch, he left his body exposed to the fury of the other black-eared dog twice his size. White spikes of teeth protruded from the brindle dog's muzzle and sank into the chunky white flank of the smaller dog. The white terrier turned his aggression on him, striking with the lightning speed of a cobra to savage the left side of the dog's head. The terrier's small beady eyes were clenched shut as his lips curled back to show curved, murderous teeth as long as a mountain cat's, the grip of his jaw slicing through gristle and bone.

The dogs suddenly broke apart; the brindle dog's left ear and a hand's span of flesh torn away from around his eye. The short white terrier latched on again to the brindle bitch, crushing her lower jaw in his curved mouth. The noise was terrible.

The men were still cheering, caught up in the bloody savagery of the fight. The terrier, with steadfast determination, remained hooked into the flesh of the bitch. Again it left him vulnerable to the greater bulk of the black-eared hound who launched himself at the terrier's neck, ripping and tearing at the flesh until the dog was scarlet with fresh blood. But the stocky white dog held stoically to his own victim, blood spuming from his jaws.

Caspar was confused by the shriek of howling screams and the rolling scrap of entangled dogs. He tried desperately to see a way of separating them but it seemed impossible. Hal stood at the edge of the pit, yelling at the warring dogs but only adding to the noise.

When the silence came, it came suddenly and abruptly. Even the men were too astonished to gasp. Brid dropped down into the snarling, snapping pit. Dragging her dislocated ankle, she hobbled awkwardly forward with her arms outstretched, feeling her way along the pit wall towards the snarling tangle of snapping jaws.

'They say cripples have God's protection but the dogs might not know that, lass. Get out of there!' yelled a voice from the back of the crowd. 'Someone get that girl out of there.'

'Brid!' Caspar started to scream, running round to wrench her out. Before he could grab her shoulder to pull her free, the wolf was beside her, growling out a low throaty snarl. The warring hounds froze. The bitch was on her side, eyes staring. Drawing quick breaths, her ribcage fluttered with the effort, but her breathing was wet and restricted by the blood that clogged her muzzle. A flap of skin dangled away from her mouth, revealing the splintered bones of her jaw, and blood pumped from her severed tongue. The terrier put his tail between his legs and whimpered whilst the big brindle hound growled and laid his bloodied lips back, jutting his muzzle forward in aggressive attack.

The wolf didn't wait for any instructions but sprang at the dog, closing her mouth round its neck, slinging it from side to side as if it were a puppy. She flung it away and the dog fell in a crumpled heap against the wall of the pit. When the hound was able to gather himself up, he didn't return the attack but leapt out of the imprisoning pit. Bolting through the ranks of callous, club-wielding men, he dashed for freedom. They were too aghast to try and stop him, though the owner half-heartedly ran after the animal. 'Hey, Throttle!' But then he stopped. 'Bah! They're worth nothing once they've lost. They never fight the same again.'

The wolf stood protectively by her mistress as Brid knelt over the injured dogs, examining them with gently prodding hands.

376

'By the truth, a bloody wolf! A wolf, I'm telling you. That's not natural.'

'I bet on that white dog. Here! Someone owes me some silver.'

The men instantly fell to squabbling over the gambling debts, completely uninterested in the fate of the damaged dogs.

Stretching up her slender-boned arm Brid called to Caspar. 'Spar, get down here with your knife. This bitch is beyond repair and she's suffering.'

He slit the animal's throat, watching her eyes flutter for a moment before sinking slowly to rest; the laboured breathing easing into a long sigh. The bitch lay in peace at last. She was shredded with fresh wounds that cut deep into the flesh but her belly and chest had long white scars where the hair grew patchily. Caspar thought with revulsion that the poor animal had suffered the barbarity of the dog-pit many times before and perhaps this death would be the most merciful thing that had ever happened to her.

The terrier was no longer white but streaked with dried blood all along his flank and a yoke of crimson covered his thick neck. An ugly puncture wound near the base of his skull pulsed dark treacly blood, but his eyes were clear and his breathing deep and regular. He didn't appear to be going into shock, so Caspar hoped the injuries were only superficial. As Brid stretched out a hand, gently and tenderly towards the dog, Hal called out a word of warning.

'These aren't pets, you know.'

She kept stroking the dog, talking in a low calm voice. 'I know you're not a pet but nor is my wolf. Now, let's see how bad your cuts are then.' The dog had an ugly bulbous face with fangs too long for his lips, rather like a cat, so that they jutted out. He had small slit eyes deeply set into his skull and Caspar thought he was quite the most ugly, vicious-looking dog he'd ever seen. Yet the animal had a certain charm. As Brid inched gently closer, he beat his rod-like tail on the ground and raised a paw pathetically towards her. She laughed and approached with less caution. With little sight in her coated eyes, she felt the dog over with the expert touch of her delicate fingers, finally returning to examining the gash on the back of his neck, brushing the coarse hairs back from the wound that was already beginning to darken and crust over. All the time the dog looked up at her with his head slightly on a tilt and devotion in his eyes.

'You'll live,' she told the terrier cheerfully and he beat his tail harder as if he'd understood her words. 'Now, dog,' she said in a matter-of-fact tone, 'you're coming with us.'

The dark-eyed man with a flat nose pushed his way through the crowd. 'You ain't taking my dog.'

'How much?' Hal grunted. 'How much does your ugly little purulent brain think the dog is worth?'

The man bristled and Hal closed his fist over the pommel of his sword. A nervous twitch of the man's eyes tracked Hal's movements and his lips curled to a snarl as hideous as his dog's. 'Bah! You're too young to even know how to handle a sword.'

The master swordsmith who forged the runesword used the same high craft to devise the scabbard that concealed the weapon's raw power. The sheath was lined with wool so that the sheep's lanolin would oil and protect the blade. As he eased the sword into the air, it whispered against the wool with none of the rough rasping of a common blade.

He spoke quietly and calmly. 'How much for the dog?'

The man hesitated, eyeing the point of the sword with a little more respect. 'Ten crowns,' he said flatly.

'Ten crowns for a dog! Ten groats more like.'

'Well, you want him.'

The wolf turned to look at the raised voices, sensing the growing tension and gurgled in her throat. Starting at her neck, the hackles raised all along the length of her spine until even her tail was a thick bush. The man looked between the point of the broadsword and the stiff-legged wolf with her eager jaws. 'Ten groats,' he begrudged.

Hal reached inside his jacket and chucked the money at him, the coins rolling on the ground.

'Let's get out of here.' Caspar urged Brid, who was trying to gather the dog into her arms. Although the dog was short, standing little more than knee high, he was thick-set with heavy bones and a bulk of muscle that made him as broad as a hound twice his height. Brid put her arms under the dog's belly and lifted him a couple of inches off the ground but unable to stand on her ankle she couldn't lift him higher. Caspar rushed to help her, heaving the front half of the terrier up into his arms and groaning under the weight. The trusting dog hung placidly in their arms. Together they swung him up over the lip of the pit. Caspar vaulted after him and Hal reached an arm down for the crippled Maiden, pulling her up with ease. She stifled a shriek as she accidentally put her weight down on her self-inflicted injury.

The dark youth lifted her up onto the cart-horse and then struggled with Caspar to hoist the awkward weight of the dog over the front of her saddle. As they rode away from the courtyard, twenty pairs of eyes burrowed into their backs. It was a relief to find the larger streets, with their welcoming open-fronted houses, where afternoon life was beginning to yawn into activity. The wolf remained briefly at their side, drawing nervous glances of disbelief and outraged shouts from a startled woman who appeared on her doorstep. When at last they turned into the broad high street the wolf had disappeared into the slinking shadows and the three companions were left untroubled by the townsfolk.

The high street was lined with swinging signs, most of which depicted wine barrels indicating the Barony's chief business. Creaking on its hinges, the sign of a bridled horse beckoned them to the ostlery at the end of the street. Hal went in first, telling Brid and Caspar to keep back until he made certain there was no sign of any Inquisitors before allowing the others to enter.

The ostler was friendly and expressed concern over the plight of their dog, readily showing them to the stables where they could tend his wounds and leave him in comfort.

'We're here to visit the holy shrine of St Anne's in search

of a miracle for my kinswoman,' Hal informed the innkeeper, who looked sympathetically at Brid's injuries, staring blatantly as he curiously inspected her face.

Brid looked vacantly back at him, showing no signs that she was being looked at, though Caspar knew she was able to see a little at least.

'It looks like you'd better take the dog along too,' the Ildrian man suggested. 'Not pretty at all them dog-fights. Brutal senseless people they are that can do that sort of thing.'

Brid sat cross-legged in the straw of the stable, cradling the dog in her lap, and carefully wiped away the blood from his scruff and flanks. As soon as the innkeeper left them she lifted her eyelids with a finger and scraped away the congealed wad of cobweb, blinking furiously to clear her blood-shot eyes. She sighed with relief. 'Just warn me if you hear anyone and I'll put them back in.' Carefully she wrapped the moulded pads of cobweb and beef fat between two moist dock leaves and placed them in her scrip for safe keeping. She fumbled through her leather pouch, choosing a twist of herbs to blend with some dried horse dung, collected from the stalls, with which to stanch the dog's wounds.

'Yellow loosestrife and water figwort,' she explained. 'They both stop bleeding.' The cut on the terrier's flank was only superficial but when the wound on the neck had ceased to ooze blood she cleaned the injury again and the skin peeled back like a toothless smile.

'Can you work some thread out of your shirt,' she asked Caspar as she delved into her scrip to produce a fine bone needle. After several attempts he managed to tear a frayed strip from the hem of his garment and tease out a thread long enough to be of use. He winced as she pushed the needle through the thick hide of the dog's neck to suture the wound. The dog, however, didn't flinch a muscle.

'The skin's very tough just here,' the priestess explained. 'He doesn't feel it. There.' She cleaned the needle and dropped it back into her scrip. 'We'll make sure he's got some water and then if we tie him up with some rope we can leave him here in the stable. You do that while I check on the Eye.'

She slid the moonstone out from beneath her jerkin and peeled back the hare's skin to feel the damp layers of petticoat covering the orb. Carefully she dribbled water from a full bucket standing near the stalls and re-moistened the cloth before carefully replacing the hare's skin. She tucked the orb back into her clothing with a dubious sigh. 'At least that's safe.'

Caspar examined the Maiden's pensive brow. 'What's wrong?'

She shrugged. 'I don't know. Just a feeling.'

'That evil presence again?'

'No, I don't think he can see us – at least not clearly. The water and the skin of the sacred hare will distort the vision, but the Eye gives me a feeling about Morrigwen.'

'What sort of feeling?'

'I don't know, not for sure, without looking and I daren't for fear of attracting the attention of that malevolent presence. I don't want to lure the Vaalakans to us again.'

Hal untied a rope from a spare halter hanging in the stalls and tied a noose round the dog's neck, making sure it wouldn't rub on the wound. He secured the other end firmly to a metal hoop designed for tethering horses to the wall.

'There,' he said with satisfaction. 'Now, come on let's go. We'd better start our search through the city. Where do we start to look for these Keepers? St Anne's shrine?'

'A shrine to a saint of the New Faith? No, I doubt that's likely.' Brid was certain that if they headed east inland from the estuary mouth they would have more chance of finding the Keepers. 'The Inquisitors are here so the Keepers must be in the port. And if they're in the port they'll need a front of some sort to hide behind. If I wanted a guise to hide a temple behind,' she said, 'I'd set up a candle shop or a flower stall, but I'd stay away from the quay and keep to the inland quarter of the town. It's too busy down by the estuary.' She couldn't exactly say why she preferred the east; she just had a feeling about it. 'It's where the sun rises, bringing hopes of a better tomorrow.'

Hal shrugged his shoulders in despair at her logic.

With a resigned sigh Brid moistened the wads of gossamer and fat. Wincing, she replaced her disguise. As they prepared to leave the stable, the dog yelped in indignation at being abandoned, dashing about at the end of his rope and over-turning a water butt. He threw himself forward and the cord snapped tight, somersaulting the dog over onto his back. He tried again.

Brid hobbled back to the dog and firmly told him to sit, whilst rummaging through the saddle-bags for some oat bis-cuits. The dog gulped them down almost without noticing, coughing on the dry crumbs, and wagged his tail feverishly. He tried to sit but was too excited and his bottom hovered over the ground. 'Now sit and stay,' she said firmly. 'You need to rest.' The dog yelped again, producing a puppyish high-pitched yelp that sounded silly coming from his deep rounded chest and thick throat.

Disgusted to the pit of their stomachs by the mindless cruelty of the dog fight, they headed eastwards in moody silence, Brid leaning on a walking stick and hobbling painfully between the two youths. The sound of the dog's indignant yapping still chased them up the street, insisting that they returned for him.

Keeping warily alert for the black tunics with the red and yellow crest of the King's Inquisitors, the questers turned away from the port and the larger houses belonging to the dignitaries of the town. Brid pointed out that the presence of sheriffs and town-elders, who would be staunch supporters of the New Faith, would hardly be a safe environment for the Keepers. She felt they were much more likely to succeed if they searched amongst the market quarters where the Keepers could hide behind innocent shop-fronts. Caspar felt dismayed by the end-less winding streets whose identical houses yielded no hint of anything unusual happening behind their innocent façades. Brid explained that even if the Keepers weren't actually within the town they might find someone who could lead them to them.

'Morrigwen believes that throughout Belbidia there are still small pockets of people who are secretly faithful to the Mother. If there are any in Ildros the Keepers may have contacted them. Of course they haven't survived for centuries by being easy to find. Without innocent disguises they'd have all faced the stake years ago.'

Brid had the end of her plait in her hands and was winding it around and around in her fingers as she peered blindly up and down the street. A tight knot of concentration drew her eyebrows together into a peak. She looked perplexed. 'Oh Mother, it's so much harder not being able to see.'

'Well?' Hal demanded. 'What's your great plan, my Lady Brid? There's thousands of houses and they all look identical.'

'Oh, shut up,' she snapped. 'I'm trying to think where I'd go if I came to this town.'

'Hm ... very hopeful, we've only got to follow the logic of a female. The Runes of War will have faded from the heartstone at Torra Alta and the Vaalakans will have reached Farona before we find them. Don't you have some sort of network to keep up with your friends?'

'Hal, you're not being helpful,' Caspar sighed.

'Are you telling me to shut up too?' The elder boy puffed up his chest and angled his nose so that he could peer haughtily over the tip at his nephew.

'Yes!'

The raven-haired youth shoved his nephew with the palm of his hand. Bristling with anger and frustration, Caspar raised a fist ready to land a punch fairly and squarely on Hal's neat nose.

'Just try it, just you try it,' Hal taunted him. 'Come on. Let's see if you've got any bigger and stronger. It would be about time, wouldn't it, little nephew? Come on then –'

With great satisfaction Caspar managed to silence his kinsman with a forceful sock into his white teeth. It was a well-placed punch, though the force of it split his knuckles. It didn't throw Hal off balance for long, however, and Caspar's world suddenly spun as if he'd been caught inside a huge church bell and thrown against its metal sides by its thrashing clapper. Hal hit him first on one side of the head and again on the other as he reeled away. He staggered back, shaking his head and getting ready to fly at the smug face of his uncle that still seemed annoyingly undamaged. Suddenly Brid was in the way, thwarting his retaliation.

'Do you two feel better now? I suppose I shouldn't expect more from a couple of kids but we have got . . .' She trailed off and the two youths were spared any more of her condescension as a cacophony of jangling metal and excited high pitched barking startled the town. With his cord flailing behind him, the white Ophidian snake-catcher bounded up the street, vigorously pumping his squat legs. The metal ring, that the dog had pulled clean out of the stable wall, clattered over the cobbles, bouncing and jarring as it skipped and snagged in the cracks between the stones. His bulbous face was pink with excitement and his tongue flapped about, sticking sideways out of his mouth.

'He's as ugly as a pig,' Hal laughed, suddenly forgetting his quarrel.

'Uglier,' Caspar corrected him.

'Mmm, more like a troll.' Brid's last words were knocked out of her by the dog's over-enthusiastic greeting as he leapt straight up at her. His forelegs punched her in the stomach as he tried to place a sloppy, dog-breathy slurp across her face with his salivary tongue. The girl staggered backwards against the wall, overpowered by the unexpected strength of the terrier, laughing and chiding at the same time. 'Ow! Mind my ankle,' she squealed. He finally released her from his embrace and leapt first at Hal and then at Caspar in exuberant welcome. Missing with his tongue he accidentally butted Caspar's nose with the bony force of his muzzle.

'Ouch! Look, stop it!'

'Down!' Brid ordered pointing at the ground. The dog turned to look at her and sank very slowly until his belly nearly touched the ground. He wagged his tail furiously, giving puppyish yips of pleasure at her attention.

'He's somebody's dog,' Hal sighed. 'That foreign wretch must have stolen him from a loving home. He's so trusting.'

'Well, Dog. I suppose you'd better come along then.'

'We can't call him Dog,' Caspar protested.

Brid looked at him in surprise. 'Why not? I call the wolf, Wolf; and he is a dog after all.'

'That's different: the wolf is wild and doesn't communicate like a dog does,' Caspar protested.

'I understand her well enough,' the girl contradicted.

'Well, he's still the ugliest dog I've ever seen – Oh, get out of it!' Hal had to side-step as the dog threaded through his legs, drawn compulsively towards some scent on a doorstep.

Following Brid's first whim they strode steadily eastwards along the narrow streets, often in single file to avoid the procession of townsmen pushing wheeled barrows of produce, and the donkey carts laden with casks of wine, rolling to and from the ports. Brid skipped and hopped along quite quickly next to the youths though she continually chewed on the willow bark to numb the pain.

Caspar lost count of the number of wine barrels that they passed and imagined that the easy access to so much of the heady southern brew accounted for the general sleepiness of the town, though as the day wore on Ildros did finally stir itself into a lazy semblance of activity. However, when they finally turned into a street lined with shops, the atmosphere was bustling with commerce. Merchants haggled over the last few groats for the wares they had brought first across vast deserts then in tall ships struggling against the ocean currents. Swaying bands of sailors peered hazily into the shops, exploring the exotica of the town. The bustle of bartering and the chorus of street-sellers rang through the air. Hal took a long stride to fall protectively into step alongside the girl as they passed a group of tanned sailors. One with heavy looped earrings raised a tankard to the sky, slopping red liquid onto the street and slurred, 'God bless the afflicted.'

'Hey, you lads, couldn't you find no lass better between the two of you?' another taunted less charitably. 'You should sail to Lonis; they've got plenty of young wenches to spare there.'

Caspar already had an arrow slotted to his bow as he swirled round to glare at the men, who laughingly put their hands up.

''Ere, no offence to your sister, laddie. Only 'avin' a lark.' One of the other sailors emptied a tankard of wine over his companion, which induced hoots of laughter from the revellers, and Brid tugged at Caspar's arm.

'Come on. Let's get moving.'

'I should have shot them all,' the young boy growled.

'They didn't mean any harm. They're just drunk.' Brid seemed totally unperturbed by the comments. 'Soldiers and sailors alike, they all get drunk!'

The youth couldn't understand why she wasn't mortally offended by their remarks but decided that Brid was too focused on their quest to be thrown off balance by the strangers. The terrier on the end of his cord towed Brid along up the street, anxious to participate in the hunt. He kept glancing over his shoulder to check he was going the right way, looking clear into Brid's white eyes for reassurance. He marched on, pushing his head down into his collar and snuffling over the ground. Every third stride Brid had to trot awkwardly to keep up with the dog's enthusiasm to pull ahead.

Hal laughed. 'He thinks we're hunting snakes.'

At the mention of the word snakes, the terrier became stiff and alert, flicking his head from side to side and pricking up his ears.

'Snakes!' Hal repeated in an excited encouraging voice and the dog rushed madly about, sniffing all across the cobbled pavement.

'Oh don't confuse the poor thing,' Brid laughed. 'We haven't got time for games.'

By late afternoon, they had covered most of the easterly quarter of the town, though they were forced to avoid a whole row of shops that contained a baker's, a silversmith, a whitesmith and a chart-maker's simply because Brid took an exception to the name of the street. Ducking-stool Lane she said was just too insensitive.

Hal was ahead of the others as they approached the next turning off the street. He abruptly sprang back and shoved Brid and Caspar firmly against the wall.

'Two Inquisitors,' he warned. 'At least I presume they are. They're in black with pikestaffs and lances, riding matching horses. They've got the King's emblem flying from the tip of one of their lances.' He crept forward again and peered down the side-street. 'They're going away from us. In a minute, it'll be clear.'

Caspar tried to slow his pulse, which pounded in his ears.

'They've gone,' Hal finally announced. 'Now, Brid, think. We've got to find these women fast; we can't risk staying in Ildros much longer.'

'As long as we keep an eye out for the Inquisitors we'll be safe,' the Maiden reasoned. 'They're not looking for us. But you're right; we've got no time to waste. We have to find something, some sort of message on the building or in the display of goods,' she muttered, but Caspar found it all meaningless. Brid dismissed all the butchers out of hand and then walked more slowly past the fishmongers, but seeing only men inside decided not to investigate further. Hal couldn't understand the difference between butchers and fishmongers. Brid explained that the association of fish with water, which was a female element, made it more of an attractive setting to worshippers of the Old Faith. They inspected five fishmongers in all. Outside each one Brid buried her head in the hood of her cloak and dabbed at one eye to briefly remove the disguise of cobweb. She hobbled disappointedly away from each stall without much more than a moment's glance.

'How can you tell so easily?' Caspar was pleased to move away from the fetid stench of the fish stalls but was becoming increasingly frustrated. Their search was becoming more and more of a wild goose chase.

'How did you know from down the street that this was a fishmonger's?' she asked by way of reply.

'The smell.'

'Don't be so smart. Why else?'

'Well, the sign of course: it's up there swinging in plain daylight.'

'Of course. And I'd leave a sign just as plain, if you knew how to read it. It would only be a matter of laying out the fish in a certain way. You can make a runic pattern out of almost anything.' Brid was still distracted, squinting up and down the street. 'It's all wrong.' They moved away from the shops towards the craftsmen's quarters, passing an apothecary. Caspar thought it might hold possibilities, but Brid turned her nose up at it because the potions were sold in premixed bottles rather than as fresh herbs and roots. She explained that too much meddling with nature diluted the efficacy of the herbs. But when she ignored a cobbler's, dismissing it without a second thought on the grounds that she didn't like wearing shoes, Hal threw his eyes heavenward and groaned.

'This is hopeless, we're just following her whims. How's she going to find anything with such an illogical, unsystematic approach?'

'I'm looking for a priestess and it takes one to know one,' Brid retorted. 'If I don't like shoes, nor will she.'

The dog circled his adopted mistress, winding the leash about her legs and so delaying Brid's response as Caspar described all the signs he could see swinging in the sea-breeze.

'There's a candle maker's at the end of the street,' he informed her as his eye fell on the picture of a candle that swung from an iron bar above the door of a shop.

'Oh dog, get out of it,' Brid complained. The dog looked up and wagged his thick short tail, which beat against Caspar's leg. But the white terrier didn't understand Brid's words and she had to swirl round to unwrap herself. The snake-catcher took this to be some sort of game and dashed in circles himself. Finally they all succeeded in disentangling themselves, mainly with the help of Hal who took the dog firmly by the collar.

'Careful of his wound,' Brid warned but somehow the dog

seemed to have a total disregard for pain. Caspar found the animal's stoicism very noble.

'Listen troll-dog, just stand still,' the dark youth fiercely ordered but the dog was unperturbed by the sternness of his voice and was still boiling over with enthusiasm.

'Anyway, as I was saying, candles are intrinsic to our sacred rites. The smoke of candles reinforces and concentrates prayers to the Goddess. We'll take a look.'

'Another wild goose chase,' Hal grumbled despondently.

Caspar watched with fascination as he looked through the open door at an old man carefully etching lines into a candle and labelling each line with a numeral. He related the scene to Brid.

'It's to tell the time with.' She looked disappointed.

'Well, we know that,' Hal retorted. 'That's obvious.'

'Yes, I know, but who needs that? I know exactly what the time is by the sun or the moon or the stars.'

'Well, you wouldn't indoors,' Hal contradicted her. 'I think it's clever.'

'I don't like being inside.'

Hal leapt at her words. 'You don't like being inside and you don't like being in towns either. Perhaps we should start looking up there on the downs.'

'But the Inquisitors are here in the town,' Brid started to argue.

'Why don't we shut our eyes, spin round, open them on the count of three and follow the first magpie we see; it would probably be just as effective.' Hal's frustration was growing by the minute. 'This is absolutely ridiculous. I'm hungry and tired. At least I could be hungry and tired in Torra Alta where I could be doing some good killing Vaalakans. Anyway, you're being ridiculously illogical. The temple in Farona isn't only in the middle of the city, it's right under the cathedral; now that's hardly in the fresh air, is it? So there's no reason why it shouldn't be here in Ildros. Women just can't think straight.'

'The temple at Farona was built in the open air,' she

389

corrected him haughtily. 'It's very old, built long before the cathedral was erected over the top to crush it.'

'Well, you can spend all night crawling over the port. I'm going back to the ostlery to get some food.'

'We'll just try the quayside, then we'll all go back to the ostlery. It'll be better to stay together,' Brid argued in one of her more cajoling tones. 'At least if we look at the port then we can discount it before trying further afield tomorrow.'

A fine drizzle blew in off the sea. They set out westwards along the widening estuary and then, as it opened out into the harbour, they turned north along the quay.

'Stop it, dog,' Brid hauled on the animal's lead as he struggled to pull ahead of them.

'Trog,' Caspar corrected her. He insisted on calling the Ophidian snake-catcher, Trog, after contracting troll and dog to form the nickname. Brid didn't approve.

The dog still pulled determinedly, his eyes fixed resolutely on the beach, and Brid simply didn't have the strength to hold him back. At first she refused to give in, strapping the lead hard round her wrist and leaning back to counterbalance the dog's force. Hal laughed at her when finally the rope began to fray at her skin and she was becoming pink with the effort of restraining the terrier.

'Look,' he laughed, 'if you wear men's clothes, ride astride rather than side-saddle and think you're tough enough to go off into the world without a chaperone, you can damn well hold your own dog.'

'Here,' the young, auburn-haired youth put a hand on the dog's leash. 'Give him to me.' He frowned at his uncle. 'That's a bit mean, Hal; don't forget her ankle.' But Caspar was beginning to regret his chivalrous offer when they reached the quay where buckets of eels were being off-loaded from the estuary fishing boats and laid out ready for auction. Trog appeared to have a taste for eels and dived headlong into the first barrel, pulling Caspar with him before he'd even realized what was happening.

Finally Caspar managed to drag him away but not before

Trog had succeeded in swallowing two live eels. He refused to abandon the one that was still clamped between his jaws, wriggling and squirming to get free. Hal busily paid off the angry eelman and the three of them shamefully retreated along the waterfront. It was a fruit stall that intrigued Brid the most. Surprisingly there weren't many fresh fruits or vegetables available in Caldea, since nearly all the farmland was given over to vines. Fresh supplies had to be imported mainly from Quertos, and the sweet scent of apples wafted through the pungent smell of fish. With a few disgusting noises, Trog had finally managed to consume the eel and his belly was looking rounder than ever. He towed them forward to the fruit stall and wagged his tail at the girl behind the counter who smiled at him. The dog yipped in the embarrassing high-pitch that he reserved for his more friendly conversations.

'Mercy, those new snake-catchers,' the girl exclaimed. 'They're just the ugliest.' She had a small button-nose with a low bridge and thick solid eyebrows, which Caspar felt detracted from her looks, but needless to say decided not to mention.

'I want some apples,' Brid said in a matter-of-fact voice.

'Yes, mistress.' The girl looked Brid up and down, the heavy brows hooding her eyes. She squinted at Brid's white eyes and grimaced, though she managed to recompose herself enough to ask quite politely, 'What kind? We've got Quertos of course and there's some imports, but the flavour's a bit woody and we even have some cookers from Caldea.'

'The Quertos apples would be fine. A pound.'

As Caspar wondered about the significance of the apples, an older woman shuffled forward from the back of the shop, carrying a basket of shiny red fruit.

The young girl turned round. 'No Ma, those are foreign ones. The Quertos ones are green.' The older woman swung back towards the rear of the shop, brushing her wide hips against a crate of pears. They tumbled to the ground. The girl sighed. 'Oh Ma, you come and serve these gentle folk and I'll put it straight.'

The older woman smoothed out her pressed apron and rolled up her sleeves. She had coarse heavy features and kept playing with her tooth as if it bothered her. Caspar felt uncomfortable in her presence but there was no doubt that she looked quizzically at Brid as if with some spark of recognition. She offered Brid an apple from the basket she was carrying. 'Try one of these red ones, Miss, you might like them better. Here, I'll fetch me a knife.'

She put the basket down. Polishing the apple on her apron, she waddled forward, twisting sideways to negotiate the gaps between the piles of fruit, determined to avoid tumbling a display of winter plums with the bulge of her stomach. Caspar suddenly realized what all the fuss was about. He'd seen Brid eat apples; it was one of the few foods she didn't refuse. The Maiden always cut them in half, not from pole to pole but through the girth, dividing them into a top half and a bottom half. It was a simple test to see how the woman reacted when the priestess sliced the apple.

Trog chose that moment to introduce himself, leaping up at the counter and producing an ear-splitting yelp.

'Ugh!' The woman curled her face up in disgust. 'Those dogs give me the jitters. Look like hogs, I'd say, but if they keep the snakes away I guess it's a good thing. Can't walk on the beaches this time of year, not with that cold snap driving the varmints out of the northern seas. And these spring tides make the beaches lethal. You can't get out there until after the next neap tide. Even then you need to pick and choose your time to walk on the sands, but of course only the locals get to an understanding with the beaches. I keep having to yell at strangers to warn them off. They don't seem to realize that the snakes are a far worse plague here than on the Causeway.' She laid down her knife and came to the front of the stall. 'Here, you see that stretch of beach. Well, last week they got thirty-three of them black sand-vipers off that beach alone, thirty-three I'm telling you. Here now, what was I doing? Ah! yes, the apple.'

She picked the fruit up and polished it again absent-mindedly. Caspar still had his eyes fixed on the apple, which the woman was now hovering over, and wondered whether she would ever offer it to Brid.

'I'm not a great apple eater myself but, they say if you put Nattarda cheese as a topping to Quertos apple tart, it's the best recipe ever. Come to think of it, Mabel – she lives down my street – Mabel puts some nuts in too. It's quite the best.' At last she raised her hand to offer Brid the apple and the knife. 'Here, bonny lady, try this.'

With great deliberation Brid held the apple on its side and sliced into the crunchy flesh, cutting it in her own peculiar way. Using the back of her hand she wiped away the droplets of juice that sprayed up onto her cheeks before offering the fruit-seller the top half of the apple. 'Let me share this with you.'

The fruit-seller raised her hand in refusal without the slightest spark of recognition. 'No, no thank you. I'm not partial to apples myself; prefer the plums. Would you like to try some of those?'

Brid didn't bother to taste the apple. She let her hand drop and said flatly, 'Yes, these are fine, we'll have a pound. Hal, you get them for me.' She limped away, pulling at her plait and stared wistfully out to sea.

'Poor lass, what an affliction,' the woman sympathetically remarked to Hal. 'I guess you're here to visit St Anne. We get all sorts here in Ildros 'cos of the shrine and of course the port brings in a lot of foreigners too. The ferry from Dorsmouth came in this morning with the funniest bunch, but they say there's trouble in the North somewhere and whenever there's trouble . . .'

Caspar was no longer listening. Dorsmouth, the ferry from Dorsmouth. With a good wind that would make the journey from Farona to Ildros in under a week. He cursed their own lack of judgement for not taking that route. Then he thought in horror that they could have been trapped on board with the enemy. But Gatto and the Vaalakans could be here now. He looked at Hal whose expression was turning to frustrated anxiety as he paid the woman but didn't wait for the change. He strode over to Brid and thrust an apple into her hand.

'Here, chew on that and come up with some ideas: we're running out of time.' There was no sympathy in his voice even though the young priestess was obviously hurt and blaming herself. She sighed. 'I wish Morrigwen were here. She'd know what to do.'

'Well, she isn't,' Hal snapped, 'and you are, so we're going to do things my way and look this city over systematically. Tomorrow we'll tie that ugly dog up, take the horses and go and look properly.'

'Perhaps I should light a beacon on the top of that wooded hill up there. Maybe then the Keepers would come to me since we don't seem able to find them.' She half-laughed and waved her hand vaguely in the direction of the rounded hill beyond the vineyards. It was veiled in evergreen yew trees.

'And draw every Inquisitor along with half the city press-ganged into a witch-hunt. Your ideas are getting almost as good as Spar's!' Hal exclaimed.

'I was joking, Hal. You remember joking don't you?'

The dark youth grunted his displeasure at her patronizing tone. He marched back down the quay and the other two followed. Trog pulled sideways the whole way, trying to get his nose into the sand.

'And keep that animal on a tight lead past the fish auction,' the older boy growled, assuming an air of authority.

Chapter 23

The girl, presumably the innkeeper's daughter, was definitely interesting. Hal watched her squeeze between two tables as she weaved through the busy room to bring them their tray of breakfast. She smiled sweetly with a healthy blushing colour to her cheeks as he looked up and grinned with what he hoped was his most disarming smile. She straightened her bodice, which had a fascinating way of stirring her cream breasts, which bulged over the top of the tight garment. He stared unashamedly and the girl giggled.

This was going to be more fun than nursemaiding his nephew and that girl. He had a momentary twinge of guilt. Yes, of course he felt something for Brid, but those eyes were so gruesome and that ankle! He knew he was being illogical, knew she was beautiful underneath, probably even more beautiful than Cybillia despite the colour of the lady's hair. But all the same he was repelled by her disfiguring disguise.

Now, what he really didn't like about Brid was the way she made him feel uncomfortable – and he hated to admit that he could be unsettled by a girl. He felt in control with Cybillia; she respected him and looked up to him, said and did what he expected her to do. But Brid! She was so headstrong and unpredictable; he didn't know how to react to her. She was only a peasant girl after all but he was frightened – no, perturbed – that she might laugh at him, or point out some inadequacy. He wondered whether Branwolf had felt the same about Keridwen. But Keridwen could never have been so wilful as Brid; after all she was Spar's mother. He wondered what his older brother felt about having Wystan's widow in the castle with him. Everyone said she looked just like Keridwen. He could see how Branwolf could be tempted.

This barmaid, now, he felt quite comfortable about her. He didn't really care what she thought of him. She was just a mere girl who would never even consider contradicting him. She was probably a little older than him and slightly plump but that added to her allure. Besides Brid might smarten her attitude up a bit if he showed an interest in this girl.

'Ow!' Something bit him hard in the shin. It turned out to be the toe of Caspar's boot.

'You're not listening to a word we're saying,' his nephew angrily accused him.

'Well, it couldn't have been very interesting.'

'We'll start at the south side of Ildros,' Brid announced with that infuriating tone that clearly implied she had made her decision and could not be contradicted.

Hal glanced towards the barmaid again who was bending over to pick up a tankard, which some sleepy reveller had dropped the previous night. He chewed thoughtfully on his lower lip.

'You can go aimlessly wondering round the town again but I'm going to preserve my shoe-leather. It'll only be another waste of time. You should know where these Keepers are. It's no good all of us trailing after you, Brid. I'll wait here, where at least it's comfortable.' He could sit in the sun, drink a few beers, wait till the maid had finished her duties ... The day looked promising. He sat back and put his dirty boots up on a chair.

'Hal!' Caspar indignantly protested.

He pouted and looked sulkily at his nephew. 'Oh, don't be so annoying, Spar. You go with her. I'll ask a few discreet questions. I'll wager I find out more than you do.'

'We're going to the shrine,' the small Maiden declared, incongruously fixing him angrily with her dead white eyes. Hal could still feel the fierceness of her eyes burning through him even though he couldn't see beyond the moist matting of cobweb.

'Good idea,' he said casually. 'It'll look good for appearance's sake. Yes, you ought to go to the shrine; it gives more credence to your disguise. But as you said yourself, it'll be the last place they'd hide, so it'll be a waste of time us all going. So you won't need me now, will you?'

'I know I said that. But sometimes what you think is the most unlikely place is often the best place to look. It's always like that if you lose something. If the shrine seems an unlikely place for the Keepers, it provides them with the best cover. No one will look there.'

Hal didn't want to contaminate his clear-thinking brain with the Maiden's convoluted logic and tried not to puzzle through her confusing argument. Girls, he thought in despair, they're all muddle-headed every one of them. He merely shrugged at her and reached for his tankard. 'Tell me what you find when you get back. I'll be here.'

Brid sniffed disapprovingly. He grinned at her and then deliberately shouted over to the barmaid. 'Here, Miss, I'll have some more bread and . . . well, whatever else is still on offer.'

'Haven't you had enough?' Caspar demanded.

'No.' Hal looked longingly towards the young woman as she turned sideways to squeeze between the tables and smoothed out her dress again. She had lovely dark eyes and rich dark brown hair. 'No, I fancy just a bit more.'

His nephew narrowed his furious eyes, appearing to be giving him a withering look. 'Oh, run along, Spar,' he grinned.

As they left the room, he winced as the priestess hobbled on her crippled ankle and clutched onto Caspar's arm for support. At least they were taking that smelly-breathed dog with them simply because Brid insisted he was some kind of sign from the Mother. No, he wasn't going to feel guilty; why should he?

They had been gone barely five minutes before he had persuaded the buxom brunette to abandon her other serving duties. She sat giggling next to him. The innkeeper gave him a grim look but what did he care? The man must have been young himself once and the girl was obviously not his daughter otherwise he would have been a little more vociferous in his objections. The barmaid, however, had little conversation of her own, which was disappointing. She did, at least, seem interested in his tale of how he had single-handedly killed a Vaalakan warrior, but after a few minutes he realized that she didn't quite believe him. That irritated him.

'Torra Alta,' she sighed. 'That's a very long way away. Isn't it cold there?'

Hal nodded. 'Yes, it's cold in the winter, but we have ways of keeping warm. Now, do you work all day or are you given some time to yourself? Perhaps you could show me some of Ildros's delights.' Things seemed hopeful, he thought to himself. So what that she had very little of interest to talk about? She was blushing again and squeezing her arms together which raised her creamy breasts and squashed them even more firmly together.

'Oh, sir, Ildros's delights, whatever do you mean?'

Hal didn't reply but shuffled a little closer to the girl's warm body, which was breathing fast and deeply next to him. Things looked very hopeful indeed.

But when the door burst open, Hal knew that he'd lost this particular opportunity. He felt thoroughly peeved. Three soldiers stood silhouetted in the doorway and the barmaid rose nervously to her feet. They were tall angular men, with black tabards, and the King's red and yellow crest of the wheat sheaf embroidered on their otherwise austere uniforms. The tallest had a yellow plume decorating his helmet and was obviously in charge of the other two. To Hal's annoyance his new buxom admirer ceased to pour her longing looks over him. She abruptly scurried off to attend to the soldiers.

They were stiff looking men, clean shaven and without a hint of a smile to share between them. Hal wondered if they felt silly wearing those ridiculous sandals with thongs that laced up to their calves. The sandals were the only bit of uniform retained in memory of the foreign soldiers who had first brought the word of the one true God across the sea. Their footwear looked quite ridiculous in Belbidia.

Though his pulse was racing, he tried to move casually and threw them a disinterested look, which he hoped verged on no more than innocent curiosity. Caspar and Brid had only just left. He wondered if they'd passed on the street. But Brid's disguise surely provided ample cover so long as she kept her mouth shut. Everyone knew witches were beautiful; it was part of their sin to seduce men so it wasn't possible for them to be ugly. And Brid looked hideous with those dead white eyes and clubbed foot.

The Inquisitor peeled up his top lip in disapproval as he stared at the naked expanse of the barmaid's cleavage that thrust up out of her tight bodice. 'Belbidia is a decent holy country; you should cover yourself a little more, woman,' he snarled grumpily.

The barmaid bowed her head and uncomfortably hitched up her bodice with her thumbs and tried to wriggle deeper down into her dress but to little avail.

'What can I get for you, sirs?' she asked without looking any of them in the face.

'It's all right, Meg.' The innkeeper left the customers he was serving and banged through the tables to greet the three austerely clad soldiers. 'I'll see to this. Now young gentlemen, I know it's early in the morning but some ale on the house? Or is there anything else we can do for you on this wonderful morning that the good Father Almighty has blessed us with, praise His name?'

'Praise His name,' the tallest of the three soldiers echoed. 'No, good innkeeper, we haven't come here for sustenance.'

'No, sir?' The squat little man fidgeted with his apron and wiped down the same table for the third time while twitching his moustache with a nervous muscle in his cheek.

'No, indeed,' the soldier replied sternly. Hal sat upright and leant surreptitiously forward trying to catch the Inquisitor's words as he lowered his voice. 'There have been sightings.'

'More sightings?'

'Not like the last time when the revellers danced in the moonlight nor the time before when strange fires glowed at

399

the beginning of autumn up on Bow Hill. No, we've seen nothing more of that up there, only hollows filled with mist. Since we burnt the vine grower's daughter that all seems to have died down.'

The innkeeper ran his finger nervously round his collar. 'Mm yes, Herwald's daughter.'

'These sightings have been even more sinister. There's a witch abroad with the power to change shapes. They say sometimes you see her and she's a deformed cripple and at other times . . .' he dropped his voice to a whisper, 'other times she's a wolf.'

'A wolf! God preserve us, there hasn't been a wolf in Caldea for three hundred years.' The innkeeper looked flustered.

'This isn't a real wolf; this is a shapeshifter. Sometimes a small woman and sometimes a wolf. It's a witch, a thing of the Devil and God has sent us a sign that a greater evil is descending on the town of Ildros.'

'A greater evil,' the other two Inquisitors emphasized. While the taller soldier had been talking to the innkeeper, the other two soldiers had prowled around the room, studying the faces of each customer in turn.

'There have been storms in flat seas and a great monster has been seen in the waves.'

Hal was trying to conceal his expression inside his tankard while his mind raced. These people were absurdly superstitious – even seeing monsters now. It was quite ridiculous, but such imagination also meant that they had seen that wretched wolf slinking in the shadows alongside Brid and now they had conjured up this tale of shapeshifting. Damn!

'I'll just stroll through and take a look at the strangers lodging here,' one of the Inquisitors muttered before strutting off to the far side of the room and lifting a few hats to peer at the frightened faces underneath. Inquisitors, even to the innocent, had a way of imbuing fear. They required no seal from a baron, no jury nor statement from a reeve, to pass a sentence of death. They were masters of the law, holding the church law higher than any other.

'Have you seen any one at all suspicious?' demanded the tallest Inquisitor, peering down his nose at the flustered innkeeper. 'Any strangers you might have noticed?'

'Well now,' the innkeeper fiddled with the end of his moustache and set to wiping the table again. 'We had a merchant here from Ceolothia, wanting to sell some of those dogs. He was a bit sinister.'

The tall Inquisitor thumped his fist down on the table and the little innkeeper leapt backwards stammering.

'I'm not interested in any dog fights. I'm not interested in the plight of a few wretched animals. I'm here to protect the people of this country from the infiltration of the Devil and his disciples. What do I care if a few dogs lose an ear or two? They don't have souls.'

'No, sir. No sir, quite,' the innkeeper muttered.

'Anyone else?'

'No, just the usual travellers going in and out of the port and the pilgrims going to the holy shrine of St Anne.'

The Inquisitors moved through the numbers in the tavern and one of them stared arrogantly down at Hal. The Torra Altan glared back, resenting the look of authority. 'Do you know who I am, youth?' the Inquisitor demanded, obviously interpreting Hal's look as an insult.

Hal was about to declare his rank and shout this soldier down but at the last second he thought the better of it. 'Yes sir,' he replied a little more meekly. 'You are one of the King's soldiers.'

'I am an Inquisitor.' He preened himself with the title. 'Have you paid your tithe?'

'My brother pays the tithe for our entire household,' Hal retorted.

'Not your own man then. Still under someone else's roof, are you?' he sneered.

Hal wondered whether he should tell this arrogant man that his brother paid the tithe on over a thousand men and their families, protecting them from the impoverishing Church Tax and shouldering the burden himself. Branwolf argued that at least paying the Tax himself avoided the expense of collecting it. The tithe, the tenth that was raised from every man in the land to pay the Church Taxes had been a heavy burden on a man like Branwolf. The tithe, of course, paid for all the priests, churches and cathedrals right down to the gold threads on the altar cloth. The moneys raised also paid for the Inquisitors. He bit his tongue and tried to think of something polite. 'Well, of what service can I be to you, sir?'

'You can tell me your business here in Ildros, since you are obviously not selling anything.'

'I'm here to escort my young kinswoman to the shrine of St Anne's where we will pray to the holy saint for a miracle.' Hal was greatly relieved that Brid had already left the tavern.

'And so why aren't you escorting her?'

'My brother is taking her.' Hal saw no reason to complicate matters by trying to explain the precise relationship between himself and his nephew.

'And how long are you staying in Ildros?'

'Oh . . . oh, until she's better of course.'

The Inquisitor seemed satisfied with his answers. 'Well, just be wary of the shadows and stay off the back streets. We're taking the news of this shapeshifter seriously.'

The Inquisitors left and for several minutes the room was silent as the inhabitants regathered their senses.

I've got to warn them, Hal thought, urgently. He shoved past the barmaid without even noticing her and hurried out into the bright street.

Chapter 24

'Who was St Anne, anyway?' Brid asked, studiously finding something to talk about other than Hal.

Caspar unhelpfully had no idea. 'Hal might know though.'

'Well, Hal's not with us, is he? Hal is *busy*.' The sarcasm squeezed through Brid's taut lips. 'Your high and mighty uncle has better things to do than help us find the Keepers. One wink from the barmaid and he's forgotten all about the perils your father is facing in Torra Alta.'

'She doesn't mean anything to him.' Caspar tried to defend his kinsman though he wasn't too sure whether Hal deserved his loyalty. He was secretly pleased that Hal was being so indiscreet because at least that meant he was alone with Brid. She squeezed his arm as he guided her through the twisting streets.

The port of Ildros was built on a slope shelving down towards the sea. In contrast to the spacious inland sector of the town none of the precious land along the waterfront had been wasted and there the people of Ildros had piled their homes one up against the other in a tightly packed labyrinth. Brid tripped regularly and Caspar reached out a hand to support her while still anxiously looking over his shoulder and down every dark alleyway.

'Stop looking so suspicious, Spar,' she warned. 'You'll draw attention.' Dipping beneath low eaves and sweeping under archways, they traipsed through the streets, taking the constant twists and turns that led them south towards the estuary. Here they found the busy ferries that prospered by transporting the afflicted pilgrims across the water to the holy shrine. Caspar paid the fare for the crowded space on the flat-bottomed boat. The ferrymen hauled on ropes to pull them out into the tide and across the brackish waters to the far side. On the south side of the estuary, they fell in with a number of other pilgrims heading towards the shrine. Trog eagerly insisted on greeting every stranger with a slobbery kiss of his tongue though Caspar struggled breathlessly to restrain him.

The town of Ildros had sprawled across onto the far bank but here the houses were poorer and less brightly painted. The shrine of St Anne lay in open country just outside the south gate of the port. A man robed in the attire of a Benevolent Friar had a satchel round his neck and a gaggle of pilgrims clamouring closely about him. He stood next to a wall where a plaque had been hammered onto the stone.

'What does it say?' Brid demanded. 'It's too blurred for me to read.'

'The shrine of St Anne. You standeth at the point that doth overlook the harbour of Ildros. Here did holy men come in tall ships from across the southern waters to bring word of the one true God to this fair land of Caldea. Of the first numbers they did convert was the pure maiden, known as Anne, who fled from her betrothed to offer herself in holy worship to the Almighty. But as she did sing the praises of the Lord across the town, her own kinsmen, vile degenerate pagans, brought her up to this very place and with their own hands did slaughter her. St Anne's blood spilt out into the waters of the spring and ever since the stream hath run red with the stain of her blessed blood.'

'More like the Great Mother has wept tears of blood ever since for the loss of the Old Faith,' Brid caustically remarked.

Caspar gave her a quick nudge with his elbow. 'Brid, be careful, you don't know who's listening.'

'No, you're right,' she whispered as they were jostled from behind by the pressure of eager pilgrims striving to hobble or crawl towards the restorative holy waters.

The sound of weeping and wailing filled their ears as stumbling cripples, some on crutches, some borne on stretchers by their friends, filed towards the shrine. Some were blind, some deaf and some shook their heads with a pestilence that ate at their brains. Some clutched at stomachs, some had withered arms and some had stunted growth. All came shuffling painfully towards the shrine.

Stumbling over Trog as he weaved awkwardly around her legs, Brid leant heavily on Caspar's arm as she hobbled blindly towards the Benevolent Friar. He smiled at their approach.

'Young sir, it is proven that the miracle of healing is bestowed with greater favour on those who have purchased a relic of the beloved martyr. A lock of her hair, a fingernail, a bone from her right arm. And most precious of all the knife with which the devil-worshippers cut her fair throat.' The friar held up in turn a few charred and fetid-looking objects.

Fortunately Caspar was spared the embarrassment of declining one of these shrivelled-looking artefacts by an outburst from the crowd ahead.

'A miracle, a miracle!' Hysterical shrieks came from the midst of the thronging pilgrims and a woman, who an hour earlier had stumbled in on crutches, now skipped and leapt about with ecstatic energy. 'St Anne be praised. Twelve times I have visited this shrine and God has deemed me too much a sinner to be cured. But today I bought a relic from the holy friar, a lock of hair, and this affliction I was born with has left me entirely. A lock of hair.' The slender woman in a long black dress pointed enthusiastically towards the holy man.

The friar staggered back under the pressure of desperate needy pilgrims begging to press gold coins into his hands in exchange for a lock of St Anne's hair.

'She must have had hair a mile long,' Brid said flatly.

'A miracle in itself,' Caspar added scathingly. 'And to think, so many different shades. I've seen people clutching black hair, brown hair, blond hair and even grey hair. How can they let themselves be duped like this?'

Brid sighed, 'Because it offers hope and desperate people will clutch at any wisp of hope however ridiculous. I pray that man isn't really a friar. It's a terrible evil to exploit these poor people.'

They waited patiently in line as the trail of pilgrims shuffled past the shrine. Water gurgling up from a spring cascaded into a pool and slipped quietly away down towards the sea. Overlooking the pool, a stone figurine of a young girl dressed in long flowing robes cast her arms down in despair. But a look of peace smoothed her face as she gazed inland across the downs of Caldea. A small creature, indistinctly carved, scrambled at her stone skirts, imploring for the touch of her sacred hand. Caspar decided it was meant to be a hare.

The pool did indeed have a reddish tinge and the slight youth clutched at his chest in amazement, suddenly realizing that the stories must be true.

With a patronizing tone to her voice, the Maiden whispered, 'Well, of course, the water is red. The hills to the south must be full of iron ore. It's as sad as those poor miners who suffer terrible hardships in the Yellow Mountains, looking for gold when all along it's only sulphur.'

Caspar felt a little sheepish.

'Brid,' he said uncertainly, peering into the depths of the water. 'I don't suppose you can see well enough but I'm sure those are letters down there on the rocks at the bottom of the pool. They're like those funny scratch marks we saw in the fire of the Halfway Inn.'

'Stand over me,' the priestess ordered, while surreptitiously pulling her hood down to shadow her face. She bowed her head and wiped a hand over just one eye to remove the gossamer strands and squinted into the depths of the pool. She dabbed her eye again before looking up, showing the ugly white congealed matter rather than the clear vivid green of her iris.

'Anu,' she whispered. 'This is a far, far older shrine than they think. The tree runes carved in the rocks simply say Anu. She is one of our lesser Gods whose tears bring healing. Ha!' she scoffed derisively. 'When they first brought the New Faith here they obviously couldn't dissuade the simple people from worshipping at the waters. So in order for the New Church to save face they must have sanitized the pagan shrine by inventing a martyr for their New Faith and changed the name from Anu to Anne. It is a hopeful sign; we must be on the right track.'

The crowd thronging around them suddenly shied away as Trog set up an excited yelping, leaping up into the air and tugging at his lead. Caspar was virtually pulled straight over. The cord snapped and, yowling like a hound on the scent, Trog parted the crowd and sprinted away from the town southwards along the sandy coast towards dunes and then open countryside.

Hobbling after the youth, Brid struggled on her distorted ankle to keep pace but soon abandoned the attempt and left Caspar alone to sprint after the dog. Trog however had lost the scent and, nose to the ground, was scampering back and forth, snuffling at the earth. Diving at the dog, the youth, managed only to grasp his tail, which slid through his fingers as Trog continued to chase in tight circles through the long grass. Brid hopped into view.

'A sacred hare,' she murmured thoughtfully. 'Perhaps it's a sign. Perhaps he caught the scent of the sacred hare and we are being led towards the sanctuary of the Keepers.'

'It's not a hare,' Caspar informed her as he examined the ground. 'Judging by the tracks it looks more like a common cat – except . . .'

'Except what?' the girl demanded, latching on to the puzzlement in the youth's voice.

'Except it appears to have six toes.'

'Definitely a sign. Get that dog back on the lead, point him in the right direction and we'll follow him.'

Caspar, however, was still unable to retrieve the dog and it took a low whistle from the Maiden to bring the white terrier to heel. Brid was quite breathless from hopping and stumbling on her twisted leg. She rested frequently while Trog strained desperately at the lead.

'I *knew* Trog was part of a sign when we first came into

Ildros. I *knew* he would eventually lead us to the cauldron. The Mother's design is in everything,' she said excitedly.

Wagging his tail furiously, Trog dragged them over the brow of a hill and down towards a small thatched cottage guarded by a picket fence and surrounded by rowans. Now in late autumn the trees bore vivid, dark red berries, much like those from a holly tree but bigger. The front entrance was made from a stable door and the upper section swung open. They just glimpsed the tail of a black cat streaking through the opening.

The cottage and its garden had a cosy, homely look about it, with a couple of spotted piglets snuffling in their pens and a cockerel balancing arrogantly on the fence. A crooked sign hung from a single nail on the low gate.

'Widow's Cottage,' Caspar read aloud for Brid's benefit.

'That's odd,' Brid mused, tugging thoughtfully at her plait.

'Why?'

'Well, we wouldn't think much of a sign at first glance now, would we? I mean we can both read so it seems absolutely normal. But how many of the ordinary folk can read, so why bother hammering up a sign? Perhaps it's a hint that this place isn't quite what it seems.' She smiled. 'Let's pray this is it. Just mind what you say, Spar; we don't want to walk into an Inquisitor's trap.' She politely knocked at the door while Caspar struggled to control Trog.

Presently a little old woman, bent double on her walking stick, shuffled round the back of the cottage, carrying an armful of late flowering borage now gone to seed. She was dressed entirely in black with a knitted shawl wrapped around her stooped shoulders. She had a broad fleshy nose, spiky eyebrows but good strong teeth when she smiled at them.

'Two young travellers,' she declared. 'Now what would you fine people be doing on the threshold of my humble dwelling?' She looked at them curiously and twitched at her shawl, betraying her unease at their unexplained visit.

Caspar remained obediently silent, wondering what Brid would say.

'We've been to the shrine of the martyr St Anne, to pray for a miracle. As I prayed I saw a vision of a cat, an unusual cat. The saint told me to follow the animal here where I might find a cure for my afflictions.'

'There's no miracles to be had here.' The woman laughed nervously. 'Nothing but hard work and a draughty cottage to be had here.' She began to turn away. 'If you want miracles go and buy a relic from the good friar down there at the shrine.'

Frustration was brewing in Caspar's mind. If this old woman was one of the Keepers' contacts surely she would recognize the Maiden but Brid, of course, looked the part of a noble-woman driven by her afflictions to a pilgrimage and like this there was no way of telling that she was a high-priestess just by looking at her. If this woman was something to do with the Keepers she would be as reluctant as Brid to reveal her true identity.

'Oh and we hoped so much.' The Maiden swished forward in her blue skirts and hooked the widow's arm. 'We've come such a long way to find someone that could give me the sight. And to straighten my foot,' she despaired. 'I'd give anything.'

She lifted her skirt and showed the ugly ankle that was swollen and red from where she had cruelly punished herself by walking on it for so long. Circling the foot to demonstrate the lack of movement, she dragged the toe through the earth. When she stepped back she left a circle in the ground. Caspar feared that marking out the sign of the Mother was perhaps a little too blatant. He blinked nervously.

The old woman stared at the ground and sucked at her lip. She turned and shuffled towards the door of the cottage. 'You'd better come in. Perhaps we'll find you some magic here after all. We can't stand out in the open. Them men with their black clothes and long spears are crawling all over the barony. All shiny and black like beetles, they are.'

This has to be the place, Caspar thought with excitement. He sensed Brid's relief as she eagerly limped after the bent old woman into the humble cottage. Small though he was Caspar still had to duck his head beneath the door lintel as they followed the widow into the poky dwelling. Brid tripped on the threshold and he hurriedly caught her. Now as they stepped out of the sunlight into the dimly lit room, the Maiden, with her eyes blinded by cobweb, could evidently see nothing at all.

'Here, sit by the fire,' the widow said warmly, though there was a touch of tremor to her voice. She peered out into the daylight, looking anxiously from side to side before swinging the stable door to and latching it shut.

Caspar found he was trembling. This must be it. At last they had found the place. The cauldron with its runes must be close by. As soon as they found it their problems would be over. They could retrieve the Egg and return to rescue his mother and overthrow the Vaalakans. His mouth was dry with the excitement of anticipation. He wondered how long they would have to keep up the elaborate pretence. Brid was obviously not yet certain otherwise she would have removed the painful veil of gossamer from her eyes.

Trog strangely ignored the cat. Perhaps now that it wasn't running away it had lost much of its tantalizing appeal. He nuzzled protectively up against the priestess's skirts and turned his back on the sylph-like lynx lying stretched out before the fire. Only the minute twitching of the tip of the black cat's tail showed that it was awake. Trog's tail was between his legs and his hackles were up. Brid patted him reassuringly.

The six-toed cat made Caspar feel uneasy. He couldn't see it as a creature from a benevolent Goddess who would give them protection. It was black with tufted ears and an unnatural number of toes; he couldn't help feeling it came from the Devil. Brid of course didn't even believe in the Devil, but Caspar had been brought up to fear him and if anything ever belonged to the sinister spirit that cat was it. He wished Hal was there with them. He felt uneasy without his uncle's reassuring presence.

'Have some spiced wine,' the humble widow implored them, ladling out liquid from a pot kept warm on the stone hearth.

'Have some wine before we talk.' Her voice crackled like the fire.

'I'd rather have something a little milder,' Brid said, still playing to her disguise as a well-bred lady of Belbidia.

'Well, that's no problem, my dear.' A hospitable tone warmed the old woman's voice. 'I'll just swing the cauldron over the flames and brew you up a cup of camomile tea in the blink of cat's eye. It'll soothe you a little and then – we'll talk.' She emphasized the last word as if implying a greater meaning.

She swung the black pot over the flames of the fire and prodded up a little more heat with a poker. When it boiled she splashed out two cups of camomile tea, one for herself and one for Brid, and ladled out some wine for the auburn-haired youth perched on the edge of his stool. Caspar twisted his feet away from the cat just to make sure he didn't touch it.

Despite the sinister animal he was certain, however, that they must have come to the right place. Any normal old woman would have been all of a flutter at the thought of entertaining nobles in such a humble dwelling. He wondered why Brid was being so cautious but he supposed after their experiences in Farona it certainly didn't pay to be open. Brid opened her hands and waited for the woman to press the cup into her palm and guide her fingers around the horn base. She sniffed the liquid and took a tentative sip.

After his experiences at Bullback's manor Caspar was wary of the potent Caldean wine, but the smell was sweet and tantalizing. He took one small sip and was pleasantly surprised at how easily the liquid slipped down his throat rather than raking over his tongue and drying out his palate like the wine in Jotunn had done. For a moment he felt impatient as he wondered when this woman would finally declare herself a pagan, as he felt sure she must; but the urgency left him. He relaxed back to watch the flames dancing in the grate.

'I've just made some honeyed oatcakes. They're flavoured with cinnamon spice that's shipped in straight from the southern seas. We're lucky here in Ildros 'cos we can get such exotic spices at a very fair price. Sometimes the sailors are a bit careless with the odd sack load.'

Caspar didn't know whether it would be impolite to laugh or not so he merely coughed nervously into his hand. He felt perplexed that even though Brid had written the sign of the Mother this old woman still hadn't declared herself. Perhaps she was more nervous of discovery than they were. Anxious to hide his disconcertion he bit into an oatcake. It was deliciously sweet with an unusual tangy flavour, smelling of exotic fruits.

Brid nibbled tentatively. She ate a couple of mouthfuls before surreptitiously slipping the rest of the cake to the dog. Trog sat up, slobbering, and begged for more.

'I won't be a minute,' the old widow mumbled. 'I'll just pop out the back and bring in a bundle of wood for the fire. There's plenty more cake, so you help yourself *then* we'll talk.'

She slipped out behind a heavy sacking curtain, covering a doorway at the back of the cottage, and Caspar sat back on his wooden stool. It was a simple room, with a table pushed up against one wall, to make room for the low stools crowding around the wide roaring fire. He decided that the old widow probably felt the cold more than they did. He wondered where she kept the cauldron. Trog was now stretched out in front of the fire, his pink belly showing through the short hairs of his coat. He was snoring loudly.

'Brid,' he whispered, taking another sip of his warm wine. 'Is this the right place?'

She reached up to her face, peeled back her eyelids and wiped away the cobwebs. 'Yes, it must be. I was worried at first when she gave us the tea because I thought she was trying to slip something into it, but it definitely smells and tastes just like camomile. I think she's only being cautious, which of course is only right.' Blinking, she looked curiously around the room while nibbling at another oatcake.

Briefly Caspar wondered why he felt so warm and drowsy, considering the time of year but gradually he decided he didn't care. The heat from the fire, the wine . . . He tried to remember what he was doing here and suddenly felt confused. What had happened to Hal? He vaguely remembered that they had gone to visit a shrine and his uncle had refused to come. Of course: the barmaid. He shook himself, trying to organize his thoughts but they wandered hazily through his mind, searching out abstracts and losing reason. He felt numb and a little sick. His hand seemed to be stretching away from him and the ceiling appeared to be falling towards him. The cat's purring throbbed in his ears, louder and louder until it came like the rasping roar of a blacksmith's bellows. The flames of the fire leapt up into sparks of green and blue, swimming out and dancing round the room. They condensed into ghostly shapes of laughing children that coiled around him, smothering him in their warm heady breath.

He had no energy. Only his eyes were able to move as they followed blurred shapes that skulked around the perimeter of the darkened room. A great weight pressed down on his chest, restricting his breathing, but he couldn't see or understand what caused it. Neither his legs nor arms responded to his will but hung limply like sodden rags from his collapsed body. He couldn't even blink. Sounds were distorted, rushing in and out like the sea. Slumped in her chair, Brid's head had fallen forward onto her chest and the horn cup of camomile tea lay spilt on the floor.

He tried to move his mouth to call out to her but only a thin moan escaped his lips.

'What did you bring them in here for?' An angry voice welled up from somewhere behind him in the darkened room. 'Can't you see they've got noble blood? Look at their clothes. You'll have that dodderer Baron Cadros after us. And the place is already crawling with the King's soldiers; what were you thinking of? We agreed we wouldn't do any more till the Inquisitors had left Ildros.'

'They came all of their own accord,' the voice of the old widow objected. 'Took me quite a while to know what to do, but I didn't think they'd be missed. That young girl ain't what she seems. She certainly ain't no noble lass from Belbidia: she drew a pagan sign in the dirt. So whoever they are, no one's going to call up no official bloodhounds if they're mixed up with her. I reckon they mistook us for someone else.'

'I still don't like it,' the man growled.

'Well, it's too late now.' The words were spoken by another woman with a soft silky voice, deep and melodiously soporific as if she was lulling a child to sleep. 'We might as well make the most of them. We'll get them tied up and down below before they regain their senses.'

Caspar's hands were wrenched behind his back and drawn tight with a rope. He tried to struggle but his limbs felt like liquid and merely lolled helplessly. The old widow was stooping over Brid and suddenly leapt back shrieking in horror.

'Satan have mercy, the Devil take my soul!'

The man grunted as he cinched Caspar's bonds tighter. 'Stop shrieking, Agnes, or you'll raise the Devil himself. Are you losing your senses, witch?'

'I don't like it. I don't like it at all. This just ain't natural,' the widow continued to mutter.

The younger woman, also dressed in black but with a tightly fitting smooth dress, swayed into Caspar's line of vision and flicked up Brid's head with a sharp snap of her wrist. He recognized her as the miraculously cured woman from the shrine. 'You said she was blind,' she accused the widow. 'This girl isn't blind.'

'Well, perhaps she really did have a miracle at the St Anne's shrine,' the man spoke harshly, laughing in his throat at his own humour.

The younger woman didn't seem to find him amusing. 'You know better than any other that there's not been a miracle in your lifetime and like as not there's never been one.' The younger woman flicked her head round to scowl at her male accomplice. No longer soft and soothing, her voice was sharp like bitter acid. 'Agnes is losing her senses, that's all. She's going simple on us.'

'I'm telling you, Puzella, that she came in here with white cankerous tissue where her eyes should have been. And now they're green but a green like you've never seen,' the widow indignantly defended herself.

'Why did they come here?' There was a touch of tremor fringing the young woman's voice. 'We lured all the others: a promise here or there to a lonely desperate pilgrim. But these two? Agnes, what did they say?'

'I didn't really listen too hard but I couldn't turn down such a gift. Like a couple of flies walking straight into the web they were. Two pilgrims alone. All pilgrims carry gold and these two look wealthier than most. I couldn't pass up the opportunity. I didn't ask too many questions, but gave them the drugged cakes, though she was suspicious of the wine and the tea. I reckoned if she realized the drink was wholesome she wouldn't worry about the cakes.'

Caspar couldn't believe that they'd been so stupid. He could only be relieved that at least they had no gold on them. Hal had insisted that he took charge of all the money save for a few groats, so at any rate they couldn't be robbed.

'Well, let's have a look at this mysterious cripple.' The man sounded both angry and worried. 'Agnes, if you've done something that'll bring us trouble, you know what Puzella here will have done to you, don't you?'

The old widow shrank lower into her shawl at this threat. Caspar couldn't possibly imagine what the younger woman would do. He could hear the footfalls of the man as he stalked across the room towards the shutters. He shoved one aside to let a shaft of daylight into the room. 'Well, let's take a better look at her.' The details of the man's robed outline were suddenly filled in and Caspar realized with disgust that he was looking at the Benevolent Friar from the shrine. 'The Inquisitors are going to take no more of a liking to us taking advantage of St Anne, bless her bleeding heart, than they will to a moon-touched woman drawing circles with her foot.'

The old woman, who had seemed so harmless, cowered behind the robes of the Benevolent Friar and the taller form of the other woman. Puzella was young, just about marrying age. Her simple black dress squeezed her bosom, clutched her waist and cascaded from her rounded hips before sweeping out around her ankles. Her hair was already silver as if it had been washed in moonlight and her eyes, set against her ivory skin, were silvery-grey like mercury.

The friar swept forwards and craned over Brid. 'Why are you so frightened of this little snippet, Agnes? She's little more than a girl.'

'You let Puzella dabble in all sorts of crafts to twist the fates for your own ends and yet you don't even recognize the significance of those eyes,' the old hag complained. 'She'll bring those Inquisitors hot on her tail and then we'll be done for.'

'Don't you get sharp with me, you old bat. It was you that invited them in and it's you alone that'll be done for.'

'They looked wealthy and there was nothing odd about her except that she was blind. But look at her now. She's one of them old people. She'll put the evil eye on us. Like as not the boy's one of them too: a warlock in the making.'

'We have our own powers,' the younger woman sneered.

'Shut up! Shut up!' The friar was beginning to crack. 'I think we should get rid of them and fast. Just get rid of them.'

'Don't be such a coward. We've got them here now; we might as well see what they've got on them.' As the woman probed the priestess's body with her long-nailed fingers, Brid twisted her head and moaned. She shook her head vigorously as if trying to bring herself to her senses and suddenly lunged forward, managing to bite the woman's hand. The woman slapped her hard and waited until the friar had Brid's jaw viciously clamped in his hard grip.

The mercury-eyed woman resumed her search. 'Now look what we've got here.' She sighed with satisfaction. 'I think she's hiding something.'

There was a sudden hiss as the bright scarlet snout of the salamander jutted out from beneath Brid's collar. The silken-voiced woman leapt back in fright. 'What the . . . ? A lizard!' The tension in her voice relaxed. She advanced and pinched the animal behind the neck and dragged it out from the layers of Brid's clothing. 'I'd say we'd get a fine price for this. Make someone an expensive purse this red skin would but . . .'

The salamander's claws were firmly clasped around the leather net that ensnared the moonstone. The orb was still wrapped in the hare's skin and the woman carefully unravelled the covering and discarded the damp cloth, which shielded the moonstone's powers.

'Wow!'

'Don't touch it,' Brid warned with pleading, her voice slurred and breathy.

The woman stared back at her and grinned. 'Now, why ever not?'

'It's evil.'

'Ha! And you think I'm afraid of evil!' She shook off the salamander that scurried away to the folds of Brid's skirt and stared into the orb.

'It's glowing, Puzella. Put it down,' the friar demanded nervously.

'It has power. I will be truly rich now, not just a few purses of gold.' She pressed her palm onto the orb and looked wondrously at the swirling patterns. 'I don't believe it,' she whispered. 'It moves.' Her eyes bulged in amazement. 'I can see things in it! There's a man. I think it's a man, wearing a mask, some sort of skull. He's reaching out towards me.' She laughed delightedly. 'Make it work for me, girl. What does it do?'

'It will show only your death,' Brid said icily. Caspar hoped the priestess's comment might warn off the sinister woman.

'Give it back to her, Puzella,' pleaded the friar. 'Give it back to her.'

'No. I'm the one that takes all the risks in our little schemes. I'm the one that sells the goods on to the merchants at the quayside. I want some reward. I'm going to keep it.'

'I think we should let them both go,' argued the old woman. 'They won't bring any harm to us 'cos they're obviously not on the right side of the law themselves.'

'I'm not afraid of this girl,' shrieked the silvery-haired woman. 'Do you think she is more powerful than me just because she has this bauble? I'm the most feared witch in all Caldea. You two can do what you like with them. I'll just have the crystal ball here and leave the rest to you.'

'No, don't leave us, Puzella,' the friar pleaded. 'You know I can't do what's necessary. We need you. We've got to get rid of these two. Agnes isn't thinking straight.'

Puzella paused in mid-stride towards the door, clutching the glowing moonstone to her bosom. The orb's silvery light accentuated her black and white colouring. She nodded reluctantly. 'I'll dispose of them as you say. You'll only bungle it and attract attention to me.' She snapped her fingers.

The noise of little scampering feet came up from below the cottage's floor. A stone flag slid back and several creatures emerged, hurrying up out of the cellars. They stared straight into Caspar's eyes and laughed hysterically. He gawped back at the thin alien faces, staring at their minute mouths, small pointed noses with slits for nostrils and their close-set eyes. They chatted and chirruped more like birds than people as their gnarly fingers clasped around him and the Maiden before bumping them along the stone floor of the cottage. They were half-sized creatures, virtually naked except for a mat of bracken and moss draped around their loins, below which sprouted spindly stick-like legs and rough barky skin. Kobolds, Caspar thought thinking of the tales his nurse used to tell him.

A little sensation had returned to Caspar's limbs so he squirmed and wriggled. It had no effect on the sprightly creatures except to increase their gleeful shrieks as the kobolds dragged them down into the cellar, thumping down the cold hard steps into a dank airless space. The tall woman swept ahead into the dark with a brand from the fire and lit rows of candles that flickered into life, bringing shape to the low-ceilinged room. Earthenware pots were stacked to the beams on shelves lining the walls and sitting on the floor was a large wicker basket full of hair. The centre of the room was dominated by a cold slab of grey stone. In horror, Caspar vainly struggled but found that he was hamstrung by the friar's knots strapping his arms and legs.

'I'm a bit short of relics,' the friar muttered, stepping back from the cackle of half-sized men shrieking around his feet. They eagerly pawed at Caspar's body and smacked their lips with little black tongues. 'Make sure they leave something for me.'

'Oh my little men always know to do that now, don't you?' the silver-tongued woman sighed and then glared at the friar. 'But you can't have the girl's heart. I want her powers.'

Oh God, help us, Caspar prayed inwardly.

'Oh Mother,' Brid implored out loud.

'She won't listen to you,' sneered the woman. Her jutting breasts were squashed up against Caspar's face as she struggled to lift the helpless boy onto the stone slab. 'I have discovered many secrets of the old ways and I draw on Her power now.'

Oh God, have mercy on me, Caspar thought. This is what we at Torra Alta have been seduced into following. Is this what happens to the Mother's followers? Is this what happens to people when they lose sight of the word of the Father? I should have listened more to Gwion's sermons. He must have been brought up with these strange beliefs in Morrigwen's cottage; he knew what he was preaching against.

'Never,' Brid spat the word between clenched teeth. 'You know nothing of the Mother. Your soul has spent too long in the worship of this new god who gives you no sense of belief or understanding. Whatever ceremonies you have unearthed without the understanding in your soul you will have twisted and contaminated with the love of opulence and lavish ceremony learnt from the New Faith. Your soul is seduced by power that shows no love of the Mother. Any tricks you have learnt have nothing to do with witchcraft.'

'High words for one so small.' The smooth-tongued woman jabbed a finger at Brid's stomach. 'Everyone knows that pagans draw on the power of the Devil and I need his help.' She tossed back her head and rolled her steely eyes, shrieking fiendishly. 'I will draw on his power.'

'Brid!' Caspar finally found his voice, though his words escaped in a thin breathy whine. 'Brid, help!' he begged, realizing how stupid he was to think there could be any evil in the Maiden's pure burning soul. He had fallen into the same trap as the woman and even Rewik, thinking the old ways were automatically tied to the Devil. 'Brid!'

Fleshless fingers dragged at the skin on his neck. One of the insect-like creatures sat on his stomach and pinched at his skin, testing his plumpness. He roared at the kobolds, stripping the skin from his throat with the fierceness of the cry. They looked startled for a second. One of them shrieked like a stuck piglet. But they soon returned to hopping and crawling all over him while the woman produced a black book from the shelf.

'If we can get his heart out while it's still pumping, the book tells me I will have further power. Is that not right, little creatures? We haven't managed it yet, have we, my little men? But perhaps now with the power of the crystal we can do it.' The kobolds' eyes followed her attentively round the room. 'If I place the crystal on his chest perhaps it will keep him alive just long enough.'

Oh God, have mercy, Caspar prayed fervently. They're going to cut us up and sell us little by little as relics from a saint.

'What do you think, little man?' The woman stroked the enlarged warty head of a kobold who clung to her skirts. 'We'll try with him first. Have a little practice on him before we give his offal to our dear friar. Then we'll be better able to get her heart. We want her power.' The kobold somersaulted in delight and looked gleefully up into her face.

There was a fiendish shriek and a howl from above their heads. The two sinister women and the friar froze while the kobolds scampered and hid under the table.

'What was that?' Puzella's voice was ice-cold with fear. There was another terrible howl.

'I forgot the dog.' The older woman relaxed, reaching for a club.

'Didn't you poison him?' demanded the younger woman incredulously.

'I gave him the cakes; it put him to sleep like the others.'

'Go and deal with him, both of you. That noise will draw the reeve as well as the Inquisitors. I've got work to do.' She reached for a silver sickle and sharpened it on a whetstone. The kobolds' heads flicked to and fro, following the rhythm of her hands.

The sound of splintering wood and a terrible shriek from the cat alarmed the relic-sellers. The widow and the friar leapt for the stairs while the devilish woman in her silky black dress stalked towards Caspar's throat.

She pressed the cool orb onto his bare skin. The youth could feel its power throbbing through him and suddenly sensed his mother desperately clawing through the layers of crushing Vaalakan ice to reach him.

'Pray, Spar, pray,' Brid screamed, trying to cut through the panic in the boy's mind. He couldn't register her words but sensed only the whispered breath of his mother coming from within the heart of the moonstone. *Pray, Spar, pray. Call on the Mother; call on her love. Worship her, love her and she will heed you.*

As the woman's sharp fingernails stabbed at his ribcage, Caspar was too panicked to think clearly. 'Hal, where are you? Hal, help me!' Hal wasn't there. Hal was too preoccupied with some plump-looking girl in the inn.

'Spar,' Brid's voice cut through the turmoil of fear. 'You can reach her. Pray!'

The ceiling above shook with the weight of stamping feet. Furniture crashed to the floor and blood-curdling screams cut the air.

Caspar stared in horror at the woman's raised hand and at the point of her glinting sickle poised above his heart. He filled his lungs and screamed. 'Mother! Mother help me! Mother!' He knew that he was thinking of Keridwen but he felt her voice calling out along with his: *Mother, Great Mother, spare my child, spare him.*

Suddenly the air was thick with expectant silence. A low growl from above disturbed the stillness as the woman's blade hovered above the boy's breastbone. He could fix only on the point. Every other image blurred. His hearing left him as he could sense only the thump, thump of his heart and the hungry tip of the sickle poised over it. A vague outline stirred in his blurred vision and his eyes were drawn to the spiky brown hand with long twiggy fingers that coiled around the woman's white arm. A sudden burst of excited chattering from the kobolds told the boy of a change in their emotions. Their eyes swung away from the tall woman to the little naked figure of a female kobold standing on Caspar's stomach. It was her hand that gripped the woman's poised arm.

Curiously the creature, with long stiff hair more like moss or old man's beard that drapes the trees in winter, was slightly bigger than the male kobolds. They all looked to her as she barked some dry commands in a fast incomprehensible diction. One of the little tree-men snatched the sickle and scurried over to Brid, slicing urgently through her bonds with rapid movements.

The others scrabbled at the knots securing the youth to the slab. Unable to prise them apart with their fingers they started to gnaw at them with pointed black teeth that looked more like the thorns from a rosebush.

The tall woman backed off, clutching the orb to her breast. 'Obey me! Obey me! I have the power. I found you. I've fed you. I've sheltered you from the Inquisitors. You are my slaves. Obey me!'

The little kobolds ignored her and continued to gnaw at the ropes, sitting cross-legged, all angles, with their knees and elbows forming a thatch like the twigs in a thicket.

The female kobold was lovingly stroking Brid's brow and turned only to spit at the woman.

The silver-haired woman raised her head anxiously towards the ceiling. 'In Satan's name what's happening?' she screamed in desperation.

There was no reply.

Her face boiled up in black rage and then suddenly she went white as the woman danced around her, gaily brandishing the sickle. The little men snapped to their feet and bristled like a thorn hedge around their matriarch. Puzella gathered her skirts and, possessively clutching the moonstone, fled towards a concealed door at the back of the dank room.

'No! Not the Eye. Don't let her take it,' Brid cried, as the kobolds sawed at her bonds.

But Puzella was gone.

Chapter 25

The streets were crawling with pilgrims. Hal thumped into the back of a one-legged man in his efforts to force his way through the constricted streets towards the shrine of St Anne. He'd been back and forth several times along the pilgrimage route but he still hadn't found them. He hoped he hadn't missed them on the ferry crossing. They had been gone hours. Where had they got to? He kicked himself for being such a fool.

How could he have left Brid with only Spar to protect her amidst all these dangers? In the circumstances Caspar wouldn't be much use; his bright blue eyes would attract almost as much attention as the priestess herself. Brid's looks were only more suspicious because she was a girl and everyone knew that the Old Faith was only led by women. He prayed Brid had kept to her disguise.

He caught his breath as he saw two soldiers ahead, both mounted on sleek horses. They were stirring the crowd with their long pikestaffs and tilting up girls' faces as the pilgrims filed past on the way to the shrine. Oh, God, help me he prayed and then wondered whether his prayers would be heard, now that he was meddling in heathen affairs. But whatever Branwolf and Spar did, he still held firmly to his faith in the Lord. He didn't worry over the contradiction in asking for the Goddess's help. The Vaalakans feared her and if those simplistic, superstitious people believed that Torra Alta wielded the power of the Great Mother then they would be easily driven back to the tundra. Personally he felt all of it was superstitious nonsense, except of course for the power in the sword: he knew that was real. He was sorry though for Caspar and Branwolf and their anguish over Keridwen. That was the one part he really couldn't understand. How could the woman still be alive? Secretly he believed that she was dead and her voice and image were part of the illusory magic of the moonstone.

But the Inquisitors were not an illusion and he couldn't bear to contemplate the thought of Brid burning at the stake. Oh God, don't let her walk straight back towards me. Please God, don't let her come straight towards the Inquisitors.

At last Caspar's bonds slid away from his frayed wrist. He leapt towards the small door, through which the woman had fled. It was bolted from the other side. He turned to race after Brid, who was already hobbling up the stairs with a stream of kobolds at her heels. It took Caspar less than a second to catch up with them.

He couldn't lose the moonstone. Morrigwen was certain they would need the orb to read the runes on the lost cauldron. They needed it to find the Egg otherwise they couldn't rescue his mother. They couldn't lose the moonstone. A red streak leapt at Brid's back and gripped her hair. Now even the salamander was separated from the moonstone and no longer fed its warmth to Keridwen. Caspar could only think of the terrible cold of the glacier, the cold of death.

He blinked in the sunlight flooding through the swinging stable door. It had been ripped open and the two grey eyes of Brid's wolf stared out from over the bloody carcasses of the old woman and the friar. Trog still held the widow's wrist in his mouth while the wolf's teeth bared as she lowered to a crouch, ready to spring.

'Quiet, Wolf,' Brid ordered urgently while the kobolds cowered behind her, chattering feverishly.

Trog was shaking. He dropped the woman's torn arm and, beating his tail nervously, he crept forward. Caspar patted him.

Brid stepped through the gory carnage without taking a second glance at the shredded skin and open wounds oozing blood from the couple's face and neck. They certainly weren't going to cause any more trouble, Caspar thought without any regret as he stared at the dead bodies. Brid was still rushing to the door in her awkward hobble. Urgently she searched left and right.

'She's gone.' She turned back towards the female kobold. 'Where has she gone?'

The barky imp gabbled and chirruped incoherently, waving her long twiggy arms in a frenzy of gesticulation and bowed low. The little men followed her example and prostrated themselves. Like quivering saplings on a breezy day, they shook before the presence of the Maiden. The little tree sprite raised her hands above her head, lightly touching her fingertips to make the circular sign of the Mother. Brid returned the sign and dropped to her knees to be level with the creatures who had streaming tears rolling down their warty cheeks. The female kobold unhooked one of her long crooked fingers and pointed at Brid's dazzling green eyes. She shrieked excitedly and leapt to her feet, hopping and skipping. The little men, who obviously looked to her for example, did the same.

'What's she saying?' Caspar demanded urgently.

Brid turned to look at him with exasperation. 'How should I know? I can't understand a single word.'

The half-sized woman threw her hands into the air in despair and looked urgently round the room. She chirruped to the excited tree-men and Caspar looked in disgust as they dipped their scratchy fingers into the pool of the friar's blood that had collected on the cold stone tiles of the floor. Then he realized what they were doing. Each of them followed the little woman's instructions and painted scratchy patterns on the ground.

'Aren't kobolds meant to live in forests?' Caspar asked as they waited for the creatures to finish.

Brid nodded. 'Yes, but deciduous ones like the oak and beech woods of northern Belbidia. Caldea's been cultivated for so long with vines that there aren't many trees left here. They can't live in yews: they're too poisonous. I imagine they've had to scrape an existence amongst the vines. Look! Tree runes,' Brid sighed with relief as she looked at the spidery marks drawn in blood.

'What do they say?' Caspar twisted his head round, trying to work out which way up to read the lettering.

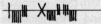

'Last moon the blood of Anu ran pure. A sign that the Mother's wounds no longer bled. We thought it was Puzella who was part of the old ways but we were wrong.'

The kobolds all hung their heads in shame. Brid reached out a hand and clutched the sensitive creatures to her. They chirruped delightedly.

The little woman scratched away again.

'You came to save us,' Brid read out loud and then nodded. 'Yes, but we have to find the Mother Cauldron first. We think it is somewhere here in Ildros.'

The little kobold scraped her bloodied fingers over the stone floor again.

'What's it say?' the boy impatiently demanded, puzzling at the shapes.

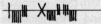

'Anu knows.' Brid shrugged and turned back to the tree sprites. 'What does Anu know?'

The kobold woman looked up quickly and drew her narrow eyes even closer together. She clawed her bloodied finger across the stones again. Brid read aloud, 'Anu looks at it.' The high-priestess sighed. 'At last we've found it. But the moonstone. Where will that woman go?'

Brid turned her head to read the lettering as the creature painted them. 'To the ships.'

The kobolds all leapt up and down and pointed northwards towards the dark green swell of the ocean.

'Get my foot straight,' Brid demanded urgently, slumping back into a chair. 'Pull it straight.'

'Don't you need to relax it first?' Caspar argued.

'We haven't got time.' The Maiden glared fiercely into his face. 'Just do it!'

The kobolds reluctantly wrapped themselves around her calf, their screechy voices even more shrill and excited as they jostled and elbowed for space. Caspar sat at the Maiden's feet, took a deep breath, snatched up her ankle and pulled really hard, bracing himself against the legs of the chair. He could feel the bones sliding over each other until they finally snapped back into place. White-faced, Brid gritted her teeth and took short sharp breaths. Her lower lip trembled slightly but then she bit it determinedly. She rose and, still limping, sped towards the door and stared towards the harbour.

'Quick, Spar! The fastest way will be back by the shrine.' The wolf had already vanished but Trog yipped and plunged after her. The kobolds also started forward around her skirts as if they too wished to help, but she halted and stooped down to them. 'No,' she ordered quite firmly. 'No, it's too dangerous for you.' They hung their heads like scolded hounds. 'Go back to the vines and the trees and the hollows. Hide from these big people until the Mother returns.' The female kobold barked at her troop of men and they scurried to gather round her. She raised her hands and sadly made the sign of the Mother. The little men bowed low and in the next instance they had faded away into the shadows.

The shrine was visible now as they leapt through the dunes and ran onto the road. A few pilgrims shuffled barefoot along the road, doing their penance, but there was no sign of the woman. Brid kept on running.

'The Eye, the Eye,' she gasped. 'We must not lose it.'

Suddenly Caspar realized that running as she was with her

leg now miraculously straight and her eyes gleaming bright she was beginning to draw attention. He clutched at her arm.

'Brid, be careful.'

'We can't be careful. We have to find her.'

Hal placed his hands on the shoulders of the man in front and hoisted himself up, trying to see above the heads of the crowd. Where had they got to? A stream of the crippled, the old, and the weak crawled, shuffled or were carried past the shrine. Each pilgrim dipped a finger into the blood-coloured water as they passed.

'There was a miracle here earlier today,' someone announced. 'She bought a relic from a friar but he's gone now.'

Hal hoped that had nothing to do with Brid. One of the Inquisitors was looking suspiciously at him and he realized that his anxious manner was attracting attention. He walked calmly past and moved away from the shrine and a little way up the hill to get a better view of the town. Suddenly he heard an excited yip. He snapped his head round. That had to be Trog. No other dog had such a ridiculous bark. He turned and ran up towards the dunes just in time for the heavy terrier to thump into him. Brid and Caspar were just below him on the other side. He waved them back, urgently hoping they were still out of view from the Inquisitors.

'Get back; keep down,' he cried urgently, but not too loudly. He realized with dismay that Brid was running freely and with the sure-footed precision of someone who could see clearly.

Caspar caught his eye and snatched at Brid, pulling her to a halt. Hal could breathe again. They had seen him. He trotted down more casually.

'The place is crawling with Inquisitors. What the hell's happened? You look like someone's tried to murder you.'

'You wouldn't believe us if we told you,' Caspar panted. 'But we've got to get to the port. A woman's stolen the moonstone.'

Hal looked at them in disbelief. Only his nephew could allow something as idiotic as that to happen. How could he let someone steal it? Didn't he realize how vital it was? He looked at Caspar and groaned, allowing his expression to say everything.

'It wasn't like that.' Caspar regained his breath, obviously interpreting Hal's expression correctly. 'We've got to get to the quay. We think she'll take a ship.'

'Well, we can't go past the shrine. The word's out. I hope your wolf's not around, Brid. They're looking for both of you.'

Wasting no time they turned off the road. Twisting back and forth down the steeply shelving hillside, they twined their way through the small terraced gardens, where the outlying townsfolk grew colewort and pot marigolds for the kitchen table. Hopping over a couple of low fences and avoiding a pen of sows they eventually found their way into the lower half of the town. Here the houses were a neglected dun colour where the original whitewash had been ravaged by the briny breeze. They had small windows compared to the big white airy villas that graced the upper town. The place stank of fish and the air was thick with the squabbles of seagulls squawking above in the strip of sky between the rooftops. At last they arrived at the lapping waters of the estuary where a row of open fishing boats tugged at their moorings. An elderly eelman raised an eyebrow at their unexpected appearance and sucked at his pipe.

'Can you row us across?' Hal panted.

The old man seemed unimpressed. 'Pilgrims, it's noon. I'm not going out again until I've had a good meal. You fine folks shouldn't be in such a hurry. It's not good for the constitution to go rushing about in the middle of the day.'

'Please,' Brid implored in her softest, most cajoling voice, instantly bringing a smile to the old man's tanned face. His long whiskers twitched upwards and his eyes glinted at her. Brid needed to say no more.

'I might be an old man but I can't refuse so fair a maiden.' He pushed himself up and moved quite smartly towards his boat, politely helping Brid to a seat in the stern, which she shared with Trog. Caspar wondered how the wolf crossed the water and decided she must run inland until the estuary became a fordable river. Both Hal and Caspar impatiently offered to row but the old man shook his head. 'It's skill not youthful muscle that gets you smoothly across, so if you don't mind stowing yourselves in the bows, young gentlemen.'

Caspar perched in the bow, craning forward to scan the approaching shore as the water slipped past the curved hull and the oars groaned and creaked against their rollocks. The rhythmical beat swept them across the estuary mouth. Hal paid the eelman handsomely, who smiled gratefully, nodding a polite farewell to Brid as he used one oar to push himself back out into the mainstream. The three Torra Altans turned to hurry towards the main harbour.

The port was bobbing with ships of all sizes, sails, hulls and keels. Bright unreefed sails flapped loose and taut ropes hummed against their masts while the tamed harbour waves constantly lapped against the ships' hulls. Further out the sea was decorated with multi-coloured sails, some running before the wind, inland towards the harbour, and some tacking away into the boundless ocean.

'Look, over there.' Caspar pointed to a woman in a black dress, moving along the quay past the fruit stall that they had visited the previous day.

But as they caught up with her she turned out to be an older, shorter woman with a round face and ruddy cheeks. She turned and looked at them in startled surprise.

'Back! Run back,' Hal urged. 'She must be on another pier. She couldn't have found a passage already.'

They ducked in and out of fishing nets, weaved through mooring ropes and scoured the decks of every vessel, but all in vain.

'We can't lose the Druid's Eye.' Brid looked forlornly at the two youths, her vivid green eyes sparkling like dew drops in a forest, 'We just can't!'

Chapter 26

He shrank into the hollow. Maybe here he could shield his scorching back from the heat in the emptiness above. He longed for the cool peace of the caves; but he longed more for the glow.

He licked at his claw, removing the last remnants of sheep. He was sick of sheep.

The glow was coming towards him. He broadened his claws and felt the tremors running through the earth. Yes, he was certain. He had nothing left now without the glow. The other Fire Beings had died in the caverns. First Grandfather. His old bones had been brittle and the flesh tough, he remembered. Then his mother. Was he the very last Fire Being?

Grandfather had said how they once stretched their wings and took to the great emptiness above and could see the mountains and the canyon and the river. He'd never seen any of it; he had only ever seen the glow.

He hated everything. He was angry that they had died and left him alone in that underworld. Even killing the sheep hadn't eased his hatred. He had eaten as many as he could but kept on killing; killing because they ran; killing because they bleated; killing because they could see and he couldn't.

But the glow was coming towards him. He would wait until the burning from above eased away. Then he would crawl out of the hollow.

He let his snout slump onto the ground and fluttered his nostrils, the breath sighing out of him. He wanted to singe all this grass, burn it until everything was a blazing fire but he couldn't. He had no fire and those hundreds of years down in the cool caverns had made him unable to bear heat. Even his mother said she had a little fire in her belly. How could he think of himself as a true Fire Being if he didn't even have fire in his belly?

Wolves! He stretched up his long neck and slipped his tongue in and out of his mouth to taste the air. No, not quite mountain wolves. He tasted the air again. In disgust, he smelt those little wolves, the ones that didn't howl, the ones that ran before the horses and were never far from the naked bear creatures. They were running this way, running in front of the glow. He had to move. He knew he had to flee despite the burning from above.

He slunk along the floor of the valley, keeping cool by splashing through a stream. The glow had turned away from him again moving southwards, further away from his ancient home.

He would follow the stream. The water was cool on his blistered claws.

The naked bear beings; he could hear them shrieking. He thumped down the stream. Water droplets now fell from the emptiness above, blissfully drawing out the heat from his scales. The glow was turning south to where the big settlement lay. He sensed the throb of thousands of naked bears. He couldn't follow it. There were lots of them behind him now, hurrying, screaming, shouting and thrashing at the ground with sticks. He wondered why they hated him so much, why they wanted to hunt him down. He thumped on.

Suddenly dazed, he recoiled from a blow to his head. Tentatively he felt his surroundings with his bruised snout. A heap of stones arched over the water, spanning the stream. Angrily he struck out with his claws tearing it apart. At least at home he knew every twist and turn in the tunnels and never smacked into things. At least at home he had possessed the glow. He had been able to see the glow.

He remembered his amazement the first time it appeared, carried by the little female creature that screamed and ran. He had even forgotten to kill her and the male naked bear that chased after her. She had dropped the glow. In the years after he had still been able to smell her in the glow, smell her fear and her pain. He hated that. But he could *see* the glow and he couldn't live without it.

He slithered over the pile of rubble that crashed into the stream and thumped on southwards. The air smelt different: fresh. It tasted like the salted sweat on a frightened animal. He liked the chase. He liked the hunt. The sheep had been dull like that. They died too easily. The salty smell excited him.

His hearts jumped and beat out their excited rhythm in his massive hollow body. He could hear a distant roar, fierce and deep from some mighty creature. He could hear it thumping along the ground, heavy thrashing beats as its tail lashed against rocks and shook the earth. Another Fire Being! He was certain it was another Fire Being.

He hurried on, hardly caring now that the scales on his back were blistering and peeling in the heat. He didn't know why he couldn't go out above ground when the emptiness above was filled with the heat. His grandfather could. His mother didn't like it but she could still survive in it but for him it was torture. Grandfather told him it was something to do with his colour. Apparently he was white, whatever that meant. He didn't understand colour. It didn't make any sense to him, but he was saddened because it was just something else that made him different. He wondered if he was a real Fire Being at all. He raced on hoping that the other being he could hear ahead would accept him even if he couldn't fly and didn't spit fire.

He lumbered to the top of the hill. He expected to smell the beast any second but the air just tasted saltier and the pounding noise seemed to come from all around. He was confused. He heard it hiss and slither over rocks and beat its great tail against the ground. He could hear it roar, but he couldn't smell it. He slithered anxiously forward. The being was enormous. The stream led him straight towards it and suddenly he was surrounded by the noise.

Water!! A vast, vast stretch of water. The water beat at the rocks and the hissing spray dragged across the sands. Not a Fire Being at all.

He slunk forward and eased into the lapping waves. The water was superbly cool. He sighed and rolled over. It stung his wounds but somehow the physical pain soothed his anguish. He rolled over, kicking and splashing into the deeper water. He was floating; his claws no longer touched the ground. Was this flying? Was this at least like flying? He twisted over and rolled in the waves, blowing out bubbles through his cavernous nostrils. He could hear and feel movements in the water. There were no small wolves and no naked bears here. It kept him cool. He need only keep his nostrils high above the waves while the rest of him wallowed through the salty-tasting water. He felt so light and agile. His great belly no longer scraped along the raw ground.

'Mother, look at me,' he crowed out, then remembered she was gone, long since gone and his only companion had been the glow.

I shall rip them apart. He gnashed his teeth at a scaly creature that skimmed past his snout. I shall tear them limb from limb, the little creatures that took my glow.

The glow was moving south. He could sense it moving, could feel its vibrations pulsing through the earth and washing through the water. He swam ashore once, realizing it had stopped but it was still in the big settlement. He couldn't go near the big settlement. The little naked bears had talons and teeth that spat through the air. He'd never worried about it before, not until they'd torn in through his neck. He'd been lucky: the thin straight talon had caused no permanent harm. That was when they took the glow. He swam out deeper into the salty waters in desperation, only returning to the coastal stretches when he sensed the glow was moving on again.

Something was in the water. Its movements were stiff and harsh. At once, he sensed it as different from the wriggling finned creatures. It was big and hard, moving in a straight line over the water. It bothered him. He wanted to get closer to

435

the glow. He sensed the glow was moving, that it was closer now to the vast stretch of salty water. But this new creature lay in his path and he didn't like this animal. It didn't wriggle, twist or dive through the water. Instead it carved through the water in a series of pulses, rhythmically beating the waves with its stiff fins. It angered him. How dare it destroy the easy peace of his cool world?

His neck thrust forward until his body formed an arrowhead and he used his thick barbed tail to power him through the water. He struck wooden boards and rocked the hard creature that swayed and tossed under his assault. He coiled up his neck and struck out repeatedly, lashing at the creature's underbelly.

He pulled away abruptly as he heard the familiar screams. Naked bears! It couldn't be anything else. Suddenly they were there in the water, thrashing pathetically, choking and spluttering. The wooden vessel glugged deep into the depths, releasing huge bubbles of air that boiled up from the hollow of its vast lungs. A few of the little creatures were pushed up to the surface, carried in the globe of a bubble. He circled the eddies where the wooden creature had gone down, waiting for them to spit onto the surface. He snapped them up as they choked and screamed. They died so easily, not like lions or wolves. He was pleasured by the way they died in such terror of his awesome presence. Here in the water they seemed unable to spit those needle-like claws.

But he eventually grew tired of the game when the screaming stopped and he sensed only a few of them moaning and whimpering. They were like sheep, he thought disgustedly and suddenly turned away. The glow was moving south.

Since he had been in the vast cool brine, the throb from the glow had washed out through all the surrounding water confusing his senses. He was no longer exactly sure where it was but he realized it was close.

He thrashed his tail, coiling his bulk through the water, outracing the long slithery, snake-like creatures and the salmon beasts like the ones in the river near his home. He dived down into the depths. His huge lungs, designed for breathing fire, gave him cavernous breaths that kept him beneath the water for long stretches at a time. Another one of those wooden beasts cut through the waves above him. He wasted very little effort, merely charging to the surface and beating against its rounded underbelly with his barbed tail. He felt a sense of satisfaction as the creature keeled and up-bellied. He swam on. The glow was calling him.

He was certain it was trying to reach him. His body thrilled with the excitement. Surely it was in the water with him. The vast salty brine was filled with its energy. The water was continually cut and broken now by the heavy rigid creatures that bobbed awkwardly on the surface. They streamed towards a certain point on the land and fanned out again from it, to-ing and fro-ing. He was nervous. Land was close and he sensed a big settlement of the wretched creatures. Too many of them. He swam back and forth, killing one or two of the big fish-type creatures that barked like the little wolves, just to rid himself of some of his frustration.

It was on the water now. He was certain. He couldn't get to it so it must be coming to him. He believed it was his soul, his lost soul, which contained the kindling of his belly-fire. He was a Fire Being, he was sure he was a Fire Being but someone had stolen the heat from his belly. He was certain it was those little screaming naked bears that lived above the canyon in the high rock towering above the Old Nest. They had stolen his home, then his fire and now the glow. He would have his revenge.

The glow was skimming over the water. Again he sensed the cutting edge of the wooden creature slicing through the waves but this one didn't have the rhythmical beat of those wooden legs but hissed smoothly. He stretched out towards it.

A deep fin cut the water. He thrashed through the waves and dived to ram his armoured head against the fin. The wooden beast splintered and rolled. The water was teeming with legs and arms, thrashing and beating frantically. Many were entangled beneath a vast skin. Quickly they stilled and floated limply just below the surface of the waves.

The glow! For a second he could see it, falling fast down into the depths. He arched his head up above the surface, flared his nostrils wide and sucked in air to fill the bladder beneath his throat. He dived down after the glow. He could see it, a pure circular light of perfection. He worshipped it.

Now he had it gripped between his mighty jaws. The glow was fading, dying down there in the cold depths. He sensed its energy lessen and dull. Two beats of his tail brought him to the surface and he erupted out above the waves. The glow didn't like the water. He must take it to the land and into a nest where he could coil around it and worship it. He avoided the waters teeming with the wooden creatures and struck out for the shore a little further south. The glow was cold and almost entirely faded now. His loneliness deepened and his sorrow was overwhelming. Was he too late? Had it died?

He crashed onto the shore and dragged himself across harsh rocks inland to find a hollow where he could rest up. He breathed onto the cold hard stone that was once the glow, warming it with his hot rancid breath. His two hearts beat furiously in his anxiety. He coiled his great body around the tiny precious pebble, trying to keep it warm, restoring it to life.

He breathed over it lovingly and at last he saw a murky glimmer. His hearts thrilled. Hope was returning. The glow filled his mind with its brilliance and the light mesmerized him. He sat in his dark lonely world, seeing only the glow.

Chapter 27

They turned the corner to be confronted by the bustling shouts of the eelmen and the competing squawks of seagulls that squabbled over fish offal and mackerel heads.

Hal suddenly froze and backed against the sea wall. Caspar peered over his uncle's shoulder and took in at one glance the lances, black boots and silk tabards of the King's men. He gulped, trying to steel his nerves against his rising panic. They couldn't risk being caught by the Inquisitors: they had to protect Brid. But what of the moonstone? He looked despairingly out into the harbour. They could do nothing while the King's Church soldiers prowled the quayside.

The eelman, who yesterday had been so affronted by Trog's greedy manners, was pointing three liveried soldiers clearly in their direction. There was no time to make a plan and Hal was the only one quick enough to think on his feet.

'Go back and round the headland.' With decisive composure, he pointed northward along the quay to the beaches and the jutting peninsula in the distance. 'Get Trog to lead you across the beach.'

'But the snakes –' Caspar started to object. His skin was already clammy at the thought.

'He's a snake-catcher, isn't he? He's your best chance. Now get out of here.'

'What about you? Aren't you coming?' Caspar asked in dismay.

'The Inquisitors can't follow you far onto the beach, but you'll need time to get a head start. I'll stall them. I'll be all right but neither of you can risk looking them straight in the eye. Look after Brid and get going. I'll go back to the ostlery, get the horses and meet you . . .' he paused, 'way up there on the highland by that ridge of dark trees, you know the ones that Brid likes so much.'

'Yews,' Brid expanded.

Hal nodded. 'Where they come to a point by that outcrop of rock pointing towards the headland. Now get going. I'll stall them.' He stepped casually out into full view.

For a moment Caspar was unable to move. He stood stock still, shocked by the idea of leaving Hal alone to face the Inquisitors, but he realized instantly that his own looks would hinder their escape almost as much as Brid's blazing eyes. She grabbed his arm and pulled him away. Though Brid winced with every step, together they trotted along the beach and slipped off the quay onto the sands where they broke into a run – but not so fast that they overtook Trog, who zigzagged in front of them, nose skimming the ground. Caspar had released him from the leash since it was impossible to keep up with the dog's changes of direction. Away from the hustle of the quay, he now felt exposed on the long stretch of open sand and shouts from the waterfront, where the lobster men mended their pots, warning them to stay away from the beach.

'Hey, you lad, it's a spring tide; the sands are crawling with vipers. Get off the beach.'

Caspar kept his head lowered, praying that Trog's teeth were sharp as he ignored their warnings and looked anxiously ahead at the ground they had to cover. Fringed with shingle, the long beach butted straight up against the quay and stretched ahead for over a mile of smooth open sands. They would have to cross all this before they would make it clear around the headland and out of sight. Only then could they cut secretly inland to lose themselves in the countryside.

Trog turned, suddenly catching a whiff of something, and dived back to a spot he'd just covered. Scratching excitedly with his front legs, he burrowed his muzzle into the ground, making snuffling grunts and snorting out sand that clogged his nostrils.

Caspar and Brid stood close to each other, trying to stand on as little of the treacherous beach as possible.

'Nobody's said yet whether these serpents are poisonous,' the boy remarked as casually as he could, expecting one of the slithering creatures to eject its head out of the sand and grab his ankles at any moment.

Trog pulled his head up and looked intently at the ground, his eyes tracking over the pale sand. Caspar detected a slight hump that rippled the ground. The dog leant his thick-skulled head sideways, with an expression of intense concentration forming on his wrinkled brow as he watched the ripple bulge towards his new owners.

'Don't move. I think they sense the changing pressure of your feet on the sand,' the girl whispered.

Caspar had no intention of moving. Not snakes, not again! The blood drained from his cheeks and he struggled to fight his panicky fear of the serpents.

'Keep still. And yes, they are poisonous, but the venom doesn't kill. It's like a spider: it immobilizes so that the snake can eat you at his leisure.'

'I don't think I wanted to know that,' Caspar remarked. He felt his tongue thicken and stumble over the words but he gouged his nails into the flesh of his arm, hoping that the pain would help him fight his fear. He could not show such fear in front of Brid. The ripple veered away from them, circled and started to head back towards the terrier. 'I hope this dog knows what he's doing; he's just standing there. Trog! Do your stuff. Get the snake.'

With imperceptible movements the terrier gradually crouched down onto his stocky legs. With extraordinary agility for such a rotund-looking animal, he leapt from all fours like a cat, jumping bodily sideways. He then immediately sprang back to his original spot. The snake trail bulged, continuing to curve back round to approach the dog. Trog barked excitedly and repeated his threatening war dance, leaping from one side to the other. Suddenly there was a rapid acceleration in the movement of the ripple and it shot like a spearhead straight at the dog. Trog froze, lowering his head, his eyes narrowing to razor slits. The ripple in the sand bulged up and a thin black line broke the surface, its trajectory aimed at the dog's forefeet.

Trog's timing was split second. He leapt backwards right at the very second that the bulbous tip of the serpent's head broke the surface of the sand. The terrier thrust forward, lips bared back to his pink gums, and sank his teeth into the neck of the snake. The mouth of the serpent sprang open, revealing hooked fangs, and venom squirted from its palate whilst the tongue flicked in and out, but it was unable to sink the deadly teeth into any flesh. Instead the tube of black scales began to retract back into its burrow, dragging the dog with it.

'Oh Mother, please no, not the dog,' Brid begged as the white terrier disappeared up to his neck in the sand.

'The snake's too big for him!' Urgent concern for the dog struggled to crush the boy's terror of the long legless reptiles and he was about to charge forward to pull the dog out when Trog regained his footing. The thick back legs were firmly sprung under his body, his deep contoured muscles taut as cord. He hauled backwards, dragging the snake from its hole like a bird pulling a worm from the grass. The serpent stretched. Once Trog was fully clear of the ground, he thrashed back and forth, beating the reptile's head against the sand. Dragging himself backwards, his whole body strained against the pull of the viper, until its entire length rushed from the burrow; several feet of snake coiling and uncoiling.

He tossed it up into the air and caught it again before repeatedly thrashing the snake back and forth until it became flaccid and the rigid twisting coils slumped into a length of lifeless rope. He flung it up into the air and let it fall to the ground. It lay still, quite dead. The dog looked at it in surprise, almost disappointment that he'd lost his sparring partner and then trotted off again, ignoring the carcass in his search for more live prey. Caspar thought how strange it was that an animal so friendly and devoted towards human beings could get so much pleasure out of killing.

Without hesitation, the youth and the young priestess trotted directly behind the dog, trying to follow precisely in his tracks and keeping a wary eye out for the tell-tale ripples. They continually looked back towards the quay, anxiously looking for any signs of Hal or the Inquisitors.

As they scurried across the sands, the town's defensive sea wall to their right above the sandy beach began to crumble and merge into the rocks and shingle of the natural shoreline. Several carcasses lay just above the high water tidemark on the rocks. The decayed and waterlogged bodies were probably goats though their state of decomposition and the number of missing limbs and crushed ribcages, made identification difficult. Although the snakes couldn't live in shingle, Brid decided to stay on the beach where they could run much faster from the threat of the mounted soldiers. But despite their desperation to make it out of sight and beyond the headland before the Inquisitors closed on them, they had to stay behind Trog. He leapt sideways again, digging furiously and wagging his tail. Seconds later he delivered a foot-long serpent at their feet as some sort of gift. Caspar crept tentatively around it. The dog was pleased with himself but soon left the infant reptile in search of larger more challenging prey. As the dog dispatched another snake, Caspar prayed that the Inquisitors wouldn't treat Hal in the same merciless manner. He prayed that his uncle's smooth charm and noble rank had managed to divert the King's officers. There was no time to speculate; they had to keep running, light-footed and with intense concentration, over the snake-riddled sands.

The headland was at least a mile down the beach from the estuary mouth and Trog had slain five snakes by the time they had covered three-quarters of the distance. But each time they had to stop to witness the violent deaths took precious time. The moment they had been dreading came when a distant cry from near the estuary alarmed the scavenging gulls. Three horsemen set off at a gallop towards them. It was going to be a matter of two short minutes before the King's men were on top of them. They couldn't run faster because of the rippling network of snake-runs. Behind them a herring-bone formation of ripples converged on their footprints.

The galloping horsemen were still closing when Trog stopped again, dancing on his toes and leaping back and forth, which they had learnt was the preliminary ceremony to another killing. There was nothing they could do but wait. Caspar unslung his bow and slotted an arrow to the string just in case the Inquisitors made it through the network of snakes converging on the galloping horses. He found his hands were shaking. These weren't his enemies; they were the King's chosen men: killing them would be high treason. He was a loyal Belbidian devoted to his country; treason was unthinkable but so was losing Brid. He raised the bow but his hand shook too vigorously for a clean shot as his conscience racked his brain.

'Halt in the name of the King,' bellowed the foremost Inquisitor across the sands.

The horses galloped on. With a mixture of dread and hope, Caspar anticipated the strike of a snake. The thunder of hooves grew louder and the men's faces drew steadily into focus until Caspar could clearly see the pointed beard and keen eyes of the lead rider. He doesn't know about the snakes, the boy thought, filled with bewildering fears about whether to shoot his countrymen or wait for the snakes to do the evil work for him. Brid grabbed the bow from him. 'Look, if you can't do it, I will.'

But there was no need. The leading horse fell to its knees and its head thumped down onto the sand, the body of a coiling snake wrapped about its hindlegs. It squealed and thrashed whilst its rider sprawled in the sand, dazed by the fall. The other two horses reared up in panic, though the riders were horsemen enough not to be unseated.

'In the name of God, what monsters has this witch conjured from the waves?' one yelled in horror, struggling to control his mount as the stricken horse in front of him was dragged by its hindleg into the sand.

The thrown rider screamed in fear as another snake seized

his ankle but he was quick with his sword and slashed through the reptile's body, cutting himself free. 'It's bitten me. Help! Help, it's bitten me,' he screamed in panic, hobbling to his feet. One of his comrades forced his reluctant horse forward and grabbed the man by the arm, struggling to drag him onto the back of his saddle before spurring his mount towards the rocks and shingle at the head of the beach.

'They didn't know about the snakes,' Caspar murmured again, watching with horror as the horse was slowly swallowed by the sand. 'They were so intent on witch-hunts that they never learnt about the snakes.' He raised the bow this time with a steady hand and shot the animal between the eyes to end its suffering. The end of yet another fine horse, he thought regretfully.

A snake, this one four feet long with a body as thick as his father's arm, was deposited proudly at the boy's feet by the white terrier, who then turned to hurry eagerly forward again. With the sand in front of them swept clear by the snake-catcher, they were able to safely run on towards the headland where the sandy beach turned to shingle. At the foot of the peninsula the shingle trailed out into a spit where two currents surged away in opposite directions and the feeling of the smooth pebbles grinding and crunching beneath their feet came as a huge relief. Brid was sure that the vipers lived only in the sands. Further up the beach the rocks became larger and Trog leapt from one pinnacle to the next like a goat, obviously totally at ease on the shore. They ran along the high water mark defined by flotsam and jetsam. Old timbers, tangled fishing nets, dried seaweed, which crackled and popped as they stepped on it, dead white-bellied snakes and crisp transparent snakeskins were all strung out along the tide-line. Wrapped in the debris were the bloated carcasses of a few unfortunate animals – several goats, two small mountain ponies and a whole skeleton of a horse. Brid stooped over it.

Caspar touched her shoulder. 'Don't worry; it's not the mare we lost. This one's been dead a long time.'

'I'm not worried,' she replied curtly, rejecting any notion

that she was suffering from sentimentality. 'I want the jawbone. There's much power in the jawbone of a horse.' She tore it free, wrenching the bone away from the few membranous tendons that secured it to the skull and stuffed it into her belt like a dagger before running after Caspar. Trog was running on ahead with a goat's cleft hoof clamped in his mouth. The terrier had stolen it from a maggoty carcass, and he carried it aloft like a trophy.

'The cave. Head for the caves round the point,' Brid shouted. 'Then we can get out of sight.'

'What caves?' Caspar panted.

'There are always cliffs the other side of a headland from a beach,' she explained breathlessly. 'Where there are cliffs, there'll be caves at the foot of them.'

To turn the corner around the headland they were forced back down onto the shingle and onto the spit. Brid was right. Brid was often right, the boy thought with admiration. The sound of the sea crashing against rocks drowned out the lapping of the waves that caressed the beach behind them and on the far side of the headland the downs plunged vertically in a wall of cliffs towards the surging green waters. As the breakers smashed against the rockface, a clap of air was forced into the back of the caves; its echo boomed out across the sea. When the water retreated back down the beach, with its sucking backwash dragging pebbles and raking sand back down into the depths, it momentarily revealed the black yawn of a cave. Then the breakers reared up again, gathering their power into the coil of their heads, before striking like a cobra at the cliff wall.

The tide was high and still rising, which meant the shingle beach was submerged under roiling water when the waves crashed in against the cliff. As the gurgling backwash retreated, an array of rocks was briefly exposed, forming a transitory land-bridge from the spit of shingle to the mouth of the cave. The steadfast coast had withstood this constant battering assault since long before man had come bare-foot and club in hand to the Belbidian shores, but now it was pitted and crumbling. Boulders, hewn from the land by the inexorable pounding of the sea, formed cruel jagged rocks at the base of the cliffs, now partially submerged in the roaring anger of the breakers.

'We can make it to the cave,' Brid said firmly. 'We just have to time it right. We wait for the breakers to hit the rocks and as the water starts to retreat we can run through the shallows and get inside the cave before the next breaker storms in.'

'Yeah, and if we don't make it in time the waves will smash us against the rocks. Brid, we can't. It's over thirty paces. There just isn't time.'

'We've got to; we can't go back.' She didn't wait for arguments, hitching her skirts up to reveal her breeches underneath. She waded out over the shelving shingle just to the point where the spit rapidly plunged into deeper water, the sea dragging and washing round her calves. She could go no further now until the waves retreated from the cliffs to open up the narrow band of beach at their foot. Caspar followed, leaving Trog whimpering on the dry spit. The dog quickly decided that he wasn't going to be left behind and plunged into the water. Brid stopped as the waves swelled up over her thighs, watching the breakers surge in. The land-bridge in front of them was swallowed up by the frothy green water that churned and roared against the cliff.

Caspar wondered whether she'd lost her nerve when faced with the seething reality of the raging water that would shred them against the rocks if their timing was anything less than perfect. The sea sucked out again, dragging around their legs, and leaving a slippery pathway clear to the safety of the cave. But it was only seconds before the breakers returned to punch violently into the rockface, soaking them in the briny spray that filled the air.

'The seventh wave. It's bigger but it gives us more time to get through. We're going, not on this one but after the next. Ready?'

'As ever I will be.' Caspar watched with dread as the waves pounded against the rocks twice more and then, just as the

447

waves sank back into the backwash, he charged forward. Trog leapt after them, sensing their desperation. The waves retreated, exposing a yawning stretch of black seabed, which bared its jagged rocky teeth. They sprinted forward, slipping and stumbling across the boulders. Briny spray filled Caspar's mouth and nostrils as he gasped in rapid breaths.

They were nearly at the entrance to the low cave undermining the cliffs when Caspar heard the rush of water as the waves snarled forward again. He flung himself into the dry mouth of the cave, scrabbling for a handhold as the breaking waves hurled him forward, ripping his skin against the rocks. The cave was plunged into darkness. His hands dragged over the boulders and foul-tasting water filled his mouth as the sea hauled at his body; but at last the waves released him and daylight flooded back into their haven. Brid cried out as the sea tugged at her body, dragging her out again under the waves. Her billowing skirts swirled out around her, their sodden weight dragging her down into the water. In desperation Caspar scrabbled for a rock and flung his free hand back, managing to grip onto Brid's shoulder. Spluttering to his feet, Caspar dragged the Maiden with him, hauling her up onto the higher rocks away from the angry reach of the sea. He coughed, gasping for fresh clean air.

'Where's the dog?' Brid cried. 'Where's the dog?'

Trog wasn't beside them nor on the rocks in front of them and they turned in horror to see the terrified animal being sucked out to sea by the retreating waves. He was curled up into the crook of the white raging breakers that paused at the height of their rear, ready to bowl the animal at the cliffs. The white foam and spray mocked the white body of the dog. The sea roared in again, catapulting the helpless animal onto the hungry rocks and sealing the cave into darkness. The dog rolled over and over, swept across the ground by the force of the waves, red blood swimming out around him.

Caspar scrabbled for the terrier but the waves were already clawing the animal out again. Trog's legs were spread wide, claws outstretched, eyes wide and frightened. Unable to scrabble for a foothold he was inevitably dragged out again. Caspar leapt at the animal, feeling a rock punch into his ribcage as he belly-flopped into the retreating shallows. His head submerged, he thrashed through the foam until finally his hand grasped something soft. His body doubled in weight as the backwash dragged at him, demanding that he obeyed the call of the sea. He lodged his feet in a crevice and suddenly he and the dog were on dry land as the water slipped out around them. Stumbling to his feet, he dug his nails into the thick layer of flesh at the base of the dog's neck and dragged him higher inland. He lay gasping on the rocks, grateful that the sea could now only just reach his feet.

The waves continued to crash in, punching air into the back of the cave and sealing out the daylight, before sucking out and letting the sun slide in under the low mouth of the opening. When at last he could breathe smoothly and had spat the salty water from his lungs, he pushed himself up to see Brid fussing over the shivering dog. The animal was streaked with blood but was managing to stand four-square on his stocky feet though he was badly frightened with wide staring eyes.

'Good plan, Brid.' Caspar was angry. 'You're as foolhardy as Hal.'

'We made it, didn't we?'

'I've heard that before too,' Caspar groused. 'And what about me? I'm covered in cuts.' Caspar felt cheated that only the dog received the girl's tender attention.

'Neither of you is badly hurt, just a few bruises,' Brid said calmly, wringing out her skirts, 'but the dog's scared. He doesn't know what's happening and you do. Anyway,' she smiled, 'thank you. You saved both of us.'

Caspar couldn't grumble at the girl for long. He dropped his head between his knees, waiting for his breath to return and for the water to drain out of his ears. They rested for a moment until Brid pointed out that the tide was still coming in and that they should find their way out of the back of the cave before the waves threatened them again.

'What do you mean the way out at the back?' Caspar was puzzled.

'Ah! Well, I'll show you if you hurry up,' she replied knowingly.

Further inside the dim cave, the noise from the sea was mostly muffled except for the rhythmical boom as the waves forced air deep into the recesses beneath the foot of the cliff. Following each deep rumbling boom a strange whistle piped out somewhere at the rear of the cavern.

'It's a swallow hole,' Brid muttered.

'A what?'

'Don't you know anything about the land?' Brid sighed. 'Come on, we'd better get moving. A dead horse won't slow the Inquisitors down for long, but hopefully they'll think we've drowned.'

It was dimmer at the back of the cave. The rush of noise, however, became more intense as the pounding waves forced air deep into the constricted caverns and funnelled it into the narrowing recesses at the back of the cave.

'Eventually,' Brid explained, 'the force of air punches a hole right up through the soil and out onto the land above the cliffs. We should be able to climb up through the hole and escape onto the downs above.'

The cave narrowed into a funnel, then gradually turned upwards and formed a vertical chimney that climbed a dozen feet or so to a pin-point of light above their heads. The rocks were slippery with the blast of spray and Caspar's worn boots slid over the surfaces, grazing his shins. A sharp yip from his feet reminded him of their other problem and he looked at the stocky dog whose loyalty had brought them safely across the sands. Then he again looked up at the shaft in the rocks.

'Oh Trog, what are we going to do with you? The climb's going to be hard enough; how are we going to get a great lump like you up there?'

'How long's the leash?' Brid answered for the dog. 'There's a ledge above your right hand; if you get him to that, can you haul him up on the rope the rest of the way?'

'I don't know if I can get myself through that hole up there yet.' Caspar was frustrated and pushed himself higher, searching for a good hand hold. He kicked his toes hard against the rock, testing for firmness. Shards crumbled away, showering the girl beneath him, but his boots held their grip. He stretched up again, wishing he was just a couple of inches taller so that he could reach the next niche in the rock with more than just the very tip of his fingers. The hole at the top was big enough for only his head. He took out his dagger and worked away at the thin crust of turf, opening up the hole. It didn't occur to him to worry that his toes were balanced on just the merest thread of rock.

Brid stood anxiously knotting the leash into a harness round the dog's chest whilst Trog enthusiastically licked her face, delighted by the attention. But he received a sharp smack when he tried to bite her plait.

Retreating back down the shaft in the rock was harder because Caspar couldn't see where to put his feet; but he made it down, slipping at the very last to fall heavily at Brid's feet. He looked at the compact form of the dog who gazed hopefully back at him, proclaiming with canine faith that his human masters could do anything and were at least magicians if not gods.

Caspar looked up at the ledge, thinking that this just wasn't going to be easy and cursing their soft hearts for rescuing the dog in the first place. He put one arm under the belly of the terrier, bringing his face close to the dog's, which invited a slurpy kiss followed by a cheeky nip on the ear. Caspar tried to lift the dog under one arm, but found he needed two to even get the bulky animal off the ground.

'I won't be able to haul him up; he's just too heavy,' Caspar said, beginning to despair for the dog. Trog had twisted round in the boy's arms and was scrabbling at his clothing with large blunt claws.

'Well, just hold him for a moment and I'll strap him to your front.' Brid drew up the dog's front paws so that they were either side of his neck and used her belt to tie them together.

Then she wound the leash around and around the dog's body to form a sling. 'There,' she said with satisfaction. 'That'll hold. Up you go.'

Up you go, Caspar thought sardonically and tried not to breathe in too much of the eely stench carried on the dog's breath. If he'd been a real hero, like in the legends, he'd have had a rope long enough in the first place . . . but then nothing seemed to work out like that. A hero's horse would be waiting nobly at the top too but, even though Firecracker was the finest horse he'd ever known, there was little doubt that he was just a horse and didn't have the magical attributes of the winged beasts and talking animals of legend. The rock on which he balanced abruptly gave way under his foot, cutting short his thoughts. He found himself hanging from his finger-tips with the struggling dog throwing him further off balance. Something grabbed his foot and he realized that Brid was right behind him, guiding his toes to a secure foothold.

'Nearly there,' she reassured him.

The last bit was easy. He braced himself with his legs against the opposing rock faces of the swallow-hole walls that were closing in more tightly around him. He reached a hand up to grip the earth and, with a little push from Brid below, he squeezed through the hole, squashing Trog against his chest. He emerged on top of the cliffs like a rabbit from its burrow and rolled over onto his back, filling his vision with the grey sky overhead and struggled to untie the dog, who was excitedly trying to kick himself free. Brid was quickly beside him, and retrieved her belt from the dog's paws.

They slumped back on the coarse grass, breathing heavily and watching as Trog dashed back and forth with the thrill of having his feet on firm ground again. Clods of earth flew up in the air from his frantic paws as he spun himself round and around. His jaws clashed and snapped, taking snatches at the thin air, as if he were sparring with a ghost. Caspar and Brid lay on their backs and laughed, half at the dog and half with relief.

They decided it would be impossible for the Inquisitors

to follow them and relaxed, looking around at the rolling countryside and letting their sodden clothes dry in the warm sea breeze. Smooth treeless downs, smeared with soil too thin to support anything more than short-stemmed grass and sea thistles, undulated in mimicry of the sea's swelling waves. To either side of them, the ground dipped away, rolling into hidden dales. A ridge led them up towards a dark strip of wood and the yew trees, which Hal had appointed as their place of muster.

'Do you think he's all right?' Brid asked anxiously.

'Well, the Inquisitors didn't stop him, did they?' Caspar said positively to reassure himself as much as the girl. 'They must have let him through the port. But how did they get on to us? That's what I don't understand. What did we do wrong?'

'Do you think there were more of them who might have stopped him at the quay? The King said there were only six Inquisitors but it looks like they've conscripted many more than that.' Brid's obvious concern for Hal brought a whole gamut of conflicting and confusing emotions to the boy's mind. Hal was his uncle, his companion, his friend; no one had the right to worry about Hal more than he did. They always stuck together; they always looked after one another. And he felt jealous that Brid's thoughts were constantly on his bold, dark-haired uncle.

'Hal will be fine. He's probably galloping out of the town right now, being given a hard time by Cracker,' the auburn-haired youth said grumpily and jumped to his feet. 'We're exposed here; come on, let's head for the trees.'

It wasn't until they started to run that Caspar realized just how exposed they were up on the ridge. From the port with its flotilla of fishing boats moored alongside the quay, from the downs to either side, from the trees ahead, and in fact from everywhere except the beach, they were clearly visible. Brid must have caught onto the same thought just a moment before him because she yelled for him to follow her over the rise and down into the dell below.

It was a more difficult route. The small valley was clogged

with brambles and gorse sprawling between rabbit scrapes and warrens. After they tripped and tumbled their way down the sloping sides into the hollow, they were faced with a steeply rising trench headed by a gorse-lined brow that obscured their view of the yew forest. The ground was stepped in a series of terraced ridges where the soil was gradually slipping towards the bottom of the valley, but at least the terracing eased the gradient of the climb. Caspar's breath was coming hard as he used his hands to pull himself up from one tuft of grass to the next. Brid was not that far behind, having kept up well on the flatter ground and only lagging behind as the going became steeper.

The terrier reached the brow first and the two humans froze as the dog set up a deep throaty bark; a tone they hadn't heard before. 'Maybe it's the wolf,' Caspar said hopefully.

Brid shook her head and covered her lips with her fingers, pressing herself low against the ground. Drawing her dusty-brown cloak over her face for camouflage, she elbowed herself along the ground and wriggled into a nest of concealing brambles. Trog barked incessantly, drawing attention, and began to growl. Caspar looked up and his eyes widened in trepidation as he realized that the dark black point he could just see above the crown of the valley was the tip of a lance. The point moved fractionally towards them and he got a glimpse of a red, yellow and black pennon fluttering in the breeze.

'We've been cut off,' Brid whispered, 'and that stupid dog is going to lead them right to us.'

The two Torra Altans sank into the protective cover of the brambles as they heard a deep voice, suddenly audible above the sea-breeze. 'A dog, Sergeant. Does that mean anything? There's a dog here, ugly brute.'

'No, a wolf, they said a wolf. Don't you listen to anything you're told, soldier? The sailor lads at the inn said the girl didn't have a human shadow but she cast the shadow of a wolf – a wolf! Small girl with characteristic sharp features. Has to be one of them. Apart from the fact she was blind, we've never had such a clear description of the Devil walking abroad before. They usually have unnaturally bright coloured eyes.' Trog growled ferociously. 'And shut that dog up, will you?' There was a yelp followed by a low series of growls.

'I can't, Sergeant: look at its teeth.'

The senior officer sounded exasperated. 'Look, she'll come up this way sooner or later. They have to come to the yews: it draws them like a magnet. We've got every approach covered, so shut that dog up. I'm not going to be the one that lets the witch slip through my fingers.'

'Scram! Get out of it!' the young soldier ordered the dog uncertainly. 'Go on, get out of here.'

Please Trog, Caspar prayed, please just leave them alone.

'Don't get off your horse, man.' The sergeant's voice was stern. 'Those dogs are bred vicious. He'll take your arm off.'

Caspar could only think that Trog was quite the soppiest dog he'd ever come across. The growling continued and then suddenly there was a heavy thud followed by a yelp and then silence. A ball of white fur tumbled over the brow of the hill, legs flailing limply. It came to rest in an inert heap ten yards away on the open chalky down. Caspar pressed his face into the earth as the tip of an open-faced helmet appeared. Dark brown eyes, glowering beneath thick brows, stared down after the dog, scanning the ground for its body. 'That's how you shut a dog up,' he grunted and disappeared out of sight.

'I'll kill him,' Caspar growled through his teeth, but Brid grabbed his shoulder and pushed him down.

'Right, young soldier, now that's how you deal with a dog. If you want to become a fully fledged Inquisitor, you've got to learn to be more direct. And in the name of the Father, don't forget to keep your eyes peeled on those yew trees, you useless lad,' the sergeant's voice warned.

Caspar nudged Brid and whispered, 'Why the yews? What do they know about the yews?'

Brid covered her lips, warning him to keep quiet, but then, ignoring her own advice, she breathed, 'Remember what the kobolds said about Anu looking at the cauldron? Well, the statue gazes at the crest of that yew-covered hill.'

'Just ride to the top of the rise, soldier, and see what the watch along is doing,' the deep authoritative voice rumbled out from above. There was a thud of trotting hooves on grass and moments later they could hear the more distant call of the younger Inquisitor coming from their right.

'They're still in position, sir. All looks well.'

'Blessed saints, soldier, don't wave,' the sergeant's voice bellowed. 'And get back here. You looked ridiculous,' the man continued in more cutting tones as the sound of the trotting hooves returned along the down. 'The King's Inquisitors must always behave with decorum.'

Brid was wriggling over the soil, skimming just beneath the Inquisitors' line of sight. Caspar kept his eyes glued to the brow of the hill as Brid's hand slid out from under her cloak and clasped the dog's collar. She froze as the voices above rang out in alarm.

'Hey, Sergeant! Look, what's that?'

'You're right. Something in the trees.'

Brid started to move again as it became clear that the men were looking away from them.

'Do you think it's the wolf, Sir?'

There was silence for a moment followed by the raucous squawk of a bird.

'Just a pheasant. We should have burnt the whole forest, like I told Captain Ranark. He's getting too soft.'

Brid dragged the body of the dog back towards the brambles and pulled him underneath her cloak, breathing hard.

'Is he dead?' Caspar whispered anxiously.

'Do you think I'd risk so much for a dead dog?' Brid answered curtly. 'They've got thick skulls. Now shut up.' Trog's eyelids drooped over slightly hazy eyes and Brid clamped her hand over his muzzle to stop the animal from whining.

Above their heads the silence was broken only by the shifting of horses' feet and the champing of grass.

'Lad, you're intolerable. When they said *fresh* recruits I had no idea. Do you have to let your horse graze while we're standing on duty? I'll have a few words to say about you in my report.'

'Sorry, Sergeant,' the younger voice muttered. There was a short silence before the irrepressible soldier perked up again. 'How do you know, Sir, that the witch is coming this way?'

'I don't, soldier. But somehow she'll make her way towards the ridge and the yew trees.'

'Why there? How do you know?'

The sergeant grumbled in his throat, seemingly irritated by his partner's constant questioning. 'Just trust me, lad. When you've tracked witches for as many years as I have, you get a feel for it. Just trust me.'

'But have you ever made a mistake? I mean have you ever burnt some girl who wasn't really a witch?'

'You have too much to learn, soldier, and too little faith ever to be a real Inquisitor. The Omnipotent Lord would never permit us to make a mistake.'

'That girl though, her father swore with one hand on the Sacred Book and one on the altar, that it was the unfermented brew of the wine that made her delirious.'

'Delirious yes, but she took her clothes off and danced naked round the fire.'

'That doesn't make her a witch.'

'But in the moonlight? A full moon too. We can't let that sort of thing go unpunished.'

Caspar looked questioningly at Brid and she whispered angrily. 'I do not dance naked anywhere. These men, these Inquisitor fools, I have feared and hated them all my life for murdering my mother. But now when I finally meet them . . . they seem so weak, so ineffective compared to the demons I'd imagined. They're just men, foolish arrogant men.'

'Anyway,' the sergeant continued, 'she confessed.'

'Only when half-drowned after three duckings in the pond and only then because Captain Ranark threatened to do the same to her baby sister.'

'I don't want to hear any more, soldier. She confessed and

that's enough. We had to free her soul from the clutches of the Devil. And fire's the only purifier.'

Caspar felt quite sick. There was a long silence before the new recruit spoke out again.

'I just thought she was too pretty to be a witch.'

'That shows how little you know. They always are too pretty. They use their beauty as a power, displaying their lustful parts. It's shameful. The very prettiest of women are often the most powerful witches.'

'So, how long do we stay here, Sergeant? We've been here ages.'

'Till someone's spotted her. It might take all day and all night but they always come up here in the end. It's our duty to cleanse the land of these vile corrupting creatures of the underworld.'

Caspar's heart sank; they were trapped. He looked at Brid who was stroking the dog's head and lifting its eyelids to examine the dazed eyes beneath. Trog began to thump his tail, showing his inbred resilience to injury. The boy couldn't understand how anyone could want to harm the beautiful Maiden.

'We just have to wait,' Brid whispered. 'They'll have to go eventually.' Her face was implacably calm as if she refused to hear the hatred in the sergeant's words, but then she sighed deeply as if a profound sorrow was welling up from her heart. She turned her eyes towards the sea. 'Dear Mother, are you still punishing me for my faithlessness in Farona? We need the Druid's Eye. We cannot lose it. Please help me.'

'I don't believe you've lost your powers,' said Caspar trying to encourage her. 'The kobolds instantly recognized you.'

She nodded and smiled. 'Yes, I know. That's true. But I'm worried. The Druid's Eye was the only thing that linked Morrigwen, Keridwen and myself: it kept the Trinity threaded together – if only barely. But now ... What will happen to Keridwen? And I can't reach Morrigwen if we need her help.'

'But you couldn't before because of that evil presence. You had to conceal the moonstone's powers.'

'That was only to dull the vision to confuse and disorientate who or whatever evil creation was staring into the other stones. But the orb still linked my powers with Morrigwen. Now I can't do that. And I'm worried for her.'

'But she'll be safe in Torra Alta.'

'Safe in a castle under siege? Don't be absurd, Spar.'

'But for nine months the Runes of War will protect them.'

'Yes, I know; you are right. But I just have a feeling. Morrigwen,' she breathed into the air. 'Mother, protect her.' The Maiden fell into a sorrowful silence while they waited for the Inquisitors to make a move.

'What's so special about the trees then?' The freshly recruited Inquisitor broke the silence. A munching noise underlaid his voice; his horse had evidently returned to cropping the grass again.

'Well, listen up lad; this is part of your training. These people have an attraction for special places. They like water and trees, certain trees in particular, and they think that there are lines in the ground that have energy. Now when you take these things into account and mark them up on a map, they form a pattern.'

Brid's face was ashen. 'How do they know that?' she gasped in horror. 'These are secret things that I'd die for rather than reveal.'

'It took many years to work it out,' the sergeant continued, 'but wherever we found them there was always a pattern. See, look. Due north beyond the horizon there's a circle of oaks. Beyond that by several leagues is the isthmus which lines up directly with Farona and that last coven we found there. So that gives you one bearing. Due west is the spit that points out towards the Hespera Isles. The largest of them is shamefully known by the locals as the Isle of the Lady probably because of the shape of those two rounded peaks. You always have to take note of anything that has the name Lady in it. They connect that with their goddess. Anyhow, that gives us another bearing. And finally south-east of us there's three long barrows and beyond that a circle of stones. Line them all up on a map and you get the centre of that hill there. There's nothing special about it in itself except that it's covered with yew trees, which don't grow anywhere else on Caldea.'

'Hal's heading up there and we're trapped here,' Caspar whispered in horror.

'How was I to know that they could work that all out? I didn't know about all those barrows and stones and the island. The yews just looked welcoming,' she sighed in dismay. 'The power in the Mother drew me to them.'

'Here, Sergeant, do you think that dog's slunk off. Should I take a look?'

Caspar curled his neck round underneath the hood of his cloak, ignoring the sharp thorns from the briar that were twisting through his hair, and tried to quiet his breathing. They were trapped here, just waiting for curiosity to get the better of the two Inquisitors.

A howl, a long low howl, echoed off the hills and filled the air. Every sound ceased; the bird song stopped abruptly; the munching from the horses was instantly silenced and in that empty pause the wolf's cry bayed out again.

'She's close, lad. She's very close.' The sergeant's voice was barely audible, quivering with excited determination. 'We'll get this witch. This one's special; I can sense it. You get a feel for these things, you know. She's a coven leader or a high witch. We've not heard of one that's half wolf for many long years now. Captain Ranark called her a lycanthropist.'

'A what?'

'A lycanthropist – a shapeshifter between woman and wolf. Now that's evil magic.'

Caspar covered Brid's hand with his own and their eyes met. 'I'll die before I let them touch you. By the love of the Mother, I'll die.'

Chapter 28

Hal marched firmly back towards the quay. Picking up a pebble he flung it out onto the beach, trying to appear as nonchalant as possible. The eelman was pointing angrily at him and shouting incoherently at the soldiers. The young nobleman rearranged his features, trying to look composed and confident as befitted his rank.

'Well, now! The King's Inquisitors,' he said, lowering his voice to disguise his trepidation. 'King Rewik mentioned that we would find you here.' He felt that an immediate reference to their sovereign could do no harm at this stage.

The three Inquisitors were sombrely liveried in black, their heads capped by open-faced sallet helmets and all mounted on sleek, liver chestnut horses. All three mounts were perfectly matched in colour except for a blaze on one and a white sock on the pastern of another. The Inquisitors' panoply of nets, hooks and cudgels were designed more for catching and maiming than for the swift dispatch of an enemy.

The leading soldier wore a scarlet sash across his shoulder and a yellow plume, which Hal recognized as an emblem of higher rank marking him out above his two associates. The officer looked at the dark-haired youth, carefully measuring him up. The Torra Altan glared back, looking him straight in the eye, knowing that he had nothing to hide in his face. He was glad that Caspar, with his violet-blue eyes, was not facing this mán. The officer of the Church with his blunt nose and broken bridge turned to the eelman.

'Is this the man you saw with the girl? And did you see a wolf?'

461

'Yes, that's him. I saw him yesterday. He was with that girl and another younger gentleman little more than a boy. I don't know about no wolves but their dog ate my eels.'

'He did, indeed,' Hal replied calmly, desperately thinking how to buy his nephew and Brid more time. 'But since I paid double for the produce, I see no crime. What exactly is the problem here?' He hoped his voice betrayed none of his misgivings at facing an interrogation from the infamous Inquisitors.

'The problem is witchcraft – witchcraft, sorcery and consorting with heathens; a capital crime and you are to be arrested on that charge.'

'Me? I most certainly am not. Do you know who I am?' Hal was determined to conceal his trepidation and decided to pull rank. He studied the man's expression and detected a flicker of uneasiness. 'The King, my cousin incidentally, will be most displeased to hear that you have been interfering with a peer of the realm in the execution of his duty.'

'The King?' The Inquisitor in charge looked more doubtful. 'Who are you? What is your name; what is your business here?'

'I am a knight of the realm and you, soldier, will speak to me with more respect,' the youth replied, feigning the deep bellowing tones that his elder brother, Branwolf, would use in such circumstances. After all nobody had ever dared accuse Branwolf of anything.

'Witchcraft is witchcraft and to keep our land free from the Devil is our highest priority. The Devil's work can infiltrate any rank of society: if you were the King himself, it would make no difference, sir.'

Hal doubted the truth in the Inquisitor's arrogant words but still felt a shiver of disquiet as the officer looked down his blunt nose, sneering out beneath the basin of his sallet helmet. He yanked the horse round by the bit, an action which Hal thought would have outraged his nephew. 'Now who are you? Lord or not, your name, sir!'

Hal lifted his hand to show the men his ring engraved with the crest of Torra Alta. 'I'm the brother of Lord Branwolf, Baron of Torra Alta.'

'You're a bit far from home, aren't you?' The Inquisitor's eyebrows rose suspiciously.

Hal's mind scrambled for a plausible explanation. 'Matters of state,' he blurted. 'King Rewik was concerned that the Vaalakans might explore the southern ports in search of a vulnerable route into the country. I've been looking for any suspicious vessels.' The Inquisitor, like King Rewik, was unlikely to know that the Vaalakans didn't have access to their warships.

Hal carefully noted the change in the man's expression as he looked uncomfortably from the ring to Hal's face and then out towards the sands. The youth thought with satisfaction that the combination of his nobility and eloquent speech had forced the Inquisitor to falter in his resolve. The blunt-nosed soldier twisted round to view the ships moored in the harbour. Hal followed his gaze, to a broad-beamed ferry with the letters *Dorsmouth Seahorse* on its low prow. He scanned the bustling decks of the trawlers, and then looked further out to sea towards the deep-draughted hulls of the merchant ships anchored off the islands. The Inquisitor's gaze skimmed over his own ocean-going vessel, with the red scythe and yellow wheat sheaf depicted against the black cloth of the loose, flapping mainsail. The sleek ship was moored at the end of a pier alongside a dozen or so small, in-shore fishing boats equipped with oars as well as sails.

'There's nothing out of place, here,' the King's Inquisitor began.

'Sir,' one of the junior soldiers interjected, 'we're losing the other two. They're going out onto the sands.'

The senior officer waved the soldier irritably aside. He looked uncertainly at the determined young nobleman standing before him then at Brid's tiny form hurrying away. He turned back to the soldier. 'Just keep her in sight; so long as you can still see her, we'll soon catch up with that one. But we'd better check first that she's the right girl and that the real witch hasn't slipped past us onto a pier.' He turned to search up and down the quay. 'I don't want her to escape us, men. The townsfolk were talking about a wolf, the girl with a shadow of a wolf. She could have gone the other way. Captain Ranark's sure the witch is heading up onto the hills, but we're going to get her first. I want this promotion. There'll be a bonus in it for all of us, men.'

Hal's relief inadvertently soughed from his lungs, but he successfully disguised it with a sudden cough before complimenting himself on doing a good job of covering his nephew's back. Brid and Spar would soon make it round the headland while these soldiers wasted their time here.

The portly woman from the fruit stall was pulling the shade of a canopy down to protect her wares whilst she retired for her leisurely midday meal. She came waddling along the quay with a fruit-basket nestled in the crook of her arm. The officer pulled his horse's head hard round by the thin bit, which cut into the corner of its mouth, and threatened the fruit-seller with the point of his pikestaff. 'Woman there, you woman, I'm looking for a girl.'

'Hey, you can't treat a Belbidian like that!' Hal objected, only to find the weapon prodding his own sternum.

'It's my duty to ask questions. You have no right to interfere; or have you got something to hide, sir?'

Hal was outraged by the Inquisitor's methods but managed to control his riled temper, deciding it would be more expedient to stand back and keep quiet.

The alarmed woman dropped her basket and pressed herself back against the sea wall, looking terrified. 'I've done nothing. I sell at a fair price. There's no potions in my fruit. I've done nothing, sir.'

'Silence, woman. The girl – have you seen a girl with an unusual shadow?'

'Shadow? N–n–no. I've seen lots of girls lately, but no strange shadows.'

'No one strange at all?'

She looked at Hal doubtfully. 'No, except for the young lady what was with this nobleman yesterday. Strange deformed eyes she had, but there weren't anything funny about her shadow.' The woman clutched at her apron and kept her head lowered, not daring to meet the Inquisitor's accusing eyes.

'Think, woman, think. You have to be sure; remember your soul may depend on it. A witch walking abroad may steal your soul. Now think. Was there anything unusual?' The Inquisitor craned forward and prodded the woman with the butt of his lance. 'What did you notice about her?'

Stricken with panic, the fruit-seller flattened her ample folds of flesh against the sea wall as if she wished for the stones to swallow her. 'N–nothing, nothing at all. No, I . . . I told you. I told you there was no wolf. She was only interested in the apples.' The woman glanced to left and right, trying to see a way of escaping from the hawkish interrogation. 'I don't know anything about no wolf, only that she wanted some apples.'

The Inquisitor sneered. 'Apples? Don't be ridiculous, woman; there must have been something else?' he persisted.

'Well, she was a bit small-like –'

A junior officer interrupted, 'That's got to be her, Sir, hasn't it?'

'Leave her alone, man; can't you see you're frightening her?' Hal demanded, trying to distract the officer from learning anything suspicious about Brid.

The Inquisitor glowered out from beneath his helmet. 'You are obstructing me in my service to the Lord. Stand back! As an officer of the church I outrank you or any other peer; you will not interfere. Now, woman, I need to know more; there must have been something else strange about her.'

She looked confused and distressed. 'W-what's to tell?'

The Inquisitor's eyes narrowed as if he were trying to pene-trate the woman's mind. She muttered and stammered. Hal guessed that she was desperately trying to think of something that would incriminate the noblewoman and so allow herself to escape from this terrible interrogation.

He put a hand tentatively onto the hilt of his great rune-sword and considered slaying all three of them; after all he carried the sword blessed with the mighty Runes of War. But if he failed and they finally overcame him . . . ? What of Spar then? The runes on the blade alone would be incriminating enough.

Go on, Spar, run. Get out across the sands, he prayed inwardly. His keen young eyes could just see that his companions had stopped but he couldn't understand why until he saw the dog thrashing something black and rope-like. Hal surreptitiously slid his hands away from the sword. It would be better to trust in the treacherous sands than fight here. He would draw every man in the town against him if he attacked an Inquisitor as well as condemn his kinsman.

'No, Sir, I told you,' the fruit-seller found her voice and wailed despairingly. 'There were nought strange about her except for her blindness and a crippling limp.'

'Limp!' the subordinate soldier exclaimed and looked out towards Brid running across the sands. 'Well, she isn't limping now!'

'Got her!' the Inquisitor smiled triumphantly. 'This is a big catch, men. She's a ringleader of sorts. One with a wolf shadow, that's rare, that's significant. Let's get her before Ranark does.' He turned on Hal. 'I don't know what part you play in all this but we'll catch up with you later. We've tracked you to the ostlery and we've requisitioned your horses. All of them are under guard. You will return there and await further questioning. Do I make myself clear?'

Hal desperately prayed that he had delayed the Inquisitors for long enough. For an instant he wrestled with his instinct to draw his blood-thirsty sword on these arrogant witch-hunters. He fiercely bit his lip, reasoning that Spar had his bow and at least that damn stupid dog was supposed to be a snake-catcher and so should look after them on the sands. The horsemen, on the other hand, would be unprotected from the snakes. No, he would serve Torra Alta better by getting the horses back from the Inquisitors and riding round to rescue his companions before they reached the yew forest. He wasn't about to let some soldiers steal his horses.

'Let's get them!' The officer spurred his horse, leaving Hal standing on the quay beside the fruit-seller's quivering bulk.

She screamed after the horsemen. 'The sand-snakes! The tide's wrong! Don't go on the beach.' Frantically yelling, she turned on Hal. 'Stop them: the snakes will take them. They can't know about the tides.' Her arms fell flat by her sides as she watched the riders charge out onto the treacherous sands.

Unable to do anything more to protect his nephew, Hal sprinted back into the main town and up the terraced streets towards the ostlery. Two liver chestnut horses were tethered to the gate and a guard of two Inquisitors, without any badge of rank, were standing duty. One soldier, his black tabard looking suspiciously new, was arguing furiously with the ostler. Hal crept slowly forward and listened to their words.

'We've requisitioned all the horses, ostler, and that's all there is to it. None can come and none can go.'

'This is not good for business,' the ostler complained, anxiously picking bits of straw from his clothing. 'It's one thing answering all your questions; it's another – '

There was a resounding thwack and a suppressed cry as a cudgel hammered cruelly onto the ostler's broad back. Hal winced.

'Silence man! We are the King's Inquisitors. We are empowered by His Majesty and the grace of God to achieve anything we see fit in the execution of our duties.' To Hal's ears, this sounded like a rehearsed speech. 'The horses are under our jurisdiction now. The witch may come back for them – or send one of her minions whose fallen under her spell.'

Hal bristled with suppressed fury. Firstly he was outraged by the Inquisitor's treatment of the ostler; no soldier had the right to treat a fellow Belbidian like that. Furthermore, he was not now, nor ever had been, nor ever would be, someone's – anyone's – minion; and lastly, he was most certainly not spellbound by Brid. Oh sure, she was not without certain desirable attributes, but she was far too full of herself and far too assertive to enchant him. Poor Spar, of course, that was a different matter: he was completely besotted. Hal felt vaguely sorry for his nephew, but supposed that was the sort of thing a boy had to go through to grow up.

His quick mind rapidly leapt through these thoughts before resettling on the Inquisitors. He was surprised to find them rather unimpressive. Their dreadful, awesome reputation might be applicable when these officers dealt with peasants and young frightened girls, but they certainly weren't intimidating to a nobleman of Torra Alta, a man such as himself. He stiffened his back and approached with his chin jutting handsomely forward.

'Well, ostler, is that one of them? Is that one of the youths who accompanied the girl, that small elven-looking girl with the limp,' the foremost soldier demanded, whilst lowering his staff to challenge the strutting youth. Rubbing his bruised shoulder, the ostler nodded reluctantly and the other soldier turned on Hal.

'You're under arrest.'

'I am not,' Hal retorted smoothly. 'I'm here on the King's business.' He was sure that such a remark would never be uttered by a pagan and felt that facing these men with a look of honest arrogance and indignation was going to produce the fastest results. 'You cannot arrest me. I am brother to a great baron and a knight of the realm.' He was quite satisfied with the deflated expressions that his words produced. The Inquisitors are too used to terrorizing peasant girls and don't know how to react when faced with someone like me, he thought.

'You've been seen with two others at this place,' the soldier accused, 'one of whom is a witch.'

'A witch?' Hal smiled gently at them, trying to look sympathetically patronizing as if he were excusing them for their ill manners towards a superior. 'Now do I look like a witch?' He knew it was a safe line to throw at them because he was quite plainly of solid Belbidian stock: dark hair, solid bones and plain earthy coloured eyes – olive eyes, like those of his brother and the vast majority of all other Belbidians he knew.

The Inquisitor raised his staff and shook his head. 'No, you don't. No, that's true.'

'Good. Now we've settled that, I want my horse.'

The man continued to nod his head even though he started to deny Hal access to the stables. 'I have my orders. Even if the Queen of Tutivillus comes begging, we're not to let any horses out of here.'

'But, I'm a peer of this land and cousin to the King. I'll see that he hears of this. What's your name, soldier?' Hal puffed himself up, speaking as grandly as he could and trying somehow to intimidate the two men.

'I'm the Inquisitor here. You will remain here until my superiors can question you.' The soldier, Hal noticed, carefully avoided looking at his eyes. Evidently it wasn't in their training to deal with the high-born nobility of Belbidia. A cudgel used mistakenly on a King's cousin might have grave consequences.

'Ostler! Ostler!' he demanded angrily. 'Am I not a respectable patron of this establishment? Have you seen devils walking abroad with me, or do I seem, as I am, a nobleman of this esteemed country? A country, I might add, which is under threat of war. And as good and loyal citizens of Belbidia you should be doing your best to aid the kingdom, rather than trying to arrest men such as myself, who are striving to protect this land and its people from the heathen Northerners.'

Hal carefully looked over the two officers and decided they were both too young to have any real position of authority. He squared his shoulders and expelled any remaining doubts that perhaps his own youth might prevent him from bettering these low-ranking, fair-weather soldiers. 'Well?' he roared, using the same intimidating bellow with which his brother controlled the stronghold at Torra Alta. 'Well, who is going to tell me what the hell is going on?'

'Witchcraft, sir.'

'I hope you're not still insinuating that the brother of a baron –'

'No, sir, no sir, indeed not, but I have my orders about this girl,' the soldier stumbled over his words and muttered to his companion. 'Cousin to the King! No one said anything about noblemen. What is Ranark doing? He'll have us all strung-up for high treason.'

Hal assumed that Ranark was the Inquisitors' officer-in-chief, but rather than dwell on that he pressed on with the task of making these men feel as uncomfortable as possible. 'You're telling me that my kinswoman is a witch? You dare say such a thing? Look; here is my ring. What does the crest signify to you?'

The first officer took the gold band, his smooth forehead gradually crinkling up into lines of perplexity. He handed it to his comrade.

'Torra Alta, my Lord. You are from the household of the Baron of Torra Alta.'

'Ah, well done, well done, we're very quick aren't we?' Hal threw in a touch of sarcasm, having always found that it worked well in his favour. 'Now, do you actually know what's happening in Torra Alta?'

'Well, yes of course, sir; there's trouble with the Vaalakans.'

'Trouble! Trouble! You idly call that trouble! They're under siege from a vast multitude that pours into the Yellow Mountains from the North. Do you know what will happen if Torra Alta falls?'

The Inquisitors looked confused. 'Torra Alta's legendary, sir. We all know –'

'You know nothing. Torra Alta cannot hold enough food to sustain the garrison through a lengthy siege. Belbidia doesn't have enough men to face the Northmen or press them back from the Pass, because people like you are arresting men like me and preventing us from protecting our homeland. Are you a loyal subject of the King? Are you a proud citizen of Belbidia?' Hal hoped that his questions would gradually wear down their guard. He looked towards the stables. Magpie's head was lolling peacefully over the stable door but he only snatched a fleeting glimpse of Firecracker's rump as the horse paced testily round in his stall. He knew that Caspar's horse could take only so much stabling and with all the raised voices he would soon be demanding to be let out – hopefully with his heels.

'We put God and country before all else,' the Inquisitor replied earnestly.

'Well, how long will the Faith survive under the rule of the Vaalakans and the oppression of their Ice-God? You are fools all of you, complacently assuming that you are safe because Torra Alta will protect you, thinking that no man or beast can get past Torra Alta. Yet you dare to attack the very heart of the great fortress by attacking me.' Hal racked his brains for a vaguely credible reason as to why the horses should be released. 'We are here looking for spies, spies that only we can identify because we've seen them in the Vaalakan camp and traced them all the way here to Ildros. I need my horse to track them.'

'We've seen nothing. We see everything that goes on in this town and there are no spies.'

'Well, of course you haven't seen them: they wouldn't be spies otherwise, would they? You'd think they were sailors or tradesman or pilgrims. Spies, for your information, tend to go round in disguise rather than in full Vaalakan battle-dress. It would be a little too obvious, don't you think?'

The Inquisitors were beginning to flush red under their black tunics. 'Ostler! What have you heard? Has there been anything unusual?'

The man shook his head. 'No, we haven't heard anything like that, but the town's been buzzing with the talk of the woman with the shadow of a wolf. They gave a description quite similar to that of the young lady who was with the gentleman here. Very small with an elfin face, though blind and crippled; you couldn't help but notice her, sir. Such a shame 'cos she would have been so pretty if it weren't for her afflictions.'

Hal had to admit that Brid, when not disguised as a cripple, was indeed quite exquisitely beautiful. She stirred all sorts of feelings within him, though he still fervently wished they had left her behind. She'd been the cause of all their troubles and really had done very little to help them find any of these obscure runes. If only she'd managed to behave with at least

471

some semblance of feminine decorum they could have avoided all this. But dashing about in breeches and galloping around unchaperoned, well, it was bound to lead to suspicious talk. Why couldn't she have continued to copy Cybillia's composure? His thoughts whirled round to his present predicament.

'Well, have you seen any wolves around here, ostler?' Hal demanded fixing him with what he hoped was an authoritative glower. 'Wolves, man. How many shadowy wolves have you seen following us?'

'Well, none.' The tall Caldean townsman half-turned towards the black tabards of the Inquisitors, not wanting to look them full in the face. 'None at all. Only that snake-catcher that they brought, sir. Ugly dog in a terrible state. They'd rescued it from a dog fight and it barked the place down.'

'And nothing else suspicious, no wolves?' Hal asked again trying to emphasize his innocence. The ostler shook his head. 'No, nothing your lordship, nothing. The only peculiar thing was a man asking odd questions.'

'A man?'

'Yeah, cloaked in a brown bearskin like yourself, sir. He was big and slow talking. A very dull look to his eye. When he ordered his meal, I couldn't make out what he wanted at all!'

'A bearskin like mine,' Hal echoed, thinking that he had only ever seen Torra Altans wearing such cloaks. He suddenly thought of the stranger Ceowulf had seen in the Faronan crowd talking to Gatto.

'What about this man?' The Inquisitor persisted in following every lead.

'Well, nothing wrong with him in himself except that he was a bit slow-like. He looked like and sounded like a straightforward Belbidian peasant. Ate a good deal too: twice as much as most fishermen. But it were a strange coin he offered to pay me with. I wouldn't have taken no foreign coinage not knowing its value, save it were silver, solid silver mind. And that's a lot for a meal in my humble tavern, so it didn't matter too much what king's head was on it. Camaalia, that's it. Camaalia. A coin from Camaalia.'

Camaalia! Gatto was from Camaalia. Perhaps this coin came from the mercenary, Hal mused. Could it mean that Gatto and his men were already here on their trail? He felt shocked and hoped his skin wasn't paling visibly as he felt a clamminess creep up his neck. What was the King doing? Why hadn't Ceowulf managed to hunt down these mercenaries?

'Was he alone?' Hal asked anxiously. 'Or were there any men with him?'

'Alone I think. He didn't actually ask a lot of questions but just looked everyone up and down. The barmaids were all having a giggle because he took such special notice of all the young girls.'

Whoever this man is, thought Hal, he's looking for Brid. He suddenly felt a huge surge of frustration at being trapped here by these bumbling Inquisitors. He needed to get away and rescue Caspar and the Maiden.

'Look, you can't hold me. There's no possible evidence against me. I've got to find this man. He's an enemy spy,' he roared at the young soldiers who anxiously held onto their lances and looked nervously at each other, not knowing what to do. 'In God's holy name, you know there's no conceivable reason to hold me for witchcraft.'

'Well, there's not a mark on him,' one of the soldiers argued reasonably as he eyed Hal. 'Not a single feature that marks him out as a witch or warlock. He's got healthy natural eyes, broad bones, a square hard chin.'

'Yeah, I'm a damn handsome specimen of a good old Belbidian prepared to fight for my country. Now let me past. I demand to have my horse.'

A sudden crash from the stables halted their altercation. An equine shriek pierced the atmosphere, followed by the rasp of hooves over cobbles as Firecracker pawed the ground. A plank of wood from the lower door of a stable suddenly splintered off and skittered over the courtyard. The ostler grimaced.

'That stallion! He's a brute and he'll set the others off. I don't want my stables and my reputation ruined. This talk of witches and wolves is bad enough but if people see that I can't look after horses – well . . .'

'You'll have to take him out and walk him up and down, that's the only way,' Hal told him firmly, whilst nonchalantly resting back against the wall. He was confident that whatever Firecracker did he was bound to cause a useful distraction. The colt had always been a troublemaker.

'I can't do that, your lordship. The young gentleman with you, he said firmly not to handle the animal.'

'Well, I can't do it,' Hal responded. 'These officers of the King won't let me past.'

The noise from the stables was growing. Firecracker had kicked another hole in the planking and even Magpie had been caught up in the excitement, roused into tossing her head and snorting restlessly like a bull.

'Perhaps you'd better,' one of the Inquisitors reluctantly conceded.

The ostler, still holding his bruised shoulder, rushed into the barn to fetch some tack. Hal shouted after him, 'You'll need a bridle not just a halter. You won't hold that horse without a bit.'

The man came out carrying Firecracker's ornate harness, jangling the double curb-chain. 'Quite right, my Lord, quite right.'

Hal grinned inwardly. The ostler was justly wary but still had no idea what he was letting himself in for. In one of these moods, that colt needed more than one man to hold him and in the three short years of that animal's life only one person had ever managed to handle him comfortably. From a very young age Caspar had always been adept at handling horses and the older boy had long since conceded that his nephew outshone him in that field. The whole matter puzzled Hal: he always thought it incongruous that Caspar, who had never matched him in any other field of hunting or war-craft, could surpass his skill on a horse. Firecracker had been the final and conclusive test: Hal found him tiresomely difficult and unmanageable whereas Caspar found the stallion responsive and fleet of foot.

'Don't unbolt the door until you've got that bridle on,' Hal offered his advice. Firecracker crushed the ostler against the stable walls and knocked his shoulder into the wooden surrounds of the door. This induced a colourful stream of blasphemous oaths and brought looks of severe disapproval as well as sympathy from the King's Inquisitors. Firecracker reared, dragging the man upwards, and kicked the stable door again.

'I need a hand here,' the ostler cried. Hal sat back and smiled, knowing he was going to enjoy this fiasco. 'The only devil I know of around here is the one in this horse.'

Until now Hal had considered the red roan to be nothing more than an unpredictable liability and had scoffed at his nephew's choice of mount, but now he found himself thanking Caspar for his stubborn, sentimental affection for the half-crazed, untameable colt. Only Firecracker could cause such a commotion and right now, he decided, such a distraction was the only thing that was going to get him out of his predicament. He noted with satisfaction the perplexed faces of the Inquisitors as they looked to each other for mutual approval before rushing to help the ostler battle with the fiendish colt.

Firecracker burst out of the stable, with the Ildros townsman barely clinging to the reins. He was a strong man used to handling horses but this animal had a fierce, unrestrainable streak. The red stallion sat back on his haunches and spun round so that the stumbling man was pulled to his knees and dragged across the courtyard. The young soldiers ran to either side of the horse, reaching up to get a hold of the steel bit, but the stallion was too quick for them. With wild eyes he reared up and lashed out with his iron-shod hooves. One of the Inquisitors ran to the barn door and grabbed a large bullwhip.

'No wretched brute's getting the better of me.'

'No, don't do that. No!' the ostler warned him.

The Inquisitor paid no attention and gave the war-horse a

crack on the rump. You've had it now, thought Hal with satisfaction; you've had it.

The heels flashed out backwards and the red colt bucked and kicked like a mule, sending the men flying for cover. Once the horse was loose, he stormed round the courtyard, taking a fierce bite out of the rump of one of the tethered horses. It didn't take long before he had stirred them to a sweating fright and they were plunging to get free. They bucked and kicked until the knots in the reins gave way and the animals were suddenly fleeing out of the courtyard. Firecracker reared and galloped after them, clattering up the street into the town, midst cries of, 'Stand clear! Ware, loose horse, loose horse!'

The Inquisitors stood dazed, foolishly looking at one another.

'Get my horse ready, Ostler. That's a valuable animal and I have to get him. You men,' Hal jabbed a finger at the two soldiers, 'I'll see that the King hears of this.'

'We had our orders, sir. Captain Ranark said no horses were to leave.'

'Well, you just about chased that colt out of here. And I'm going to fetch him.'

The two men stood brandishing their staffs but seemed totally undecided about what to do. Hal suddenly realized how hopeless soldiers could be if left without the guidance of their leader. Left only with orders that now seemed quite impossible to follow, they were totally flummoxed. The King's regular Inquisitors, he knew, were very few in number, yet Ildros seemed to be crawling with them. He decided that these extra inexperienced rank and file soldiers must have been hastily drafted after their superiors had evidently anticipated a need for a greater force of numbers. Hal was furious. What was Rewik doing? How could he waste good men on such a fanatical hunt, for what were really no more than a few batty women, when soldiers were desperately needed on the northern frontier?

The large Caldean threw the youth up into Magpie's saddle. Hal had no difficulty following the trail of the horses. All along the streets, men, women and children were pressed back against the walls. Baying dogs galloped up the alley ahead, and upturned barrows and spilt carts littered the cobbles. 'Loose horse, that way, that way!' the cry went up. He had the vivid impression that he was following a hurricane.

Some enterprising wagoner had turned his cart across the narrow street to bar the way and it had indeed stopped one of the liver chestnut horses, though there was still no sign of Firecracker. A young and very proud boy firmly gripped the reins of the lathered-up horse.

'Get the cart out of the way,' Hal yelled, seeing the obstacle too late with no time left to manoeuvre. None of the townsmen moved but gawped speechlessly at the thundering approach of the piebald mare. 'Come on then, Magpie, let's see what you're made of.' Gathering her up, he steadied her pace and gave her a sharp thwack of encouragement with the end of the reins. Despite her ponderous weight and the heaviness of her feathered legs, she flew smoothly over, just clipping the back of the cart with a hoof. 'Good girl. Now, get up,' Hal encouraged.

A toddler ran out into the street and a woman scrambled after the child and clutched him in her arms. Hal narrowly missed them both and galloped on with her angry words ringing in his ears. 'You stupid, reckless fool!'

My God, I could have killed her child. The youth guiltily tried to wipe the accusation from his mind. Why am I here on this crazed wild goose chase when I should be in Torra Alta killing Vaalakans? He was beginning to lose faith in Brid and her magic and talk of Goddesses. If she was such a powerful priestess, one of the select three, why didn't she know where the Egg was? Maybe it wasn't her fault; maybe it was all the bitter old Crone's fault; but all the same Brid had to be partly to blame for this madness that turned his own countrymen into his enemy.

There was a fork in the road ahead. 'That way, that way,' a boy shouted as Hal approached.

His directions were unnecessary since the spill of white milk trickling in runnels through the cracks in the brick cobbles, made it quite plain. Only Firecracker could cause so much havoc. Thank God Bullback had the sense to stable reliable animals like Magpie. The street climbed eastwards out of the town towards the downs and the tree-covered ridge. Firecracker was instinctively galloping for open ground and Hal hoped that once the horse struck the soft turf and smelt the grass he would slow up. The animal would be impossible to catch otherwise, but at least he was heading in the right direction towards the yew trees. He prayed Brid and Spar would be waiting for him.

The road ahead was blocked. A crowd stooped down over an old man lying on the ground. Hal dragged on the reins, bringing Magpie to a halt. There was no way he could get past. The man was sickly white; a trickle of blood oozed from a cut on his temple. The voices in the crowd were angry and there was nothing Hal could do but barge his way through, using the horse's brutish size to force the townsfolk apart.

'You mad man, was that your horse? Look what he's done!' a woman howled at him.

Hal felt a huge sense of guilty remorse tighten around his gut but he refused to dwell on such thoughts. How was he to know that Firecracker would cause so much damage? What he was doing was trying to save Belbidia and what was one old man to the fate of the whole country? A strip of green beneath an archway ahead led him out towards the open countryside where a dirt track, cut up with hoof-sized crescents, climbed towards the yew forest.

The other liver chestnut horse was idling grazing on the first tufts of grass beyond the town. Its saddle had swung round under its belly and the sleek animal had stepped through its reins, which dragged through the grass. There was still no sign of Firecracker though, and Hal urged Magpie on. She thundered stoically over the ground at a steady, reliable pace. As they passed over the first rise Hal began to sense that something was wrong. He couldn't work out exactly what was bothering him so he slowed up to take in his surroundings.

The yews lay about a league ahead to the left, a dark strip against the dusty green downs, rising above the road that led to the court of Baron Cadros at Tartra. Everything looked peaceful, though there was something distracting about the attitude of the workers who pruned the vines in the vineyard to his right. They appeared to have a marked lack of enthusiasm for the day's work. Hal didn't expect much else: there was a general air of lethargy here in Caldea compared to mainland Belbidia, but it was the expectancy in their idleness that caught his attention. They had downed their shears, which were used to prune back the vines after the harvest, and were grouped at the ends of their rows, staring up towards the ridge. They momentarily looked towards Hal as he approached but quickly turned back to their vigil. He trotted over to the first vine-worker who nodded his head and respectfully straightened up a little. He was short with pronounced bow legs.

'A horse, have you seen a loose horse?' Hal enquired.

The peasant nodded.

'Didn't you try to stop him?' Hal asked with an edge of irritation in his voice.

'Well, yes, we did, sir, but he galloped straight by.' The peasant kept glancing up towards the ridge.

'What's going on?' Hal demanded.

'Witch-hunt, sir. Them black-clothed Inquisitors rode by at dawn.'

'It weren't dawn, Ludd: we didn't get up here till two hours after,' a round-faced man contradicted his friend.

'Well, thereabouts, early this morning,' the bow-legged peasant conceded. 'All mounted and all serious like. They're staking out the woods up there. Set a trap we think. The word in town is that there's a wolf-woman abroad. Some chief witch they say, but I hope it's not a mistake like last time. They burnt old Herwald's daughter, you know.'

One of the others laughed sardonically. 'She weren't no witch now. Just a bit free with her favours. It's the wine, you know, made her a bit too spicy, but the Inquisitors had just

479

arrived then. It was a horrible sight to see her burn. Horrible. Never heard a wench scream like that. Poor Herwald threw himself into the sea.'

Hal felt quite revolted and the image of Brid sizzling in flames crept into his mind. He was flushed with rage and anger. Brid and Caspar were walking straight into a trap; he had to get to them before the Inquisitors did.

'Where are these men then?' Hal pressed on with his interrogation.

'Oh, they're all over, all round the woods. We watched them for a bit then went back to work. The vines need a lot of tending.' This short bandy vine-worker is as bad as the fruit-seller, Hal thought in frustration; he can't stick to the point. 'Well, as I said, we went back to work till the other men rode by, quite a few of them in two separate groups – but these ones weren't Inquisitors. The last lot stopped to ask questions, just like you, and the minute I mentioned a witch-hunt on Bow Hill there, they turned up towards the yew trees.'

Alarm bells clamoured in the youth's ears. 'What were these men like?' he demanded.

'Well, let me see,' Ludd pondered in slow unhurried tones, making Hal want to strangle the words out of him. 'The first lot were soldiers of sorts.'

'Black cloths over their mail-suits,' the round-faced vine-worker added. 'But no emblems nor badges. They were foreign-looking too but that ain't nothing. We get lots of different folk being so near the port and all, and we guessed they were off to Tartra to see the Baron.'

'It were odd though, weren't it lads, that peasant being with them.' Ludd looked up at his companions for agreement. 'Very big man. He didn't look comfortable on a horse at all. And there were another like that in the second group an' all. Very thick forearms – I thought to myself that none of us vine-workers get forearms like that. They had Mainlander's smocks on, like the harvesters wear, and they looked real odd in the company of those soldiers.'

'And the second group, the ones that asked the questions?' Hal demanded.

'I don't remember much about them but we all talked about their weapons and horses. Never seen anything like it. Clinking coats of metal, long spurs and their horses all prettied up like ladies going to a dance with all their finery on. Quite a sight,' Ludd exclaimed.

'Quite a sight,' his comrades agreed, still looking northward towards the yews.

'How many?' Hal questioned, determined to arm himself with as much detail as he could.

Ludd raised his shoulders and looked up to his round-faced companion for an answer. The taller peasant chewed on his lip pensively. 'Not counting the two peasants I'd say there were three or four soldiers in each party maybe – and I'm nearly forgetting the man without armour, the one in the fur cloak.'

'Yes, him, all smothered in a cloak,' a younger peasant interrupted, eager to join in the conversation. 'And he looked like he'd got something or someone hidden under it too.'

'No, he didn't, Herbert, that's you just being fanciful.'

'He did so! You were just too busy looking at the glittering armour,' he wailed indignantly, but Hal wasn't listening.

I've got to get Spar out of there, he chafed with worry. Where's that crazed horse of his?

He cantered further up the Tartra Road, eyeing the distant, dark green band of the yew trees on the horizon and hoping that his nephew was there, hiding safely. Around him on the lower slopes, the rutted highway cut through trailing brambles then rose to squeeze between the striped vineyards, which stretched away to pattern the higher downs. Breaking over the top of the third rise he skidded urgently to a halt, immediately pulling Magpie back and out of sight. Firecracker was there all right, not more than three hundred paces ahead, but there were also five dark men trying to catch him. Two were on foot with their arms stretched wide, trying to usher the colt towards their companions, who remained mounted. Hal nudged the piebald into the cover of some vines, which were as yet untouched by the vine-workers' pruning shears. He coaxed the animal deep into the vegetation so that he could get a good view of the shallow valley without being spotted himself. Firecracker was still causing a furore, skittering away each time the armoured men came in close. But it was the muffled cry, coming from a bundle of cloak thrown across one of the horses, that drew Hal's attention.

The two men trying to catch the stray horse were clad in black hauberks. Their angry shouts drifted across the downs and Hal instantly recognized Gatto's gravelly voice. 'I won't forget that horse if I live to see a thousand battles. That's the brute that set on us in the forest. It's definitely one of their horses. We've got them now, Tasso. These fool Inquisitors will corner them for us.'

'Don't any be forgetting that the Belbidaks is to be alive. You hears me.' Hal's blood ran cold as he recognized the ugly Vaalakan accent. 'Special the girling. We needs her. She will lead us to this thing of power, to this Egg. No forgets, Morbak wants the Egg.'

'And Master. Morbak wants the Egg for Master. Master must have the Egg.'

Hal was shocked. He knew that voice too: it was strangely familiar. It came in a deep Belbidian accent from a man in a bearskin cloak but he couldn't quite place where he had heard it before. 'Master says when we have the Egg no one will call me kitchen-fool no more.'

Hal was certain he knew that voice but here out of context, so unexpected, the identity of its owner eluded him. The man slowly turned and beneath the hooded form of his cape a broad fleshy nose jutted out from a moon-shaped face. Ulf, from Torra Alta's kitchens; a traitor before his very eyes! Hal couldn't think. All rational argument deserted him; and with the white metal runesword high in his hand and the battle-cry of Torra Alta raging in his throat, he kicked Magpie forward and charged at the group.

'You traitorous dog!' Outrage, fury and disgust swamped his

senses; his focus narrowed in on the once-trusted servant who had now turned traitor. Hal gave no thought to the Vaalakan and the three mercenaries with their sabres and short swords. He knew who had betrayed his homeland and he had only one intention as he narrowed his vision onto the knobbly Adam's apple in the oaf's throat as he swallowed hard at the sight of him. 'I'm going to tear your throat out, spineless traitor!'

His furious attack of blind rage was intercepted by a hefty blow that smacked him full in the chest and knocked the wind out of him. He fell back onto Magpie's hindquarters but pulled himself upright only to be coshed on the side of the head. He rolled forward, tumbling from the war-horse's secure back, and landed face down in the dirt. For a second the world went black and his breathing was smothered by clods of earth. The jarring shock of the second blow scattered his senses. Someone kicked him in the side. He could hear a distant moaning sound, but it was a moment before he realized the noise was coming from his own mouth. He turned his head sideways, trying to shake off the grogginess that was sucking him into unconsciousness. He blinked. Everything was a swirling red blur with pinpoints of light flashing across his vision. He managed to drag a hand up to wipe his eyes. A blood vessel by his temple must have ruptured: his head was sticky with blood. His right eye cleared but his left eye was peering through a cloudy sanguine veil.

Lying flat on his side, his clear eye focused on the fetlocks and hooves of a horse. Then a pair of black boots filled his vision and Hal doubled up as he felt the boot kick into the soft tissues of his stomach.

'Get up, boy, and fight.' Gatto's voice was mockingly confident without any trace of fear.

Hal rolled over onto his front and hauled himself up onto his hands and knees. He struggled to his knees and dizzily tried to follow the blurred shape circling him.

'I'll have this one, Boss.'

'All yours, Tasso.'

The blur moved aside and Hal's eyes were drawn to a black shape moving in from the left. He shook his head vigorously to clear his senses and focused on Tasso's sleek black skin, his sinister black clothing and his black steel mail, as the mercenary circled him. The crescent curve of the foreigner's sword threatened Hal's neck. The man lunged forward, almost playfully with no serious intent, merely taunting the boy like a cat taunts a mouse. A mocking smile split his black face with a white slash of teeth. Hal saw the image of the man flicker in bursts through his distorted vision. He could only see half of the man clearly. He frantically wiped away the blood from his face, trying to regain his focus.

'Stand up, boy, and fight,' he snarled. 'I'm going to enjoy this after what you did to my comrades, especially Bolga.'

'What makes you think I won't do the same to you?' Hal gasped, trying to steady his breathing and spitting dust and blood from his mouth. He staggered to his feet, bearing the humiliation as Tasso bowed with mock gallantry and permitted the inexperienced youth time to rise up and meet him. Turning slowly on his heels, letting the point of the great runesword pivot in the dust, Hal tried to follow the man's movements. He grasped his sword firmly in two hands. His body was still hunched with the pain in his stomach and he tried to shake off the dull fog that befuddled his senses. Tasso swam in and out of focus.

'You are the worst sort of slime.' Hal spat the words trying to buy himself time to gather his faculties. 'You fight for no reason – not for faith, nor belief, nor country, nor honour, not even for a woman.'

The lithe mercenary feinted forward, flicking the sabre in a quick rising arc and catching Hal's cheek. He nicked the flesh with a razor cut before the Torra Altan youth had time to raise the weight of his great sword.

'Hah! The innocence of youth,' Tasso scoffed.

Hal touched his cheek and felt the fresh warm blood on his fingertips. His heart raced, frustratedly aware how his blind anger had led him recklessly into the centre of these men. He felt like a baited dog trapped in a pit with no escape. Reckless! He vainly berated himself. If anyone sings my praises in a ballad to the heroes, I shall go down as Hal the Reckless. He faced the battle-hardened veteran, knowing he was totally out-matched.

The injured Torra Altan realized that his expression must have betrayed his sudden misgivings. He tried to screw the momentary look of horror that flickered across his face into a sneer – or what he hoped was a sneer – of contempt. But the mercenary had marked the suspicion of doubt on his face.

Tasso stood back and smiled pitifully at the Belbidian youth, displaying his healthy white teeth. 'You didn't really bargain for this did you, boy? Let your temper rule your head. That's it, take a good look around you.' Through his blood-smeared vision Hal saw a distorted view of Gatto's scarred face, the sadistic sneer of the Vaalakan, and the treacherous eyes of Ulf the Torra Altan traitor. All of them wished him evil. 'Bitten off more than you can chew, as they say in this castrated, butter-soft country.'

The whispered grating sound, as Tasso pulled his vizor down and clicked it into place, signified that the man had finished gaming and was ready to assault in earnest. Hal braced himself. Come on, clear your head, clear your head. How's Spar going to cope without you? Watch that sabre, watch the point of the sabre; it's going to come at you any second. The sinews in Hal's hands tightened round the reassuringly solid grip of the sword hilt. He stiffened his back, slowly drawing his own sword into a position of readiness. The broadsword gave him a long reach but Tasso was well built and as agile as a mountain cat. He moved with well-trained confidence and natural grace.

They circled each other round and around. Hal focused intently on the sabre that swirled in and out of the clear sight of his unbloodied eye. He twisted his head to wipe the trickle of blood onto his collar and Tasso seized the distracted moment. He drew the serrated edge of his sabre back and

lunged in with the speed of a pouncing panther. Hal anticipated the movement and flung himself sideways, feeling only
the rush of air past his ear. The mercenary feinted in again
on the same side. Hal rolled away again, but through the dim
muddiness of his left eye he didn't anticipate the threat of
the dagger that Tasso snatched from his knife-belt and thrust
forward with his other hand. Twisting away from the slicing
cut of the sabre Hal drove himself directly onto the spiked
point of the dagger. Tasso pressed his face up against Hal's
and twisted the blade with a satisfied growl. 'You didn't bargain
for that now, either.'

The blade slid beneath the buckle of Hal's baldric, slicing
into his side and puncturing the flesh at his waist. Hal looked
down in disbelief as red blood moistened his skin and soaked
a broad patch of his leather jacket in a swath of warm liquid.
The unexpected shock of the blade-cut was sudden and fierce.
He anticipated an acute pain. He had always imagined that
the injury from a sword cut would burn with a pure raw agony.
As Tasso withdrew the blade and stood back, breathing heavily
in satisfaction, Hal pressed his left hand against his side,
reassuring himself that it wasn't his heart or lungs, still waiting
for the onslaught of the pain to scream into his flesh. But
numbed by the rage of battle, the anticipated pain never came.
All he felt was a dull nagging stitch as his muscles cramped
up around the wound. He clutched his left hand over the gash
as if trying to catch his blood before it seeped out onto the
parched ground. All he knew was anger and hatred. He looked
from the oozing wound up at the satisfied face of the mercenary.

Tasso was sneering at him, smiling at his suffering while
the older mercenary was cheering, 'Go on, finish the little
weasel off, or are you going to leave it to an old man like me
to do your work?'

Rage screamed in Hal's ears. How dare they mock me? He
raised the sword and, without thought of tactics or technique,
launched his assault. He swung from left foot to right, spinning
round and around, the great runesword slicing the air in a

greater arc around him. And like a whirlwind, a circle within a greater circle, Hal's fury burst onto Tasso.

The clash of steel on steel rang out across the downs.

Chapter 29

'The runesword!' Brid tightened her hand on Caspar's arm until her nails cut into his flesh. 'It's Hal; he's in trouble.'

Caspar looked at her in bewilderment.

'Can't you hear it?' she insisted. 'Its song fills the air.'

He shook his head.

'Hal's in trouble; I know he's in trouble. We've got to help him. There isn't time to lie low and wait for these men to go. We've got to help Hal.'

'What are you doing?' Caspar was suddenly afraid that Brid was about to behave rashly as she began to wriggle forward through the ensnaring brambles.

'I'm going to cause a distraction so that we can get away.'

'No, you're not; that's utterly hare-brained. You can wait here and I'll deal with them,' he announced decisively as he disentangled his bow of holly and antler from the thorns.

The Maiden raised a hand to silence him. 'Now listen to me, Spar; there's at least two of them and the next watch is in shouting distance. You're not going to be able to get both of these men without one of them raising the alarm, are you? No, I need to throw them off balance first before you can do anything. A little feminine charm and a couple of potent berries should do the trick.'

'I can't let you do it,' Caspar persisted. 'It's not right: you're a girl.'

'I'll be all right, I promise. The Mother will protect me.' She reached for her scrip and dangled a spray of shiny white berries in front of his face. 'Tempting but deadly, quick-acting mistletoe will do very nicely – if I can get close

488

enough. And you'd better look after this. It might make them suspicious.'

She slid her hand down the front of her dress and wriggled through the loose layers to extract the red fire-drake. The animal spat angrily and clawed at her as she tried to shake it off into Caspar's care. Grimacing, he goaded it into the warmth of his own clothing. He expected it to be damp and slimy but found that it was pleasantly warm and its little claws tickled as they hooked into his skin.

Brid fixed him seriously with her eyes. 'Cover me just in case, but I don't want any arrows loosed. If they cry out it'll alert the others. At the moment they're looking for a wolf-woman not an archer. They heard the wolf close by now and, with help from the Mother, they'll be distracted by her and she'll throw them off our trail. Now, I'm going to concentrate on the sergeant – the younger soldier doesn't know what he's doing. When I've got the sergeant where I want him you can rush forward to help me with the other one – but not until I'm ready.'

'It's too dangerous for you,' Caspar vainly protested, feeling inadequate and lacking in manly assertion when faced with Brid's diamond-edged determination.

'Promise me you won't do anything. Just keep icy quiet. Don't move, don't do anything except keep Trog quiet,' she ordered, slinking out from the cover of the brambles and creeping up the grass bank towards a thicket of gorse bushes.

Caspar wouldn't promise; he grabbed hold of her arm just as she turned to crawl out from under the brambles.

One by one she prised his fingers off. 'Trust me, Spar; I know what I'm doing. These men have spent their lives hunting half-crazed girls and using diseased women as scapegoats for bad-luck and ill crops. I'm not afraid of them and they won't expect that.'

She froze perfectly still, listening intently. Her lips parted slowly to murmur, 'Hal. We haven't got much time. Oh Mother, help him; even though he isn't truly one of us, help him.'

'Where is he?. What's happening?' Caspar fretted for his uncle.

She looked at him in exasperation. 'I don't believe you can't hear it. Have you inherited so little from your mother?' She pointed southwards. 'Way over there. He must be on the road out of Ildros. Now just keep this thick-skulled dog quiet, Spar.' Trog wagged his tail furiously as the girl looked into his eyes. 'Yes, you dog, keep quiet,' she instructed, 'and stay low.' Her whisper was quieter than the breath of the wind in the still of midsummer. She turned to leave but at the last second stopped to kiss her fingertips and pressed them onto Caspar's forehead.

'May the Mother protect you,' she blessed him and turned to crawl out of the bushes.

Again the wolf howled and, through the thatch of bramble fronds, Caspar could just make out the tip of a yellow plume flicking round towards the irksome noise. He could plainly hear the nervous stamps of the horses as they snorted and swished their tails, agitated by the scent of the prowling wolf. He had to risk creeping forward: he couldn't possibly leave Brid to go on alone and unprotected. With one hand firmly on Trog's collar he wriggled out of the brambles and crept towards the cover of the gorse bushes on the brow ahead, following stealthily some distance behind Brid. With his heart pounding in his ears he slithered closer, pressing himself into the thorny cover, until at last the Inquisitors came into view. One wore only a plain black uniform whereas the older man's uniform was emblazoned with Rewik's yellow and red crest. They were both staring away from him towards the dark shadows lurking beneath the skirts of the yew forest.

He scanned the ground ahead for the Maiden but she had vanished. He scoured the grass with his eyes, noting only tufts of gorse, twisting brambles with rabbit holes pitted around them and chunks of broken flint lying in the numerous sheep scrapes that dotted the chalky down-land. He shook his head. It was impossible for her to disappear like that: there was nowhere to hide. The brambles and gorse were sparse on the top of the downs and only a soft shading in the folds of the earth's crust offered any refuge in the short cropped grass. A movement suddenly caught his eye. What he had thought was a clod of mud turned out to be a rabbit as it bobbed to the next clump of grass, keeping one ear warily cocked. She's there somewhere in the grass just like the rabbit, he thought, straining to catch any signs of movement.

The Inquisitors still stared fixedly towards the forest. The sergeant, beneath his plumed helm, shifted the lance in his hand, bringing his grip back to its balance point, ready to throw the weapon.

'Do you think that's her?' his junior asked. 'Or do you think it's an ordinary wolf?'

'It's her. There are no wolves in Caldea,' the man said matter-of-factly.

'Are you looking for me?' The ground appeared to speak in a soft lilt, like a summer brook gliding over smooth cool pebbles.

Both men whipped round in amazement. What seemed to be a patch of dry soil turned into a cloak. The brown bearskin was pushed back by delicate hands to reveal a small woman sitting on the ground, twiddling a daisy between her fingers. Slowly she eased the cloak off her shoulders, winding her fingers tantalizingly through her thick plait and shaking out her camomile-lightened hair. The wolf's howl curdled the air, sending the rabbit bolting to his hole and both horses half-reared. The men jerked round, following the eerie sound as it drifted through the trees and blended with the breeze. When they looked back again the girl was gone. They wheeled their horses round, searching frantically with their spears held aloft. The wolf bayed once more almost as if she were laughing at them and when Brid spoke again she was standing right behind them.

Caspar was gripped with panic. The sound of the wolf would surely draw the other Inquisitors staked out around the forest. Perhaps he could jump these men from behind. He bit his lip, trying to stave his natural instinct to protect the girl, but she

had insisted that he stayed put. Trust me, she had told him.
He had to wait for her signal.

The two men were staring at her in disbelief. The sergeant
looked her up and down, nodding gormlessly, his clean-shaven
face frozen in horror.

Brid smiled. 'Well, soldier, you didn't expect this. You've
been terrorizing half-witted girls all these years. They were
frightened just to look at you just because you hide behind
that uniform, but you didn't expect me, did you?'

The younger one was edging his horse backwards and the
older man with the black helmet and plumes slowly began to
raise an ox horn to his lips as if to summon help.

The beautiful girl tantalizingly slid her dress from her shoulders to expose a glimpse of sandy skin. 'I wouldn't do that if
I were you.' Her voice was like silk caressing the man's ears.
She slid her hands down the front of her soft blue dress, easing
open the buttons to reveal the silk and lace of her bodice
moulding her breasts. She loosened the top laces. Caspar had
no doubt that any soldier who was even half a man would be
disarmed by her fresh beauty. 'Think; if you call the others
you won't be able to take the glory for catching me alone. Two
big men like you can surely handle one little maid between the
two of you, can't you? And if you call the others I won't be
able to tell you where my coven is hidden. Think of the
honour if you unearthed an entire coven on your own.'

The sergeant thoughtfully dropped his horn.

'Here, soldier-boy,' she laughed at the younger one, 'I bet
you've never seen a witch before. Do you know what happens
to your soul if you look into my eyes?'

'Don't look at her eyes,' the older man growled in warning,
as he struggled to unhook the net looped over the pommel of
his saddle. 'Witch-woman of Satan, your lustful charms won't
touch us. We are men of God.' The man's fingers were trembling as he struggled with the knot that secured his net. She
reached up her hand and covered his coarse hairy knuckles
with her soft touch.

'But you're still a man and you're afraid of me,' she taunted, probing his smooth clean-cut face with her deep forest-green eyes that shone in the sunlight. 'You're afraid of me.'

The sergeant seemed incapacitated; his jaw lolled gormlessly towards his sagging chest. As she carefully fixed him with her mesmerizing eyes, her hand slid down her shirt, easing it under the cotton. Gradually teasing back the material, she exposed more of her smooth skin. No man on earth, thought Caspar, could do anything now but watch her, transfixed by her magical beauty. The soldier gawped, hopelessly tracking the movements of her hands as they caressed her female curves.

'You don't need the net,' she whispered, drawing his hand away from the mesh and sliding her fingertips over his thigh. 'You don't need it; I'm not running away.' Brid was no longer the young stubborn girl that Caspar knew; the one who argued with Hal, the one who had screamed in the Jotunn Manor, the one who spitefully sneered at Cybillia: this girl had power. A strengthening energy seemed to be gathering in around her. She was maturing into the mortal form of a goddess, someone to be obeyed instantly and without question.

'If I'm going to tell you my secrets you'll have to come closer to me, or are you too afraid?' Brid teased in the same soft timbre.

The man's lips were dry as he ran his tongue over them, his glassy eyes settling and finally fixing on Brid's bosom. Slowly he began to stoop towards her from his horse. Brid stroked her hand over his tense thigh. 'Closer,' she demanded in a soft teasing voice. The man was trembling. Caspar felt himself tremble too.

The young soldier gawped helplessly for several moments before scrabbling for his horn, uselessly dropping his pikestaff in his clumsy efforts to raise the clarion to his trembling lips.

'Don't do it, lad. We'll get the glory ourselves,' the sergeant hissed, without taking his eyes from Brid.

Caspar prayed that Brid's plan was working. She only needed to get a little closer to the sergeant. No man would be in too much of a hurry to call his comrades with Brid like that and it would give enough time for the poison to work. With his sergeant incapacitated the younger soldier wasn't going to be much trouble.

'Come down to me,' Brid implored.

The experienced Inquisitor grinned and inched fractionally closer. But then in one instant his face blackened and his left hand snatched up his net. He cast it expertly into the air, entangling Brid's shoulders and flailing arms in the ensnaring ropes.

'Call the others, lad. This woman is going to burn.'

Brid's plans had gone cruelly wrong; she had over-estimated her spellbinding allure.

The younger man filled his lungs and the haunting wail of the ox horn filled the air. An answering cry came from the distant rise. Caspar released his grip on Trog's collar and the dog spurted forward in front of him as they both raced to save Brid. The soldier blew again but this time the deep notes were shredded by the growl of a wolf as the great shaggy beast leapt at the man's back. He screamed horribly but only for a split second as the noise was swallowed by the snarling wolf. The sergeant spurred his horse forward to try and spear the animal with his pikestaff.

With supreme self-control Brid mastered her instincts to struggle frantically in the ensnaring net. She rolled clear of the stamping hooves and wormed her restricted hands through her clothing to reach for her knife, still stuffed in the belt of her breeches beneath her dress. Sprinting from the cover of the gorse bushes, Caspar's lungs were bursting with his efforts to reach Brid, but she had already cut herself an opening and was squirming free of the net. Just before he reached her, she was on her feet. Snatching up the tangled net, she ran forward, tossing it over the head of the sergeant's horse. It reared in panic, wildly bucking and throwing its head, trying to free itself from the netting about its throat. The Inquisitor crashed heavily to the ground.

Caspar dived for the pikestaff lying in the grass, ready to use it as a cudgel on the Inquisitor's skull. Just as his hand closed around the shaft, a flailing hoof caught him on the back of the hand and sliced up the skin of his arm. The sharp corner of the metal shoe hammered against his elbow, sending a screaming pain through his nerves. He rolled over in agony on the ground.

The younger soldier was lying on his back, his hands trying feebly to keep the wolf from his throat. Huge blood-filled furrows sprang in slits across his arms where the wolf had raked with her teeth. The thrown sergeant had finally gathered his senses and leapt from his floundering horse to hook Brid under his arm, holding her in a strangle-lock around her throat. 'You'll burn. We've got you now.'

Caspar shook himself and stumbled to his feet but Trog outpaced him as he sprinted to help the Maiden. The terrier latched onto the man's forearm, his powerful jaws slicing into flesh. Caspar heard the bones crunch as they splintered in the vice-like grip of the dog's mouth. Instantly the man's hold loosened on Brid's neck and she slipped from his grasp and ran towards Caspar. 'We'll leave them to the dogs,' she cried, dragging him round towards the trees. 'We've got no time.' Even now they could hear the thunder of hooves from beyond the rise and the pipe of the answering bugle, echoing across the grassland.

'Run! Into the trees,' Brid urged the boy. 'Don't wait for me.'

Caspar, however, slowed his pace slightly to stay level with the girl and together they dived under the drooping skirts of the yew trees and into the murky shadows. A moment later a troop of horsemen thundered over the down.

Trog tired of his quarry's dull response and bounded after his adopted mistress. But the wolf stayed out in the open. Brid wrung her hands, seeing the snarling wolf standing over the soldiers and turning to face the approaching horsemen. There was a shriek of triumph as the cry went up. 'There she is, men. May God preserve us, she's in her full bestial form.' The wolf bared her teeth, peeling back her serrated lips to show red gums and the shards of flesh dripping from her hooked fangs.

'Get out of there, Wolf,' the priestess urged under her breath.

The wolf snarled deeply in her throat, growing larger and fiercer as her mane ruffed up into a yoke of hackles.

'Don't let her get away. A hundred guineas to the man that spears her.'

The soldiers gave a delighted cry as they galloped forward with their light lances up, ready to spear the animal. For a second, Caspar thought the wolf was going to lead the horsemen right to them as she lunged towards the wood. The whole line of Inquisitors wheeled round after her but then the animal lurched the other way, fleeing down towards the cliff. 'Run, Wolf, run; get away from them,' Caspar cried, clutching at the stinging skin of his arm. 'She'll easily outrun the horses, won't she?'

Brid didn't answer.

When the horsemen had galloped from sight, they rose from their crouch in the shadows. 'Come on; Hal needs us,' the girl spoke heavily. For just a split second she stared towards the two mauled soldiers lying inert on the ground. 'I failed. My powers have weakened. The Mother is still punishing me for my faithlessness.'

Caspar dragged at her arm. There was no more time for words. They ran along the edge of the trees, keeping to the shadows. Trog, who had seemingly boundless energy over short sprints and fierce fights, was beginning to flag. Caspar was amazed at how quickly Brid covered the ground. Like the dog, he could outrun her over a sprint, but now, with a stretch of down-land to cover, she kept up a steady pace with fluid strides and light breaths despite the pain she must have suffered in her ankle. After the third rise Caspar's lungs hurt. The dog had long since ceased to bound ahead or skip in front of them, trying to trip them up. Instead he kept up a quiet trot at Brid's heels, his bright pink tongue lolling sideways, dripping saliva from the tip.

Running hard alongside the girl, Caspar covetously watched as she skipped lightly over a hummock of grass and leapt like a doe over a low gorse. Unbroken in her stride, she was as free and as wild as any creature of the wood. He couldn't help remembering the expression on the soldiers' faces as they had leered at Brid. How could she have let them look at her like that; how could she have lured them on in such a way? A tightening knot of jealous anger gripped his throat and he ran harder, leaving the girl behind as he tried to escape his feelings and outrun his envious possessiveness of the girl.

His lungs began to rasp as he sprinted on and on, but the pain numbed his mind and drove his thoughts back to Hal. Brid could be wrong; maybe he's not in trouble, maybe the sound she heard was the victorious cry of triumph from the sword and not a song of defeat. Brid wasn't always right. He still felt bitter towards her for flaunting her body at those men. It was crude and offended his senses.

Gradually the physical exertion dulled the burning anger of his jealous frustrations and the nagging voice of his conscience forbade him to run further. What if she were ambushed by a lurking Inquisitor? He pulled up smartly, drawing in fast hard breaths and clutching at the stitch that jabbed in his side while he waited for her to catch him up. At least his elbow no longer throbbed.

Ahead of them rose a smooth curving hill. Its sparsely covered brow obscured the view of the fields beyond. Brid slowed, putting her hand to her chest to calm her breathing and suddenly stared down at the ground where she stood. She looked to her left into the yew trees and then right, out to sea. A tongue of grass pushed into the woodland, forming a horseshoe-shaped curve in the outline perimeter of the wood. Standing alone in the middle of the curve was a solitary yew with space to stretch its branches. It was so old that the lower branches dipped right down onto the ground, resting its tired weight on the earth while the tips of the boughs turned up again with renewed vigour. Mosses and lichen knitted the join between tree and earth. The bark itself was a dark greyish brown and the trunk seemed to be made of knotted cords wound together, giving the appearance of huge twists of rope. From the yew tree a narrow ridge of land broke the smoothness of the downs like the ridge of a shinbone contouring the roundness of a leg. Brid stood on the ridge and traced a line from the roots of the yew to her feet and then out towards the sea. It led her gaze directly to the spit and on towards the twin peaks of the largest of the Hespera Isles. She glanced quickly at the sun.

'On midsummer's eve,' she panted, trying to catch her breath, 'the sun will set directly between those peaks.' She drew another sharp breath. 'The place we're looking for is directly on this line. If we follow the line of this natural cursor into the woods, I'd stake my scrip of herbs, we'll find the Keepers. They're in there.' She knelt down and touched the soil with her palm, then took the horse's jawbone from her belt and scratched a circular pattern of runes through the grass. Finally she drove the curved bone hard into the soil, right in the centre of the pattern. Leaning forward she murmured softly as if talking to the bone and then rose. 'If they are there, they will hear me.'

Far out on the western horizon a great bird rose up from the peaks of the Hespera Isles. It soared into the heavens as if it had felt the disturbance in the lines of energy running through the earth's crust.

They paused for a moment more before pressing on with renewed haste. Caspar and Brid panted across the rolling dales of scrubby gorse and the well-drained slopes with their ordered strips of vines until they came to a rise above the Tartra Road and stopped abruptly. Below them they could hear distant shouts, jeers and the jarring clash of metal.

'Hal!' Brid cried in dread. They ran on faster but when they reached the next brow and looked down into the far side of the valley they were too late: the battle was over and the men had gone. A distant thunder of hooves lay testament to where the warring men had galloped southwards. Two horses stood close by, one standing awkwardly with his hindleg crooked under him as if he didn't want to bear any weight on the ground and the other grazed a little distance off by some overgrown vines. Caspar instantly recognized the second animal as Magpie.

The sickening signs of bloody combat lay in broken fragments, forming a rough circle centred on the Tartra Road. A man's body lay staring upwards; his tongue thick and purple, slipped out between his parted lips. Blood congealed in a crust across his belly and the white knuckle of his shoulder socket lay open to the air where the flesh had been sheared away to the bone. The chain-mail of his hauberk had torn and crumbled like ancient parchment.

'A mercenary,' Caspar croaked through his dry throat as his eyes skimmed over the black surcoat. 'Only the runesword – only the magic in the runesword could have done that to the steel mail, but where's Hal? They must have taken him!'

Trog lumbered over the hill behind them and immediately sprinted forward to attach himself to the dead man's boot, worrying at it until Brid gave him a sharp clip on the muzzle. He dropped his quarry contritely. Snuffling the ground, he scratched at the earth and buried his nostrils into the dirt where it was dark and moist with spilt blood. The two Belbidians continued to search the terrain; the young boy covering his mouth to try and stem the nausea, which he felt rising in his maw. He was sickened, not so much from the distasteful task of looking through the remains of butchered humans but because of his fear for Hal.

Fragments of metal and the splintered teeth of saw-edged blades lay amidst a powdery dust, showing all that was left of the forged sabres that the mercenaries had dared to raise against the shattering power of the runesword. Patches of dark blood soaked into the ground like bruising, and a deep score in the earth showed where a sword had missed its fleshy target and sliced into the soil. A circle of hoof-prints marked out an arena littered with splintered weapons and a broken limb.

Caspar threw himself onto his knees to examine an entire severed arm. The young Torra Altan was relieved; it wasn't Hal's. It was broad with dark hairs sprouting from black knuckles. The fist still gripped the hilt of a sword. A short length of jagged blade lay midst a swath of grey dust, which had fallen in the pattern of a curved sabre and showed where the weapon had been shattered. A gristly flap of greyish flesh lay nearby, which on closer inspection appeared to be the lobe of an ear. Caspar felt sick.

'There's nothing here to say that he's hurt,' he announced, trying to allay his fears.

Brid shook her head, cradling a small white object in her hand.

This was distasteful work and only his fear over Hal's safety drove the young boy to examine the human debris so closely. It was a finger, someone's little finger.

'Is that Hal's?' she asked, whitening.

Caspar looked closely, trying not to retch. 'I couldn't say it was, but I couldn't say it wasn't.'

Something glinted on the earth, shining through the blood-caked mud. Caspar's eyes seized at the tiny speck of gold. He brushed away a clod of earth to discover a plain band of gold with a flattened side engraved with the speared dragon of Torra Alta. The boy looked at his own ring as he slid Hal's gold band alongside the adjacent finger. He felt a huge surge of guilt and cried out against the fates that had separated him from his uncle. 'We should have all stayed together. Now he's taken. It's my fault. We should have stayed together.'

'Look, he might have lost a finger, but that doesn't mean he's dead.'

'Hal would fight on; nothing would stop him whilst he still had strength to fight. Nothing! They've taken him.' Caspar couldn't think straight for his anguish. 'I'll kill all of them, every last one.'

Brid was white and trembling slightly as she slid Hal's severed finger into her leather pouch. Caspar thought that was a particularly morbid and distasteful thing to do, but Brid was apt to hoard the grotesque and the macabre. 'Come on,' she said more calmly, 'we'll have to catch up with them.'

'At least we've got Magpie now,' Caspar agreed and was rising to his feet when he saw a handful of yellow hair lying nearby. 'Oh no, Brid look. It's Vaalakan. Look, blond hair. Those butchers have caught up with us.'

She snatched it from his grasp and pouted thoughtfully. 'It's too golden: Vaalakan hair is nearly white and dead straight; this has a curl to it. They've got someone else with them but not Vaalakan. Now let's get going before Hal loses any more fingers.'

They ran to Magpie and Caspar threw Brid up into the saddle before trying to vault up himself. The mare was so tall that it took him two attempts to kick himself up. He folded his arms protectively round Brid and turned the mare southwards, giving her a firm kick to get her up to a pace. She cantered on willingly but in comparison to his red colt, Caspar found the pace cumbersome and frustrating. If Hal had managed to ride up here, the freckled youth wondered why he'd taken the piebald mare and not Firecracker. Fiercely he drummed the mare's sides, urging her to a faster and faster pace. Nobly she gave more and more, leaving Trog far behind, struggling after them. The boy was distraught with fear and castigated himself over and over for ever allowing Hal to remain alone to cover their backs.

As they galloped across the broad stretch of down they were alarmed by the pounding of hooves over the parched soil, closing from their right. The horse was moving fast and since the youth couldn't see who was approaching, he reached for his bow. Two rust coloured ears tipped over the horizon, then the white blaze on a dished face and finally the whole of the red roan stallion galloped into view, his tail held high and nostrils flaring. Firecracker whickered and Magpie returned the greeting. Caspar could only think that Hal had brought Firecracker with him and abandoned the animal on the downs for some inexplicable reason. The sound of Magpie's galloping hooves must have drawn the colt to them. He was closing from behind and Caspar was puzzled to see that Firecracker was without a saddle but yet was bridled. The reins flapped treacherously around his high-stepping knees.

'Cracker, steady,' he shouted, hoping the horse would respond but knew the animal wouldn't. He was a horse not a dog.

Firecracker drew level and Caspar nudged Magpie towards the stallion, stretching his arms out, trying to get a finger to the reins. The red roan surged effortlessly ahead, kicking his heels. The boy thought that the colt would surely put a foot through the reins any moment and, at that speed, break his neck in the fall. The stallion slowed again, taking a sideways snatch with his teeth at Magpie's neck as if telling the mare he was in charge. Just as the piebald shied away, Caspar managed to snatch at the loose reins. He stuffed the mare's reins into Brid's hands and released his grip round her waist.

'Don't do it, Spar, don't,' Brid pleaded with him as he applied pressure to the stallion's bit, pulling him alongside the mare so that the horses' flanks banged together.

'I'll make better time.' Caspar looked down at the blurred ground that was skimming beneath them, brought his left leg up so that he balanced on Magpie's rump and leapt across onto the red roan's galloping back. Without a saddle there was little to grip onto and Firecracker's hide was smooth and glossy. He felt himself sliding sideways, being bounced precariously with each stride, the angular bones of the horse's surging shoulder-blades grinding against his chest. He grabbed a handful of mane at the horse's withers and pulled himself upright, gathering up the reins and settling comfortably into the curved hollow of the horse's back.

Once his master was securely seated, the horse seemed to know it was time to race the wind. He stretched his neck forward with the boy hunched over his withers, every muscle of the pair working in unison. Caspar urged his faithful colt to a speed that left Brid and the heavy-boned piebald charger far behind.

As he broke over the rise, Caspar charged full into the view of his enemy. He was galloping too fast to halt immediately, since that would have pitched him over the top of the horse's pricked ears, and he had to turn Firecracker in a wide circle. The stallion reared, raking the sky with his hooves, but without a saddle Caspar had to grip fiercely with his knees and snatched at the mane to avoid being thrown backwards. He looked beneath him at a semi-circular group of free-lances and saw with horror the war-like band of more than half a dozen men clad in black mail. They stood guard around Hal. His eyes skipped over the details of a cloaked figure and two ruffians, their importance blurred by the threat of the armoured men. The mercenaries stared up at the rearing horse as if they'd been expecting him.

A girl's terrified scream shrieked out from beneath a bundle of heavy cloak. Golden hair spilt from under the hood.

Chapter 30

The bright golden metal of the sabre shattered into particles of dust, dry and powdery like flowers of sulphur. The great runesword sliced on through the blade and hacked into Tasso's arm just beneath the elbow. A jet of blood spurted from the severed artery and the mercenary clutched at the stump, doubling over and sagging to his knees with the shock. He didn't scream. His eyes merely looked up at Hal, and he shook his head in disbelief. 'My arm, my arm,' was all he said before passing out. Hal stared back at him, stunned by the violence of his own attack, and wiped the mercenary's blood from his face where it had sprayed from the stump.

His vision was still blurred and he turned just too late as a mounted mercenary leapt to the ground to make his challenge. 'Here, Belbidian, taste this.'

Warned by the whir of a blade cutting the air, Hal pivoted round on his back foot, flicked his head to one side and raised his arm to defend his head. The cut was fierce, yielding a searing pain, first to his ear and then to his hand. Ignoring the raw pain, he swung round, bringing up the runesword so that it arced in a rising curve. He yelled out in the rage of battle, putting all his weight behind the swing, only satisfied as he felt it bite into flesh, hacking up through the man's ribcage and shoulder, and coming to rest just below his collarbone. The mercenary staggered back from the blow, the butchered section twisting grotesquely away from his body as his legs buckled beneath him. Hal drew up his sword and plunged it into the man's gut, sliding it into his entrails as if they were nothing more than a bucket of worms.

Suddenly the hysterical shrieks of a woman pierced his blind rage and he faltered in his attack. Ulf, the moon-faced kitchen knave, struggled with the figure trussed in the cloak and threatened with his butcher's knife. 'You'd best stop now, Master Hal!' There was an upturned sneer to his face as he licked his slobbering lips.

'You'll all die first, traitor,' Hal returned with venom.

'I don't think so,' Ulf shrieked maniacally. 'Or do you want to see the little lady scream some more?' He ripped off the cloak from the struggling bundle that he clutched in his arms and pulled a cloth hood off the captive's head. 'Ain't so pretty now, is she? But I can mash her up a bit more if you likes, Master Hal.' The kitchen-hand held a short knife to the maiden's throat and pressed it against the white flesh until a red beaded choker added a splash of gory colour to her pale neck.

Hal dropped his sword and Gatto leapt at it.

'Cybillia?' he asked uncertainly.

'Don't look at me, don't look at me! Let them kill me, Hal. I've got nothing left to live for.' She tried to turn her face away from the injured youth, but Ulf grabbed what was left of her hair and wrenched her round to face Hal again.

He sniggered, 'She ain't so pretty now, huh?'

Two ugly black bruises closed up her eyes and her hair had been cropped short with a ragged knife so that it spiked out, stiff with grime. Her clothes were torn, half-revealing a naked breast, and her chest was raked with scratch marks, which had healed into knobbly stitches of darkly crusted scar tissue. The moon-faced oaf slid his fat fingers down inside her ragged gown and cupped her breast with his hand. She struggled, but with her arms tied and her neck stretched back in the man's strangle-hold, there was nothing she could do.

'How dare you touch a lady of Belbidia like that!' An overwhelming sense of impotent outrage cramped the muscles around Hal's heart.

Ulf shook his over-sized head. 'She ain't no lady no more.' He tutted as if he was scolding the girl and smiled. 'The Vaalakans learned me a lot. They knows how to keep their womenfolk tame, not like the great Baron Branwolf.' The slobbering man ripped her bodice open. A five-pointed star had been gouged into the pale soft flesh surrounding her left breast. 'It were four men they needed to hold her down, you know.'

'You're a Belbidian.' Hal was sickened to his soul and revolted by the sight of Cybillia's injuries. 'How could you do that?'

The man merely gave him a sideways leer. He slid his hand up Cybillia's neck and grasped her chin, forcing her face round to show Hal her left cheek. 'Look. Another to match.' The lesion had healed into an ugly raised red weal. The sign of the pagan was permanently etched into her face. Silent tears rolled from the girl's swollen eyes.

'Don't look at me, Hal,' she begged. 'I'm ruined. I'm lost.'

The kitchen knave laughed. 'A shame, ain't it, Master Hal? Such a pretty wench.'

They roughly bound Hal's arms behind his back while the youth stared with hatred at the treacherous Belbidian. His intense anger masked the pain in his hand and the throb of his smarting ear and he was only dimly aware of the wet stickiness of his oozing blood. The bald-headed Gatto goaded him in the back with the point of the runesword and kicked him in the direction of a horse. Thick arms crushed Hal around the waist as he was thrown into the saddle and the mercenary heaved himself up behind him. A gauntleted hand clamped Hal's upper arm, cutting off the circulation.

A smock-covered Vaalakan wrapped a strip of cloth around Tasso's arm and bound it tightly with a length of cord, before hefting the mercenary onto his horse. The injured man hung over the horse's withers, slumped with the pain and shock through loss of blood. Hal had time to examine the Northman's pallid skin and dyed hair, which was knotted into war plaits. He was small for a Vaalakan and, with galling rage, the boy recognized him as the shaman, Kullak, who had been part of the troop that had captured him in the Yellow Mountains.

Gatto looked satisfied. 'Good, now we can join the others. Now we've got this little heathen trapped, he'll draw the others to us. We need the girl. But we'd better put some more distance between ourselves and that yew forest. We don't want those fool Inquisitors spoiling our fun now, do we? If they get the little witch first we won't be able to sell her to your fine Vaalakan countrymen now, will we, eh Kullak?'

'What did they promise you?' Hal asked Ulf bitterly. 'What could the Vaalakans possibly give you that makes such evil worthwhile?'

The kitchen boy laughed. 'They won't call me oaf no more. They'll be bowing and scraping at me like they did for you and the Baron and all.'

'You are quite mad,' Hal said coldly and with dignity as the traitor inexpertly yanked his horse round to slap him hard across the mouth. He was careful not to show one twitch of reaction to the man's heavy-fisted blow.

They galloped up to the top of the rise and the Vaalakan shaman pulled to a halt to assess his surroundings. The eerie bay of a wolf echoed through the rolling landscape; the deep, hollow wail carried on the sighing sea breeze.

Ulf smirked in satisfaction, his fleshy lips turning up at the corners. 'He'll come looking for you now, eh Master Hal? Little Master Spar ain't never that far behind you. Maybe we'll kill him for you. Everyone knows you want rid of him; everyone knows you wants Torra Alta for yourself.'

Hal spat at the man.

In retaliation the cloaked peasant cuffed Cybillia. 'You can't do that no more, Master Hal. She'll pay for everything you does.' A bugle cry from the distant hills piped through the air, shrill and harsh after the ghostly howl of the wolf.

Gatto squinted towards the horizon. 'The Inquisitors will do our work for us. She'll flee from them and run this way.'

Ulf grimaced with the sweet pain of anticipation.

Gatto studied the ground ahead. 'Come on, men, over the next rise. Morbak's men will be impatient. They've had to wait a long time for this witch.'

'Master has waited longer.'

Master? Hal pondered to himself. The Vaalakan Guth-kak had muttered about the Master too, but he had assumed he meant Morbak. Obviously he had been wrong. Too stricken by more immediately pressing thoughts, he could only dwell briefly on the problem. He was sickened not only by the sight of Cybillia's wounds and her cruel suffering at the hands of these men, but also by his own throat-tightening guilt. *I shouldn't have left Spar; only I thought I'd be more useful stalling the Inquisitors.* He had a vivid recollection of looking up at Branwolf and the Baron's face bloated with anger, telling him that he should never leave his nephew.

The image was one from the past when his brother had been so angry that he hadn't even punished his young raven-haired half-brother but merely turned his back on him. Hal had been ten or thereabouts and Spar only seven. He'd been given his first hunter, a sleek quick-footed bay and in the excitement had chased after a fox, forgetting his nephew on his short shaggy pony. Caspar got left behind and lost. It had taken five hours for the garrison to find him. On that day, numbed and riddled with remorse and guilt, Hal swore his first oath, giving Branwolf his word that he would never again neglect Caspar's welfare and now all these years later he still had the same feeling that he was letting the Baron down. That sense of failure numbed him, deadening the pain in his side and hand.

The soft thud of hooves turned to a clipped drum roll as they crossed the Tartra Road. They cantered through the vineyard, scattering startled peasants and crashing through the rows of vines, before breaking out onto the far rise and coming to a halt by a copse of blackthorn. The other troop of mercenaries awaited them. Hal looked in bitter disgust at the group of mounted men and the huge muscular bulk of the Vaalakan warrior who rode with them. Despite the peasant's smock, the wooden clogs and the muddy brown hair, Hal instantly recognized Scragg and he felt his eyes burn with hostility. Ulf shoved Cybillia fiercely in the side, dragging her sideways by her hair until she fell to the ground. Her arms were bound, making her unable to break her fall, so she landed awkwardly on her shoulder. Hal could feel the ground shake with the fall.

'You'll rot in hell!' he snarled through gritted teeth.

'Me? Hah! Master will protect me. I'm no heretic like you and that girl is.'

'And what heresy is this poor girl supposed to have committed?'

'Master learn me that women have the devil close in their hearts. Then after what them Northmen did she had no right to the love of God when she were no longer pure. It were her own fault 'cos she were a woman. She had to be punished.'

'You are quite evil,' Hal said simply, trying to obliterate Cybillia's pitiful whimpering from his mind.

A mercenary, protected only by a quilted knee-length gambeson, unslung his sabre and pressed the point into Hal's back, prodding the wounded youth in the direction of a gnarled blackthorn. He slashed through Hal's bonds and the youth looked in horror at his mutilated hand and severed finger. They roughly pushed him towards the bole of the tree.

Gatto mockingly shook his head at him. 'You're a sorry sight, young nobleman. And to think you were trusted to safely escort this lady to Farona. We knew that you must be going to Farona even though we couldn't find you on the road. But then you see you made a mistake. We didn't know where you would go after Farona, but luckily you left Cybillia behind. That was a big mistake.' His ugly face puckered into a laugh. 'She couldn't tell us anything at first though even after the men had – how should we say – subdued her, tamed her a little, but then Ulf turned up, looking for his Vaalakan friends. He gabbled something about his own shaman seeing vague images of you going south and he brought with him this little stone. Show him, Ulf.'

Delightedly the kitchen-hand dangled a small orb before Hal's eyes.

'Well, poor Ulf of course didn't know how to use it. Apparently this pagan magic doesn't work for everyone, but fortunately, as I said, you left Cybillia behind. We held her hand to it and, despite her shrieks, she conjured an image in the crystal. It was very vague but every now and then it sharpened into glimpses of road and then we had a flash of the isthmus. That was enough. The ferry from Dorsmouth to Caldea was quick and easy and it took us directly to Ildros. When we arrived here, there was such a commotion about sorcery and witchcraft it didn't take much to put two and two together.'

'Her face were so funny.' Ulf jumped up and down delightedly at the thought, a ridiculous sight in such a heavy-limbed man. 'You should of seen her face when the magic wouldn't work for no one but her.'

Gatto continued with more sombre self-control than the demented Ulf. 'You see, Kullak said she had to be a witch too, despite her prayers to the Lord Almighty, otherwise the stone would have kept its secrets. Well, once we knew she was a witch we had her marked as one. And all because she wanted another dress. Vanity must be a sin after all. It was the only time we saw her away from the palace. Now, up against that tree. And you girl, move.'

Helpless, Hal had no choice but to obey and let himself be bound hand and foot to the trunk of the blackthorn. Cybillia was tied next to him. Her convulsive sobs had ceased and she hung her head shamefully. Hal felt a deep pity for her. She was no longer beautiful, either inside or out. She had been ruined for any man, but she was still innocent and still a Belbidian even though he couldn't bring himself to look at her mutilated face. He had few spare thoughts for her now though, as his rising panic grew over Caspar's safety.

Triumphantly, as if claiming the glorious weapon for his very own, Gatto thrust the point of the runesword into the soil where it stuck, casting a long thin shadow like a sundial. Hal wondered how long it would be before Brid and Caspar came to search for him or whether the Inquisitors had already captured them. He had never before felt so hopelessly power-less. In his desperation he had to pray. Dear God, he began, the conditioning of a lifetime bringing the words automatically to his soul, are you punishing me for taking up with these heathens? But I must, I must to save Torra Alta. Please Lord, miserable sinner that I am – his thoughts stumbled over these self-effacing words that he knew he was supposed to use in a prayer – please help us.

He looked at the runesword, looked at the shadow creeping round, showing the inexorable passage of time – time that ran rough-shod over their lives, marked by the passage of the sun in his great circle. He looked at Cybillia; her life, her hopes, above all her honour and dignity destroyed and yet she had devoutly trusted in the omnipotence of the one true God. She had been faithful and unwavering in her commitment and yet he had abandoned her. Since the one true God had forsaken even Cybillia in her plight, he consciously steered his thoughts to the ancient religion of his ancestors. Mother, help me, Mother, he prayed inwardly though a little uncertainly. My own God will not answer me; please hear me. He pressed the soles of his feet into the soil as if trying to reach her comfort. He didn't know how to summon her help, didn't know what powers Brid called upon but suddenly he wished that the Maiden was here with him.

Tasso looked sick beneath the thick layers of his black skin as a comrade helped to unwind the tourniquet from the stump of his arm. The wound was clean; the bone sliced keenly through to expose the spongy texture of the marrow and the ends of circular grey tubes where the arteries were severed. One of the mercenaries reached for his saddle-bag and dragged out a flask. The cork popped as he unstoppered it. 'Sorry, Tasso but we'll have to stop maggots getting in it.' He sloshed the liquid over the raw stump and for the first time the injured mercenary screamed. The reek of neat alcohol filled the air.

Hal looked back at the runesword where the chief mercenary had jabbed it into the earth. The shadow had shortened. For a moment Hal thought his blurred vision was deceiving him. The sun couldn't have moved that much. He looked hard at the sword and realized that slowly, imperceptibly, it was sinking into the ground. The weight of the hilt was driving the sharp point down through the soil as if the sword were being sucked into the earth.

'When are they going to kill us?' Cybillia asked. Her voice was raw as if it hurt to speak.

'Kill us? They're not going to kill us.' Hal tried to sound reassuring. 'We're not done for yet. Now, just don't worry. We'll think of something.' It was an absurd thing to say: what could he possibly hope to do trussed up like a festival goose. The wolf, he thought again linking his thoughts, trying to catch onto anything that might bring them hope. The wolf; maybe she'd come to their rescue – but that was absurd: wolves were miserable creatures with a hatred of man. It was hopeless. He was bound and weaponless; their only real hope was Caspar – and Brid, of course, but he didn't know what such a small damsel could hope to do against the vicious brutality of these armed men. No, their hopes rested on Spar. He pictured his nephew battling against this band of cruelly war-hardened warriors, all probably twice his weight and strength, and despaired.

'So Camaaliak, your men is not look so good now.' Hal knew that voice too well. 'You careless with your men. Your man is bigger careless with his hand. Little Belbidak fiercer than you thoughts. You give me knife. I has a score to count with this boyling.'

Hal looked in disgust at the thick bull neck, the ash white skin, those watery ice-blue eyes. What should have been long, straggling blond hair was a strange flat brown with a hint of green tingeing the edges where the dye was beginning to fade. The clothes were Belbidian, plain weave cloth with distinctive smocking around the yoke but everything else about him was Vaalakan. Hal wondered sorrowfully how on earth this man had travelled so far through Belbidia without being challenged. His country had been at peace for so long that the people just didn't understand suspicion; they thought only of the crops and the oxen and the market prices.

Hal's ready defiance came rolling off his tongue. 'I hear an infusion of blackroot tea is very good for dyeing hair, but I think your serving girl has used the wrong potion. I'm flattered though.' Hal smiled wrinkling up his nose into a sneer, despite the pain that it produced around the swelling in his eye. 'It's very touching that you want to copy my own hair colouring. Your ears though – I'm not sure about the ears – the elven look is perhaps a trifle too fey.' It seemed like centuries since Hal had faced Scragg across the Vaalakan arena and, with Brid's help, defeated the man and sliced off the top of his ears.

'You speaks too freely, Belbidak. Me thinking I is cutting your ears, now me thinking your tongue. Bah! You is dead anyway and it is the girling we wants.' There was a hiss from behind the bushes and Kullak, the Vaalakan shaman, slid forward.

'We is catching the girling alives and she is leading us to the Egg – the Egg that conquers all.' The shaman had a leather pouch similar to the one that Brid always carried. He reached in and drew out a fistful of short bones, each one no more than an inch long. It took Hal a moment to work out what they were. As he saw them measured in the palm of the Vaalakan's hand, he realized that they were knuckle bones, human knuckle bones.

Kullak looked at Hal and the Torra Altan could not hide the horror written on his face. 'Ha! You is right.' He rattled the bones in his hand as if they were gaming dice. 'Thingers from Belbidaks. Special Belbidaks, you marks. Virgin girlings. We cut their thingers from right hand, one by one as they screaming. The power in the virgin is strong, much magic there. Has to be virgins.' He began to scatter the bones in a circle around the blackthorn to which Cybillia and Hal were bound. 'Has to be virgins otherwise being no power against the virgin priestess.' He looked in satisfaction at the ring of bones. 'I can makes circles of power too.'

Hal felt a sudden coldness creep up through his feet. His toes felt numb and his shin bones began to ache. It was like standing on the glacier again.

'Vaal-Peor is mighty,' the shaman sighed. He knelt down to rearrange the bones, making sure they formed a perfect circle, carefully forming his pattern so that the runesword remained on the outside of the ring. 'Has to be virgins,' he muttered.

Scragg smiled, showing his ivory teeth. 'Morbak is to be proud. Not easy to know if girling is woman or no. Kullak says has to be sure. Every one of bones was come from little girling, no higher than here.' He held his hand out with the palm facing downwards, lifting his hand level with his hip. Hal felt sickened. Churning nausea swelled up from his stomach, producing an acid taste in his throat as he envisaged the little five or six year old girls that must have suffered at the hands of these men. He'd expected Cybillia to scream or swoon. The thought of such horrors was surely too dreadful for the delicately-natured girl to bear, but her head hung passively and when she spoke it was with sorrow and not with shock.

'I watched them. They made me watch. These demons from hell hacked their fingers off. If I'd been a man I'd have killed them all.'

Hal shook his head. 'No, it wouldn't have made any difference. Lady or not, you couldn't have stopped these fiends. They are mad.'

The shaman seemed satisfied with his arrangement and delved into his scrip again to retrieve dark red flaps of something that looked like raw flesh. They wriggled as he moved.

'Tongues, tongues of woman. Belbidia be a quieter place now. You should be thanking me.'

Ulf's eyes bulged with insatiable blood-lust as the shaman laid out the flaps of tongue that curled on the ground. The Vaalakan priest crawled round on his knees, muttering charms in his guttural language, every vowel half-swallowed as he spoke, while Scragg stared down the valley towards the dirt track, thumping the handle of his axe into his palm. The shaman, growling in his northern tongue, irritably tapped the Vaalakan warrior's leg as he came up against his boots. The warrior stepped sideways away from the circle.

Finally satisfied, the shaman stood up. 'Circles within circles. The trap for the girling shaman is set.'

Hal looked into the man's eyes and saw a deeper colour in the iris and remembered how the shaman was smaller and darker than the usual Vaalakan warriors. He had put it down to being a priest and not a warrior; but he reconsidered as he watched the man's practised rituals, which like Brid's ceremonies, focused on the elements. He wondered whether, some way far back in time, the Vaalakan had sprung from the same seed as the old tribes of Belbidia.

'She is no ordinary priestess, you know,' Hal said as casually as he could. 'Not just a wise woman, not just a herbalist, not just a half-crazed woman who sees circles and patterns in everything; she is One of the Three, one of the high priestesses.' He searched his memory for Brid's title, which he'd always thought rather ridiculous. 'As Daughter of the Moon, and One of the Three, her magic is far greater than yours, journeyman priest. You think your circles will hold her. Bah! Her power is strong.' He tried to sound convincing but in his heart he only thought of Brid as a stubborn and arrogant girl. All the same he could see that his words were disturbing the priest of Vaal-Peor.

'Necessary for her being strong. She is the one to be finding the magic Egg,' the Vaalakan retorted, continuing to crawl round the circle, muttering more urgent invocations to his macabre sacraments. 'Morbak has heard of Egg and when we has girling we has Egg.'

'Eggs, tongues of women, bones of maidens, circles within circles. You call yourself men of a great male god? All your tools are female; all your power is stolen from women. Do you think that will destroy One of the Three? Her power is strong, shaman.' Hal tried desperately to undermine Kullak's confidence. He didn't know what he was saying or whether it made any sense but he knew that Brid classified everything as male or female and it seemed to be of great significance to her. His knees ached and his bones felt brittle with cold. Cybillia was shivering.

The Torra Altan kitchen-hand was staring fixedly down into the valley, watching carefully for any movement. Hal stared at his back with loathing. This was the man whom his brother had cared for and protected, given a job and given shelter despite his ham-fisted manner and lack of sensibilities. He upset the cook and molested the scullery maids but Branwolf had still defended him, saying we must look after those less fortunate than ourselves. Branwolf had been cruelly repaid for his kindness.

'Traitor!' Hal hissed at his back.

'Cut his tongue out,' Ulf screamed with rage. 'Give me his tongue and I'll grind it into the dirt with the others.'

The shaman stood up and pushed the oaf-faced man backwards. 'You is mad like the Belbidak says. Mad as troll; touched with fire of hatred in your brain. His tongue, the tongue of a boyling, will ruin the enchantment.'

Greatly relieved, Hal swallowed hard and for the moment he decided it would be better to keep quiet. Time seemed to be dragging by and he fretted that something must already have happened to Caspar. Those Inquisitors must have got them, he thought in despair. We're surrounded by enemies in our own land.

Kullak was becoming impatient, striding back and forth, muttering in Vaalakan. Hal couldn't understand a single word except for the name Morbak midst his agitated mutterings. He looked at the sickening circle of human detritus around him and then despairingly at his sword. It was beyond his reach and still appeared to be gradually sinking. All I need is the sword, he thought, and then I can take all of them, everyone. The sword is mine. Without the great weapon he felt naked and vulnerable, nothing but a Belbidian youth more skilled with a hunting bow than a sword. The bow, he leapt at the thought. Caspar at least had his bow.

'It's time to pull back,' Gatto ordered, hooking Tasso under the shoulder and helping him to stagger into the cover of the thicket. 'Get out of view, you fool Ulf, and start saying some prayers. We're not letting this girl get away a second time. I'll have that sword.' He bent to retrieve the weapon, putting his hand on the hilt and trying to ease it from the ground. It wouldn't move. He wrenched at it, trying to work it back and forth but the soil wouldn't release the blade, as if the Mother were reclaiming it for herself.

'Hey, look out! Look up there!' a mercenary warned, pointing at the ridge on the far side of the down. 'The other boy!'

'On horse of devil,' the Vaalakan shaman muttered. 'Colour of fire.'

Oh no, Hal thought in dismay. If Spar's on Firecracker, he'll have left Brid miles behind. Suddenly he was afraid that, without Brid's clear-headed guidance to control him, Caspar would be blindly reckless and thunder straight into the enemy trap.

Gatto abandoned the struggle to extract the sword and dived for the cover of the blackthorn thicket. On the far horizon the horseman broke over the brow; his red roan reared, striking the air with its hooves. The rider briefly took in the scene of the valley below, before charging down towards the grit road and following the swath of splattered mud. It led him straight towards the blackthorn thicket where the mercenaries and the Vaalakans lay in ambush.

Beyond the rise, a bugle horn, insistent and penetrating, blasted through the air. The horn of the Inquisitors, Hal thought, listening in horror. They must have captured Brid and still be chasing Spar. He's going to ride into this trap alone. He started to yell, trying to warn his nephew. 'Spar, get out of here get away; it's a trap. Save Brid and get out of here.' His lungs hurt with the effort. He stopped to draw breath; all he could hear above the frantic drumming of his heart was the pounding of hooves galloping towards the thicket. Scragg's axe was held out sideways, knee high to a horse, ready to cleave into Firecracker's forelegs the moment the stallion broke into the thicket.

'Scream on, Belbidak,' Scragg sneered. 'Scream on. It drawing him more faster.'

'Spar, look out! Look out! It's a trap! They're in the trees,' Hal frantically yelled.

Caspar was riding with his reins knotted, the bow in his hand and an arrow already slotted to the string. Still at full gallop, he raised the bow and pointed the barbed shaft directly at Hal. The captive youth stared straight back in astonishment. His mouth dropped in disbelief. Caspar was pointing an arrow directly at him whilst galloping straight onto the axe of a Vaalakan. 'For the love of Torra Alta, he's going to shoot me,' Hal murmured in that brief second as his nephew drew back his arm to fire the arrow.

The slap from the bow-string that skimmed Caspar's forearm was drowned out by the thud as the arrow embedded into the black bark of the blackthorn tree. The vein-biting ropes slipped from Hal's wrists as the arrow split the tethers that bound him and Cybillia to the trunk. The blond-haired girl swooned to the ground and Hal struggled to free himself from the ropes, which still entangled him. The next second there was a roar from the huge bulk of the Vaalakan warrior as he swung his axe at Firecracker's legs. The horse leapt sideways, tripping in the undergrowth and sprawling to the ground, throwing Caspar to the Northman's feet. Hal watched helplessly as his nephew stared up at the thin, cutting edge of the blade suspended over his head. Urgently the unhorsed boy rolled to the left away from the crunch of the blade as it gouged deeply into the ground. Scragg worked the cleaver back and forth and raised it again in preparation to strike at the boy's feet. He straddled the Torra Altan, pinning the boy to the ground, making it impossible for Caspar to roll beyond the axeman's reach.

'Spar!' Hal's voice was strangled with anguish. 'Spar, no!' Caspar turned his head and for a second their eyes met. Hal crawled towards the edge of the circle but found he was moving slower and slower, as if his joints were beginning to freeze solid. He could hardly see; a curtain of icicles seemed to drip from his eyelashes and his vision was distorted, swirling in and out of double focus. The great runesword lay only a pace in front of him but his arms moved so painfully slowly that he couldn't reach it. It's only in my mind; if I don't believe in the spell, in the power of the shaman's circle of knuckle and tongues, I'll be freed, he thought. This is superstitious nonsense. This is only the blow to my head taking its toll.

And then he felt he was falling, falling through time and space as if he'd stepped off the top turret of Torra Alta. He seemed to be drifting painlessly through the air, taking for as long as a winter season to plunge towards the canyon floor. Don't let me lose consciousness, he begged himself, but somehow he couldn't get his body to move. His will was being sapped from him, dragging his sense of reality beyond the grasp of his mind.

'Spar,' he tried to yell as he struggled to break free from the rigor that clawed at his bones. His voice was thin and brittle, cracking into fragments like falling icicles splintering to the ground.

Scragg lurched forward, heaving the great double-bladed axe over his head. Slowly it swung into motion and gained momentum as it reached the zenith of its arc and turned to bear down on its desired path to split Caspar's feet from his ankles. The Vaalakan, however, lurched again as someone shoved him hard from behind and the axe slipped forward, scarring the earth a hand's width from the Belbidian's thigh.

'He's mine,' roared Ulf. 'I want him! I want him!'

Scragg swung round furiously to confront the fleshy-faced kitchen knave. Caspar wasted no time waiting for the men to resolve their quarrel. He kicked his heels hard into the chalky soil and wriggled free, escaping from between the Vaalakan's calves where he had been pinched in a crushing vice of solid muscle. He dived towards his uncle.

'Hal, get up! Get up!'

'Stay out of the circle.' Hal looked up with pleading in his eyes. A heavy blanket of bloodied eyelid hooded his vision. 'Stay out of the circle.'

Hal watched helplessly as his nephew struggled to find his bow.

'The sword,' Hal tried to say but he didn't think his words were audible. The hilt was now all that was visible above the tufts of grass and his nephew couldn't have seen it. Firecracker was still down, one foot caught through his reins and kicking with both his back legs. The faces of cruel, evil men, with no morals or mercy were closing in on the young boy. His eyes scanned the ground, looking for where the bow fell.

'He's mine. Don't touch him,' Ulf howled in demented rage.

'I not listens to your madness,' the bear-like Vaalakan bellowed, wasting no effort in arguments. With the straightened knuckles of his free hand, he punched the treacherous Torra Altan full in the face. Stunned, Ulf staggered backwards. The huge axeman drew his teeth together, the muscles on his cheeks contracting with the concentration of effort, but his next blow was thwarted by the shaman who confronted him. They growled in their ugly language and eventually the warrior relaxed his grip and left Caspar to the shaman.

'We thinks better you is alives, better to catch the witch. You gets into that circle now too. The circle is binding you with the breath of Vaal-Peor.' The smaller, darker Vaalakan grabbed the red-haired boy by the collar and began to drag him across the ground. The heels of Caspar's boots left two score marks on the grass as he dug them down, while ripping at the man's wrists and gouging his nails deep into the pale Vaalakan flesh.

A raucous trumpet blasted out alarmingly close. It stopped Kullak in his tracks. He dropped Caspar to grip his axe with both hands and turned to face the attack. Hooves, Hal thought, hooves drumming on the surface of the ground. He could feel their vibrations pulsing towards him. Hooves, a trumpet, more than one set of hooves, like a rolling drum, like thunder after sheet lightning, the thunder that rumbles on the edge of the horizon. He could no longer raise his head from the ground and was only aware of the drumming in his ears. Faltering on the edge of reason, he could only believe that it was the Inquisitors. His hopes were lost.

Chapter 31

Above the warriors' heads, two black hooves savaged the sky. The mass of Magpie's hefty body stormed into the midst of the enemy circle, carrying the diminutive form of the Maiden. Perched on the solid breadth of the war-horse's back, Brid wielded the reins with the feather-light touch of her hands. Her penetrating eyes focused with brave fury on the faces of the enemy. In comparison to the bear-like strength of the men and the great bones of her charger, she looked like a small frail child, as incongruous as a coracle on a storm-ridden ocean.

Huge gauntleted hands clawed at her from all directions, grappling for her legs and feet. She kicked back viciously and reached within her torn dress for the herb scrip that she always wore about her neck. Snatching out Hal's severed finger, she was ready to hurl it into the circle of knuckle bones formed by the Vaalakan shaman.

'Hal,' she cried. 'Hal, breathe fire into your heart; think of flames; think of the heat of life.' She concentrated her flow of energies towards the prostrate youth, wounded and bleeding his life away into the soil. Only the great piebald mare, wheeling and kicking, kept the enemy from her.

Grovelling towards the fronds of bracken that had swallowed his bow, Caspar felt the collar of his shirt snatch at his throat and his breathing grated through his constricted wind-pipe. He writhed and twisted until his bulging eyes caught at the triumphant face of the shaman. He struggled frantically to free himself from Kullak's grip and his breath came back in a rush as the wool shirt rent and released him from the garrotte, which bit into his neck. He curled himself up into a ball and kicked out straight to connect hard with the man's knee cap. The shaman gave a stifled grunt of pain before kicking the small youth forcibly in the stomach with the wooden toe of his sabot boot, probably stolen from some unfortunate Belbidian peasant. He drove it deep into the boy's unprotected abdomen and Caspar doubled up, gulping air. The Vaalakan caught him in a relentless throttle, twisting the collar of his shirt into a knot around his half-strangled neck. With the youth hamstrung, the shaman turned towards the girl on the great Jotunn charger.

'Witch, you is here at last,' he hissed, his tongue flickering. 'I can taste you in the air. We haves you now. You does as we say or blond girling dies and then leg by leg, arm by arm, the Belbidak boylings dies. Dies very slowly. The screaming eat up your mind.'

'Never! It's you who will die!' Small though she was, her voice was serene with all the potency and command of a warrior queen. She no longer looked ineffectual or incongruous on the back of the great war-horse, but was both a lioness and a she-dragon at once. A bugle blast shattered her words, sending her voice to the four winds, more in accord than disharmony, lifting and enhancing her cry to fill the heavens.

A white plume tipped the crown of a shining helm, the knight's face hidden behind the muzzle of a dog-head vizor. His burnished plate armour was draped in silk tabards adorned with the crest of Caldea and the red and white chequered emblem was repeated on the pennon of his lance. A broadsword, buckled to his saddle, balanced the weight of the kite-shaped shield that covered his left side. A further array of deadly weapons was buckled to the high-cantled saddle, including a mace, several daggers and a throwing axe. The full bard of horse armour protected the heavy-boned destrier and the broadsword clanked against the metal plates of the flanchard that guarded the horse's flanks. With metal antlers protruding from the protective chaffron – the metal mask shielding the horse's head – the armoured destrier looked like the devil's own war-horse. Even the experienced mercenaries in their plain hauberks took a step back from the fearsome sight of the knight in full armour before bracing themselves for his assault.

Powered by the thundering charge of his black war-horse, the knight lowered his lance and tilted it at the first mercenary who barred his way. Bravely the soldier raised his sword to defend himself but it clattered to the ground as he howled in agonized pain. The lance speared his shoulder, puncturing the chain-mail as if it were nothing but lace, and lifted him bodily off his feet. Spitted to the lance, the bones in his shoulder splintered with a snapping crunch as his body rammed into the spiky branches of a blackthorn. The man kicked and writhed for a few seconds, his body thrown into convulsions, blood spewing up from his pierced lung and trickling from the corner of his mouth. At last he slumped into the quiet release of death. Still lanced to the tree, his feet dangled lifelessly in the air.

Abandoning his lance, the knight wheeled the black destrier and reached for his broadsword, which screeched against the metal trimmings of its scabbard before flashing in the afternoon sunlight. The thicket was dense with the clash of steel on steel as the noble knight cut through the men, hacking at the limbs and heads of those who dared to oppose him. With his right arm he slashed the sword through the mail and hacked deep into the shoulder of a black mercenary who attacked from the thicket. With his shield-arm the knight fended off the hammering blows from an axe, which bit into the central boss and embedded itself in the shield.

A third mercenary attacked from the same quarter and in desperation the knight hurled the shield at him before reaching for his mace. The club bore down towards the attacker's head. The soldier flinched sideways to protect his skull but he couldn't save his body. The blow hammered into the mercenary's shoulder, crushing the bones and splintering his upper ribcage beneath the flexible mail of his hauberk. The links in his mail were designed to protect against piercing arrows and slashing swords but could not prevent the blunt trauma caused by the hammering blows of the mace. The knight wrenched the horse round by the bit to seek out his next opponent.

The grip round Caspar's throat was suddenly released. Dazed by the immediate confusion of battle, his wits were thrown into chaos. Hal was lying motionless on the ground; blood covered his clothing. His arm stretched forward for the hilt of the runesword. Above him hooves stamped and pawed the ground, threatening to crush the youth under foot. Firecracker was on his feet, shaking but unable to move, and Brid . . . where was Brid? He couldn't see her in the writhing mass of limbs and swirling cuts of axe and sword. He couldn't see her . . . He rolled clear into the thicket, raking through the ferns to find his bow. He had to have his bow. He couldn't tell how many men were raging in mortal combat around him. He didn't know nor did he have time to think who the red knight could be. He only knew that Brid was lost somewhere in the midst of the mêlée and Hal was lying half-dead on the ground. He must have his bow.

There! His hand fell on the smooth carved wood and he snatched at the weapon, pulling an arrow from his quiver with a trained automatic response. A black boot appeared by his hand where he knelt in the bracken. He didn't pause to think but flung himself over, sunlight blinding him, and released the arrow into the dark shape silhouetted against the sky. With an agonized groan the man fell to his knees, doubled up clutching his stomach, and crumpled onto the boy, pinning him to the ground.

The mercenary's blood filled Caspar's mouth as it gushed over him and the boy spat out the salty liquid as he heaved off the body and raised his bow, ready to shoot again. Suddenly Brid was in the midst of the scene, half-dragged from her horse by a large brutish man, his muscular fury mocked by the peasant's smock that was stretched across his back. Caspar raised his bow again but Magpie was twisting and pulling round and the young Torra Altan couldn't be sure of his aim.

'Hal!' Brid cried out. 'Hal, this will save you!' She flung something from the palm of her hand and it fell into the circle marked out by the knuckles and tongues. Instantly the Vaalakan released his grip on her. Howling with rage, he flung himself into the circle, grovelling for the object. Hal's hand slid across the ground, crossing the line of knuckle bones and tongues and reached for the hilt of the sword. The moment the blood-smeared youth touched the weapon he seemed to gather strength, staggering up onto his feet. With the ease of drawing water from a stream he lifted the mighty blade and broke free from the binding magic of the ice-circle. The Vaalakan shrank back from the power of the weapon and with a quick look at the carnage inflicted on the hired mercenaries, slipped away into the thicket.

A yell on Caspar's right alerted him to the red knight who was battling hand to hand with a mounted mercenary. The moment the fully armoured knight had burst into their midst, one of Gatto's faithful followers had dragged a horse from the cover of the thicket to meet the knight's attack on more equal terms. A small sunburnt mercenary, with looped earrings and a scavenging look to his eye wielded the curved blade of a sabre with serrated teeth along its cutting edge. Instinctively the Torra Altan heir released an arrow that embedded deep into the mercenary's shoulder blade.

A movement in the corner of Caspar's eye caught his attention; he whirled round to see Hal stumbling forward, supporting himself on his sword. With great effort he raised the weapon and advanced to strike at a fur-cloaked man who had seized Magpie's reins. Caspar immediately noticed the heavy bearskin draped over the man's shoulders. A Torra Altan cloak. His mind reeled. Why would a Torra Altan be here in Caldea so far from the northern borders? The man turned and for the first time, Caspar looked in horror and disbelief at Ulf, the simple kitchen-hand. 'Don't.' The word formed on his lips. 'Don't kill him, Hal – he's one of us. He's from the castle.'

Hal screamed with rage. 'You traitorous man of the Devil.'

The runesword swung through a horizontal plane, level with the man's ear.

'No, Hal, don't do it!'

The urgent cry from his kinsman momentarily distracted Hal's attack, giving Ulf that split second of grace to throw himself to the ground. The huge bulk of the ice-blond Vaalakan warrior charged aggressively forward to stand over the limp body of the whimpering peasant. He raised his double-bladed battle axe to bar the vicious slash of the runesword. The cleaver in Scragg's experienced grip shattered into filaments of iron dust that scattered in the breeze.

'You should have known better than to face me again, Vaalakan dog!' Hal spat. He deftly wielded his weapon, twisting the edge of his honed blade. It carved through the air and sliced towards the head of his victim. 'And now, I wield the death-dealing runesword!'

The physical exertion of raising the sword opened up the wound in his side but he gritted his teeth against the pain and drove all his force into the swing of the runesword. As it whistled through the air, its victorious song of savage blood-lust shrieked out across the down-land.

'Fear me for I will kill you all!' Hal cried in crazed battle-lust as the weight of his runesword lurched him slightly off balance.

Scragg's face gawped helplessly at his shattered weapon and the remains of the broken axe-handle held impotently in his fist. He blinked and the fleeting look of horror was gone. Before Hal could regain his balance for the final stroke, he ducked to the ground, scooped up a fistful of the powdered filaments of his shattered axe and flung them in the youth's face.

Hal screwed his eyes up and scrambled to wipe the stinging dust from his eyes. When he opened them again Scragg was gone and the snivelling form of Ulf was stumbling before him on his knees. His dull eyes held a blank expression like those of the Torra Altan donkeys that had spent too many days trudging the treadwheel in the well-room. They still gawped with an empty uncomprehending look as the sword sectioned his sweated scalp. The top half of his skull spun through the air like a discarded cap, spraying the debris of his brains out into the air.

Continuing his swing, Hal dextrously whipped the blade round and sliced the edge back into the thick trunk of Ulf's neck. The remains of the kitchen-hand's head splattered to the ground even before his decapitated body rocked on its feet and sagged into its blood-soaked cloak. Without hesitation, Hal heaved his sword into the air and hacked the side of Ulf's face, splitting the severed skull. 'Faceless traitor!' Hal raged in maddened hatred.

Ulf! Caspar couldn't believe it. Ulf, the simpleton from the kitchens, a traitor? It seemed absurd.

Hal clutched at his side. Still incensed with the madness of war, he spun round to seek out further sacrifices for his deadly runesword. Only Hal, the red knight and Gatto stood in the centre of the field. Caspar rushed forward, bound by duty, honour and the bond of fraternal comradeship to stand beside his kinsman.

The Caldean knight in his casing of glistening armour dismounted with a jarring crash of metal. 'Stand back! This one is mine.' His spurs clinked as he manoeuvred round onto his right foot, ready to meet his opponent on chivalrous and level terms.

Ceowulf! Caspar thought in amazement. Ceowulf! Dutifully he obeyed, respecting the man's wish to pay his own debts.

'Yield up your sword, Gatto, or I am forced to kill you,' the red knight commanded.

'Yield to the man I trained myself? Never!'

Caspar recoiled from the thundering clap of metal on metal as both swords clashed above the knight's head. Ceowulf grunted with the effort as he bore down on Gatto, beating the sword time and time again against the man's shield arm. A quick jab knocked Gatto's helm sideways, obscuring his view and, with the proper gallantry of a knight, Ceowulf paused to allow his old leader time to sling the damaged helm from his shoulders. Gatto acknowledged the gesture with a nod of his bald head, then stiffened the contours of his scarred face as he braced himself for the next blow.

'Come, old man, yield,' Ceowulf demanded again. 'I'll give you safe passage back to Camaalia.'

'A free-lance owns nothing but his sword and his pride, and I will give you neither.' Gatto's deep voice ground over the words as he lashed forwards with his sabre, only to be beaten back with Ceowulf's heavier broadsword.

The old mercenary was a survivor of many hard-won battles and his experienced sword-arm parried every stroke. But each of Ceowulf's hammering blows drove the old mercenary further onto his back foot, allowing him no opportunity to flaunt his offensive skills against the knight's obdurate assault. The veteran could only block a strike or shield his skull from the furious blow. Gatto was breathing hard, snatching at his breath in short gasps, as he stoically endured the punishing weight of his adversary's blows. Gradually his movements became slower and more laboured. Another shock wave from the clash of swords jarred his arm and the pounding weight of the metal hammered him to his knees.

Ceowulf struck again and again at the man's right side, repeatedly forcing him to the same guard, beating the balding man further and further back with each stroke. The red knight drew back his sword to hack down against that same side once more while Gatto was backed up against the trees, his eyes wide with concentration. The scar that lifted one side of his face enhanced the grim look of determination, as he followed the knight's movements.

The Caldean nobleman drew back his arm as far as his shoulder-socket permitted then spun away from his quarry like a whirlwind. Twisting onto his back foot he continued to spin in a full circle and slashed sideways into Gatto's unguarded left side. It bit into the flesh beneath his armpit where the chain-mail gaped, finding flesh and bone. The sword sliced deeper, splitting apart the rib-bones as it carved into the cavity of the mercenary's thorax. There was no change in the expression on Gatto's face; he died instantly without any re-cognition of the skill and unexpected nature of the fatal blow.

The red knight looked down at his former chief and raised

his vizor almost in tribute. 'There is only one death, Gatto,' he said between quick breaths. 'There is only one road to death for such as you or I.'

With their leader felled, the few remaining mercenaries ran for their horses and retreated at a breakneck gallop, westwards to the port. Looking around him, Caspar could see nothing but limbs torn and shattered from their lifeless bodies, strong healthy men hacked to their deaths. The enemy were either dead, dying or fleeing. This, he thought, is the glory of war. We fought hard, fought nobly and this is our victorious award – to bear witness to carnage and destruction. He felt a heavy weariness dragging down on his soul.

Hal slumped to his knees, swooning with the loss of blood, but he staggered up again and stumbled towards the support of a tree-trunk. Instantly, Brid was beside him and caught him under his arm to help the youth gently to the ground. From somewhere close came the soft sound of sobbing; a girl was weeping, her head slumped in her hands, spikes of golden hair standing upright on her scalp.

Ceowulf was checking through the bodies, nudging each one carefully with the point of his sword, turning them over to check that each body was truly dead. To make the task of stooping easier, he unbuckled the yoke of armour from his breast, revealing a grey netting of chain-mail. Vaguely Caspar wondered how the man moved at all beneath the weight of such metal.

A throttled gurgling noise from a mutilated foreigner bubbled up from what was left of his mouth. Ceowulf rolled him over with his boot and plunged the sword down into the man's chest. He placed his heel in the pool of blood and withdrew the sword, the metal sucking and slurping through the soft bloody tissue. He strode on to dispassionately examine each of the remaining bodies. A black boot protruded from the brown winter ferns and he knelt to grab the ankle and drag the body out into the clearing. Its arms were stretched up out of view and were the last to emerge from the concealing cover of the vegetation.

'Look out . . .' Caspar's warning cry was too late. The body suddenly curled up, brandishing a throwing axe in its one remaining hand. The axe hacked forward to bludgeon into Ceowulf's collar bone, severing the mail shirt and embedding into his upper ribcage. Caspar was too slow with his bow. He had it raised with an arrow slotted but the damage was done before he could fire. The barb found its mark, puncturing the centre of Tasso's forehead, but it was too late to save Ceowulf. Brid was across the clearing and beside the knight as he fell.

'You're not dead yet,' she cried, pressing her palm directly down onto the wound. 'Ceowulf, fight! Hold on! Listen to my words. You're not going to die.'

'War is death's feast,' his trembling lips quoted as his eyes looked up at her in startled bewilderment. Slowly they darkened as the shadow of death crept through his body, flickered and closed.

'Get me a cloth, Spar. Get me anything – anything to pack the wound.'

Caspar ripped the shirt from his back, frantically struggling to wrench the cuffs over his wrist and thrust it at Brid. He looked at Ceowulf's closed eyes and the axe embedded in his chest. He shook his head doubtfully. 'Brid, he's gone.'

'Shut up, you fool,' she murmured. 'Now Ceowulf! Keep fighting. Hold on to us. Think of the beautiful things in your life; think of your homeland; think of Caldea; think of roast venison and hunting in the crisp winter frosts, think of anything! Think of us and how much we need you.' She was packing the cloth around the blade, pressing firmly to stem the flow of blood.

'Brid,' Caspar tried to say as tenderly as possible, 'he can't hear you.'

'His mind, maybe not, but his soul is hovering uncertainly over him. He doesn't have to die. You don't have to die,' she said more firmly at Ceowulf's face. 'The arteries aren't severed; you're not losing much blood; you don't have to die. Believe in life, believe in me: I can save you.'

The girl put her hand on the axe and took a deep breath

as if to steady herself. She relaxed again and looked across at the boy who knelt anxiously by her. 'Put your hand here and do exactly as I say. When I say now, pull the blade out fast, really fast.'

Caspar reluctantly nodded, though he felt their sad labours were in vain.

'Ready?' Brid raised herself up slightly to kneel over the man's chest and held the cloth ready in anticipation on either side of the blade.

'Ready,' Caspar nodded again.

'Now!'

A jet of blood sprang up from the gash as it opened up, squirting straight into the priestess's face, but the girl was quick to press the lips of the wound together. The white cloth was sodden with blood and she pressed more firmly until the sudden rush of blood was stemmed.

'Ceowulf,' she pleaded. 'Ceowulf, listen to me. Don't leave us.' She was no longer looking at the man's face but upwards above them. 'Ceowulf, don't leave us; you can live. You have much to live for.'

Caspar sensed that they had already lost the battle to save this knight, who had ridden so nobly to their aid, but to ease Brid's anguish over the man's death he wanted to do anything he could to help.

'Ceowulf,' he added his own voice to the girl's plaintive cries. 'You owe it to us to live. Ceowulf, we need you.' He took the man's hand and pressed it between his own. 'We need you.' Suddenly a fierce grip crushed the bones in his palm as the man's body went into rigid spasm. Caspar didn't know if it was the spasm of death or the racking pain that comes with the return of consciousness. He looked at the knight's ashen face and the blue lips. As the eyes flickered open, hazily centring their vision on Brid, Caspar's heart burst with thankfulness.

'Sweet, sweet maiden,' the knight murmured. His eyes closed again but the boy could still feel the tenacious grip on his hand, the grip that held determinedly to life.

Stroking Ceowulf's forehead to wipe the blood from the man's eyes, Brid looked into his face. 'Stay with us now, Ceowulf. It hurts, I know, but I'll purify the wound, stop the poison from blackening your blood and you will live. You fought well. You fought like a king.' It didn't matter what she said, it was just the comfort in her voice, that soft, quiet, untroubled lilt that brought comfort to Ceowulf's ears. She had a gentle nurturing confidence that assigned the will of others into her care. 'Spar, keep that pressed there,' she ordered, 'whilst I make some preparations and tend to Hal. I can't do much more until the bleeding's eased.'

Lying on his back staring up at the sun, Hal's breathing was quick and shallow. His hand was pressed to his side and he was biting his lip but some of the colour had returned to his cheeks. 'It hurts, doesn't it?' Brid said soothingly. 'Now, let's have a look at that.' She indicated the crusty mat of dried blood caked to his side. He shook his head.

'I can't feel a thing.'

'You're a rotten liar,' she laughed. 'Here, take some of my willow bark and chew it because it's going to hurt a lot more when I clean it up.'

'Well, anything not to offend you,' he half laughed. 'My hand though, Brid.' He held it up with dismay. 'Look at my hand.'

'I know,' she replied matter-of-factly.

'But my finger, I've lost my finger. Will Ceowulf live?' he added immediately, his fears for the brave knight overshadowing the loss of his digit.

'I don't know,' she replied sadly. 'There's a time for all of us.' She rose to retrieve a canister from Magpie's pack before concentrating on her herbs. She ground a handful of tough yarrow stems with the hedge woundwort into her palm and drizzled drops of water over the powder to form a paste for packing over the wounds. 'I haven't got any loosestrife left,' she explained, 'but these are as good if not better. They stop the bleeding as well as prevent infection.'

Hal paid no attention to the details of her remedies,

accepting her knowledge without question. 'I was dying in that circle. There was an evil spell that produced a voracious coldness, so cold it was eating through me. I couldn't even reach the sword. The mercenaries couldn't get the sword either though. It sank into the ground and they couldn't retrieve it.'

Brid nodded in understanding. 'The Mother was claiming it for her own.'

'You broke the spell,' he said wearily.

'I know. It was a basic spell. The Vaalakan used simple charms, concentrating them through the purity of a confined circle. They are very effective but easy to break if you ruin that purity. But he wouldn't have known that I'd found your finger. When I threw it into the circle, it broke his spell. He must have been careful to choose only virgins when he hacked off their knuckles.'

'How did you know – ouch! – they were virgins? How did – did you know about the knuckle bones?' Hal was speaking through gritted teeth and wincing as she bathed his wounds and bound his hand. He began to relax a little more as she used the blue juice of woad to paint the runes of healing around his injuries.

She looked at him with condescension. 'I am One of the Three; I know these things. The aura of magic, the smell of power was thick and turgid in the air. But the tongues? I don't know what he was thinking of; they added nothing to the spell. They were probably just there to horrify and so weaken your will.'

Listening to them talk about the shaman, Caspar looked anxiously round the scene of bodies looking for the Vaalakan carcasses. Panic swirled through his brain like a storm whipping up the dark waters of the open sea. 'The Vaalakans. Scragg and the Vaalakan shaman, they're not here. They've gone!'

Brid nodded as if the news came as no surprise. Amidst the fury and chaos of battle, Caspar had only fleeting views of the warriors pitted against them. Too much had happened all at once for him to do anything more than concentrate on the immediate threats confronting him. Even the girl still slouched by the blackthorn tree had only just registered in his mind, which had been too preoccupied by fear for Ceowulf's life and Hal's welfare. Caspar flicked his head round, scanning the bushes, stripping the shadows with his gaze. He searched for any sign of movement, or a place of likely ambush. His heart pumped wildly against his chest.

'They've gone,' Brid said flatly, tilting her head towards the sea. 'A spy knows when to cut loose rather than be caught by his enemy. The moment I used Hal's severed finger to break the spell on the circle, the shaman fled and Scragg followed soon after. They'll have gone straight down to the port and bought themselves passage on a merchant ship by now.' She glanced towards the distant harbour and the tall-masted vessels anchored off the Hespera Isles. 'They've gone,' Brid reaffirmed. 'The air is already clearing from the stench of Vaal-Peor's priest. We've got enough worries now with Hal and Ceowulf and that girl.' She nodded towards the sobbing noise that wracked Cybillia's body. 'Listen, young lady.' Caspar detected less resentment in Brid's voice and more gentle sympathy towards the Baron's daughter. 'Of course you're going to feel bad if you sit on the roots of a blackthorn. Now come away from that tree. It has no love of people and will wish you only strife and discordance. Come away and help me tend the wounded.'

Cybillia shook her head, keeping her face buried in her hands. 'I cannot. I wish they had killed me,' she sobbed bitterly.

When Brid had finished applying salve to Hal's wounds, she rose and moved towards Cybillia. Putting her hand firmly on the girl's wrist, she yanked her upwards. Cybillia, though tall, was light and her hand came easily away from her face in Brid's positive grip, revealing the hideous scarring. With a feather-like touch the priestess soothed over the raised weals of the pentagram that was etched onto the maid's fair face. Suddenly all Brid's envies seemed to melt. She put her arms round the girl, stretching up on tip-toe to offer her comfort.

'Come on, come away from the tree, come out of this circle. I promise you things will get better.'

Cybillia was rigid, silently rejecting the offer of succour from the priestess.

'You're a witch. You're a witch. It's your evil that has brought these fiends upon us. It's you who has ruined me. Take your hands off me, witch.' The girl was panicking but there was no will left to fight off the confident composure of the small priestess.

Cybilla's accusations of witchcraft abruptly reminded Caspar of the Inquisitors. He looked anxiously over the downs but there was no sign of them and he presumed they were still distracted by the wolf.

'Shut up, Cybillia,' Hal groaned unsympathetically. 'Shut up. Everything hurts too much as it is, without your screeches adding to it all.'

'Don't worry, Jotunn lady. You'll be thankful I'm a witch, as you call me. At least I have the power to do something for your face, though it'll be a long hard cure.' Brid looked with concern at the knotted scars. In the aftermath of the harrowing battle, Brid was the only one left now capable of calm rational thought.

'No one can cure me: look at my face,' Cybillia wailed in despair.

'If you truly believe that then you are right, but trust me and I'll help you. Look at Ceowulf and pull yourself together. Yours is only a flesh wound.'

'But my face . . .' she touched her cheek but as her eyes fell on the injured body of Ceowulf and the six-inch gash on Hal's side her hand fell limply away. She stood stupefied for a long breathless moment and then stiffened with resolve. 'Can I help?' she asked, sucking in a deep breath to compose herself.

Following Brid's instructions Caspar and Cybillia dressed and redressed Ceowulf and Hal's wounds. Brid busily ground herbs and applied poultices until she was satisfied with her powders and began to search through the undergrowth for dry wood. She stripped off the bark and cleared away any leaves or green shoots to make a fire. Once Caspar was content that his uncle was comfortable, he hurried to attend to his horse, delaying the evil moment when he alone would have to bury the dead. He couldn't exactly ask the two girls to help him.

'The smoke though, Brid,' he warned, as he soothed Firecracker and applied one of the priestess's poultices to a swollen gash above the colt's knee. 'The Inquisitors – the smoke will draw them to us.' He was worried that the frenzied panic of the battle had driven all thoughts of the King's soldiers from her mind. 'Why haven't they followed us?'

'They won't follow us now,' Brid said.

Caspar waited for her to explain but the girl was silent with her head bowed over the flints, which she struck together with vehemence. Tendrils of her long lightened hair had escaped from her plait to conceal her face. 'Why won't they follow us, Brid?'

She still didn't reply and Caspar left his horse and sat down beside her. After all the fury of battle and the worry over his severely injured fellows, there was suddenly nothing left to do. Caspar felt flat and deflated. He gloomily looked at Hal and Ceowulf slumbering in their drugged sleep and the realities of the day's events loomed large and real. He didn't know what to do. He knew Brid was upset but didn't know how to comfort her nor how to coax the reason from her. At last he summoned the courage to tentatively touch her lightly on the shoulder. She looked round at him with swollen eyes and silent tears streaming down her cheeks and rolling off her jaw, dripping into the soil at her feet. Their eyes met. Caspar felt his own eyes pricking and he instantly knew what she was going to say. Brid pushed his comfort away, preferring to mourn alone.

'She's dead, my wolf is dead. She's been with me all my life and she's saved me by giving up herself. They'll burn her tonight.' Brid nodded in the direction of the port. Her voice was harsh and broken, racked by gasps between the swallowed sobs. 'We'll see the smoke over that hill. They're not looking for me any more: they think I'm dead.'

'But you don't know she's dead,' Caspar tried to reason,

hoping to bring Brid some rational comfort. 'We haven't seen her or heard her; maybe she's hiding someplace.'

The priestess looked at him bitterly. 'You of all people, Spar, should understand. Do you really think I wouldn't know if my wolf were dead or not?'

Caspar felt humbled and rather inadequate, unable to know what best to say. A rustle in the bushes provided a distraction and the white terrier, long since forgotten, sneaked out, whimpering and wagging his tail. He nuzzled Brid, demanding affection, and she flung her arms round the dog, hugging him closely. Finally the silent tears broke into heavy sobs and she rocked back and forth, cradling the dog in her arms.

Caspar felt a light touch on his shoulder and he looked round to see Cybillia. 'I've checked on Hal and Ceowulf and they're both sleeping.' She lowered her anxious voice. 'I didn't know witches cried.' Her hand was pressed to her cheek and she sat down, carefully placing herself so the scarring wasn't directly visible to the youth.

'She's not a witch, Cybillia, she's a priestess, a high-priestess and she's crying because she has lost something dear and loved.' Caspar could understand because he knew how he felt about his old deer-hound, Wartooth. 'She's crying because her heart is full of love, pure and simple and unselfish, and yet you still condemn her as evil.'

'She's a heretic and should be burned,' Cybillia said flatly. 'But who am I to say when I am lost and ruined, doomed to eternal damnation by this scarring on my body.'

'But you can't think she should be burned? Not when she fought so fiercely against the Vaalakans.'

'I don't know anymore, Spar. I cannot hold my head up high and say I believe this or I know that. I am faceless, an outcast. I can never return home. Do you know what my father used to say? He would tell me I was beautiful enough to marry a prince?' She laughed at the sheer folly of the idea but her laughter soured into tears.' Now I shall go mad. I shall stay here and die of madness.'

Caspar felt helplessly trapped between the two weeping

females but now, at least Brid's racking sobs had calmed to silent tears and only the occasional shudder. The small Maiden, still hugging the dog, pulled her head back and wiped her nose on the back of her bloodied sleeve. 'I should not mourn. The Mother will have her sacrifice and we must all suffer. I will do my mourning when we have fulfilled our promise to restore the Trinity.' She turned her head and looked directly at Cybillia. 'And you, girl, are also too full of self-pity. I told you I can cure you.'

Caspar looked around at the gruesome scatter of mutilated bodies and dragged himself to his feet. He couldn't put off the evil moment any longer. He used an abandoned Vaalakan axe to hack out a shallow hole beneath the roots of the black-thorns. One by one he hauled the bodies through the bracken and slung them into the broad grave. He kicked them in with his boots, trying to avoid touching them with his bare hands.

Eyeing Ulf's bloody body, he left it until last, finding the quartered head particularly gruesome. With the help of two sticks, which he used as tongs, he manoeuvred the segments of skull to the grave. Then he returned for the rest of the butchered remains. Dragging the body by the boots he became aware of a strange tingling energy in his fingertips. Instantly he thought of the moonstone. Forgetting his repulsion, he rifled through the corpse's blood-soaked clothing. With great satisfaction he found the soft white glow of the orb; but he was instantly disappointed. Although this stone was similar, he knew immediately that it wasn't the Druid's Eye. It lacked the intense energy and power that radiated from the moon-stone that trapped his mother's thoughts in its crystalline heart.

Swiftly he finished his distasteful task and hurried breath-lessly back to Brid. He held out his outstretched palm and presented her with the small moonstone. 'Ulf, the traitor from the castle kitchens, had this on him.'

Brid's big green eyes sparkled for a fleeting moment, then her head dropped as she also realized it wasn't the Eye. 'But your father said they were all gone. They searched the tunnels beneath Torra Alta after the explosion and the Baron said they couldn't find any.' She grasped at the moonstone and looked into its heart. 'It's telling me nothing,' she said with disappointment. 'This small stone on its own is too weak and, wherever Puzella is, she must have the Eye concealed – probably in water since that's the simplest way.'

'But I don't understand. How could Ulf have got hold of a moonstone? What would he want with it? The man was always a bit strange, even twisted, you might say, but he just didn't have the wit to know what this was in the first place. He'd more likely just smash it with his kitchen-cleaver for the fun of it.'

Brid shrugged and tossed the moonstone into her scrip. 'So it seems Curate Dunnock had an ally, but the combination of the two seems absurd. One a devout but rather weak man and the other a half-crazed oaf. Would these two men really conspire against the might of Torra Alta? It's absurd. We're only seeing half the picture.' Brid wrinkled her nose as she puzzled over the thought and then wiped away the crusted tears that had dried at the corners of her eyes as if dismissing the problem. 'Well, Cybillia, shall I take a look at your face?'

'You are a witch, a heretic. Brother Rufus will have me excommunicated if I willingly let you touch me.'

'Well, Brother Rufus isn't here and doesn't have to know, does he?' Brid pointed out realistically. 'And that face of yours, as it is, won't allow you back home even if the Vaalakans haven't overrun the border yet.'

'There were some things done to me that can never be undone. It's no use, even if you can heal my face.'

'Well, Brother Rufus certainly doesn't have to know that. No one is going to tell him. We'll heal your face for you.' Although small and child-like herself, Brid offered the comfort of mature words.

The promise of restored beauty was beginning to woo Cybillia and she glanced uncertainly at the pagan priestess.

'You know,' reasoned Brid, 'it's not your fault they marked you. It's because they are evil people. It's not your fault; it's war. And the markings? The pentagram isn't so dreadful. It won't do you any harm and may even have protected your life. There is design in all these things. The fates have allowed your true nature to be declared to the world.'

Cybillia looked shocked. 'What do you mean? I have been devout and holy, always following the ways of the one true God, in awe of his presence and obedient and compliant to his will and the will of my parents.'

'Well, they obviously didn't know what they were doing when they named you Cybillia. Your name means little witch,' Brid informed her.

Cybillia was silent for a moment, then turned her face to show the girl her disfigured cheek. Red ugly weals and keloid scars formed bright ridges of knotted flesh on her smooth pale flesh. 'Can you really heal this?' Her question was more of a challenge. 'And why should you? You never liked me and I betrayed you to Rewik.'

Caspar was wondering the same thing. At least Cybillia presented no rivalry for Hal whilst she looked like that and Brid could have no reason beyond sympathy. He couldn't think that was enough for the priestess whose thoughts were invariably set on higher goals.

'I can do it for you, yes; but it'll hurt ten times more than it did when they cut you. You'll look worse too – far worse – to start with; but in the end it will heal. And I'm only going to do it for you as part of a bargain. You will learn from me and follow my ways and thank the Mother everyday for her mercies and her blessings.'

'I've got nothing to lose anymore,' Cybillia sighed, 'and everything to gain.'

'I'll have to find some leaves of Ophidian pennywort first as well as the red stems of dragonsfire, but you might change your mind when you find out how much it hurts.' Brid raised her eyebrows in warning.

'I might only be a girl,' Cybillia replied taking up the challenge, 'but I am a Belbidian and no Belbidian of either highborn blood or of peasant stock will balk at the threat of pain.'

Brid laughed. 'I never said I didn't like you, Cybillia. I just thought you were silly – all ribbons and dresses and golden hair. I thought you proud and overbearing because you were spoilt and soft and had no belief in yourself; but now, without the trappings and meaningless ornaments, you're still proud – and that I admire. You are proud not because of superficial titles and grandiose ornaments but because of the strength in your soul. But enough of all that; I've got work to do.'

Brid stripped off the tattered remnants of the blue dress they'd bought in Bleham to reveal her more practical breeches and spun silk shirt. She rose and returned to the blackthorn tree, carefully picking up Hal's finger and all the knuckle bones and dropping them into her scrip so that they rattled as she walked. She turned the tongues over in her hand, selected one and discarded the rest. She had to pull Trog away from them, giving him a sharp crack across his muzzle to keep him from scavenging after them.

'I'm going to be sick.' Cybillia covered her mouth and swallowed hard. 'How could she do such a thing?'

Caspar was equally revolted but was more familiar with Brid's ways. 'She's like a magpie with certain plants and objects. There is power in many things and she collects them wherever she can. She needs them.'

Sitting by the fire, preparing the tinctures and pastes under Brid's ever vigilant supervision, Caspar had little time for sleep that night. Occasionally, while watching over Hal, he lolled into a near dream, his head floating downwards, drifting in an ever decreasing spiral like a feather falling in the breathless air. Each time his forehead eased onto his knees he snapped his head back up again to anxiously check on Hal's breathing. He had no need; Brid knelt continually by his uncle with her hand resting lightly on his forehead. She was murmuring softly and painting more runes of healing across his brow.

When she had finished, she paused for a lingering moment, anxiously studying him in his deep, drugged sleep before gently easing herself up and starting to creep away from the blackthorn thicket. Caspar jumped up and caught her arm.

'Where are you going?'

'I won't be long. I'm going to find those herbs for Cybillia.'

'In the moonlight?'

The priestess nodded. 'The Moon strengthens all magic and her blessed light will guide me to them.'

Caspar anxiously watched over his uncle and the short rasping breaths of the injured Caldean, while he waited through the quiet of the night. The familiar noise of the horses stirring in their sleep made him feel only a little more comfortable when he thought of the body of the headless traitor lying in its shallow grave. He struggled to shake away the nightmarish image that crept into his mind. It was trying to persuade him that the decapitated body would creep out of the earth and hack him limb from limb if he slept.

Caspar was saved from his imagination by Brid's light footsteps, padding back through the blackthorn thicket. In the light of the fire he could see the look of triumph blazing in her eyes.

'I found the herbs.' She produced the sprigs of Ophidian pennywort and the red-stemmed dragonsfire.

The resin that Brid prepared stank and brought tears to their eyes as she painted it on Cybillia's cheek. The Baron's daughter went rigid with pain, her fingers hooking into talons with the tendons like iron bars ridging the back of her hand. Caspar had to hold her arms to stop her from tearing at her face; but she didn't scream. True to her word, she gritted her teeth and shook with the pain, but she didn't scream.

'It hurts too much to scream,' Brid said quietly. 'We call it dragonsfire; it burns with an ever increasing heat that will dissolve away the top surface of the skin. I can only apply it little by little, day by day. The quantity has to be just right. Too much would take away her whole face, too little will have no effect on the scarring.' After five minutes Brid painted on a separate mixture to neutralize the first and then washed them both away with water.

'These pastes are like two armies, the one as fearsomely acid as the other is caustic; but when the warring is done we must have the neutral and balanced water to maintain the equilibrium. Too much of the caustic paste would be as harmful as too much of the acid.'

Ceowulf hardly stirred. His breathing was shallow and his pulse rapid but Brid said that was the normal effect of the drugs that strengthen the heart and purified the blood. 'If he survives the wound, which he will, his danger is from poisons entering the blood,' Brid explained.

'You're a great healer, Brid,' Caspar asserted as the bright stars dimmed in the violet light before dawn.

'I am as the Mother made me.'

As the morning sun brought the colours of the Caldean countryside to life and danced in the dew drops beading the gossamer, Brid rose and climbed to the top of the down away from the blackthorn bushes. She turned east with her arms outspread and lifted her voice in a song of sad lament. Its tone was eerie and mysterious, gilded with a sense of beauty and hope; a song to the Mother, begging her to cherish the soul of the wolf so that it might be reborn to a happy life. Caspar's cheeks were wet with silent tears. The priestess turned westwards towards the hopes of the future. As a distant cock crowed, proudly declaring the joys of morning, a thin wisp of smoke curled up from the port of Ildros, spiralling heavenwards.

Brid froze as the first rays of sunlight brightened the contours of her face and sparkled in her vivid green eyes. 'Can you feel it, Spar?' she whispered, dropping to her knees and pressing her palms to the ground.

He shook his head blankly.

'That evil woman never made the port. The power of the Druid's Eye still trembles through the Earth.'

Chapter 32

A jagged explosion of yellow flashed past the crack in the shutters.

May no longer flinched as the sulphur-bombs crackled and exploded on the valley floor though she still couldn't help looking nervously towards the blackened recess of the arrow-slit. The shutters were firmly clamped to muffle the noise and help seal out the sickening smell. When the wind blew up from the north it carried a stench worse than that of winter cattle confined to a windowless barn. A pungent, rancid fetor.

May stroked the Crone's thin scalp, brushing away the loose hair that fell away like downy feathers from an old bird's nest. Her breathing was fast, shallow and rasping and she hadn't spoken now for three days. May had tried to trickle broth, laced with the restorative herbs into Morrigwen's limp drooling mouth, but the woman's old and withered body didn't seem to respond. Her skin was the colour of ash and bore a frightening resemblance to Catrik's just before he had died. Once or twice she cried out in her sleep, calling for Brid and Keridwen. 'I am poisoned. The Trinity, the Trinity is lost. Brid, answer me; Brid, I need you. Look into the Eye. For the Mother, for the love of the Mother look into the Eye.'

Once she awoke with almost vivid clarity in her sunken eyes and stared straight at May. 'Child, the smell. Put juniper on the fire to mask it.' The young girl looked at her with delight, feeling certain that she had regathered her senses but the old priestess slumped back again and had lain in icy silence ever since.

'All hands! All hands! All hands to the west tower. Fire! Fire! Fire!'

May leapt to her feet and ran to the door. Maud, Rosalind and the other women were fleeing the keep, loom and spinning wheels scattered to the ground in their haste to help. A human chain formed across the courtyard from the well-room to the west tower. A tongue of angry red flames lashed out of the top turret and spat at the sky. Dense black smoke billowed up in a thick column, blackening the crisp blue heavens. A hungry cheer wailed up from the valley below, chilling May's heart as she snatched at the slopping bucket and thrust it into the outstretched hands of the woman in front. More trolls had mustered in the valley over the last few weeks, dragging war-engines. Now their missiles fired impotently at the castle's steadfast walls. But one lucky shot . . .

'It must've been one of our own sulphur bombs,' a soldier explained to the anxious women as he tried to organize an orderly line. 'We must've fired one out onto the road where they've stationed them infernal machines. It must've landed unexploded at their feet. I guess they hurled it back. But how it hit the tower . . . ?'

'No, it couldn't have done,' an archer reasoned. 'That tower's far too high and way beyond their range.'

'But there's naught else to set it aflame. No one's lived up there for years.'

May couldn't contain herself and her voice piped out shrilly into the smoke-choked air. 'But, sir, there was a strange man in the turret right at the top. Pip and I saw him with Ulf the day before he disappeared.'

'No, lass, no one's been there for years. You couldn't have done.'

'But if Ulf'd been hiding there all this time?' the other soldier pondered. 'A mule-brained man like him, maybe he would have set it alight?'

The men hurried forward along the line and May's arms rapidly tired as she heaved the leaky buckets forward. The women and children formed the chain from the wellroom to the courtyard, leaving the soldiers to brave the fierce heat nearer the tower and up into the spiralling staircase. As they laboured May thought back on that day she'd spied Ulf through the keyhole. With hindsight she began to have niggling doubts that the voice of the black-cloaked man had been Father Gwion's. But it seemed so unlikely. She didn't dare mention it for fear of upsetting everyone with such outlandish accusations.

The sound of clattering buckets and sloshing water was barely audible beneath the roaring rage of the flames above. They couldn't save the top rooms, that was clear, and the Baron had ordered them to contain the fire and stop it spreading. Sentries were placed about the castle to spot for sparks spattering down from the tower but they hit only bare stone and quickly dwindled.

A heat haze shimmered around the tower as May looked up at the raging ball of red flames that engulfed the turret room. She felt her face glowing in the heat and the women around her had to shout above the roar of the flames. The slushy snow under foot was soaking up through her threadbare leather boots but she hardly noticed for the effort of lugging the heavy buckets to the woman in front. She thought of Pip down in the wellroom, small but determined, heaving at the buckets, struggling to keep up with the older boys. She looked ahead down the line, quickly picking out her mother's bright red hair from the row of dark chestnut heads. Elaine's anxious eyes sought out her daughter and nodded reassuringly as she saw she was safe.

But the runes, May thought. The Runes of War were meant to protect the walls of the castle. She looked towards the heartstone and immediately felt the uplift in her soul at the sight of the blood red ruby with the circular sigil of the Mother embedded in its crystalline structure. She knew the runes were fading. Before succumbing to the fang-nettle, Morrigwen had explained it over and over to her. The runes would fade little by little, month by month and it was now already Fogmoon. By the last day of Fallow the runes would be gone.

At Morrigwen's request she had studied them after the snow

had been brushed aside and the edges were rounding and the grooves less defined. But still while they were etched on the heartstone they would protect the solid walls of the fortress. How then could the tower be burning? If only Morrigwen would wake up she would know. Why had the Mother forsaken the top turret of the western tower? May remembered that horrible day when she and her brother had peeked through the keyhole at the hideous rites of sacrifice and heard the blood-thirsty insanity of the demented Ulf and his devilish companion. Was the Mother cleansing her castle of this evil? May prayed that was true. Then at least the runes would not be failing.

The women scattered and cringed beneath the overhang of the keep as the tower above creaked and groaned. Men poured out from the roots of the tower just before a splintering crash announced that one of the floors had given way. A shard of wooden buttress peeled away from the outside of the tower and crashed down into the courtyard, spraying sparks and sizzling embers into the crowd. The women hurriedly brushed down their skirts and leapt forward with their buckets to douse the fire. Smouldering timbers and a flurry of grey ash seeped into the snow.

As twilight doused the brilliant blue of the winter sky into a mysterious purple the flames calmed to a flicker and a glow. Then finally only the thick noxious smoke pumped out to augment the darkness of night. Branwolf walked up and down the line, nodding his thanks to the castle folk and checking that all was well.

The young soldier who had helped organize the women into lines stepped forward and saluted the Baron. 'My Lord, I fear that Ulf, the kitchen lad who disappeared, may have been holed up in the tower.'

Branwolf nodded. 'We'll form a search party.' He looked round with a frown creasing his face. 'Anyone else missing?'

'Well, no sir, not that I'm aware.'

Branwolf pouted and scuffed his toe through the compacted snow, which was hardening to a slippery layer of ice over the cobbles. 'Captain,' he bellowed. 'Get all your sergeants together. I want them to account for every man in their company. And report back immediately.' He moved forward to examine the roots of the tower and waited for the captain to shout out his orders and return with the information.

'All present or accounted for, sir.'

Branwolf marched up and down the lines, looking for any face of authority. 'Cook, are all your women here?'

The broad woman, with her sleeves rolled up over her shiny red skin, polished from years of scrubbing and scouring in the kitchens, looked efficiently around her and nodded.

The Baron's face remained twisted into lines of perplexity. 'All of you, look around at your friends and family. Is there anyone missing?' There was a buzz through the crowd. May looped her hand through her mother's, who was hugging a weary and drenched son to her sides and rubbing his frosted hands. Eyes searched over the crowd but there was a general agreement that no one was missing. Branwolf tapped his foot in frustration. 'Someone's missing. I'm sure there's someone missing.'

The tall rangy captain looked thoughtfully around him. 'Sir!' he exclaimed in sudden revelation. 'It's Father Gwion, sir. I haven't seen him all day and he would normally be the first –'

Branwolf threw his eyes up towards the charred remains of the tower. 'Men, back to your posts. Women, back into the keep,' he ordered as he grabbed a pitchfork and marched determinedly towards the tower. The captain snatched at his shoulder.

'The stairwell, sir, it'll be unstable. Charred timbers could give way any moment.'

Branwolf brushed him off. 'He's my wife's brother, damn you.'

The women huddled round the open keep door and waited impatiently. Torchlight flickered in the arrow-slits high up in the blackened remains of the west tower and no one spoke as they waited for their lord to return. After many anxious minutes Branwolf's commanding voice bellowed out for assistance. Presently a sombre procession filed out from the lower arch door, reverently bearing a stretcher. The soldiers formed a ring around it and pressed the women back, but May couldn't contain her curiosity. Ducking under spread arms and rigid shoulders, she wriggled to the fore of the hushed crowd.

'I cannot hide this from you, men,' the Baron said steadily, though his face was white in the firelight. 'There was very little intact to recover; the heat from the fire was so intense.' May gaped at the smouldering heap, which lay discreetly covered in a blanket and covered her mouth to block out the acrid smell and fight back the bile rising in her throat. 'The whole body is crisp and blackened. I would not have recognized him but for this: a boot, a strip of satin cowl and this.' A tiny gold object glinted in the Baron's fist as he raised up his arm. 'This is Father Gwion's ring,' he said heavily. 'That was all I could find. Everything else in the room was ash.'

The church bell solemnly tolled out the death knell in honour of the Baron's brother-in-law. But May felt no sorrow at the loss, certain now that it was Father Gwion she had seen with Ulf. Still, it didn't matter anymore, not after the fire, and no one would believe her, anyway. So she said nothing, but her mother stooped down and whispered in her ear. 'Perhaps the Great Mother is cleansing her domain of the New Faith.'

'No, Ma,' May contradicted her without even knowing where the thought came from. 'No, she is cleansing the *evil* from her domain, purifying her castle with fire.' She fled back to check on Morrigwen, leaving the other castle folk to mourn.

She had left the old Crone too long and she was worried. Bursting open the solar door she stopped short at the sight of Morrigwen standing by the open shutters. Her eyes were glazed and she was staring with a stupefied expression into the distance.

'Brid,' the old hag murmured. 'Brid, help me. Hurry, child, find the cauldron. I need your powers or the Trinity is lost.'

May tugged at her hand. 'Back to bed with you, Morrigwen.' She tried to sound authoritative but her voice squeaked out, distressed and piercing. 'How did you get out of bed?' When the old Crone didn't respond, the young girl realized she wasn't awake but had been driven to the window by her delirium. She tugged nervously at the woman's thin hand, grimacing at the feel of her raw bones beneath the barest shreds of her wafer-thin skin. 'You must get back into bed.'

Morrigwen slowly turned, blinked and then collapsed into a heap at her feet.

'Ma! Ma!' May shrieked.

Several of the women from the lower keep came running at the sound of May's urgent screams. Effortlessly, they lifted Morrigwen's scant frame back onto her pallet. Elaine felt for her pulse and listened to her breathing.

'She's very weak. What on earth drove her to the window?'

Maud, the fat old woman with ruddy cheeks who kept company with them in the keep, stared over the widow's shoulder and announced with characteristic bluntness, 'Whatever, she won't last much longer.'

'Don't you dare say that!'

The women leapt back at the sound of the Baron's stern voice. His face was black with smuts and his hands were red raw with burns and cuts. He knelt by the Crone's bedside and all the women save May and her mother fled from the chamber. 'I came to tell her about her foster-son.'

'I don't think she can hear you,' Elaine said sadly. 'Her body is still with us but her mind is wandering.'

'She must live. If she dies I will lose my Keridwen.' He crouched by the woman and whispered in her ear. 'Come on, old woman, pull through. You know you have to live. You have to live for the sake of the Mother and for Keridwen. You have to live. We need you.'

Morrigwen's flecked blue eyes stared unseeing up at the ceiling. 'Brid. Tell Brid to hurry,' she muttered weakly and fell silent.

Chapter 33

Looking out towards the Hespera Isles, the sea was green, peaked with foam. White horses surged up from the depths and reared into the air, their long manes spraying out in a proud crest before diving back down again. In the shelter of the harbour waters, deep-draughted merchant ships dragged at their anchors and, alongside the quay, squat fishing boats tugged on their moorings. Jutting between two flat-nosed lobster-boats, the Inquisitors' sleek ship was clearly discernible, pushing its bows out towards the open sea. The black ship, its red and yellow crest ballooned on its dark sail, buffeted northwards against the waves, taking the King's Inquisitors back to their monarch.

At last it was safe for Caspar to return to Ildros. He bridled Firecracker and rode back to the inn to retrieve the last of their packs, his saddle and the cart-horse. He paid the ostler handsomely, turning the man's suspicious mutterings into a partially satisfied grunt.

'You've been away, young lord,' he said pointedly. 'You missed the wolf-witch being burnt. I doubted you would return.' His voice was lacking the warm hospitality and it was clear that he was glad to see the back of him.

As he rode out through the town he drew up sharp at the sight of the charred and shrunken remains of a wolf's head. It was stuck on a post in the middle of the town square. A little boy was throwing stones at the head to pass the idleness of his childhood.

'Get away from it, boy,' Caspar yelled angrily, turning his high-stepping horse threateningly towards the child. The mother rushed from her doorstep where she was scrubbing the stone slab and hugged the boy to her.

'I only wanted to see the demons come out,' he wailed. 'The men in black said when it burned, devils would come out of its mouth and fly away. There weren't any though, were there, Ma?'

No, thought Caspar, there weren't any demons. Rewik's superstitious fears caused too much suffering in an otherwise good country.

Caspar didn't mention the wolf's head to Brid when she greeted him on his return. Hal was fully dressed and the black charger was saddled. Ceowulf was still propped up next to the campfire, being nursed by Cybillia who patiently offered him another spoonful of rabbit broth. Brid was very skilled at snaring rabbits but over the last four days Caspar had become entirely sick of the meat. He dismounted and strode across to the knight to see how his wounds were healing.

'Now remember, Cybillia,' Brid instructed, 'every two hours replace the bandages and apply more paste, and get him to eat as much broth as you can.'

Cybillia nodded, her face too swollen to allow her to speak.

'Ready, Spar?' she turned to face the younger youth, the morning sun catching the fire in his red hair.

He too nodded; words seemed unnecessary.

As the two of them rode out over the downs, he looked back uncertainly at the thicket where they had left Cybillia tending his wounded uncle and the Caldean knight and grunted in satisfaction. At least they were well hidden. 'How do you know we're going in the right direction?' he asked Brid as she rode purposefully forward. 'I don't see how you can tell where the moonstone is?'

'Sometimes I wonder whether you're Keridwen's son at all,' Brid despaired.

Caspar didn't know whether to be relieved at the thought or angered. If Keridwen wasn't his mother, at least he wasn't so intrinsically entangled in this network of paganism. On the other hand he knew deep in his heart that he loved her and yearned for her motherly protection. The second he had seen her trapped in the ice he had known her as his mother. He sucked in a deep breath, steeling himself from the superstitious fears of his childhood. Yes, he was proud to be the son of a high-priestess. He was proud to be the son of Keridwen.

'You just have to open up your heart and feel what is really happening around you. Man seems to be so wrapped up in his own little world now that he can no longer feel the presence of life all around him. There is magic everywhere in the rocks and streams and plants and animals; you men just can't feel any of it.'

Caspar reflected that he could at least feel the magic in Firecracker's graceful speed, but thought that wasn't much of an argument. 'I can feel more than Hal can,' he lamely defended himself.

'Ah well, that's saying a lot,' Brid retorted tartly. 'Hal's as sensitive as a cudgel.'

Caspar grinned inwardly at the thought of Brid condemning his uncle but then relented as he remembered Hal's wounds. 'But how do you know the moonstone is over to the south? It seems so unlikely that she should have headed north and then turned south again,' Caspar argued.

'I don't pretend to know the ins and out of it, Spar. I can just feel it. That's all that matters, surely.' Expertly she pressed Ceowulf's sleek black charger to a thundering gallop. The horse curtsied deep onto its hocks and arched its proud neck, bowing to her will. She soothed his glossy mane. Faced with a choice of Magpie or Ceowulf's black destrier she had chosen the latter. Being slightly shorter and heavier he wasn't so difficult to mount. She also liked the name. The animal was so black that he'd been named Sorcerer.

They cut round the edge of several walled vineyards before finding open dunes and dusty grassland that led them out towards a headland that jutted into the sea. Without hesitation Brid guided Sorcerer westward towards the roar of breakers pummelling against cliffs. Firecracker bucked and fought against his bit, determined to stay ahead of the black stallion and Caspar was caught off balance when the Maiden deftly wheeled the mount in a tight circle. Tufts of earth spun off the red colt's hooves as Caspar circled him round and drew to a sharp halt. Brid was already on the ground, tentatively feeling the earth.

She looked up at Caspar. 'It's under here.'

'You mean she's buried it?'

'Oh don't be daft, Spar. We're right by the cliff face; there are bound to be caves undermining this peninsula. I should think Puzella fled the port when she saw all those Inquisitors and is still hiding from them. Perhaps she took a boat from the estuary and sailed out here to hide in the caves.'

Caspar looked around him at the ridge of land. 'We'd better go back to the bay and then along the foot of the cliffs. We won't get down to the sea from up here.'

Brid wasn't listening; she had already set off back towards the bay he was pointing to.

A thick layer of shingle fringed the beach. They tethered their horses and scrambled over the rocks, keeping well above the high water mark where crisp blackened seaweed and shrimp pools clearly marked the boundary of the sea's domain. Caspar swore as he caught his shin on a jagged rock. When he looked up Brid was some way ahead. She had an uncanny ability to move quickly over difficult terrain, leaping from rock to rock with the precision of a mountain goat. Suddenly she stood stock still.

Sensing her panic Caspar strung his bow and ran on faster to protect her. 'What is it?'

'Listen.'

He stood still, calming his breathing. Gulls mocked at a cormorant diving into the sea. The boom of breakers clapping against rocks and the hiss of spray filled the air. Beneath that he could hear the shuffling rasp of sands sighing in and out, dragged back and forth by the motion of the sea. But he could hear nothing out of place.

'What?'

'Breathing.'

'That's the sigh of the sea.'

'Is it?' she said flatly, implying that it most certainly was not. 'Look at that cave there.' She pointed to the black mouth, swallowing the air at the foot of the white cliffs. Terns shrieked from the crevices in the rock high above their heads. 'The noise is coming from there and the sea is behind us.'

'That's an echo,' Caspar explained reasonably.

'Humph!' Brid crept forward more carefully until they both stood in the half-light at the edge of the cave, slipping on the slimy, moss-covered rocks. 'Do you still think so?'

Caspar could hear the whispering sigh of the shifting sands mingled with a hollow echo, like the sound from the inside of a shell, reverberating through the cave. But there was something else, almost like a deep snore. And the smell!

'Ugh! It's like rotting fish. A high tide must have washed something in there. Are you sure the moonstone's here?'

Brid nodded. 'Yes, I'm sure.'

Caspar put his hand to his chest and felt for his mandala. It throbbed with great energy but at the same time was cold with warning. He felt confused.

Soundlessly Brid moved forward while Caspar crunched at her heels over the cave's pebble-strewn floor. At last sand moulded to his worn boots and muffled his footfall. All daylight was swallowed in the depths of the cave and they found themselves inching forward by feeling along the eroded walls.

'Through here,' Brid whispered.

Caspar couldn't work out where she had gone until his hand explored a crack in the rock. The Maiden had disappeared through a fissure that led deep into the back of the cave. The low, long rumbling roar of the sea, like distant thunder, echoed down the tunnels. Gradually the noise became louder. He decided they were in a narrow fissure that linked two caves.

His heart thumped. Suddenly he could feel it; the throbbing energy of the moonstone. His nerves tingled and thrilled with the excitement of its presence. A dim glow filtered through the crack ahead, casting angular shadows over the broken rocks. He could feel the power calling him. He ran forward.

His mother needed him. He could almost hear her crying out from her entombment in the Vaalakan glacier. Brid caught his arm.

'Careful. You don't know what Puzella has in store for you.'

Caspar pulled up short and stole stealthily forward.

'Oh Mother, help us,' Brid prayed, the words barely escaping between her tight, pallid lips. She clutched at Caspar. The sense of her distress and her silent plea for protection made the noble boy swallow his own fear and gather his courage.

'What is it?' He found his own words trembled from his lips but as he heard the rasp of scales grating over rock, he didn't need an answer. The thump of elephantine feet pounding the earth and the irregular slap of a tail crashing against the cave walls induced a gripping fear. Stupefied for a blind second, he stared helplessly at the crack before determinedly mustering his nerves.

'Don't worry; he can't reach us in here.' He tried to sound reassuring as he drew his bow.

Involuntarily he flinched away as the gnarly form of a sickly-white snout penetrated the tunnel entrance. The long, whip-like tongue lashed forward, tasting their scent, and its cavernous nostrils flared in and out. The trapped humans felt the air being sucked away from them as the dragon inhaled volumes of the dank atmosphere to swell the bladder of skin beneath its throat. The bladder bloated until it was transparent and turgid, the network of purple capillaries throbbed visibly through the white skin. The monster exhaled a blast of hot wet breath. Coughing and spluttering to expel the revolting stench from their burning lungs, the two companions retreated backwards.

Caspar's step momentarily faltered and then, with one hand clasped over his nose to filter out the foul-smelling gastric gases, he threatened with his bow. It was a pointless gesture since the lizard was blind, though the vestiges of one eyeball still rolled beneath a greyish veil of skin. The other eyeball was a weeping gelatinous mess, crushed and torn where the leathery eyelid had been hacked away to reveal the blind dead-white tissue beneath. One of Branwolf's arrows was still embedded in what was left of the glazed eyeball. Caspar needed the animal to raise its head and so expose the soft membrane beneath its armour-plated snout but it kept its head tightly arched, protecting its gizzard.

With great relief Caspar let out his long held breath, as the white-faced monster withdrew its snout from the tunnel. 'Stay behind me.' His voice was high and strained but he still stood his ground, determined to protect the young girl.

The relief was short-lived as he stared in wide-mouthed horror at the massive claw groping towards them, like a cat reaching into a mouse-hole. A tumble of rocks gave way under the pressure of the dragon's weight as it pressed its armoured shoulder into the narrow entrance, straining to reach them.

'Here!' Brid pressed a sickle into Caspar's hand. 'Use this. We've got to get the Druid's Eye.'

The hooked claw uncurled and lashed at them again, stretching out three barbed talons. Instead of cringing back against the tunnel walls, Caspar lunged forward, swinging the sickle. The point snagged in the reptilian scales and the boy raked viciously. The needle-sharp tip pierced the dragon's armour and dragged through the flesh, before embedding in the sinews and being smothered in a rush of purplish blood.

The monster gave out an earth-shaking roar and retracted its claw. Enraged and distressed, the mindless beast lashed out viciously with its other uninjured claw. It smashed into the tunnel walls with such strength and fury that rocks crashed from the walls, splintering into rubble on the floor. Caspar attacked again, piercing the animal in the crevice between two toes, thrusting the sickle under the slate of a scale to penetrate the flesh beneath. The boy's brave battle-cry was drowned by the roaring howl from the beast. Stepping backwards onto his rear foot, the young nobleman wrenched out the curved blade and a jet of blood spurted from the wound, covering them both in a splatter of thick warm liquid. The dragon retreated and the tunnel was filled with the rumble of deep groaning followed by the echoing slap of a wet slurping noise.

The youth listened intently, trying to decipher the strange sound.

'It's licking its wounds,' Brid decided. Her trembling hand clutched on to Caspar's arm.

'How do we get the moonstone?' Caspar despaired. 'We must have it. My mother . . .' He couldn't put his desperation into words. Charging forward into the cave with a maddened dragon lying in wait would be suicide but to lose the moonstone would mean losing his mother. 'I'll have to go in there,' he declared. His mindless bravery was engendered from fear for his mother, though his voice began to lose conviction. 'Maybe, if I'm quiet and he's busy with his wounds, perhaps . . .'

'Don't be such a fool.' Brid pulled him back.

'But the moonstone . . .'

The young Maiden ignored him as she prodded her garments. She reached her arm into the depths of her shirt to retrieve the salamander whose scarlet scales glinted like rubies in the whispery light of the moonstone, filtering through from the far cave. She tipped the lizard onto the ground and it scurried away in short bursts, abruptly stopping in the dark crevices and niches before fleeing forward in jerky fits and starts.

'It has an affinity for fire and the blazing heart of the Druid's Stone,' Brid murmured as she looked anxiously after her pet.

The deep rolling moans of the white leviathan rumbled on, interspersed by the slurp of its syrupy licking. The mutant dragon still guarded the tunnel, like a giant terrier watching a rabbit hole, whilst it tended its wounds.

'Won't it get eaten?' Caspar was concerned that the pet reptile was about to become a tasty morsel and vanish into the monster's fetid maw.

The waiting seemed interminable. Caspar was close to despair when he felt a sudden rush in his veins. The mixed sensations of fear and excitement overwhelmed him. His hand was trembling even though his fist was closed tightly around the hazel mandala, so tightly that the tips of the five-pointed star dug into his flesh. Only when the walls of their narrow fissure were fully washed in the brightness of the glowing moonstone did he relax, knowing that it was the power of the orb that had disturbed his senses.

'Well done, my little dragon,' Brid mumbled as the salamander appeared, backing up the tunnel in a curious waddle and dragging the ball of white flame. The moonstone was still girdled in the leather netting and the creature gripped the straps firmly between its teeth. 'I knew you'd find it. I knew you'd find the stone of white fire.'

The ground shook as falling boulders crashed about their ears. A spray of caustic slime spat from the gaping maw of the dragon as its tongue lashed out towards them. Its shoulders rammed into the fissure walls, which were crumbling beneath its pressure. The furious scream hammered at Caspar's ears sending him reeling and senseless.

He snatched an arrow from his quiver and fumbled to notch it to his bow-string. The Vaalakans had brought this animal down once before, piercing the soft tissue beneath its throat. All he needed was the right opportunity and a lucky shot. Brid sheltered her head from falling debris as dislodged dust and shards of rock showered down from the roof of the caves. She shouted at him to flee the caves but Caspar wouldn't. He had this one opportunity to finally slay the beast.

The dragon howled, frantically thrashing its head back and forth, its white scales tearing away more and more of the rock. Its falcate claw stove through the jagged hole and raked at Brid, shredding a gash in her leather breeches before hooking into her boot and pinning her leg to the rocky floor. Caspar raised his bow as the monster flung back its snout, preparing to use its warty nose as a hammer against the rock.

'No!' Brid suddenly shouted. 'No, don't do it, Spar.' She flung her hand towards him and he grabbed her, pulling hard. Her body was drawn taut between him and the dragon's claw. 'Don't kill him, Spar. He's kept Keridwen alive all this time with his heat. He got the Eye back from that evil woman and kept Keridwen alive. We can't kill him.' She fumbled for her scrip and reached for the smaller moonstone that Ulf had carried and flung it at the monster's lidded eyes. It thudded against the scaly snout. The animal sharply withdrew and poised its flaring nostrils over the small moonstone lying at its feet. Wrapping his tongue tenderly around it he drew back, gripping it delicately between his vast saw-teeth fangs. A soft purring fluttered in his craw. An instant later he roared with rage, spitting out the orb and crushing it beneath his disappointed feet but Brid had already wriggled back beyond his reach.

'Quick, he's already realized it's not the real Druid's Eye,' Caspar warned.

Brid stooped quickly to reach for the larger moonstone, only to be repelled with a snarling hiss from the salamander. She snatched back her hand in surprise.

'Give it to me!' she demanded as if she were talking to an untrained puppy. 'Drop it! Now!' The spiny ruff around its neck bristled threateningly and with its grim red snout clamped to the leash of the moonstone, the salamander stared back defiantly.

'It loves fire.' Brid shrugged apologetically to the impatient youth. 'And the pure white fire of the orb is its greatest prize.'

'Well, we can't wait for an over-grown toad,' Caspar objected, shouting above the roars of the dragon and looking fearfully along the crumbling fissure. Why didn't she let me kill the monster? I might have killed it once and for all.

Brid pounced at the fire-drake but this time the salamander rapidly retreated, dragging its passion with it. At least it scurried further away from the frenzied roar of the leviathan lizard. 'Come on, little fellow.' Her voice was sweet and enticing, though she spoke through tight, unsmiling lips. 'Come on, give it to me.' The creature backed off.

Caspar solved the problem by taking a headlong dive at the animal and just managed to grab its squirming tail. The tail was all the boy could get a firm grip on and he needed both hands to stop the salamander wriggling free. He lifted it up into the air and its red body was stretched taut by the weight of the moonstone, which it stubbornly refused to relinquish. With the creature in one hand and the incandescent globe in the other, Caspar ran after Brid as they fled from the fissure and sprinted towards the safety of the bright daylight.

'There little fellow, I won't take it away from you,' Brid soothed as she took the moonstone from Caspar and hung it round her neck. The salamander wormed into the folds of her shirt to snuggle against the orb.

By the time they reached the horses, Caspar was panting breathlessly and his lungs hurt with the effort. He flung himself into Firecracker's saddle and led the other horse the few paces back to reach Brid. Within seconds they were in the broad open daylight where they knew the dragon with its sickly-white scales couldn't follow, as they raced over the down-land above the cliffs, strips of turf flying from the horses' hooves. The sound of an earth-shaking roar and then a heavy splash far below made Caspar wheel his colt in a tight circle. He turned to see the white humps of the dragon's back porcpiscing through the waves and one last flick of its barbed tail before it dived down into the depths of the sea and was gone.

'I had a chance. I had a chance to kill it once and for all.' Caspar turned furiously on the Maiden, as she drew up next to him, panting heavily. 'Why the hell did you stop me?'

She was unruffled by his anger. 'I didn't think it was right.'

'You didn't think it was right! That evil monster has tracked us all the way from Vaalaka just to get the moonstone. How it got it, I can't imagine.'

'I should think bits of Puzella are somewhere inside its belly,' the girl remarked lightly.

'How can you be so unconcerned about the beast? I should have killed it.'

Suddenly Brid shouted at him, 'I just didn't think it was right. I'm sorry, Spar, it just seemed he'd rescued it for us. He nested with the Egg, giving his heat to Keridwen, keeping her alive. I couldn't repay him by killing him.'

Caspar was shocked into silence. Brid had never shouted at

him before and it made him feel small and insignificant – just like Hal did sometimes. Sulkily he turned his back and rode northwards.

Hal's olive eyes met his, brimming with questions. With his hand clutched to his injured side, the raven-haired youth raised himself up, wincing. 'Well, did you get it?'

Caspar grunted and dropped off Firecracker's back. 'Yes,' he panted, and briefly explained about the dragon.

'It's gone now, hasn't it?' Brid added in relief. 'It plunged away into the sea.' She dropped down to sit cross-legged with the moonstone cradled in her lap.

Suddenly all thoughts of the dragon washed away from Caspar's mind. Throughout their journey the moonstone had been shielded in cooling cloth or shrouded in smoke, its full energy kept contained, but now the pulsating rays reached out to touch him.

'Are you going to look?' he whispered, sitting next to Brid.

A pout formed on Brid's dark red lips. 'We'll wait until nightfall and the magical protection of the moon, just to be on the safe side.'

The Maiden rose and went straight to attend to Ceowulf. With his right arm in a sling, taking the weight off his splintered collar-bone the knight was now at least able to sit upright. Ceowulf accepted without question that Brid's herb-lore was far beyond the capabilities of any physician they might find in Caldea and they all agreed it would be safer to stay hidden in the thicket.

'And I'm not presenting myself to my father weak and crippled and penniless like this,' the knight declared defiantly. He pushed away Cybillia's hand and the spoonful of rabbit broth that she was trying to coax into his mouth. The bramble-strewn valleys of the downs were riddled with warrens and, with her mountain-lore and natural stealth, Brid had proved far better than Caspar at snaring rabbits. The priestess seasoned the meat with her healing herbs but left the patient task of feeding the injured knight to the golden-haired Cybillia.

Caspar looked from the black destrier to the chequered red

and white war-cloth rolled up as a cushion beneath the knight's head. 'But I presumed you had already been to your father's . . .'

Ceowulf shook his head. 'With nothing to show for myself after all these years? Never! No, I went to an old friend, an old retainer in the marshes. He slipped into Tartra for me. I still have some friends there, but I couldn't face my father, not any more.'

'No,' Cybillia murmured with understanding.

Caspar sat back against the bole of a tree and sucked at a dry stem of grass, passing the hours until sundown. 'And what made you track us down and follow us to Caldea? I mean how did you know we needed help?' he asked, hoping that Ceowulf at last felt well enough to answer his questions.

The knight smiled and started to laugh but the movement stabbed at his wound and he spluttered for a moment before regaining his composure. 'Two hare-brained, reckless lads like you and Hal, you were bound to run into trouble. I thought you'd kill each other first with your heady tempers though, rather than wait for Gatto and the Vaalakans to get a good swipe at you.'

'No, seriously,' Caspar insisted.

'Well, Cybillia suddenly vanished, and the King never found Gatto so I guessed he was still after you.' Ceowulf fingered the bandage strapped across his upper ribcage and shifted himself round to lie on his other hip to avoid cramp. 'I knew Hal's mother was in Farona so I tracked her down, and I'm telling you, it took me ages to get her to say where you'd gone. She's very protective, Hal.'

'I'm surprised you managed at all,' the dark youth laughed.

'Maybe I've got more charm than looks. She made me promise to keep an eye on your affections for a certain young lady,' Ceowulf lowered his voice and nodded towards Brid. Hal flushed. Caspar swallowed hard, trying to disguise his jealousy as he caught his uncle's eye.

The dancing reflection of the moon shimmered on the rippling waves. Brid murmured a prayer towards the light, her face like ivory bathed in the silvery beams. Reverently she lifted the opaque sphere of the Druid's Eye to her mouth and spoke into its heart. 'Morrigwen!'

Whenever Caspar had touched the bare surface of the stone, a blinding flash like lightning had punched into his brain, seizing his mind with a shattering pain. But Brid showed not even the barest signs of discomfort and he was surprised at how confidently she handled the magical orb. Silver rays from the moon overhead stretched down and blessed the surface of the stone. Slowly the creamy surface rippled and melted away to reveal a clear watery scene. At first, Caspar thought he was seeing the reflection of the Caldean moon in the translucent surface but gradually the outline of craggy peaks and the spiralling towers of a fortress formed in the image. He was glimpsing the northern moon above the towers of Torra Alta.

In the black night, dark orange flames lapped at the buttresses that anchored the castle to the peak of the Tor. Billowing smoke drifted up to cloud the face of the moon. The west tower was a giant torch of flame.

Talons of fear seized Caspar's heart.

'Morrigwen, hear me.' As Brid summoned the old Crone, the image in the moonstone swept up through the canyon. The boy felt his eyes were being carried on the wings of a hawk as they swooped through the air towards a low arrow-slit in the central keep. The vision slid through the narrow window and fell on the haggard face of the old Crone, which glowed and flickered in the reflection of the fire. Her speckled-blue eyes seemed huge as they stared out of her withered face. Her parchment skin was stretched over the jutting ridges of her cheekbones and deep hollows had formed beneath the thin skin at her temples. Caspar thought, with horror, that she looked a hundred years older than when he had last seen her. Brid's eyes filled with tears.

Have you found it yet. The Crone's mouth moved but Caspar heard the words only in his mind.

Brid shook her head.

There's been a fire. I'm weak, too weak. You must find the cauldron quickly. I will not last much longer; I need your power, Brid. I need your herblore to save me. Vaalakan fang-nettle. I fear I am poisoned.

'Fang-nettle! Are you sure?' The Maiden sounded shocked and disbelieving as she addressed the Crone's image in the moonstone.

Morrigwen merely nodded heavily.

'Then take some bladderdock and foxleaf,' Brid advised urgently.

I have, child, but I need more, much more and we have run out of foxleaf. The poison is deep in my veins. Hurry, child, hurry. Find the cauldron and return with its secrets before it's too late.

As Brid nodded, the vision in the moonstone shimmered and faded. Desperate not to lose sight of his homeland, Caspar snatched the white sphere from Brid's hand. A searing white bolt of light shattered his thoughts; the muscles in his body seized into spasm, arching his back with the pain but he fought back against it.

Brid touched his arm and the blazing white agony dissipated like lightning being absorbed into the earth. 'Spar, be careful; you're not trained for the power in the stone.'

'Mother,' he pleaded, looking deep into the heart of the sphere. 'Mother, where are you?'

The fine-boned features of a beautiful woman with violet eyes and a wealth of rich auburn hair curling to her shoulders smiled out of the stone. *Spar,* she whispered in his mind. *Spar, my child.* Her soundless words were filled with love. *Find the cauldron; uncover the runes, Spar.* The clear image lasted only a second before it gradually frosted over. As the colour sapped from her cheeks her eyes glazed to a deathly grey. Her hands shrivelled up into pain-racked claws and her mouth opened in a muted scream. The agonized echo of her pain shrieked through Caspar's brain and tore into his heart.

The image faded from view as ripples of white smoothed over the stone's surface.

Caspar choked back the tears that stung at the corners of his eyes, while Brid slid the moonstone back into its pouch and hung the precious sphere around her neck. She let out a deep breath as if to forcibly expel her terrors before fumbling with the ties on her herb scrip. Tipping out the contents, she searched through her supply of nettles, henbane, comfrey, fennel, feverfew and rue along with many other plants and roots that Caspar did not recognize. 'Bladderdock but no fox-leaf,' she announced with forced calm. 'I'm going to look for some in the moonlight.' She coughed to chase away the sobs that threatened to grip her throat. 'We must go on at first light. Morrigwen is dying.'

Chapter 34

The glow was wrong. It smelt wrong.

The small dimly glowing pebble had confused him for only a moment. He thought it was his glow but it wasn't. It didn't have the same power or energy. There was no woman inside who spoke to him. It was empty and lifeless. He sniffed at the remains of the pebble he had ground to dust beneath his mighty weight. His glow had gone. The naked bears had taken it again, out into the scorching heat that fell from the great emptiness above.

He threw his snout up and bellowed until the earth trembled around him. The cave was cool but restrictive and lacked the freedom of the big wide water. He sniffed the air and tasted the salt. The sea was calling to him.

He could track the little bears but that meant forever hiding in the caverns and stealing out to scavenge for what little food there was here. The waves at least were teeming with life. He didn't need the glow out there in the cool freedom of the vast water. And in the water he could almost fly.

Suddenly he yearned for the waves and the freedom of the deep.

He knew the other beings were out there, somewhere far from the shore in the deep waters. The big monsters called to him. He had heard their wailing song sough through the ocean. He would be free at last out there where the naked bears couldn't go. He pushed the thought of the glow from his mind. He couldn't reach it. The burning in the emptiness above thwarted him. Now the freedom of the cool waves beckoned him. There were big creatures out there, maybe not Fire Beings, but there were other big creatures out there like himself.

He slid into the water and struck out for the western oceans.

Chapter 35

From afar the dark impenetrable green of the wintry yews had seemed untouchable, unreachable, as if the shrouds of mist surrounding the ancient forest had stolen away the intervening ground. In its place swirled the insubstantial stuff of dreams. On the higher ground, tails of mist were fleeing before the warmth of the morning sun only to be scattered by the briny breeze murmuring in whispers off the sea. Now only the occasional drifts of wraith-like mist remained trapped in the glades and along the paths of the forest. Where the wind snatched at the ground-hugging cloud, it whirled up into plumes like the manes and tails of ivory horses galloping into the wind. To Caspar it was a world of phantoms and will-o'-the-wisps.

Accompanied by the faithful Trog, the three Torra Altans had left Ceowulf in Cybillia's care and headed up along the downs towards the forest. At first Hal had taken the lead as they threaded through the vineyards but when they began to skirt the edge of the dark yews he had relinquished the initiative to Brid. She seemed anxiously pensive and kicked impatiently with her heels, distracted by her thoughts. She usually rode gracefully, hardly disturbing the horse in its natural gait, but now she fidgeted fractiously on the back of Ceowulf's black destrier.

When they reached the place where the peaks of the Hespera Isles aligned with the wide-spread boughs of the yew, Brid dismounted. Kneeling on the ground, she closed her fist around the horse's jawbone that she had struck into the soil several days beforehand. She paused, listening, then pressed her palms to the ground. Like a physician feeling for the beat in a patient's heart, she turned her head sideways in concentration, listening for any mystical vibrations pulsing through the energy line in the Earth's crust. Pouting with displeasure, she wrenched the jawbone from the earth and tucked the toothed bone into her belt like a dagger.

'There's no one here,' she said flatly, trying to hide her disappointment behind her loose hair that curled about her face. 'Not a soul.' She remounted before nudging Sorcerer between the dark green branches and led the two youths into the dark of the forest.

Caspar glanced anxiously around him, suddenly aware of the hushed stillness in the ghostly mist-shrouded woods. He felt like an intruder hammering on the doors of a temple of silent worship.

'What do you mean, there's no one here? Are you saying this is just another wild goose chase?' Hal asked irritably, shattering the silence.

'I don't know; we have to look. But if there were anyone here with the mystical knowledge to read the runes they would certainly have sensed the power in a horse's jawbone cutting into a cursor like that. Either they've fled or the Inquisitors have found them.'

'Or more likely they were never even here in the first place,' Hal remarked sceptically.

'Your wound is making you bitter, Hal,' Caspar rebuked his uncle. 'We've got to look.'

'You haven't lost a finger; you've got no right to judge my wounds.'

'At least you slew that vile Ulf; that's got to be worth losing a finger for.'

Hal grinned. 'I'd have given my whole hand to kill him.' His smile flattened. 'But I'd give my whole *arm* to kill the man behind him. Ulf never had enough wit to team up with the Vaalakans on his own initiative. Someone else was directing him.'

'Dunnock?' Caspar didn't need to wait for Hal to dismiss the idea. He knew the curate was not a strong enough character to incite such malice.

'Too much has happened since he died. Too many things that can't be explained. There's someone else behind it all.'

The woods were silent. The oppressive stillness railed against the muffled thudding of the horses' hooves on the soft leaf mould. Brid was silent too. In the dark of the forest, the path ahead was obscured by the twisted boughs that coiled and spiralled out from the corded trunks. The roots of the oldest yews were split, revealing their hollow dying cores, and they rested their tired branches on the ground like drowsy old men leaning on their elbows.

'Old, old trees,' Brid sighed, 'thousands of years old. They remember how the world used to be.'

It was slow going brushing through the trees, meandering between the coiling boughs, turning and twisting, weaving back and forth, on and on through the deepening umbra. The silence prickled at Caspar's neck. He wished they'd stumble on a trail with at least some sense of direction rather than maundering helplessly at the whim of the forest's secret ways. Still he trusted Brid enough to follow her as she chose each turn with confidence. Trog trotted devotedly at her horse's heels.

'Are you sure you know where you're going, Brid?' Hal asked for the third time, in one of his more acerbic tones. 'I'm sure we've passed this tree before.'

'Have we?' Brid demanded, turning on Caspar. 'Or are we still going due east?'

'We're going east,' Caspar affirmed, reluctantly being drawn in as arbitrator.

'You always take her side and you're only saying that because you want to please her. None of us can see the sun so you can't know. I think we're lost.'

'Well, you're wrong,' the freckled youth contradicted.

'Brid might be wrong. She's not always right, you know, nephew.'

'She's more right than you are.'

'Everybody knows that men have a better sense of direction than girls,' the darker youth retorted.

'Well, when you become a man we'll put it to the test, shall we?' Brid said lightly.

'Well, at least I will be a man, but you'll always be a maid. No man would take your lashing tongue and pig-headedness.'

Brid just laughed, carefree and untroubled by the youth's denigrating scorn. Her laughter seemed to be trapped beneath the canopy of dark, thickly meshed leaves. The branches intertwined as if shielding the travellers in their haven, like fledglings beneath the wing of a great bird, guarding them from the harshness of the outside world.

A musty smell was shortening Caspar's breath. In the lull of the forest he felt drowsy as if there were no urgency, no pressing need. He felt seduced into believing that they could wander through the trees forever and that it simply wouldn't matter – that nothing would ever change.

'I know,' Brid said, swiftly tuning in on his thoughts. 'It's hypnotic. The breath from the yews steals your mind. You can get drugged asleep by it. You don't even need to eat their berries to lead you quickly to Annwyn. The yew is the tree of eternity, the everlasting tree that leads us through the full cycle of life to be reborn again – and so on and on, forever. Time moves more slowly here. Yews do not understand that time passes, that there is a today or a tomorrow, because when tomorrow comes it is not the future but the present relived. Tomorrow is just today again.'

The ground dipped gradually away but the slope was so shallow that Caspar was unaware of the gradient at first. As the slope steepened, Firecracker picked up his hooves to avoid the exposed tree roots where running rainwater had leached away the soil. Caspar had a definite sense that they were descending into a dell even though the closeness of the trees made it difficult to orientate himself. The further they penetrated the dell, the more Caspar felt uncomfortably trapped. Born and raised in the heights of Torra Alta, he had a natural affinity for high places in the wide-open air and his instinct made him distrust the confined valley.

The trees seemed to be getting older. Their dusty brown bark was peeling away in long strips and, where their boughs lazed on the ground, they had re-rooted to rise up into fresh branches. Caspar could sense the life-blood of the trees pumping out into the forest, a very slow, deep, booming pulse that seemed to vibrate through his whole body. The air was gradually thickening as drifts of cloud lazed along the path. He pulled up sharply: a wall of mist barred the way ahead.

Without hesitation Brid slid into the mist, as if slipping through a veiled and secret doorway. Within seconds she was absorbed into the esoteric heart of the ancient wood. Totally trusting, the white terrier plunged in after her but Caspar hesitated. He saw the mist as an impenetrable shield. The air around the white shroud was cold and seemingly unnatural. It lurked like the breath of a ghostly dragon, drugging them and luring them forward to be swallowed up and lost forever in its timeless obscurity.

'I don't like the smell of this place,' Hal whispered, his breath chilling on the cool air and mingling with the white fog before them. 'The air tastes stale and it feels like the fog is hiding something.'

'Something big – and fierce – and sleeping. And the fog is warning us to keep away lest we wake the thing into wrath,' Caspar suggested, tightening his rein on Firecracker.

'I didn't say that,' Hal protested with a half-laugh. 'It just smells of death.'

'Like walking into fog and being caught in the spirit-world between life and death, forever trapped and lost in this timeless forest. That's what it feels like to me.'

'Well, nephew, you always were excessively fanciful. I personally don't want to walk into a trap; I can't see anything through *that*.' The dark youth waved his hand towards the dense mist. 'There could be a whole troop of Vaalakans for all we know.'

From somewhere far away, Brid's voice called out like a song from the speck of a lark singing high up in the sky, the

573

clear notes soaring in the wide heavens thrilling the air. Her voice was beautifully clear yet mysteriously distant. Hal and Caspar looked at each other and then tentatively pushed into the mist; but not before Hal had drawn his runesword.

The fog muffled every sound so that only Caspar's immediate world was audible. Firecracker's hoof-beats were dampened and distant, like the slow beat of a drum from beyond the horizon. But in comparison the horse's breathing was loud, smothering his ears as if the sound was unable to escape through the dense fog, clinging to him as they glided through the damp cloud. The boy turned his head to look for the reassurance of his uncle's presence but he could see nothing but a faint glowing line. The runesword, he thought. The mist seemed to go on forever. With no reference to time or distance he felt as if he'd been swimming through it for hour upon hour; but at the same time it might have been no more than moments as each step seemed to cover identical ground.

Was the fog getting thicker, he asked himself, beginning to have the eerie feeling that he wasn't passing through the mist but that it was passing through him. The vapour seemed to fill his mouth, probe his nostrils and worm into his tear ducts. It crept behind his eyes to wander and swirl through his mind, exploring the possibilities, the thoughts, the meanings.

Eerie feelings and strange emotions suddenly possessed Caspar's mind and he struggled to gain control of these irrational thoughts. He felt as if he had fallen asleep and a strange nightmare had flooded into his mind. He shook his head vigorously to rid himself of the images, but the thoughts remained. Suddenly he realized that they didn't belong to him at all. Someone else's thoughts intruded into his head, as if they had crept in with the mist, sliding into his brain and dancing unbidden with his own thoughts to disturb his mind. He couldn't recognize the pattern, didn't understand the words, until suddenly he realized they weren't words at all but sensations, savage broken snatches of thought rudely formed into an idea. The thoughts were too basic to describe in words but he understood them to be something like panic, hunger or lust. But all the ideas captured something driving or searching: an urgency, a determination, a wildness of spirit; the yearning to be free like water pouring from a fall or the wind sweeping over plains. The thoughts were blunt and harsh. Their savage intensity had the same depth of emotion as anger or hatred but these wants and desires pertained only to a determination to be free.

Caspar could hardly grasp the simplicity of it, the purity of the thought, until gradually it drifted into his mind that the ideas weren't from Hal or Brid but came from Firecracker. He smoothed the horse's mane. For a very fleeting moment he sensed a flicker of communication as the horse's mind acknowledged something weak and burdensome, something that the animal didn't understand. There was no resentment and yet no love. Nothing as complicated could be formed by these wispy thoughts. They were too simple, too plain, just basic acknowledgement, nothing more.

In an instant the thoughts were gone. The animal's mind was away, struggling against the close confinement of the woods and the fog, crying for wide hot plains that swept from one horizon to the next. Caspar realized with amazement that the image couldn't have come from the horse's memory but was something even more atavistic, carried in his instinct from the distant homeland of his fore-sires.

A burst of rushed ideas, one pouring in on top of the other, scrambled the simplicity of the horse's nebulous notions. These ones were involved, asking questions and answering them in the same shred of mist. Where? When? Why? How? Over and over again, puzzling and explaining, as the tumble of reasoning formulated full and structured patterns. There was fear, as with the horse, but fears of many things complicated by a perception of time – fears from yesterday, fears of today and more, many more, fears for tomorrow. What will happen if we fail? What will happen if we succeed? Is there danger? Why is the fog here? Why are these alien thoughts in my head? There was a realization, a comprehension there as if Hal's mind had said: 'Oh, it's you.'

Caspar understood these thoughts. He instantly knew it was Hal. He wasn't surprised by the cold jealousy; the hard driving force; the speed at which one emotion rolled over in Hal's mind to become another. He understood the mercurial, ever-changing shape of his uncle's feelings. There were feelings of resentment and gratitude, jealousy and love, an overwhelming protectiveness that hugged and embraced him. Yet there was bitterness, unresigned and unresolved that galled and soured the edges of his shield of guardianship. Their thoughts touched in simple recognition – hello friend – warmth in the recognition and comfort in the familiar.

A different character of thought pattern was easing into Caspar's mind. There was a complexity, a churning whirlpool of thoughts, much like Hal's with each thought tripping over another – except these didn't ask questions. They had no need to ask questions, as if all the answers in the world were already known. But like Firecracker's, the hectic thoughts were impossible to bind into words, seemingly immeasurable and irresolutely wild. They were savage, like a carnivore living on the hungry borders of the wastelands in the downside of winter: a dreadful fearsome savagery sharpened by desperation. The power of such, natural, basic instincts was not born out of fear or the need for freedom, like the instincts of the horse, but out of love. The love was so pure, so uncompromised and so fulfilling, a love that overwhelmed all other thoughts swimming through Caspar's mind. It was so vast, so bright and – to him – so unimaginable that the shock of its force seemed to burn his mind. He reeled away unprepared for the enormity and strength of the girl's mind.

The intense searing whiteness faded and was replaced by laughter as happy and as carefree as a stream in a meadow, gaily wending towards the waters of the sea. It gave the sense that, like the stream, there were no doubts in her future. Come waterfall or weir, mill or maelstrom, the stream would return to the sea, just as she would return to the womb of the Mother. The ideas laughed, suddenly moulding into comprehensible thoughts and with a soothing stroke Brid whispered in his mind, 'I'm sorry; I didn't mean to hurt you. I never want to hurt you. Come on, hurry, hurry through the woods. Morrigwen needs us and we must reach the cauldron before it's too late. Hurry, for Morrigwen's sake, hurry.'

Again he felt the love of companionship and protection but nothing fiercer, nothing hotter. Her love was smooth and warm, deep and comforting but not the love between man and woman. She whispered again, 'I'm sorry, Spar; I never meant to hurt you.' And then the thoughts danced away into their savage wildness, too close to nature and the elements to be understood by the boy.

Firecracker abruptly halted, making Caspar lurch forward onto his red mane. The stallion snatched at the bit and threw his head up, flattening his ears as if startled by something in the mist. The horse's panic flared up into the boy's mind and through Firecracker's nebulous images he touched the ghost of a savage thought that snarled up out of the mist. The untamed savagery of the thought was too bestial for him to comprehend but, he felt the mind of his domesticated horse shrink from the barbaric brutality of the threat.

A flash of claw and tooth, of thunderous hooves, vast wings and conical horns leapt into Firecracker's mind. The panicked colt threw up his head and shrieked, his muscles trembling as if he had sensed a pride of starving lions. Caspar felt they were being stalked. That same eerie feeling had crept through Caspar's bones once before, when he had been unnerved by the cackling magpie in Oldhart Forest. Again he sensed he was being followed but he told himself firmly that the feeling was too distant, too insubstantial to be anything more than the fear created in his horse's mind.

'It's probably only a branch or something, Cracker. You're always mistaking them for monsters,' he told the horse decisively, whilst struggling to shake away the haunting sensation that something hovered just behind his back.

The unearthly feeling was exorcized by a scatter of playful thoughts that leapt and danced in his mind, chasing and snuffling through his own ideas and embracing the comfort of close companionship. 'Trog?' Caspar murmured in his head and the thoughts raced with excitement. Compared to the untamed heart of his horse, these thoughts delighted in human contact. Though the boy couldn't form the thoughts into language, he clearly understood the emotions of the animal and sensed a mutual communication. A flash of a curved tree-root formed a picture in his mind and the dog's thoughts leapt to examine the suspiciously snake-like object. Disappointed, Trog's mind infused back into his thoughts to curl up alongside the boy's warm emotions.

The images drifted away like a dream falling to the back of the mind, stowed into the deeper lower layers to sleep whilst the rest of the mind woke from its slumber. The mist was clearing ahead. Nebulous drifts and curling fronds formed swirling veils of haze, which were dispersed by the stirring of cool fresh air, and suddenly he passed out of the cloud and into a large clearing. The mysterious mist still surrounded them, but here in the glade the air was clear. Caspar drew his sleeve across his face to wipe away the foggy dew, which had condensed on his skin and soaked his hair, before taking in his surroundings.

Sealed in secrecy by the forbidding mist that encircled it and cradled right in the heart of the ancient yew forest, the clearing held at its centre a wonderfully diverse collection of trees. The circular grove was stocked with various trees of power and magic, resplendent in their late autumn robes before the bare starvation of winter: holly, hazel, alder, ash, hawthorn, oak, honeysuckle, willow, furze, rowan, blackthorn, birch, and beech. Simple trees, which through his childhood Caspar had hardly considered, but now he was struck by the symmetry and proportion of each specimen as his senses awoke to their natural powers.

Within the circle of thirteen trees and placed toward each of the four winds, smoked four cauldrons. Each poured out a thick cloud that blended into the mist surrounding the clearing, effusing the air with a heady smoke of hazel and rowan. He knew the rowan was there for protection against evil enchantment, but struggled to remember what power was locked in the hazel. Brid had told him once. That was it: intuition, for enhancing the inner power of the mind. Maybe that was what stirred the mysterious blending of thoughts in the mist.

In the centre of the clearing, suspended from the ancient boughs of an oak, swung an immense cauldron. It was not a kitchen cauldron, nor even a herbalist's cauldron, but a vast vessel so full in girth that if all three of them were to join hands they would only just encircle it. The supporting oak was bowed under the weight, creaking and moaning as the great cauldron rocked on its handle. A single spray of mistletoe dangled above it and gouged into the bark of the oak were ugly designs, depicting the faces of trolls and goblins that glared accusingly at Caspar.

The cauldron was richly decorated with a frieze, etched and moulded on the black metal. Its rim recorded a chase: a wild stag, with antlers lowered, coursed hounds that fled before him around the pot. But as Caspar paced around the cauldron, the hunted turned hunter, and the hounds snapped at the stag's heels in an eternal circle of life and death. Below the stag and hounds ran the symbols of the sun and the moon, in her many phases; and carved around the sun and two full moons was a series of runes.

Below the celestial Gods a simple circle of waves girthed the pot. Cramped up and crushed beneath the waves, another frieze of animals was immortalized in the design. All were legendary beasts: dragons, wyverns, griffins, sea serpents, trolls, winged horses, unicorns, all battling and tearing at each other.

Beneath the monsters an etched pattern of flames leapt up from the base of the pot, like tongues of fire, so that the beasts were imprisoned between the two opposing elements. The bottom of the pot was smothered in a thick layer of soot. It smeared and coated the etched images in the metal where the real flames had leaped up from the fire and lapped at the underside of the cauldron.

From beneath the roots of the willow a shallow stream

slipped out of the mist to enter the secluded grove. It explored the foot of the oak before winding towards the beech and flowing gracefully back into the shrouding mist. Alongside the stream a wooden spoon, the size of a stave, lay discarded on the ground. Its handle was decorated with runespells whittled out of the wood and the discoloured head of the ladle showed where it had been dipped into a deeply coloured brew. Beneath the singed cauldron lay a bed of grey cinders on blackened charcoal. Brid knelt to put her hand into the ashes.

'They're cold,' she said flatly. 'I told you they'd gone.' As she looked at the complex patterns on the cauldron her face showed the first signs of trepidation. 'How could they have abandoned their holy duty? Even faced with the Inquisitors, they should have remained to the last to protect the cauldron. I need them to help me understand the runes.'

All three stepped slowly round, their disappointed eyes searching forlornly for any signs of the Keepers in the deserted grove.

'They can't have gone long; the other cauldrons are still smoking,' Hal said logically.

'Those fires will burn for many days yet,' Brid corrected him. 'They're smothered in moss, which means there'll be a lot of smoke but no fire.'

'Why on earth would anyone put wood in a cauldron rather than burn it underneath?' Caspar asked, as he tried to fight down his disappointment.

'Why?' Brid repeated incredulously. She seemed too distracted to bother with unknowledgeable questions. 'To make the smoke of course. But now we will just have to decipher the symbols for ourselves. But first I must see to Morrigwen before we worry with the runes. One of you fetch me a log to stand on so I can see into the cauldron.'

Standing on tip-toe on her yew log, she peered into the depths of the black pot. 'Morrigwen,' she whispered. Her voice was distant and hollow as it echoed through the vast belly of the cauldron. She struggled with the salamander and finally managed to break its grip on the moonstone's leather leash.

She slipped the orb out of its latticed net. 'Here, Hal, I can't reach. Place this in the bottom for me.' The youth leant over into the black depths of the pot and placed the moonstone on the smooth rounded base. It rolled back and forth for a moment, its white light illuminating the girl's anxious face. Caspar had found his own log and stared into the depths expectantly.

Though none of them touched it, the moonstone was already alive with images.

'It's the power of the cauldron,' Brid whispered reverently. 'It reaches out along the lines of power that run through the Earth.'

'That's the glacier,' Caspar cried. 'The glacier in Vaalaka, where–where– ' His voice faltered. Where his mother was entombed, he thought bitterly.

'Of course. Keridwen is incarcerated right by that cairn, which marks a confluence of power lines.'

'And Torra Alta,' Hal murmured as the image swooped away from the ice-bound north, south towards the snow-capped Yellow Mountains.

'Mmm, Torra Alta lies on one of the same major cursors, of course. All places of significance lie on energy lines. Just like this spot here. That's one reason why the Keepers would have chosen it.'

As the image hovered above the smoking tower of the fortress, Brid's eyes narrowed with concentration. 'Morrigwen, hear me.'

Caspar found his eyes drawn to the seething mass of warriors howling around the foot of the Tor. Teams of trolls strained at their harnesses as they struggled to drag vast wooden war machines, slings and catapults towards the outer ramparts. They were not short of ammunition. Blocks of masonry dragged from the cathedral foundations seemed almost tailor-made for their purposes as the shot was fired at the castle walls.

Caspar had the uncomfortable feeling that the one true God was conspiring with the Vaalakans against the stronghold of the Mother. Though clouds of dust spat from the mortar, no masonry fell away from Torra Alta's protected walls. The Runes of War held fast. A burst of yellow sulphur-bombs and a hail of arrows drove the troll teams and siege-engines back beyond their effective range.

Caspar sighed with relief. He looked up to study Brid's face to share his sense of victory but the girl's face was deeply perplexed. 'She won't answer me. Morrigwen!' she shouted. Her voice hammered the walls of the cauldron like a metal clapper. 'Morrigwen, hear me.'

The image swooped towards the lower arrow-slit in the buttressed walls of the keep. The shutter on a latched window suddenly burst open. They looked into a dimly lit chamber where a girl sat on the edge of a fur-covered pallet. She snapped up her head, her rich brown curls dancing around her shoulders, and stared wildly around the room, clutching a shawl fearfully around her neck. 'Who's there? What do you want?' Her big, darting eyes were startled.

'May. It's Wystan's daughter, May,' Caspar exclaimed. The girl's eyes flitted round the room as if sensing their presence.

Brid pouted thoughtfully. 'Merrymoon, can you hear me?'

May suddenly stared straight out of the moonstone into their eyes as if she had finally located them. Her mouth moved and Caspar heard her words in his head. *How do you know my name? Brid? Brid, is that you or am I dreaming? Brid, help us: Morrigwen is dying.*

'Hold her hand, Merrymoon and turn her face towards me.'

Caspar's eyes stared in horror at the shrunken skeleton. The old Crone lay so lightly on the pillow that she hardly left an impression. Dark blue bruises covered her eyelids and every bone of her jaw and cheeks strained through her gossamer skin, like a rotting corpse. Her thick silvery hair was now a thin wispy straw, the ash-white scalp of her skull glowing through what was left of her tattered strands. There was no colour in her skin and her forehead was beaded with a cold sweat.

'Morrigwen,' Brid called out softly. 'Morrigwen, reach out to me.' Her voice caught in her throat and her green eyes sparkled with tears.

She hasn't spoken for days. May looked at them heavily. *The bladderdock and foxleaf have done nothing. They didn't save Catrik either.*

'Catrik?' Hal asked urgently.

May nodded. *He's dead.*

Dead. The word dragged like a lead chain around Caspar's neck, drawing him further into the depths of despair.

Brid wriggled to reach her herb scrip and fumbled to open the ties. With a shaking hand she extracted the broad, pale green leaves of bladderdock and the soft-stemmed foxleaf with its distinctive feathering of reddish hairs on its falcate leaves that she had gathered the previous night. Caspar sensed her urgency: Catrik was already dead.

'Hal, reach the Eye for me again and, Spar, stand directly opposite me.' She tied the herbs into a chain and crowned the orb with them. 'Spar, help me hold the Eye here in the cauldron and summon your mother.'

Caspar hesitated, fearful of raising his mother's half-dead image in the ghostly orb. He remembered the pain it induced in the depths of his mind.

Brid held the sphere in her palm. The white surface shimmered with raw energy as the Maiden lightly touched her fingertips to the Druid's Eye.

'Keridwen, Keridwen, hear me!' she demanded impatiently, not waiting for Caspar's help. The white clouds scudded furiously over the surface of the stone, as if driven by a storm, but the magical orb remained cloaked in its dead-white pall. 'Quickly, Spar; Morrigwen is dying!'

With his fingers feathering Brid's hand, the pain of the white hot energy that would have seethed through his brain was channelled away by Brid, freeing his mind to pierce the depths of the crystal. The likeness of his mother was immediately vivid and her frozen face leapt out at them, her whole screaming mouth filling the image and they stared deep into her blue throat. Her scream shrieked out like an agonized vixen from the depths of the crystal and Caspar recoiled from the pain.

'Keep calm, Spar,' Brid urged him fiercely. 'Keep calm. It's the power of the cauldron intensifying the image.'

'Mother, Mother,' he cried, tears rolling down his nose and sizzling on the surface of the stone.

Her frozen face suddenly blinked and the image shimmered and softened. Her frosted hair melted to radiant locks of fiery red, which swirled around her shoulders. Abruptly her violently blue eyes struck out at them. Caspar felt he was staring at his mother's soul, the real woman beneath the exterior shell of her entombed body.

Spar, Spar. Her voice filled his mind with wonder and love.

'Keridwen.' Brid intruded into the bond between mother and son. 'Keridwen, we need you. We must call on your power: Morrigwen is dying.'

I have very little strength left, she murmured in their minds. The image flickered between the vibrant, full-blooded woman and a frozen corpse. Caspar flung his will out to her, urging her to grasp onto him.

'Morrigwen is dying,' Brid said more insistently. 'You must help us.'

Keridwen's eyes clung to her son and she nodded.

'Morrigwen,' Brid whispered again, a hint of relief soughing in her voice. The Eye's image soared away from the glacier and sped through the chill air. Caspar could feel his mother's presence there beside him as they burst through the window of the Crone's chamber. His mother's lilting voice sang out, sweet like summer flowers, rich and silky smooth like warmed honey. *Morrigwen, my Morrigwen, hear me; it's me, Keridwen. Fight off this poisoned sleep.*

The old Crone's heavy eyelids dragged open across her hazy eyes, revealing a clouded, dull glaze. As blank as the eyes of a stuffed stag decorating a castle wall, Caspar thought in horror.

Keridwen? Keridwen, my child? There was a flickering sense of recognition and a glimpse of intense joy before the old woman's soul sank back into black oblivion.

Morrigwen, reach out to us. We three are one. The Trinity can heal you here in the ancient magic of the Mother Cauldron. Bladderdock and foxleaf to drive away the evil poisons. You will heal. You will heal. The Mother will heal you . . . the Mother . . . the Mother . . . Keridwen's voice slipped far away into the echoing depths of the cauldron, fading rapidly as her strength eluded her. Slipping back into the agony of her entombment, the thin trailing echo became an agonized scream. The fearful noise turned to hollow silence as if the lid of a lead-lined coffin had suddenly been hammered shut over it.

Huge, empty despair swam up into Caspar's mind at the sudden, tearing loss of his mother. His hands slipped from the orb and he clutched faintly at the brim of the cauldron for support. 'Mother, don't leave me. Mother, . . . Mother . . .'

Brid stared deeper into the orb. Around the rim of the images, runes were sparkling like slivers of silver. They spiralled downwards falling towards May who stared up out of the heart of the moonstone. They drifted down into her grasp and she gaped at them in bewilderment and wonder. Her brow furrowed and she looked up at Brid in confusion.

'You are seeing them through my mind, Merrymoon. They are the runes of healing. Paint them on Morrigwen's skin and she will heal.' The priestess stared at the herbs twisted around the crown of the orb and Caspar saw their ghostly image filter down into the depths of the moonstone. 'Bladderdock and foxleaf to drive away the fang-nettle. Heal, Morrigwen, heal.' Clutching at the moonstone, Brid staggered back and fell to the ground. Caspar sprinted round to her but Hal already cradled her in his arms.

Chapter 36

May felt overwhelmingly alone. She stared at her hands, expecting to see the strange silver shards that had fallen into her lap, but there was nothing. She blinked uncertainly, wondering where so strange a dream had come from, but in her heart she knew for certain it wasn't a dream. It was far too vivid, perhaps even more vivid and real than life itself, which didn't make sense to her. She had felt so much closer to the real truth, to the real pulsing energy of life as if . . . as if she had touched on the power of the Great Goddess. Surely that was what happened when the three priestesses were united? Isn't that how Morrigwen explained it? And hadn't they just been here with her in this solar?

She struggled to remember the image of the runes, which Brid had freed into her mind. But the more she fought to remember, the more they eluded her, dipping into the feathered edges of her conscious mind. She exhaled deeply, expelling her thoughts and tried only to picture the fiery red-haired woman, so much like her mother, and the so vivid green eyes of the uncomfortably perceptive Brid. They had all been here in this room, she felt certain. A teasing image crept into the edge of her thoughts, glinting in the light and gradually took form. The runes danced through her mind, a procession of strange characters, each almost with a life of its own.

Snatching up the quill, she dipped it in the woad that still lay at Morrigwen's bedside. Carefully she began to paint the mysterious angular shapes on the woman's neck and peeled apart her night-dress to daub her ribbed chest with the enchanted sigils. At first her characters were wavery and uncertain but, as she gained confidence, her writing gradually smoothed into fluid lines.

'These are the runes of healing,' she murmured, remembering what Brid had whispered in her mind. 'Great Mother, heal your daughter Morrigwen.' The prayer came unbidden to her lips, giving her an unnerving feeling of surprise as each word slipped out with her breath.

The old Crone lay still with her sunken eyes closed and her gnarled hands lying limply open by her sides. But there was a perceptible change in her breathing. May held her own breath and listened intently. She didn't dare hope . . . but yes, surely she breathed more deeply. The young child sat by the ancient woman through the long hours of the day, murmuring the prayer over and over. Her eyes never strayed from the priestess's face, watching, hoping and praying. Even the rabid hunger that gnawed at her stomach was forgotten in her vigil. Gradually Morrigwen's breathing became stronger and more even and finally a healthy pink blush flooded up into her face.

Her eyes blinked open. She smiled weakly.

'Merrymoon, my child.'

May's heart rejoiced. She knows me at last, she thought with utter gratitude.

The Crone's hand gripped her wrist with a firm warmness. 'Keridwen was here; I remember she was here. Did you see her?'

May didn't think she had actually seen her but she had been aware of her presence. To avoid any complicated explanations she merely nodded. 'And Master Spar and Brid. They were all here.' She had a strange feeling as she remembered the presence of the Baron's son, his mind mingling with the charged atmosphere. It wasn't at all what she had expected; so full of compassion and sensitivity. There was no arrogance or cold superiority as she had imagined. She felt she had wronged him with her judgement.

'Keridwen,' Morrigwen smiled. 'I knew she was here. But I feel so weak. Have I lain here long?'

Again May nodded. 'It must be weeks. It was the fang-nettle. I'm afraid it killed Catrik.'

'Was anyone else poisoned?' Morrigwen asked, though she slumped back and closed her eyes as if the effort of speaking was becoming too much for her.

'No, just the two of you.'

Morrigwen nodded thoughtfully. 'Someone was afraid of my power but Catrik? It could be to do with the well or maybe he knew something – something that someone didn't want found out.' She sighed, drawing deep heavy breaths to regain her strength. 'But Vaalakan fang-nettle. Slow acting, virtually tasteless in this foul well water and it merely makes the person look as if they are wasting with age and weakness. No dramatic convulsions or purging to arouse anyone's suspicions. Very clever. But it's a rare herb, not something that those of the New Faith would know much about . . . except for . . .' She slumped back and closed her eyes, exhausted by the burden of her thoughts.

'Except?' May was too curious to let the sentence go unfinished.

'Well, you wouldn't know of it unless you were either Vaa-lakan or came from the Boarchase, like you and I or your mother, where the seeds of the herb may have been blown from the Dragon Scorch. And to use it you would have had to have a strong working knowledge of herblore, like I taught my foster-children.' Morrigwen frowned suspiciously. 'Gwion knew almost as much as Keridwen about such things.'

May stroked her knotted hands, trying to think how best to break the news of her foster-son's death. The plain truth seemed the only answer. 'Father Gwion is dead. The west tower burnt and all they could find to identify him was his ring. I – I'm sorry, Morrigwen. I know –'

'He was like a son to me once,' Morrigwen said with more resignation than sadness. 'But the New Faith lured him away when Keridwen vanished . . .' Her voice trailed off and her eyelids sagged heavily onto the crepey skin of her hollow cheeks. 'Fang-nettle . . . Gwion . . . and he's dead.'

May was shocked: there was almost a sense of relief in the hag's croaking voice.

Morrigwen's eyes snapped open. 'Now stop prattling at me, child. I need to think and rest. Go and fetch me some food; I feel like I haven't eaten in a year.'

May ran out into the courtyard, oblivious of the hammer blows that shuddered the castle walls and the gurgling shrieks from beyond the battlements as the archers thinned the Vaalakan numbers howling round the Tor. She no longer cringed as the great catapults strained against their ropes and crashed into the crossbeams, spraying out nails and shot onto the barbarians below. She ran straight to the heartstone, her eyes brimming with tears of thankfulness. Morrigwen would live, Morrigwen would live and she had to thank the Mother. The heartstone would be the right place to worship Her.

The snow had been swept aside, revealing the circle of runes stamped around the perimeter. The evening shadows no longer cast such a deep straight line as they fell across the lettering and the edges of each rune were just a little more rounded. She fell to her knees and stared speechlessly at the heartstone.

The ruby had vanished.

Chapter 37

Brid sat with her head in her hands, looking dazed and drained.

'Is that it then?' Hal demanded. 'Will Morrigwen live?'

Brid lifted her head wearily and pushed her hair off her face. 'Yes, that's it.' Her eyes turned and blinked at the mysterious design of the cauldron and she drew a deep breath as if summoning her strength. 'Now for the cauldron's secret.' She turned slowly round, absorbing her surroundings. Infused with the smoke from the smaller smouldering cauldrons, the wall of mist still encircled the grove.

'The four cauldrons,' she declared, as if talking to herself and working things through in her own mind, 'could represent the four magical cities of the world, each at opposing points of the compass. They still burn with life. The central cauldron could be the ethereal city, the city of spirits, the city of faerie, the place where no one knows, that cannot be located in this world but from where all magic emanates. And that cauldron is lifeless, empty, dead. No magic brews there anymore.' Her face dropped with the flicker of defeat. 'The Keepers have gone – left us – and the secrets of its runes have gone with them.'

'Now what?' Hal asked, grumpily scuffing his heels in the ground and kicking up a dust of leaf-mould. 'Do we return to Torra Alta empty-handed?'

'No,' Brid said. 'No, but –'

'But what?'

Brid looked blankly at the cryptic design of the cauldron. 'But without the Keepers it's going to be difficult.'

'Can't you summon up Keridwen and Morrigwen again?

No doubt they'll understand it better than you.' There was a terseness to Hal's voice that betrayed his frustration.

The Maiden shook her head. 'I have no doubt that you're right,' she retorted with dignity, 'but I know how much the spell-casting sapped my energy. The other two will be gravely weakened and neither of them were strong to start with. I cannot drain any more of their strength without first trying everything else.'

Hal looked at her uncertain face. 'Don't tell me, please don't tell me, we've come all this way for you to be defeated by the cauldron.'

'No!' A look of self-reproach scolded Brid's face and her mouth set into hard lines of determination. 'No. We rekindle the fire and awaken the magic in the great pot. I'm sure there must be enough power in this place to bring forth the memories in the cauldron. I want only dead wood for the fire, clean, dead wood with no green shoots or leaves.'

'That's all this is: so much dead wood,' Hal complained. Nevertheless he slouched off to do the priestess's bidding.

Caspar leapt after him to gather bundles of kindling. His uncle murmured under his breath, 'Do you really think she understands it all and knows what she's doing?'

'Yes, I really do,' the younger youth replied with sincerity.

'She's wild!' Hal said unexpectedly, his voice tight with excitement. 'Wild and free.'

'So you felt her mind too,' Caspar replied, coldly aware of Hal's mercurial emotions.

'She might be difficult and think she's in charge but there's still something beautiful about her.'

'And you needed to pass through the fog to find that out? If you didn't know it already you'll soon forget it again.' The boy felt a bitter resentment towards his uncle though he pushed away the thoughts, aware that the time and the place were too sensitive, too inappropriate for such emotions. Secretly Caspar had also learnt something new about Brid: she had dreadful power, a strength that gathered the elemental energies to her. He flicked his eyes towards the Maiden, watching as she traced the designs around the brim of the cauldron with her fingers. Hal was resting a moment from his task and openly admiring Brid.

Why, Hal, why are you always here to put me down and belittle me? He instantly tried to rid himself of the thought and sought to concentrate on the higher matters at hand. With his arms fully laden with logs, he stumbled across the glade to the cauldron and presented the firewood to Brid, who sorted through the material, discarding the ones she didn't like.

'The canisters,' she ordered. 'Get them from the packs and fill them from the stream.' Brid didn't even look up but kept circling the cauldron, tracing the patterns in the metal with her fingertips. Her forehead puckered into a knot of concentration. He handed the first of the water containers to Brid and she splashed the clear liquid into the bottom of the blackened pot. Standing on tip-toe she peered into the black depths. Her voice was deep and echoing as it explored the inside of the pot.

Filling the cauldron was wearisome work and it took many trips back and forth to the stream. Hal seemed reluctant to participate in the labour, preferring to study Brid as she sloshed the water into the swirling depths of the cauldron. At last she seemed satisfied with the volume of liquid. The branches of the overhanging oak tree arced into a fuller bow.

'That's enough. The circle is already drawn. The womb of spell-weaving is prepared.'

Caspar stared into the black well and saw his own curious expression staring back at him. A trickle of sweat rolled from his forehead and rippled the dark surface below. He stepped back from the great pot, amazed by the intricate work of the carvings and the fascinating patterns, which he couldn't understand. Brid had been silent for many minutes and rose again to carefully examine the writing on the pot. She sighed in frustration at the complexity of the characters.

She ran her hand over the moulded metal. 'I can read the

glyphs and understand their meaning but I'm sure the picture's incomplete. It tells only fragments of a story.'

Caspar waited patiently, restraining his curiosity with great effort so as not to interfere with the girl's concentration. He felt like Firecracker fighting against his jangling curb chains.

'Well,' Hal demanded bluntly. 'What does it all mean? Does it tell us about the Druid's Egg?'

Caspar pressed the side of his crooked nose and looked disapprovingly at his uncle for interfering with Brid's train of thought. The girl, however, seemed unworried. 'Well, I don't know,' she admitted. 'I've always known about the existence of the Mother Cauldron, but nothing about the meaning of its design.'

'Why is it called the Mother Cauldron if it doesn't have a representation of the Earth on it?' the younger boy asked. 'I mean, there are Suns and Moons but no Earth.'

Brid smiled indulgently. 'No, of course not, Spar. The whole cauldron represents the Earth. Look, this oak is the king of trees and he gives protective support to the Great Mother suspended in the universe.' She pressed her palm into the etched bark of the tree, carefully avoiding the grotesque carving of a hobgoblin that leered out at her. 'Here at the top of the cauldron is the wild hunt, the eternal chase that keeps the cycle of life spinning. Here is the Sun and the Moon and beneath them the elements. And trapped between the fire and water are the ancient animals of power suppressed and tangled because the time is yet unready for them to walk freely abroad in the world. And here, of course, is the fire of life lapping up from the base.' She indicated the tongues of fire that lapped up from the underside of the pot.

'So what?' Hal said bluntly. 'There isn't any magic in it. It's just the representation of the world as you see it.'

'You think I don't know that?' Brid snapped back, revealing the first signs of frustrated anger. 'You think I don't know these things better than either of you? These things are more important to me than they are to you. You might lose your precious Torra Alta, or your country but I will lose my world, my faith.' She wrapped her body in her arms, fiercely gripping her forearms; crescent-shaped marks from her fingernails left deep imprints in the flesh. 'I don't know what it means but this is a powerful cauldron and it won't yield up its secrets just because we want it to. No one said it would be easy.'

'Well, could it be in the runes around the Sun and Moons?' Caspar feathered his fingertips over the charred metal, feeling the ridges and etchings. He tried to sense an aura of magic, searching for a revelation of insight and understanding. But he felt nothing.

'When faced with a riddle of enchantment, you have to approach the questions from the right angle, with the right frame of mind,' Brid sighed. 'And I'm not looking at it right. We'll light the fire and see if that brings an image to the water inside the pot and so draws us towards the answers.' She stirred the embers and to her amazement a spark leapt up. It caught the tip of the dry wood and, after a moment's fanning, burst into flames. The fire reached up and teased the base of the cauldron. The flames swirled on the underside of the pot, sending long tongues flickering over the fire-carvings in the metal of the Mother Cauldron.

'What do the runes say?' Caspar demanded, feeling that Brid was keeping something back. Perhaps if she voiced her thoughts she might clarify a nebulous idea that would otherwise remain just beyond the reach of her consciousness.

'They tell of all the creatures of the Earth; the new creatures like you, me, Trog and the horses. And of the old animals, the mythical animals that have been suppressed into the world with the dying of the understanding of nature. But here around the Full Moon it tells of that time when we passed from one age into the next.'

'A thousand years ago?' Hal asked.

'No, a thousand, thousand years ago, longer ago than can be remembered in tales or passed down from mother to daughter. It tells of that time when the spirit of the animals was locked up in a single microcosmic world, containing the matter for their entire existence, and their secret was hidden from the new age. Why it's written around the Moon, I'm not sure.' She circled the cauldron again and again. Following the pattern of the Moons as they waxed from a slit crescent and waned to the Full Moon. Suddenly she cried out with revelation, 'It's not the Moon, not the Moon at all. I wasn't thinking straight: they wouldn't carve two Full Moons. One of them is the Egg, the Druid's Egg. The runes tell us of the seeds locked within it.' Her eyes shone with excitement, mysteriously bright like the heart of an emerald touched by starlight. 'But where? Where on Earth is the Egg? There has to be another clue.' Brid looked at the cauldron, drumming her clenched fists on the brim. Then she looked at the four smaller cauldrons at the edge of the glade. 'Perhaps it's more simple. Perhaps the Egg here on the metal is related to the position of the other cauldrons. There, the cauldron to the North represents the northernmost of the four sacred cities, Farona; the one in the South, Salixa; the one in the West, Waerloga; and the one in the East, Oriaxia. That would place the Egg centrally to those four. The Egg would be in the ethereal city.'

'You mean the Egg is somewhere that doesn't exist, only exists in the imagination? Oh come on, Brid; that's just crazy.' Hal placed his hand sympathetically on her shoulder. 'Think again. None of this makes much sense but that makes the least sense of all.'

'No, I meant it showed the real position. Here, Spar, where's that map of yours?'

Caspar wondered how Brid knew about the chart he had hidden. He felt each one of his pockets in turn, patting the outside and went round again. Finally he laid his hand on the folded piece of parchment that he had slipped into his jacket on leaving Legros's library. 'Here,' he said excitedly, 'here it is.'

Unfolding it carefully, Brid laid the map out along the ground, elbowing Trog in the chest to stop him from walking all over it. The terrier managed to get a quick slurp at Hal's nose before receiving a sharp smack and being banished to a more respectful distance. The four cities were clearly marked in illustrated capitals, each with a symbol of a cathedral next to the name.

'No longer the four sacred cities,' Brid said bitterly, 'but the four cathedral cities.'

Hal elbowed his way in between them so the map was the right way up for him and pushed the other two aside. Using his hand to span the distances between the cities he located their central point. 'Well, somehow, Brid, I don't think that's going to help us very much.' He nailed the map with his index finger. 'Look, it's dead in the centre; here in the sea.'

'Well, it was only a thought,' she retorted, 'only an idea. I didn't say it would be there; I just said it might be possible. But it's too pat, too easy. It wouldn't be safe to leave such an obvious clue. It's here, I know the answer is here. The Goddess will lead me to the Egg. We need to weave the spells of releasing, the spells of understanding, the spells of clarity. But we will start with the spells of intuition – a simple enchantment. And if that doesn't work, well, we will just have to lead on from there.'

She drew out a small golden sickle from her belt. The crescent blade was no more than the size of her palm. Faithfully followed by the white terrier, she went first to the blackthorn tree and without touching the plant stepped sunwise to the next tree. She stroked the smooth bark of the beech. Murmuring a polite word to Phagos, the tree of knowledge and learning, she sliced a twig from its branches before moving to the next tree. She went right the way round the perimeter of the grove until she returned to the blackthorn and, again without taking a sprig from that tree, returned to the cauldron. 'Straif, the blackthorn is the tree of fates: it strives to deny us any choice or control in our future. It prevents magic, wards off foreknowledge and bids people to step away, step back from the powers of nature,' the Maiden explained. She dropped the sprigs into the water and stirred it with the spoon, waiting till the water boiled up and frothed in the cauldron. She stood back and critically walked around the pot again, studying it in detail. Trog curled up by the fire, just out of spitting distance of the flames.

'Well, is there anything different?' Caspar worried.

Brid shook her head. 'I was hoping that the heat and the characteristics in the trees would change the metal – develop its properties – and that some new runes would appear on the surface.' She reached up and stared into the pot. Hal and Caspar did the same. No longer was the boy staring at his own reflection but at a boiling, writhing sea. He felt giddy with the fumes; the image seemed to dance and mutate before his eyes and suddenly he could see Torra Alta. The rest of the image was unclear, suggesting only a chaotic sense of raging turmoil at the foot of the Tor. The boiling froth surged up the pinnacle of rock and engulfed the castle, sucking it into the gruel. Caspar felt tears pouring off his cheeks and they dripped into the liquid. The image instantly dispersed.

'You fool, Spar.' Brid pierced him with cold eyes. 'Anything, any tiny little thing will change the spell.'

He looked at her meekly and apologetically.

'How could you cry?' Hal mocked under his breath.

'But Torra Alta, Father, Morrigwen . . . all drowned in the chaos of the Vaalakans . . .'

'What are you blathering about?' the older youth demanded.

'In the pot! The image in the pot.'

'It's only boiling water with a few bits of tree in it, Spar.' Hal shrugged, dismissing his nephew's foolishness.

'We need a stronger magic,' Brid decided. 'That spell wasn't working anyway, so it's not your fault.' Taking her sickle, she went round each of the horses and cut three hairs from their tails and three from their manes. Then carefully, after Caspar had flustered warnings about his horse's heels, she pinched the skin on Firecracker's neck and punctured the nipped hide with the point of her sickle, squeezing the wound to release a trickle of the stallion's blood. Carefully she collected precisely three drops on the flat blade of the sickle. Deftly avoiding Trog who was weaving round her legs, she stepped towards the fire and offered the bloody sacrifices to the boiling cauldron. The simmering liquid frothed up in a rush of effervescence, foaming to the brim of the pot before subsiding to a rolling boil. Trog scurried away from the spitting liquid to curl up in the roots of the hazel. Brid again paced around the cauldron, carefully re-examining the runes.

'Anything?' Hal enquired.

She shook her head and began plaiting and unplaiting her hair as if trying to soothe the rhythm of her thoughts.

'We will put in everything of power, everything to hand that wields magic.' She cut three strands of hair from each of them, and after a moment's hesitation took three strands of coarse hair from the snoozing dog, who raised a heavy-lidded eye and thumped his tail in appreciation of her attention. 'I've never heard of dogs having any magic but just because I haven't heard of it doesn't mean it doesn't exist.' She emptied her scrip and picked out the tongue, which was beginning to look a little green at the ends, and thirteen of the virgins' knuckle bones. She searched deeper into her herbalist's bag and extracted a cutting of belladonna, a kernel of nutmeg and some poppy seeds all of which, she explained, were hallucinogenic and might loosen an image from the cauldron. Ceremoniously she let the herbs sift through her hands into the pot, which swung from the branches of the bowed oak. The base of the cauldron was beginning to glow a bitter orange, highlighting the frieze of flames that writhed up above the black smoke, coiling up from the tongues of live fire.

The runes remained stubbornly unchanged.

Brid's cheeks glowed red from the sweltering heat of the flames and the rage of her frustration. She fell to her knees and beat the earth with her fists. 'Mother, Mother, my powers are too diminished to release your secrets. Don't punish me anymore for my crimes in the cathedral at Farona. Give me my full powers. We do this for you at your bidding; Mother, help me in our quest.' The only reply was the sizzling hiss of the fire as the boiling cauldron spat drops of liquid out into the crackling flames. Hal was coughing to clear his lungs from the thick acrid smoke that had wafted in his direction.

'There must be more I can add.' She felt her neck and ripped the symbolic charm, hidden beneath her shirt from its cord. She stretched out a hand to take Caspar's mandala as well.

He covered his hazelwood pentagram protectively with his hand. 'But Morrigwen gave it to me as a special gift.' He felt a sense of panic at the thought of losing the charm.

A touch of irritation frayed the edges of Brid's smooth cool voice. 'The greater the loss, the greater the sacrifice, the greater the potency of the magic!' She snatched at it and with one fierce tug snapped the cord and tossed it into the cauldron. Caspar ran to the brim of the pot and leant in, mourning the loss of his mandala. Seething liquid spat up and burnt his cheeks but the image that appeared before his eyes in the fuming, aromatic and drugging vapours was far more painful. He stared at the eyes of his mother, eyes of deep blue, almost the violet of midsummer twilight, watery with tears. Her hand stretched up, reaching out of the fumes to almost touch him but she was being dragged away. An axe blade hooked into her shoulder and pulled her down into the evil brew.

'Spar, don't breathe the fumes.' Brid's hand was on his shoulder, pulling him back from the pot. 'Didn't you heed what I put in there? Much of it is instantly lethal!'

Caspar's eyes gushed with razor-hot tears that streamed unbidden from his tear-ducts. His throat was tight and he couldn't draw breath as if his lungs were contracting and squeezing the air out of his body.

'Hal, keep him away from the pot and put his head in the stream to clear his eyes.'

The older youth quickly steered his nephew towards the brook. 'Try and keep calm, Spar. I don't think your excitement is helping Brid.' The cool water eased the smarting and, as Hal pulled the boy's collar up, Caspar coughed, splattering out the lining of his throat. He drew harsh rapid breaths until finally he felt released from the constricting clutches of the vapours. Brid still paced up and down, with the dog following every step, waiting for the boiling potion to take effect.

The cauldron remained defiantly immutable.

Suddenly Brid looked up towards the sky. 'We will wait,' she announced firmly. 'The magic will be stronger when the moon rises. Then we will try again.' She sat down by the roots of the oak tree, hugging her knees but when Trog's muzzle squeezed under her arm she lay back and cuddled the dog. He was too big to sit on her lap but contented himself with lying on the leaf-mould and resting his head on her knee. A deep throaty breathing, almost like the contented purring of a cat, ruffled his throat. Brid closed her eyes, looking frail and drained, and seemed to fall instantly asleep.

'The spell-casting takes so much out of her,' Caspar whispered. 'Do you think this spell is too big for her? Maybe she needs the Three; maybe she can't do it without Keridwen and Morrigwen.'

Hal shrugged. 'I don't know. Maybe.' He was distracted and looked wistfully at the girl. 'Why is it that in this place nothing seems to matter?'

'It's probably the poison from the yews filling the air and drugging us,' Caspar suggested, feeling exhausted himself. Wearily he tended to the horses. When he had finished unsaddling them he furled up Firecracker's war-cloth and mane-sheet into a wad and eased it under the Maiden's sleeping head as a pillow. 'Brid, when this is all over,' he promised himself in the lightest of whispers, 'you'll see me differently.'

A light touch squeezed the boy's forearm.

'No, I won't, Spar. There's a thousand years' difference between you and me – too great a void to reach across. In a different life maybe ... but not in this one.' Her voice was blurred and drowsy. Mortified, Caspar retreated and returned sulkily to examine the cauldron.

'If she can't fathom its meaning, what makes you think you can, Spar?' Hal remarked scathingly.

'Why do you have to be so sharp?'

The raven-haired youth sighed. 'Because I'm sick of this witchcraft. I want to go home and fight. Maybe I'd die fighting but at least I would be doing something. Here I feel as useless as Cybillia.' He sighed wistfully at the serene face of the sleeping

Maiden, nestled by the roots of the hazel. 'By truth and honour, she's beautiful!'

'Who? Cybillia?'

'No! Well, she was of course; she was, very. No, I meant Brid. She's different when she's asleep, looks more gentle and compliant, less angry with the world and definitely less bossy.'

Caspar sighed and turned back to the cauldron. 'What do you think the animals represent?'

Hal shrugged again and looked at his hand. 'Don't ask me such fool questions. I don't know. I've lost my finger and half my ear and it hurts. So just shut up.'

Above the clearing, which remained free of the circling mist, the blue of day slipped deeper into the violets and indigos of dusk. The first ripples of moonlight teased through the branches of the leafless oak tree and kissed the Maiden's face. Her eyes flickered open and with renewed vigour and enthusiasm she returned to the cauldron.

'It's here, I know the answer is here: I dreamt it. We're just not trying enough, not giving enough, not sacrificing enough.' She turned on Hal. 'And you're too negative: you don't believe enough. For the love of Torra Alta, if not for anything else, apply your will to the magic.' Hal took a deep breath as if preparing to make some sarcastic comment but Brid touched his hand and whispered softly, 'Please, Hal, for me, please.'

'You've never said please before,' he grinned co-operatively. 'Well, come on then. What now? What's the next spell?'

'We'll add more water and ... Oh it'll take too long to explain. Just fetch me some fresh water to start with.'

In the pitch of night, the stream was black, dark and mysterious. A beam of moonlight touched the surface and the water was shot through with dazzling silver.

Brid scooped out the silvery liquid once they'd returned. 'The touch of moonlight in the water is an auspicious omen,' she murmured, trickling the water drop by drop into the cauldron. 'Now, Hal, you watch this side and, Spar, the other. Tell me the instant you see any change in the surface of the metal.'

Caspar fixed his eyes on the image of the Egg, which initially they had mistaken for a full moon. He traced out the glyphs, trying to remember the pattern so that he would know if it altered.

'First water then earth.' She scraped a handful of soil into the palm of her hand and sprinkled it over the liquid. 'Then fire.' She selected a branch from the ancient oak and drove the end of the staff into the fire. It caught life from the embers and danced into a flame that crackled and spat on the sap of the unseasoned wood. Trog cringed from the sizzling smuts spitting from the brand. 'Now fire.' She poured a vial of winter bark oil over the surface and dipped the burning staff into the liquid. Blue flames of a cool heat skimmed over the surface. The potion began to stir and froth until it surged up into a rolling boil, churning the contents of the brew and throwing them up to the surface. Knuckle bones and tongue mingling with the offerings from the trees, seethed in the agitated waters.

'Is there anything?' Brid demanded anxiously. 'Anything at all?' Her voice was hollow and distant, booming inside the cauldron.

'Nothing.' Caspar felt a heavy disappointment. They could not fail. They must not fail. Keridwen – Mother – help us, he thought despairingly. Mother, this has to work: we must find the Egg. Tears of frustration pricked at the corners of his eyes. He brushed them away with his sleeve lest they interfered with his vigil over the runes.

'More heat,' Brid cried, her presence and her power growing. 'More heat. The runes may be cast in a special metal that will only be revealed by excessive heat, like the tree-runes in the Jotunn hearths.'

Hal and Caspar sifted through the undergrowth again, careful not to stray too far into the fog that still surrounded the clearing. They returned with bundles of kindling, which Brid tossed into the fire, murmuring her incantations to the Mother Goddess. The flames engulfed the bottom third of the giant pot and the metal began to glow a bright orange. The potion boiled furiously, drumming the ingredients against the walls of the cauldron.

'It's glowing,' Hal said uncertainly, 'glowing but not changing.'

Brid stirred up the fire, agitating it with the staff of the spoon, so that it roared and hissed. Pockets of air trapped in the wood whined before exploding in a shower of sparks. The flames roared higher.

It'll catch on the trees and then the whole forest will go up and we'll all be burnt alive, Caspar thought apprehensively. His cheeks were raddled and scorched from the heat and he covered his mouth with his sleeve to filter out the acrid smell of the smoke. The bright flames, reflected in the wall of fog around the edge of the grove, produced unnatural orange shapes that stirred in the veil of mist. Caspar tried to cut the unnerving images out of his mind and fixed his smarting eyes on the runes. Near the base, the pot glowed white hot, blending through golden orange, burnished red, smoky dun and finally the dull black of soot where the metal was cooler near the brim.

'There must be a change now,' Brid almost pleaded. 'There has to be.' She circled the pot and flung the wooden spoon down on the ground in disgust. 'More magic. I need stronger spells.'

The priestess searched through her leather scrip and withdrew Hal's severed finger, which was beginning to putrefy. She tossed it into the cauldron and the liquid foamed and roared to the top and then abated again. 'Your sword,' she demanded. 'I will stir it with the sword.' The white metal hissed as she plunged it into the seething liquid. When she withdrew the blade, blood-red stains coloured the runes that were etched into the central groove of the sword.

'My sword!' Hal protested.

Brid leapt to examine the runes on its fuller. Her mouth dropped open and her hands went limp. She looked lamely at Hal.

'What have you done to my sword?' he thundered, snatching it out of her hands.

'The runes have changed.'

'You mean you've destroyed the Runes of War?' Hal stared at the indecipherable blood-red sigils.

'No,' Brid said uncertainly. 'They're still there.'

Caspar's eyes brightened. 'You've found them, then. You've found the lost runes.'

Again Brid shook her head. 'No, it's a warning. The sword was etched with the Runes of War. Their powerful spell has stirred up a deep magic from the heart of the cauldron. I've made a mistake.'

'Brid!' Hal shouted at her roughly. 'You're blathering. You're not making a single grain of sense.'

She drew in a deep breath. 'The Mother is still punishing me. She let me stumble through the dark and now I have inadvertently awoken a new spell.'

The two youths looked at her blankly and even Trog pricked his ears and cocked his head, worried by the anxious sound of his mistress's voice.

'What spell, Brid?' Hal asked coldly.

'The ancient runes of sorcery. They awake the old powers.'

'Well, will they help us find the Egg?' the youth demanded more practically.

The Maiden shook her head and stared at the unyielding pot with new determination. 'No, no they won't. Mother!' she cried. 'Mother, we must have the cauldron's hidden runes. Mother, we beg of you! We must have the lost runes.'

The pagan high-priestess tore at her hair and at her clothes in rage and frustration before delving into the scrip again. Frustrated with searching in the darkness, she scattered the contents on the ground and rummaged through them. Without selecting anything she stood up and kicked at her precious sacramental herbs in disgust. 'Nothing! I must give of myself! I must create a higher magic, a moment of great power. The moon is right; I am the Maiden, One of the Three. Mother, my powers I relinquish. I give up my office. I sacrifice myself as a virgin – as the Maiden – in return for the runes.'

She ripped the shirt from her torso, the moonlight highlighting the pink tips of her breasts. Her bronze flesh was decorated in white painted symbols. Reflected in the star-light and the glow from the fire were the images of crescent moons, stars and the circle of the full moon, which accentuated the oval curve of her smooth belly. She slid her breeches down over her lithe thighs and stood in the midst of the glade, utterly naked. She cut a spray of mistletoe, from the oak tree and shaped it into a circlet to crown her flowing hair, the opal spheres of the white berries glistening in the moonlight. As if possessed, she whirled round and around so that her long hair flung out in a wide skirt. Caspar felt his chin drop to his chest and stirrings disturb his body.

'I am the Maiden,' she shrieked. 'I am the Maiden. I can use this magic only once. I pledge the magic of the first conjunction.'

Hal was stepping eagerly forward and caught her in his arms.

'We give this magic only once. Mother, bring forth the runes,' Brid demanded in wild cries.

The younger, less forceful youth damned himself for being too slow as he looked on in astonishment and unbridled jealousy. A deep raging pain, like a self-consuming canker, gnawed and tore at his insides as Hal, after gaping in astonishment for a moment, seized his opportunity and struggled to rid himself of his belted jacket.

'No!' he cried above the furious roar of the fire and Brid's hysterical chanting. 'No!' He beat the cauldron with the staff and kicked at the flames in his raging anger and jealousy. He wrenched back and forth at the lip of the cauldron so that it swung on its handle. The branches of the bowed oak tree creaked and moaned. 'No!'

Rage boiled in his eyes as he watched Brid roll out the caparison. Firecracker's war-cloth, the cloth that Branwolf had presented to him, Caspar. Now she was going to lie on it with Hal. Hal! It had to be Hal! 'No!' he cried, his rage, like the seething liquid in the cauldron, turning his ugly emotions over and over. The pot swung precariously.

Brid lay on the blue and gold cloth, her long hair curling

round her breasts, whilst Hal struggled with a boot that refused to come off his foot.

Caspar beat against the cauldron, oblivious to the pain from the heat. 'Runes! Give me the runes now. Give them now, so I can stop this.' He wrenched back and forth against the scorching handle, railing and screaming in his jealous rage. The tree creaked and groaned in protest. 'Hal cannot help find the runes; the shamaness of Oldhart Forest said I was the Seeker, not Hal. Not Hal!'

Suddenly there was a splintering crack as the branches of the old oak tore and snapped. The cauldron crashed to the earth, spewing its contents over the flames and dousing the fire to smouldering ashes. The pot rolled over and over towards Brid, who lay naked and helpless in its path. Caspar looked on with shock and dismay. His anger, his jealousy had created the momentum behind the great cauldron. And now it was going to crush his beautiful Brid.

Half-dressed, Hal dived at the pot, caught it by the handle and dug his toes into the ground. He swore from the burning heat of the metal but nevertheless clenched his fists determinedly tight. Score marks scraped the earth where his feet skidded over the soil, as he strained to arrest the cauldron in its thunderous roll.

Brid was on her feet with the caparison wrapped around her body, swaying unsteadily as if she weren't in full control of her senses. The base of the cauldron rolled round to face her and juddered to a halt as Hal's back muscles rippled with the strain. The Maiden pointed triumphantly at its base. 'Look!'

The two youths ran to her side and stared at the base of the cauldron. 'They're not flames at all!' Caspar spoke in wonder.

'Snakes' tails,' Hal said simply as he blew on his scorched palms. He didn't bother to disguise the black look of disgust that he shot at his nephew, venting his frustration at being thwarted from his pleasure. The muscles tensed along the line of his jaw as he bit his lip and hitched his belt with a dissatisfied grunt.

Caspar's eyes slid along the snakes' tails towards the very bottom of the pot, which was decorated with a band of twenty-one square tablets. The serpents squirmed between the gaps in the collar of tablets and the boy followed the length of their bodies to their fanged heads and flickering tongues. The fork of each tongue pointed towards the very centre and a solitary egg. The central egg was bare of any message but each of the surrounding tablets bore a broken disjointed pattern. Caspar was certain they were neither spell-runes nor tree-runes and he felt his mouth sag in disappointment.

Brid however glowed with elation. Snatching up the moonstone she placed it over each sigil in turn. She clutched at the orb and smiled lovingly into its heart. 'Morrigwen, Keridwen, I need you now. I need the power of the Three.' She turned to Caspar. 'Touch the orb; help me summon them.'

The white patterns of the moonstone scudded aside, as if a bright summer breeze had whipped away the dusty, lazy mist of early morning, to reveal two faces. The old Crone looked stronger now. Though her hair was thin and ragged and her eyes still dark with bruising, there was a healthier tinge to her skin. She embraced the frail, frosted-white image of Keridwen, stroking back the icicle-bound tresses of her hair and breathing warmth onto her deathly-blue face. Caspar felt his heart thump in his throat.

'We are Three, here joined at this focus of power,' Brid declared. 'Mother, give us the runes.'

A sense of blinding energy, which made him feel at once both terribly afraid and yet overwhelmed with joy, flooded into Caspar's soul. He felt free and wild; invincible and comforted. An all encompassing love embraced them.

'Mother, Great Mother,' Brid murmured reverently.

The central image of Morrigwen and Keridwen distorted and swam aside to curve around the rim of the crystal, where they became thin and transparent like hazy ghosts. The moonstone became liquid clear with only a thin mercurial sheen sliding just beneath the surface. Caspar squinted at the orb; it was like looking through a prism. As the high-priestess guided the moonstone over each tablet, its liquid curves distorted the image carved into each tablet. The fragmented lines focused together to form clear angular spell-runes.

Brid's eyes sparkled with triumph. 'We have them. We've found the lost runes.'

Glossary

MONTHS OF THE YEAR

December	*Wolfmoon*
January	*Snowmoon*
February	*Horning*
March	*Lenting*
April	*Ostara*
May	*Merrymoon*
June	*Fallow*
July	*Mellowmoon*
August	*Harvest*
September	*Shedding*
October	*Hunting*
November	*Fogmoon*

THE LORD OF THE RINGS
J. R. R. Tolkien

Part 1: The Fellowship of the Ring
Part 2: The Two Towers
Part 3: The Return of the King

The Lord of the Rings cannot be described in a few words. J. R. R. Tolkien's great work of imaginative fiction has been labelled both a heroic romance and a classic of science fiction. It is, however, impossible to convey to the new reader all of the book's qualities, and the range of its creation. By turns comic, homely, epic, monstrous and diabolic, the narrative moves through countless changes of scenes and character in an imaginary world which is totally convincing in its detail. Tolkien created a new mythology in an invented world which has proved timeless in its appeal.

'An extraordinary book. It deals with a stupendous theme. It leads us through a succession of strange and astonishing episodes, some of them magnificent, in a region where everything is invented, forest, moor, river, wilderness, town, and the races which inhabit them. As the story goes on the world of the Ring grows more vast and mysterious and crowded with curious figures, horrible, delightful or comic. The story itself is superb.'
– *The Observer*

'Among the greatest works of imaginative fiction of the twentieth century.' – *Sunday Telegraph*

'The English-speaking world is divided into those who have read *The Hobbit* and *The Lord of the Rings* and those who are going to read them.' – *Sunday Times*

The Lord of the Rings is available as a three book paperback edition and also in one volume.

David Eddings

The Shining Ones

Book two of
The Tamuli

HAVOC AND WAR

Prince Sparhawk is pledged to fight the enemies of the
Tamul Emperor Sarabian with all the skill and cunning of a
Pandion Knight. Meanwhile his Queen, Ehlana, educates
Sarabian in the art of ruthless statesmanship. Sarabian is
transformed from a mere puppet ruler into a formidable
politician. But still Trolls, vampires, werewolves, zombies,
ghouls and Ogres form a vast conspiracy to take over the
Empire. Most disturbing of all are reported sightings of the
Shining Ones amongst the hordes. These luminous beings
inspire more fear than the rest combined. And Sparhawk
and his companions must resurrect the sacred jewel of the
Troll-Gods to combat them.

The enemies of the Empire know that possession of the
jewel makes Sparhawk as dangerous as any god. But gods
are among his foes. And while Sparhawk defends the far-
flung Tamul Empire, he cannot also protect his beautiful
Queen.

David Eddings, the greatest of modern fantasy writers,
unveils the hidden powers at work in the story of Sparhawk
and the Tamul Empire, an epic for our times.

ISBN 0 586 21316 3